THE NORA ABBOTT MYSTERY SERIES BOOKS 1-3

HEIGHT OF DECEPTION, SKIES OF FIRE, CANYON OF LIES

SHANNON BAKER

Published by Severn River Publishing.

ALSO BY SHANNON BAKER

The Desert Behind Me

Echoes in the Sand

The Nora Abbott Series

Height of Deception

Skies of Fire

Canyon of Lies

The Kate Fox Series

Stripped Bare

Dark Signal

Bitter Rain

HEIGHT OF DECEPTION

A NORA ABBOTT MYSTERY

To Dave, may the adventures keep coming.

1

Frigid air ripped down her throat, searing both lungs as her heart threatened to burst through her rib cage. Heavy panting announced the pursuer, one step from overtaking her. A final leap put her safely on the ledge.

He blew past her, not seeing the sheer drop-off beyond the ledge.

"Abbey!"

Skidding on his butt, two legs dangled over a 300-foot drop to rocky ground. Nails scrabbled on the cold stone.

Fear and adrenaline shot through Nora Abbott's body. She dove toward the edge, her fingers frantic to find purchase. Using all the weight in her lithe frame, Nora flung herself backward to jerk him to safety. Then she closed her eyes.

"Stupid dog," she whispered, as she released his collar and hugged the aging golden retriever. Why couldn't he stay home, snuggled into his warm bed, as Scott had?

Holding his panting body close in the muted light, Nora turned to the east. She'd nearly missed it. Fearing that failure to be here on time would jinx the day, she half ran the entire three mile uphill hike, something she wasn't really in shape to do. With just minutes to spare, she knelt on the rough volcanic stone, recovering her pulse and breathing.

Wait for it. Wait for it.

Bam!

Sunrays burst over the silhouetted ridge of Kachina Mountain, warm and welcoming, like a mother greeting her child.

Joy filled Nora's mind and heart. This was the mountain's gift to her. "Thank you." Her whispered words drifted over the tree tops and the ski lodge below. The sun and the mountain took care of her spirit, and she'd do her best to take care of them.

Maybe the run up the trail hadn't brought her as close to death as she felt at the moment, but her heart and lungs still complained, so she decided to sit a bit longer. Abbey, however, stood and shook, moving away from her to sniff and pee.

Nora rolled her eyes, "Sacred moment terminated." But the gratitude lingered, throwing a soft blanket over her anxiety.

She drew in a deep breath and tilted up her face, letting the sun soak in as fortification for today's battle. How could she not triumph? She was right, and right always won.

Didn't it?

Nora blew out a last breath, then stepped back from the ledge and along the precarious footing that would lead her back to the main path. If she slipped, she'd crash six feet onto the trail. Probably not enough to kill her, but with her luck, she'd strike her head. They'd find her broken and in a coma, and her mother and Scott would fight over her brain-dead body for the next twenty years. Or until Scott gave up.

Sheesh, Nora. Over-dramatize much? She steadied herself against a chilly rock.

Woft, woft, woft. Above her head, wings beat the air. Nora looked up and spied an enormous raven sailing over her. Despite the natural glory of her mountain, ravens always seemed sinister. Circling in a wide arc, the black bird came at her like an alpine kamikaze.

Nora scrambled down to the trail, heart racing once again. Halfway there, her foot slipped and she smashed her tailbone against a rock, sending a shower of knives up her spine, then she slid the rest of the way to the dirt trail, back scraping on a stone.

Nora groaned in pain. Abbey meanwhile barked like a terrier on meth. His outburst added to her jitters and she started to quiet him. But he wasn't looking at the vanishing raven. Abbey focused on a point farther into the pine trees and closer to ground level. His hackles rose as he bared teeth,

Nora turned her head, her hackle-less neck raising hairs of its own. A man stood in distant flittering light. Even from far away the bright blue that accented the stranger's clothes flared in the forest.

Nora jumped to her feet, ready to bolt down the trail for the safety of home. She blinked. The figure was gone.

Nora squinted and drew in her brows. "How in the . . .?" Abbey had stopped barking and serenely picked his way down the steep ledge to the trail. He trotted past her, tongue lolling and tail wagging.

Nora shook her head. That wasn't a person, couldn't be. She glanced around again. Her heart rampaged, even though she told herself her imagination and the spotty light had turned a really big blue jay into a threatening predator.

A cloud covered the newly risen sun, blotting out the warmth, just as the stupid raven and huge jay had blotted out the peace of her spirit. Didn't the Navajo believe ravens were a bad omen? Maybe that's why she didn't like the things.

She let out a disgusted breath. Prophecy, bad luck from a broken mirror, and omens existed only in people's imaginations. She really needed to be more practical than that, especially today.

But if she didn't believe in omens, why did she race to within an inch of her life this morning just to greet the sunrise?

2

The judge, in his polyester robe, slammed the gavel onto the podium. "Court dismissed." Wordless prattle erupted in the back half of the room.

Nora's attorney, Raymond, jumped from his chair and slapped her back hard enough to knock her into next week. "Congratulations!" His arm reared back for another celebratory smack, but Nora sidestepped out of his reach.

Not sure she trusted the verdict, she asked, "No more appeals?"

Raymond's guffaw drowned out the excited chatter of the people exiting the room. "Next stop is the Supreme Court, and that's as unlikely as snow in July." A cheesy grin spread across his face as he looked sideways at her. "No pun intended!" He burst into exhilarated laughter.

Snow in July... The future opened before her, ripe with possibilities, rotten with pitfalls. *Focus on the possibilities, Nora.* Snow. Wet, life-giving. Not only to her ski business but to the drought-stricken mountain.

"That's a good one," Raymond said. "Now that we won, you *can* have snow in July, if that's what you want." He stepped close again, and his heavy paw landed so hard on her back that her children—if she ever had any—would be born dizzy. "It's okay to whoop a bit. You just won a landmark case, missy."

Raymond had worked tirelessly for almost four years, through appeals and setbacks and the same threats and harassments she'd borne from activists and hell-bent enviros on a mission. This landmark win would skyrocket his career. That made her smile. She raised onto tip toes and kissed his cheek. "You're brilliant. Thank you."

Raymond beamed at her. "Coming from a sweet young thing like you, that makes it all worthwhile."

So why didn't she feel the victory with as much enthusiasm?

Because Scott wasn't here to share it with her. Being too tired to catch the sunrise with her hadn't stopped him from leaving the apartment before she and Abbey returned from the mountaintop.

He said he'd be here. She glanced at her watch. He was late. Surely that was all.

Raymond directed her toward the courtroom doors. "The press is gonna set up outside. We gotta get you out there for a sound bite. This will make it all the way to the *Today Show*, I guarantee it." He whisked her through a jumble of bodies clustered in the hallway, muttering, "Excuse me, excuse me."

More thumps on the back—thankfully less heartfelt than Raymond's—and congratulatory exclamations followed her. Not watching where he walked, Raymond pulled her directly into the path of a man striding down the hallway.

Her shoulder accordioned into him.

Raymond released her arm and continued toward the media frenzy, not noticing the lost contact.

A tall, athletic man with sandy blond hair and a serious face reached out to steady her. Her eyes rolled down his plaid shirt, fitted jeans, and worn hiking boots. Not normal dress for the courthouse. *Great. An enviro, here to berate me for unnatural acts against the world.* She tensed, ready for a fight. People like him didn't understand that conservation and business didn't have to be mutually exclusive. She'd prove it to them.

"Sorry, ma'am." He hurried past her and down the hall.

Nora grimaced and glanced over her shoulder at his receding back. She didn't believe the contact was an accident.

Still, she'd endured worse than an ignorant shove. Others of his ilk no doubt waited to hurl insults, and hopefully not sharp objects, at her. Tire-slashers, window-smashers, activists who protested each court appearance and sent her death threats lay in wait somewhere outside the courthouse. She scanned the faces in the lobby. Mostly white, well-dressed. Flagstaff's mayor and business leaders clustered together.

The court decision to allow manmade snow on Kachina Mountain outside of town ensured the success of Nora's skiing business, but it would bolster all of Flagstaff's winter income, too. To some, Nora was a hero.

Knots of supporters dotted the courthouse lobby. Raymond waved and shouted comments to several. He leaned close to Nora. "Why don't you slip into the powder room there? The cameras wash you out and you'll want to put on lipstick and spruce up a bit."

Cameras? Sound bites? Slick sweat appeared on her upper lip. She was a business person, not one of FOX's foxes. "Can't you do the talking?"

"I could, but you're much prettier." He nodded and grinned at a rotund man crossing the tiled floor. "Get going. You don't want Big Elk to get all the attention."

She lost her breath as an anvil dropped from the sky and pounded her into a nervous mush. Of course Big Elk, the Al Sharpton of Native Americans, would be around for the decision. He'd be rousing the rabble outside, wooing the media, and working someone into a froth so fiery they might not stop at threats this time.

Raymond gave her a shove. "Off you go."

Nora pushed open the bathroom door and let it bump shut behind her. She peered under the cream painted doors, making sure the space was her own. For added privacy, she stepped into a stall and slid the lock closed.

If I spontaneously combust I won't have to do any of this. No speaking to news crews. No facing Big Elk. No fighting to come up with money to fund an expensive snow making operation. And no finding out why Scott didn't show up today.

She braced her arm against the door and dropped her chin to her chest, letting coppery hair curtain her face. The court's decision was a victory. She deserved to relish the achievement, damn it. *Go ahead. Relish.*

A hand shot under the stall door, driving at her ankle. A glint of metal flashed. Nora leapt back instinctively, slammed her calf into the stool, lost her footing, and fell against the toilet seat. *Good God, was that a knife?*

Rage fueled her scream. "Hey! Stop!" She heard the door thump closed. She fumbled with the stupid metal lock on the stall. This weapon-wielding psychopath was getting away and her fingers acted like water balloons. Finally released, she lunged toward the bathroom door and burst into the lobby panting.

People in the lobby closest to her stared at her abrupt entrance. Raymond boomed midway across the space. "And here she is."

Her eyes darted to dark corners and the busy hallway. He couldn't disappear, not in this crowd. Blank expressions met her glance.

A hand rested on her arm. "Miss."

Nora launched to the ceiling.

"Missus."

Ready to waylay her attacker, she turned to find a withered slip of a Native American gazing up at her with the darkest eyes she'd ever seen. Come to think of it, his soft voice sounded more tentative than deadly. Deep wrinkles lined his face like wadded parchment and skin sagged around his eyes. He must be a hundred years old.

This had to be an elder, still embracing the traditional ways. He probably lived in a pueblo with no modern conveniences and spurred younger people to protest snow making. He looked too frail to be the bathroom knife-sniper, but he could have encouraged someone else to attack. The threats and insults of the past months had taken their toll, and trust wasn't something in Nora's backpack anymore.

She pulled her arm away.

"Missus. I brought you my kachinas." Though barely reaching her ears, his voice held a strange combination of sadness and strength. He pulled a dusty canvas bag off his shoulder and reached inside.

A kachina salesman? He wore a long, threadbare tunic and what appeared to be ancient leggings and moccasins that reached to his knees. He could easily fade into the desert with his beiges, browns, and deeply tanned skin, except he wore a bright blue sash around his tunic. The old guy must be poor and desperate. Her heart thawed a bit. Nora understood desperate. Her checking account contained fourteen dollars and

Kachina Ski was so far in the hole she'd need carabiners and ropes to get to the surface.

She slid her hand into her pocket for her last twenty. The one her mother tucked into personally embossed stationery with the admonition to take herself for a nice cup of coffee after the hearing. Nora hoped to use it for lunch with Scott, to celebrate their court victory and new beginnings.

She sighed. Bravo for the court victory. Too bad Scott wasn't really on board with the new beginnings part. "I don't want a kachina, but take this."

The little man avoided her money and shoved a small wooden doll into her hand. In an accented voice shaky with age, he said. "Not for sale. For you. For the moun-ain."

She looked down. With its slit eyes and plug nose, the masked face of the doll looked creepy. The doll wore a tunic, the same blue fabric as the sash of the old man. He held a hatchet in one hand, feathers in another.

Raymond startled her with a whack on her back. "It's showtime."

Nora looked up to return the kachina doll, but the little man was gone. She searched the crowd for sign of his thick, black hair like a bowl he tied to his head with a weathered red strip of fabric. He'd disappeared. First the apparition in the woods, then the phantom bathroom stabber, and now a harmless kachina salesman. No doubt she was headed for the loony bin.

"Big Elk's got the crowd all fired up. You gotta get out there and have your say or the media will take his side."

Ben Hur's chariot race couldn't thunder louder than the thoughts in her head. Where the hell was Scott? Kachina Ski was his business, too.

Her slick dress shoes offered no traction to fight Raymond as he propelled her toward certain doom.

Raymond inspected her. "You didn't put on lipstick. And what happened to your ankle?"

Nora followed his gaze and was surprised by the thin line of blood oozing from the slash just above her ankle bone. She felt the sting for the first time.

"Ms. Abbott," a voice spoke with unquestioning authority, drawing her attention. With the confident air of success and an impeccable

Western suit and ostrich-skin cowboy boots, Barrett McCreary looked every bit the part he played of an international icon in the energy business.

Raymond clucked like a hen, pulled a handkerchief from his pocket and bent to dab at the sliver of blood on her ankle.

Already breathless, Nora was now tongue-tied. In business school, she'd written a paper on McCreary Energy and its owner. Barrett McCreary was her ideal role model: a tycoon with an environmental conscience.

He held out his hand. Raymond elbowed Nora. She transferred the kachina and crumpled twenty to her left hand, wiped her sweaty palm on her dress, and grasped Barrett's hand.

"I'm Barrett McCreary. Congratulations on your victory."

Through the rush of blood in her head, she managed not to stammer or choke. "Thank you."

The sandy-haired man she'd bumped into earlier advanced on Barrett as he moved away from her. She'd read in the paper that Barrett intended to resurrect uranium mining in the area, and she was somewhat grateful for the diversion. Now the enviros would have their pick of causes to attack.

Raymond tugged Nora toward the door as she tried to invoke Barrett's spirit of confidence. She stepped through the courthouse door...

And the confidence evaporated. Nora fought the urge to dive back into the courtroom and slide under a table. The blast of high altitude sunshine didn't blind her to the crowd gathered in the courthouse plaza. Sure, it was Flagstaff, so the plaza wasn't large and it didn't take a lot of people to fill it, but a hundred angry protesters increased the churning in Nora's gut by two hundred fold. The tire-slasher, the rock thrower, and probably the ankle-slitter loomed somewhere in the crowd.

A voice issued from a bullhorn with nauseating familiarity. Big Elk. He stood on the steps, his back to her, screeching to the angry mob. "Kachina Ski will pump 1.5 million gallons of water per day during the ski season. That's the blood of our Mother splattered on the ground."

The crowd was mostly young natives, eager for Big Elk's speech. A few gray heads dotted the bunch. Nora called them the Guilty White People. They followed Big Elk around the country, living off their trust funds and trying to make up for their ancestors' exploiting the indigenous people of the world.

She needed her husband now; she shouldn't have to do this alone. Where was Scott? A trickle of sweat rounded the small of her back.

Big Elk's beak-like nose rubbed on the horn as he spewed vitriol. "It's regrettable that the courts place profitability of a playground over the deeply held religious and cultural convictions of hundreds of thousands of indigenous peoples."

Where was that spontaneous combustion?

Since she couldn't attain incendiary suicide, she took a deep breath. It didn't calm her. She squeezed sweaty palms around the crude doll and twenty dollars.

Raymond gave her a gentle shove. "You've done tougher stints than this. Go get 'em, Tiger."

Nora's blood pressure spiked another twenty points as she readied to thwart Big Elk.

With his skin looking more sunburned than Native red, Big Elk squawked like an injured chicken. "Why is there global warming? Why 9/11 and the hurricanes, tsunamis, floods, earthquakes? Because we are allowing our sacred mountain to be desecrated. The mountain is home to the kachinas. We must protect their sacred place." His limp gray ponytail whipped side to side when he raised a fist and started a chant.

Many of the people shouted their agreement.

I can't listen to another plea to keep Mother Earth cloaked in her burkha and hidden from the modern world. Nora loved her mountain as much as any Native and would never do anything to harm it. Spraying water meant an end to its suffering from drought and a return to biodiversity. The runoff would eventually filter back into the underground aquifer so there would be very little net loss to the water table. She'd vowed to fight for her mountain when Kachina Ski became hers. She couldn't back down now.

Like the Leonard Bernstein of activist rallies, Big Elk conducted the crowd to a crescendo. "The courts gave her permission to destroy the home of the kachinas but there is a higher judge. We must fight for the kachinas of the mountain."

Raymond nudged her. "You need to make a move here."

Now that Big Elk whetted the crowd's bloodlust, she was supposed to speak reason? Right. Nora couldn't present an argument to Native Americans and enviros who thought today's decision was akin to granting her legal right to blow up the Washington Monument. She'd be lucky if they didn't shoot her full of arrows.

She needed a savior but Scott riding in on his white stallion to save her seemed about as likely as the sky opening up and ending the drought. Nora took a deep breath. *Be Barrett.*

She marched straight to Big Elk. If her legs trembled, she didn't acknowledge it; if her heart hammered, she ignored that too. No one needed to know her fear loomed so large she barely kept from peeing her pants. With her head erect, she called forth the dignity and poise of her mother, Abigail.

Ignoring Big Elk's murderous glare, she stepped in front of him and noticed for the first time that he stood several inches shorter than her five seven. No wonder he had the vicious bark of a little dog. She shouted, "Thank you, Mr. Big Elk."

She had testified in the courts, given interviews for the media, put her money and life on the line for this. She could certainly overcome fear of public speaking. "I'm Nora Abbott, owner and manager of Kachina Ski."

Boos and hisses.

"How would you like it if I pissed in your church?" someone yelled at her. Nothing new. Tainted water on a holy site. The analogy made sense to them.

People shouted in a jumble of heat and temper.

"Go back to your white world and leave us alone!"

Two cops in uniform stood at the back of the crowd. They looked alert and focused on the steps.

More people joined in the insults and soon distinct words disintegrated into swelling outrage.

Was it her imagination or did the crowd inch up on her?

They'd settle down and act civilized any minute now. Sun penetrated her skin, singeing her insides. Up on her mountain it would be cool with a slight breeze, the pines letting off their summer tang.

Just then Scott rounded the corner of the courthouse plaza, his dark curls as reassuring as a troop flag. Her cavalry of one. Nora nearly collapsed with relief.

A tall Native American with blue-black hair down to his waist stepped forward, his blazing eyes scorching her. "Get the hell out of our sacred places."

The cops waded through the knot of protesters in slow motion. Others jeered and shouted in a confusion of voices.

Scott wasn't even looking her way now. Nora's courage dissolved like a tiny levy in a big flood. Instead of cutting through the crowd like a knight on his charger, Scott hurried in the wrong direction toward someone else.

Barrett McCreary? The older man strode away from the courthouse. Scott bee-lined for him, an uncharacteristic frown marring his mischievous face.

The scene around her deteriorated as her eyes came back to the people in front of her. The livid young man climbed a step, his face like the fires of hell. "You can pack up and leave on your own or not, but you will leave."

Others stepped up, and Nora's fear shot from her heart and climbed her throat. What had she planned to say?

The man climbed again, and a pretty girl followed. His teeth looked like the fangs of a wolf, ready to shred her flesh. "You don't belong on the mountain."

The cries from the crowd grew even louder now. "Save our Peaks!" "Don't desecrate the sacred Mother!" "You don't belong here!" Eyes full of vengeance, mouths opened in escalating rage, they shouted at her.

And Scott was off on his own mission. Cops only halfway to the steps. No help in sight.

The young girl's pretty eyes shone with excitement and she placed her hand on the angry young man's muscled shoulder.

He looked ready to tear out her jugular with his hands.

Nora backed up, panicked and frozen in place.

The guy leapt up the last step and advanced on her. "This mountain was given to us to keep sacred for the whole world."

The girl jumped up on the step, close behind him.

Nora took another step back and bumped into the courthouse wall.

The cops couldn't get to her in time. More people pushed toward her, forming a wall of bodies that blocked her from sight. Scott couldn't see her now even if he looked.

Malevolence shooting from his eyes, the tall Native American pulled something from his pocket. Impossible against the riotous clatter of the surging crowd, Nora heard the *swisht* of a blade jumping from a handle.

—

3

Barrett McCreary III slid his Serengeti sunglasses over his nose, cutting the glare from the plaza. Too damn bad the glasses couldn't hide the sight of Big Elk and his rant.

"Barrett."

Shit. Another idiot holding him up.

Cole Huntsman. For a smart man, an expert on uranium mining, he sure dressed like an illiterate granola. Cole pushed his shaggy pale hair from his forehead. "I found that study on the in situ mining in Canada you asked me about."

"It hasn't been five minutes since we spoke."

Cole held up one of those fancy phones that could contact the moon and download an encyclopedia, if anyone knew how to use an encyclopedia anymore. "I emailed it to you."

Even if he looked like a tree-hugger, this guy impressed Barrett. He was smart, efficient, and not one to waste Barrett's time. "Nice work."

A woman's voice sounded from the courthouse steps, startling Barrett with its clarity. Across the courtyard, Nora Abbott stood on the steps, looking remarkably cool for the mess she'd put herself in. Both Barrett and Cole focused on her addressing the hostile crowd. That coppery hair and bright eyes made her cute as a penny but she had to be smart, too, to keep that ski area running through this drought. She should know better than to throw herself in front of that mob.

That was not his problem. He hurried across the plaza while Cole was distracted. Barrett wanted nothing more than to get home, shed this stupid suit and tie and get down to business. With the congressional hearings on uranium mining set for next week, there were palms to grease, weight to sling around, and dirt to dig.

He hadn't been quick enough. Around the corner popped Scott Abbott. Just who he didn't want to see. And certainly not in public.

"I need to talk to you," Scott said.

"Not here."

Crowd clatter rose from the platform.

"Tomorrow, then. On the mountain," Scott said.

"Six a.m. There shouldn't be anyone on the trail that early."

Scott squinted toward the noisy courthouse. His eyes widened when he saw his wife and without another word to Barrett he elbowed his way into the crowd.

Barrett didn't want to wait around for the finale. Big Elk had succeeded in his typical mischief. The brothers and sisters to the moon and sun were storming the steps. Par for Big Elk's course.

Wait.

He spun toward the steps.

It was her.

How could she be standing there? A train wreck of memory slammed into his gut in an explosion of excruciating pain followed by an arctic paralysis. His mind spun back forty years. He saw the woman he loved smiling at him, her shining black hair and turquoise necklace catching the sun and tossing it back for everyone's delight.

Ester.

He sucked in air, fighting for reality. Ester, in her velvet skirt, silver earrings, Concho belt...

But this girl on the steps wore jeans. No turquoise and silver glinted.

Ester would never set foot in this plaza or anywhere else again.

Slowly it started to make sense. The girl amid the mob advancing on Nora Abbott was his Heather. He didn't know the black-haired delinquent she followed, but he would find out. No Native American jerk-off, angry at the world and looking for a hand-out, was going to get near his Heather. The boy would disappear from Heather's life.

And that damned Scott Abbott needed to disappear, too. All in a day's work for Barrett.

He was a virtual magician when it came to vanishing people.

4

His hand shot out, the blade aimed for Nora's belly.

She lost her balance. One foot slid and she crashed to her knees. It saved her from that thrust but she had no hope of avoiding the next.

She squeezed her eyes closed, expecting the burn of flesh as the knife sliced between her ribs into her lungs. Instead of the pain of the blade stabbing through her skin, a hand closed around her wrist and jerked her to her feet. She opened her eyes and looked into the face of the enviro who'd knocked her in the hall and accosted Barrett McCreary. Probably some Earth Firster who would turn her over to Big Elk and his henchmen.

He shoved her behind his back and faced outward. "Back off!" he yelled at the crowd.

The cops finally infiltrated the mob and shouted orders to move back. The slasher was nowhere in sight. He vanished from the courthouse steps as completely as he had from the bathroom. Hate-filled faces glared at her, still thirsty for blood.

The enviro pulled her through a break in the crowd and down the steps. They ran across the street and she stumbled on the curb, reaching for his arm.

The kachina doll splashed into the gutter and her twenty dollar bill fluttered away on a breeze. Nora's fingers clutched at the sudden emptiness in her hand. Losing her last twenty stung, but seeing the kachina, its mask broken and floating in the filth of the gutter punched a hole in her heart. Even if she didn't believe in its supernatural powers, the old man probably carved his heart into the doll and it felt wrong to abandon it. She pulled against the enviro, determined to save the kachina.

He closed his hand around hers and dragged her down the street into a parking lot. He gently pushed her into the shade next to a building and stood in front of her. "Are you okay?"

If okay meant terrified, shaken, and mad enough to spit bullets, then yes, she felt dandy. She nodded, trying to catch her breath.

He studied her and bent down to wipe the line of blood from her ankle with the cuff of his sleeve. He stood. "I'm Cole Huntsman."

From murder attempt to garden party introductions in a matter of seconds. The day added weird onto bizarre. Oh well, the impeccable manners she was raised with surfaced. "I'm Nora."

"Hey!" Scott shouted.

Cole swung around, stepping in front of Nora.

Scott strode up to him. "Who are you?"

Of course Scott would be protective against a stranger. Nora hurried to explain. "He helped me get away."

Scott didn't look pleased but he wouldn't start swinging. "Well, thanks. But I was on my way."

"Cole, this is my husband, Scott Abbott."

Cole squinted as if assessing. "Scott Abbott." He stood in awkward silence for a moment then said, "Well, you don't need me hanging around here so...." Cole started to walk away.

Nora jumped forward. "Wait."

A smile, more in his eyes than on his lips, lit Cole's face.

"I just wanted to say thanks."

He put a finger to his forehead as if tipping his hat, a boyish grin spread across his face. "Good to meet you, Nora." He strode out of the parking lot and around the corner.

Nora switched her attention to Scott, eager to feel the safety of his arms around her. He'd come for her. Late, but he was here now.

Scott's eyes flashed with anger. "Have you had enough, yet?"

She'd expected support and his reaction smacked her upside the head. Scott's anger burned against her again. And once again, her struggle to please him backfired. She masked her hurt. "As a matter of fact, I have. Enough of struggling to make Kachina Ski earn a living in a drought. Enough of religious freaks and rabid environmentalists and Crazy Horse wannabes sticking their nose in my business. And I've really had enough of you acting like I'm the devil."

His face didn't soften. "Then walk away from it."

Scott might as well suggest they buy a ranch on Mars. "I didn't want to run a ski area. But we're in it now. We can't just give up."

He shrugged. "I thought it would be a fun."

When she'd been offered Kachina Ski she wanted to turn it down. But he practically begged her, promising they'd do it together. The picture he painted of growing a fruitful business together and raising children free to roam the mountain had faded with the drought. "When we have reliable snow it will be fun," she said.

He frowned. "We have no right to alter the natural environment for profit."

What? Mutiny now they'd just won their victory? He had been on board with the fight for snowmaking in the beginning. She opened her mouth to remind him of the drought relief snowmaking would bring to the mountain. She closed it. It didn't matter what the issue, he never agreed with her anymore. He never laughed with her. She couldn't remember the last time he even kissed her.

The stress of the ski business killed their hope. The drought not only sucked the land dry, but her energy and resources as well. If she could get a good year or two, pay down the debt, ease up the pressure on them both, they'd be okay together. Maybe they'd slow down enough to have a baby. Making snow meant making money and that meant saving their marriage.

"When we started this fight you were all for doing whatever it took to keep Kachina alive. What's changed?"

His eyes darted away from hers. "Things."

Controlling her impatience was like trying to keep a tree upright after they'd yelled "Timber!" "You said you thought snow making was a good idea."

Scott shook his head. "That was before."

"Before what?"

He shifted from one foot to another. "You wouldn't believe me if I told you."

Sudden tears burned. He used to tell her everything. She remembered sitting in a mountain meadow, their packs discarded under a tree. They held hands and Scott told her how he never loved anyone as he loved her. When he laid her down with her back against their mountain and the sun in her eyes, it felt to her that their souls joined in their lovemaking. Now she struggled to get him to talk about his day.

"When have I ever not believed you?" she said.

"Since you stopped believing in anything except cash flows and lines of credit."

A nice one-two to the heart. "Kachina Ski won't run itself."

He glared at her. "See what I mean?"

Idiot. She always said the wrong thing. "I'm sorry. What changed your mind about snowmaking?"

"You won't get it."

"I want to get it. Tell me."

He leaned against the building. "Okay. Up on the mountain yesterday when I ran the Ponderosa trail, about four miles into it, near the summit..." He paused as if reluctant to go on.

She and Scott used to run the trails together. Now, walking Abbey from the lodge down to Mountain Village constituted a big outing.

Scott started again. "I saw something blue in the trees and I stopped to get a better look."

Chills vibrated down her spine.

"It was a guy. I mean, he had arms and legs. He was all decked out in some kind of costume and had a mask. He had a blue sash and held feathers and a hatchet."

Like her kachina, the one broken and abandoned in the gutter, or the guy she didn't see in the forest. A hard pit formed in her stomach. "Maybe you caught a Native American in the middle of a ceremony."

"Yeah, that's what I thought. But I got the feeling he was expecting me."

She ignored the hairs that stood on her neck.

A thin sheen of perspiration formed above his lip. “It was like the whole forest stopped moving and held its breath.”

“What happened?”

“I started walking toward him and he raised his hatchet.” Scott’s eyes lost focus. “He didn’t say anything. But I felt that he was warning me.”

“Warning you?”

“He was telling me not to make snow.”

Her willing belief lost its suspension and crashed to the ground. “What happened then?”

“I took another step toward him and he ran away. I chased him and he darted behind a tree and then... he was gone.”

“Gone?”

“Yeah. Vanished. Like he was never there. I searched all over but never found a trace of him.”

“Let me understand this. Some guy dressed in a kachina outfit met you on the trail and you got the feeling he was giving you a message from Native American mythical gods to sabotage your means of livelihood.”

His face closed up.

“And you believe this?” She cringed at the incredulous tone of her own voice.

“See? That’s why I didn’t tell you.”

“Why, because I have a firm grip on reality? Because I have some perspective?”

His eyebrows drew together. “Because everything for you is black and white.”

“The only reason you can give me for ruining our chance at success is a phantom visit from a mythological spirit?”

His ears turned red, a sure sign he was losing his temper. “If you insist on snowmaking something bad is going to happen.”

“Why are you suddenly so against snowmaking?”

He bristled. “I told you why.” He stared at her a moment. "But there is something else.”

Her teeth clenched so tight against a retort her jaws hurt. “What else?”

"If you don't believe the kachina, why should I bother you with anything else?"

"What else?"

"It's best if you don't know."

Gut wrenching dismissal. "Or what? You'll have to kill me?"

He looked worried. "Just don't make snow, okay?"

Nora ached to give Scott everything he wanted and she would, as soon as they started making money. "It's our only chance at survival." She wasn't talking about the business.

"Then I'm outta here." He spun around and took off.

She agreed to Kachina because he wanted it and fought four years to make it work. All for Scott, to somehow make him happy enough he wouldn't leave her. She even forgave him for what he did two years ago. She couldn't let her marriage end in a parking lot. "Wait!"

When she burst around the corner onto the sidewalk Big Elk and his usual knot of devoted stared at her from across the street. Cole stood between her and Big Elk's contingent with his arms crossed. She and Scott were afternoon street entertainment like the noon shoot-out reenactment in Tombstone.

She couldn't worry about that now. "Scott! What did you mean?"

He turned around. "I mean I'm done. Finished. Through with Kachina and through with you."

She negotiated and worked deals in business, fought daunting court battles and created business plans to make Donald Trump weep. But Scott always managed to have the upper hand with her. She wouldn't beg. Couldn't let herself. "Please, Scott." *Damn it, have some pride.* "Don't go."

Thank goodness her mother, Abigail, still lived. If not, there would be major grave-rolling-over at this Jerry Springer Road Show.

His gaze made her feel like a hairy spider crawling across the kitchen floor. "You're strong. You don't need me." No more shouting and red ears, just a disgusted shake of his head as he turned.

She watched his back retreating down the sidewalk, her heart dragging on the pavement behind him.

5

Barrett McCreary III did not like mountain hikes. But he'd learned early to do whatever it took to keep his family and McCreary Energy safe. If that meant meeting this earth muffin in secret on a mountain, then he'd do it.

While they climbed he let Scott yammer about protecting the environment and people's health, as if the bonehead knew anything about saving people. Life, liberty and the pursuit of happiness probably came next on Scott's list of talking points.

Barrett was beyond happiness and pursuing it for himself would be a waste of time.

Scott strode along the trail ahead of Barrett. "I appreciate you meeting me."

Barrett thought about swattting the back of Scott's head. "You said you wanted to talk about ground water on the Hopi reservation."

Scott stopped and waited for Barrett. "Did you know this mountain is sacred to fourteen tribes?"

I even know why. Barrett stepped around Scott and kept walking.

Past sixty and overweight, Barrett's main exercise consisted of riding his champion quarter horses on his ranch. His monthly hiking meetings with Scott over-stretched his patience as well as his stamina.

Scott followed closely on Barrett's heels. "You read the last report, right?"

The trail rounded a curve and Barrett saw what he looked for, a sheer drop on the side away from the cliff. A boulder field bottomed on jagged lava rock 100 feet down.

Barrett struggled to get his air. Flagstaff sat at 7,000 feet above sea level. They must be a good 10,000 feet on this mountain. That left little oxygen. He hated the sweat dripping down his jowls and couldn't wait to get back to a shower and wash the slick film covering his body.

Scott's breath sounded soft as a sigh. "We need to go public with this information right away."

Barrett saved his limited air.

"I know something this big will impact McCreary Energy."

Impact it? You cretin, it would destroy it.

Scott fidgeted, as if unsure what to do next.

Barrett leaned against the cliff wall.

Scott stared at him, voice incredulous. "You aren't going to do anything about it?"

"Why yes. You're lovely wife is going to make snow on Kachina Mountain."

Scott shook his head. "That's not cool.

Barrett pushed away from the cliff wall and took a step forward. "Making snow is good for business. Making snow will eliminate our little problem. Everyone is happy."

Scott looked wounded and stumbled back a step. "I thought...."

Barrett narrowed his eyes. "What evidence do you have about this?"

Scott gazed toward the distant meadow hundreds of feet down. "I submitted the well logs to you. You wouldn't hide that, would you?"

"Did you make copies?"

"You can't cover this up." A spark of panic lit Scott's eyes. As Barrett suspected, Scott was too much of a dolt to keep copies.

Barrett took another step toward Scott. "The problem is being taken care of."

About now Scott probably regretted trusting Barrett and not making copies. He glanced down the trail, no doubt searching for escape. "Pumping water on the peaks is no solution."

Barrett hadn't wanted it to come to this but the moron left him no choice. He might be old and out of shape but his extra weight wouldn't hinder him now. Without another word, Barrett lurched toward Scott and slammed into the fool, launching him over the edge. Barrett walked to the edge of the cliff.

The granola cruncher had been paid well to keep his mouth shut and up until now, hadn't had any temptation to open it and spoil his good deal. The only person who might know about this was his wife and if she spoke up, the whole snowmaking deal would be off. She struck Barrett as too smart to let that happen.

Barrett glanced over the side of the cliff.

Not much blood, but the angle of the neck proved just how dangerous it was to cross Barrett McCreary III.

—

6

Nora stood on the wide lodge porch and gazed across the empty expanse of the ski run. So few summer mornings to savor on her mountain, and this one withered away in worry, meetings, balance sheets and business plans.

Abbey trotted up the lodge steps, tongue lolling.

Nora scratched his ears. "You don't care if the bank is skeptical about snowmaking and Scott walked out. As long as there is a rabbit on this mountain and food in your dish, you're content."

He slopped in his tongue, wagged his tail and sat to survey his mountain.

Her restless night alone pounded in fatigue behind her eyes. With her closest neighbors in Mountain Village, nestled three miles down the winding road at the base of the mountain, Nora felt isolated at the lodge. She'd jumped at every noise, afraid Big Elk or Knife Guy would come back to finish her off. Hoping maybe Scott would return.

The nip of pine wafted in the air and the sun filtered through the branches creating a camouflage of cheer on the grass. Normally, the fiery penstemon, the violet flax and sunny cinquefoil made her heart light. Today, she forced appreciation for the beauty of her mountain.

She stared at the rocky, red dirt parking lot about 200 feet down a path from the lodge. She imagined snow piled on the periphery and happy people shrugging into ski togs. She loved those days. Everyone excited and busy, laughter chasing around the mountain. Unfortunately, too many days the parking lot sat dry and empty.

Nora allowed herself memories of early morning skiing with Scott. They often checked the slopes before allowing skiers on the runs. Sharing the thrill of their mountain, the morning run felt as intimate as lovemaking.

Enough emotional torture, business beckoned. This morning's meeting in town with her banker yielded mixed results. Despite her impressive charts and projections and armed with the court's decision, her banker considered her already sizeable operating loan and the refinanced business loan. Kachina Ski's lifeline showed minimal activity. But making snow would not only speed recovery, it would guarantee robust health far into the future. At least, that's what Nora told the banker.

In the end, the banker offered enough to pay for initial construction of the snowmaking equipment, providing she came up with investors to furnish the remaining capital.

Set my hair on fire, pull my toenails out with pliers, bury me to my neck in hot sand, but don't make me call Abigail for money.

For the thousandth time since dawn, Nora scanned the forest behind the lodge. Scott might traipse back after camping in the forest. It wouldn't be the first time he appeared after a night away and they went along as usual with no mention of the argument.

A ridiculous notion. Failure of their marriage had threatened for months, maybe years. Despite all their efforts, they'd never really recovered from... her mind automatically shifted away.

A flash of bright blue drew her attention deep into the forest. Scott? But then, it might be Knife Guy, back to finish her off. Isolated out here, he wouldn't have to wait for the cover of darkness. A fat, mean blue jay flew from the forest

Logic did nothing to stop the electric flash of nerves.

A crash behind her sent another zing of fire through her chest. Abbey barked. Nora spun, and fell against the railing, arms up, ready to defend against Knife Guy.

She drew in a breath, probably her last. A figure lurched from the gloomy lodge.

Oh. She slowly exhaled, allowing the panic to dissolve. This heart fibrillation needed to stop or she'd keel over dead.

Charlie, gray-haired hippy, survivor of the summer of love and whatever Jesus freak, earth-loving, peacenik movements surged in the old days, stood in front of the screen door he'd let bang closed. His rusty voice brought his usual good cheer. "You are beauty and grace and give me reason to live."

Viva normalcy—at least Charlie's version. "I'm here just for you," she said.

Pabst Blue Ribbon beer can clutched in his hand, Charlie made his way to her, Abbey dancing at his feet. His grizzled face wore his usual grin and his faded eyes crinkled with affection. "I heard what happened in town yesterday. You ought to keep the back door of the lodge locked."

"I thought it was locked." Her inadvertent vulnerability shocked her.

Though they called the rambling building a lodge, it resembled an insulated barn with a few dividing walls to separate the small snack bar, rental and locker area, and her office. On snow days crowds packed the small place, making it hot and stuffy. The rest of the time it echoed and a constant chill filled the air. With a dependable snow supply, they could expand. Why not build a restaurant and get a liquor license? Possibilities and plans sprinted against her worry.

"Might think about getting a gun, too." Charlie lived in Mountain Village, edged up to the forest, probably born of the pine needles and cinders after the last volcano erupted. He stopped in with his beer to visit Nora a couple of times a week then headed up one trail or another to perpetrate his brand of eco-terrorism.

"What's the good news today, Ranger?" Nora asked her usual question.

Charlie gulped his beer and gave his expected response. "Looks like rain." Charlie hung teapots, kettles, coffee cups and water buckets in a tree in front of his house to encouraged rain.

"A gully washer."

He guffawed. "I like an optimist."

With his unflappable attitude and his quirky outlook, Charlie often felt like her only ally. Even if he objected to snowmaking, he never argued with her about it. She felt slightly uncomfortable that he spent his days dragging logs across trails to thwart the wheels of hated motorized vehicles in his forest. But he did give up stringing cable from tree to tree when he nearly decapitated a dirt biker and ended up with a month's jail time.

He reached into a pocket of the oversized army jacket he always wore, probably the one issued to him in Viet Nam, and pulled out another PBR. "Care for a beverage?"

Nora laughed. "That stuff tastes like gasoline."

He popped the top and took a swig. "Coming from anyone else, I'd say that was an elitist comment made by an exclusionary capitalist out to exploit the underclass. A real Barrett McCreary."

"I wouldn't mind being compared to Barrett McCreary."

Charlie shook his head. "Child, you don't know what you're saying."

Charlie tipped his head back and drained his PBR in one long chug. He crushed the can and slipped it into a pocket. "Got work to do. You be careful and lock that door."

Abbey, tail wagging, joined Charlie and they ambled across the grass, disappearing in the forest. Nora wandered into the dark lodge. She checked the back door. No wonder Charlie walked right in. Scott must have broken the mechanism and forgot to tell her. She needed to rework her revenue projections and then she'd head back to town for repairs. No way did she want to spend a night here without sturdy locks.

The sound of a chair scraping over the floor startled her. Her head whipped around and she searched the vast darkness. "Who's there? Charlie?" Her pulse pounded in her ears, blocking any other sound. Movement next to the white stone fireplace caught her eyes.

"If you're one of those activists, you'd better get off my property." She stepped toward the door. "I'm calling the police." Another step. No replies. Maybe her overloaded mind blew a fuse and nobody was really there. She hurried toward the door anyway. In the dim lodge her eyes strayed to a hulking shadow jutting from the wall. Breath caught in her throat.

Knife Guy glared at her from behind the rental counter.

No debate between fight and flight. She took off for the screen door.

Nora barely cleared the rental counter when a brick wall slammed into her back, sending her crashing to the floor in a crush between concrete and two hundred pounds of lean, murderous Indian.

Fingers raked her head and grabbed a handful of hair. He jerked her around and pounded her down, the back of her head cracking on the floor. Fissures of pain blinded her. He straddled her chest, letting only the barest stream of air into her lungs, hatred shooting from his eyes. "You won't destroy our sacred moun-ain." His words slinked between clenched teeth.

She struggled for breath. "I..."

His hand smashed into the side of her face, grating her cheeks and tongue against her teeth. Agony exploded through her temple and a copper wave of blood filled her mouth.

"Shut up."

His hands wrapped around her throat, squeezing as if her neck were nothing more than a wash rag. Rage turned his dark face into a mask of destruction, eyes glinting with absolute power.

She kicked for her life, fought to buck him off, struggled to shake her head. She barely moved, despite adrenaline pumping through her. Impossible that death could find her so easily. It shouldn't happen this effortlessly. Someone shouldn't simply walk in the door and kill her. No preamble, no preparation. Hardly any struggle. Dead.

Pain. Real, excruciating, burning her lungs as they dried up, turning in on themselves, begging for air. Blackness seeped into her vision, closing in, shuttering life. Her arms dropped to the floor; her body no longer obeyed her dying brain. The twisted face hovering over hers faded into darkness. This was it.

Death brought instant relief. The weight on her chest disappeared. It felt as if air actually raked against her raw throat. There shouldn't be pain in death, right? Great gulps sent coughs scraping delicate tissue. She wasn't dead! But Knife Guy wasn't on top of her.

Black receded from her eyes and sound returned in the form of grunts and pounding flesh. Two men grappled on the floor next to her. Knife Guy, larger and heavier, took a fist to his face. The other man moved with grace and agility, planting another blow and another.

Knife Guy shoved the thinner man off balance and settled himself in an attack stance. And there it was. The knife appeared and the blade emerged with a *schwit*.

Jump, scream, or at least run. She could do nothing more than wallow as though buried in tar. The man, her savior, jumped to his feet. Cole Huntsman crouched, his eyes burning into the attacker's, calculating, calling him on.

The heart-stuttering siren of an emergency vehicle sliced through the air.

Knife Guy hesitated only a second then bounded past Cole and out the screen door.

Before the door banged closed Cole knelt beside Nora. "Are you okay?" He put an arm under her shoulders and helped her sit.

She swallowed fire. Her voice sounded raspy and weak. "Yes. No."

"Can you stand?" She nodded and he pulled her to her feet.

Her core shook, radiating out to her arms and legs. She leaned on Cole. "He's gone?"

"The siren saved us. Our odds took a bad turn when he pulled the knife." He took her weight and helped her toward a bench.

Sirens. Police? Ambulance? Charlie. How long since he left her, minutes, a half hour? He might have been careless, fallen and broken a leg or crushed a foot with a heavy log.

Who else? Scott always teased Nora for over reacting. A hiker probably twisted a knee or something.

Cole lowered Nora to sit. "Where is your husband? You shouldn't be out here alone."

But she wasn't alone. Cole was here. A dangerous environmental activist. Her heart accelerated again. Fear made for a terrific aerobic workout. She glanced at the door, wondering if she could get outside before he caught her. Cole Huntsman couldn't be any more pleased with her making snow than Knife Guy. "What are you doing here?"

He looked startled at her accusing tone. "Well," his Western drawl sounded as if he just stepped in from the range. Even in the dim light she saw a blush creeping into his cheeks. "I couldn't help but notice that things didn't go that great between you and your husband yesterday. I don't mean to butt in but I just wanted to check to make sure you were all right."

Likely story. He and Big Elk had to be in cahoots and he was taking the "good cop" role. Maybe he came to Flagstaff to stop Barrett's uranium mining—why else would he be hounding Barrett—but he'd obviously joined Big Elk's camp. Still, he saved her life.

Her life. Her throat and neck ached with bruises inside and out and her tremors intensified. She nearly died. And the man who wanted her dead lurked out there somewhere.

Cole's hand rested on her shoulder and rubbed slowly across her back. "Let's get you into the sunshine."

Good guy/bad guy. Right now, Cole was the only guy. He'd kept her alive so far. She let him help her stand and stagger to the deck. As soon as possible she ducked from his supporting arm.

The lodge squatted halfway up the mountain. Two short flights of wide metal stairs led from the ground to the deck. Five giant picnic tables spread out on the expansive redwood platform that faced the lift. Nora and Scott's tiny apartment sat on the second story, accessed by a steep outside stairway climbing on the front of the lodge.

A police cruiser pulled into the parking lot and stopped.

Someone called the cops? How did they know about the attack? Odd they showed up so quickly.

She and Cole watched as the cop walked up the path and clumped up the stairs. Nora recognized him as the same officer who investigated her slashed tires and the broken shed window. Gary Something or Other.

Gary glanced at Cole then settled his focus on Nora.

"Hi, Nora," Gary looked down at his shoes then up at her again. "I'm afraid I have some bad news."

It suddenly dawned on her this wasn't about the attack. The ambulance. Charlie.

"We just brought Scott down."

"Scott?"

"I'm sorry," he said.

Scott? Brought him down? Down from where? The ambulance. Not in town but on the mountain. Scott.

Her eyes lifted to a hint of red glow through the trees. Scott was there.

Her husband had been hurt on the mountain. He needed her. She sprinted past Cole and hit the stairs two at a time.

Gary called to her but she dashed on. Scott needed her.

The ambulance sat at the trailhead across the road from the parking lot. Its red lights flared off the pines.

"Scott!" Her screams echoed off the mountain.

No, oh no. He's got to be okay. He's fine.

Then she saw it. The gurney. Two people wheeled it toward the back of the ambulance. There was no face. It couldn't be Scott.

No face.

Because it was covered with a sheet.

7

Barrett stood at his office window assessing the view. His home commanded the countryside from atop a hill that looked over an expanse of juniper, scrub and desert. Across the valley the San Francisco Peaks rose in splendor.

The mystery and power of the peaks still had the ability to awe him, despite his years in the sordid energy business. God, how Ester had hated the ski resort. He barely remembered his own disgust in those earlier times. Ester wouldn't understand why he'd had to do what he did to Scott. What happened on the sacred mountain this morning would break her heart, if he hadn't destroyed it forty years ago.

But Ester wasn't here to rail against him. Her sacred kachinas hadn't saved her. He lifted the faded photo and stared at the happy young family. Ester, with her black hair falling over one shoulder to her waist, bent toward their two-year daughter at her feet, his darling Soowi. She stood next to someone who used to be Barrett. He was thin and sunburned with a baby resting on his arm. His son, Manangya. In the photo, Barrett's head tilted back, his mouth open in laughter. He couldn't remember what his daughter said that morning to make them laugh. Just one more thing that haunted him.

The sun slipped below the tallest peak.

Heather skipped down the stairs, the short skirt flipping, a bare strip of brown belly showing. Instead of the usual burst of love and joy at the sight of his daughter, he girded himself for battle. Being a father required more courage, strength and sacrifice than running a multinational energy corporation.

She ran to him and stretched to kiss his cheek. This affection used to be her normal state. Now it was usually sighs and outbursts, tears and slamming doors. There should be an Alcatraz for teenaged girls. You sent them there at thirteen and picked them up when the hormones settled, whenever that might be. In the meantime, a vast moat would protect them from sniffing and groping men.

"I'm meeting some friends in town. I won't be late."

A rock sat in his gullet. "You're not going anywhere."

Quicker than a teenaged boy's orgasm, she whipped toward him, her eyes heating with temper. "Why?"

"Because I said so."

"That's not fair."

Bad start, but he was committed. He motioned for her to enter his office and she flounced in front of him. "I saw you at the courthouse yesterday."

She thrust her chin in challenge. "So?"

Screw it. "You will stay away from Big Elk."

Heather leaned back on his desk and faced him as he dominated the room. She folded her arms, that impenetrable look on her face. She'd never met her, yet Heather's expression matched Ester's. It still took Barrett's breath away. "Do I have your word you won't have anything to do with Big Elk?" He wouldn't bring up Alex Seweingyawma. Barrett had no trouble finding the hoodlum's name, or making sure the cops locked him up.

She stared at him, emotionless except the flash of defiance in her eyes. "You have no right to keep me from my people."

Surprising that his clenched jaw didn't pulverize his molars. "Your people are the McCrearys."

"My *adopted* people." Her nearly black eyes glistened with contempt.

He glared back. "McCreary's don't carry signs and stop economic progress. We don't spout fairy tales of sacred mountains."

Though she assumed an icy attitude, she hadn't established Ester's stamina to hold the calm yet. She broke and shouted. "You bigot! You think your Christian doctrine, the one that says the world was created for you, is the only viable religion on the planet. It's never occurred to you that you were created to protect the planet. That's what Hopi believe. To you, the whole world is here for you to rape and pillage."

Now Barrett had the upper hand. "I know what the Hopi believe. I spent a fair amount of time on the rez. I've even been inside the kivas during certain ceremonies."

She laughed in disbelief. "When were you ever open-minded enough to learn the true Hopi way?"

"I was young once." It sounded cliché even to him.

She narrowed her eyes as if detecting a lie. "Maybe. But you don't get it."

Déjà vu sent a chilly wind over his skin, raising goose bumps. He stood outside their home on Second Mesa, the ancient bricks crumbling beside the newer stone repairs and cinder blocks. Heat radiated from the empty plaza and created a haze across the landscape below the mesa. Sweat drenched his body under his dashiki. His heart broke but he made sure Ester didn't see the fracture.

Ester stood in front of him in a colorful peasant dress he'd bought for her in a Flagstaff boutique. It was one of the few gifts she'd let him buy, always insisting she didn't want anything that cost him mere money. If her heart broke too, she did an equally good job hiding it. She said those same words to him that Heather said. "You don't get it, do you?"

Barrett's heart had pounded in desperation to make Ester understand. As much as she talked about responsibility to her people, the world and respecting the Hopi way, she should know he had a responsibility to his family.

Ester left him sweating on the blazing plaza. Barrett never saw her again. They didn't even tell him when she died.

He couldn't let Heather slip from him like that. "The Hopi are wrong. Their claims to being able to save the human race are nothing but false hope and giant egos. All they amount to is trying to control their youth, ban world progress, and keep the people living in poverty."

"The simple life brings us into balance, let's us focus on what's important."

This, from the iPod princess with the plasma TV, driving a new Toyota SUV and charging gas and lattes on his card. "Ask some of your new Hopi clan how they like living in squalor, not having money for food or clothes and the sorry state of their medical care."

"A spiritual person doesn't need much to be happy."

"A poor person has to be spiritual because that's all he has."

Heather jumped from the desk and started for the door. "If you can't touch it or put a price tag on it you don't believe in it, do you?"

Barrett grabbed her arm and forced her into a chair. "There you are wrong, little girl. Show me where I can touch our heritage and the essence of McCreary. And yet, I believe in family above all else. And show me where I can touch the love I feel for you. Because, Heather, THAT is the most important thing in my life."

She ignored his exposed heart. "Hopi have a special bond with the forces of nature. If we don't pay attention, the world will be out of balance." Heather glared at him. "And then it will end."

Barrett's frustration threatened to break loose. "Hopi are like children. They don't know how to function in the real world and are afraid of it. We, the McCrearys you think are so evil, have been taking care of them for three generations."

Heather's voice rose to a shriek. "Taking care of them? Is that what you call strip mining their coal and pumping water for a coal slurry? And you paid them a pittance."

Acid ate Barrett's stomach and he wondered if he could mainline Rolaids for the next few years. "You call 25 million dollars a pittance? That's what it cost to seal 900 mines. McCreary Energy reseeded thousands of acres."

Heather swiped at her tears. "Yeah. You hauled off the radioactive tailings and boarded up the bad wells and water holes. But Poppy, before you did that, people died."

His heart went dry and cold as the mesa in winter. It continued to beat even so. Just as he still breathed and walked around. He couldn't stop the image of the twinkling brown eyes, the soft skin and baby fat thighs, the gurgle of delight from Daddy's embrace. The son that would never swim in the creek, eat a popsicle, or even go to school. Barrett saw Ester's eyes burning with love and passion the last time they made love.

Barrett drank in the sight of the beautiful girl in front of him, his last chance at redemption. He'd lost everything but her. "You are forbidden to see Big Elk. You will not go up to the Mesas."

Heather pulled her hand back and swung, smacking Barrett on his cheek with such force it snapped his head back.

They stood toe to toe, breathing hard and staring at each other.

Heather's lips peeled back in a snarl. "I hate you."

Even taking into account her teenaged hormones, the words hurt far worse than his stinging cheek. "I love you. More than you can know."

She walked slowly out of the room, leaving the door ajar.

Barrett sank to his desk chair. He felt her tugging at the blood that bound them together.

Keeping Heather safe right now carried urgency, but her long-term security depended on uranium. Individually, the problems didn't amount to much, but each cog had to work or the whole thing would fall apart.

The Congressional committee needed to release the lands they'd temporarily withdrawn. Huntsman had the cred to give convincing testimony but he had a troublesome individual streak. Even if he performed for the committee, he might give Barrett problems later on. He was much smarter than Scott, after all.

Protesters, specifically that loose cannon Charlie Podanski and the troublemaker Big Elk, constantly got in Barrett's way. Barrett would love to smash them but had to tread lightly to keep from creating a public relations debacle. Big Elk was a smarmy fake and Barrett could dispatch him easily enough with cash. Barrett knew Charlie to be relentless and once he got started, he wouldn't quit.

Then there was Nora Abbott. Tough in business but young and easy to manipulate. Now that her husband was gone, she'd need strong guidance. Who better than a wealthy mentor?

The Hopi had agreed to recommend mining on their lands, but he couldn't count on them until their x was on the line.

"Barrett." Cole Huntsman's voice startled him.

"Jesus." He had a meeting. Completely forgotten. Barrett was losing his fucking mind. He never used to forget anything.

Barrett rose from the desk and waved Cole in. "Just finishing an overseas call."

"Thought it might be something like that when no one answered the door. Hope you don't mind that I let myself in." Cole had a country bumpkin face that made him look harmless. It didn't fool Barrett.

"Glad you did," Barrett said. "I've been working on our testimonies for the hearing."

One eyebrow arched on Cole's forehead. "Our testimonies? I figured on speaking for myself."

"Of course. These are just some thoughts to coordinate our message."

"Right." That sincere drawl and perpetually friendly face would play nicely at the hearings.

Barrett picked up a stack of papers from his desk and handed them to Cole. He lowered himself back into his chair. "Sit down and we'll get to work."

Cole took the papers and wandered over to the window, his eyes on Kachina Mountain. He acted as if he had all the time in the world, like he operated on Navajo time. Cowboys and Indians--with their disregard for time, it was a wonder the West was ever settled.

Cole glanced at the pages Barrett prepared for the hearing. "Releasing those claims might be a tough sell to the committee."

Another shovelful of coal to his heartburn. God damned Interior Department withdrawing lands he needed for expansion of uranium mining. "That's why we've got to coordinate our efforts."

Cole nodded. "Be easier if we had a champion."

Barrett could ease Cole's mind by telling him about a guaranteed vote or two, assured by Barrett's behind-the-scenes tactics. But the less Cole, or anyone else, knew, the safer for Barrett.

Cole read silently for second. "What do you know about a Charlie Podanski?"

Barrett's neck hairs bristled. "He's a kook. Why?"

Cole shrugged. "I hear he's a radical and can disrupt things like hearings. And that he doesn't like you. Is there anything he can use against you in this?"

Despite himself, Barrett laughed. "He's past his prime. Keep tabs on him but I doubt he'll amount to much."

Cole didn't seem to mind chunks of silence in a meeting. Finally, he said, "I've got a concern about the ground water."

Barrett's balls sucked into his belly. "Ground water? How so?"

Cole continued to look at the mountain.

Did he know something? Impossible. Did he suspect?

"I'm not convinced about the stability of the breccia pipe formation. Even with the in situ method, there is risk of crumbling and some of the debris leaking into the ground water. I'm wondering if anyone on the other side will challenge it."

Barrett leaned back in his chair, the well-oiled springs silent. "This has all been researched. Hell, you did most of it yourself."

The shaggy head nodded. "Might be something I missed someone else caught."

Cole moved in slow motion to a leather Morris recliner and sat. He slouched, his long legs stretched in front of him. "When's the last time you logged the water? Wouldn't mind updating our records."

Christ. No one needed to find what Abbott's logs revealed. "We've got surveys up the ass, most of which you conducted, that say mining uranium up here is perfectly safe. We had functioning test wells and the green light on everything until this god damned moratorium. In a few days we're going to give sincere and heartfelt testimony before the congressional committee and get them to release the claims."

"There's no evidence to contradict those surveys?"

Barrett didn't need an employee questioning his decisions. But he did need the esteemed Cole Huntsman on his side. "Surveys are up to date. Let's just get past this hearing. Then you can do more testing. If we see it isn't safe to the groundwater, we'll back off. I'm not interested in polluting the whole Colorado River, for Christ sake. I've a proven track record with respect to the environment."

No change in expression. "Track records don't mean much against knew information. We need to be extra careful."

Cole had joined McCreary energy two years ago. He was a damned good miner and carried a lot of weight in the industry. For some reason, people respected that "aw shucks" personality. He acted humble and down home, but his brilliance in matters of mining and his reputation for environmental ethics were legend. It surprised Barrett that he wanted to work for McCreary since he leaned more toward granola sensibilities than the hard reality of big energy. Maybe he decided it was time to make some money.

And maybe Cole had another agenda. Barrett studied him. "Why all the questions?"

"Can't go into combat without bullets."

The day suddenly piled up on Barrett. He stood, signaling the end of the meeting. "Look over those notes. Be sure to hit the talking points in your testimony."

Cole rose slowly. "Sorry I was late getting here. Had something come up this afternoon."

Barrett walked toward the door, trying to usher Cole out. He wanted nothing more than bourbon and Patsy Cline.

"You know that ski area owner, Nora Abbott?" Cole asked casually.

Barrett's skin pricked. Cole may sound offhanded but if he mentioned the Abbott woman, there would be some thinking going on under that hillbilly mask. Barrett tilted his head to indicate slight interest.

"Her husband fell off a cliff and died this morning. I was out there when they found him. I took Nora to the hospital."

"What a tragedy." What was Cole doing out there?

Cole wasn't making much progress toward the door. "Just before that, some Native American guy attacked her."

This was news. "Attacked her?"

Cole nodded. "Yep. Came right in the lodge and tried to kill her. It was that same guy that pulled a knife on the courthouse steps. Big guy."

"Did she report it?" It had to Alex Seweingyawma. He was supposed to be locked up on Barrett's orders.

"Did you know Scott Abbott?"

Shit. Why would Cole even ask? Barrett shrugged and stepped into the hallway, making it plain he expected Cole to follow. "No."

Finally Cole made moves to wrap up the meeting. He offered Barrett the manly western handshake and walked away, business conducted.

Barrett pivoted, already focused on fixing the Alex Seweingyawma problem. He was halfway to his desk when the thought struck.

Scott Abbott had accosted him at the courthouse. Cole was there, too. Did Cole see it? Did he just catch Barrett in the lie?

But Cole had run off to rescue Nora Abbott on the courthouse steps. He hadn't seen Barrett's encounter with Scott. Probably.

God damned loose ends.

8

Raw, throbbing and aching for relief. But it went on and on.

After two hours of standing on the side of the mountain listening to Scott's friends tell stories and give tribute, Nora's pain had reached maximum force. Her agony had little to do with the bruise on her cheek, sore throat, and black and blue neck from the attack. The beer, lugged in coolers from the trailhead of Kachina Ski, dwindled to a few bottles and the speeches gave way to anecdotes.

At least Abigail wasn't here to hate this casual funeral, or whatever she called it. Nora wanted to honor Scott and give his friends a chance to say good bye. Now, at the end of her ability to maintain control, she simply wished it to end.

Nora leaned against Charlie, glad for his loyal, if a little beer-bleary, support. Abbey lay at her feet, content to snooze in the dappled sunshine from the pines.

Charlie put his arm around her shoulder and squeezed. "Mighty fine send off. Scott had a boatload of friends."

People flocked to Scott. He knew how to have fun. It always amazed her that someone so full of life and mischief would hook up with someone serious like her. At first she hadn't trusted it, hadn't trusted him.

But he charmed her and won her over so completely that after seven years she didn't know where he started and she ended. So many women wanted to be with Scott but he'd chosen Nora to be his wife.

One of Scott's buddies finished his story. "Scott pointed his skis down, took that jump and landed like a giant snowball. He rolled down the mountain. We thought he at least broke twenty bones. But when we got there he was brushing snow off. 'Dude, what took you so long?' he said." The friend raised his bottle. "You got there first again, man. Guess you couldn't wait."

A few people murmured, most raised their bottles at the simple hat-sized pine box Nora had picked out for Scott's ashes.

After a moment of silence Nora sucked in a breath. She planned to dump his ashes over the side of the mountain and leave him in a place he loved.

Charlie's watery eyes filled with compassion.

How could she let him go? She could scatter Scott's ashes anytime. It didn't have to be now. Nora stepped from under Charlie's arm and turned to the knot of people. Since trekking up the mountain, Nora had drawn in her body tight so she wouldn't fly apart. She knew his friends had gathered by the sounds of shuffling feet and murmurs. She hadn't been able to turn and see them all.

She inhaled deeply and swallowed. "Thank you for coming. This is the way Scott would have chosen that we celebrate his life." *Celebrate his life. Who came up with this crap?*

Abbey stood and stretched. He settled his silky head under Nora's dangling fingers.

They stepped forward, hugged her, kissed her, told her "if there's anything I can do—." She smiled and accepted that they loved Scott and cared for her. But she wanted to be alone.

Charlie and Nora stood by the box as everyone else wandered away. God, when would this end? A mass of blonde drew Nora's attention to the edge of the clearing where people started to make their way down the trail.

A big-assed, ugly mule kicked Nora's belly, followed by instant nausea. That face always caused the same reaction.

Charlie followed Nora's line of vision. "You got something against that girl?"

The blonde threw her arms around one of Scott's cycling buddies. She sobbed into his chest and he patted her back.

Already tender, Nora's emotions shredded into piles of gore. "I can't believe her nerve."

Charlie took a step down the trail. "If you don't want her here, I'll send her on her way."

Nora didn't want to remember two years ago, the night she'd driven to town for a beer. Alone because, supposedly, Scott competed in a bike race in Utah, she stepped into the bar. She expected happy greetings from friends but their faces froze. It took about two seconds to see Scott cozied up to that athletic blonde at a back table.

Just seeing that bleached head of spun shit brought back the pain, humiliation and betrayal. Nora wanted to honor Scott today, not relive pain.

Charlie put a hand on Nora's arm. "Looks like she's ready to leave."

Nora stomped to the rock and picked up Scott's box. "She's got no breeding." The comment sounded like Abigail. *Gaa!*

The tethers of her control snapped. She sprinted toward the blonde, weighted down by the heavy pine box.

Abbey let out a bark and raced with her.

"Hey. Honey, wait," Charlie called.

Outrunning Charlie wasn't hard. Nora's vision narrowed to a red laser focused on the tacky blonde. The bimbo turned just as Nora slammed into her side, driving her into a tree like a croquet ball.

The girl regained her balance. "What the hell?"

Abbey bowed his front legs and barked, tail wagging.

The two guys with the bimbo stood back. Just the cowardly sort of friends she deserved.

"How dare you show up here today!" Nora fought the urge to slam Scott's box into the girl's nose.

Silence fell for a moment while the woman stared at Nora.

Charlie caught up to them. He waved his arm at the blonde as if she were a wasp. "Go on. You're not wanted."

Nora's words spit at her. "Don't you have any pride? I'm his wife." *Was his wife.*

Abbey circled around. He sat and panted.

The girl narrowed her eyes and glared at Nora. "How long do you think he stayed away from me?" When Nora didn't answer, she said, "Try two weeks."

Blood rushed through Nora's ears. This wasn't true. It couldn't be. They'd been trying to put their marriage back on track for almost two years.

The bimbo nodded. "That's right. There is a lot about him you don't know."

Breathe. Stand up. Do not fall apart. Pride was all that kept her alive.

"He used to call you Mom. You squeezed the life out of him. That's why he came to me."

Despite Herculean effort, Nora slumped against Charlie.

Charlie held out his palm. "You stop talking now."

Bimbo stuck the dull knife in further. "He planned on leaving. He almost had enough saved for us to leave together. But you found out and you killed him!"

Money? "Liar." She pulled away from Charlie. "There was no money."

The smug look on Bimbo's face infuriated Nora. "Maybe Scott felt sorry for you and didn't want to hurt you. But I won't protect you."

Charlie shooed her away. "You're out of line."

Bimbo shouted at Nora. "You didn't know anything about him. He had a job, his ticket to freedom. That's what he said. And he was finally to leave." Suddenly she broke down in heaving sobs. "And now he's gone."

Nora couldn't feel her own body.

Tears streaked Bimbo's makeup. With her red eyes and dripping nose, she looked more like the grieving widow than did Nora. Bimbo shrieked and ran at Nora. "And I know you did it! You killed him. I know it!"

Bimbo drew her arm back and swung toward Nora's face. Just before her palm slapped Nora's cheek, a hand shot out from behind Nora and caught Bimbo on the wrist.

Abbey set up a string of agitated barking.

Cole Huntsman lowered the woman's arm, giving her a fierce look. "Leave her alone."

No one moved for a full three seconds. Then the two guys, Bimbo's cowardly friends, shrouded her and spirited her down the trail.

Abbey stood in the middle of the trail and watched them go.

Nora's knees trembled. She bent over and heaved, the acid of bile burning her sore throat.

Charlie appeared at her side, grabbing a handful of her hair and patting her back.

Strength trickled back. It didn't matter how many deaths Scott died to her, she would have to keep breathing. She stood and stared into the forest, gathering her forces.

The branches, logs, flowers and shrubs shifted from fog to focus and she realized she was staring, not at a Ponderosa, as she'd expected, but at a man. Or at least he seemed like it. He wore a mask, the scary kind with the slit eyes and plug mouth. His clothes and body paint jumbled in a tangle of blue and red. This living vision of the kachina doll the little man forced on her sent chills racing over her skin. He only had to spring forward and raise his hatchet to hack her to pieces.

Nora cried out.

Charlie patted her back. "Let it out."

She glanced down, backing away . When she swung back to avoid his attack, the man was gone. She pointed. "Where did he go?"

Cole whirled around and studied the forest. "Who?"

"That guy. That Native American." Even to her it sounded crazy. But there were plenty of people who would like to harm Nora. Seeing strange men--and then not seeing them--in the forest freaked her out.

Cole pushed his hair from his forehead. "I'll check it out." He started away.

The whole thing stank. "What are you doing here?"

Charlie swayed slightly. "Cole was keeping that girl from clocking you."

Wait a minute. How did Charlie know Cole's name? "You know him?"

He shifted and mumbled. "Why wouldn't I? Working for the enemy, out to cause mischief."

Not unusual for Charlie to head off on a tangent that made no sense.

Did Cole's face turn red? Probably a sign he was hiding something. Why did he always show up to save her? Was he keeping her safe so the masked guy or Knife Guy could get her later on?

The red deepened on his face. "I was... wanting to pay respects to your husband."

She scowled at him. "You didn't know him."

He stammered. "But I sort of know you and it seemed like something I should do." He looked at the ground as if he were an embarrassed kid. No wonder Big Elk sent him. He played up a boyish charm. It might fool some people but Nora had dealt with threats and harassment for a long time. She was no sucker.

"I'll go see if I can find the person you saw," he said.

"You do that." She watched him walk away.

And now I will put my life back together. I will run Kachina Ski and do all the things I need to do. She marched down the hill ahead of Charlie.

Scott and Bimbo. Together. Molten lava exploded inside. Nora heaved the pine box. It sailed up and crashed to the forest floor. The top landed three feet away and the plastic bag of ashes flopped out.

She sank to the ground. Every cell in her body weary, Nora said to Charlie, "What am I going to do without him?"

Charlie gathered the bag of ashes and placed it back in the box. He slammed the lid on. "You'll do what you've been doing all along. You'll take care of everything and everyone around you."

Nora shook her head. "Scott gave me courage. And now I'm all alone."

"That boy didn't give you anything."

God, she was tired. Nora pulled herself up and trudged down the trail.

Charlie followed her, carrying the pine box.

They walked in silence. The ache in Nora's heart pounded in her brain. She'd never feel good again. The last curve rounded into a long straight decline to Kachina Ski's parking lot.

All Nora wanted to do was climb the stairs to her apartment and fall into bed.

She looked down the trail and froze. The worst day of her life just cranked up another full turn.

Bimbo and her friends were gone.

But something far worse waited for her down there.

9

Like strategizing the next chess move, Barrett chose the exact words to reassure the Congressional committee members. He maintained relaxed body language and a sincere expression, leaning slightly forward in his chair and looking each vote-hungry vulture in the eye.

Since the meteoric rise in uranium prices recently, McCreary Energy, among others, had filed hundreds of mining claims in the vicinity of the Grand Canyon. Environmental alarmists scurried to block them and repeal the 1872 mining laws that made mineral rights king over every other public lands use. Climate change, clean fuel, faltering economy—all of it stood squarely in Barrett's way as he readied McCreary Energy to go after the uranium windfall. Now this hastily convened Congressional committee thought they had the power to pull Barrett's plug.

They wouldn't stop him.

Wheelan Deavonshire, Senate representative for northern Arizona, hosted this on-site hearing. Barrett owned Deavonshire, which meant this asinine mining moratorium would go away. Or else.

Christ, he hated squeezing his feet into the fancy ostrich-skin boots and confining himself to a suit and tie. Didn't matter if it happened to be the finest fabric, tailored to fit his growing bulk. He might despise this and other actions, but it was a small enough sacrifice for family. For Heather.

Barrett studied the Congressional panel while keeping a keen ear out for the media and other participants filling the conference hall behind him. He spoke with authority. "Withdrawal of these lands from mining is unnecessary and if enacted will degrade the environment of the Grand Canyon, reduce public visitation to the area, increase America's dependence on foreign energy and negatively impact the economy of both the region and the country."

He paused to let that digest. "With China and India pushing for nuclear reactors, it's our patriotic duty to develop uranium here and reduce our dependence on foreign oil. If you withdraw this land from uranium development a valuable resource capable of producing clean electricity for millions of people will be sacrificed to appease the emotions of a few special interest groups."

He sounded reasonable. "This union of special interests is attempting to justify withdrawing lands by attacking the mining industry. They grossly exaggerate environmental damage of an operation closed for more than 40 years. They assume we'll use the same outmoded techniques today we used in the 1970s. I can assure the American people that McCreary Energy has cleaned any contamination that remained from earlier operations and today's techniques are far safer.

"If this attack is successful, you will send a clear message to the American people that the federal government doesn't care about the price of fuel, domestic jobs or the environment."

Barrett thanked the committee and the chairman declared a break.

Before Deavonshire could escape, Barrett gave him a hearty slap on the back and directed him toward the senator's office.

Once inside Barrett settled into the comfortable client's chair and waited for Deavonshire to close the door and seat himself behind the glossy desk. Even in a district as cash-strapped as northern Arizona, the senator managed to surround himself with tasteful and expensive trappings. All on McCreary's dime.

"The opposition's lined up an impressive roster for testimony today," Barrett said, eyeing the glad-handing, ingratiating slime.

The senator nodded his head with annoying enthusiasm. "Thank goodness there aren't more people like that Charlie character badgering the committee."

At least Charlie had kept his heckling outside the courtroom and behaved himself in the hearings. In their youth, Charlie carried more threat. His bark, as well as his bite, weakened with age. "Charlie's made a career of being a pest."

Deavonshire matched Barrett's insincere smile. His tanned face, wavy hair and toothpaste-ad radiance didn't quite hide his discomfort. "Uranium mining close to the Grand Canyon is a hot button issue. At the end of the day, people are concerned with preserving the beauty of one of the Eight Natural Wonders of the World."

Seven, you idiot. "The committee was receptive to Huntsman's testimony about the safety of modern mining techniques. With your support, Senator, they'll have no problem giving us the go-ahead."

When Deavonshire's only response was an uncomfortable silence, Barrett hardened his voice. "You understand McCreary Energy is responsible for putting you where you are now."

Good. The grin slipped from the senator's face. "You know I'm grateful for your support."

"Bring home the votes. We're set to start drilling immediately."

Was Deavonshire's smile the tiniest bit shaky? "It's a tough issue, Barrett. I'll do what I can."

Barrett rose. "Deliver."

The senator held out his paw for the firm politician hand job. "Big Elk sure isn't helping our cause. The Hopi council was ready to recommend the mining but they cancelled their testimony for this afternoon. Rumor has it Big Elk convinced them to change their position."

Fire blasted through Barrett at this unexpected setback. "I'll take care of Big Elk."

"I'm sure the committee is going to call for another environmental impact study."

God damn it. "You'll convince them it's not necessary and a waste of taxpayer dollars. Last year's EIS is sufficient."

There was that patronizing attitude, as if Barrett didn't know how the system worked. "This is a small issue and might be something we can concede to appear cooperative."

"Another EIS is non-negotiable. No new studies, no delays. Get the vote."

"Absolutely." Could teeth get any bigger or whiter?

Barrett wasn't convinced of Deavonshire's sincerity. "How rude of me. I haven't asked about your wife and adorable daughter, Angela, isn't it?"

The senator grinned. "She's a corker."

"The world can be a dangerous place for a three-year old, don't you think?"

Deavonshire's face froze. He might be stupid but, apparently, not retarded.

Barrett showed his teeth, only slightly resembling a smile.

The color drained from the Deavonshire's face.

Barrett patted the senator on his shoulder. "I'm looking forward to the committee releasing those claims." He sauntered down the hall, spying Cole chatting with, of all people, Charlie Podanski.

Cole spotted Barrett and ambled over. A young reporter scurried to them, her notebook and pen poised. "What do you say to those who are worried uranium mining could destroy the landscape and pollute the water? That ideally, mining should be forever banned in this region?"

Barrett barely kept himself from growling at the ditz. Obviously, he shouldn't talk to the press now. "Let me introduce Cole Huntsman. He's McCreary's expert on uranium mining."

Barrett stepped back and let the ever-charming Cole disarm the reporter.

"Mining techniques have changed dramatically since uranium was mined around here in the seventies," Cole said. "The typical footprint of the mine is smaller than a Wal-Mart parking lot. Each mine would only last about five years and as it closed, a new one would open. So we're not talking about hundreds of mines operating at the same time."

The co-ed scribbled and nodded. With the reporter occupied and the hearing room empting, Barrett moved on to his next problem. He needed Nora Abbott under his thumb. Not necessarily out of the picture as her meddling husband, though if it came to that he wouldn't hesitate.

Cole continued with his smooth press voice. "Uranium is deep underground so mines won't be exposed to wind and water. The water table is way below mine level. There will be no blasting, no unsightly pits, and no lasting contamination."

Problems roiled in Barrett's gut and he swallowed acid. Was this how his father felt before he keeled over from a heart attack?

"The Arizona Strip, a land area of 1.7 million acres, contains one of the richest uranium resources in the world." Cole was wrapping up the soft sell. Touting the benefits of nuclear energy wasn't difficult. Barrett, himself, was a true believer.

Barrett slipped away. He pushed open the smoked-glass courthouse doors, stepping into the blinding sunshine of the courtyard.

How could he expedite snowmaking? Left to her own devices Nora Abbott might not get around to it this year, what with mourning the loss of her husband.

He tossed Nora to the back of his brain and shuffled the next issue to the top. Big Elk. Didn't that asshole ever quit? Like an annoying gnat under Barrett's nose, he meddled with the Hopi Tribal Council and stirred up do-gooders who didn't have lives of their own. Barrett could neutralize him and it would only cost money. Lots of it.

So deeply into his plots, Barrett paid little attention to crossing the street and arriving at his shiny black Escalade. He pushed the unlock button on a key he didn't remember pulling from his pocket. Damn, age whittled his awareness. Used to be he could manage McCreary Energy's five-year plan, train a quarter horse to pace and enjoy Heather's preschool antics, all at the same time.

Focus, you old fool. Barrett drew in a breath and glanced across the park at the edge of the courthouse parking lot.

A gunshot through his temple wouldn't have been a bigger jolt.

Cuddled under a tree, Heather leaned forward and shared a sloppy kiss with that fucking Indian.

God damn it. He'd paid good money to send that thug to jail.

Barrett wanted to kill the boy, tear him apart and watch wolves fight over his flesh. He wanted Heather safe at home in a ten-year time out. Red hot rage coursed through his blood. He couldn't get to Heather fast enough. His hands ached to close around the boy's throat and see the life drain from him.

Heather's eyes flew open when she saw Barrett. She recovered and jumped to her feet, hardening her face in challenge.

Suddenly it was Ester in front of him with that same expression. "I have made my choice, Barrett."

Barrett froze.

Heather stepped in front of him, chin raised. "Hi, Poppy."

Not Ester. Heather. Years ago he'd wrap his arms around her and take her into his lap, her little pony tails bouncing. Like Ester, his sweet little cherub didn't exist, anymore. The teenager in front of him burned with enough anger to heat a Siberian village for a week.

Barrett took Heather's hand. "It's time to go."

His touch hit her like acid. "I belong with Alex. With my people. Honoring Mother Earth and the kachinas of the sacred mountain."

The stinking pile of shit dared to speak. "She is finally with her people. Don't try to corrupt her with shiny toys."

This scum didn't understand the thin ice he skated on. "Shut up."

Alex tossed his veil of black hair with an aggressive thrust of his shoulders. "You can't talk to me like that. I got friends. More powerful than you."

Barrett barely held on to his rage. "What friends?"

"Big Elk. Don't fuck with him, dude."

Nice nail to your coffin, asshole. Barrett pulled Heather's hand. "Let's go."

The young man's shifty eyes focused across the park and he took a step back.

Heather resisted. "I've tried to talk to you about this and all you say is about cost of living and making money. You don't listen."

Heather's brave boyfriend took another step back and hurried away.

Heather watched him with a puzzled frown.

A man's voice sounded behind Barrett's shoulder. "Mr. McCreary?"

He turned to the gray-haired uniformed cop and flipped through his mental Rolodex. "Mike Tomlinson, isn't it?"

The cop returned his smile, probably impressed Barrett could come up with his name. "That's right."

Heather retreated.

Before she could take another step, Barrett put his arm over her shoulders and drew her to his side. "Have you met my daughter, Heather?"

Tomlinson lost his smile and hesitated a moment.

Ice floes threatened Barrett's heart. There was a reason Alex disappeared, a reason the good officer approached and it all had to do with Heather.

Tomlinson looked Barrett in the eye. "Actually, Mr. McCreary, we have a situation involving your daughter."

Heather stiffened next to him but kept an implacable expression.

Moisture evaporated in the arctic chill of his body.

"There was an incident here a couple of days ago at the courthouse that involved your daughter."

"What sort of incident, Mike?"

Tomlinson shook his head. "That activist, Big Elk, stirred up a bunch of people and things got out of hand. The owner of Kachina Ski, Nora Abbott, was threatened."

"That's terrible."

"Afraid so. Anyway, several witnesses identified your daughter as one of the assailants."

If he'd had any doubts before, this sealed Alex's death warrant. "How is Ms. Abbott?"

"She wasn't injured. Unfortunately, the next day the main assailant, Alex Seweingyawma attacked Ms. Abbott at her home and nearly killed her."

Heather drew in a sharp breath. At least this news surprised her.

"Attempted murder? And this criminal is at large?" No need to tell Tomlinson that Alex had been here. Barrett was more efficient and lethal than the legal system.

"We've got leads but frankly, when these people retreat to the rez, it's hard to get our hands on them."

"I understand, Mike. This is a disturbing situation and I promise we'll take care of it."

Tomlinson nodded. "Seweingyawma is a dangerous man. Your daughter needs to keep her distance."

"Of course. Thank you." Barrett started to walk away.

"There are consequences, you know," Tomlinson said.

Barrett clenched his teeth. "Consequences?"

"To your daughter's involvement. Heather will have to appear before a judge. In cases as serious as this, juvie lockup isn't out of the question. But sometimes, if the family can come up with suitable restitution and the youth shows appropriate remorse, probation is a possibility."

Heather didn't balk when Barrett led her to the Escalade.

A black wave of panic gathered at the back of Barrett's brain. He forced calm waters. He'd made a fortune turning problems into opportunities. He needed to think like Barrett McCreary III, not some addled peon.

How could he stop Heather from this teenaged rebellion stage and get her back on track? When Heather threatened Nora Abbott she also threatened her own future. Fear of her next self-destructive move terrified him. At the very least, she'd made his next move trickier.

If Nora had resentment for Heather's part in the attack, Barrett would have a hard time manipulating her. He needed Nora Abbott on board.

Barrett cleared his mind and waited. He put his trust in the wheels and cogs of his brain that operated on the other side of his consciousness.

It happened again, as it always did. A solution sprang into his head, fully formed like Athena bursting from Zeus's temple. Barrett hadn't lost his touch, after all.

By this time tomorrow Nora Abbott and Heather would both be under his control.

10

Charlie bumped into Nora on the trail, Scott's pine box stabbing her in the back. "Oh man, it's The Heat."

She thought the death of her husband, revelation of his betrayal and looming financial ruin might be more than she could take in one day. And yet, the black cloud just got darker.

Maybe she could walk back up the trail like the Von Trapp family at the end of the Sound of Music. She'd trudge onward until she found sanctuary.

"You go," she said to Charlie. "I'm heading up the mountain to find a place to sit until I petrify."

Charlie frowned down the trail. A crowd milled in the lot but Charlie's sole focus was Gary Something-or-Other in his uniform.

Cole Huntsman stood next to the cop and probably spilled his guts about Bimbo accusing Nora of murder. Any other time, that might worry Nora.

Big Elk stood in the middle of a circle of protesters like a ring master. With the righteous following, this circus wasn't short on clowns. Not even the dozen or so Native Americans and the Guilty White People chanting "Make love, not snow" frightened her.

As bad as all that seemed, what froze Nora's blood and made her want to swallow the cyanide pill, stepped from a taxi.

Abigail.

Charlie sucked in a breath of awe. "I am in love."

Cold sweat slicked Nora's forehead. "Forget it, Charlie. Abigail is like carbon monoxide. You don't realize how deadly she is."

"Abigail. The name sings as if spoken by the hosts of heaven."

Right on schedule the news van pulled up and a camera woman jumped out. Big Elk had to be disappointed the crew was local. Still, a network affiliate left hope for national exposure.

Charlie all but floated down the path. "Who is this vision?"

Reluctant, Nora followed. "My mother. Abigail The Perfect."

Abbey trotted down the trail as a one-tail welcome committee.

Big Elk held his hand out to quiet the chanters. "This is our sacred mountain, home to the kachinas since the beginning of the Fourth World. When our Hopi brothers and sisters received responsibility to balance the world, they agreed to protect the Mother and this sacred home."

The mini-van that served as Flagstaff's taxi sat in the parking lot. As if spotlighted by the sun, Abigail stood in her beige silk suit and gold sandals, her arms crossed, scowling at the demonstration.

The sanctuary of the lodge sat across the mine field of the parking lot.

Run back up the trail while you still can. But she couldn't hide on the mountain forever; they'd already hauled off the beer.

The taxi driver reached into the back of the van and brought out an enormous tapestry-covered suitcase. He hefted it onto his shoulder, picked up a smaller bag and started up the path to the lodge. Two other large suitcases and a couple of smaller bags sat on the deck.

Charlie's joy was unmistakable. "It appears she's here for a long spell."

"Hard to say how long she plans on staying. Being fabulous requires supplies." A tiny Abigail troll appeared at the base of Nora's neck and turned a control knob from 0 to 1. The headache started in Nora's temples. Big Elk raised his arms like a televangelist. "The fire-bearer of the mountain is demanding we listen to him. If we don't stop the desecration he will bring fire to the mountain."

Charlie didn't take his eyes off Abigail. "I only want to bask in her presence."

"You don't know what you're in for." Nora set a determined pace and Charlie fell in beside her.

Together they walked across the parking lot. Involved in his performance, Big Elk didn't notice Nora. Too bad. She'd rather face Big Elk and his evangelistic army than greet Abigail.

Nora took a deep breath and braced herself. "Hello, Mother."

Abigail spun around. A reactionary frown flitted across her face. She quickly rearranged her face in a show of sorrow, probably practiced in front of a mirror. Abigail opened her arms. "Baby! Oh, baby. Mother's here."

Nora stopped just outside her mother's reach. She wondered how much rehearsal Abigail had done to get her words and facial expression just right. The parking lot full of protesters might have thrown a less experienced performer for a loop but Abigail excelled at improvisation.

Nora rubbed her temples. "What are you doing here?"

"Excuse me." The authoritative voice behind her could only belong to a cop. Gary Something or Other approached Nora.

Abigail looked confused that Nora hadn't run into her arms. "Where else would I be when my baby needs me so."

Hawaii? Italy? Outer Mongolia? "I thought you were on an Alaskan cruise?"

Officer Gary stepped closer. "May I have a word with you?"

Abbey pushed his head under Abigail's hand. Abigail's upper lip curled slightly and she pulled her hand away. "I caught a plane at the first dock as soon as I heard. I knew you'd need my help planning the services."

Welcome to the Abigail Show.

"I'm sorry to disturb you today." Gary's official formality grated on her nerves.

Cole inserted himself between the cop and Nora. "Then why are you? I asked you to come back tomorrow."

Enough of Cole's rescuing. Even though she didn't want to talk to

Gary, she said, "What about Alex Sewe-something? The guy that attacked me."

Obviously, this wasn't the topic he came to discuss. He hesitated. "Alex Seweingyawma. We're sure he's hiding on the Hopi reservation."

"He's still missing?"

"We don't consider him a threat to you at this time."

Charlie nudged Nora with the pine box and gushed at Abigail. "How kind of you to fly to your daughter's side."

What a rat to jump ship like that.

Abigail's Mary Kay smile froze on her lips.

The cop interrupted. "This is an urgent matter."

"And a murderer running lose isn't?" Nora asked.

"...fire on the mountain." Big Elk's bleating ceased making sense.

After depositing the last of the matching baggage on the deck, the taxi driver returned to Abigail as if approaching a sacred altar. "That about does it, Mrs. Stoddard."

Abigail pulled a bill out of a small bag dangling from her shoulder on a long gold chain. With both hands she pressed it into the taxi driver's palm. "You must call me Abigail, Ted. Thank you so much for all your help. I would have been lost without you."

Shoot me now. The troll at the base of Nora's head clicked the knob to three and her headache traded in amateur for professional status.

Cole lowered his chin, a big horned sheep readying for battle with Gary Something-or-other. "Why not make yourself helpful and get rid of that asshole." He pointed to Big Elk.

Gary glared at Cole and shifted his focus on Big Elk. "He is an asshole." He marched to the protestors and raised his voice above Big Elk's, ordering them to disperse.

Of course Big Elk wouldn't take that lying down. "The whole world will shake and turn red and fight against those hindering the Hopi."

The picketers took up their stupid "Make love not snow," refrain while Big Elk and Gary had words. Bless Cole's heart for calling off Big Elk and Gary with one remark. Now, if he could just make Abigail disappear Nora might forgive his environmental activism and even promise him her first born. Not that she'd ever have a first born with her husband gone.

Abigail flashed Cole a dazzling smile. "Could you be a dear and take my bags up to the apartment. That dog of Nora's is likely to get underfoot and those stairs are so treacherous. I'm afraid I'll fall and break my neck."

"Mom! Cole is not your servant."

Charlie started up the path to the lodge. "I'll haul your bags to heaven if that's your wish."

Cole smiled. "It's okay."

Nora looked straight ahead, her neck stiff. "It's not okay."

Abigail's tone set Nora's teeth on edge. "Really, Nora. There's no need to be so prickly. Here is this young, strapping man willing to help us out."

"I'm capable of dealing with your bags. It doesn't make me more of a woman to act helpless and stupid."

Abigail drew in a breath of offense. "Same Nora, always cutting off your nose to spite your face."

The scene in the parking lot, the arrival of the Wicked Witch, the presence of this Cole person, piled on to the devastation of her husband's death. And his betrayal.

Balancing the pine box with one arm, Charlie pulled a Pabst Blue Ribbon from a jacket pocket. He held it out to Abigail. "Can I offer you a beverage?"

Abigail stood as if she'd turned to a pillar of salt.

Cole strode ahead. Lean and tall, he looked like he spent more time outside than in, probably camping and living off the land. A younger, and less crusty, version of Charlie. Nora imagined that, like Charlie in his radical days, Cole wouldn't hesitate to protect nature with violence if he thought it necessary. He kept turning up and acting helpful but she figured his agenda dealt more with finding her vulnerabilities. But if his issue was uranium mining and his nemesis Barrett McCreary, why would he be stalking her? Nora couldn't begin to sort that out.

Undaunted by Abigail's rejection, Charlie pulled the tab on the proffered beer and took a gulp. He smiled and delivered his normal opening line. "Looks like rain."

Abigail jerked her head to the cloudless sky and shot Charlie an offended look.

Nora felt an almost imperceptible decrease in the pounding in her temples. "A toad strangler."

He guffawed. "I like an optimist."

Abigail walked next to Nora and put a hand on Nora's arm. She kept her voice low and barely moved her lips. "Who is this person?"

"This is my friend, Charlie."

It didn't take Queen Abigail long to assert her authority. She eyed Charlie. "I'm Nora's mother and this isn't a good time for a visit. She's suffering stress and needs to rest."

If what Jim Bowie went through at the Alamo was called stress, maybe you could say Nora's day was stressful. "Charlie is my friend and he's always welcome." *Even if he is struck with momentary insanity and thinks you're a goddess.*

Officer Gary temporarily won the battle with Big Elk. Either that or the news crew shot their footage and sound bite and Big Elk had no more incentive to hang around. The chanting subsided and the protestors climbed into their vehicles, slammed doors and started engines.

Nora trudged up the stairs to the deck. Abigail tapped up behind her, probably struggling to keep her sandal heels from getting stuck in the metal grating. Charlie followed them.

Cole waited next to the luggage. "Where do you want these?"

"Timbuk-three." Nora headed for the apartment stairs. The world could turn or stop for all she cared. She wanted to climb into her bed. "Abbey, come."

Abigail folded her arms. "I wish you hadn't named that dog that way."

"He's named...."

Abigail's annoyed voice finished, "I know, after Edward Abbey. An anarchist."

Charlie perked up. "Ed Abbey was a god!"

"A great environmentalist, Mother."

"Now she calls me Mother."

As opposed to Queen of Darkness?

Abigail tried to enlist Cole to her side. "I think she calls him Abbey to annoy me. I don't know why she couldn't call him Rover or Spot."

With a straight face and slow, serious drawl Cole said, "He doesn't really have any spots."

For the first time in forever, Nora almost laughed.

Abigail smiled at Cole. "You can take those upstairs to the apartment. I need to get settled in so we can discuss the funeral."

Here came that troll again. "We had the ceremony today."

Abigail's eyes widened. "Today? What church?"

Nora squared her shoulders. "No church. We did it up on the mountain. We just got back."

"What?"

Nora didn't reply, sort of enjoying the strangling sound coming out of Abigail.

"Did you say you just came back?" Abigail sputtered.

Nora nodded "Yep."

She couldn't have sounded more shocked if Nora had murdered Scott. "And you wore...jeans?"

"It's hard to wear heels on the trail."

Abigail waved in Charlie's direction, indicating the box. "And that...?"

"Is Scott's ashes." Nora stomped over and took the box.

Though Scott's unusual ceremony must have thrown Abigail's world off kilter, she recovered quickly. She tossed her head, sending her bob fluttering. "You look tired."

My husband is dead. I just found out he was cheating on me, again. My business is drying up and I'm not sure I care. I'm being stalked by an abnormally large and angry Native American who would like to see me dead. A rabid activist calls me names on the news. Some strange masked man appears and disappears in the forest. And now, the woman who tortured me all my life, the one who makes me throw up and have diarrhea at the same time, the diva of demons, just dropped in for a visit. "I haven't been sleeping," Nora said.

Abigail hurried to her bags.

Fatigue overrode Nora's urge to run.

While Charlie and Abbey watched, Abigail bent to one of the smaller bags and rummaged inside. She held up a small bottle. "This is absolutely the best concealer on the market." She handed it to Nora. "We'll have you looking decent in no time."

The troll gave the knob a good crank.

Cole picked up a suitcase. "I think Nora looks great." An obvious lie, but greatly appreciated.

Abigail smiled at Cole. "It's a woman thing."

Cole started toward the stairs. Nora shouldn't allow him up to her apartment in case he wanted to plant a bomb or something. But it seemed that being blown up might actually be better than lugging her mother's bags up the steep flight. Exhaustion didn't begin to cover what she felt. Nora moved aside to let Cole pass.

Thudding on the metal stairs alerted her to Officer Gary. He stepped onto the deck and walked to Nora.

Cole stopped. "Didn't we decide you'd come back tomorrow?"

Gary spared him a stern look and turned to Nora. "I know this is a bad time but I need to ask you to not leave town for a few days."

"Sure. I'll cancel my Mexican vacation." Stupid to be belligerent with cops but Nora was beyond reason.

Charlie held his fist in the air, some hippy symbol of power to the people. "If you don't have a warrant you're harassing my friend."

Abigail put her hands on her hips. "You stay out of this." She flashed Gary a smile. "I'm sorry, Officer. It has been a trying day, what with a funeral and those people in the parking lot and I don't even know why they were here. Nora's nerves are shot."

Cole descended a stair.

Okay, maybe Abigail had her usefulness. She spoke with a tone of warm tea. "Nora doesn't intend on traveling, of course. Can you tell me what this is all about?"

Gary studied Abigail and let out a deep breath. He addressed Nora. "There is evidence of foul play in the death of Scott Abbott. As his wife, you are an official person of interest."

The deck tipped and swayed. Scott's box hit the deck and for the second time that afternoon, ejected the bag of his ashes.

"Scott was...?" she couldn't say it.

"Murdered," Gary finished.

A suitcase hit the stairs behind her and tumbled after Scott's ashes just before Cole's arms closed around her and kept her from doing the same.

11

One was not required to bang the frying pan on the stove, slam the cupboard door, and clang the lid to make eggs. Yet, Abigail never mastered the art of making breakfast with the volume turned down. Nora wanted nothing more than to sleep again.

She rolled over and squinted her eyes. The vast empty bed bored an equally barren hole into her heart.

But if what Bimbo said was true, Scott had posted the vacant sign over Nora's bed long ago. She'd been one argument away from sending him packing herself. It didn't stop the pain welling in her chest, nearly stopping her heart.

Murder. Her eyes flew open with the thud in her chest. It made no sense. Suspecting Nora as the murderer would be logical, though. No one else was ever angry with him. If Cole told Officer Gary about Bimbo's accusations, that would make him even more suspicious.

Had someone really killed Scott? It had to be Alex. After all, he'd attempted to murder Nora two, maybe three times already. Scott had died as collateral damage, an exchange for Nora.

The door swung open and Nora held her breath. Maybe Abigail would see her sleeping, take pity and leave her alone.

No such luck.

"It's eight o'clock. You can't stay in bed forever."

Nora rolled away. "Yes I can."

The blinds zipped up, the window slid back, and the cawing of a crow exploded into the room. "I know it hurts, baby. But you have to put your life back together and the sooner you start the better."

"Why do you hate me? I tried to be a good daughter."

Abigail tsked. "None of that self-pity."

Even if she wanted to, Nora couldn't rise. Her body morphed into something made of an alien substance more dense than lead.

"It's a new day. You can't hide away."

"I'm not hiding, Mother. I'm mourning."

Abigail sat on the side of the bed and patted Nora's shoulder. "I'm sorry about Scott's passing, of course. But he wasn't the quality person you deserve."

Nausea welled in the pit of Nora's stomach. "I expected too much from him."

"I tried to keep it to myself but you never should have married him."

Nora sat up, toppling Abigail from the bed. "Keep it to yourself?"

Abigail managed to keep from splatting on the floor and smoothed her shirt.

"You've never missed an opportunity to trash Scott," Nora said.

"You should have married someone like Cole Huntsman."

Age slowed Abigail not one bit. She still held the Flabbergaster Master world title. "What?"

Abigail stooped and whisked Nora's jeans from the floor. "He stopped by this morning to check on you. Now that's considerate."

Nora swung her legs out of bed and snatched the jeans from Abigail. She stared at her mother and dropped them back on the floor. "You're sticking up for an environmentalist?"

Abigail let out a superior chuckle. "He's not an environmentalist. He's from Wyoming. Besides, I embrace the green movement. I recycle."

"Do you eat local, too? Ride your bike instead of drive? Or do you just throw your empty water bottles into the correct bin?"

Abigail put a hand on her hip. "Again with plastic bottles in landfills? I'm not a fanatic like you, if that's what you mean."

"For the love of Pete." Gaah! She used one of her mother's favorite clichés. "Would you go away?" She needed Scott. He provided Abigail Protection. His deficiencies deflected Abigail from Nora's failures.

Scott. She saw his dark eyes twinkling with humor and heard his deep laughter. A slap of pain as sharp as a thousand needles hit every inch of her skin. She sank back to the bed.

Abigail grabbed her arm. "No you don't."

How was it possible her cheeks were wet with tears? Scott didn't deserve her tears. But he hadn't deserved to be murdered, either. "I can't do this without him."

Abigail put her arm around Nora. "Of course you can. You've always been able to do anything you set your mind to. You've got decisions to make."

"Like what?"

"For one thing, you'll need an attorney."

Oh. That.

Abigail picked up the jeans and folded them. "Sooner rather than later. That po-dunk Officer Gary said you haven't been accused of anything yet but we need to be in control."

"When they have Alex in custody, it won't take them long to prove he pushed Scott and then he came after me."

Abigail tilted her head. "Of course. But in the meantime, you need counsel. I've watched enough Law and Order to know that without a lawyer you could be in trouble."

Nora tugged against her mother. "I want to sleep."

"I know you do. What you're going to do, however, is brush your teeth. Then you'll come out to the kitchen and eat the omelet I'll make for you."

Nora wouldn't admit it to Abigail but once she showered and dressed she felt better. She took the omelet to the deck and only worked through a fourth of the conglomeration before it fell to her stomach floor. Leaning her head against the wood siding of the lodge, she closed her eyes to the sun and rested her hand on Abbey's head.

Bubbles of worry fought the murkiness of her brain. They needed to begin construction on the pipeline immediately if they—she—was going to make snow on the main run by Christmas. And what about money to pay the attorney?

Jail and/or bankruptcy loomed unless she drummed up the courage to ask Abigail for a loan. Impossible to calculate the years of verbal sniping ahead of her for failing badly enough to beg Abigail for money.

The screen door of the apartment opened and the black cloud of doom, the keeper of Kachina Ski's financial future, the heel that would grind Nora to emotional dust, descended delicately to the deck. "I was thinking we should get spiffed up and go shopping. New clothes will cheer you up."

"My clothes are fine."

Abigail didn't vanish, despite Nora's fervent prayers to any and all spirits of the mountain. "I don't want to be indelicate but you must face the reality of your situation. You're no longer an attached woman. If you don't make yourself attractive you may spend the rest of your life alone."

"I'm not in the market for a new husband."

"You say that now but loneliness sets in surprisingly fast and it's not fun. I miss Howard terribly."

Nora stopped herself before saying: *Good thing he left you with yet another fortune to help you heal.* Nora was wicked and no doubt heading for the fires of hell.

Abigail's eyes filled with tears and as if she controlled it, one single drop spilled from her eye. Not enough to ruin her makeup, just enough to make her appear vulnerable and strong at the same time. "It has been an extremely difficult year. I've fought every day to remain true to the Stoddard dignity."

"You've been strong."

Nora's husband died just four days ago and yet, all sympathy and attention needed to focus on Abigail's loss. Situation normal.

While things were bad, Nora girded herself to ask Abigail for money.

"Good morning, lovely ladies!" The shout came from across the ski run.

She blessed the kachinas for their mercy in sending Charlie.

Abigail's hiss reeked of disapproval. "Honestly, Nora. I don't think you should allow that man around here."

"I like Charlie."

"But, dear, he's not really..."

Nora waited while Abigail trailed off, and then finished for her. "Our kind?"

Charlie stepped on the deck.

Abigail let out a deep sigh. "You know what I mean."

Charlie walked over to Nora. "You are the sun and moon and bring meaning to my life."

He bowed to Abigail. "Your glittering visage takes my breath away."

Abigail clasped her hands behind her back. "Oh posh."

A black SUV crunched the cinders in the parking lot. *Great. Visitors.*

12

Barrett shut the door of the Escalade and waited.

After a moment he opened the door and put his head inside. "Staying in the car won't make me change my mind."

Heather glared at him from the passenger side. "I don't see why I have to do this."

"Be on your best behavior or Nora Abbott can make your life difficult."

Heather didn't move.

Barrett shrugged. "You don't need to go with me to ask Nora Abbott's forgiveness and offer your services."

She smiled and sat upright. "Thank you, Poppy. I'll be good. I promise."

"You can wait for the judge to send you to juvenile detention." Boom.

Out came that lower lip. "The judge might come up with something besides jail."

Barrett raised his eyebrows. "We are McCrearys. We don't wait for others to decide our future. We take control."

She crossed her arms. "What makes you so sure this Nora woman will hire me?"

"I've got ways."

"You mean you've got money."

"Something like that."

She grabbed the latch and shoulder checked the door. "Someday you're going to come up against a situation where money won't buy you out."

She didn't know he couldn't buy the one thing he ever truly wanted.

Heather came around the Escalade and together they walked across the cinder parking lot and up the path to the lodge.

Heather stopped at the top of the stairs and Barrett gently pushed to move her forward. An attractive blonde about Barrett's age stood next to Nora Abbott and a few feet in front of the woman a decomposing mountain man gulped from a beer can.

God. Charlie. That dried up piece of idealist turned up everywhere.

Barrett reached for Nora's hand. "How are you, Ms. Abbott?"

He'd read her profile. Graduated at the top of her class, smart, ambitious, not a bad looker. But she'd certainly struck bad luck with the drought. He'd seen her around town. She carried herself well, her coppery hair usually shiny, bouncing around a cheerful face with intelligent eyes. The last few days had been hard on her, making her pale and adding a shadow of grief to her eyes.

Barrett couldn't afford to feel guilty for causing her pain. Heather's well-being and protection came first. It was Scott's own fault he got in the way.

Nora gave Heather a stony expression but her face softened when she shifted to Barrett. "I'm fine, thank you."

Charlie sipped his beer and narrowed his eyes at Barrett. He sank to a bench beside an old dog. "She's a woman of uncommon strength and breeding."

Barrett looked away from Charlie without comment. It was just like Charlie to use that phrase, the old joke the three of them had shared about Ester.

The classy looking blonde smiled at Barrett.

Now here was a woman worth looking at. He held out his hand, enjoying the rush of pleasure when she placed her delicate fingers in his. "I'm Barrett McCreary," he said.

Her lips were full, inviting. "Nice to meet you, Mr. McCreary. I'm Abigail Stoddard, Nora's mother."

"Barrett, please." His blood pumped to places he'd ignored for too long.

"Barrett," she repeated, looking into his eyes.

13

The Legend. Barrett McCreary here at Kachina Ski. What was he doing with that Native American girl? She was the one at the courthouse with Alex. Should Nora run from her or slap her? Either way, Nora wanted the girl off her property.

Barrett put a hand on the back of the girl and brought her forward. "I'd like to introduce my daughter, Heather."

Daughter? She was more the age of a granddaughter and clearly not his European background.

Barrett shot a pointed look at the girl and she glared back. The standoff felt as familiar to Nora as an old movie. Although Barrett and this girl—was Heather her name?—didn't look at all like Nora and Abigail, the body language was their same tango from fifteen years ago.

Finally the girl turned her attention to Nora. "I'm here to apologize for my part at the courthouse. I'm sorry."

Maybe the girl lost the silent battle with her father, but she didn't shirk her duty. She impressively held Nora's gaze and her voice sounded strong.

What do I do with that? Maybe Heather hadn't actually harmed Nora, but she'd been with a very dangerous man. Her friend had pulled knives and strangled Nora and probably killed Scott. "You're hanging out with bad people." Nora said.

Barrett nodded in satisfaction, apparently approving Nora's firm stand.

"Nora!" Abigail sounded as though Nora scalped the poor girl. "Heather came to your home and humbled herself. She deserves your gracious forgiveness."

Abigail didn't need facts. She made them up for herself.

Barrett shook his head. "Nora's right. An apology isn't sufficient."

Heather inhaled. "I know there's nothing I can do to change what happened. But I can make restitution by working for you the rest of the summer."

No way. "That won't be necessary."

"Actually, it is," Barrett said. "If you'll agree to Heather working here it will probably save her from time in juvenile detention."

Not only no, hell no. Maybe locking her up would teach her a lesson.

"While she might deserve that treatment," Barrett said. "I believe in rehabilitation."

And I get to have The Murderer's Apprentice on my property?

Barrett continued his sales pitch. "She's a good worker."

Heather obviously fought to keep her dignity in the face of what amounted to a slave auction. Abigail in all her evil glory couldn't have been any worse.

Abigail focused her feminine attention on Barrett. "What a caring father you are. Raising children isn't easy."

Abigail probably didn't know Barrett McCreary steered the course of one of the largest energy companies in the country. But she had the ability to smell money, even in the fresh mountain air. It was a valuable skill, much cheaper than Nora's MBA.

Charlie crushed his can, put it in a pocket and stood. Surprising bitterness crisped his voice. "You'd have to look far and wide to find a more caring father than Barrett McCreary."

If Nora could harness the frosty look her mother shot Charlie she wouldn't need snow making equipment.

Barrett addressed Abigail. "I think Nora is an inspiration to young women."

Abigail beamed. "Well, growing up she gave me some challenges but she turned out well."

Just like that Nora felt like the prize pig at a stock show. In the newly revised History According to Abigail, the only reason she'd achieved anything was due to Abigail's steady parenting. What credit would her mother accept for the financial ruin of Kachina?

Nora couldn't help feeling a connection with the sullen teenager. While Barrett and Abigail focused on each other, Heather and Nora made eye contact.

Charlie produced another beer from a jacket pocket and popped the top.

Abigail took a step closer to Barrett. "Now dear," she said to Nora. "Didn't I teach you about giving back?"

What you taught me was to smile, keep my nails painted, and if I acted really pleasant, I could marry rich. Well, it had worked for Abigail—three times. Her mother lived a life of leisure with no worries.

"I believe your mentoring would be a turning point for my Heather," Barrett said.

The poor girl was doomed. With this bull of a father it's no wonder she raced down the wrong path. Nora looked at her with a smidgeon of compassion. "I really hope you don't have to spend time in jail. But I can't help you out."

"Nora!" Abigail said.

Nora shook her head. "To gear up for snowmaking I'll be devoting all my time to raising financing and I can't take on mentoring."

Barrett's smile reminded her of Dracula. "If it's a matter of money we should be able to work this out."

Incredible. She'd spent years straining for ever more creative ways to keep Kachina solvent and suddenly, money was as easy as turning on the faucet. Even more incredible, Nora felt a real aversion to obvious salvation. "Actually, I'd prefer to keep this a family business."

Abigail's eyes looked wide in her pale face. "Nora, honey. Can we talk?"

Leave guests unattended? This must be serious. "I'm sorry you came all the way out here for nothing," Nora said to Barrett. She nodded to Heather. "Good luck."

Abigail placed her hand on Barrett's arm. "Would you mind waiting while I talk to Nora?"

She couldn't tell if Barrett was pleased with Abigail's attention or angry with Nora. "Of course."

Abigail took hold of Nora's arm and pulled her into the lodge.

"What's this about?" Nora said.

A bead of sweat appeared on Abigail's upper lip. "You have to take Barrett up on his offer."

Confused by her own reaction, Nora could only say, "Something about it doesn't feel right."

"What other options do you have?"

This wasn't how Nora hoped to broach the subject. *Here goes.* "I thought you might want to loan me the money for a few seasons."

Abigail's voice squeaked. "You have to talk to Barrett right now, before he changes his mind."

"Mother, you aren't listening to me. I don't want to work with Barrett."

Abigail paced across the room and back to Nora. "You can't get any money from me."

Ouch. Abigail had no faith in Nora. She scrambled for other options.

"You have to keep Kachina and I'll help you run it," Abigail said.

"What?"

"I'll be living with you anyway so I might as well earn my keep."

"You are not living with me."

"I have to. I sold my house in Denver. I sold the condo in Boca."

Nora's stomach started to churn. "What are you saying?"

Abigail stared at her.

"Are you out of money?" Nora hated asking such a ridiculous question.

"I met a man at church. He had this idea of a great investment and it was making money hand over fist. Even in this crazy market."

Nausea pushed at the edges of Nora's belly.

"Have you heard of the name Madoff?" Abigail said.

"Madoff? As in Ponzi schemes?"

Abigail looked sick. "Something like that."

Nora sank onto the bench. "You're broke?"

"We need to take care of each other. We're family."

14

For the third time in less than two weeks Nora wore her business suit and played the professional entrepreneur. Today, the uniform felt more like a collar and leash, complete with muzzle. Seven years ago she sold her soul to Kachina Ski for Scott. Today, she mortgaged her future to Barrett for Abigail.

Barrett shook the attorney's hand while everyone gathered papers and pushed back from the conference table. Power and money created efficiency Nora only dreamed about. In an hour they'd seen two top attorneys that Barrett had flown in from his law firm in Los Angeles. One was a corporate tax expert who had magically drawn up partnership agreements ready for Nora's blood signature. The other was a criminal attorney prepared to shield Nora from any inconvenience associated with being a person of interest in the murder—*murder*—of her husband.

In a few short days she went from destitute and alone to secure under the wing of Barrett McCreary's millions. Her life careened downhill like a sled on an icy luge run.

Abigail, perfectly coiffed and looking every bit equal to Barrett's bank account, smoothed her skirt and lifted the chain of her slim bag over her arm. "We should have lunch to celebrate this happy arrangement."

Happy. Yep. All Nora's heavy money problems were over. She should be floating like a helium balloon, instead of sinking like a bowling ball on a lake. "You and Barrett go ahead," she said. "I've got to call the snow sprayer contractor."

Barrett gave a final back pat to the tax attorney. "Don't worry about that. I contacted a firm in Colorado and they've expedited the equipment. Should be on its way."

"You ordered it? Without talking to me? When?" Heat rose from her belly to her face.

"Work crews are due by the end of the week. We'll have snow by Christmas."

Abigail already had a soft hand on Barrett's arm. "I was thinking Thai."

Barrett walked toward the door. "I'll take care of the snow making and leave you to the rest. You've got enough to do with operations."

Nora pressed her foot to the brakes but Barrett had cut the lines. "You said you'd be a silent partner and let me run things. I know what kind of eco-friendly equipment I want up there."

Barrett barely slowed his exit. "We have a limited window to get the equipment functioning. I've got contacts and, dare I say, some weight to throw around." He winked at Abigail and patted his belly.

"For once let someone help you," Abigail said.

Help or take over? "We can't put just any equipment up there. It has to be energy efficient and work with the environment."

Abigail scowled at her. "Don't be so controlling. Barrett hasn't gotten this far by making poor decisions."

Frustration twined through Nora. Abigail was right. Barrett had created an empire, while Nora succeeded in nearly destroying one small business. She could use a mentor, not to mention a bank-roller. She waved them off, keeping her temper in check. "Go ahead. Enjoy the Thai. I'll see you later."

Abigail took Barrett's arm. "If you're sure..."

Nora waited a few moments before leaving the conference room and stepping into the hall. Her high heels sank into the plush carpet of McCreary Energy's corporate office. After years of struggle and worry, snowmaking was a reality. The sunrise of opportunity shone just below the horizon, too bad it felt more like an alien spaceship aiming its laser.

Nora used to be happy and hopeful. Challenges sparked her blood and the possibility of winning thrilled her. Somewhere, in the seven years since meeting Scott, obstacles had become mountains that required exhausting effort to scale. Gone were the hurdles she sailed over on her sprint to the finish line.

The hallway led to the finely appointed reception area, escape only a few feet away. She'd head up to the mountain, get Abbey and hike away this growing dread.

Abigail stood with arms crossed by the front door, her face impatient.

Nora followed her gaze to a conference room where Barrett's muffled voice sneaked out. The door to the room stood ajar a few inches. Now would be a good time to tell Barrett to cancel the equipment he ordered. She needed to stop his intrusive management before it went any further. Since the receptionist no longer manned the desk, Nora veered around the corner, heading for the conference room.

She stopped outside the door to gather courage. A deep chill hardened Barrett's words. "How trustworthy is this information?"

Nora froze at the ice in Barrett's tone. Through the slit of the open door, she saw Cole Hunstman's lean form.

"Pretty reliable," Cole said.

Something crashed like a chair thrown into a table. Barrett sounded as if his temper barely held. "Fucking Devnonshire. He said he'd get the votes."

Cole's drawl contrasted with Barrett's heat. "Doesn't look likely. We'll need to switch gears. Do you have something up your sleeve?"

"Like what?"

Cole paused. "Favors to call in, maybe? Cash to spread around? Congressmen aren't angels."

Cole worked for Barrett and advocated bribes to Congress? This blew her theory that Cole was a righteous enviro out to get Barrett. He was far more dangerous than she'd thought.

Barrett's voice became clearer as he headed toward the door. "I'll get that greaseball Deavnshire to pony up the votes."

"How are you going to do that?" Cole hung back.

Nora hurried away from the door, slipping into the restroom across the hall.

She leaned against the door.

There was no hint of Barrett's anger as he obviously rejoined Abigail in reception. "How about that lunch? I'm hungry enough to eat a bear."

Abigail laughed, her impatience vanishing along with Barrett's terrifying threats. "Bear curry with Thai spice. Sounds yummy."

Nora waited until Abigail and Barrett had time to leave the building. She moved as quickly and silently as possible from the restroom to the front door. The receptionist was back at her desk and issued a pleasant good bye as Nora exited.

Nora hurried past the courthouse, her Jeep in sight. Barrett and Cole had to have been talking about the uranium hearing and the vote to withdraw lands from mining. Cole must be some sort of double agent working for Big Elk and Barrett. He advocated bribing Congressmen. She should tell someone. Who?

What a power-hungry maniac. Barrett tampered with Congress, ran a multi-billion dollar company, raised a teenage delinquent and still had time to mess up Kachina Ski. The man was like a chainsaw juggler.

"Nora."

Cole's voice slashed across her thoughts. He must have followed her out of Barrett's offices. She pretended not to hear him. Only two blocks down the sun-drenched sidewalk to the parking lot and ten miles north to the serenity of her mountain.

"Nora, wait!" Cole trotted to her.

He was a ruthless criminal who might hurt her if he suspected she knew about his duplicity. She froze and waited for him.

His face lit in a boyish smile. "Good to see you." That flush started up his neck again. "Have you had lunch? Would you like to?"

What was his game? "I'm on my way home."

"Oh." He looked disappointed. "So, what were you doing at McCreary?"

"What were you doing there?"

"Business."

"Same here."

He studied her face. "What's your business with Barrett?"

"He's my partner."

He scowled at her. "You and Barrett partners? I don't like this."

"You don't like it? I'm sorry to hear that." She took a step away.

"That didn't come out right." His face flared as if he really were embarrassed. "Obviously you can do what you want. But getting involved with Barrett isn't a good thing."

A few minutes ago she'd thought the same thing but she wasn't about to let one more person tell her what to do. "I see. It's okay for you to work with Barrett on whatever you do. But not okay for me to work with him and make snow."

He didn't seem the least upset that she'd discovered he worked for Barrett. "It's not about snowmaking."

"Of course not. Suddenly you're all for desecrating the sacred peaks and ripping uranium out of the Grand Canyon."

"I don't necessarily think we should mine uranium at the Grand Canyon. There are places that should be left alone. I'm not sure we should risk this important watershed." He stopped when he noticed Nora staring at him, probably with her mouth open.

"If you were any kind of environmentalist, you'd be screaming about uranium mining up there. But you're not cheering for Barrett, either. What team do you play for?"

He stared at her as if she'd gone bonkers. Finally he shook his head. "We're talking about you and the fact you shouldn't be involved with Barrett."

She was as involved with Barrett as a person could get. Not only was he financing and making decisions on her business, he might be courting her mother, as well as placing his daughter in virtual daycare under Nora's watch. Having Cole confront her on it only made it worse.

Cole frowned and leaned forward. "You're in all kinds of danger. You've got Barrett with a hidden agenda. Alex Seweingyawma has already tried to kill you. And Big Elk is out to get you. Who is he, anyway?"

"Big Elk is exactly what he seems. A fake chief, beating his drum and creating attention for himself. Other people, on the other hand," she glared at him, "are not at all what they say."

Cole didn't respond to her accusation. He was one smooth player. If she didn't know better, she'd think he had nothing to hide. "But where did Big Elk come from?"

Her Jeep sat a mere few feet away. "He's Sioux. From Nebraska, I think."

Cole shook his head. "That's just it. I have a Hopi friend who's pretty tight with several people up around Rose Bud in Nebraska. They don't know where Big Elk came from. He never spent time up there. He just came on the Native American activist scene working for other tribes, saying he was Sioux."

"I don't care," she said. "I just want to run my business and be left alone."

He shook his head, his eyes full of concern. "That's not going to happen. You're in the middle of this mess and I'm worried about you."

This was too much. "Worried about me? Maybe you should quit lying to me. Why not tell me what you really want?"

Dumbfounded. He stood mute for several beats. "You saw the meeting with Barrett just now, didn't you?"

Good one, Nora. Now he knows and he'll have to kill you. "The one where you and Barrett plotted to bride Congress?"

He grabbed her arm. "Forget about what you heard."

"You'd like that, wouldn't you?"

"You don't need to put yourself in any more danger. These people don't mess around."

"Sure. I should forget about it to protect myself. Right."

He let go of her arm and ran a hand through his hair, agitation coming from him in waves. "Hell, Nora, someone killed your husband. Do you know why? Who? How can you ignore the danger you're in?"

Her knees buckled. *Scott murdered.*

Cole put a hand on her elbow to steady her. "I'm sorry."

She tried to pull on her armor. "Leave me alone."

Cole led her to a bench and they sat. The heat of the sun-warmed concrete soaked through her dress.

He looked her square in the eyes. "The woman at the funeral said Scott was working for someone. Do you know who it was? Maybe that has something to do with his murder."

What was wrong with her? Cole might be all nice and warm and kind on the outside but he'd already proved he had a dark side. It might be blacker than she thought. She jerked away. "I've got to go."

Cole jumped up. "I didn't mean…"

She let her panic pound in her heels clicking on the sidewalk. Just before jerking the door open on her Jeep she saw Heather in the park, leaning against a tree, scanning the area as if waiting for someone.

Nora glanced behind her and didn't see Cole. She headed toward Heather. "Aren't you supposed to be shoveling dirt from around the lift house?"

Unruffled, Heather waited for Nora to get to her. "Abigail said since everyone else was going to town, I could have the afternoon off."

Two days on the job and already Nora had lost control. "Abigail's not your boss."

"Your mom's cool."

"Yeah. I thought that once, for about two seconds." Now who was being a bratty teenager?

Bitterness tinged Heather's words. "You don't even appreciate what you have."

As if Abigail couldn't irritate her enough, now her mother had her very own groupie . "I suppose you think your father is cool, too?"

Heather's eyes narrowed. "My adopted father."

Uh oh. From out of nowhere the pressure overwhelmed Nora. It had nothing to do with Heather; the levy simply gave way. No more banter, no more holding it together. Nora fought one last moment and the tears overtook her. "What am I doing here? I never wanted any of this."

Heather's eyes opened in alarm "Whoa. I can go back to work if it means that much to you."

"I mean the whole thing. I never wanted the ski area or Flagstaff or snow making."

Heather relaxed a little. "Then why are you here?"

Nora sank to the grass, getting control of her sobs. "It was for Scott. And for Abigail. And for Berle."

Heather sat across from her. "Who's Berle?"

"Berle was my mother's second husband. I loved Berle and he was good to my mother. I think maybe she really loved him."

Heather's gaze encouraged her to talk.

"Not long after Scott and I married, Berle developed stomach cancer. I was finishing business school and had some nice offers. I was anticipating living in a plush high-rise condo in Chicago or L.A. and vacations on sunny beaches."

Heather sat quietly, waiting for her to continue.

"Berle went from healthy to almost dead in two weeks. One of the last days, he begged me to promise I'd always take care of my mother. He had a fortune and it would all go to her but he worried. He owned this ski area in Flagstaff. Kachina Ski. He said he'd give it to me, free and clear, with the one caveat that if my mother ever needed financial help, Kachina would be her safety net."

Heather's eyebrows drew together as she worked it out. "This was before any drought. I can see where that would be a good move."

"I told him that, of course, I would take care of my mother but I didn't want Kachina Ski. I assumed I'd have a great career in finance."

"But you ended up here."

"When I told Scott about it, he latched on to the idea and couldn't see anything else. He was full of dreams of us running the place together and spending our days on the mountain. He wanted it so badly I couldn't say no."

"But it didn't work out as you'd planned."

She shrugged. "I was naïve to think Scott would enjoy the business side."

"Your mother says he played and you worked."

"It was more than that. I couldn't have done any of it if he hadn't been with me. Scott made me feel ..." she searched for the right words. Being Scott's wife made her feel special. If he loved her, she must have worth. Sheesh, it sounded so Abigail. Since Bimbo's appearance in their lives, she'd lost even that confidence.

She shouldn't be talking like this to a teenager. Heather might seem mature and, well, like a friend. But this kind of sharing with a sixteen year-old was inappropriate. Nora wiped her eyes. "Enough of this. Tell me something about you."

Heather shrugged. "What do you want to know?"

"Why don't you tell me about what interests you?"

"Hopi."

"Okay. Tell me about Hopi."

Heather eyed her and began slowly, as if testing her. "On either end of the Earth's axis twin brothers sit and hold down the head of the serpent. They are the balance of the world. If they let go, the Earth will tilt and there will be chaos. Hopi are responsible for keeping the brothers there."

Nora nodded.

"Every Hopi belongs to a clan, sort of like families, and each clan performs ceremonies that together maintain balance of the natural forces. See, each of us has a good side and a bad side. Like an elder told me, 'black and white threads wind together in our ceremonies.' So we have to balance our two selves to protect the world."

Nora wanted clarification. "Hopi are in charge of the whole world?"

Heather's shiny black hair bounced to her nod. "We're the smallest tribe but have the biggest job."

"Balance in life is important," Nora said, wondering what it would feel like to be balanced. "Really, the *whole* world?"

"We do the ceremonies and that's what keeps the balance."

Why not? "So tell me about kachinas."

"Kachinas are spirits. They aren't like saints or things like Christians have or like the Greek gods. It's kind of weird. They can help people or cause problems or just sort of be there."

Nora thought of the doll the old man had given her. What spirit did he contain?

Heather held Nora's eye. "Thanks for not laughing at this. Poppy won't listen. But your mom, she's great."

"You're talking about Abigail? You told her this?"

"Yeah. She's really interested in it. I just picked up a bunch of library books to take to her."

Could it be her mother's mind had expanded a notch or two since Nora was young?

Heather stiffened and her eyes hardened to flint at something behind Nora. "Douche bag."

An oily voice floated over her shoulder. "If it isn't Ms. Abbott. Taking a break from destroying Mother Earth?"

Big Elk.

Nora ought to climb into her Jeep. But her dander was running high and she took a step toward Big Elk and his usual entourage of Guilty

White People. "Face it, you lost. I won. Go pick another fight somewhere else."

"The courts granted you permission to gut the Mother. But they aren't the ultimate law."

His followers murmured assent.

He raised his voice in evangelical excitement. "The kachinas promised fire on the mountain if you continue your destructive path."

Heather shifted her hips and crossed her arms. "Knock it off, Big Elk."

Venom filled his eyes.

Nora jumped in to distract him from Heather. "Go ahead and send someone else to kill me. But snow making will happen. Kachina Ski has a partner now, McCreary Energy."

Dismay washed across Big Elk's band, but his arrogance never wavered. "I haven't sent anyone to kill you, Ms. Abbott."

"Don't bother lying to me."

"Lying is the way of the white man. Native Americans don't hide behind falsehoods."

Rage erupted in a fiery furnace. "Is that so? You haven't been behind all the vandalism and protests? You didn't send Alex to murder me?"

Heather blew a disgusted breath. "He wasn't going to kill you."

Big Elk remained irritatingly calm. "You're the one spreading untruths. Alex, our brother of the Hopi, went out to the sacred mountain to pray and offer gifts to the kachinas. When you attacked him, he had no choice but to defend himself."

"Defend himself with his hands around my neck!"

"The Hopi value peace and he wouldn't react unless threatened."

Unchecked words shot from her. "You and your bullshit! What do you know about any of this anyway? You're not even Native American."

"My ancestors..."

Her blasters were fully lit and take-off initiated. "Your ancestors were probably European farmers. You aren't any more Native American than I am. Where are your records, huh? You're not Sioux."

He may or may not be indigenous but his face turned a violent red. "My people were with Dull Knife at Fort Robinson. I..."

She stepped forward and pointed. "Yeah? No one up there knows you or your family. You're a fake."

She'd gone too far.

She thought she felt hatred from him before, but that was mild displeasure compared to the noxious wave that knocked the wind from her. He looked at her with Charles Manson eyes. "You'll regret uttering those words. The kachinas protect their own."

He turned slowly, his murderous eyes lingering on her.

15

Brooding again. Barrett leaned back in his custom-made leather desk chair and gazed at Kachina Mountain.

McCreary Energy was one very profitable privately owned company. Thanks to Barrett the Third. But he wouldn't have had the opportunity if his grandfather hadn't planted the family in Northern Arizona and if Barrett's father hadn't seen the benefits of mining.

It's what McCreary's do. Grandfather started it. Father almost lost it but if he hadn't died young, he probably would have turned it around. I staunched the hemorrhage and turned it into a powerhouse. But I have to strengthen the family chain even more. Heather needs a company with wealth and a diversified position. McCreary Energy has to move into the future.

Uranium.

Northern Arizona is the Saudi Arabia of uranium and that's Heather's future and my legacy. If I let this opportunity slide by, McCreary Energy will become a third-rate has-been and Heather will have nothing.

A lesser man might fold under the forces against him: Enviros hated the idea of mining close to the Grand Canyon. Those radical long-hairs wouldn't go away quietly. Native Americans feared uranium mining on their lands. He didn't blame them. They suffered from the industry's earlier ignorance. But none suffered more than Barrett.

He grabbed the Rolaids from his desk drawer. Below the bottle, Ester and their children smiled at him from the Kodachrome memory. He slammed the drawer closed.

Mining techniques had improved. That disaster would never happen again. He had to move forward. He owed it to Heather. *Forget the past.*

Like a cool breeze on the desert, the image of Abigail wafted before his eyes. She had class and intelligence and a fine ass for a middle-aged gal. Maybe when this was all over they could be together.

No time for romance. Right now, Abigail was good cover so he could keep an eye on Kachina Ski.

He'd like to get rid of Nora. Her balkiness over snowmaking irritated him. But it would look suspicious if Nora disappeared and for now, he had her under control. Her life expectancy would change, though, if she ever found out Scott worked for him.

Barrett sank back in his chair. Abigail was a fount of disturbing information at their lunch. For instance, Barrett learned about Scott's affair. *Another loose thread to take care of.*

Dust on the road signaled an approaching car. He glanced at the clock. Right on time. That proved Big Elk was no real Indian. He was nothing but a damned mercenary.

Big Elk's black Escalade, now dusted with dirt, braked in front of Barrett's house. He turned off the ignition and sat behind the wheel talking on the phone.

The irksome imposter drove the same vehicle as Barrett. Before he rose to answer the doorbell, Barrett sent a quick email to his assistant at the office in Phoenix telling him to trade the Escalade for one of those Mercedes SUVs.

"Nice place," Big Elk said when Barrett opened the door.

Barrett led him to the great room. "It's home. Drink?"

"Whiskey, straight up."

Barrett poured two fingers and handed it to him.

Big Elk settled himself on the leather sofa. "What's on your mind?"

Barrett wanted business with this varmint concluded quickly. He stood by the window. "Stop influencing the Hopi council against uranium mining."

Big Elk sighed. "The Hopi are a simple people. I'm merely a voice for them to the outside world."

Barrett knew more about the Hopi and cared more for them than Big Elk ever would. He knew what served their best interest. "Convince them of the benefits of mining."

"I see no benefit to raping and mauling their pristine lands to satisfy your avaricious desire."

Good thing for Big Elk that Barrett's gun rested in his desk drawer across the room. Too bad for Barrett the Rolaids sat in the same place. "The benefits of mining royalties to the Hopi are something I'm sure you can imagine. What's more important for this discussion is the benefit to Big Elk."

Big Elk sat back with satisfaction. "Go on."

"What's your price?"

Big Elk feigned shock, coming closer than he knew to Barrett's fist in his face. "This is about an ancient people's land and their right to sovereignty."

Barrett waited.

"I can't say you're much fun to do business with."

"I don't like you."

Big Elk's eyebrows shot up. "Ouch."

Again Barrett waited.

Big Elk stood. He reached in his back pocket for his wallet. "Two million. Deposited to these accounts." He pulled out a handwritten note.

Barrett didn't move. "One."

"With uranium selling at an all-time high and you panting after one of the world's largest deposits, you won't miss two million, my friend."

"I'm not your friend." Barrett let the clock tick. "One point five."

Big Elk took a moment as if weighing the decision. "And a warehouse in Flagstaff."

"A warehouse? I won't be involved in drugs."

Big Elk laughed. "Nor would I. I'll spare you the details but saving Mother Earth isn't the only game in town for this Indian."

Barrett snatched the paper containing the bank accounts from Big Elk's hand.

Big Elk smiled. "I'll let myself out."

"One other thing," Barrett said. "Keep Alex Seweingyawma away from my daughter."

An oily smile slid onto Big Elk's face. "I can't control him."

"If I find out he's been anywhere near Heather, the deal is off and you're going to jail."

Big Elk shrugged. "I'll do what I can to protect your innocent daughter. But understand this, Barrett, I have as much on you as you have on me."

Barrett glared at Big Elk until the small man snorted with arrogance and sauntered down the hall.

Barrett craved a disinfectant shower. It sickened him the way Big Elk had no principles.

Big Elk tossed off words over his shoulder. "You don't have any attachment to Nora Abbott, do you?"

Barrett waited while Big Elk faced him.

"I've heard she's accident prone," Big Elk said.

An accident, such as a fall from a cliff? Maybe a malfunctioning Jeep engine. The lodge apartment ran on propane and those pesky fuel bottles could blow under heat or pressure. It would be nice to have the Nora Abbott problem eliminated.

Barrett bent to pick up the empty whiskey glass so Big Elk wouldn't see his smile. Good. Let Big Elk take care of her.

The front door opened and closed as Big Elk left.

Barrett headed to the kitchen and realized he hadn't heard Big Elk drive off. One glance out the window made his veins feel like a river in January.

Heather stood next to Big Elk's Escalade. He sat behind the wheel with the window down.

Damn it. She said she'd be gone all day riding her horse and here she stood, talking to Big Elk. Heather seemed to have a talent for finding trouble these days. Maybe Barrett should install a tracking chip under her skin.

Heather's eyebrows drew together the way they did when she made a serious point.

Barrett stomped onto the front porch. "Heather."

She jumped and turned toward the house, not finishing her sentence.

“Come inside, now.” Barrett glared at Big Elk while Heather pounded up the stairs and into the house.

If Big Elk didn’t stay away from Heather, he might make Barrett angry. A very bad position for Big Elk.

16

Watching the truck loaded with pipeline inching up the slope should fill Nora with triumph. Three months ago, she feared she'd end up selling the ski lift on E-bay and peddling used rental skis on the street corner.

Back then, Scott was still alive and planning to leave her. The 9th District court weighed its decision on snowmaking. Abigail shopped in New York and though Nora fretted about losing Kachina Ski, she hadn't learned real fear, yet.

A ski area in Arizona sounded crazy. But Kachina Ski opened in 1935 and was one of the oldest ski slopes in the country. Sure, the drive to a desert took only an hour, but this mountain rose to nearly 13,000 feet. Though the runs didn't rival Colorado or Utah resorts, Kachina Ski held its own, and even managed to be profitable. That is, until Nora took over, which happened to coincide with a five-year—and counting—drought.

But this pipeline proved she conquered the drought, and with Barrett's help, she'd have Abigail shopping for shoes in no time. By Christmastime this mountain would be covered in snow, whether Mother Nature felt up to the task or not.

Why did it make her stomach ache to think of it?

The sun glared overhead, heating the pines and releasing their pungent perfume over the mountainside covered in June's wildflowers.

Enormous black ravens cawed and glided from treetops and over the wide swath of grass-covered ski run. The day sparkled brilliantly on her mountain but it might as well have been sleeting.

Nora plodded up the slope, following the truck with its load of pipe rolled like giant spools of fire hose. Its tires tore the ground like the Jolly Green Giant's golf divots.

A quiet voice filtered through the truck's struggle. "Miss."

The slip of a man, the kachina salesmen from the courthouse, stood behind her. His approached must have been masked by the roar of the truck. He stood without moving, his black eyes focused on her face.

If he breathed, Nora couldn't see the movement. Though nothing about him threatened, Nora's pulse quickened. Maybe he brought Alex with him. "You. What do you want?"

His eyes shifted slowly to the truck which stopped at a level place to unload the hose. The sorrow on his face felt like fingers squeezing Nora's heart.

The rolls of hose stacked on the flatbed would be unrolled and laid on the ground alongside the run. The pump would shoot water and air through the hose to the sprayers. Snow, directly from the abundant aquifer. God, it was good to be an American.

What a triumphant day on her mountain—well, her sliver of it, anyway. *I will not feel guilty, damn it.* This guy needed to go away.

He brought his gaze back to her. "Are you gonna...?" He spoke in clipped words, as if English wasn't natural for him. He pointed to the hose.

He didn't look like the placard-bearing, rally-calling, hysterical religious fanatics that fought her for years. That didn't mean he wouldn't turn on her any minute. "It's for snow making, yes."

He nodded so slowly he barely moved. Those eyes carried deep sadness.

Nope. Not feeling bad for bringing water to the mountain. Nora hiked to the truck. She waved to the driver when he climbed from the cab. "We want to stack the rolls right here."

He pulled a clipboard from the cab. "I gotta do the paperwork."

Nora walked next to the rumbling truck, ignoring the diesel fumes.

She put a hand on the sun-heated hose, the veins that pumped the blood to keep Kachina Ski alive.

"Miss."

Nora jumped. His gentle voice raised the hairs on her neck. Why did he seem to belong here more than she did?

He pulled a ratty bag from his back. "I brought you my kachinas."

The crude doll with the blue mask, broken and floating in the gutter flashed in her mind. "No thanks. I lost the last one."

While his hand rummaged in the bag, he stared into her face.

The two top rolls shifted. Nora jumped back.

They settled. The driver must be ready to unload. "Excuse me," Nora said to the little guy. She strode away to talk to the driver.

Holding his bag in front of him, the man stared up at the hose.

Something moved on top of the truck.

The top two rolls of hose shifted again and straps holding the stack upright slipped to the ground. Lightening flashed inside Nora as she realized the hose was no longer strapped to the truck. If the little man didn't move now, the hose could fall and flatten him.

The unstable roll slipped from the top.

Why didn't the little man react?

The whole pile started to topple. The Native American man stood motionless.

A normal person would run. No one would stand there doing nothing.

The top of the load rolled, followed by the others. Her body took over, legs pumping up the slope, perhaps her voice shouting, hands in front of her.

The man stayed rooted to the mountain.

Nora smashed into him like a defensive tackle, pushing them out of the way of the crashing hose. She landed on top of him. The ground vibrated with the impact of falling freight.

Still pulsing with adrenaline, Nora dug her feet into the dirt and tried to scoot them away.

Too late.

A heavy weight crushed her ankle, sending hot waves of pain

shooting up her legs and spine. Several more hits felt like someone with a sledgehammer pounding her shin.

Silence. Not even a raven cawed.

Nora opened her eyes and pulled her face from the ground. She still lay on top of the little man and tried to move but the hose pinned her calves. She managed to shift enough for him to wiggle out. Throbbing pain made everything below her waist ignite in flames.

Behind her, the truck bed sat empty except for two rolls of hose. The remainder of the load spread across the slope, with one roll on her legs.

"Nora!" Cole appeared next to her head. He reached for her hand, his eyes searching her face. "Are you okay?"

Her throat tightened and she fought panic. Somehow Cole caused this accident in an effort to shut her up about the bribery. Her legs hurt, pain piled on all the misery of the last week, topped off with fear for her life.

Cole shouted at the driver. "Help me get this off her."

The overweight driver scurried around Nora's head and grunted. The weight on her legs lightened and Nora held her breath against the throbbing. It hurt like hell but she could move her legs. Celebrate life's little victories.

Cole knelt beside her. "Can you stand up?"

She struggled for strength but her voice sounded weak. "What are you doing here?"

"What are you thinking jumping under the hose?"

"That man..." Yee-ow! No way could Nora stand. "Ankle," she said between clenched teeth.

Cole bent over to examine the foot she raised. His lean fingers gently tested the purpling flesh.

The raw agony nearly made Nora pee. "Stop it!"

"Sorry."

She rotated it slowly, the pain galloping all the way up her leg.

"It's sprained. I can wrap it," Cole said.

"Just leave me alone!"

"Hey, buddy." The driver stood next to the hose. "What do you want me to do?"

Cole shrugged. "Finish unloading the truck and stack it."

The driver shot Nora an annoyed look. "I was told there would be help."

Maybe the kachina man could use a few bucks. "What about that guy?"

Both men gave her a puzzled look.

She scanned the slope, suddenly worried he'd been injured. "Where did he go?"

Cole followed her gaze. "Who?"

"That Native American guy I was talking to."

"I didn't see anyone," Cole said.

Nora looked at the driver. "You saw him. I tried to shove him out of the way of the falling hose."

The driver shrugged. "I was doing the paperwork."

The aching in her ankle overrode everything else. "Load it, leave it. I don't care."

Abigail appeared out of nowhere, like she used to whenever Nora was in some kind of mischief. "What is going on?"

Cole put Nora's arm around his shoulder. "Stack it. You've got a dolly on your truck."

Nora shrugged, trying to back away from Cole.

"I gotta get back on the road, man," the driver said.

The little guy had been right here. Where could he have gone? Was he working for Cole and Barrett, too?

The expression Abigail turned on the trucker would make a werewolf whimper. "If you looked before you unstrapped the load, you would have seen Nora and not released the strap. I'm sure your supervisor won't like that report."

The driver jutted his head. "Hey lady, I didn't unstrap the hose. I was in the cab."

He might as well start stacking hose.

Abigail pulled a cell phone from her pocket and looked at the phone number of the company advertised on the side of the truck. "Why do you suppose the hose suddenly let loose?"

The sun beat on Nora's head, giving her maybe two minutes before her hair burst into flames. "It doesn't matter whose fault it is. Let's just move."

Controlled anger tightened Abigail's voice. "You might have been killed." She glared at the driver. "Your negligence caused bodily harm, so be helpful or you could be in worse trouble."

Nora felt sorry for the driver. He probably had nothing to do with the accident. Cole, the man who held her upright, was Nora's main suspect.

The driver puffed up his shoulders. "I ain't in any trouble, lady. I checked out at the yard. You don't have nothin' on me."

Nora's head and ankle throbbed in syncopation. She wanted off the slope. "Lawsuit is her middle name."

The driver's shoulders dropped slightly. "Whatever."

Cole helped Nora take a step and spoke to the driver over his shoulder. "I'll come back and help."

In the presence of witnesses, Cole might as well help her to the lodge. He couldn't make another attempt now, could he?

The slope opened wide before them with the lodge looking like it sat in another country. Each step wiggled her ankle and sent waves of hot lava shooting through her. *Another day in paradise.*

They hadn't gone but a few steps when the driver called out, his tone smug. "Hey, lady. Take a look at this."

Abigail marched to him.

The driver held one piece of strap and tugged the end from under a roll of hose. He held up both pieces.

Abigail snatched one from him. After inspecting, she dropped it and stomped toward Nora and Cole.

"I need to call the police." She marched closer. "This will convince Officer Gary that your life is in danger and you didn't kill Scott for the life insurance."

Ankle, head, now all nerves. "What do you mean convince him I didn't kill Scott?"

Abigail waved her hand at the annoyance of it all. "Gary called on your cell and I answered. He wanted to know about Scott's life insurance so I found it. Your files are a mess."

What about Barrett's expensive lawyer? Nora was pretty sure he wouldn't want Abigail handing over anything to the cops. Nora gritted her teeth at the pain in her ankle. "I don't know who killed Scott but I've got a good idea who is behind this accident." She glared at Cole.

He acted as if he didn't know what she meant. "Use that cell phone in your pocket," he said to Abigail.

"Battery is dead. It's this high altitude. Nothing holds a charge for long."

Cole laughed. "Good thing Mr. Truck Driver didn't know that."

Nora planted her good foot. "What is going on?"

Abigail squinted in rage. A steam engine couldn't have been hotter. "Someone sliced the straps."

"Cole sliced the straps, Mother."

He froze.

Abigail laughed. "Don't be ridiculous." She marched ahead then turned around. "Let's go. Nora can't stand out here in the sunshine on that bad ankle."

17

Nora leaned her head against the warm siding of the lodge and closed her eyes to the sun. Resting on an old lawn chair Abigail scrounged up, her foot elevated on a stool, she reached down and patted Abbey's head.

The peaceful setting warred with her emotions. Sitting on the deck felt like prison. She needed action to calm the growing panic.

"There you are." Abigail came from the lodge.

"Right where you left me."

"What a beautiful day. I've made mint iced tea and we can sit here all afternoon and talk."

Was it possible the falling hose actually killed Nora, because she had to be in hell. She closed her eyes again. "When are you going to find a new home?"

Glasses clinked on the bench next to Nora. "I couldn't think of leaving you now."

"Abbey and I can get along fine on our own."

"Don't be silly. Your dog can't fix you tea and provide conversation."

"No. But I like him better." Why did she say things like that? Abigail didn't cause the problems, not directly, anyway. Her mother needed Nora's help and protection, not her hurtful comments.

Charlie's voice boomed from the base of the deck stairs. "Greetings mountain nymphs."

Abigail froze momentarily. She sprang to her feet and leapt to the apartment stairs.

Too late. Charlie bounded onto the deck, not like a graying, hippy alcoholic, but more like a teenager in love. Abigail was caught.

Despite Nora's earlier resolve to be a kinder, gentler daughter, she cracked up.

"Look who I found on the trail," Charlie said.

Cole appeared behind Charlie. His sandy-colored hair fell across his forehead. "How are you feeling?"

Cole pretended to be charming and Abigail obviously bought into it. He'd acted all shocked and hurt when Nora accused him of slicing the straps but maybe he was an excellent performer. She should go to Gary with her suspicions, and tell him--what? That she overheard a conversation between Cole and Barrett about illegal things? That would hardly prove Cole tried to smash her and it would only make her sound like a hysterical pea-brain.

But he was always around to "save" her.

Exactly. Why was he always around when things went south?

But everything was going bad lately. If he was going to be around at all, he'd be witness to bad.

"How thoughtful of you, Cole," Abigail said.

Nora waved a hand at her foot propped on the chair. "I hate to disappoint you but the falling hose gave me a sore ankle. Not even sprained."

"Nora!" Abigail acted predictably aghast.

"Come on, Abigail. Why was he here when the hose fell?"

Cole looked embarrassed. "I wasn't stalking you. I was at Scott's murder site looking for some clue to who killed him."

Charlie nodded. "That's right. We've been over that place again and again. Cole says you don't know who Scott worked for. 'Spose he left some papers or something around so we can figure out who offed him?"

Charlie and Cole working together? Abigail trusted Cole. Charlie always protected Nora. Cole gave off honest and kind vibes. Trust him or not? "If you believe the cops, I did it," Nora said.

Cole sighed. "I don't believe the cops and that means you're in danger until we figure out who did it and why. Just look at what happened with the hose."

"And you care?"

"Of course, he cares," Abigail said.

Abigail was in full match-making mode.

Cole stared at her ankle. "Someone has to take care of you. You won't do it for yourself."

Nora closed her eyes and leaned her head against the lodge. "Are you taking care of me or planning to kill me?"

Charlie and Abigail both laughed.

No one took her seriously.

"You could talk to the police," Abigail said to Cole. "That Gary Something or Other said they'd look into it but he's incompetent at best. And I'm sure he's out to get Nora."

Nora threw daggers at Abigail with her eyes. Now Cole knew the cops had no leads. "Charlie, didn't you tell me columbine's blooming behind the lodge? I'm sure Abigail would love that."

Charlie had Abigail's hand tucked into his arm before she could break and run. "It is beauty to rival mortals, though it doesn't come close to your heavenly dazzle."

There was no escape. Abigail's eyes pleaded with Nora for rescue as Charlie led her away, extolling her beauty with each step.

Nora looked at the iced tea and up at Cole. "My mother just made tea. Please have some."

He sat next to her on the bench and took a glass.

Nora watched him raise it to his lips, weighing whether setting him up like this was cruel and unusual punishment for him nearly killing her.

He took several gulps, his Adam's apple bobbing. When he lowered the glass his eyes grew wide, his mouth contorted. "Your mother made this?"

Nora gave him her sweetest smile and nodded.

"And you think I'm trying to kill you?" He picked up her glass and ran to the rail, dumping both glasses. "You don't need to thank me."

Nora fought giggles.

Cole sat down and leaned forward, eyes intense. "Who do you think cut the straps?"

"You."

His eyes crinkled with laughter. "Seriously."

"I am serious."

He stood up and paced the deck, long legs striding. He stopped in front of her. "I'm trying to keep you alive but you're not helping. Get out of this deal with Barrett. Quit snowmaking. You know it's not good for the mountain and hooking up with Barrett might get you killed."

"You're in Barrett's back pocket. Suddenly you're all environmental and down on McCreary?"

"You don't know what's going on."

"Enlighten me."

He stared at her, an obvious battle waging in his mind. Finally he puffed out air. "Please. Just trust me. In the meantime, you and Abigail should move to town."

"We're not going anywhere. All your scare tactics won't work to stop snowmaking." *Forget about stopping it. With Barrett at the controls I can't even slow it down.*

"I don't care about the snowmaking. I mean, I don't think it's a good idea. But that's not the point. Barrett is dangerous."

She batted her eyes at him. "I get it. You don't want Barrett to be my partner because you're concerned for my safety."

"Of course I am."

How could he confuse her so much?

The putter of a car floated to the deck.

A soft tinkle of Abigail's laugh preceded her arrival from the back of the deck. When she caught sight of Nora, she sobered. "I didn't appreciate you sending me off with that Gonzo."

Charlie appeared with the satisfied grin of someone awarded a blue ribbon. He winked at Nora.

Abigail hurried to the rail. "I wonder who this could be?"

If the current trend held, it wouldn't be good news.

Abbey let out a mild woof. They all stared at the stairs and waited.

In a moment a young, heavy-set woman with too much eye make-up trudge up the stairs. She sidestepped Abbey. "Are you Nora Abbott?" She carried a cardboard box which looked heavy.

Nora nodded.

The girl plopped the box on the bench, knocking over one of the iced tea glasses. "Sorry." She didn't look sorry. Despite the heavy black outlining her eyes, they were red and puffy and her whole face looked swollen. Her thick lips turned down at the edges.

Abigail hurried over and picked up the glass. "We haven't met. I'm Nora's mother, Mrs. Stoddard." She held out her hand as if meeting a dowager at a garden party. "This is Cole Huntsman." The warmth in her voice plummeted to subfreezing. "And this is Charlie."

The girl looked confused. "I'm Teresa. Maureen's roommate."

A garrote sliced through Nora's neck.

Abigail smiled warmly. "Maureen? I'm sorry, I don't..."

Nora held up her hand and interrupted. "Never mind, Mother." She looked at Teresa and made her voice as unwelcoming as possible. "What do you and Maureen want?"

A little hiccup of distress slipped from Abigail.

With surprising speed, Teresa's eyes filled with tears and they gushed down her face, revealing the amazing quality of waterproof makeup. "Maureen would want to be alive."

Silence. The confusing sentence started to make dreadful sense. Nora would rather sprint to the other side of the mountain on her painful ankle than ask. "What do you mean?"

Teresa wiped a pudgy arm under her nose. "She's dead. I don't know what to do with this stuff and since it belonged your husband I thought you might want it, but if you don't I'll take it away." Teresa dissolved into great heaving sobs.

Always ready, Abigail pulled a tissue from her trouser pocket. Of course, it was unused. "You poor dear."

It seemed hard to recall that Abigail was Satan's handmaid. She didn't know Teresa or Maureen, had to be repulsed by Teresa's physical appearance, and yet, here she was, all comfort and grace.

Unlike Nora, who hadn't the slightest idea how to react. What do you say when your husband's mistress (now that's an old fashioned term) dies? Maureen wasn't her bff but she didn't wish her dead. "I'm sorry."

Charlie and Cole couldn't even drum up that much.

Teresa lifted her head from Abigail's shoulder. The black smear on Abigail's dry clean only shell proved that water-proof make-up wasn't perfect. "It's just not fair, you know? Not long ago she was so happy. She was planning on getting married..."

To my husband. Nora's stomach lurched.

Another sob. "You can't imagine how hard it was for her when he died."

Can't I?

Abigail patted Teresa's back. "I'm sure it was awful."

Teresa nodded. "At least she's not in any more pain."

What a stupid thing to say. Nora would learn to live without Scott and she was sure Maureen could have gotten over him, too. But Maureen would never have the opportunity to love again. She wouldn't feel the sunshine on her face or eat a bite of dark chocolate or even be annoyed by a deranged mother.

Nora's throat closed and an artesian flow rushed through her head, forcing tears. "I'm sorry," she said again.

Cole sat next to Nora and put a hand on her back. Surprisingly, Nora didn't want to brush it off.

Teresa gave Nora an appraising look. "You don't seem like such a bad person. I mean, you don't know what goes on in someone else's life, but you don't seem as cold as he said."

A javelin through the heart pinned her to the deck.

Cole stood up. "Do you need anything else?"

"Well, there's that box of stuff and...I guess that's all."

Cole held Teresa's arm and walked her away.

Abigail took over from Cole and ushered Teresa down the stairs. "Thank you for bringing his things," Abigail said. "I'm sure you understand. Losing a husband is one of the most difficult situations to endure. I, myself, buried two husbands..." Their voices thankfully faded.

Nora struggled to remember something she'd thought earlier. Yes. Sunshine on her face, dark chocolate, annoying mothers. Small things. She lifted her face to the sun, reached down and patted Abbey's head.

Light footsteps tripped across the deck and stopped in front of her. "You need to develop dignity," Agibail said. "You can't fall apart at every revelation of Scott's secret life. You are above that tacky display. Now pull yourself together because Barrett is on his way up the trail."

"Barrett McCreary?" Nora leveled her head and looked at Abigail.

"How many Barrett's do you know?" Like a general dismissing his troops, Abigail nodded at Charlie and Cole. "We have issues to discuss regarding Kachina Ski. Thank you for stopping by."

With her arms outstretched, she herded them toward the back of the lodge. She returned to stand in front of Nora. "You should go inside and put on some make-up but I suppose you'll do."

Nora took the offered tissue. Did Abigail have a never ending supply in her pockets? And yet, her slacks had no tale tell bulges. Too bad she didn't use her magic for good. "Thanks for the compliment."

Abigail patted her own hair and applied lipstick from some other hidden pocket. "He's important to us."

"Us?"

Abigail faced the stairs, flexing her shoulders like an athlete stretching for competition. "Don't forget it's his funding that's keeping this place alive."

Right. Nora studied her leg propped up on the bench. Kachina Ski might survive, but would she and her mother?

Abbey's tail thumped the deck and Charlie trudged around the corner from the back. "Hidy ho, ladies."

Abigail rolled her eyes. "You couldn't just go?"

He sidled over and sat next to Nora in a puff of beer and forest scent. "I've got interests to protect."

Abigail turned her back and flounced to the rail.

Nora welcomed Charlie's warm hand over hers.

18

Barrett slammed the door of his new Mercedes. Damn Big Elk. Barrett had really liked the Escalade. Maybe it wasn't the new car that had him irritated so much as it was the meeting with Heather's school counselor.

Heather clicked her door closed "Grades are just white man's way to control and catalogue people."

He ground his teeth. "You have to at least pass to make it into community college."

She shrugged. "Even if I wanted to go to college, which I don't, all you have to do is build a science building and I'm in."

His jaw clenched. The women he loved most in the world could always launch his temper. But not Abigail. He may not feel the same passion for her as he did Ester, but passion was overrated. Just the thought of her feminine and pleasing ways soothed him. "Bring your grades up next year or we'll be looking at military schools."

Abigail waved from the deck. Her soft blonde hair glimmered in the sun and her trim body draped in well-fitting slacks. So unlike Ester, but he found her immensely appealing. He allowed the five second fantasy full run.

By the time he and Heather climbed the stairs he had his imaginary climax and stubbed out his cigarette.

Abigail took Heather's hand. "How was the meeting with the counselor?" Abigail was a good influence on Heather and measured up as a suitable companion for him.

While Heather complained about the unfair American educational system, he turned his attention on Nora. She sat on a bench with her foot elevated. Ignoring Charlie he said, "Feeling any better?"

Abigail pulled herself away from Heather. "She's in some pain, of course. But she's managing with over-the-counter painkillers. She was lucky."

"The company agreed to give us the hose at half price." Barrett had argued a half hour to convince them the discount trumped a lawsuit for negligence. "Of course, it's not worth the pain you're going through."

She didn't seem as pleased as he expected. "It wasn't their fault. They should get the full cost."

"The hose didn't jump off the truck on its own. There must be recourse for poor safety procedures," he said.

Abigail's pleasant smile slipped from her face. "No, Barrett. It wasn't an accident. Someone cut the straps."

Heather's small gasp said it all. Alex was at it again. It wouldn't hurt Barrett's feelings if Alex eliminated Nora.

"Did you talk to the police?" Barrett asked.

Abigail folded her arms and even that gesture appeared feminine. "Of course. But that Gary is more interested in Scott's life insurance, which was paltry by the way, and some alleged threat Nora made to Scott's mistress at the funeral."

His deepest protection instinct kicked in. Abigail needed the shelter he could provide. "I'll hire a detective and get to the bottom of this."

Nora gave a weary sigh. "Great. What I'm really concerned about is the snowmaking. The pipe is fine. But the sprayers you ordered are all wrong. I stopped the order this morning."

Abigail drew in a breath. "Won't that slow the process?"

Nora nodded, keeping her focus on Barrett. "I doubt we'll get delivery until early spring."

Temper swirled below the surface of his control. "That's ridiculous. Do you realize how much that delay will cost us?"

Nora bristled. "I've been running this place for a few years; I think I know the costs. But the sprayers I ordered are more fuel efficient, less noisy, and generally more environmentally friendly."

"Don't give me the fuel efficiency line. And the noise issue is moot since they run at night when no one is here. You're afraid to move forward." It was hard to stay calm when he'd rather smack her.

"We do not cave to terrorists," Abigail said.

At least Abigail stood on his side. "You've had threats for years."

Nora struggled to her feet. "I won't deny I'm scared and worried about protecting Abigail. But this mountain needs care, too. I'll do what's right for it."

Charlie raised his fist. "Right on."

"For once just listen to someone else, Poppy," Heather said.

Barrett sent Heather a scathing glare. "You're in enough trouble right now." He looked at Nora and tried to sound soothing. "You're obviously distraught. Let's give this a day or so and we'll discuss it again. If you still want to delay snowmaking by changing the equipment, of course, I'll abide by your decision."

Big Elk's little buddy better hurry up or Barrett might have to take care of Nora himself.

Charlie narrowed his eyes and stared at Barrett. *What a waste of skin.*

Abigail brushed her hands together at the job well done. "Letting it sit for a while sounds reasonable. I've got a pitcher of iced tea. Let's enjoy the beautiful sunshine."

To make Nora feel less attacked, Barrett backed off a few steps. He glanced down into a large cardboard box. He had a meeting with Big Elk tomorrow and would encourage the Alex situation—

His mind registered what his eyes had been reading for the last seconds. Logging records. Water composition. Well numbers. Signed by Scott Fucking Abbott.

Proof. God damned evidence that Scott worked for Barrett and exactly what he discovered. Ice and fire and more ice raced through Barrett as he struggled to hide all emotion. He had to get that box, destroy it. Right now.

"Iced tea sounds nice but Heather has already missed several hours of work. She needs to earn her keep." He gestured toward the box, concentrating on not letting his hand shake. "This looks like a box of old records that needs burning."

Nora collapsed to the bench, all fight sucked out of her. "Yes. Burning."

He reached down and picked up the box. *Slowly, no rush. Don't act desperate.* "I'll help Heather take it around back."

Nora looked like a whipped dog. "Good idea."

Abigail nodded approval.

Barrett hefted the box. "Let's go, Heather."

"Wait." Nora looked up.

No! Burn it now. Do it.

Nora stood and hobbled across the deck. "Leave the box."

Abigail rushed to throw Nora's arm over her shoulder for support. "You need to let it go."

Nora's face was little more than enormous, tortured eyes. "Leave it."

Barrett inhaled slowly. *God damn it!* "Of course. Where would you like me to put it?"

Abigail frowned, arguing wordlessly with Nora. Just as mute, Nora held firm.

Barrett wanted to close his hands around Nora's scrawny neck and wring the life from her.

Abigail finally relented and sighed. "Let's put it upstairs for now, shall we? In the back of a closet perhaps."

Way to the back, where Nora wouldn't want to retrieve it and where he could snatch it before she ever got the courage to look.

19

Nora rolled over for the billionth time, her wrapped ankle wadding up the sheet. Across the hall, Abigail slept like a baby. Except babies don't snore like lumber jacks. Maybe she exaggerated. Abigail's snoring sounded more like a soft purr.

Nora couldn't sleep anyway. Like worms chewing into her guts, apprehension gnawed at her. She felt a growing resistance to making snow and the only reason she could name was that it felt wrong.

Of course having Barrett on her side was a good thing. He knew how to make money. She should be grateful for his help. But he wasn't helping. He was running things. And the closer they got to pumping water onto the mountain, the more uneasy Nora felt. At least she got the right sprayers. One small victory.

Abbey woofed on the deck below the apartment. His claws scratched the wood as he scrambled to his feet.

Nora tossed off the covers and stumbled to her bedroom window. Her ankle still throbbed but felt stronger all the time. She slid the window open further and leaned out to see Abbey. He barked again, focused on the woods.

Resting her hands on the ledge she stared into the dark forest. It was as if electricity didn't exist and the stars jumped from the sky like footlights on a stage.

How many summer nights had she and Scott cuddled in a sleeping bag on the slope and stared at those amazing stars? They'd talked and laughed and made love caught up in the magic.

Just as the chasm in her heart started to crack and bleed she hardened. How often had he done the same thing with Maureen? The stars were just cosmic facts, not divine sparks, and Scott proved to be nothing more than a common cheater. She loved them both once but she knew better now.

Nora lowered her eyes to the forest and that's when she saw the distinct flicker of fire.

Abbey barked for real now. He ran down the stairs, high-tailing it for the forest.

Nora's skin froze. Maybe the pinpoint of light deep in the trees was Alex's dying fire and right now he snuck through the forest, planning to slit their throats.

"Abbey!" Like the well-trained and obedient dog he was, Abbey kept barking and running across the slope.

Abigail snored on. Should she wake Abigail and head for town? But they would have to get to the parking lot and Alex could jump them on the way. Should she call the cops? And tell them what? That someone was camping in the woods, on public lands, for which they have every legal right.

She strained to see the flame but lost sight of it. In the old days--just 2 weeks ago—when she'd taken the time to look at the mountain, the sky or the forest, she saw nature's beauty. Now it seemed she constantly squinted into the shadows looking for danger.

Abbey stopped at the edge of the trees and kept barking.

The campfire either flickered its way out or was deliberately doused. The only lights came from the stars and they refused to help Nora.

Without warning a fireball ignited at the edge of the slope.

Nora gasped. The flames leapt higher than a man. But there was nothing except green grass where it burned, no fuel to feed a fire. It looked like an independent monster, living on its own.

Abbey dove into the shadows. A moment later, his bark turned to a yelp of pain.

"Abbey!" Nora spun from the window, her heart pounding like an unbalanced washing machine. She pulled on her jeans and shoved her feet into shoes, grabbed the flashlight by the door and took the stairs two at a time. She paused at the deck railing and stared into the trees. Abbey made no sound.

The fireball slipped up the slope for several yards and then turned into the forest. It moved with the jerky gait of a runner, but quicker than any sprinter Nora had ever seen.

Was it Alex? For all she knew, it could be Cole out there running up and down with some high tech eco-terrorist lantern. Except it didn't look like a real person running. It moved too quickly, with random fits and starts.

Nora raced across the open ski run, dew quickly wetting her shoes. Despite the chilly mountain air, a film of sweat covered her body and her heart rampaged against her ribs. After several yards, she didn't feel the pain in her ankle.

Nora searched the forest ahead but didn't see Abbey, a flare, dying campfire or anything except thick darkness. Picturing the fireball, she slowed her paced and tried to figure where it would have gone. She entered the trees, her breath sounding like a freight engine.

The moon gave scant light. She was no stranger to nighttime on the mountain, but this was no jaunty moonlight hike.

Nora gripped the flashlight, expecting Alex to jump from behind every tree, his butcher knife poised for her throat.

"Abbey." To her left the night lit up. Abbey barked. Fire. It blazed too far away to make out any details but the ball of flame appeared to be about the size of a laundry basket and it hovered six feet off the ground. It was definitely not a campfire because it moved, winking in and out behind trees. The flame slipped through the forest about 50 yards uphill and Nora took off after it, following Abbey's excited bark.

Nora chased the fire through the pines, stumbling over fallen logs and piles of brush, wondering what the hell she'd do if she caught up to it. Not even sure what "it" was. Did she expect to beat it to embers with her flashlight? Was it Alex with some Native American flame carrier?

She followed the light uphill until her thighs burned, turned back toward the ski run and downhill, executing a circle. Abbey barked occasionally but now it sounded more like play. The closer she came to where she entered the forest, the more nervous Nora grew. Just before the flame stepped—if stepped was even the right word —out of the trees, the light disappeared.

Nora stopped and Abbey trotted out of the trees, nose to the ground. He whined and sniffed at the edge of the clearing.

Nora knelt and ran her hands over Abbey. He licked her face once but had more interest in smelling the forest. He seemed in one piece.

"*Pas pay um waaynuma.*" A quiet voice made Nora gasp and spin around.

The little kachina salesman stepped out from behind a tree, the top of his head nearly two feet lower than the fire ball.

Nora tried to keep from bolting. "Who are you?"

He shrugged. "You must protect dis moun-ain."

Abbey shoved his muzzle in the man's hand. The little man greeted Abbey as if they were friends, speaking to him in a quiet, guttural speech.

Nora gripped the flashlight, doubting she'd need to defend herself physically from this gentle man. But he was just plain scary in the forest in the middle of the night. Strangely, she felt like she needed to justify herself. "I'm not out to ruin Kachina Peak."

He spoke in soft, halting accent. "You can do much good. Or you can do much harm. You choose."

The fear and anger that propelled her on this foolhardy journey clung to her. "What is that fire? Why are you here?"

"You love dis moun-ain. You mus' care for it." His words fell to the forest floor with no inflection.

She turned away from him and searched the trees for Alex.

"Bad men are here." A speck of sadness shone in his eyes in the moonlight. "Dey don't understand Hopi way."

"If slicing me with knives, strangling me and crashing freight on me and general terrorism is the Hopi way, I think they understand it just fine.

"Hopi is balance," he said.

The fireball was gone, she didn't see Alex anywhere, and cold seeped under her skin. She wanted to go home. "Are you here to tell me not to make snow?"

His eyes showed intensity not evident in his voice. "You are protector of our moun-ain."

"I'm not Hopi."

He shrugged. "You love our sacred peak."

Was she really having a conversation with a shriveled Native American in the forest in the middle of the night?

"Watch for da spirits of the moun-ain ," he said. "Beware men speaking for Hop.i Dey do not speak da true way."

"You want me to watch for kachinas?"

If doing the kachina's bidding made her end up living like this little guy did, no thank you. Impossible to tell when he'd showered last, if ever. Come to think of it, he had no smell. Dust covered his black hair down to his thick moccasins. He looked nothing more than skin and bones and bad teeth, a walking lifetime of malnutrition.

He inclined his head and words formed in slow succession. "Watch for giver of fire, da spirit of death and owner of da upper world. He has no hair, no eyelashes and his skin is marked with scars of many burns.

"Sounds like an attractive guy."

The little man didn't acknowledge her sarcasm. "He should not be living on da moun-ain dis time of year. But dere is loss of balance."

"Is he the one running around here with the fire?"

"Do not meet him face to face. No man may look upon his face."

With no eyebrows and scars, who would want to?

"Nora." The sound of Cole's voice boomed in the still night. He jogged down the trail from deeper in the forest.

Nora sucked in a breath to quiet her startled heart. "What are you doing here?"

He stopped in front of her. "You shouldn't be out here alone."

"Why? Are you here to hurt me?"

Cole clenched his teeth. "I'm out here trying to protect you. Apparently, from your own stupidity."

She needed to get out of here, away from Cole. "I don't need your protection. I've got this guy here keeping watch over the forest."

"What guy?"

She knew before she turned that the little man had vanished. "Never mind. I may not understand what this fireball thing is or how you're doing it, but I want you to stop."

Cole pushed his hair off his forehead. He stared at her a few seconds and let out a breath. Good. He was going to confess. "I saw it, too. What do you think it is? I followed it but couldn't catch up to it."

"Right."

His head shot up as if she'd slapped him. "I'm not your enemy, Nora. I've been camping out here for days keeping watch. You don't seem to understand the danger you're in."

Damn right. She needed more protection than a flashlight if she continued to stand in the forest with a dangerous man who admitted to spying on her.

"Big Elk is doing mischief up here on the mountain. I think it has something to do with the lava tubes."

She stared at him.

"You know about them, right?"

"I know about the opening next to the crash site. There are more?"

He nodded. "The tubes crisscross the mountain and have openings all over. It's like a tunnel system. My Hopi friend told me about them. I'm not sure what Big Elk is doing with them, though."

"What could he be doing with them?"

"Most people think there are one or two isolated tubes. Like you know about the one at the crash site. Benny told me it's more like a subway system with connecting routes. It's another secret of the tribes and they can use them to move around the mountain."

"If they are lava tubes, though, aren't they sharp and dangerous, like the lava fields." She tried not to think about the razor edges of the lava rock where Scott fell.

Cole shook his head. "Actually, the stone is smooth in the tubes."

"So you think Big Elk has his Native American gang running through the tubes to jump out and scare people?"

He frowned. "It's got to be something bigger than that."

She backed away and started for the lodge. "I'm calling the cops."

"Good. Tell them someone is using the springs for a camp. I think it might be Alex."

Her heart leapt to her throat. "What makes you think that?"

"I saw Heather leave some food and supplies there a couple of days ago."

He'd been in the woods for days, watching, waiting.

"Come on, Abbey." Nora backed away, ready to sprint for the lodge.

Cole's hand shot out and grabbed her arm. With Hulk-like strength, he jerked her back into him.

Nora pushed against him but he didn't give.

A loud shshshsh hit her ears. She followed the sound to the lift house halfway down the mountain. Cole stared in the same direction.

She didn't have time to focus her eyes when the world erupted around her.

Light exploded and her eardrums boxed with pressure. A blast of heat added confusion to the fire at the lift house. The jet engine roar of the explosion echoed across the mountain.

Nora fell against Cole or he might have pulled her to him. He shrouded her, blocking the heat of the explosion with the cocoon of his body. Yellow flames danced in the distance.

20

Nora stared at the gnarled metal that used to be the lift house, now drenched in water from the fireman's hose. The grass and top soil around the lift base washed away, leaving a red muddy sludge of rocks and cinder. The cables weighted down with bent and twisted chairs eventually rose to the next pole, heading up the mountain into the gray dawn. The lift house sat as a bent shell, blackened with soot.

Abigail shoved a steaming cup of coffee under Nora's nose. Nora couldn't think what to do with it.

Abigail picked up Nora's hand and wrapped it around the cup. "Drink this, dear. It will help."

Help what? It wouldn't rebuild the lift or save them from Big Elk and his gang. She longed to feel Scott's arms around her, let his warmth reassure her. The last bit of blood drained from her heart, knowing if he lived Scott wouldn't be here with her.

Abigail stepped back. She might have jumped to Tibet for all Nora knew or cared. She couldn't pull her eyes from the wreckage and her vision narrowed to block everything else.

The police had scrambled over the area, taking notes, asking her questions, and stringing yellow crime scene tape.

Cole answered police questions but asked a lot more. He finally tromped into the forest grumbling about incompetent police investigations. The cops left a while ago. Now the mountain rested in early morning silence.

"Those sons of bitches." Nora shouted, feeling some life at the echo of her words on the mountain.

"Nora, language." Armageddon could strike and Abigail would demand linen napkins on her luncheon table.

Nora turned to Abigail and was shocked out of her stupor. Abigail stood next to Charlie wrapped in his army jacket. It enveloped her so she looked like a camo version of SpongeBob Squarepants. Her hair and make-up, of course, were perfect.

Charlie appeared scruffier than usual, probably because he hurried over when he heard the explosion and hadn't supplied his jacket with beer. "This is not cool," he said.

"We can't stand around here all day staring at this mess." Abigail took her all-business tone. "I'll fix some breakfast while you shower and dress. You'll feel better."

"No, Mother. I don't think putting on a happy face is going to fix this."

"For heaven's sake, of course not. But action is better than moping around."

Charlie rubbed his hands together. "Breakfast with you two lovely ladies would be the highlight of my life."

Abigail huffed in disgust.

"You go ahead. I'll be right up," Nora said.

"You're just saying that to make me go away." Nothing escaped Abigail.

Nora's head felt filled with tiny, fire-breathing dragons, their sharp tails stabbing her brain.

Abigail sighed in an injured way. "Stay out here staring at the ruin all day then. I'm going to behave in a civilized fashion." She stomped toward the lodge.

Charlie put a hand on Nora's shoulder. "Do you want to be alone with your thoughts?"

The old rascal. "Go get some breakfast."

"I could stay with you."

"Better take advantage of this opportunity. Breakfast is her best meal."

Charlie bowed as he backed away. "It's not just the food, you know. I'd eat sand if she prepared it for me."

"She's so mean to you. Why do you adore her?"

Charlie's eyes got a soft, faraway look. "You think she's all sharp angles and cold surfaces. But I see the light in her eyes that opens the way to her loving heart."

Nora blew air out her mouth. "Come on."

She changed the subject to what really nagged. "Don't you think it's suspicious that Cole is always around when things go bad?"

Charlie's eyes lost their floating quality and sharpened. "You noticed he's hanging around?"

"Here's the thing, you and Abigail act like he's this great Wyoming guy. But he works for Barrett. He's against snowmaking but for uranium mining. Sort of, I guess. And I swear I heard him and Barrett planning to bribe Congressmen."

"Bribery, huh?"

"He's full of contradictions. I don't think we can trust him."

For a moment Charlie looked like a general planning strategy. Then he glanced at Nora and a lopsided grin crept onto his face. "You coming to breakfast, darlin'?"

Nora watched his lurching gate as he hurried across the grass to the lodge. Even Charlie, her one constant, seemed off his norm.

The rumble of an engine brought Nora back to the mountain. Barrett's black Mercedes slid on the cinders. The slamming door rebounded around the empty forest. With powerful strides, Barrett hurried up the trail and across the slope.

Maybe he'd been her idol for years when she thought he was the compassionate entrepreneur. Now she knew him for a controlling jerk.

"What the hell happened here?" Barrett bellowed.

"When the spaceship landed it crushed the lift." Ask a stupid question....

He glared at her. "Is that supposed to be funny?"

Irritation blasted into her brain. "Someone blew up my lift to stop snowmaking. My mother and I could be the next target. That's not a real knee-slapper."

An angry storm clouded Barrett's face as he focused on the smoking debris. "This is the work of cowards. You aren't in any physical danger."

"Thanks for the words of comfort."

Footsteps crunched in the cinders behind Nora. "Good morning, Barrett. Isn't this awful?" Abigail said.

Like an eraser on a schoolroom chalk board, Barrett wiped anger from his face and replaced it with sorrow. "Despicable. I'm just glad you and Nora weren't injured."

Abigail pshted as if it were a silly idea. "Oh we aren't in any danger. Cowards did this and they wouldn't dare mess with me and Nora physically."

Déjà vu or simply hell?

Charlie sauntered up behind Abigail and she looked surprised, as if he hadn't been at her side all morning. She shrugged out of his jacket and shoved it at him.

"How was breakfast?" Nora asked Charlie.

His adoring gaze never drifted from Abigail. "I made sure to turn the burner off after she rushed out."

"You need to abandon ship, Charlie. Throwing men overboard is what she does best."

Charlie's mischievous grin lit his faded eyes. "I'm tied to the mast, sweetie. Don't worry about me."

An Escalade, as ostentatious as Barrett's Mercedes, cruised into the parking lot, followed by a ratty pickup and finally a compact car.

Welcome to the circus.

All the doors of the Escalade swung open and people spilled out. Big Elk climbed out of the passenger side and the whole troupe headed up the slope.

Dorothy Black, the incredibly young reporter from the Daily Tribune popped from the little car and quickly passed a few Guilty White People, catching up to Big Elk, her notebook and pen leading the way.

Satisfaction and self-importance swarmed around Big Elk like flies on a corpse.

"Do you think he did it?" Abigail asked.

"Of course he did it," Nora said. Or maybe it was Alex. Or whoever sent the death threats. Or maybe the little kachina salesman. Or whoever carried the fireball. Or maybe Cole.

Abigail's eyes flashed with that mother bear intensity. She glared at Big Elk as he approached but she spoke to Nora. "Pull your shoulders back, lift your chin and put a confident smile on your face. Why didn't you listen to me when I suggested you clean up for the day?"

Charlie stepped next to Abigail and faced Big Elk and his entourage.

Over the shoulders of the invading hordes, Nora caught sight of a police cruiser easing into the parking lot. They must be tired of traipsing out here for fires, riots, murders. It would be fine with Nora if police-worthy events stopped happening to her.

Big Elk gazed at Nora. "Are you okay?"

You'd think Mr. Soundbite would come up with something more original. Maybe, "Ha-ha" or "Take that."

Abigail raised a regal chin. "Turn right around and march down this mountain. You are not welcome here."

He ignored Abigail and addressed Nora. "I didn't mean for this to happen but I warned you."

Barrett's low voice carried threat. "If you don't want a restraining order, I suggest you leave."

"And I suggest you keep on my good side, Mr. McCreary."

Barrett narrowed his eyes in a look that foretold epic destruction, torture and mayhem.

Enough of this. Nora didn't need others to protect her. She eased in front of Charlie and Abigail and opened her mouth.

Dorothy Black, who had interviewed Nora on several occasions, slid from behind Big Elk and into Nora's personal space. Perhaps sensing she held center stage, Dorothy spoke with volume and drama. "What is your response to this morning's Tribune article?"

As if Nora had time to peruse today's paper. It didn't matter what Dorothy asked, Nora had a few things to say she'd kept bottled up for too long. "In Arizona and New Mexico at least 40 to 50 mountains are sacred to tribes. There are over 40,000 shrines, gathering areas, pilgrimage routes and prehistoric sites in the Southwest, all of which someone claims are sacred. We want to spray water on one fourth of one percent of this mountain."

Dorothy brushed that aside. "In light of this destruction, can you respond to today's article in which Big Elk calls for the Hopi and other pueblo tribes to rise up in rebellion against you?"

"He called for what? Against me?"

Big Elk raised his voice. "I was speaking metaphorically."

Dorothy scribbled away, eyes jumping from her small notebook to Nora's face. "You're familiar with the Pueblo Indian Rebellion of the 1600's? He compared snowmaking to the missionaries quelling the culture and enslaving the Puebloans."

Charlie put his arm around Nora's shoulder and turned her away. "The press, man. Use them, don't let them use you."

The reporter took another step toward her, speaking to her back. "The Hopi, known for being a peaceful tribe, actually rebelled against the Spanish priests and flung them off the mesas to their deaths. Big Elk said the Hopi should do something similar to stop snowmaking."

Big Elk sounded desperate. "I did not call for violence against Kachina Ski. I merely said we need to recapture that spirit."

"Bullshit!" Nora spun around and let her anger shout back at Big Elk.

Abigail spoke quickly, maybe to save Nora from poor press. "If you think your terrorist shenanigans will stop us, Mr. Big Elk, you have greatly underestimated our fortitude. We won't run away like frightened field mice."

Good one, Abigail. Your ability to throw an excellent cocktail party will protect us from murderers.

Gary and another uniformed officer finally arrived and pushed past the reporter. Gary's freckles nearly disappeared in his flushed cheeks. "All right, everyone calm down."

Charlie whispered to Nora, "You can't trust the heat."

Nora's stomach tightened and sweat slimed her underarms. The last two times Gary showed up he brought news of Scott's death and accused her of murder. Maybe now he'd haul her off to jail for blowing up her own lift.

Behind Big Elk the small knot of followers started to chant. "Make love, not snow, make love, not snow."

Gary spoke to Big Elk, his voice barely discernible above the activists. "What are you doing here?"

With a glance at Dorothy, who moved closer and stood ready to scribble a quote, he said, "We came to assure Ms. Abbott that violence is not what we stand for. We want to demonstrate our solidarity to peaceful means, even as we vehemently disagree with Ms. Abbott's determination to disrupt Mother Earth's balance by making snow and send us on the path to certain destruction."

Blah, blah, blah in capitals and quotation marks.

Gary's face remained expressionless, despite the red slashes high on his cheeks. "I see." He unhooked handcuffs from his belt. "You're under arrest for the destruction of property."

Whoa! He wasn't going to haul Nora away? Maybe her luck was turning. Well, aside from the blown up lift, the death threats, and financial failure.

Big Elk held his hand up. "I had nothing to do with this, even if I'm not sorry to see it go."

Gary interrupted. "You've got your press coverage. Let's go."

"You have no proof." Spittle flew from Big Elk's lips as he shouted.

Gary shrugged. "Anonymous tip from a reliable source. I consider you a flight risk so I'm not taking chances."

"What about my rights?"

"You'll get the spiel on the way to the car," Gary said.

"You're behind this." Big Elk's finger pointed at Nora. Death. Violent, painful, endless. That's what Big Elks eyes told her plainly. Eyes able to command from prison. She'd never seen so much hate. Her knees wobbled.

"You won't get away with this." Though said under his breath it floated with Black Death through her veins.

Gary pulled Big Elk's hands behind him and clamped on the handcuffs.

The other officer took Big Elk by the arm and directed him across the slope. "You have the right to remain silent..."

"False accusations," Big Elk launched into one of his famous rants. He twisted his head to shout at Nora. "Your prejudice against Native Americans is well documented and now you're tainting Flagstaff's finest with your lies. My people will carry on this battle in my name for our Great Mother."

Gary looked as if a headache of Biblical proportions banged behind his eyes. "Knock off the histrionics."

Evidently deciding Big Elk was the more dramatic story, Dorothy scurried to his side.

Abigail stepped close to Barrett and put a delicate hand on his arm, looking into his face. "Can't you do something about him?"

Though his features seemed calm, there was something about Barrett's face that brought to mind scorched fields of ash and death. "He won't bother Kachina Ski again."

Somehow, that didn't make Nora feel safer.

Gary exhaled as if exhausted. "Nora. I need to talk to you."

Scott was dead and she'd been accused of his murder. Not to mention Gary's suspicions about insurance fraud. What other disaster could Gary bring?

"Do you know a Maureen Poole?"

The name stabbed a gusher in her heart and she couldn't begin to pull apart all the emotions connected. Betrayal, sadness, tragedy. Anger or compassion. She nodded.

"She was recently killed in a one car roll-over accident. We discovered a connection between your late husband and Ms. Poole."

Nora tried to swallow but her mouth was too dry. She barely squeaked out, "They were having an affair."

Gary studied her face. "We suspect her death wasn't an accident."

Knife to the lungs, air gone. Murder. Gary was saying someone killed Maureen. Unthinkable. Things like this didn't happen in real life. At least, not in her real life. Nora needed to get Abigail and her out of here. Someplace safe. People were being killed and Abigail or Nora would be next.

"As a person of interest in the murder of your husband, this obviously makes you," he hesitated. "More interesting."

Like a fish jerked toward the pole by the painful hook in its mouth, Nora reeled toward disaster.

21

Barrett's boots thudded on the yellowed industrial linoleum. He'd orchestrated Big Elk's arrest to illustrate that he was CEO of more than McCreary Energy. Noble Sergeant Gary had no idea who gave his chief the reliable tip. Now Barrett and Big Elk would have their Come to Jesus meeting and Big Elk would deliver the Hopi Tribal Council.

Three small barred cells left room for a walkway in the cinderblock structure. Dull yellow paint covered the walls.

Big Elk had the only cot, in the cell farthest from the door. A bleary-eyed drunk hung his head in the next cell. Other than that, they had the place to themselves.

Barrett's steady footsteps down the linoleum corridor didn't disturb the prone figure of Big Elk. He lay on his back, arms under his head, staring at the ceiling.

Barrett stopped outside the cell. "Enjoying your stay?"

Only his lips moved. "Not five-star quality, but what can you expect for the sticks?"

"As a native person of the land, one funded with the hard-earned donations of a faithful following, isn't five stars out of your league?"

Big Elk chuckled and sat up. "Mr. Barrett McCreary. How good of you to call. And how generous to arrange my release."

Despite the difficult things he'd been forced to do in his life, Barrett didn't like violence. However, he might enjoy ripping this guy's throat out. "At least you understand the chain of command here."

The smirk on Big Elk's face stretched Barrett's control. "So you got the local yokels to toss me behind bars. Good for you. Now get me out."

"Not until you guarantee prompt delivery of what I paid for."

Big Elk rose from his cot. He stretched his arms overhead, took a deep breath, exhaled and bent over in downward dog. When he stood, he ambled to the bars and faced Barrett. "I'll get the Hopi counsel's endorsement for uranium mining, but not because you think you have power over me."

"I do have the power. This incarceration is a warning. If I decide to let you out, understand that any delay in the Hopi agreement will result in something much more costly than repairs to the ski lift, which you'll reimburse me for, by the way."

Big Elk's arms went overhead and he bent to his left, inhaled up and bent to the right, eyes full of malicious humor. When he straightened he said, "People of the Earth feel strongly about white men desecrating their sacred lands. But I won't be giving you a dime, Barrett. In fact, I want another mil deposited in that account."

Ripping out his throat might be letting him off too easy. "Do you have a death wish?"

"Like Scott Abbott?"

This prick didn't know the first thing about Abbott. He was fishing.

When Barrett didn't react, Big Elk narrowed his eyes and considered. "I don't know how or why, but I'll bet my best horse you have something to do with that."

"Get the job done and get the fuck out of my playground or rot here in jail."

"You don't want to threaten me, Mr. McCreary."

"That's not a threat."

Big Elk appeared as casual as if he relaxed at a picnic. "Your daughter might not be happy to see me abused like this."

It took all of his control not to fly at the bars and smash Big Elk's skull. Through a jaw locked as tight as Attica, Barrett said, "Leave her alone."

Big Elk shrugged. "Okay. You ought to know, though, that I'm the only thing standing between her and considerable jail time."

Barrett's lungs hardened to stone.

Big Elk chuckled again. "The authorities you think you hold in your pocket might be interested to know the name of the brave eco-terrorist who blew up that ski lift."

Boots of iron riveted Barrett to the floor and his ears rang with the words he didn't want to hear.

"Heather set that explosion and her prints are all over the evidence."

22

Nora's ankle throbbed as she stepped on the clutch of her old Jeep and downshifted. Maybe running all over the mountain, standing in front of her burned-out lift and driving to town for supplies wasn't the best recovery plan. Abbey rode shotgun, head shoved from the passenger window and tongue hanging out. The Jeep swung from the highway into Mountain Village.

During the court battles, she'd thought about the financial benefits of snow making, not only to Kachina Ski but to the whole town. She had sincerely believed in the advantages of making snow. But now wasn't so sure. Was it right to create a playground, rip out more trees and scour the mountainside so more skiers could spend their weekends and their cash tearing up the wilderness? Would unnatural snow benefit the mountain as she'd thought? After four years of the battle, the victory came at her too fast. She addressed Abbey. "Scott was right. We should get out while we're alive."

Abbey pulled in his tongue, glanced at her, swallowed, and hung his tongue out again.

Wish I could find something to bring me as much pleasure as riding in the Jeep gave him. Pleasure, my ass, I'd settle for a little less pain and fear.

She coasted into the parking lot of Kachina. Barrett's black Mercedes reflected the late morning sunshine. The metal cordon defining the edge of the lot lay on the ground and a set of deep wheel ruts ran over it.

At the far side of the slope, next to the gnarled remains of the lift, several pickups parked and a dozen men in hard hats milled around. Barrett stood with a man who had to be a crew foreman.

"That son of a bitch." Nora sprinted across the slope. About halfway there Barrett noticed her and he walked away from the men to meet her. She held his gaze as she slowed and stomped toward him. The ache lingering in her ankle fueled her determination.

"What is this?"

"The contractors to start trenching for the sprayers."

"The sprayers won't be here until spring. We'll trench then."

Barrett put a hand on Nora's shoulder. "I reordered my sprayers. They'll be here next week. It's been a tough day for you. Go on back to the lodge and get some rest."

She felt like smacking him. "You can't do this."

Condescension oozed from Barrett. "I understand jitters. This is a big step. It's the beginning of taking Kachina Ski from a one run mom and pop operation to a resort rivaling Lake Tahoe. It's scary and you're understandably nervous. But you're up to the task and I'll be with you every step of the way."

"I don't have the jitters. I will not allow this."

His steady gaze held a hint of danger. "Bigger and more powerful people than you have tried to stand in my way and they were crushed. One thing you should know about McCrearys, we get what we want."

"Really?" Volcanoes of molten rage made her face burn. "One thing you should know about me, I won't be railroaded."

"Glad to hear it. That kind of determination will transform this mountain into a destination resort. There is no limit to the winter Disneyland we can create."

"I don't think you understand. I mean I won't fold before you, the Crown Prince of Assholes."

"You're overreacting." He spoke as if quieting an unreasonable child

Nora raced away, heading to the foreman. He looked startled. "We'll never get these trenches done if..."

She ran behind the men and herded them toward the pickups. "Get out of here. Now. Go!"

Confused, they stared at her. She probably seemed deranged to them. She didn't care. Eventually, the foreman must have decided she was crazy enough he didn't want to argue. He motioned for the men to leave.

As soon as the men began loading up she stomped across the slope and up the stairs to the deck. Voices came from inside the lodge. She slinked outside the screen door and looked in.

Abigail, Heather and Charlie gathered around the large front window. Charlie stood on a chair and hammered something above the corner of the window. Heather carried a waterfall of bright yellow fabric with tiny blue flowers. Abigail stood with arms folded supervising.

Heather rambled on her favorite topic. "When the first people climbed from the Third World to the Fourth World the leaders gathered and each choose an ear of corn. Other tribes quickly grabbed the largest ears, leaving only the smallest for Hopi. According to their choice, each tribe went on their way to settle in their lands. Because the Hopi chose the smallest ear, we were told our lives will be difficult and we'll always be a small tribe. But we'll survive the longest."

Abigail handed something to Charlie. "But why here? Why didn't they settle where survival is easier?"

"The Hopi clans migrated for a very long time. We left behind maps and histories in the rock paintings that are all over. One day the Bear Clan made it to the Mesa and they met a powerful spirit. They wanted him to be their leader and stay with them. He refused but said they could stay as long as they lived in his way. As time went by, other clans settled on the mesas and were accepted into Hopi."

Abigail nodded to Heather. She stepped toward Charlie. "If you raise that bracket a smidge you'll have better luck getting that nail in."

Nora opened the screen and stepped inside. "What's going on?"

Heather looked over her shoulder, the expression on her face like a child at a birthday party.

Abigail didn't turn. "We're sprucing up the place. Don't you think these curtains add cheer?"

Maybe her head would just explode. "No. What I think is that they'll turn into a giant Kleenex for skiers with runny noses."

Abigail clucked. "Heather and I spent the morning sewing these and you could at least say thank you."

Speechless. Good. Because anything she said would be bad.

Abigail gasped. "Not like that. Charlie, you must measure so they'll be even."

Charlie smiled at her, sweat dripping from his face. "Aw, Ab. No one will ever be able to tell."

Heather laughed. "They'll be too busy blowing their noses."

Abigail gave her a playful swat. "You dickens."

Just one happy party until Nora, The Big Green Ogre, entered.

Barrett walked into the lodge.

Nora strode to Barrett, put a hand on his massive chest and gave it a shove. "Get the hell out of here."

"Nora!"

Barrett held up his palm. "I can see you're upset."

"Upset?" She sounded shrill. "Why should I be upset?"

Abigail faced Nora. "I don't know what this is about but hysterics will get you nowhere."

"Be quiet, Mother."

Abigail stomped her foot and clapped her hands. "That's enough! You will not speak to me that way."

Heather's eyes widened and she stared at the scene.

Charlie climbed down from the chair. "This sounds like the kind of discussion best undertaken with beverages. Might I suggest a trip to the Mountain Tavern?"

Nora stared at Barrett. "I don't care what agenda you plan. This is my business and I'll run it my way."

"If you'll recall," Barrett spoke with infuriating calm. "The deal was that I'd give you money to make snow. An ethical business person doesn't renege on a deal."

"Using responsible methods is not reneging."

"Will you sit and we'll talk about it?"

Abigail drew in her chin and straightened her shoulders. "Of course she'll discuss this in a rational manner."

Nora took another step toward him. "Why are you pushing this? It's not as if you need money."

"Nora, really. Barrett is our benefactor."

Barrett's voice dripped with false kindness. "You have the brains and savvy to steer Kachina to the success it can achieve. But you're overwhelmed with the burdens thrust on your narrow shoulders. I'm only here to help."

Her brain felt dry as a desert, all the neuro-pathways like sandy washes. Let him handle the details, why not? She and Abigail could move into town for a while. Nora would recover from Scott's death and betrayal, though she didn't see how. The business would thrive and she'd pick up her life again. Alex would eventually make a stupid move and end up in jail. A smooth transition orchestrated by the great Barrett McCreary himself.

Her term paper research told her he cleaned up uranium contamination, built clinics and schools, all while increasing profits and moving McCreary Energy into the forefront of the industry. He'd achieved success more complicated than running Kachina Ski.

Abigail put her arm around Nora, her hands cool and soft. "There now, you see? Barrett is trying to help."

Nora looked up, exhausted. "Fire that contractor. Cancel the sprayers."

Barrett shook his head. "It's not good to make rash decisions right now."

"This is not a rash decision."

Abigail patted Nora's shoulder. "You won't have to do it alone. Barrett is going to help you, aren't you, dear?"

Dear? Abigail took to rich men like foie gras to Champagne.

Barrett looked pleased with himself. "People will be here tomorrow to begin the lift repairs."

"What?"

"Leave it to me. I'll take care of everything."

Blood pumped back into her brain, flash-flooding the synapses. "No. I'll make the decisions about snow and the lift."

The p-shew of a beer can opening broke the silence. Charlie slurped then said, "Perhaps Miss Abigail and I can wander down to the Tavern and reserve a table. You could join us later."

Abigail let out a deep sigh. "No, Charlie. Barrett and I are on our way out."

Charlie didn't sound daunted. "Okay, then. Might I interest you in an evening stroll?"

Nora and Barrett faced each other. Nora breathed fast and shallow.

"I'm sorry," Abigail said, sounding anything but. "I'm not interested in strolling with you, having supper at the Tavern with you, sharing a six pack with you or doing much of anything with you except wishing you a nice day."

Charlie chuckled. "I like a woman with some vinegar to her."

Barrett's smile looked benign enough, but something nasty lurked around its edge. "You're still general manager. In fact, I'd planned on giving you an actual salary and benefits, like a real corporation."

Nora put her hands on her hips. "Unlike Abigail, I'm not interested in being your kept woman."

"Hear me roar," Charlie said.

Abigail glared at Nora, color high in her cheeks. "That was uncalled for and cruel."

Guilt felt like tar in Nora's throat. "I'm sorry, Mother. I didn't mean that."

Abigail's gold lame sandals clicked across the floor and she grabbed her bag by the front door. "Are you ready for lunch, Barrett? I'm half starved."

Barrett hesitated a split second and started after Abigail. "There's a quaint bistro in the old mining town of Jerome."

Nora spoke to Barrett's back. "Cancel your equipment."

Just before he walked out of the lodge, Barrett said. "Don't try to stop me, Nora."

She followed them onto the deck, seething. They strolled down the path to the parking lot. Charlie and Heather stood behind her not making a sound, as if in thrall at the climax of an adventure movie.

Barrett opened the Mercedes' door for Abigail and helped her to settle inside.

Without much thought Nora raced down the steps to the parking lot. Two pickups full of trenchers idled in the lot and she ignored them. Nora jumped into the Jeep, cranked the key, and slammed it into gear. The Jeep lurched backward, spraying cinders as she popped the gear shift from reverse into second and aimed for Barrett's Mercedes poised to turn onto the road. She braced herself on the steering wheel and stomped on the gas. The Jeep shot forward and crashed into the bumper of Barrett's gas-guzzling black monster.

She grabbed the gear shift and shoved it into reverse, backed up a few feet and slammed it to second again, giving it gas. The impact created a satisfying explosion of taillights.

The Mercedes' driver side door opened and Barrett jumped out, motivating his bulk with impressive speed.

While he approached she backed up again, put it in neutral and revved the motor.

Barrett put a hand on the door as if that could stop her. "What the hell are you doing?"

She faced the rage in his eyes. "I don't know but it feels good."

Ram into gear, stomp the gas, slam into the bumper.

"You're crazy!"

"That's right."

Abigail appeared next to Barrett. She put an elegant hand on his massive arm and turned him toward the Mercedes.

The fire inside Nora died as Abigail saw Barrett into his seat, gave him an endearing smile and turned to walk like a queen to her side of the vehicle. She opened the door and just before stepping in, looked at Nora.

Instead of anger and disappointment, Nora saw pain and confusion.

The trenchers idled in their pickups.

Barrett and Abigail drove away.

23

What did that prove? Only her incredibly unstable imbecilic nature.

Heather and Charlie gave her a standing ovation.

First one pickup, then the other inched toward the road. No doubt the trenchers would be called as witnesses at the murder trial of Scott and Maureen. They'd testify to Nora's deranged actions. Maybe insanity would be a good defense.

Charlie walked over to her window and reached in, tilting her chin to look at him. "You are a magnificent woman."

At that, a sob escaped her. "So magnificent that I poured the last five years into a doomed business that led to the death of my husband. A husband, by the way, so impressed with my magnificence he was boinking some other woman. And I just went berserk and smashed my Jeep for nothing!"

Charlie shrugged. "Sure. But you're not passive. You've got life and passion and that's a great thing."

Heather stood at the trail to the lodge. "That was some crazy shit."

Nora climbed from the Jeep and plodded past Heather. "I'm sure that's not the example your father wants you to emulate."

Heather turned and followed her. "No one ever treats Poppy like that. Whatever he says goes."

Charlie followed them up the path, popping a beer and slurping. Abbey trotted along behind.

"If you really believed he's invincible you wouldn't be getting in trouble and doing time with me," Nora said.

Heather shrugged. "Okay, so I'm fighting uranium mining and snow-making. It won't make any difference. Poppy always gets his way."

"Not this time."

A light sparkled in Heather's eyes. "Maybe not this time. Too many forces are against him."

"Thanks for the vote of confidence. I'm only a small force but I've got controlling interest."

"It's not only you."

"If you think Big Elk is a douche bag why are you helping him?"

Heather's face turned as blank as a pack mule's. "I don't work for him. We just happen to support some of the same causes."

"I support Ponderosa pine and Mexican spotted owls, and no motor-ized vehicles in my forest," Charlie said.

I support staying alive. "Okay. Let's see if we can salvage anything of this day."

Heather sounded eager. "Charlie and I could finish hanging the curtains and surprise Abigail."

"To see her smile I'd hang a curtain to China," Charlie slurred.

"Much as I'd love to please my mother," sarcasm injected Nora's voice, "I think we can finish inventory of the rental stock. Besides, Charlie shouldn't be climbing chairs."

Heather walked next to Nora. "How come you don't like your mother? Abigail is so cool."

"Abigail the Horrible? Abigail the Intrusive, Controlling, Disapprov-ing, Demanding Mother From Hell?"

Heather's eyes took on a hard glint. "She's really proud of you. You should hear her talk about all the great things you've done."

"You're kidding."

Nora stopped and looked at Heather. "Abigail went to bed for a week because I wouldn't attend my undergrad graduation. She was so busy planning a month-long cruise after my step father's death she never noticed I took Kachina Ski. By the way, between graduation and Kachina, she barely spoke to me in protest of me marrying Scott."

"You have to admit she was right about that."

Now Abigail was recruiting troops? "I suppose she spent the morning gossiping about my marriage and how she tried to save me."

"She cares about you," Heather said.

"Cares about me." Noxious memories of Abigail's care swirled in Nora's brain. What about the preppy outfits Abigail bought, purely out of concern for Nora? It had nothing to do with Abigail's friends' disapproval of Nora's hiking boots and flannel shirts. Abigail's concern overflowed when Nora struggled the last semester of her senior year of high school. She said Nora simply had to be valedictorian because Abigail invited so many people to the reception. The list of Abigail's loving concern was endless.

Nora inhaled to begin her litany of abuse but Heather's sad face halted her momentum. "I'd give anything to have a mother."

Nothing like a tire iron to the temple. God, Nora acted self-centered, insensitive and calloused. She put her arm around Heather. "I'm sorry. From now on, I'll share her with you. Maybe you'll get a little of that doting mothering you've missed and I can get a break."

This felt kind of good to Nora. She'd never had a little sister and she liked talking with Heather. Maybe this whole mentor thing would work out for both of them. "Look. I know I've been hard on you. I don't mean to be. I just don't want you to get hurt."

Heather's eyes misted. "That's nice. But I can take care of myself."

Nora gave Heather's shoulders a squeeze and felt her tense. The girl stared at the corner of the lodge.

Nora followed her gaze. Straight into the jaws of death.

Alex leaned against the lodge, arms folded, a smug smile on his lips.

Nora dropped her arm from Heather's shoulders and fought to keep from screaming. "What's he doing here?"

"I don't know."

Nora spun and sprinted for the apartment and her phone.

"Wait!" Heather called. "He's not going to hurt you."

There wasn't a wait bone in Nora's body. She hit the stairs and took them two at a time. While her heart threatened to explode, she told the 911 dispatcher that Alex loitered on her property.

Heather spoke to him right below the apartment window.

Somewhere Charlie had found a shovel and stood a few feet from the couple, the shovel poised to attack.

Whatever Heather and Alex discussed, it wasn't roses and sunshine. Their body language shouted anger. Alex grabbed Heather's arm and pulled her a step toward the forest.

Nora didn't hesitate. As quickly as she'd flown to the apartment she doubled her speed to get back. By the time she arrived, Charlie moved closer and held the shovel like a javelin.

Heather held her hands up in a calming motion. "It's okay, Charlie. He's not going to hurt me."

"You'd best clear out of here, young man."

Nora stepped next to Charlie. "Why not stick around a few more minutes. The cops will be here by then."

Heather turned on her. "You called the cops? You bitch!"

Alex laughed. "Go ahead and call the army for all I care. They can't save you." He waved at Charlie, dismissing him. "This old man won't help. If I wanted to kill your lily white ass, you'd be dead now."

In another couple of minutes her heart would burst from fear and save Alex the trouble of killing her. "Come on, Heather. Let's go back to the lodge and wait for the cops."

Alex flipped his hair back. "You gonna let that white bitch tell you what to do?"

Heather narrowed her eyes at Nora. "I can't believe you called the cops. I told you I'd take care of it."

"He's a murderer, Heather."

She shook her head. "He never killed anyone."

"Yet." Alex grinned at Nora.

Nora grabbed the shovel from Charlie. "Damn it, Heather. Get away from him!"

Heather shook her head, tears accumulating in the corner of her eyes. "He's the only one who loves me." She took Alex's hand and together they ran into the forest.

24

When Sergeant Gary suspected Nora of murder he drove to the mountain. But a threat on her life only warranted a junior Mouseketeer who took notes. He never even scouted around the property. Finding Alex on the mountain probably presented an impossible mission. The officer flipped his notebook closed and headed toward his cruiser.

Heather hid somewhere alone out there with Alex. With all the confidence of youth, she thought this bad-ass loved her and wouldn't hurt her. What a mess Heather created for herself.

Evening pushed around the corners of the afternoon. She wanted Abigail home and safely locked inside before darkness covered them all. Abbey and Charlie provided some comfort but not any real protection. Both of them dozed by the lodge, in the last strength of the sun.

A middle-aged couple with daypacks strapped on their backs appeared near the top of the run and tramped across the slope, disappearing into the forest. At the peak of hiking season, today couldn't be any more perfect. The forest might seem empty but Nora counted four or five hiking couples that afternoon.

Cole swung into the lot on his mountain bike. He braked by the cop and climbed off the bike.

Great.

Nora turned from the railing. "I've got to do something about Barrett."

"Hmm." Charlie picked up a beer from the bench beside him. It might be the same can sitting by him for two hours. Maybe he didn't drink as much as she thought. Could be he carried around an open can out of habit. "I hate to see you leave this mountain, sugar. But she needs a rest from the skiers."

Nora stared at the grassy slope. Instead of enjoying a mountain lawn, as she used to, she cringed at a bald swath once covered by pines. To add insult, the tire tracks from the trenchers left muddy scars. "I thought making snow would fix all my problems. We'd have money, Scott would be happy. I'd be the success my mother always wanted."

"Hold on there, honey." Charlie sounded almost energetic. "Your mother is proud of who you are, not what you've done." Super. Now Charlie and Heather tag-teamed for Abigail.

"Anyway," Nora said. "Nothing has changed about making snow. Kachina Ski won't survive without it and with it, I'll be rich in a matter of a few years."

Charlie's voice settled back into half consciousness. "True."

Her mouth almost couldn't form the next sentence. "But it's wrong."

"Now you're talking."

"The arguments are still valid: Kachina Ski only uses less than one fourth of a percent of the mountain, more moisture would be good for biodiversity and vegetation; more commerce would help the local economy. It's all there."

"Yep."

"Why have I changed?"

"You're seeing the light."

She wouldn't admit the little kachina salesman held any sway over her but his words about her protecting the mountain sank deep into her heart. "It's Barrett. He's desperate for snowmaking and I don't know why. It's like he's sprinkled evil powder over it all and now it feels bad."

"Mac has that effect on life."

Mac. It sounded too familiar. Nora left the rail and sat next to Charlie. "There's something between you guys, isn't there?"

Charlie stared at the beer can. "Not anymore."

"What happened?"

"It was a long time ago, honey. All I can say now is don't trust him."

Nora waited while he gulped his beer. "Come on, Charlie. Tell me."

He considered a moment. "We were all young and out to save the world."

"Who is 'we'?"

His eyes gazed decades into the past. "Me and Barrett and Ester."

"Ester?"

"A woman of uncommon strength and breeding. The only woman on this green earth that could rival your queenly mother for beauty, grace and intelligence."

Nora rolled her eyes.

He patted her knee. "Pain is best left to the past."

They sat together for a few moments letting the last of the day's sun soak the rawness from their hearts.

Cole climbed up the stairs to the deck. "Hi, Nora. Charlie."

Charlie stirred and stood, crushing his can and dropping it in a pocket. "Got some recon to attend to."

Nora jumped up. "Wait. Don't go."

Charlie glanced from Nora to Cole. "Aw, he's okay."

Cole raised his eyebrows at Charlie as if asking a silent question. Charlie answered with a slight shrug and walked down the steps.

It surprised Nora that evening advanced so far she needed to squint to see Cole. "What's up with you and Charlie?" Abbey trotted over to Cole with a wagging tail. Too bad Nora couldn't trust the dog's character instincts. On the other hand, Abbey had never been all that fond of Scott.

"We have a pact to keep an eye on you."

"I trust Charlie. You, not so much."

He gazed off toward the mountain. "Lots of people out here this evening."

She shrugged. "It's a good time of year for hikes and camping."

He considered her for a minute, a slight lift to his lips. "That stubborn streak of yours is hard to get around sometimes."

"I'm not stubborn."

He laughed. "Right. What do you call fighting an uphill battle for years just to get the right to do something you don't really believe in."

He was treading on dangerous emotional turf. "How do you know I don't think snow making is exactly the right thing to do?"

His shrug said her defensiveness sounded too silly for him to argue. "And you stuck by a guy for a long time that didn't deserve your loyalty."

"You don't know anything about it."

"I know enough. He worked for someone else, lied about the money and cheated on you."

Thankfully dusk was far enough along he couldn't see her face flame with embarrassment and anger. "You never met Scott. Maybe he had reasons for what he did."

"A man can't justify betrayal."

"I guess bribing Congressmen doesn't qualify as betrayal in your book."

Cole let out a sigh. "You don't know what you're talking about."

She stood up and turned her back to him, crossing her arms against the chill of the night. "Maybe not, but you're lying to someone about something."

He'd moved beside her without a sound and his warmth radiated to her back. His voice rumbled low. "I'm not lying about wanting to protect you."

She thought about what he said and her temper ignited. "I can take care of myself."

"Really? How prepared are you to face Big Elk?"

She waved him off. "Big Elk's in jail."

"Was in jail. He's out and the cops lost track of him already."

Nora quit breathing. Big Elk out and at large? She wanted to jump in the Jeep and roar away. She gripped the rail. Hang on. Big Elk wouldn't attack her. He might send someone else after her but he wouldn't expose himself that way. She faced no more danger than she had when he was in jail.

Probably.

Cole took hold of her arm and turned her to face him. "Benny said--"

"Benny?"

"My friend on Second Mesa."

"Second Mesa as in Hopi?"

"Yes. He said the kachinas are supposed to be off the mountain and on the mesas this time of year. But they are still here."

"You believe they're real?"

Cole pushed his hair from his forehead. "Hell, I don't know what is real. I know Benny believes and that's good enough for me."

Nora had felt the same way when Heather spoke about Hopi. "You think if someone else believes it that makes it true?"

"What I think is the Hopi have traveled throughout the Southwest way before our ancestors knew a continent existed here. They built shrines and worshipped and along the way developed a relationship to the land or Mother Earth or whatever you want to call it. The Hopi communicate with the world in ways others can't."

"You may be better looking than Big Elk but you speak the same language."

Frustration built behind Cole's words. "Believe what you want but I'm saying that everything is off kilter. People are upset. That translates into you and your mother being in danger. You should stay in town until this is over."

Nora swallowed the lump of fear rising in her throat

Dangerous liar with a clever delivery or nice guy who cared about her?

"Okay?" He insisted.

She nodded. "Yeah. Soon as she gets back."

Cole stood for another moment looking as though he might add something more. Then he plodded down the stairs.

Cole's friend said Big Elk planned something. Hadn't there been an unusual number of hikers today. And hadn't most of them been gray-haired, like many of Big Elk's groupies? In Charlie's words, something was going down.

Heather was out there somewhere alone with Alex.

25

Nora had to find Heather. Okay, she didn't have to. Heather did everything she could to push Nora away and she excelled at it. But the girl needed help and Nora felt responsible. Cole suspected Alex camped at the springs. They nestled at the base of a rock pile a fifteen minute hike from the lodge. Nora hollered for Abbey.

True night settled in. Like fireflies, lights flickered here and there. These weren't awesome fireballs like the night of the lift explosion, but ordinary flashlights. Maybe the activity was nothing more than teenagers out for a party and not some dastardly plan of Big Elk's. Heather might just be drinking with a bunch of friends. Which was dangerous in its own way but not in league with Big Elk's murder campaign.

Heather tugged at Nora's heart in an unexpected way. Nora didn't owe the girl anything and yet, she felt connected. It was probably some stupid transference of affection for the little sister she never had and always wanted. Or the baby she thought she'd have with Scott. Whatever. She'd confront all that wishy-washy malarkey later and figure out a more appropriate relationship with her employee. But right now, Nora wanted to make sure Heather was safe.

Nora sucked in a deep breath and hurried deeper into the forest. Not far ahead, three people scurried along, their voices close to a whisper.

Nora reached down and grasped Abbey's collar to keep him from joining the others.

The distant boom, boom, boom of drumming thumped in Nora's head.

"They've started. We're going to be late," an older man in the group ahead of her said. Definitely not an underage drinking party.

A thin woman with stringy gray hair breathed hard but managed to whine. "It wasn't my fault. The fuse wouldn't stay connected."

The third person, a woman, jogged a few paces to keep up. "I think there are other sites so even if it doesn't work, it'll still be spectacular."

What were Big Elk's Guilty White People so worked up about? Something with a fuse. The ski lift wasn't enough, they planned to blow up something else.

Nora followed as the three veered onto an uphill trail. A short but strenuous hike brought them to a clearing. The drumming beat loud enough now that Nora didn't worry about being heard. They gathered at the site where a plane crashed into the mountain in the early 1970's. Some of its wreckage still rested in this spot next to an opening to the lava tubes. An easily identifiable landmark, it was a popular place to gather.

And gather they were. A bonfire flared next to the bit of fuselage and Big Elk stood on a flat rock, facing a growing crowd of Natives and Guilty White People. The Flagstaff jail must be a Holiday Inn. They sucked at keeping prisoners locked up.

With Abbey's collar firmly in her grasp, Nora crouched in the shadow of trees.

Big Elk raised his hands and brought the drumming to a halt. "People of the mountain. Holy people. It is time for us to gather in strength and do what the spirits of the mountain demand of us. The Hopi have responsibility to care for the world and that starts with this mountain. We are joining with our brothers and sisters to take a stand for our Mother when she can't defend herself."

The drums pounded and people shouted.

"A powerful kachina came to me last night. He stood outside my shelter with his fire and told me to gather the people on the mountain. He wants to show us his displeasure with what is happening and make us understand that we need to stop the white rapists from destroying our Mother."

Nothing but a summer repeat. Nora needed to find Heather and get off the mountain.

Big Elk raised his arms. "Show us, great kachinas. What would you have us do?"

Nora took a few steps into the forest. Vibration in the ground shocked her feet before her ears caught the roar. An astonished gasp rose from the forty or so people around Big Elk.

A ball of flames burst from the lava tube making Big Elk's bonfire looked like a campfire next to the impressive inferno. The Wizard of Oz couldn't have created a better illusion.

"He is with us!" Big Elk shouted. "He's giving us a message."

Another explosion erupted from the forest below. Flames leapt above the trees and escaped into the air. The flash barely extinguished when yet another flare and rumble surged from several hundred yards to the left. Another exploded toward the top of the peak. The crowd gasped and applauded at each successive fire burst.

Big Elk had cleverly staged his mystical pyrotechnical theater from the lava tubes. Maybe he'd rigged fuses through the tubes to connect with each other or maybe he used timers. The balls of flame would ignite the night but since they originated in the rock openings, the risk of forest fires would be slight. The show exhibited drama and flare (literally). But who really believed mountain gods created fire to demonstrate their wrath?

"Are you going to allow Nora Abbott to desecrate the kachina's home?" Big Elk might be a thin, short man, but next to the fire, with the momentum of the supernatural display, he resembled a roaring lion.

The shouts and enthusiasm of his followers left no question they hungered for blood. Or at least, more destruction of property.

"She ignored our pleas. She plunged the needle into our Mother's veins and will pump her blood to stain the scars she cut into our Mother's flesh. Brothers and Sisters of the Earth. I beg you. The spirit commands you, don't let this happen."

She had to get out of here before Big Elk's rant gained critical mass against her. Nora raced down the path, hoping she could make it to the springs to get Heather. That is, if Heather was even at the springs. She crashed along the trail, stumbling over rocks and roots. Each step ignited more fear for Heather.

Finally she made out a weak light shining from the springs. Alex and Heather stood in a clearing, surrounded by the forest on three sides. A huge boulder pile created the fourth boundary. A flat granite rock looked almost like an altar at the base of the boulders and to the side of this, green ferns and yellow flowers ringed a small spring about the size of a child's backyard wading pool.

"I don't trust Big Elk," Heather said. "Don't do what he says without talking to the elders."

Alex picked up a wad of bright turquoise colored cloth. A dead animal lay next to a half empty bottle of Wild Turkey. She'd caught them in the middle of a ritual animal sacrifice.

Wait. The dead animal turned out to be some sort of costume with leather and feathers. It didn't take a genius to spot Scott's mystical kachina.

"The kachinas want us to act now."

Heather put a hand on his arm. "I'm just asking you to wait and talk to the elders. Do it for me."

He kissed her and smiled. "Only for you."

Nora crashed into the clearing with Abbey following.

Like a squirrel chased by a dog, Alex spun and fled without stopping to see who attacked. He dove for the rock pile...and disappeared.

Heather turned to the forest and scowled. You'd think a sixteen-year old would be skittish in that situation but she acted more put-out than nervous.

"We need to get out of here!" Nora grabbed Heather's arm.

Heather pulled back and glared at her.

Wherever Alex had gone he might reappear with his tomahawk and scalp her. Nora didn't want to wait around for that.

Abbey climbed around the boulders and whined. The lantern only cast enough light to create shadows that danced with menace.

"Let's go."

"You shouldn't be here. This is a sacred place."

Abbey still worried over the boulders.

Nora didn't want to go near there. If Alex disappeared, he could reappear.

"Lava tubes," Heather said.

The rock pile. Stupid! "Here?" She grabbed Heather's arm and jerked her away.

Heather pulled back. "Leave me alone."

"The tubes. Big Elk. We've got..."

A click and whoosh came from the direction of the rocks. Whatever high tech device Big Elk commissioned must be engaging. It was going to blow!

Nora dove for the dirt.

Armegeddon broke loose in the clearing. Flames engulfed the space then rose before igniting her skin. She felt as if her eardrum's burst. Incredible light and heat flashed and Nora knew she'd be nothing but a sooty skeleton scattered on the forest floor.

Then it ended.

She couldn't hear anything. Acrid fumes burned Nora's nose and her face burned. Heather had been closer to the opening. Was she okay? In the blindness from the flash and smoke, Nora rose to her knees and searched for Heather.

Oh god, where was Heather? She should be close to Nora. She must be flash fried with no trace.

Movement next to the springs drew Nora's eye. Through smoke, Nora watched Alex heft Heather to his shoulder and disappear into the trees.

26

Nora ran across the slope, slipping on the wet grass. Abbey galloped behind her. Heather had looked like a Raggedy Ann draped on Alex's shoulder. Please let her be no more injured than Nora had been. Even if Heather survived the explosion, Alex might be the bigger danger.

Behind her, the mountain erupted with bursts of flame. Drums pounded and people cheered.

Nora raced by the lodge. Abigail still hadn't made it home. Nora didn't like Abigail being with Barrett, but it beat getting caught in the middle of an incendiary riot. Whatever, Nora couldn't take care of Abigail tonight.

"Nora!" Cole's shout stopped her before she made it to her Jeep. "Thank god you're okay." He sat in his Toyota Tacoma pickup, the engine running. "I saw flames and was afraid..."

She jumped into the pickup and Abbey scrambled in after her. Nora scooted over to share the bucket seat. "Go! Alex has Heather. We need to save her."

He backed out of the parking lot. "He has Heather where?"

"The rez. I don't know. Somewhere. The lava tube blew and he took Heather."

Cole drove down the mountain. "You aren't making sense. Start from where I left you at the lodge."

Nora told him about Big Elk and the explosions and the kachina costume. She explained everything.

He braked as he pulled into town. "We're going to go to the police station and tell them what you just told me."

Nora shook her head. "No. We should go to the rez. I'm sure that's where he'll take Heather."

"Which rez?"

"Hopi!"

"Do you know which mesa?"

Nora hadn't been to the tiny reservation completely surrounded by the Navajo Nation. She didn't know all the details but the Hopi had been in this part of the country for centuries before the Navajo made their way to the area. The Navajo tribe grew and little by little moved onto traditional Hopi lands. When the United States government, showing their usual even-handed, understanding ways, divided up the area for reservations, they reduced the amount of land the Hopi considered theirs and placed the reservation smack in the middle of the immense Navajo Nation.

The Hopi lived on in a remote part of the desert on three mesas north of Winslow. About 2 hours drive from Flagstaff.

Cole pulled into a parking space in front of the police station. "If we don't get any satisfaction here, I'll get Benny to help us."

Benny? Oh, Cole's Hopi friend. Okay. She'd give the cops a chance but if they didn't do something immediately, she and Cole would rush to the rez.

She didn't get the action she'd hoped for. Every spare hand patrolled the mountain to create order after the amazing fireworks show. Worse, the cops dragged their feet before even talking to them.

They took Cole one way and escorted her to a room where they told her as soon as someone was available, they'd take her statement. Hours passed. Twice Nora tried to leave and uniformed officers led her back to the room. As a person of interest in two murders, the cops didn't feel magnanimous toward her.

Finally Gary showed up, took notes, told her not to worry and let her go.

Not to worry that Heather could be injured and in the clutches of a murderer?

A grumpy cop relented and let her use the office phone to call Abigail. The apartment phone rang uselessly. Nora slammed the receiver down. Her mother wasn't home.

Either Abigail held a grudge at Nora for her demolition derby or she experienced a romantic encounter with Barrett that stretched all night. Staying at a hotel to indulge a snit seemed far-fetched, even for Abigail. But Nora couldn't calculate the cost of therapy to cope with the image of Abigail in Barrett's bed.

Where was Abigail? What about Heather? Getting home to a mountain pocked like incinerated Swiss cheese presented a problem. She stepped out of the police station into the inky predawn quiet.

Cole popped out of his pickup, followed by Abbey. They hurried toward her. "I'm sorry. I had no idea they'd keep you like that."

She glared at him, patted Abbey and marched toward his pickup. "Did you find Heather?"

He shook his shaggy head. "I checked the hospital and she's not there. I talked to Benny. There's a public dance out there today at Second Mesa. Alex is supposed to dance so there's a good chance she'll be there."

Nora opened the passenger door and let Abbey in. What if Heather was hurt in the explosion? "Let's go to the rez."

"You can't just go out there. There are certain rules."

"Like what?"

"It's sort of like a church service and you're supposed to dress nice."

"You're taking me to church?"

He opened the door and settled in. "I'm taking you home. Benny will help Heather."

She jumped into her side. "We've got to go out there now. Heather needs us."

He started the pickup and maneuvered through the silent town. "Benny has a better chance of getting her home than you or I."

Nora argued and reasoned and still Cole held firm. He might be right. Nora wasn't exactly Heather's best friend and she'd fight coming home.

It didn't matter. The stubborn girl needed someone to help her. The cops didn't care and if Barrett found out he would crush Heather's spirit. She might not want the responsibility of Heather, but Nora couldn't turn away.

Cole pulled into Kachina's parking lot. "There is something else."

She hated those words and the serious way Cole dropped them.

"I found out the cops were about to extradite Big Elk to South Dakota when he disappeared."

Stupid cops. "Only to reappear on my mountain. What did he do in South Dakota?"

"His real name is Ernie Finklestein. He's wanted for a scam that stole the investments of a bunch of retirement home residents. They lost his trail several years ago. Turns out Ernie got a sunburn and changed his name and now he's into something here."

"Aside from destroying my property and threatening my life?" Nora asked.

Cole nodded. "Looks like he's importing cheap crap from China to sell as authentic Navajo crafts."

"A real hero." She stared out the window. "Maybe he knows the cops are on to him and after last night's Bonfire of the Kachinas, he'll go underground."

"He doesn't strike me as the underground type." Cole pulled up in Kachina's parking lot.

"Don't worry about us." Abbey scrambled from the cab and Nora followed. She was a few steps up the path when his door slammed. She whirled around. "I can handle it from here."

"I'm not leaving you out here alone."

Punching him might feel good. Not that he'd blown up the mountain or caused Heather to run away but because of him, she'd lost precious time. "Just leave me alone."

He paused. "Have you found out anything new about Scott?"

Why would he ask unless he wanted to know how close she was to finding out he was the murderer? Except he'd have no possible reason to kill Scott. Unless he felt far more strongly about no snowmaking than he let on. Her suspicion must have scrolled across her face.

His face hardened. "I'm only trying to help. The key to everything lies with figuring out who killed Scott. Once I know that, this nightmare will be over for you."

Which nightmare did he mean? Alex's hands crushing her larynx? Big Elk blowing up her property? Barrett ruining the mountain? Or Abigail taking up residence in her home? She stomped up the path.

After a few moments she heard his pickup door open and close. He didn't start the engine of course.

Nora slid her hand into her pocket for her key but when she held the knob to insert it, she realized the door was unlocked. She locked it last night. She knew it.

What to do? Something caught her eye. The screen on the window next to the front door was bent. It looked as though someone peeled it back. The sliding window was open just a crack. Someone had broken into her house. She should run. Cole sat in the lot waiting to rescue her once more.

Rescue or attack?

A slight shuffling sounded behind the drawn blinds. Someone was inside!

Damn it. No more being a victim. She would fight back this time. Casting about wildly for a weapon, Nora grabbed an old ski pole she used to shoo raccoons that occasionally climbed the stairs.

Nora held the pole like a bayonet and reached for the knob. One, two, three....

With a mighty leap she opened the door, lunged inside and stabbed into the kitchen where she heard the shuffling.

"For heaven's sake, Nora! What are you doing?"

Nora stopped mid-attack, confused. "Mom?"

"Whom did you expect at this hour?"

Abbey trotted inside, his tail wagging.

A silent figure stepped from the hallway. Nora raised the ski pole again, sure this was the intruder who used Abigail as a hostage.

"Hey, Nora," Charlie said. He walked from the bathroom.

Nora lowered the ski pole.

Abigail tied an apron behind her waist. She opened the refrigerator.

What the...?

Charlie fumbled for a chair at the table and her mother banged a fry pan onto the stove.

Abigail glanced up. "If you're going to join us for breakfast, at least comb your hair."

Nora turned questioning eyes toward Charlie but his head rested on his hands, gazing adoringly at Abigail.

"What is going on?" Nora managed to ask.

Abigail didn't look up from beating the hell out of the eggs. "I refuse to talk to you until you make yourself presentable."

"Oh for the love of Pete." Nora went off to change clothes and brush her teeth.

Bacon sizzled and coffee dripped, which seemed fairly normal. What made Nora wonder if one of the Hopi warriors had let go of a serpent head and thrown the world off its axis, was the way Abigail sat at the table across from Charlie and spoke in a soft voice.

Keeping an eye on them, Nora snagged a cup of coffee.

Abigail turned to her. "Please pick up your feet. Shuffling is low class."

The mug warmed Nora's hands. "Where have you been? Why did you break into my house? What are you doing with Charlie?"

Abigail raised her eyebrows. "The tables are turned and she's giving me twenty questions."

Charlie looked up at Nora and grinned. "I've been taking good care of her."

Nora ran a hand through her hair. "Excuse me, Charlie. But you can barely take care of yourself. Why would you overwhelm yourself with Queen Abigail?"

Her mother giggled. "See?" She said to Charlie. "That's why I like to be around her. She's always so witty."

"Not witty, Mother. Tired. Worried. Confused. And just a little freaked out."

Abigail and Charlie exchanged a look that said "isn't she cute?" Abigail patted Charlie's hand and got up to fiddle with the bacon and start the eggs.

Nora sipped her coffee, trying to clear her head. "I thought maybe you were staying in a motel or something."

"Why would I do that?" Abigail poked a strip of bacon with a fork and transferred it to a paper towel-lined plate.

Her mother practiced her typical form of punishment. She'd force Nora to detail the offense and Abigail would demand an apology.

Frustrated, Nora took a breath. "I'm sorry I called you a kept woman. I didn't mean it."

Abigail nodded and continued with the sputtering and popping bacon.

"I'm sorry I ran into Barrett's bumper and probably ruined your lunch date."

Abigail grabbed the eggs and whisk and let them have it again. "You didn't ruin our date. We had a lovely time."

Nora couldn't fathom what a lovely time with Barrett looked like. Her imagination balked at anything romantic with that man, and thinking of her mother that way was just plain sick.

"You're not mad at me?"

Abigail poured the eggs into the warm pan. "I'm not pleased with your performance. You should see a therapist for your anger issues."

Nora looked at Charlie, hoping for some help.

He dozed, head resting on his hand.

Nora fortified herself with coffee. "Where have you been and how did you end up with Charlie?"

Abigail folded the omelet, a skill that impressed Nora. "I was understandably upset when I got back to Mountain Village. Honestly, Nora, you wear me out sometimes."

"So what about Charlie?"

"When Barrett dropped me off I went for a stroll instead of going directly home. I ran into Charlie and he took me for a cocktail at the Tavern."

Nora choked on coffee. "You went to the Tavern? With Charlie?"

Abigail shot her a withering look. "Really, Nora. I'm not an ice queen."

Nora tried to keep from laughing. "No, go on."

"We had a few drinks and he bought me supper..."

"At the Tavern? You know they only serve fried food there."

"I had a fairly nice salad."

"Okay, salad. How did you get from drinks and salad to spending the night with Charlie?"

Abigail's eyes blazed. "I DID NOT spend the night with Charlie."

Nora grinned. "You're right. You're home before dawn."

Abigail pulled the skillet from the stove. "Sometimes you're so crude."

"So what happened?"

"You know I'm not much of a drinker..."

Nora laughed, "You have a cocktail or two every night."

Abigail gave her a warning look. "While we were walking home I felt queasy and Charlie gallantly took me to his cabin. He gave me seltzer and aspirin and I'm afraid I fell asleep."

"You passed out at Charlie's house?" This was getting better and better.

Abigail slid the omelet onto a plate and picked up a knife. "Would you please try to act like an adult?"

Nora drank her coffee to hide her amusement. "Sorry. Go on."

"That's all. There's nothing more. I woke up, Charlie walked me home, and I promised him breakfast."

Nora followed Abigail as she carried the plates to the table and set one down in front of Charlie.

He opened his eyes and smiled at Abigail. "This looks perfect."

Abigail sat. "You need some companionship, Nora. Charlie and I think you should start seeing Cole Huntsman."

Nora nearly spit her coffee. "Good idea. It will make it easier for him to kill me."

Abigail laughed.

"You agreed with this?" Nora asked Charlie.

Charlie smacked his lips, loving the omelet. "He's a fine man."

"Well, if you love him so much, why not take him a cup of coffee to make stalking me more comfortable for him."

"What do you mean?" Abigail said.

"He's sitting in the parking lot right now making sure I don't get away."

Abigail smiled. "That's so sweet."

Nora wanted to go to bed forever. She glared at Charlie. "You approve of what he does for a living?"

Charlie sat back and patted his belly. "Nuclear is cleaner and more efficient than coal but I don't think they need to gut the Grand Canyon for uranium. But Cole's a good man and he's working on other things. "

"What else? Murder?"

Abigail set down her coffee cup. "Really, Nora. You should get more rest. You sound confused."

Charlie stuffed a giant bite in his mouth and closed his eyes in ecstasy. Or was he hiding something about Cole?

When he swallowed and opened his eyes, he saw her staring at him. "You ought to get that front window fixed," Charlie said.

"I'll get to it later." She sipped her coffee. "Did you rip the screen or just bend it."

Abigail got up for more coffee.

"Why didn't you use your key?" Nora asked.

Abigail filled Charlie's cup and gave Nora a puzzled look. "I did."

Nora reached for a piece of bacon from Abigail's plate and received a slap for her effort. "If it was so easy for you guys to break in maybe I ought to put bars on it."

Abigail's head snapped up. "We didn't break in, Nora. I told you, I used my key."

27

She left Charlie to repair the window and as soon as Cole drove away and Abigail turned her head, she jumped in the Jeep and started for the rez. Maybe Cole could sit around and wait for his friend to intercede but Nora needed to help Heather and do something to stop Alex before he broke into their home again. This time, when they were home and ripe for murder.

Nora traveled as fast as she dared the nearly seventy miles to Winslow. She turned off the Interstate onto a two-lane paved road and pushed the accelerator even more, the bumps and swells of the poorly maintained surface creating a sway like a sailboat. The sign to Second Mesa said sixty miles on a road that ran straight to the horizon.

She headed toward the three Hopi mesas, each with some villages. Nora had heard that Old Oraibi, on Third Mesa, was the oldest constantly inhabited village in North America. Cole said today's dance took place on Second Mesa.

Poor farms and ranches of the Navajo Nation dotted the roadsides miles apart, each compound with a hogan.

After what seemed like five hundred miles, the road ended with a T. On the right, a mesa rose and Nora barely detected the symmetrical lines of structures on the flat surface above her. The buildings blended with the yellow dirt of the desert, effectively camouflaging the town. A sign pointed left to Second Mesa. She passed a large, new school and turned right on a road leading up the side of Second Mesa. Around a switchback the road tilted sharply upward. It continued to get steeper with two more switchbacks. Shanties and worn buildings with signs identifying them as tribal and U.S. government and health facilities squatted alongside the road.

The third switchback, about halfway up the mesa, brought her to a stretch of road occupied with cars, people and several card tables set up under bright awnings. The tables displayed food and crafts.

Whatever Nora expected of the ancient village, the truth disappointed her. The settlement looked like a third world country. Dirt dominated everything. Yellow dust covered the paved strip of road, which broke off in uneven edges and dropped to windblown dirt shoulders. Houses made of cinder block, rock, and cobbled-together materials clung to the bare dirt hillside.

Nora stepped out of the Jeep. A candy wrapper fluttered under her feet. Feeling uncomfortable and unsure, she headed for the sound of drums.

Several groups of Native Americans meandered up a trail etched into the side of a nearly vertical mesa. Nora crossed the road and started onto a rocky trail that switchbacked up the steep mesa. The path ground to fine yellow powder by centuries of feet trudging through the village.

From time to time bunches of weeds survived, covered in yellow dust. A few food wrappers and other trash flitted across the ground on the dry, hot breeze. The sun beat on her and with no sunscreen or hat, she'd crisp in a matter of minutes.

She topped out on the mesa and the savory smell of roasting meat struck her. Muffled sounds of men singing joined the constant beating drum. The people on the roof of a two-story building looked down the other side at whatever activity caused the singing and drumming.

She assumed the building held two stories because it rose that high above the mesa, but no windows showed on this back side to indicate its structure. Built of natural rock it became a part of the mesa as if it had been uncovered by shifting desert dirt. Cars and pickups ranging from shiny and new to rusting heaps, all under a coating of dust, crowded the narrow alley behind the building. Smatterings of Native Americans moved in and out of the confusion. Like any other outdoor celebration, they carried camp chairs, water and bags full of necessities.

Nora approached a friendly looking older woman. "Is this the way to the dance?" A few heads turned toward her but Nora didn't feel hostility or even much curiosity.

The older woman eyed Nora's jeans and though she didn't change expression, Nora felt chastised. "This your first time?"

How could she tell? Nora nodded. "I'm not sure what I'm supposed to do."

"Follow me," the woman said. She led Nora to the corner of the solid structure, where another building stood at a right angle leaving a narrow passage. People crowded into the opening all facing toward the drumming and singing. A young woman with a little girl about ten-years old shuffled aside and made room for Nora. She nodded her head at the older woman.

The two buildings comprised half of the parameters of a village square, with an identical set of buildings making up the other half. Nora stood transfixed by the scene in front of her.

The plaza measured about as wide as a basketball court and twice as long. Color, drums, and singing whirled around her as she tried to sort out the images. A circle of bare-chested men lined the length of the plaza, all wore masks, their long black hair falling down their backs. In a symphony of feathers, paint, leather, bells, plants and animal skins, the men danced in their vibrant costumes, each one different from the others. Or maybe some looked similar to another. The alien mix made it impossible for Nora to capture all the details.

The fifty or so men chanted and stomped their feet. Some held rattles they shook in rhythm to the drumming. It sounded like unintelligible syllables to Nora but apparently they were singing words and verses because suddenly they all stepped back and turned in a line dance more synchronized and impressive than in any cowboy bar.

"Wow." She couldn't muster more intelligent words.

The older woman didn't take her eyes from the dancing.

The dancers continued to sing and move in unison. The drums pounded, rattles kept time, spectators sat quietly and watched. Time and place vanished from her normal life of businesswoman in the middle of American society. Through the space between the buildings across the plaza, the desert stretched from the mesa into eternity. The sky offered bunches of clouds in the expanse above.

"What is this about?"

The woman whispered. "Those are the kachinas. They come from the sacred peaks every spring. They perform dances; most of them secret in the kivas. This is a summer dance. Just a celebration."

"What, exactly, is a kachina?"

The old woman considered before answering. "The kachinas represent things that are important to Hopi. There are more than 300 of them. They act as a kind of go-between for Hopi and the supernatural world. Mostly, they are spirits like animals or ancestors or plants, clouds, stuff like that." She shut her mouth as if the conversation officially ended.

The celebration resembled a Fourth of July picnic. Smells of cooking wafted around the plaza. Women in aprons moved in and out of the houses, taking a moment to sit and watch the dance, then going back to attend to whatever caused the wonderful aromas. Unlike the American holiday where children ran and shot off fireworks amid a buzz of activity, for the most part the crowd focused on the dancers. It seemed a mix between church and bar-b-que.

With a final hard pound of the drum the dancers stopped chanting and stamping their feet. The bells and rattles ceased and the kachinas took up a moaning sound. Perhaps it was in lieu of applause. Their chorus sounded strange like deep cooing of doves, low whine of dogs, but not really any of those, maybe a combination. Maybe it was a Hopi amen.

A man in the middle of the circle shouted and the cooing accented whatever he said. Sometimes the drums beat or the rattles sounded. Several men moved from the circle to the crowd distributing parcels of food. Nora couldn't unravel the mystery why certain women received these. They offered no exchange of smiles and thank yous, as she'd expect. The women simply accepted the food, passed it back to other women who disappeared through the doors with it. It looked like an arbitrary mixture, store-bought white bread, homemade cakes and pies, fresh vegetables, cooked ears of corn, melons, bags of chips, all gathered in various containers such as cardboard soda flats, plastic storage containers, baskets, and bowls.

The food distribution and the oration went on for a while. Nora tucked herself next to a building taking advantage of a sliver of shade. Time became irrelevant. How long did she stand watching the dancing and gift giving?

The kachinas formed a line and exited the intersection of the buildings opposite Nora.

Whatever the ceremony meant the Hopi had performed in almost the exact same way for centuries. The masks and costumes might have added a few modern touches over the years. The jingle bells on the dancers' legs wouldn't have been available until after Europeans brought trade goods, and there were probably other bits and pieces constructed of synthetic fabrics, though none were obvious to Nora. How was it possible that these customs, older than the castles in Europe, survived intact?

The heat and yellow dirt yielded the answer. The mesa didn't welcome stray visitors. Outsiders that did venture up here didn't want to stay. Even early settlers coveted rich farmland and easy water sources. The harsh environment kept the Hopi isolated and able to focus on the old ways.

Her gaze wandered back to the crowd. She couldn't waste time on a cultural mission. She needed to find Heather. With a thudding heart, Nora scanned the plaza. She finally spotted Heather on a rooftop across the plaza. At least she appeared uninjured from the lava tube blast.

Heather stood with folded arms, her body rigid. She had no interest in the plaza. Behind her, a figure moved into sight. He towered above Heather. His hand shot out and he grabbed her shoulder.

Alex.

Nora gasped and ran several steps across the plaza. A glimpse of a familiar beaked nose and sunburned red skin stopped her dead.

Big Elk.

28

A regular convict convention. With no law enforcement to protect them.

Alex stood within clubbing distance of Heather.

And Big Elk. He hated Nora enough her white hide would be worthless as soon as he saw her.

Alex reached out and Heather let him touch her arm. Nora had to get up there. Even though she didn't see any horses, if Big Elk spied her, being drawn and quartered seemed possible.

Big Elk held several young women in thrall. He could look over here any time. He'd sic his minions on her and she'd disappear without a trace.

Sweat dribbled down Nora's spine. Big Elk spoke to a middle aged woman. She considered, shook her head and walked away.

Big Elk scowled after her. He glanced in the other direction and hurried from the plaza. Today's faithful following was noticeably devoid of Guilty White People. He must have thought they'd bring down his cred out here and asked them to stay away from the rez.

Alex pulled away from Heather and she reached to stop him. He shrugged her off and left the roof top.

Nora lit out after Heather.

A hand on her arm made her squeal.

A man decked out in yellow mud with facial features painted in black, frowned at her. "You can't go back there. That's for the kachinas."

Heather disappeared down the back side of the building

"But a bunch of other people went that way."

He stared at her. "Only Hopi are allowed. The next dance will start pretty soon. You can go down and look at the art or try the piki bread."

"Sure. Thanks"

She felt his eyes on her as she sauntered toward the displays. She had to find Heather before the girl got into trouble. But Nora couldn't traipse off anywhere. Obviously, a white woman wandering by herself over the mesa spelled trouble.

The mud-caked man watched her. Many of the spectators had disappeared and those left in the plaza visited with each other. Nora acted as if she intended to wait for the next dance.

She glanced behind her. The alley was empty. Wherever the audience went, they weren't loitering there. She looked back to the center of the plaza, her guardian nowhere in sight. What to do? The rez was foreign territory and she could get herself into trouble and not help Heather.

But Big Elk shouldn't be here. Whatever he had planned might involve more explosions. Nora stepped out of the shade into the alley. Helping Heather couldn't wait.

A hand clasped her arm squeezing her heart into her throat. Expecting Alex or another of Big Elk's foot soldiers to drag her off and dismember her, Nora threw herself out of his grasp.

Someone hissed into her ear. "Come on. We've got to stop Big Elk."

Heather! Nora sucked in a breath. "Are you okay? Where's Alex?"

Heather pulled in a breath and straightened. She arranged her face into a calm mask. "I'm fine. You didn't need to come rescue me but since you're here you can help. "

"How did you know I was here?"

Heather gave her an "oh, please" look. "You don't stand out at all."

Nice. "Let's get out of here before someone decides to kill me."

"We can't go. We have to save the dance."

Teenagers and their distorted sense of proportion. Big Elk plotting murder constituted a crisis; Alex attacking Heather reeked of disaster; one ruined performance didn't really matter. "It's just a dance."

Heather glared at her. "You don't get it. Nothing is 'just' anything up here."

"There will be other dances."

"Maybe there won't be any more. Maybe this is the last test and we fail."

"What makes you think this is a failure?"

"Big Elk. The guys need to be in their kivas doing whatever they do and he's got them listening to his stupid shit."

"Kivas? What do they do?"

They wove between a rusty Ford pickup and a newer compact car. Heather said, "Every clan has a kiva they get into by a ladder through the roof. It represents the way people climbed from the Third Word to this one. I don't know what they do in the kivas. Each clan does their own secret ceremonies. And now they aren't doing it because of stupid Big Elk."

A young woman walked by with a baby on her hip. She nodded to Heather.

They rounded a corner and Nora saw the backs of three or four young men, Alex among them. Big Elk spoke, his face red.

Big Elk was nothing but a poseur out trying to stir up trouble to make himself important. As much as she'd like to charge into the center of the circle and wring his neck, her coward's heart balked. Nora pulled back, trying to slow Heather. "What do you want me to do?"

"I don't know. I saw you ram Poppy's car to prove a point. I thought you'd come up with something."

Nora felt her face flush in embarrassment. "That wasn't one of my best moments."

"We've got to do something." Heather took Nora's hand and dragged her forward.

Bad idea. Big Elk hated Nora. He would identify her as the Devil of Kachina Ski. "Let's just..."

"Hey!" Heather yelled.

Clever plan, Heather.

Big Elk barely glanced up. "The way to power is wealth. White people with money crave the spirituality and connection of the Hopi. They'll buy a kachina doll or pottery in hopes some of your wisdom will rub off. We can give them what they want and help the tribe at the same time."

His eyes rested on Heather and he lowered them to the men, never ceasing his sales pitch. His gaze swept over Nora and his lips stopped moving. He straightened.

The men in his circle turned to see what distracted him. Alex stiffened like a dog with raised hackles.

"Well, well." Big Elk swaggered past his posse to stand in front of Nora. "It's not enough you desecrate the sacred peak, you have to bring your vileness to the mesas?"

Heather shook her hair back. "I brought her here so she can understand the Hopi way. You're the one destroying the ceremony."

Big Elk raised his eyebrows. "Miss McCreary, Uranium Princess. Maybe you look Hopi but we all know you're Daddy's little pawn. You want to rape this land and disrupt the balance."

The exchange drew a group of women. Except for the four young men with Big Elk, the other men must be in their kivas.

"I belong here," Heather said with a touch of defensiveness.

Big Elk turned to Alex. "What do you think? How dedicated is she to our cause?"

Alex's face looked as hard as his fingers around Nora's neck, his voice as sharp as the knife that sliced her ankle. "I'll take her back to Flagstaff."

"You want me to leave?" Heather's eyes couldn't hide the betrayal she felt.

Alex looked at Big Elk, waiting instruction.

Heather scowled at Big Elk. "The Hopi way is not one of inhospitality."

"How would you know the Hopi way?" Big Elk spat out. "You're smoking the peace pipe with the enemy, baby."

"She's not the enemy," Heather said.

Big Elk shifted his malevolent force on Nora. "You killed your husband on sacred ground and the kachinas are punishing you."

The young men with Big Elk looked like a pack of hungry wolves waiting for their Alpha to turn them loose.

"She's here to bring discord to the peaceful dance of the Hopi," Big Elk said.

Alex revved like a racecar at the starting line.

Nora hoped her words wouldn't stick in the dry desert of her throat. "Big Elk has been desecrating the sacred peak himself."

"Enough talk," Big Elk said.

The young men crowded behind him.

Nora heard a quiver in her voice. "The kachinas weren't up there last night 'bringing fire to the mountain.' Big Elk manufactured the whole thing with some explosives and a couple of old white people."

Confidence oozed from Big Elk like blood from a tick. "You don't know what you're talking about."

"You made a good living by pretending. Why not tell them your real name, Ernie."

Big Elk stepped closer to Alex. "Don't listen to her. She's a deceitful *pahana*."

Her hands shook and her stomach churned. "Big Elk doesn't know about Hopi or respect for your land. Before he became Big Elk, champion of indigenous people, he was Ernie Finklestien, robber of the helpless."

Heather made a fist. "I knew it!"

Big Elk turned on Heather. "Go back to your white mansion. You have no business here."

Alex's anger roiled like a thunderstorm about to break loose.

Nora pointed at Big Elk. "He's importing fake Native American art he plans to sell to line his pockets and ruin your reputation. Talk about angering the kachinas."

Destruction flashed in Big Elk's eyes. "I gave you a chance to walk away. Now it's too late."

The mud-caked clown who had accosted her in the plaza pushed his way from behind Alex. "What are you doing here?"

"She's disrupting the dance. Spreading lies and discontent," Big Elk said.

Heather's calm exterior melted and she sounded like a volatile teenager. "He's the bad one. The kachinas won't like what he's doing."

Big Elk directed Alex. "Get her out of here or I will."

Heather folded her arms. "I'm staying."

"Do it," Big Elk said.

"All right." The clown held up his hands in a calming gesture. "Let's settle down." He pointed to Heather. "She's from a powerful clan and has a right to be here." His gaze swung to Alex and the other young men. "I see some of you are Hopi. Go to your kivas." He addressed the others, including Big Elk. "The rest of you are from other tribes. You're welcome to observe the dance. But please stay in the plaza. This area is reserved for Hopi only."

He turned to Heather. "Sikyatsi, I'm glad to see you." His gaze held affection then he shifted gears to business. "You're welcome here but bringing her," he nodded in Nora's direction, "wasn't a good idea. She should go now."

Gladly. With relief, Nora took a step backward.

Heather didn't move. "She's not leaving until he does." She pointed at Big Elk. "He shouldn't be here."

The clown sighed. "He's helping us to save our sacred mountain."

"He's ruining the dance and messing up the balance." She might as well stomp her feet and cry.

Since Heather wouldn't allow them to get while they could, Nora added, "And he's using Hopi beliefs to manipulate you."

Big Elk's face turned redder than his usual sunburn. He looked over the clown's head to the young men behind. "We can't let this evil *pahana* destroy Hopi. Where will the kachinas live when the mountain is clear cut for skiing and water is pulled from the veins of the Mother and She is trampled on by white men's skis?"

When had the crowd multiplied? Where there had been four young men and some curious spectators, now a group of Native Americans glared at her.

"Everyone calm down," the clown said again.

His voice disappeared in Big Elk's bellow. "Our ancestors didn't allow the *pahana* priests to destroy our way of life. In this time, when the Fourth World hangs in the balance, we need to have the courage of our grandfathers."

The clown held his hand up to silence Big Elk. "Hopi people value a humble life, self-respect, respect for others, compassion, integrity, self-control." He inhaled. "We are not activists in the white man's way. We protect the world by carrying out our clan responsibilities."

Nora took hold of Heather's arm. "Let's get out of here."

Heather pulled loose. "I'm not going." She raised her voice. "I belong here and I won't let Big Elk ruin it."

Big Elk's shout rose above the mesa. "Lies from the rich white girl! This is foretold in prophesy and it's our duty to stop you."

"Now," Nora said.

The clown's calm drowned in Big Elk's ranting. Of course the people listened to Big Elk. In their eyes, the money-chasing whites—that would be Nora and Heather—set out to destroy their sacred lands. They had lived and worshipped here for over a thousand years. The courts wouldn't listen, the governments wouldn't listen. Now frustration built to the breaking point.

Add a dance that was deeply rooted in religious significance, being on their own ground with their own people, and a talented instigator. This combination could lead people to forget their normal sensibilities, embrace the mob mentality and ...

Kill Nora and Heather.

Big Elk continued to stir the pot. "We need to take extraordinary steps, like our grandfathers did when the white priests tried to ruin Hopi with their baptism. If we don't, it will be like the time of Lololama, when they took our children to their white schools and tried to wipe us out. But we won't let them this time."

Nora grabbed Heather's arm and tried to run.

Heather pulled back. "We're responsible for the balance of the world. I can't let this bastard ruin it all!"

Alex lurched forward and grabbed Heather around the waist. He jerked her backward, pulling her into himself and off her feet.

Heather's arm wrenched from Nora's grasp. "Heather!"

Alex backed into the growing crowd. They closed ranks and Heather disappeared. Two of the young men moved with purpose toward Nora.

29

"You shit!" Though Nora couldn't see Heather, there was no mistaking her fury.

Nora lunged after Heather only to face a wall of Big Elk and his thugs. No way could she get through them. Rescuing Heather became impossible. Rescuing herself was up for grabs as well.

"You disrupted our sacred ceremony and brought evil to the mesa." Big Elk's words diced the air like a razor through flesh.

One young man pulled back like a ball in a pinball machine, ready to fly forward, grab Nora by the neck and draw her into the pack to be torn limb from limb.

She spun and shot away before he could spring.

Nora wove through the cars and bumped startled women, certain she outpaced the younger, stronger men by only a few steps.

She raced to the path, dodging rocks and pits, praying she didn't slide off the side of the steep slope. Her legs stretched and she felt the impact of each footfall up her back. Her blood pounded, "Faster, faster."

Shouts melted into a roar. Even though she ran past the vendors and crafts booths, no one tried to stop her. Nora dashed forward, not knowing where she headed.

Pot holes and ragged concrete made the road treacherous and she concentrated on each step to keep from landing on a rock or hole and crashing into the dirt. She dared not slow enough to look behind her but she heard feet pounding and heavy breathing. Any moment a hand would slam on her shoulder, grab her shirt and drag her to the ground.

Then what? They'd take her to the mesa ledge and toss her over to dash on the rocks below. Maybe Hopi believed in peace and hospitality, but some of Big Elk's guys belonged to less friendly tribes. Her shattered death would bookend Scott's.

Nora turned off the main road onto a path that narrowed into an alley between two stone houses. This part of the village looked as if it had grown from the desert of its own volition. Ancient, crumbling, ashes to ashes, dust to dust. She'd never be able to escape the thugs chasing her. No one in Hopi would help her. Nora's last moments on this earth would be spent running for her life.

The dirt path of the alley t-boned and Nora ran to the right. The houses crumbled away until there was only a low wall on either side. The last turn proved to be a fatal mistake.

The walls ended. Nothingness lay beyond them. Nothing, except the edge of the mesa... and death. She faced the same fate as those priests four hundred years ago. Broken and bleeding under a culture they didn't understand.

She ran on, hoping to see a path down the side of the mesa. Some escape. Sheer cliff wall dropped impossibly far to murderous rocks below. Like a cornered dog she turned to face her enemy. Panting and frantic for some way out, Nora could do nothing but watch them approach.

Two young men stopped about fifteen feet away. The taller one squinted at her. "Now where're you gonna go?"

The other one, sweat dripping through the dust on his chest, said, "She's goin' down."

"You insulted our Mother."

They walked toward her. "You shouldn't of messed with our peak."

They blocked the path of retreat. The mesa formed a point and she stood at its apex, with nowhere to go but splattering on the rocks below. "This isn't the 1600s. You guys will ruin your lives if you kill me."

The tall one shrugged. "If we let you make snow, our kachinas will turn their backs on us. The lives of all the people will be ruined."

The sweaty one took two quick steps, his arms up, ready to push her.

Nora swung to the side and he missed, losing his balance. He didn't go down, but humiliation burned in his face.

He let out a growl and lunged for her.

Nora sidestepped but he wasn't fooled again. He crouched like a football linebacker and moved with her. His hands connected with her shoulders.

She couldn't scream. Could only understand that her life was over. Her body anticipated free fall. The painful crush of pointed rocks. Blood, broken, death.

But she didn't fall backward. Strong hands on her back held her upright.

The man in front of her staggered backward as if she shoved him.

The little kachina salesman stepped from around her. He glared at the two younger men and spoke in a quiet voice. His Hopi words carried an obvious message of shame.

They paled. Stepped back. Lowered their eyes.

The little man barely moved his head but he made eye contact with Nora and in a gesture so slight she wasn't sure he did anything, he indicated she needed to follow him.

Nora struggled to keep up with his sure-footed gait, especially when she kept turning around to see if the men chased them.

This little man must be a revered elder to have such an impact on the thugs. Maybe he could make Alex let Heather go.

The kachina man trotted around the last corner and pointed to Heather's Rav4. Alex must have driven Heather out here in her car.

Heather paced in front, looking the opposite direction. Like warm honey, relief spread through Nora.

He nodded in dismissal.

Nora bowed her head, not sure how to express gratitude to him. "Thank you."

He nodded again.

"What did you say to them?" she asked.

He spoke slowly, his words halting. "I said dis is not the Hopi way, to harm people. We are a people of peace."

"That did it?"

"They are not Hopi. Navajo."

"And they obeyed you anyway?"

He shrugged. "Our mother villages have mysterious powers to protect. If someone defies the power, we all suffer. Maybe all mankind."

This guy should be president. He should be mediating in the Middle East. Such simple words and she wanted to spread peace and harmony throughout the world. She believed it could actually make a difference.

"Nora!" Heather ran toward her. "Where were you? What happened?"

Heather launched herself into Nora's arms and exploded in a monsoon of tears.

With equal relief at Heather's safety, Nora hugged back. "I'm fine. Are you okay?"

But Nora couldn't make sense of the sobs. Something about Heather's embrace and tears tapped Nora's heart like a tiny jeweler's hammer. This girl with the courage of a lion owned the vulnerable heart of a child.

When was the last time someone had touched her with this much raw love? She'd suffered her mother's dutiful hugs, the well wishes of Scott's friends. She'd appreciated Charlie's affectionate pats. But this girl cracked open the shell of her heart and it gushed with pain and loss, but also hope and healing.

Nora let loose with her own storm of tears, pulling Heather close.

30

Barrett's Hopi contact leaned against the black Mercedes with his arms crossed. The shade of the juniper concealed the meeting from the Interstate but didn't do much to buffer the roar of semis running down I-40.

Barrett had faced any manner of business problems in the past and overcome personal tragedy that would leave a lesser man a puddle of slush. But the last few years he had relaxed into complacency. He relied on the easy pickings of the energy boom and the domestic tranquility of a daughter that adored him.

All that changed in the last six months. His emotional and intellectual softness had to harden into granite again. He needed to be the Barrett McCreary III he used to be.

He gave the councilman a steady stare. "You said the Tribal Council was on board. They've got to know uranium mining will make the Hopi a rich tribe."

The man shrugged. "Rich don't always matter to Hopi. The elders don't want nothing to do with mining after the sickness last time. But the younger ones, some of them want the electricity and water lines brought to the mesas."

"Big Elk said he was making progress with the elders." Scalding blood pumped into Barrett's brain. Just the opposite of his cool-headed trade mark.

The cadence of the councilman's voice sounded as if a drum beat in his head. "Benny, he's against uranium and lots of guys listen to what he says. Big Elk ain't convincing no one to go for uranium. He's just gettin' the younger ones mad."

"Doesn't matter now that Big Elk isn't around anymore."

"I don't know who told you that. He's out at the rez now. He's got them so's nobody's even thinkin' about uranium."

Barrett had sprung Big Elk from jail and had hoped he'd hold up his end of the Hopi deal. He should have known Big Elk wouldn't act with any honor. "What's it going to take to change a couple of votes? Another clinic? A school? Untraceable cash? What does Benny want?" There was always a price and this one wouldn't be cheap.

The Hopi man's face showed little emotion. Indians hardly ever did. "I can ask but I don't know how far I'll get. The people are gettin' pretty worked up now, with the government okayin' the snow making and the woman layin' pipe and all."

"Get me the votes and you'll be a rich man."

Barrett slid behind the wheel of his Mercedes, leaving the Hopi man to his dilapidated pickup. He drove over the hill and out of the juniper.

The peaks commanded the landscape. His peaks. Barrett ticked through the issues needing his attention.

Deavonshire assured him the committee leaned toward allowing existing claims to go ahead. Barrett could start work on the current mines but that wouldn't make major expansion possible. He needed the Hopi endorsement. Barrett shunted the uranium mining issue to the bottom of his agenda.

Big Elk had become too much of a liability. He punched in a number on his phone and when a low voice answered, Barrett gave the details.

Now, the next problem. Water had to be pumped onto the mountain immediately. More importantly, he needed to find and destroy Scott Abbott's papers before someone figured out why.

He turned the Mercedes onto the highway and headed for the mountain.

Next. He had to check on Heather. Without looking, he took his phone from his shirt pocket, flipped it open and pushed speed dial for the house. No answer.

God damn it. When she'd called last night and said she was staying with her ditzy friend, Sheryl, she'd promised to be home early to clean horse stalls. This rebellion phase of hers had to stop.

Barrett simmered in a stew of problems, making phone calls to lobbyists and staffers the whole trip to Kachina Peak.

Sun sifted through the pines and dappled the hood of Barrett's Mercedes. He pulled into Kachina Ski's parking lot. Good, the decaying wreck of a Jeep was gone so he assumed the raving redhead wasn't home.

He stepped out of the Mercedes and started toward the lodge, pasting on a pleasant face and formulating a plan of attack. He'd put off getting rid of Scott's papers too long. He didn't usually let loose ends dangle like this.

Maybe after the pumps were up and running here and he'd made a start on the uranium mines, he'd take Heather on an extended vacation. Get her away from everything Hopi.

His chest loosened slightly. Good plan.

He clumped up the deck stairs and into the lodge. "Hello." He waited for his eyes to adjust to the gloom.

No one answered him. He tried again. Silence.

Barrett knew a gift when he received it. He retreated, heading for the deck. Seemed strange Nora would keep Scott's things. If it were him, he'd have sifted through the leavings looking for anything of value and destroy anything else. But women thought differently. Nora would probably cry over it for years.

Barrett planned to grab the box from the bedroom closet and reduce it into ashes within an hour. He reached for the screen door but it opened, startling him.

Abigail looked up and yelped. She sucked in a breath and let it out, a welcome spreading across her face. "Oh. Barrett. You scared me."

Barrett met her smile, feeling that goofy balloon in his chest. What an exquisite woman. Her face glowed smooth as porcelain. Her eyes lit up with an enchanting sparkle. He felt foolish and delighted in a way he hadn't felt in years--no, decades.

Right now, though, he needed to find Scott's papers and get rid of them. "Abigail. It's wonderful to see you."

She gave him that inviting smile he longed to see in his bed. "It's always nice to see you. What are you doing all the way out here?"

He stepped outside. "I wanted to see if the sprayers had been delivered. We've got a tight schedule if we want to have snow for Christmas."

Abigail followed him. "You could have called. But no sprayers, it's been quiet out here."

She usually offered him something to eat or drink by now. What was the holdup? "Could I trouble you for a glass of water? I am really dry."

"Of course. Come up."

He followed her up the stairs, enjoying the gentle sway of her hips. His blood rushed to pleasant places. Yes, he'd have to find a way to keep Abigail.

Not an item seemed out of place in the little apartment. Abigail hurried to the kitchen. "I'm afraid we don't have bottled water. Nora insists it's environmentally abusive. But I made mint tea this morning."

"That would be wonderful." At least he didn't sound as frantic as he felt.

She handed him the tea and he took a sip. "That's great."

She seemed pleased. "I picked the mint behind the lodge so I suppose it would pass Nora's test for natural."

"You aren't having any?"

"I hate to fill up on too much tea. I'll have to excuse myself all afternoon if I do." The way she said it made him think she was trying to tell him something.

He noticed her handbag and a notebook sitting on the table. "I'm sorry. I should have asked sooner, are you on your way out?"

She smiled in that enticing way again. "It is my club afternoon. I'm secretary, which is funny, really, since I'm the newcomer. But I wanted to get involved in the community and this club does such good work."

"Oh, I'll get out of your hair." Where was Nora?

She gestured toward the sofa. "Don't be silly. Please sit and enjoy your tea. I've got a couple of minutes."

She pushed him to sit and perched on the sofa arm, swinging her foot.

He started to get up. "I'm keeping you."

She put a hand on his shoulder. "You just sit. Finish your tea. But I do have to run downstairs and get something. I'll be right back."

Barrett couldn't have written this. "Thank you, Abigail. You're amazing."

"Oh, you." She giggled like someone thirty years younger and hurried out the door. He wanted her. No reason he couldn't have her.

The door clicked shut and Barrett moved as quickly as his bulk allowed. He dumped the disgusting tea down the drain and returned his glass to the coffee table, only losing twenty seconds. Another couple ticked away as he hurried into the bedroom.

They lived like mice in a box. Abigail would love his spacious home with its open floor plan and towering windows, plenty of closets and cabinets to store all the pretty things he'd buy her.

Barrett opened the closet and plunged into the back where he and Heather placed that stupid box.

Gone! She'd moved it.

He spun, frantically searching the room. A filing cabinet shoved into a corner. What was stored inside? Did Scott keep copies? He ought to blow up the whole place to make sure there were no loose ends. This slum would be no big loss.

A memory blindsided him. He'd lived in more cramped quarters than this. It had been the happiest time of his life. Their bed was nothing but a mattress on the floor, the crib crammed next to the threadbare sofa. Fliers for the next rally sat on a Formica table. He stretched out on the rumpled sheets with his daughter sitting on his flat belly chattering about sister stars. Ester clattered the dented coffee pot and lit a match to the rusting stove. He loved to watch her naked body move with such fluid motion. His son made sucking noises from the crib.

Ester insisted they rise and greet the sun on the mesa so she could offer corn dust and prayers. In those moments he had everything he ever needed.

"Barrett?" Abigail's voice jerked him from the mesa.

Damn it. He'd lost time and opportunity. Was he losing his mind, as well?

"What are you doing?" she asked, her eyes sweeping the bedroom for clues.

He cleared his throat. "I'm sorry. I know this is rude. I have to confess I didn't come up here because I was thirsty."

"Oh?" Her eyes narrowed in suspicion.

Barrett tried not to look at the closet door; instead he walked to the window. "I wanted to see the view. I think this lodge could use an overhaul. Maybe even a scrape off and start over."

Her eyes lit up.

If spending money made her glow like this, he'd make sure she never had another bad day. "That's a good idea."

At least he hit upon a decent excuse and maybe not such a bad idea after all. "If we incorporate a living quarters in a new lodge what should it look like?"

She joined him at the window. "It should be much larger. And more secure. I feel completely exposed up here."

Her soft scent tickled his nose.

"I hate to chase you out, Barrett, but I need to get going if I'm going to be on time."

He nodded. "What about storage? This apartment doesn't seem to have much closet space."

Her laughter tinkled. "Closets are a myth here."

"It must have been cramped with Nora and Scott here. There can't be much space for your things."

She blushed, probably thinking he made an overture about moving her out. "We manage."

"Are all of Scott's belongings still here?"

She led him from the room and sighed. "I've urged Nora to clean it out. I've been through this before and the sooner you bring yourself to discard the belongings, the sooner you move on."

"How is she doing?"

"She's made little progress, I'm afraid." Abigail picked up her handbag from the table and reached for a peg by the door. "Oh, poo."

Poo?

"I forgot Nora's gone with the Jeep. You wouldn't mind taking me to town, would you?"

He held the door for her. "Of course." It felt right having this attractive, charming woman in his life. She might provide the missing piece to settle Heather and give her a true sense of home. With Abigail they would be the family Heather longed for.

Abigail descended the apartment stairs and didn't hesitate before stepping across the deck. He followed her to the parking lot, the idea sounding better with each step.

The iron seemed hot enough for him to strike now. "Abigail, there's something I want to say."

The slightest impatience darted in her eyes, the color of the aquamarine ring he'd buy for her.

He reached out and took her delicate hand, youthful passion tingling in his veins. "I've grown more than fond of you."

A rosy blush appeared on her cheeks. "Barrett, I..."

He squeezed her hand. "Let me finish. Since I've met you, I can think of little else. I hope I'm not out of line when I say I think you feel the same way."

For the first time he saw her control slip. That he could catch her off guard and send her heart racing made him bolder.

"We're not youngsters and I'd like to spend whatever years we have left together. Will you marry me?"

The roses vanished from her cheeks, leaving a floury shock. Her lips lost the lift of her perpetual smile revealing crevices in her cheeks and wrinkles around her mouth. He'd made a terrible miscalculation.

Her hand jerked as if she'd like to pull it away. "Barrett. That's sweet..."

He wiped the sappy look from his face. "I caught you by surprise." He laughed. "To tell the truth, I surprised myself. I got carried away by the moment. Please excuse my impulsiveness."

"I don't know what to say."

"Let's just forget the whole thing."

"This is unexpected. And I'm flattered, of course. I am terribly fond of you."

A police cruiser turned into the parking lot. That put an end to the conversation. The officer climbed from the car and approached them. He nodded to Barrett and addressed Abigail. "Is Ms. Abbott around?"

"Good afternoon, Gary," she said, always the perfect hostess. "Nora isn't home."

"Do you know where she is?"

"She left early this morning to bring Heather home from the reservation."

Heather on the rez? A sledgehammer crashed into Barrett's brain.

Thoughts might be processing in Gary's head as he stood looking up at the lodge. "I have a warrant to search the lodge and apartment."

Abigail gasped. "You will do no such thing. What possible reason would you have for this outrage?"

"As a person of interest in two homicides, searching her home is routine."

Searching this place, with Scott's papers somewhere inside, could not happen.

Abigail lifted her chin. "I won't allow it."

Gary let out another exhale. He seemed to have a lot of air in him. "I need to ask you a few questions, too," he said to Abigail. "Can you come down to the station?"

"Now?"

Gary nodded. "Now would be good. You can ride with me."

"I'm sorry. I have a previous engagement."

Gary held up his hand as if directing traffic toward his cruiser. "I'll bring you back when we're through."

Barrett's jaw ached where he clenched his teeth. *What the hell was Heather doing on the rez?* But more urgently, he had to make sure the cops didn't find Scott's fucking papers.

Barrett stepped close to Abigail and put an arm around her. "I'll call my attorney and have him meet you there."

Now came the grateful eyes. He felt tides shifting inside Abigail as it became clear to her what Barrett could do for her. She was a bright woman. "Thank you, dear."

He nodded in his most protective way.

She leaned into him. "Could you please follow us to the station? I don't want to be there alone."

Before she slid into the cruiser beside Gary, she sought Barrett's eyes. "The answer to your question is yes."

He watched them drive away, his mind shifting into overdrive. Even if he didn't have to go hold Abigail's hand, he wouldn't have time to search the apartment and no telling what he'd leave behind for the cops to find. Scott's papers. Heather on the rez. Big Elk fucking up his plans. Alex, too. Barrett had business to attend to.

31

The horizon stretched across sparse grassland. Rain clouds threatened a patch of desert miles away. The speedometer of Heather's SUV wavered around ninety. Nora wanted to put miles between them and the mesas. She hated leaving her Jeep on the rez but Heather was in no shape to drive herself.

Heather's head rested in Nora's lap. They'd barely made it to the highway before Heather fell asleep.

Nora stroked Heather's black hair, soothing the child as she slept. What a fiercely courageous girl with a committed heart. But so blind.

At sixteen Nora had been full of insecurity and angst. Abigail circulated in a world of Junior League fundraisers and cocktail parties. She introduced Nora to preppy boys in Izod shirts who were going places.

Nora snuck out the back door during formal dinner parties to hike in the foothills. She wore jeans with holes in the knees and Birkenstocks. Maybe to the world she looked committed to saving Earth as she passed petitions for Green Peace and protested Rocky Flats Nuclear Facility outside of Denver. She listened while friends ranted about the evils of capitalism, took hits off the passed joint and nodded her head when they complained about how grades were society's way to control the creativity of youth.

Then she went home and did her homework, studied college catalogues and dreamed of a corner office on the 18th floor. Valedictorian pleased her mother, disgusted her friends and left her feeling as she usually did, without a place.

Nora couldn't offer any advice or answers to Heather. She was still a misfit—a nature lover trying to make a living off exploiting the land.

But making snow responsibly wouldn't ruin the mountain. Would it?

Heather stirred and sat up. "Where are we?"

"About ten miles from the Interstate. Fifty miles and counting from the rez."

Heather nodded and stared out the window. "He said I was from a powerful clan."

"Who said?"

"Benny. The clown. He knows who I am. He knows my mother. Children take on their mother's clan."

"Is Cole's friend the same Benny as the clown? How would he know about you?"

Heather smiled with satisfaction. "I'm going to find out who I am."

They rode in silence for a while.

"Alex said he loves me." Heather's voice sounded weak as a melted ice cube.

Nora thought about not answering but couldn't keep her mouth shut. "Kidnapping you isn't a good way to show love."

Heather swallowed hard. "I would have gone with him even if I hadn't been out of it."

"He didn't seem to have any trouble stealing your car. You sure he didn't hurt you?" Nora asked for the hundredth time.

Heather shook her head and studied the passing landscape. "Not this time."

That stabbed at Nora's gut. "What do you mean?"

"He's scary. We had a fight about Big Elk earlier and he told me he'd do whatever Big Elk told him to do, that it's time for Hopi to quit being passive and take charge."

"Was that on the roof today?"

Heather nodded. "I tried to break up with him but he wouldn't let me."

Nora shifted her glance from the road to see Heather's frightened eyes.

"I don't know what he'll do but he scared me."

"You have to stay away from him."

Heather sniffed. "He's changed."

"Maybe you're getting to know him better."

Heather's voice hardened like cooled lava. "It's Big Elk."

"Alex was probably a creep before Big Elk, but Big Elk knows how to bring out the asshole in people."

"I think we were warned about Big Elk. The prophecies say a *pahana,* a white guy, will try to destroy Hopi and we have to be strong and not follow."

"What prophesies?"

"We have all these amazing prophecies from over one thousand years ago and they've all come true."

"Such as?"

Heather counted off on her fingers. "Roads in the sky. Those are jets' contrails. They say there would be moving houses of iron, and those are trains. Horseless carriages are cars. They said we'd be able to speak through cobwebs. Pretty descriptive of phone wires, don't you think?"

"How do you know these were given a thousand years ago?"

"They've been passed down in the stories. Here's a scary one. They said that an upside down gourd of ashes would explode in the sky and cause rivers to boil and bring disease medicine can't cure. That's the atomic bomb."

"Okay, so back to the *pahana* one."

"I always thought it meant Poppy. It says the *pahana* will gather us under his wings and feed us and care for us because he sees something underneath that he wants. And soon we'll be dependent on him and act like his servants and give away the Mother."

"I can see Barrett in that."

Heather shook her head. "But it could be Big Elk, turning the young men away from the true way. Even if he's not the evil one in the prophesies, we need to stop him."

Except he slithered away from restraints like a snake. He stole pensions and stirred normal people to criminal acts and still, he sashayed out of prison like a prom queen at her coronation.

"He needs to be stopped. But not by you," Nora said.

"Then who?" This girl may be adopted, but her determination and the look in her eyes made Nora think of Barrett.

"What about the clown? He tried to talk reason to them," Nora said.

"Benny? Look how much good he did."

"But weren't the other elders in the kivas? There's got to be enough of them to calm the young ones down."

"The thing is, Big Elk has a point. We need to protect the peak for the kachinas. A lot of people are getting frustrated. They might see this as the time to act."

"What about the whole Hopi concept of peace?"

Heather's voice rose in frustration. "What has that gotten us? Sure, Hopi believe in peace but we also need to keep balance and take care of the land."

"I thought you were against Big Elk?"

Heather slammed her palm onto the seat. "That's just it. I know Big Elk is wrong. But everything is out of control and something has to happen. We need guidance."

"Don't you have a Tribal Council?"

"The Council can't agree on anything."

"What about a chief?"

"A *kikmongwi*? Each village has its own. In Hopi, every person gets to make their own decisions. The government doesn't make laws. People use persuasion and discussion to get agreement."

"What about that old man who helped me?"

"What old man?"

Nora felt a growing irritation, as if Heather wasn't trying to find a solution. "That old guy who walked me off the mesa. He's the same one who keeps trying to sell me kachina dolls."

"I didn't see anyone with you."

"He is little and wrinkled and old. He wears knee length moccasins and a long tunic type shirt."

Heather raised her eyebrows at the urgency in Nora's voice. "I haven't seen him."

How could she be oblivious? The man had been right there. "He wore his hair in a bowl cut and it looks like he used a dull knife to trim it. He looked so odd I can't believe you didn't notice him."

Heather shrugged. "Sounds like a real traditional guy." She hoisted herself to her knees and reached into the backseat. "I got these for Abigail." She turned around with a library book, plopped it on her knees and started flipping pages.

A whole array of black and white photos passed under Heather's fingers.

Heather stopped at a picture of a little man standing in front of a dusty stone house. "Here is how they used to dress."

Nora glanced at the photo. "That's him. That's the guy."

Heather rolled her eyes. "They all look alike to you, huh?"

This kid could be so annoying. "No. They don't all look alike. This is the guy. He's got that unique look in his eyes."

Heather stared at the book. "Can't be."

"Why not?"

"This is Nakwaiyamtewa. He's one of the greatest *kikmongwi's* the Hopi have ever known."

"That's what I mean. You need him to straighten out the Hopi."

"Nora, he died like in the late 1800s."

Karate chop to the gut. Nora pressed the breaks and pulled the Toyota to the side of the empty road.

"What?" Heather's eyes opened wide in alarm.

"Let me see that." The book lay on Heather's lap and Nora pulled it close, studying the little man. No doubt. This was the same man, except in the picture, he didn't wear the blue sash.

That proved it. She was crazy. She dropped the book back into Heather's lap and stared into the sandy desert.

Heather touched her arm. "What's the matter?"

Nora didn't understand it and didn't want to tell anyone in case they locked her up. "I swear that is the guy."

Heather looked at the picture, then back at Nora. "The spirits of ancestors can become kachinas."

Great. Now she was being haunted by an old chief. No, not chief. Heather called him a *kikmongwi*. Much better than an ordinary chief.

"I'm sure there's an explanation. Like, maybe Scott's kachina was Alex. And he didn't really disappear, he went into the lava tubes."

"What do you mean?"

"Before he died, Scott said he saw a kachina in the forest who warned him not to make snow."

Heather stared at Nora. "It wasn't Alex. He just made that costume yesterday."

Some tinny rap song blared from a bag in the back seat.

Heather jumped and reached for her bag. "It's probably Poppy. What time is it?"

Nora glanced at the clock in the dash. "Three ten."

Phone in hand, Heather plopped back in the seat. Worry creased her forehead. "That's not his number."

Damn it. Nora knew that expression. "Where does he think you are?"

The phone continued to blare and Heather gave her a mischievous grin. "Spending the night with a friend. It's okay, I told him I'd be home early and I'm just a little late. No biggie."

That tops the day off with whipped cream. Nora put the car into gear and pulled back onto the road.

Heather thumbed a button on the phone and held it to her ear. "Hello."

"Hi!" Heather settled back. "You won't believe what happened. This guy on the rez called me by a Hopi name. Sikyatsi. I think it means little bird or something like that. Anyway, he knows who I am. When I asked him about it he wouldn't tell me any more but I'm going to find out. Maybe from Charlie."

She listened a moment. "Because Charlie said he knows a lot of Hopi. Said he spent lots of time there when he was young. He's got to know my mother."

While Heather chatted in her animated way, Nora resorted to her constant state of worry. First, there was Big Elk and his followers. Should she go to the cops? They had no jurisdiction on the rez and they proved they couldn't keep hold of him. Then there was Nakwaiyamtewa, or whatever his name. And that was too bizarre to figure out. Now she'd probably have to face a livid Barrett, not her favorite thing.

Heather tapped Nora's arm with the phone. "It's for you."

"What?"

"Your mother."

The cherry on the top of a disaster sundae. Nora took the phone. "You have Heather's number?"

"Of course I have. I also have her email and have friended her on Facebook. She's my friend. You remember about having friends, don't you?"

The little Abigail inside Nora's head banged a sledgehammer against the backside of her forehead.

"It's a good thing Heather had her phone. Yours is in the apartment," Abigail said.

One hand on the wheel and her eyes straight ahead, Nora said, "What do you want, Mother?"

"Oh. Well. I just wondered when you'd be home."

The sledgehammer thudded inside her head. Dick Cheney and his gang had nothing on her mother. They could have conserved buckets of water if they'd used Abigail instead of water boarding.

"Cole called this afternoon. He's such a nice man and so concerned about you. Really, Nora, he's quite a catch."

"Mother." The word packed so much warning Heather raised questioning eyebrows.

"All right."

"If you only called me to matchmake with Cole, thanks. I'll be home later."

Abigail drew in a breath and let it out. "I have something I want to discuss with you."

"I thought you had your club meeting today."

Abigail let out a sigh. "I did. But your officer friend, Gary, decided to search your apartment."

"What?"

Abigail lowered her voice. "Don't worry. I put him off and he ended up taking me to town for questioning."

Thud, thud, thud. The tiny Abigail fiend worked in Nora's brain.

"Barrett sent his attorney to help me and when he showed up I excused myself to go to the powder room."

"That's good, Mother." Big Elk was probably gathering a force to track her.

"I didn't have to use the facilities, Nora."

"Okay."

She paused. "I snuck out and ran to the club meeting and had Marilyn drive me home."

Nora snapped to attention. "You left a police interrogation?"

"Just like Emma Peale. Now I'm home. What do I need to hide before the cops get here."

"You think I've got something to hide? You think I murdered Scott and his girlfriend?" Even calling Maureen Scott's girlfriend made her heart feel like a bruised pear.

"Don't be ridiculous. Of course you didn't murder anyone. Everyone has something to hide. Like maybe," she whispered, "a vibrator."

"Mother!"

"Oh please. We're both grown-ups. I don't know where you keep yours and I thought you might want me to get rid of it."

The Abigail in Nora's skull found another sledgehammer and delightedly slammed them both into Nora's head.

"Wait." Abigail said.

Nora waited.

"Someone is outside," Abigail whispered.

"Mother."

"Shhh."

"Mother!"

"I'm going to hang up now." Nora strained to hear Abigail's words. "Hurry home."

"Call the cops," Nora said.

"I can't honey. They think I'm in interrogation."

"I'm on my way home."

"One more thing," Abigail still whispered. "Don't tell Heather, I'm sure her father wants to be the one. But congratulations are in order."

Nora's stomach now throbbed too.

"Barrett asked me to marry him and I've accepted."

32

Maybe Abigail thought she played some Cagney and Lacy game but life didn't mimic TV where everything always worked out. Scott and Maureen's murders proved that. An hour ago Abigail told Nora someone lurked at the lodge. Abigail's phone put all messages to voice mail since then and Nora had raced to Flagstaff with growing concern.

They sped up the mountain road toward home.

A hint of anxiety crept into Heather's voice. "Poppy's going to be mad."

"Because you ran off with your boyfriend and ended up in the middle of a lynch mob?"

"Ex-boyfriend."

"Parents can be so unreasonable." *Was Abigail all right?*

Heather rolled her eyes.

Nora whipped into the Kachina Ski parking lot and jumped out of Heather's car. "I don't blame him."

Heather followed. "Now you're going to go all adult on me."

Her heart hammered while she rushed up the path. "Being irresponsible is not cool."

"That sounded just like your mother."

The mother she hoped would be waiting with musty mint tea and tales of outwitting the cops.

Heather hurried beside Nora. "I really like your mom but this whole dating thing with Poppy is creepy."

Even if it meant Abigail moving out, taking all her perfectly hung clothes on newly purchased hangers, packing the potions lining the bathroom counter, and eliminating processed foods from her refrigerator, the idea of Abigail with Barrett gnawed at Nora, too. "Why do you say that?"

"He's my father and I love him and all that, but...." A raven cawed while she hesitated. "He's like a king. People always do what he says, even if they don't want to. I'm afraid he'll change Abigail. She'll turn into a robot, like everyone else around him."

"Are you afraid that's what will happen to you?"

Heather laugh. "Poppy won't ruin me. I'm worried I'm so much like him I'll ruin other people."

Heather and Nora climbed the deck stairs.

Charlie and Cole stood by the lodge door so immersed in their conversation they hadn't heard Heather and Nora. They looked up, startled.

"What's going on?" Nora asked.

Cole pushed his hair from his forehead. "Benny said you cause all kinds of trouble at the rez."

Nora shrugged. "I brought Heather home in one piece." Barely.

"Damn it, Nora. Why didn't you tell me you were going to Hopiland?"

"Like you and Charlie tell me everything?"

"Now, honey," Charlie started.

She interrupted him. "Where's Abigail?"

Charlie looked sad. "She's at her club meeting. You didn't notice the muted colors of the mountain?"

It would break Charlie's heart when he found out Abigail was engaged to Barrett.

"She didn't go to the meeting," Heather said.

Nora looked up at the apartment and a jolt of fear hit her. "Didn't you fix that window?" she asked Charlie.

He followed her gaze to see the edge of the screen peeled back.

Cole's head whipped toward the window.

A crowbar lay in the shadow of the deck railing, as if dropped from the window. Why hadn't she seen that before? Nora sniffed the air. "Propane."

Charlie cocked his grizzled head. "You smell gas?"

"Where's the tank?" Cole already moved to the back of the lodge where Nora pointed.

Heather sniffed. "Now I smell it."

Charlie inhaled deeply. "Nose ain't been the same since the Radio Fire in '99."

Nora leapt for the apartment stairs. "Mom!"

Charlie pushed Nora back with surprising force for a degenerating alcoholic. He cleared two stairs with his first leap, Nora on his heels. "Abigail!"

"Mom!"

Charlie reached the landing while Nora was only halfway up the stairs. It felt as if cement filled her shoes. She imaged Abigail collapsed on the living room floor, her face contorted in agony, gassed and left for dead.

Charlie pulled the door. Locked! Someone snuck in the window and locked the door on the way out. They had probably hid inside before Abigail got home. And Abigail, pumped from her jailhouse escape, never noticed a crowbar or wrecked window.

"Abigail!" Charlie's voice sounded like Nora's heart, splitting with fear. He lunged for the window, wrenching the screen. Nora grabbed a corner, her hand ripping on the sharp metal. She braced herself and pulled it back and Charlie dove inside.

"Mom!" Propane wafted around Nora.

"I've got her," Charlie yelled. "Stay back." He coughed. "There's too much blood."

Blood? "No!" Nora fought the screen. *What blood?*

Charlie coughed again.

"I'm coming," she yelled.

"Don't..."

Ka-whump!

The world erupted in fire and sound.

Blinding light seared Nora's eyes. Shattered glass and other airborne objects crashed into her, stinging and bruising. The stairs disintegrated and suddenly there was nothing under her feet. The sickening drop of her heart and stomach ended when she crashed onto the deck amid shards of glass, splinters and burning debris. Pain exploded along her spine and she couldn't breathe. It seemed like forever before her mind caught up to her body and she sucked air into her lungs.

Flames leapt from the window and stretched out the apartment doorway which now tilted off its hinges. Smoke scorched the blue sky and blistering heat seared Nora's face and legs. She jumped to her feet wishing she could leap to the upstairs apartment. She screamed before she was aware she'd opened her mouth.

"Mom!"

She charged for the ragged remains of the stair railing and tried to climb the wobbly structure to the apartment. "Mom! Charlie!"

Rough arms pulled her back.

Through the roar of the flames Heather yelled. "You can't go in there!"

She fought against the arms but they dragged away. "Mom!"

Heather stepped in front of Nora. "Charlie will get her out."

The arms around her felt like iron but Nora fought to escape. She had to get to Abigail.

Nora succeeded in twisting away long enough to see that Cole held her. She didn't get more than half a step away before he latched onto her, pinning her arms to her sides and lifting her off the ground.

She kicked and jerked. "Abigail needs me!" Nora had to pull her mother and Charlie out of the apartment before they burned. God, why wasn't her mother on a cruise somewhere? And Charlie, he didn't deserve to be hurt.

"Call the fire department," she screamed at Heather.

Panic ringed Heather like a sulfuric aura. "They won't get here in time."

It didn't matter how hard Nora fought, the arms around her didn't weaken. "Help them! Don't let this happen."

Her mother was vital and beautiful. Abigail couldn't burn up. She had too much to do. She had to stick around and straighten Nora out.

She had to keep breaking men's hearts and spending too much money. *Oh please, let her be okay.*

"If you quit fighting I'll go get them," Cole said, his mouth close to her ear.

Nora remembered a self-defense class she'd taken and with the one move she'd actually practiced, she lifted both arms.

Not prepared, Cole lost his grip.

Nora lunged for the railing, determined to save Abigail.

Heather shouted something, probably trying to get Nora to stop.

Nora launched her flight, aiming for a spot several feet up the railing where a small portion of a step remained, hoping momentum would carry her to the entryway of the apartment and the wall of flames.

She flew by Heather before she registered that Heather had the crowbar in her hand. That was a blink before it smacked into the back of her head.

White pain exploded and the world disappeared.

33

Nora surfaced to the sway of Heather's Rav4 and the thrump-thrump of wheels flying across seams on the highway. Where was the cannonball that struck her head? Her skull throbbed.

Abigail!

Nora tried to sit but her arms wouldn't push her off the back seat. "What the hell?" Pain shot across her back and every muscle felt like a giant pulsing welt. Her arms and face stung with an army of cuts.

Heather glanced over her shoulder then back to the road. "Good. You're awake."

"I'm tied up. What's wrong with you? Let me go." The pounding in her head made her want to throw up and she'd gladly aim for the back of Heather's neck if she could sit up.

"If you didn't wake up, like in the next five minutes, I was going to take you to the hospital in Winslow. And I didn't want to do that."

"Where's Abigail?" Nora tugged at the loose knots trussing her wrists to her ankles.

Heather didn't respond.

"What happened? Is she alive? What about Charlie?" The knots loosened more.

"I don't know. Cole pulled them out of the apartment and then we got you to the car. After that he went back and I tied you up and took off. The ambulance was there before we got off the mountain. I'm sure she's okay."

Nora slipped her wrists out of the rope. What was Heather doing with rope in her car anyway? "You're not sure of anything. Take me to the hospital."

Heather shook her head. "Cole is there. He'll take care of them."

Nora sat up and reached over the seat. She wanted to grab the wheel and stomp on the gas but they were traveling down the Interstate at ninety miles an hour. "Did it ever occur to you Cole might have set the explosion? Where the hell are we?"

"Twin Arrows. Cole is on your side, Nora."

Half way from Flagstaff to Winslow. "Turn around."

"Cole told me to take you to the rez."

"No."

Heather's phone jangled with that rap bullshit. She pushed it to her ear and mumbled. She shoved the phone at Nora. "It's Cole."

Nora grabbed it. "How's my mother?"

At the sound of Cole's Wyoming drawl she wanted to reach through the line and pull the words from him. "She's in the emergency room now. I don't have any information. She's burned but I can't tell much. She was unconscious and has a big gash on her forehead. They don't know if there's any internal damage from the explosion."

"What does that mean?"

He let out a breath. "We just don't know."

She shouted above the rush of blood in her ears, fighting to stay focused. "Charlie?"

"He's at least got a concussion and burns on one of his hands. They're working on him, too."

Nora slammed the back of the seat with her palm. "I need to be there."

Cole's reasonable tone tethered her. "Listen, Nora. You have to stay away. The cops—"

"I don't care about the cops."

"Okay, how about: Someone tried to kill you. It might be Big Elk, might be someone else. Whoever it is, they aren't going to give up. The rez is the safest place for you right now."

"The same rez where they tried to shove me off the cliff?"

"Nora, trust me. I wouldn't put you in danger."

"I can't hide out there when my mother's in the hospital."

"Just until tomorrow. I'm close to figuring this out."

"I won't stay there."

"Heather can make sure you do."

"Right. She can't tie a knot to save her skin."

Exasperation crept into his voice. "Don't force it, Nora. Heather knows enough people at the rez that keeping you won't be a problem. And if you'd like another knock to the head, my guess is that it can be arranged."

"Kidnapping."

"If that's what it takes to keep you safe."

"Did you try to kill my mother?"

"Damn it! Quit being stupid."

She breathed fire into the phone, imagining it branding the side of his face.

"Nora?"

"What?"

"I...we care about you. I'll take care of Abigail and Charlie."

She didn't answer.

"See you tomorrow." He hung up.

Nora slumped in the back of the Toyota. She spent the remaining hour and half ride churning. They drove to a different mesa than where they'd gone to the ceremony that morning and turned onto a dusty road. Heather pulled in behind a dilapidated shed and cut the engine.

"We'll hide the car here and walk the rest of the way. There's a village at the top of this mesa. We'll stay there tonight."

Nora folded her arms. "I'm not moving from this car. Take me back."

Heather pulled the keys from the ignition and shrugged. "Whatever." She climbed from the car, slung her leather slouch bag over her shoulder, and slammed the door.

Nora wasn't going anywhere without the keys. Maybe she could steal them. That being her only plan, she needed to stay with the keys and wait for an opportunity when Heather was distracted. Nora climbed from the vehicle and they tromped up the trail in silence.

The sun hovered over the western horizon, casting ominous shadows filled with Big Elk and hostile enemies that wanted Nora dead. She didn't see anyone lying in wait for her, but that didn't mean they weren't there.

She followed Heather up a worn yellow dirt trail, switchbacking along the side of the nearly vertical wall. A paved narrow road wound its way up the mesa some distance from the trail. Too bad Heather hadn't felt it safe enough to drive up; it might have saved Nora from marching in rhythm to the pounding pain in her head, the ache in her back, and the dull throb of her ankle. She named the peak-sized lump on the back of her head Mount Heather.

Once the trail intersected the road, where at some time in the last two centuries some hopeful Native American had built a structure, long since abandoned. "Why didn't you park behind this place? Your car would have been hidden and we wouldn't have to walk so far."

Heather grinned. "I could have. If I'd remembered it was here. Sorry about that."

"You're sorry. Right."

They topped the mesa not far from a tall structure with a flat roof similar to those in the village they'd been in earlier. They walked around the edge of the building to the plaza. Buildings, like aboriginal pueblos constructed of desert sand, created the enclosure.

Heather looked over her shoulder and knocked on one of the doors. Without waiting for an answer she opened it and directed Nora inside.

A ruin of a couch covered with a pale yellow sheet furnished the cramped room with cracked linoleum floors. One single bulb hung from the low ceiling, casting shadows from the round kitchen table and three chairs. Two folding lawn chairs, a stack of boxes and general clutter clustered in one side of the room. A small refrigerator and stove--several decades old--shoved into a corner of the room next to a long table that served as a kitchen counter. Everything looked shabby and second, maybe even third, hand.

"How's your head?" Heather asked.

Nora wanted to pummel the girl. "How's Abigail?"

Heather plopped her bag on the table. She rummaged in it and brought out a bottle of pain relievers. She poured water from a pitcher into a plastic cup and brought it to Nora. "I only hit you to protect you"

"You didn't enjoy it a bit?"

Heather scowled at her. "I didn't hit you hard."

Nora's neck felt like cement. "Take me to Flagstaff."

"I can't. It's for your own good."

Nora struggled not to choke on the pills sliding down her throat. "I've got to see her."

"See? I knew you love Abigail." Heather's eyes filled with tears.

"She's the most annoying and strongest woman I know. She's made my life hell. Of course I love her."

"You don't show it."

Nora couldn't deny her guilt. The dim space closed in on her. "Who lives here?"

"Benny." Heather looked around and headed for a closed door. "I've got to pee."

The leather bag didn't quite cover the car keys. As soon as the door clicked shut Nora snatched them and sped out of the house, sprinting for the Toyota.

It would take a couple of hours to return to Flagstaff. She'd go straight to the hospital and make sure Abigail was okay. Of course Abigail was fine. Nora couldn't allow herself to think her mother might be seriously injured.

Nora rounded the corner of the building and raced for the trail. She needed to get a head start on the Heather. Crashing down the path, she rounded a switchback to the ruins that intersected the road. She spotted a sparkle of metal behind the pile of stone and stopped to listen. Someone else was out here on the mesa. Alex? Big Elk? Some other Native American who would love to see her disappear. She slowed her breathing, hoping to be invisible and tiptoed closer.

A black Mercedes. Barrett. Maybe not her favorite person but at least he'd take her back to town. He was probably out here looking for Heather. Maybe Nora would rat Heather out and Barrett would lock her up. Might not be a bad way to keep the fool out of danger.

Voices floated to her at the same time the top of another black vehicle came into view. Didn't really matter who Barrett spoke with, at least he could take her back to Flagstaff. Nora started forward, opening her mouth to call out to him.

Something slammed into her face and wrapped around her mouth. A hand. An arm pulled her against a hard body and dragged her back into the shadows of the crumbling rock wall.

Alex found her and he would slit her throat. Nora bucked against the immovable captor, who seemed not much taller than herself.

Heather stood in front with sweat running down the side of her face. Her eyes wide, she pointed toward the vehicle and shook her head in frantic insistence. "Big Elk," she mouthed.

Nora stopped struggling.

The man's hand clamped Nora's head in a vice with her lips pressed into her teeth. Her head smashed into his chest, pressing painfully on the lump from Heather's batting practice.

"And Poppy," Heather whispered. She nodded to the man holding Nora.

The pressure lessened as if testing Nora and when she didn't scream, the arm fell away. She spun around to see the clown, still covered in yellow mud and black face paint. He stared at her with no expression.

Fight, run, scream. Or stay here and hide. Nora had to choose. Benny or Big Elk? Big Elk definitely wanted her dead. Benny seemed slightly less dangerous.

Heather dropped down and crept to the edge of the ruins. Nora followed. They peered around the rubble. The sun sucked daylight from the mesa, taking it beyond the horizon, leaving Nora and Heather in deep shadow. Barrett and Big Elk stood between Barrett's black Mercedes and Big Elk's black Escalade, a convoy of death.

34

"Bottom line is that you didn't deliver." It had been surprisingly easy to contact Big Elk to meet him here. Where the possibility of extortion existed, Big Elk would be first to the party.

Big Elk faced Barrett with the insolence of a terrier unaware he's about to be ripped to shreds in the jaws of a Rottweiler. "I'm waiting for the balance to go up in that bank account. When that happens, you'll get your vote."

Barrett was going through the motions. He only had to keep Big Elk talking for a couple of minutes. "Too late."

"You might change your mind when I tell you I've figured out you killed Scott Abbott and his girlfriend."

Bluff and bluster. Barrett remained expressionless.

Big Elk grinned. "You covered your tracks pretty well."

The back driver's side door of Barrett's Mercedes whispered open and two black cowboy boots stepped into the dust. The rest of the rough-looking dark man seemed to float out of the vehicle like an oil slick on the ocean. He moved like a shadow, silent, out of Big Elk's periphery.

Barrett kept his eyes riveted on Big Elk's eye while the dark man slipped behind Big Elk. Barrett would enjoy seeing that smug look fade from Big Elk's face.

"Okay, you got me." Big Elk laughed. "I don't have proof. I don't even know why. But I can get the cops sniffing around. You don't want that, do you Mac?"

Barrett didn't move. *Enjoy your last seconds, little man.*

As if the shadow man worked magic, Big Elk seemed unaware he existed. "Don't play games with me, McCreary. Either that money hits my account or I expose Heather as an eco-terrorist. Sure, she's a minor, but she'll do time somewhere, I guarantee. Blowing up a ski lift is serious business."

Barrett's self-control strained to the breaking point. He should have saved his money and killed Big Elk himself. On the other hand, it was almost comic how Big Elk didn't even sense the black menace behind him.

"That's where you made your big mistake, Mr. Elk." Barrett heard the sneer in his voice. "I could tolerate your low class ways. I would even pad your accounts. But you should know to never, ever threaten my family."

Barrett dipped his chin slightly like Caesar giving a thumbs down. The dark spirit behind Big Elk raised his hand and drew it in a fluid movement across Big Elk's throat.

Big Elk made a sound like a gag, then slid to the yellow dust.

It looked so easy and clean, aside from the gallons of blood gushing into the dust. No struggle. No last words. One second alive, the next... dead. Expensive, but you got what you paid for.

Barrett pulled a thick envelope from his pocket and handed it to the phantom. "Tempting as it is to keep the Escalade, get rid of it as completely as you do the body. You'll get the rest when I read the next obit." What a waste of a great vehicle. He stepped briskly to the Mercedes and climbed in.

Scott Abbott: check. Big Elk: check. Abigail: check. Alex: soon to be a check. All that remained was getting the Congressional committee lined out, getting snowmaking up and running, and finding Heather and corralling her.

Cole was a wild card. Nora needed to go.

35

They closed the door and all three took the first deep breath since the black man severed Big Elk's jugular.

Heather finally spoke. "Poppy and Big Elk were working together?"

With his yellow body paint streaked with sweat, Benny nodded. "Charlie and I suspected it. Big Elk was secretly buying up the council to vote for uranium mining."

"That was worth his life?" Nora asked.

Benny shook his head. "Don't think that's what Barrett said."

What Barrett said was that Heather blew up the lift. Nora stared at Heather. "Did you really do it?"

Heather froze. "Well, sort of. Yes. I helped."

"Why?"

Heather looked lost. "I don't know. I got all caught up in saving the mountain and doing the right thing and Charlie kept talking about all the cool stuff he'd done. And your mom said you'd been such an activist when you were young. It was a mistake."

Mistake didn't begin to cover it but Nora couldn't confront Heather today. Not with the smell of Big Elk's blood swirling in her nostrils. "We'll talk about this some other time. Right now, we have to figure out what to do about Barrett."

Heather sank to the couch, tears falling without care. "He's a monster."

Nora nodded. "And Abigail just agreed to marry him." The words tasted sour.

Heather's head shot up. "Poppy and Abigail are getting married?"

"Over my dead body," Nora said, knowing that phrase might be too true.

"I gotta clean up," Benny said and disappeared into the other room, clicking the door closed.

Heather curled up on the couch and in seconds she fell asleep. A psychologist would probably say sleep was her coping mechanism. At least Heather could find a moment's relief.

Nora wanted to pace but the small, windowless room wouldn't allow much movement.

Benny emerged in ten minutes looking like a normal person. The yellow mud and makeup gone, his hair damp and combed, he wore jeans and plaid western shirt. Though dressed in normal clothes and larger all around, he reminded Nora of the little kachina man. Maybe it was dark eyes that didn't seem to miss much.

Nora's insides twisted so tight she could barely breathe. "I need to know how my mother is."

Benny nodded. It seemed to take him forever to answer. Did he rehearse everything he said before it came out of his mouth? "It's best if you stay here tonight."

She couldn't twiddle her thumbs out here when Abigail was in the hospital. "At least call and find out how she is."

If he spoke any slower she'd need someone to translate. "Can't call. No cell service and we don't have land lines here."

Frantic now, Nora wanted to punch something. "How can you live like this?"

He watched her with annoyingly calm. "I have everything I need."

Sure. If you're an aborigine in the outback. "You live in isolation with no phone, no television. You use kerosene for light and haul water. Maybe you're surviving but what kind of quality of life is this?"

Pause, pause, irritating pause. "Tomorrow I will greet the sun and the Creator with prayers and thanks. My family and neighbors will be happy to see me. I have enough corn to last until harvest. I have the work of farming to keep me busy. The simple life avoids waste and misuse. There is no over-production. I live in harmony and balance."

This philosophy wasn't new to her. She'd grown up in Boulder, Colorado, after all. Communal, back-to-nature living and all the new age spiritual stuff drifted off the foothills with the pine pollen. But she noticed when even dedicated hippies reached middle-age most had real jobs, mortgages and health insurance like everyone else.

Benny's words beat in cadence to a rhythm in his head. "We live like this to develop a strong spiritual life so we can care for the land and protect it. Our spirit people looked after the people and taught us many things. They gave us language and our ceremonies and many sacred and secret things. But with this knowledge came great responsibility. When we live as instructed, we are happy and the world stays in balance."

Benny inhaled deliberately and let it out slowly. "Taking water from our sacred aquifer and spraying it on the sacred moun-ain is disrupting the balance. You shouldn't do that."

Sacred Everything. "There have been scientific studies that show making snow will not harm the mountain." Even as she spoke, it sounded flat and unconvincing.

Benny shook his head as if sad at her ignorance. "Western science compartmentalizes. We know everything is connected. To say taking water from the ground and spraying it on the surface won't change anything is denying the relationship. It's like saying your thumbs are not connected to your toes."

"You know the court ruled that Native American religious rights are not harmed by making snow as long as there are other places on the mountain where you can perform your ceremonies."

If she'd been trying to goad him to temper, she'd failed. He considered what she said. "Everything depends on the proper balance being maintained. The water underground acts like a magnet attracting rain from the clouds. The rain also acts as a magnet raising the water table under the roots of our crops. Drawing water from the aquifer throws everything off. Our elders tell us if this happens everything but Hopi will disintegrate. They warn us that time is short."

Suddenly exhausted, Nora sank to the couch. What she wouldn't give for a bath and to change from the sooty, dirty, sweat-soaked clothes.

Heather didn't stir. "It would be great if the Indians could live the way you did two hundred years ago and have all your sacred places and follow the buffalo and smoke peyote and all that. But this is the real world and you can't halt progress. Indians need to stop living in the past and acclimate to the modern world."

"We need to live our way. It is what we are made to do."

Nora kneaded her forehead. "And destroy or kill anyone who gets in your way."

"That is not the Hopi way." He didn't move, simply watched her with his unreadable dark eyes.

Nora couldn't argue with his logic. If he wanted to live in poverty and believed it saved the world, she had no right to tell him any differently. Heather's soft snoring filled the room. "Sleep will do her good," Nora said.

Benny pulled a folded blanket from the back of the couch and laid it over Heather. He walked to the door with his steady pace. "You can stay in my cousin's house tonight. She works in Winslow as a night clerk at the Holiday Inn."

Nora didn't follow him. "I want to see my mother."

"It's across the plaza."

"Can't you take me back to Flagstaff?"

He held the door open for her. "Do you really want to go back tonight?"

"Of course I do."

His deadpan expression didn't change. "Someone, maybe Barrett, killed your husband and tried to kill you. The cops think maybe you're a murderer and suspect you're trying to swindle the insurance companies so going to them won't help you."

Someone wanted her dead. Even if that someone was Big Elk and he couldn't get her any more, his faithful might not want to call it quits. If Barrett killed Scott, maybe he'd kill Nora, too. She couldn't go home. Couldn't check on her mother. Like Fay Ray in King Kong's grip she felt trapped. "How do you know so much about this?"

Benny waited by the door, letting cool night air into the cluttered room. "Cole told me."

"What does he have to do with me?"

One of Benny's eyebrows lifted slightly, what for him was probably a hissy fit of some kind. "He cares about you."

Not sure what that meant and too tired to figure it out, Nora gave in. She'd go to Flagstaff at first light.

She plodded across the plaza. The pitch-black night closed about her and she stayed on Benny's heels. Even if she didn't believe in spirits and ghosts, which she reminded herself she definitely did not, she could imagine the place teemed with malevolent forces that knew she intended to desecrate their home.

Benny walked her out a small arched entry to a dark door. He pushed it open and pulled the little chain to the light hanging from the ceiling. The place looked similar to his.

"I hope you don't mind staying alone. My house doesn't have another bed." He slipped behind an old door, the kind that easily broke if someone fell against it or, as this one looked, accidentally kicked it. He emerged with a blanket.

She took the blanket. "This is fine, thanks." Not sure if he kidnapped or saved her but, as Abigail taught her, it never hurt to be polite.

At the thought of her mother, Nora's throat tightened and tears pricked her eyes. Burns were painful. And what about disfigurement? Was her face ravaged by flames?

"Are you going to be okay?" Benny asked.

She swallowed. "Yeah. I'll be fine."

He nodded and left.

The quiet of the village, along with all the creepiness of the night and the native-ness of the whole place pushed against her. She hugged the blanket and sank to the couch. The light would stay on.

36

Sometime later, the chill forced her to move her stiff muscles and wrap the blanket around her. And later still, she must have dozed.

Panic blasted through her sleep and vibrated in the blackness. She gasped and sat up. Darkness covered the room so deeply she barely made out shapes of furniture. The bare bulb she consciously left burning no longer glowed.

There it was again. A terrible crashing on the roof must be what woke her. It sounded like a boulder dropped overhead with shower of smaller rocks and pebbles following.

Nora huddled into the blanket, imagining Alex outside. Of course he knew she hid on the rez and came to terrorize her. It was only a matter of time before he burst through the front door with a knife. Or maybe only his bare hands to shut off her wind pipe. How stupid to think she was safe here. Maybe Barrett lurked outside. Probably not. His style called for a silent assassin or a quick shove. He had no interest in toying with his victims.

The noise stopped. Nora waited. And waited. Apparently, Alex only wanted to scare her because no one stormed through the front door.

How she could have dozed despite the anxiety over her mother, the threat of death, the very real attack by Alex with his rocks and boulders, surprised Nora. But she jerked awake to more of the rocks crashing on the roof and windows.

It happened two more times before the first hint of dawn penciled the horizon. Each time Nora clutched the blanket to her and stared at the front door, expecting Alex to break it down and kill her. But the attacks broke off abruptly and eventually, she dozed.

With a shaking hand, Nora eased the doorknob and creaked open the door. She imagined Alex on the other side, ready to wring the life from her. But no one stood outside.

Nora crept from the house, sure there would be a pile of loose debris and rocks from last night's assault. But the dirt surface in front of the house sat empty. She climbed a low stone wall and worked her way up another ancient building until she surveyed the roof. No rocks. No pebbles. Just a flat roof.

The sun slept below the horizon casting enough light to convince her the morning would arrive. She had to get out of this place before Alex, or someone like him, killed her and tossed her somewhere in the wilderness never to be found. Maybe that wouldn't be such a bad thing, at least if Nora were gone, her mother would be safe. That was assuming Abigail recovered from the blast.

But if Nora never made it back to Flagstaff, would Heather warn Abigail about Barrett? Her empty gut clenched at the image of Big Elk's surprised eyes, his last gurgle, all that blood.

Nora ached with worry for Abigail and Charlie. Maybe she couldn't make a difference if she were at the hospital. But she needed to be there.

As soon as she saw her mother was okay, she'd report Big Elk's murder and get Barrett locked up.

Nora barely discerned a footfall, a tiny scratch of sand on rock. Her heart leapt up her throat and she swallowed it, fearing she'd look down and see Alex with a hatchet ready to chop her into bits.

But that's not what made the noise.

Standing below her was the little kachina man. What had Heather called him? Nakwaiyamtewa? He looked up and his calm, deep eyes searched hers. Without a word, he walked away. He made no sound and Nora suspected he purposely made the earlier noise to get her attention.

Like a kitten in a tree, Nora found climbing down much tougher than climbing up. She searched for each foothold and eventually got low enough to drop the rest of the way. Her landing in the dawn sounded like a buffalo stampede.

She hurried after the little man. As if he'd been waiting for her, she caught sight of him as he rounded the corner in what appeared to be an alley. Although she saw newer buildings in the first village yesterday, some made of cinder block, some framed and covered with cheap government siding, this village consisted of stone structures snugged closely together. It felt ancient and primitive.

The little man continued toward the edge of the mesa at his calm pace, limping a bit on his left foot. She shouldn't go out there. Maybe it was a trap and Alex waited to jump out and shove her off. But then, the little man had saved her before. He never made her feel threatened, a little freaked out, but not in danger.

She wondered if she was acting like the stupid waifs in the black and white horror movies, stepping up to the attic in the dead of night while Count Dracula waited in delight. But she felt compelled to follow.

The sun inched toward the horizon, taking the chill off the frightening night.

The little man stopped at the edge of the mesa. He reached into a small leather pouch hanging around his neck and brought out his thumb and forefinger pinched together. In a quiet voice he made strange noises.

Sure, he would probably say he sang, and it did have a certain rhythm, but Native American songs never really sounded like music to Nora. His voice wavered with age and he dipped his head to the east. Just then, the sun burst in surprising warmth and fire over the horizon. He held out his hand and let whatever he held in his fingers loose into the calm air. It looked like a fine dust.

Tears sprang to Nora's eyes. She might not understand what he said or all the implications, but she knew he prayed with thankfulness for the new day. It didn't matter to whom he addressed the prayers, the gratitude and beauty of the dawn seeped into Nora's heart.

He motioned her forward.

Nora obeyed without worrying about how close to the edge she stood.

He held out the pouch and nodded to her, indicating she take whatever it contained.

She reached inside, felt a rough powder and pulled out what looked like a pinch of crushed corn.

The little man did the same. He sang again in a quiet voice and tossed his pinch toward the sun. His eyes urged her to her own prayer.

His eloquence, though she didn't know his words, made her feel like a galumphing elephant. Stiff with embarrassment at her inability to say a simple prayer of thanks, she felt her face grow red.

The little man began his song again. The quiet bleating of his old voice sounded like a lullaby.

Nora's tears flowed, melting her reserve. She longed to sing, to offer thanks for another day. But she didn't know who to thank.

What was she so damned thankful for, anyway? Another sunrise and a chance for whoever wanted her dead to succeed. A day of painful recovery, at best, for her mother. The first day of the rest of her life fighting battles alone.

"What are you doing here?" Benny's voice made her jump. She spun around to see him frowning at her.

Her mind felt muddled and she realized the old man's song ended. "I came out here with him."

"Who?"

Of course the little kachina man didn't stand next to her. Obviously, Benny hadn't seen or heard him singing.

Remember when the most horrendous thing I could imagine was Scott having an affair? Now her life revolved around murder, terrorists, mothers in hospitals, and some ancient Indian chief, *kikmongwi,* only she could see.

"What are you doing here?" she said instead, to turn the challenge around.

He stepped beside her. "Offering my morning prayers."

She stood next to him as he took a pinch of corn from a pouch he carried. He ignored her and sang his song, bowing and tossing his offering over the mesa. He sang faster and louder and without the holy feel of the older man, but it felt like church, all the same.

He finished and stood straight.

Nora bowed her head slightly and let go of the corn she'd taken from the little kachina man's pouch.

Benny eyed her curiously.

She lifted her chin. "Nakwaiyamtewa gave it to me." She waited for his reaction.

He nodded, not looking the least surprised. "That's good."

Dirty and sore, Nora faced the warmth of the sun. "Someone waged a war of terror on me last night."

Benny laughed. "How is that?"

Maybe it sounded funny to him but he hadn't sat through hours expecting to be murdered any minute. "Probably Alex trying to scare me and he succeeded."

A glint of humor showed in Benny's eyes. "What exactly did Alex do?"

"He threw rocks at the windows and roof."

"Rocks?"

Anger and embarrassment heated her face like the sun. "Big rocks. Boulders from the sound of them."

Benny raised his eyebrows. "I didn't see any boulders when I walked by the house."

Infuriating, rational man. "I don't know what happen. He must have cleaned them up."

It sounded lame to her but what other explanation was there? He'd attacked her four times, that wasn't something a wild imagination conjured up.

Finally Benny seemed to take her seriously. "I wondered if they would come visit you."

"Who?"

"The kachinas."

"Funny."

"I'm serious. This house is on one of the energy lines. The highways of the spirits. You aren't the only one to hear them."

She gave him a skeptical look.

"Just because you don't believe it don't mean it doesn't exist. There are certain lines of spiritual power that run across the world. One happens to pass through where that house sits. Lots of people hear the spirits when they pass. Even a few white ones."

"You had me stay there on purpose."

"I wondered if they'd pass by."

She didn't believe him, of course. The idea of kachinas or any other spirits knocking on the house was ludicrous. There had to be another explanation. But who could have done it and where did the boulders go?

Benny meandered down the path.

Day or night, the village, with its crumbling and ancient buildings felt creepy. She trotted to catch up. "Where are you going?"

He didn't look at her. "Breakfast."

In normal life she wouldn't be the least bit curious about his prayer or what it might mean. But normal life ended with Scott's death and spiraled into Bizarro Land since then. Her mother lay in a hospital nearly two hundred miles away, murder du jour served as the main fare, and last night, spirits from some other world played Bowling for Sanity on the roof.

"What did you say over there? To the Creator or whatever?" Okay, that was the epitome of rude. Heart-stopping fear caused her to lose the manners Abigail had tortured into her.

"I thanked the Creator for another day and gave him some corn meal. I said, 'It is your way to live the simple life, which is everlasting and we will follow. I ask that you speak through me with prayers for all the people. We shall reclaim the land for you.'"

"Yay for the simple life of hoping the generator holds out."

A smile touched Benny's lips. "If the rest of the world faced disaster and there was no electricity or running water, they would perish. Here, we would go on as usual."

"You've got all this talk about keeping the old ways and ceremonies and poverty that, for some reason, balances the world. It's as illogical as one man's death accounting for the sin of mankind. Where is the proof that would make any of this reasonable?"

They crossed the plaza, less menacing in the morning light and more third world without a dance crowd filling it. He held the door of his house open for her. "You want proof as obvious to your senses as this door is to touch. I think maybe you need to expand your perceptions and develop new senses."

She couldn't come up with a polite response and blowing air through her lips while rolling her eyes would be wrong.

The blanket sat folded on the back of the couch. "Where is Heather?"

Benny's face showed no emotion. "She left."

A tide of salty anxiety surged into Nora. Without Heather, she was a prisoner on the rez. "How will I get to Flagstaff?"

"I can give you a ride." Benny opened a cupboard and pulled out two granola bars. He handed one to Nora. At least breakfast wouldn't be a painfully slow-cooked meal.

"Let's go." She hurried out the door, hoping to get Benny moving.

He drifted into the daylight of the plaza and stopped, his face to the sun. "You've heard of the Anasazi?"

Who blew up my apartment? Barrett? One of Big Elk's followers? What did Alex have to do with any of it? Was Cole a good guy or Barrett's henchman?

Benny stopped talking and waited for an answer.

She backtracked to his question. "The Anasazi are the cliff dwellers. The people at Mesa Verde and Walnut Canyon. They disappeared and no one knows what happened to them, right?"

He stretched as if urgency didn't thunder in Nora's blood. "It isn't a mystery to us. We are the ancient ones. They didn't just happen to disappear in 1100 A.D. like the archeologists say. Each of our clans was instructed to migrate and we did. For centuries we wandered over this country, up to the glaciers, down to South America. We left our history etched in stones along the way. We left our broken pottery and homes made of stones and mud. When we reached the mesas, clan by clan, we settled in the place chosen for us."

She took several steps and waited for him to meander in her direction. "If you're a chosen people, why would you get this hard country where you can barely survive?"

"This is the center of the world. All life depends on what happens here."

By the time he plodded to his vehicle and drove at an idle down the mesa, Nora would need a walker and adult diapers and her mother would be dust.

"Many of our young people are not keeping to the Hopi way. They want all the material things of the white man and it's causing disturbances."

Nora nodded and hoped she looked thoughtful. She'd get a ride out of here sooner if she didn't irritate Benny.

"Now Mother Earth is in pain. McCreary is taking her guts for money. Coal is her liver and uranium is her heart." They walked out of the plaza to the alley.

It felt like her skin stretched too tight for all the anxiety popping inside her. Benny's molasses pace made her want to scream. "You're against mining on the rez?"

He nodded. "Don't matter what McCreary says or how clean it is or how many jobs and royalties it will bring. Would you cut out your mother's guts for money?"

Barrett seemed to be involved in everything. Snowmaking and uranium mining. Other than both being damaging to the religious sentiments of the Native Americans, what did they have in common?

Benny's old Ford pickup used to be white. Now it was tied-dyed with waves of rust and dirt. Bright Indian blankets covered the bench seat that broke down toward the door. A large crack split the dash, showing yellowed foam rubber filler. Enough dirt accumulated on the floor he could probably plant a garden.

Despite seeming like an odyssey, they eventually made it down the mesa and a few miles south on the highway. Benny turned onto a trail hidden by tall summer grasses.

Worry twanged through Nora like an out of tune ukulele. A Hopi shortcut didn't seem like something that would get her to Flagstaff quicker. "Where are we going?"

Benny didn't look at her but maneuvered the truck down the bumpy trail. "I have to see to my corn."

"I have to get to the hospital!"

Benny shrugged.

"What about my mother?" She had to protect Abigail from Barrett.

Benny braked the pickup and got out. He headed to the side of the road beyond the tall weeds and started singing in Hopi. His low guttural consonants made a beautiful ringing on the desert floor.

Nora jumped out and ran to him. "Please. I've got to get to my mother."

He stopped singing and turned to her. "All your worry and impatience won't make your mother well. Let go of your stress and listen to Mother Earth." He continued on his way.

Arguing didn't turn Benny back to the pickup. And his stubbornness didn't halt her arguing. She followed, topped the ridge still making her case and stopped, amazed. In the dry desert, surrounded by hills of sand and scruffy weeds, Benny's cornfield grew lush and green.

He turned to her. "Do you know why I sing to the corn?"

She shook her head.

"The corn is like children. I sing to the seeds when I plant them. I sing when I tend them, bringing water or thinning the weak plants. That way, they learn my voice. They will grow toward it, wanting to please me the way a child would."

Nora wondered if she finally suffered the effects of too much stress. Benny's mystical gumbo sounded logical. "How do you get the corn to grow with no water?"

He smiled proudly at the bushy plants, so different from the endless fields of corn encompassing all of Nebraska and Iowa. "The cloud people have been good to me this year. They have given enough rain but not too much to flood the young plants."

"Why do you plant them spread out like this and not in straight rows?"

He reached down and pulled a weed growing close to one of the leafy stalks. "I don't use a tractor so there is no need to make straight rows. And spacing the corn like this confuses the cloud people. When you plant in rows all close together, the cloud people know where the corn is and they rain and leave quickly. But when you plant like this, the cloud people must look around and they stay over the field longer, giving more rain."

Cloud people—really? But he spoke as if he believed it and she didn't think he was a stupid man.

He focused on her. "We've been growing corn here for a thousand years. The cloud people live on the sacred peaks. If you destroy their home, there will be no rain for my corn."

"You don't really believe this, do you?"

He walked between the plants, touching their leaves in a loving caress. "Hopi have a respect for life and trust in the Creator. We were told that white men would come and try to take away our lands. But if we cling to the ancient ways we will prevail."

"Seems like you could grow more corn if you used a tractor or irrigation sprinkler. Why would your spirits want you to do everything the hard way?"

Benny straightened and brushed his hands together. "Making things hard prepares us for what may happen. Like a runner practices every day, building strength and endurance so he can run the marathon, we Hopi live a meager and hard life so we're ready to survive when the time comes."

He handed her a stick about a foot long and thick as a broom handle. He reached into his pocket and brought out a small plastic bag of corn seeds. "You stay here and plant these seeds over there." He pointed to a sandy spot next to the outer corn plants.

Nora's frustration boiled over. "I can't plant seeds when my mother is lying in a hospital and I don't know how she is."

He nodded. "I have to tend to another field then I'll take you to Flagstaff. You plant the seeds and if you can, sing to them."

"I don't have time to plant corn."

He shook his head. "I won't tell you what to do, that isn't the Hopi way. But I urge you to plant these seeds. Do something good for Mother Earth and it will go well for your mother."

"Like a prayer?"

He nodded. "Yes. Like a prayer."

She dropped the stick. "I don't believe in prayer."

Benny started walking toward a low hill, presumably to another cornfield. "Since you've got nothing to do until I'm done you might as well plant the corn. No one is around to hear you so go ahead and sing to the seeds. It will help them grow."

She followed him. "Please, I need to go."

He topped the hill. "I'll be back soon."

She trudged back and picked up the planting stick. Might as well, Benny had said. Planting corn was a stupid idea and she didn't want to do it. Just because Benny told her to plant was good enough reason not to plant his stinking corn. She ought to sit down in the dirt and wait for him to come back. If he came back.

She squatted down and thrust the stick into the ground.

Action might help her frustration.

It surprised her the dirt held moisture a couple of inches below the surface.

Planting corn while Abigail lay in a hospital. As if that would help anything.

She dropped in a few seeds and packed the earth around them. She took four steps away, the distance she estimated Benny's other plants were spaced, and squatted down again.

What if Barrett comes after Abigail or Charlie?

The seeds dribbled from her hand into the hole she dug and she covered them with dirt. She thought of Abbey, patting him on the head and seeing the devotion in his eyes.

Oh, God. Abbey. Had he been caught in the fire?

Hands shaking, she scraped out the next hole, carefully selected the three largest seeds. Scott. Abigail. Abbey. She dropped the seeds into the hole and patted the loose soil on top. She saw Scott's sweat-drenched face as she climbed from the SAG wagon at an Adventure Race last year. He grinned at her as she handed him his Gatorade and fresh inner tube for the flat he just had. She'd taken care of him for years, holding back the real world by finagling the finances and keeping Kachina Ski running, making sure he had time for hiking, biking and outdoor play that seemed to keep him alive.

She'd wanted to care for him with all the love in the world. Love he sucked up without thought. Barbed wire wrapped around her heart and squeezed with every memory of Scott. She'd given him all she had and he hadn't wanted her. Tears dripped into the mound of dirt she pushed back into the hole.

She straightened and stepped sideways, falling on her knees to dig a new hole, dropped in the seeds and scooped dirt. Patting the dirt reminded her of tucking a child into bed. A child she didn't have but one she wanted with all her heart. Was this what Abigail felt? She loved the seeds and wanted them to grow into strong plants, to tassel and create life-sustaining corn. Her mother wanted that for her. But like Scott rejected Nora, she'd been pushing Abigail away.

Nora rose from the ground, feeling love for the seeds, for her mother, for a child she hoped to nurture someday. For her old dog who might be alone and frightened on the mountain. The earth gave life to the corn which nourished the people here in Hopiland. It was this way all over the world. Abigail gave life to Nora and loved her, tried to make life good for Nora, teaching her and protecting her. And if she were lucky, someday Nora would be able to do the same with a child of her own.

Words wouldn't form but rhythm and sound grew naturally, boiling up her throat and erupting from her mouth in a song. She danced, tears falling from her face, her voice loud and deep with love for the corn, the earth that would nurture it, for her mother, and even for Scott.

Seeds planted, Nora dropped to the ground, her back against a weathered fence post. Her eyes drooped and her mind floated.

When she opened her eyes a man stood in front of her. Two slits served as eyes in a face flat and smooth. A cylindrical peg looked like a mouth. His bare chest showed zigzags of blue, like lightening. He wore a woven white cloth around his middle like a kilt and carried a hatchet in one hand and feathers in his other. Why she didn't scream at this apparition she couldn't say. It should have scared the be-jeesus out of her. But she wasn't scared. The kachina, and that's what it had to be, didn't frighten her, despite his bizarre appearance.

He didn't speak but pointed to the mounds she'd planted. Small puddles pocked the field where she'd put her seeds. The kachina told her plainly, though he used no words and she didn't know how she knew what he meant, that he'd brought the rain.

"...brought rain."

Nora blinked at the words that seemed to be as real as the desert under her. She turned to the sound. The voice belonged to the kachina man but he didn't stand there.

She rubbed her eyes and stood, focusing on a lean figure silhouetted on the ridge. Cole trotted toward her. "Nora. What are you doing?"

Thank kachina or luck or whatever power brought him here. She stood up, her legs weak and waited for him. "How's my mother? How's Charlie?"

"She was sleeping when I left and the hospital staff wouldn't let me see her. They wouldn't tell me her condition because I'm not family." He stopped in front of her, just inside acquaintance distance.

A tremor of despair began at the base of Nora's head and tears flooded her eyes.

Cole opened his arms and stepped forward. Without hesitation Nora leaned into him and poured her anguish, fear, regret and sorrow into his beating heart. His arms closed around her, temporarily shielding her from any harm. He felt warm and smelled of sun and pine and safety.

When the worst of her storm passed, she pushed against him. "Okay. I'm done with that. Now, let's get to Flagstaff."

He shook his head. "I just came out to see you. I'll go back and check on Abigail and Charlie. But you've got to stay here."

"I need to protect Abigail."

"This is the safest place for you. I'll take care of your mother."

Nora grabbed his arm. "It's Barrett. She thinks she's going to marry him and she can't. He's a killer. He killed Big Elk."

Cole stared at her. "Big Elk? When?"

"Yesterday." Nora started to tremble and tears spilled from her eyes. "My god, he had a man slit Big Elk's throat. Big Elk was working for Barrett."

Cole grabbed her by the shoulders. "I've got to go. Please, just stay out here for a while longer."

She shook her head. "I have to go with you."

A flash of anger lit his eyes. "You're going to get yourself or someone else killed."

"I've already caused murder. If I would have stopped snowmaking, Scott would still be alive."

"If you had stopped it, you'd be dead."

"What do you mean?"

He stood up, all business. "Never mind. Just stay here." He strode up the ridge. "I'll get this taken care of and be back for you. I promise."

She watched him disappear down the other side. When an engine started she raced up the hill, desperate not to be alone. She sprinted up the next hill and stopped short.

The whole time she planted corn and let her imagination run in hysterical circles, Benny's pickup sat a short trot away.

She ran to the rusted hulk of a pickup and jumped behind the wheel, pulling the door closed with both hands. It wasn't very smart of Benny to leave the keys in the ignition, but then, he probably wasn't used to taking hostages.

37

Nora spent the next two hours with her right foot pushed to the floor, trying to make Benny's old pickup move faster. It drove like he talked.

Nora fidgeted. Barrett could be with Abigail this very moment. Maybe he didn't have a reason to harm her but maybe he did.

Then there was the dicey situation that if Gary found her before she got to Abigail, Nora would spend too much time trying to convince him of Barrett's guilt, leaving Abigail on her own, unaware of the evil monster she planned to marry.

She finally puttered into the hospital parking lot and parked at the far edge. Nora jumped from the pickup, slamming the door. She struggled not to race to the front door.

Her nerves strained like rubber bands stretched throughout her body, twisting tighter and tighter.

A vehicle moving way too fast caught her attention. In the next row Heather whipped her Rav4 into a parking space and jumped out. She'd changed from yesterday's clothes and from the look of her wet hair hanging down her back, had the luxury of a shower. She slapped toward the entrance in her flip flops.

"What are you doing here?" Nora called to her. Despite everything, she envied Heather's shower and clean clothes.

Heather whipped around, obviously surprised. "I thought Cole wanted you to stay on the rez."

Cole could issue orders, but it didn't mean Nora had to obey. "I need to see Abigail and Charlie."

Heather hurried toward the hospital entrance. "He called me and asked me to be here with Abigail because he had to check something out."

Nora outpaced Heather. "Why didn't you wait for me this morning?"

Heather's face looked gray and cold as granite. "I've got to talk to Poppy."

"Stay away from him!"

"Benny won't tell me who I am. He said I have to ask Poppy."

Nora grabbed Heather's arm and made Heather face her. "You saw what he's capable of. Don't go near him."

"Whatever he is, he's my father, even if I am adopted. He would never hurt me."

Nora opened the door of the hospital and let Heather in front of her. The cold of the air conditioning smacked her skin after the heat of the parking lot. She hesitated, not wanting to ask the pink-coated volunteer Abigail's room number.

Heather strode passed the front desk. "She's on the third floor."

Heather had more confidence than a normal sixteen-year old. Nora wouldn't have thought to call hospitals and remember to get room numbers and generally take charge. At that age, passing out flyers about environmental issues or volunteering to plant trees ranked as her biggest accomplishment. And though blowing up the lift was definitely not a good thing, it demonstrated Heather's ability to act.

Nora leaned over and spoke in a near whisper. "Try to look casual and not draw attention. Keep an eye out for the cops."

They bypassed the elevator and opted for the stairs, hoping to avoid as much human contact as possible. At the third floor, Nora poked her head out the door and surveyed the hallway. Nothing but shiny linoleum, cream-colored walls and bright lights. She slipped out with Heather behind her. The room numbers led them down the hall and to a nurses' station situated in front of the elevators. Abigail's room sat on the corridor on the other side of the nurses' station.

Nora took a breath, straightened her shoulders and glanced at Heather. She had no choice but to march confidently by the nurses and hope they didn't take note of her shabby appearance and smattering of scabs from the flying glass.

Heather met her eye and gave a nod.

Nora stepped out to round the corner. A splash of dark blue stopped her. She turned and shoved Heather back around the corner.

"Hi, Laurie." Gary's voice greeted someone who replied with her own hello.

Nora didn't know she recognized Gary's voice but then, he represented a major menace in her life and Nora was gaining survival skills. He must be here to interrogate Abigail. Maybe he set a trap for Nora so he could snap the cuffs on her and drag her to a dungeon.

Nora leaned against the wall and strained to hear, but her beating heart made it difficult.

Heather tossed her hair and stepped around the corner.

Nora wanted to pull her back but Heather moved so unexpectedly she lost her chance.

"Hi," Heather said as if she hadn't witnessed a murder yesterday or blown up a ski lift. Whatever the female version of ballsy was called, that was Heather. "I'm looking for Abigail Stoddard. She's on this floor, right?"

The nurse, or whoever Laurie was, answered. "She's in room 321. But you'll have to come back another time. She needs to rest now."

"How is she?"

Gary interrupted, "Heather McCreary, isn't it?"

Nora imagined Heather turning a royal countenance upon him and barely acknowledging his question.

"Your father said you were on vacation in Mexico." Suspicion sprinkled his voice.

"I came back when I heard about Abigail." She never missed a beat.

"Do you have time for a few questions?"

Now Nora knew Heather's plan. She would distract Gary so Nora could see Abigail. The girl was cunning and, in her own way, sweet.

Heather sounded annoyed, exactly as Gary would expect. "I don't have time now. I've got to be somewhere."

"You came to visit Ms. Stoddard. I think you've got a few minutes." Some whelp wouldn't get the better of him.

"Fine." Heather sighed with supreme teenage superiority. "But only a couple of minutes."

"We can use the lobby downstairs," he said. His black police shoes squeaked and Nora figured he moved to the elevator and pushed the button.

"Great. Let's do it in front of the whole world so everyone thinks I'm a criminal." Easy, Heather.

A ding, soft rattle, a little shuffling, a swoosh, and Nora assumed they were on their way down to the lobby. She poked her head around the corner in time to see who she thought was Laurie, scoot down the corridor on the other side of the elevator.

Nora stepped out and strolled past the station. She didn't see anyone behind the counter. Nurses were busy people.

Nora read the room numbers as she hurried down the hall. She smelled like fire and fear, and had to look like a homeless person. If Abigail felt anywhere near herself, Nora braced for an epic lecture.

Laurie's friendly but firm voice floated out of what ought to be Abigail's room. Damn. Nora glanced in the door of the room next to Abigail's. The patient inside lay flat on her back with her eyes closed. With any luck, she—or he, it was hard to tell with all the white hair and sagging skin—was asleep. Nora slipped inside the room, into the bathroom next to the door and waited.

"I'm going to ask you to come back another time," Laurie said. "Ms. Stoddard has had visitors all morning and she really needs to rest."

"Oh posh." Steel bands loosened around Nora's lungs. Abigail sounded like her regular self. "I'm not the least bit tired. Having visitors makes me feel better."

"That may be, but I'm going to insist." Laurie obviously didn't know who she dealt with.

"If you're going to be that way, at least give me a couple of minutes to finish our conversation." Now Nora detected fatigue in her mother's voice. To allow someone to tell her what to do really clinched it. Abigail hurt. Nora fought not to run to her mother's bedside. But doing that might get her hauled away and she couldn't protect Abigail then.

"Just a couple of minutes," Laurie said from the doorway. "I'm checking my watch and I'll be back down if you don't come out."

Abigail's visitor could be one of the women from her service club, but Nora hoped for Charlie. If so, it would mean he was okay. More than anything, she wanted her people safe and healthy and away from Barrett.

Laurie's shoes squeaked with infinite efficiency as she hurried down the corridor.

"Are you the nurse?" A crotchety voice called from the bed.

The voice jettisoned Nora into the air and sent her nerves jangling. She'd guessed incorrectly. The patient was a man.

Nora tried to be calm. "No. Just the wrong room."

His voice carried much louder than necessary. He probably didn't hear well himself and compensated by shouting at everyone else. "What did you say? I asked if you are the nurse."

She couldn't shout back. What if Abigail's visitor wasn't Charlie? What if Laurie came back and caught her? What if Heather broke under Gary's interrogation and told him Nora lurked on the third floor? What if a meteor struck the Earth and they went the way of the dinosaur?

Sheesh. She always accused Abigail of exaggerating life to follow a movie script; it must be an inherited trait.

Still, Nora hurried to the old man's bed and spoke quietly. "I'm sorry I disturbed you. I'm in the wrong room."

His hand shot out from under the blanket, his grip surprisingly strong on her wrist. Nora's heart kicked in at the nightmare aspect of this frail-looking man actually being a demon. Or maybe a kachina, out to stop her from creating more chaos.

"The nurse hasn't been here for two days. No one gives me food. I haven't had a drink of water. She's trying to kill me so she can have my money."

His lunch tray sat on the windowsill, the gravy not even coagulated, yet. An insulated pitcher with condensation from fresh ice water sat on his bedside table. He wasn't an evil sprite or Big Elk's faithful. He was an old, sick and confused man.

Would life ever be normal again?

Nora reached over to grasp the pitcher, her other arm still in the old man's clutches. A bendy straw stuck from the top. "Let me help you," she said, grateful when he released her.

She put the straw in his mouth and he drew in the water, his rheumy eyes focused on her. The drink quenched his hostility and his eyes filled with the trust of a small child. He finished drinking. "You're the best nurse I've ever had."

She set the pitcher down and patted his hand.

His voice changed. "You are here to do good."

Moisture vanished from Nora's mouth and reappeared as cold sweat on her forehead. The old man's eyes closed and his mouth opened a bit, letting out soft snores as he immediately fell asleep.

The voice hadn't been that of the patient lying in front of her. He spoke with that hesitant and abrupt cadence of the little kachina man.

Certifiably nuts. Probably paranoid and delusional. She tried to take inventory of what was real. Scott lay dead. Heather, and probably Alex, had destroyed the lift. Barrett had murdered Big Elk. Someone blew up her house along with Abigail and Charlie.

Her mother rested next door. Nora had to touch her and know she was alive. She rushed toward the door...And stopped dead when she heard the low rumbled of a man's voice. It wasn't Charlie in Abigail's room.

"You should get some rest now. I'll be back later." Barrett sounded sincere and tender, all the wonderful things a man should be to the woman he intended to marry.

38

Barrett softly stroked the back of Abigail's hand. It might be the only spot on her that wasn't bruised or cut. He would prefer to take the pillow she rested her bandaged head on and smash it down on her face, grinding it until the life left her body.

"That Laurie is so bossy." Abigail pouted in a way he once thought attractive. "I want to spend more time with my fiancé."

He dodged stitches on her forehead and brushed his lips on her skin. "You've been through too much. First the gas leak and explosion itself, then to find out Nora is responsible." If Abigail hadn't turned at the last minute and ruined his aim with the tire iron, she wouldn't be lying here worrying at all. She'd be stretched out on a slab in the morgue.

Abigail's eyes sparked with indignation. "Nora is not behind this, despite what Gary says. He's determined to throw her in the clink. I'm glad she's on the lam, hiding from the heat." Since Abigail's brush with the law she'd taken on a whole new language.

Why had he found her so appealing? She looked like an old woman and sounded like a harpy. The stitches and dried blood along the eight inch gash on her forehead made her look like Frankenstein's monster. "I know it's hard to consider but if the police are convinced Nora is at fault, no doubt they have strong evidence."

Barrett hadn't planned on killing Abigail. He'd left her at the police station in the care of his trusty attorney and rushed back to torch the apartment. But she'd shown up unexpectedly. After he decided killing her was the most expedient solution to the problem, it struck him as justice for rejection. She'd said yes to his proposal, but only for his protection.

God damn Charlie for his meddling. He'd somehow rescued her and now Barrett had another loose end.

A lioness protecting her cub would be no more ferocious than Abigail, even injured as she was. "It's Big Elk and his gang of thugs, maybe that big Indian friend of Heather's."

Barrett tried to soothe her. "You're probably right. At the very least, poor Nora has lost everything. Not even a memento of her husband is left."

Abigail sniffed in indignation. "Not that she needs to be reminded of his low character. The awful irony is that box of Scott's did survive."

This couldn't be right. "I'm afraid nothing is left of the apartment."

"It wasn't in the apartment. I didn't want Nora to have to face it again so I had Heather load it into her car to take to the dump."

Scott's fucking logs were still around. Fiery claws ripped at Barrett's gut. Heather had the logs. Nora was with Heather. He had to find them. Now. "I can protect Nora until we get this all straightened out. Where is she?"

"I don't know. What if Big Elk has her?" The final word squeezed into a sob. He'd thought she was so dignified and classy. Her sniveling made him want to slap her face.

He had to convince Abigail of his grave concern for Nora's safety. "Big Elk isn't a threat. But I really need to find Nora if I'm going to help her."

"The last I knew, she and Heather were coming back from the Hopi reservation. Heather was really excited because she found out something about her family."

Her family! Barrett was her family. Some big-mouthed Indian was filling her head with bullshit. Barrett couldn't allow this. "What about her family?"

Fatigue crept into Abigail's voice. "She found out her name and is going to ask Charlie. Charlie knows a lot about the Hopi people."

Again her words tailed off into tears. "But now he's here because of me."

Barrett clenched his teeth. "Or because of Nora, if the police are right."

Abigail's indignation burst out. "They are most certainly not right. I won't have you casting aspersions."

Charlie's brain was probably so pickled he couldn't remember his last name but what if it wasn't? He might know about Heather. Barrett couldn't risk Heather finding out. Charlie had to go. "I'm sorry, Abigail. Don't worry about Nora. I'll find her and protect her."

The last spurt of anger must have drained Abigail. She sounded exhausted. "Thank you, dear."

Barrett pulled her hand to his lips. "You said Charlie is in the hospital, too?"

"He'll help her if he can. He's very fond of Heather." Abigail closed her eyes, already drifting off..

Barrett strode toward the door. "It's time Charlie minds his own business and leaves my family alone."

39

The same gaping slit across Big Elk's throat awaited Charlie unless Nora could save him from Barrett's plans.

Barrett's cowboy boots clacked under his bulk and he exchanged friendly remarks with Laurie at the nurse's station.

Nora snuck into Abigail's room. Her mother lay like a corpse, pale and lifeless, her eyes closed. One eye puffed in a bed of purple and pink, a stapled gash with blackened blood lined the eyebrow. If Nora had given up the idea of making Kachina Ski a money machine, if she sold it or closed it and walked away, none of this would have happened. Scott would still have left her, but he and Maureen would be alive. Abigail would be flirting and probably planning her next wedding to some tycoon she met on a cruise. Nora caused this disaster with her greed and pride.

She tiptoed to the bed.

Abigail opened one eye, the other swollen shut. "Oh, Nora." Tears spilled down the side of her face. "You shouldn't be here."

Nora took her mother's hand and leaned close. "I'm so sorry."

Abigail blinked, the struggle to be strong obvious. "Gary was here. He wants you for questioning. He thinks you killed Scott and blew up the lift and apartment for insurance. I know it wasn't you."

"Shh."

"He thinks you were in the apartment when I got there and snuck up behind me, hit me with something hard then turned on the gas so the place would explode. Only you were on the phone with me. But I can't tell him that because he'll find out where you are."

"I'm sorry, Mother."

The fear that rode shotgun with Nora colored Abigail's words. "You've got to find Barrett. He'll protect you."

Abigail was so worried already, Nora couldn't scare her more by telling her about Barrett. "Don't worry, Mom. I'll figure it out." Nora smoothed the hair on Abigail's forehead, avoiding the raw spots. "How are you?"

"Look at my face. This will leave a scar. This is where I hit the table when I fell. At least the blow on the back of my head will never be seen. But I'll heal. The real concern is for you."

No. The immediate threat was for Charlie. Barrett wanted something hidden from Heather and he wouldn't hesitate to silence Charlie. She had to save him.

Abigail patted Nora's hand. "I'm glad to see you but you have to go before Big Elk or Gary find you."

"I love you, Mom."

Tears returned to Abigail's eyes. "Well, I know that."

"No, I really mean it. You're a wonderful woman."

Tears left trails through her make-up. Of course nearly dying would be no excuse not to put on her face. "That's nice of you to say, but we both know it's not true."

Nora pulled a tissue from the box by the bed and dabbed Abigail's eyes.

Abigail sniffed. "I'm not strong and smart like you. I so admire you."

"You admire me?"

"I wish I were more like you. You aren't afraid to be on your own. Look at me. I'm terrified of being penniless and alone." She sobbed.

Nora's bruised heart ached at the sight of Abigail's tears. "You're not alone."

"If I were more like you I wouldn't be marrying Barrett. I know he's the kind of man I appreciate. But this time," she sobbed, "this time I wish I had more courage to do what my heart wants."

Why wouldn't Abigail want to marry the man she thought Barrett was? "What does your heart want?"

"Charlie." Abigail dissolved into heaving sobs.

Blow someone up and the strangest things seeped from the cracks. Abigail and Charlie? That might be even crazier than a century-dead man showing up on Nora's doorstep.

"If you want Charlie, why not be with him?"

Abigail sniffed and wiped her eyes. "What security does he offer me? A decrepit cabin in a rundown mountain village. No shopping, no vacations, no retirement."

"Do you love him?"

Abigail looked at Nora in surprised. "No one has ever made me laugh the way Charlie does. He makes me happy just walking in the woods or sitting on the porch in the sunlight. I've never had that much fun at Macy's, even during a sale."

Nora smiled and shook her head. It would be great to stay with Abigail and continue the most genuine conversation they'd ever had. "I've got to go," Nora said.

"Yes. Go. Be careful. Be safe."

If Nora didn't save Charlie, Abigail's dreams of enjoying the mountain with him would never come true. She'd already given Barrett too much of a head start.

Keeping one eye out for the industrious Laurie, Nora strode as quickly and silently as possible, straining into every room, desperate to see that grizzled head she loved so much.

Up one corridor. Nothing but strangers in each room. Nora felt sad for every patient in every room and all their loved ones. They lived out their own stories of misery, woe and hope. Hospitals are normal life amplified. In here a headache doesn't mean two aspirins and a nap. It means a life-threatening tumor. A bruise becomes cancer. Affection is passion, anxiety is terror. Watching, waiting, praying. Life on the precipice. She hated hospitals.

At the far end of the hall a service elevator sat at the intersection of the two corridors. Nora hurried up the other side, checking each room.

Charlie wasn't on this floor. Barrett could find and kill Charlie in slow torture by the time she checked each floor manually. Time for bold action.

Laurie and another staffer discussed a teacher at Laurie's daughter's school. Apparently, the teacher was the Anti-Christ.

Nora inhaled, straightened her shoulders, smoothed her clothes as much as possible and ambled to the station as if she felt no pressure. She smiled in what she hoped appeared natural, wondering if it looked like a desperate woman fearing for her life and that of everyone she loved. "I'm lost, I guess. I'm looking for Charlie Podanski. I thought he was on this floor but I must have the wrong room number."

Laurie looked at her with the deep eyes of a Native American. She didn't return Nora's smile. Maybe she recognized Nora. Maybe she just didn't see the need to smile.

The other woman, a petite blonde, grinned, her teeth white in her tanned face. "Sure. Let me look it up."

The younger woman punched a few keys on the computer. "Here's the problem, you've got the wrong floor. He's in 408."

Laurie hadn't said anything. She studied Nora as if she were a new disease.

"Thanks," Nora said and tried to walk away when she wanted to run.

"You can take the elevator," the young woman said.

"It's only one floor. I'll walk." And hopefully avoid Gary when Laurie called him, which she would certainly do.

Nora rounded the corner and lunged for the door. She bounded up the stairs, taking off for room 408.

Charlie's room was on the same side of the floor as the stairs and Nora didn't encounter any staff as she dashed down the corridor. She glanced behind her to make sure Gary and Laurie didn't trail her before she ran into his room.

Charlie lay on his back, eyes closed. A white bandage wrapped around his forehead. White cotton swathed his left hand and looked like a puff of snow lying on his chest.

He should be out creating environmental mischief on his trails, not wrapped in disinfected sheets under artificial lights. Nora hurried to the bed.

"Charlie?"

He opened his eyes and focused them with effort. "An angel of the first degree."

Nora put a hand under his shoulders. "Are you hurt? Can you sit up?"

He grunted. "For you, darlin', anything."

He didn't weigh much but felt like a hundred and fifty pound sack of sand. "I've got to get you out of here."

He gave her a blank smile. "You're breaking me out. I knew you were a good one."

Nora succeeded in sitting him on the side of the bed but his speech and movements blurred around the edges. "Come on, Charlie. This is important. Barrett is coming after you."

He turned an amused face to her. "He better watch out. I'm coming after him."

"Are your feet or legs hurt? Can you stand?"

"Oh, sure. I can stand. I can take you dancing. I used to dance. Did you know that? I was dashing and the sweet girls lined up."

"Good, Charlie." He was so drugged up his arms and legs had less body than the hospital sheets. He'd never make it out.

Nora ran into the hall. There had to be wheelchairs somewhere. Two doors down a loud female voice, the tone perfect to get the attention of a deaf two-year old, hollered. "Hello, Mrs. Robinson. I need to take you down for some tests. Let's just get your vitals."

The figure on the bed didn't respond. Nora wouldn't have responded, either, unless it was to tell the woman to speak like an adult.

The wheelchair sat by the door waiting for Mrs. Robinson to have her pulse and temp taken.

"I'm Debbie, Mrs. Robinson. You chart says your name is Deborah, so we're both Debbies. Debbie Robinson."

Amid the annoying and senseless chatter, Nora stole the wheelchair. Guilt nagged at her for not stealing Mrs. Robinson from darling Debbie's clutches, but there was only so much saving she could do in a day.

She rushed back to Charlie's room, expecting Gary to be standing there with his gun drawn.

Charlie sat on the bed humming, arms out, swaying as if on the dance floor. "Do you suppose Abigail would like to dance with me?"

"Into the chair." Nora hefted him from the bed and plopped him into the chair not as gently as she'd have liked.

He grunted and tried to grab the chair rails but his mittened hand bounced off and landed in his lap, where he let it stay.

She inhaled. "Here we go. Act natural."

"Darlin', I'm the master at deceiving The Man."

She whisked him out the door and flew past Mrs. Robinson's room, where Debbie hadn't noticed the missing chair yet. No wonder hospital costs are so high with idiots like Debbie at large.

Chances were Laurie was no idiot. She probably put in a call to Gary before Nora had even hit the stairwell. Why hadn't he shown up yet with his handcuffs and billy club?

Nora stopped short of the corner where the nurses' station faced the elevator. She couldn't wheel Charlie in front of the nurses and get on the elevator. Even good ol' Debbie would have a better handle on her patients than to let strangers take them away. Any second, said Debbie would burst from Mrs. Robinson's room and send the SWAT team after the missing wheelchair.

The elevator door whooshed open and Nora shrank to the wall.

Feet stepped out of the elevator onto the linoleum of the hall. Nora calculated the distance back to room 408. Maybe she could make it back to Charlie's room. And then what? Wait for Barrett or Gary to finish them off?

Footsteps approached the corridor. She lunged across the hall to the nearest room. She could shove Charlie into the bathroom and hide like she did next to her mother's room.

She didn't move fast enough. The footsteps sounded behind her.

If those feet carried Gary, the jig was up. She braced to swing the chair back, maybe charge into him and throw him off balance. That was a stupid idea. She gave Charlie's chair a massive shove and dove into a room, not quite clearing the doorway.

A hand landed on her shoulder. She gasped. Heather's voice sounded irritated. "What are you doing?"

Charlie gave her a lopsided grin. "My beautiful Indian maiden. You make the world a better place just by being alive."

Heather raised an eyebrow and looked at Nora. "What kind of drugs is he on?"

Nora shook her head. "Can you distract the nurse so I can get him down the elevator?"

"That's a stupid plan."

"What do you suggest? We've got to get out of here before Gary finds us."

"No lie. But he took off for your mother's room and it won't be long before he figures out you're up here. When he does, he'll be on the elevator, or he'll have someone watching the lobby." Heather took hold of the handles of Charlie's chair, shoving Nora out of the way.

Charlie tilted his head back to look at Nora. "How is Abigail, that vision of grace?"

Nora patted his shoulder, trying to dam the panic flooding her brain. Think. There had to be another way to get Charlie out of here. Debbie was a blink away from storming out of Mrs. Robinson's room or a nurse would round the corner. They had to get moving.

Lightbulb. Nora hurried back the way she came. "There's a service elevator this way."

Heather spun the chair around and sailed down the corridor past Mrs. Robinson's room, where Debbie shouted her sing-song nonsense.

Charlie's head listed to the right. "Like a chopper over the Mekong. Wind in my face."

No way would they get out of this. Gary or Debbie or Laurie or some other authority would find them, send Charlie back to his bed where Barrett would kill him like shooting a fish in a barrel. Nora would spend the rest of her life in jail for killing Scott and Maureen.

The hallway ended with a narrow corridor leading to the other side of the floor. The service elevator doors faced the corridor. Heather punched the buttons.

"Where are we goin'?" Charlie asked. He hummed a Doors tune circa 1972.

The numbers above the elevator marked the floors while her heart threatened to pound through her skin. Two, three.... She held her breath, waiting for the doors to open on death.

The light stayed on four and the clank and settle of the gears and cables signaled the arrival of doom. The doors slid open.

There he stood. She'd been right. They were caught and it was all over.

The young Native American man in blue scrubs looked up and gave them a distracted smile. He carried a plastic tray full of vials and other lab paraphernalia. "How're doin'?"

Heather shoved the chair into the elevator. "Good."

Nora stood paralyzed while the young man stepped out. He didn't give them a passing glance as he hurried away.

"Let's go, Laura Croft," Heather said.

Nora stepped into the car and the doors shut. They descended to the ground floor and out the back hallway to a courtyard with flowers, grass and benches. All lovely, normal, no police chase, nothing but Charlie humming tunes from his psychedelic phase—his earlier one, that is.

Nora still couldn't breathe and her heart might quit any time. But they strolled at a normal pace along the paved path, passing other patients enjoying the summer sunshine. Although Nora could only follow dumbly along, Heather even smiled and nodded at people.

A sidewalk veered off the garden path between two buildings. It must lead to the front of the hospital and the parking lot. Without altering their pace, Heather directed the chair into the deep shadows between the buildings. She reached into the pocket of her jeans and pulled out the car keys.

"Bring the car up and we'll load him in. Easy as pie."

Nora snatched the keys and scrambled for the car. Running through chocolate pudding would be easier. With every step she knew Gary closed in. When he discovered Charlie had disappeared he would call for backup. Police would be circling. They might have already captured Charlie. Eventually she reached Heather's car. It seemed like two moon cycles but it probably took thirty seconds.

She fumbled to unlock the door and shook so badly it took three tries to slide the key into the ignition. She fired the engine and made herself take a deep breath to get control. Peeling out of the parking lot might draw attention. She started to count. If she pronounced each number slowly, maybe her movements would slow to the beat and help her calm down. Thirteen, fourteen, back up, brake, sixteen, seventeen, put it in gear. Twenty two, twenty three, drive slowly down the row, turn. Thirty five, thirty six, pull up to the slit between buildings, put it in park.

Heather appeared with Charlie. Beyond all odds, Gary hadn't found them, yet.

Charlie's chin rested on his forehead. His mittened hand dangled from the side of the chair. Passed out or fallen asleep. He was alive though. Right? He didn't move.

What if they had killed him?

Heat rose from the pavement. Nora opened the back passenger door and she and Heather lifted and shoved Charlie into the backseat. Nora grabbed a jacket and other clothes in the backseat to make a pillow and settled his head, arranging his legs.

"Let's go." Heather said then shouted, "Now. Now!"

Nora jerked her head up. Heather bounded around the front of the car, and into the driver's seat.

Over the rumble of the idling engine, Nora heard what she'd been expecting all along. Gary yelled, "Stop!"

She still crouched over Charlie, his feet hanging out the open door.

Gary ran from the front of the hospital reaching for the gun strapped to his side.

40

Heather rammed the Rav4 into gear and stomped the gas, sending Nora tumbling across the seat. She bounced off Charlie and wedged between the floor and seat. Her head slammed against the frame as the door closed, catching her hair in the jamb. The door hit Charlie's feet and bounced open again.

Nora pulled herself up in time to see Gary raise his gun. She hoped he aimed for the tires, or better yet, shot like bad guys in movies, and missed them entirely.

Heather raced from the parking lot, squealing a right onto the street, throwing Nora to the floor and sending the door swinging again. It took out another clump of Nora's hair and gave Charlie a new set of bruises.

Nora struggled to right herself and pull Charlie's feet inside. The vehicle swayed around corners and bumped through rough intersections, tossing Nora from side to side. With difficulty, she managed to catch the door on one of its swings inward and snick it shut. She checked Charlie.

With his eyes closed he hummed tunelessly. He was conscious again, so they hadn't killed him. Enough pain medication flowed through him that the car door didn't seem to hurt him. For right now, he floated in a happy place.

Much more than could be said for Nora. She climbed to the front seat and looked out the window. They sped down a forest road, packed smooth but unpaved.

Heather stared down the road. "One thousand, two hundred, eight-two what?"

Nora didn't have the patience for a game. "What are you talking about?"

"What are you counting?"

She didn't realize she still counted. "Moments until I lose my grip on sanity."

"You could have stopped at five."

A giggle welled from somewhere in her gut. It rose, to a full boil of belly laughs.

Heather swung from the packed dirt road onto a trail and they slammed into rocks in the road, bouncing high enough to make Nora's head bang the roof.

Nora laughed harder. Tears cascaded down her face.

Heather ventured a glance at her, then quickly back at the road. She swerved, throwing Nora against the door with a crash.

Nora's sides hurt. Hysterical. Soon she'd come completely unhitched.

Heather braked hard, made a nearly ninety degree turn, drove into a thicket of pines and killed the engine. "Knock it off," she growled at Nora.

Nora sobered. There was nothing funny about this. What was the matter with her, anyway? She looked back at Charlie.

He knelt on the floor of the backseat. His voice sounded like he spoke around a mouth of cotton balls. "You girls know how to stage a jailbreak."

"You're a freak," Heather said to Nora, with as much irritation as a teenager can pack into a few words. And Heather was particularly skilled in that area.

Maybe they weren't exactly safe, but Barrett wouldn't find them here. They needed a plan.

Nora took a breath but instead of words, she let out a laugh and started again.

Heather rolled her eyes. Then she smiled, chuckled and soon, her laughter joined Nora's in a tango of hysterics.

After a time, they settled down, wiped the tears from their eyes and grew quiet.

"How're doing, Charlie?" Nora asked.

"Don't suppose you grabbed some meds on your way out the back door?"

"Sorry."

"Ah, well," he said.

Heather turned to the back seat. "You said you know a lot about people on the Hopi rez."

Charlie sounded fuzzy. "I spent a fair amount of time out there when I was young. Good people."

"Benny said I was from a powerful clan."

Charlie's words slurred even more than usual. "Are you Hopi? You look Hopi."

Frustration edged Heather's words. "Benny knows me."

Charlie's eyes drooped closed. "To know you is to love you."

Heather reached over the seat and took Charlie's hand. "Do I look like anyone you know?"

Charlie struggled to open his eyes. "You're a vision. A beauty."

"That's not what I mean. He called me Sikyatsi."

Charlie's head dropped back and he mumbled something that might have been a name but it strangled in a deep snore.

Heather twisted in the driver's seat and glared at Nora.

"I'm sorry. Maybe he'll remember when he wakes up," Nora said.

Heather looked toward the forest, then back at Nora. "Are you going to tell me why we kidnapped Charlie and what we're running from?"

Nora opened her door and stepped into the forest. She had to think.

Heather got out and walked around to her. "I saw Poppy coming out of the elevator while Officer Buttface interviewed me. Was he visiting Abigail?"

Nora nodded.

"Did he see you?"

Nora shook her head. "He was nice to Abigail but he wanted to know where I was. When he found out you were going to ask Charlie about your family he got upset."

Heather raised her eyebrows, adding insult to the sarcasm of her tone. "Oh good, she does something more than nod her head and laugh."

"Can you stop with all the smart-alecky attitude?"

Heather plopped down on a rock. "Sorry. I'm scared, okay? I don't know what to do about Poppy and I'm probably in trouble with the law, too."

"You? Scared?" Nora sat down next to her. "You can blow up my lift, run in and out of the rez, and do the Starsky and Hutch through town and you tell me you're scared?"

Heather put her chin in her hand. "I do what I have to do."

Nora stared into the silent forest, the Pondersoa pine thick and dark.

What was that? A flash of blue? Her heart lunged, followed by a flare of anger. No. This was crazy and she wouldn't look, wouldn't let her imagination and more hysteria make her believe the kachina man followed her.

"We've got to figure out what to do." Nora's voice sounded harsher than she expected.

"About what? Charlie in the backseat of my car? Poppy wanting god only knows what from you?" She licked her dry lips. "Poppy... Poppy ordering that man to kill Big Elk? Ordering Gary to arrest you?"

Nora rubbed her forehead.

"You know, when you do that, you look just like your mother," Heather said.

"Wouldn't it be nice if someone said something today that wasn't disturbing on some level?" Nora glared at Heather.

"And that's her look, too."

"Gaaa! Stop it." Nora couldn't help her outburst.

Heather laughed. "Really. You're almost as good at that you-low-life-scum look as Abigail."

"I'm an amateur compared to her."

Heather nodded. "Abigail is good. She's got that Queen Abigail attitude, you know. But you're like the Lady Di of the family. You're classy and royal and sort of above everyone else. But you've got that soft vulnerable thing going on."

Nora narrowed her eyes in irritation. "You're full of shit."

Heather burst out laughing. "Not Lady Di at all."

A small grin tugged at Nora's mouth before she remembered what a terrible mess they were in.

"We had to get Charlie out of there because your father threatened to hurt him."

The teasing smile vanished. "Not Charlie! Why would he do that?"

"Whatever Charlie might know about your family is something Barrett doesn't want you to find out."

"And he is going to hurt Charlie to keep him from telling me?"

"I think so."

Heather looked at her skeptically. "Where did you come up with this?"

Nora told her about the conversation she'd overheard.

Charlie mumbled from the back seat, his eyes still closed. "A cold, wet can of liquid painkiller might keep me alive."

Nora put a hand on Charlie's forehead. He didn't feel feverish. One good thing. "I'm sorry, Charlie. It's almost dark. Maybe we can do something soon."

Heather leaned over and gently kissed Charlie's cheek. "I'll protect you from Poppy."

After Heather's calculating and calm attack of the situation, this tenderness surprised Nora. Just when Heather seemed nothing but a Barrett clone, she flashed a human side.

Charlie took hold of Heather's hand and patted it. "You gotta stop trying to clean up Barrett's messes. He's a big man and he makes big problems. You can't make up for him and you're going to kill yourself trying."

Heather's eyes shimmered with tears. "You're probably right." She cleared her throat. "He's not even my real father so I don't know why I feel responsible for the evil he creates."

Nora stepped up to form a circle. "Whatever Barrett is up to, it's not your burden. It's hard enough living your own life without having to make amends for someone else."

Heather nodded. "I know you're right. But in Hopi, we believe in balance. I should be able to balance Poppy's bad with my good."

Nora put an arm around Heather's shoulders. "Are you telling me that because Abigail is my mother I am responsible for all her actions? That's a chore I'm not willing to take on."

"The Hopi elders say that two or three righteous people are enough to fulfill the Creator's mission. Some say even one truly righteous person can save the world."

Charlie smiled at Heather. "You are good, no denying that. Let your goodness shine and leave Barrett off your scales."

Heather looked at the ground. "It would be different if he were my real father, I guess. Are you sure you don't remember Sikyatsi?"

Charlie shook his head. "It sounds familiar but my memory isn't as good as it used to be." He looked stricken. "We should have brought Abigail with us. She's not safe when Barrett is on the loose."

A spear of apprehension shot into Nora. "This is insane."

Charlie said. "Let's get the goods on Barrett and we'll all live happily ever after."

Nora took a deep breath. "I'd settle for all of us living."

Charlie's head fell back and he snored.

After several minutes of silence, Nora shrugged in frustration. "Cole thinks Scott's murder is at the crux of everything."

Heather considered. "Okay. We need to do some research."

"What do you mean?"

Heather walked to the back of the Rav4. "Don't get mad at me."

Cold stone hit Nora's belly. "Did you blow something else up?"

Heather shot her a withering look. "I'm sorry about that. I didn't know you very well then."

"I'm not forgiving you yet. When we're safe from Barrett and your environmental and ethnic brethren, you and I are going to have a talk."

At least Heather looked contrite. She opened the back of the vehicle and reached inside to pull out a box.

That stupid box contained grief, anger, pain, and rejection. Nora remembered when Maureen's roommate brought it to the lodge. Why hadn't she burned it?

Heather looked at her with a mixture of embarrassment and guilt.

"It's okay. I know you have the box," Nora said.

Heather carried the box to a flat rock and bent over it. She rummaged beneath odd items and pulled out a sheaf of paper. "Why was Scott working for Poppy?"

"Barrett? He worked for Barrett?"

Heather waved the paper. "This is from Southwest Consultants."

The box held her dead husband's possessions from a life she didn't know existed. The thought stunned her like a draught of hemlock.

"Southwest Consultants is Poppy's uranium company."

Nora hadn't known that. But then, why would she care? "I don't know why you'd think Scott was working there."

"He's got a whole stack of papers from them."

41

Nora stirred herself and took the sheet of paper from Heather. It bore Southwest Consulting's logo. A matrix covered most of the page with printed column and row headings and Scott's scribbled figures in the boxes. "I don't know what this is," Nora said.

She stomped to the box and peered into it. Just what she wanted, to paw through remnants of Scott's life with another woman. Her stomach flipped and landed with a dull ache.

The first few items looked innocent enough. Racing magazines and old bike gloves. Under that she extracted a framed snapshot of Scott and Maureen standing in front of his backpack tent with a river in the background. Nora tried not to remember lying in that same tent next to Scott on so many of their own camping trips. When had she stopped backpacking with him? Two years, three? Something at Kachina always needed attention and even if she found down time, the thought of strapping on a forty pound pack and traipsing into the woods exhausted her.

She'd been stupid to think Scott, the man who loved an audience, would be happy alone while she worked. The pain of her loss made her want to fall to the ground and curl into a tight ball.

She started to put the frame on top of the magazines but she didn't drop the frame as she intended. Instead, she raised her arms over her head and brought the frame straight down on the edge of the rock, shattering the glass and breaking the frame into two separate pieces held together by the photo inside. She picked up the mess and ripped at the picture and with a final violent flourish, threw it into the trees.

"Wow." Heather said. "I never heard anyone scream like that."

Nora turned around, suddenly aware that her throat hurt. "I screamed?"

Heather nodded. "Feel better?"

Nora swiped at tears. "Not really."

"Want me to go through that stuff?"

Nora shook her head. "It doesn't do any good to deny the truth. I need to face it and put it behind me."

Heather's mouth twitched.

"I know. It sounds like Abigail." Nora scowled at her.

Seeing his things so neatly in the box hurt nearly as much as noticing Maureen's arm around Scott's waist in the photo. Scott didn't organize or keep anything neat. This had to be Maureen's doing. She took care of him, nurtured him. Nora forced herself to think the last...loved him.

Nora pulled out the stack of charts wrapped in a rubber band. The pages showed dates for twice a month. She flipped to the end of the stack. Over three years! He told her the affair ended two years ago. It had never ended. Damn it. Damn him.

Giant tentacles with razored claws serrated her chest, leaving a gaping, bleeding mess. She sank to her knees and gasped for air.

Heather materialized at her side, stroking Nora's back. "I'm sorry."

Nora struggled through the haze of anguish. She had something to do, exactly what, she didn't know. She couldn't fall apart. The world slowly took shape around her.

Heather stood next to her, uttering soothing words.

Nora pulled herself to her feet and cleared her throat. "Abigail called that one right. I wasted seven years on Scott."

Focus, Nora. Take care of business. It's what you do. She picked up the pages again. "What could these be?"

Charlie croaked from the backseat. "Bring them here and let me look."

Nora jumped. Charlie was like some spook that raised himself from the dead to spout prophecy and then disappear, only to rise again.

She hurried to him to see if he looked close to death. His face showed a healthy bit of color and his eyes sparked with life.

Charlie pushed himself to sit with his back against the door. With his good hand he took the page Nora held. He stared at the paper for a full minute, maybe willing his eyes to focus. Finally he handed it back to Nora. "Those are well logs. Scott was a logger for Barrett. He was checking ground water."

"How do you know all this?" Nora asked.

Charlie smiled with reminiscence. "Protested a coal mine a couple of decades ago. Right before I lit the fuse in the office, I saw some logs like that. The company wanted to prove the water content."

The situation mushroomed in her mind, overwhelming her. "Who was Scott?"

Heather stepped back and watched.

Nora spun from Charlie and paced the clearing, anything to drag out the gremlins gnawing at her sanity. "I knew our marriage wasn't as good as it used to be. I didn't know how to make it work but I tried. Everything I did backfired. I should have known he had an affair. I probably did on some level. But how could I have known he worked for Barrett for three years?"

Charlie studied the page. "Did Scott know anything about water?"

Nora couldn't stop pacing. "He had an undergrad degree in environmental science. He knew a little about a lot of things. And yes, I think he had some hydrology classes."

"So Barrett hired him to track ground water," Charlie said.

"Why would he want to do that? Why not hire him outright with McCreary Energy?" Heather asked.

"There's something in the ground water that interests Barrett and he doesn't want anyone to know about it," Charlie said.

Heather considered this. "Wouldn't Scott have needed an office and a lab to do the testing?"

"Maureen was a graduate teaching assistant at the university," Nora said.

They both looked at her.

"She worked for a biologist."

"You knew her?" Heather asked.

Nora tried not to think about it. "She had a project tracking a vole or something out here a few years ago. She and some field techs camped on the meadow on the other side of the mountain. Scott probably met her there. Or maybe she chose to come here because they were already together."

Gradually Nora forced her mind from her Wronged Woman track. She didn't have time to mourn for a husband or life she never really had.

Heather frowned. "Poppy hired Scott on the side. Looks like Scott took samples every two weeks from," she counted on the page, "ten wells. He hired Scott on the sly to keep the findings secret."

"And Scott found something he couldn't keep quiet about," Nora said.

"This is it! Got a phone?" Charlie sounded suddenly alert.

Heather found her bag under the back seat and grabbed her phone. When she handed it to Charlie he waved his bandaged hand.

Nora snatched the phone. "What's the number?"

Charlie recited and Nora punched, no clue who she dialed. She didn't wonder long. She recognized Cole's voice immediately.

Cole sounded frantic. "Where are you? Never mind. Stay put. The cops are everywhere looking for you. Charlie is gone and they think you kidnapped him."

"I did."

Silence. Big inhale. "Okay. We'll figure this out."

"Charlie's here. He wants to talk to you." She held the phone to Charlie's ear.

"We got it. Proof that Scott worked for Barrett. Well logs, pay stubs." He paused while Cole responded.

"Not sure where they're located. Got to be maps at Barrett's office with the wells numbered." Again he waited.

"No. You gotta stay with Abigail. I've got Heather and Nora with me. Take care of my girl, man."

Charlie nodded at Nora. "Wants to talk to you."

Cole spoke quietly. "I don't know if you want to tell Heather but they found Alex. Cops think he stole Big Elk's Escalade, rolled it outside of Winslow and he's dead."

Big Elk and Alex both dead, along with Scott and Maureen. Corpses were piling up on Barrett. Nora had to make sure there would be no more.

Even though panic clutched at Nora's lungs, she pushed the words from her mouth. "You and Charlie are working together on this, aren't you?"

"We're going to stop Barrett. I promise."

Nora swallowed. "Just keep Abigail safe."

"I'm on my way," Cole said. "Be careful."

Careful. As in, don't let the bad guys kill you and the people you love?

"Nora," Cole paused. "It will be okay."

"Okay." It sounded more confident than she felt.

"I really care about you," he said, his voice low and urgent.

She hung up the phone and turned to Charlie.

He nodded with conviction. "We're going into enemy territory."

42

Heather climbed into the driver's side. "This is a good plan. Poppy will be all relieved to see me. I'll get him to walk to the stables. He thinks we always bond over horses. And you and Charlie can read the logs and maps and find the wells."

Fear lodged in the pit of Nora's stomach. "This seems ludicrous to go right into Barrett's grasp."

"He'll be so happy I'm home it won't occur to him that I brought you with me."

It might work in a perfect world. But the last few weeks proved how imperfect her world could be.

Charlie lay down in the back seat and before they even hit the main forest road his snores echoed in the vehicle. Nora watched the road behind for headlights, swiveled and stared down the road ahead, turned to the side, then back.

"You're making me nervous," Heather said.

"Maybe we should go to the cops. I'll turn myself in. They don't have any evidence on me because I didn't kill Scott or Maureen or blow anything up."

Heather rolled her eyes. "Sure. Let's do that. You can convince them you didn't kidnap Charlie. Then, you can tell them that Poppy really killed all those people and blew up your house, and you have a theory it has something to do with groundwater. That will fix everything."

"Okay. But this is stupid. What if we figure out what wells he's monitoring. How will that tell us anything?"

Heather shook her head. "I don't know. But it's all we've got."

Normally, the drive would take them back to the highway, through town, out to Interstate 40 and ten miles on the other side of the peaks, a forty-minute commute. But going through the peaks on a curvy, steep dirt road took much longer. The night grew darker and more sinister. Heather didn't spare the tires, suspension or comfort of the passengers as she sped down the rocky mountain pass. Two hours of driving tied Nora so full of knots her blood pressure nearly popped the veins in her forehead.

Still, when they turned down the one-lane blacktop road leading to the McCreary headquarters, Nora found her right foot pressing phantom breaks, dreading entering the lion's den.

They rounded the last corner to the imposing ranch house.

Heather frowned. "He's not home. Where would he be?"

"Maybe he's home, he's just trying to fool you."

Heather pulled up in front and put the Toyota in park. "What's the point in that? If he were home, the lights would be on."

Charlie stirred in the back seat. "Got a powerful headache. Sure could use a cold one."

Heather pulled the keys from the ignition and dropped them in the console. "Let's get that taken care of."

Nora got out and grabbed the well logs. "It's after ten. You're sure he's not in bed?"

"Poppy hardly ever sleeps."

Nora and Heather helped Charlie out of the back and up the porch steps. Heather opened the door and turned on the hall light.

"If he wasn't here, he'd have locked the doors," Nora whispered, already pulling back.

Heather led them through the front door, past an entryway and great room with enormous windows looking across the valley to the peaks. A three-quarter moon rose, brushing the tip of Kachina Peak. "Poppy doesn't lock doors. In his world, no one would dare cross him. Maybe he's right. He's never been robbed."

Heather left Charlie supported on Nora. She walked to a wet bar at the edge of the room and opened a small refrigerator. She pulled out three cans of beer and, lodging two between her forearm and belly, she popped the third open. She held it out to Charlie.

"Jewels in your crown, darling." He took it and tipped it back, chugging it down.

She opened another, handed it to him and took his empty. "Feel better?"

"Immeasurably."

"Barrett really believes he's above it all?" Nora asked.

Heather stopped at a closed door and punched a code into the lock. "Yes."

"He doesn't lock the door to his house but he locks his office?" Nora asked.

Heather grinned. "That's to keep me away from his guns." She opened the door. "People hardly ever say no to him and when they do, he's got ways to deal with them."

"Like Big Elk and Alex."

Heather froze. "Alex?"

Ugh, what an idiot. Nora put an arm around Heather. "I'm sorry. I shouldn't have told you like that. Cole said they found him dead in Big Elk's vehicle."

Heather stood motionless for three seconds, then took one deep breath. "Poppy needs to be stopped."

Nora shivered. "Thank god Cole is with Abigail."

Heather switched on the light, illuminating the office. She walked to the wall opposite the desk where a four foot by three foot framed map hung next to a full gun cabinet. "Okay, what are the well numbers?"

Charlie dropped into the leather desk chair and opened the third beer.

Nora spread a few logs on the desk and studied them. She listed off well numbers.

Heather turned around. "There are so many maps here. I don't know where to start or even what we're looking for."

"Do you have your phone?" Nora asked Heather.

Heather handed it over and Nora hit the last number. After two rings Cole picked up. "How's Abigail?" she asked.

She heard the smile in his voice. "Sleeping."

"Good. Is U the symbol for uranium?"

"Yes."

Nora leaned over and looked at the well logs. "Now that I can read the logs I see that uranium levels are increasing in the last few months. We can't figure out where, though."

"What are the well numbers on the logs?"

She read off the list.

He paused. "Those are water wells on the Colorado Plateau."

Nora passed that along to Heather, who flipped charts. While Nora explained about finding Scott's logs and the increase in uranium counts, Heather located the wells on Barrett's maps.

"Uranium levels are increasing. It must mean McCreary Energy didn't do such a grand job of cleaning up their spills," Charlie said. He sipped instead of gulped his beer. A good sign. "But why would Barrett kill Scott because he discovered the contamination? Someone was bound to do a study and find out sooner or later."

"Unless he wanted to clean it up before anyone found out," Heather said.

Charlie shook his head. "You can't suck uranium from water in the middle of the night. It's a big operation and he'd have to get permits and jump through EPA's hoops."

Cole listened, and then said. "The wells are in Hopiland."

"Scott knew it and was going to say something at the hearings," Nora said.

Heather nodded. "And Poppy found out about Maureen and figured she knew, too."

Charlie rose from the desk. "Barrett thinks you know and maybe Abigail, too."

"Barrett is getting desperate," Nora said. Cole didn't weigh in.

Charlie leaned back and picked up one of the log sheets. "My ancient eyes can't see this miniature log."

Heather leaned over the desk. "I think Poppy keeps a magnifying glass in the drawer."

Charlie opened the drawer and rummaged around under a few papers. He pulled out the glass, then stopped and stared. He took out an old snapshot of a woman, little girl and a man holding a baby.

He held the picture under the glass and stared at it. "Oh! How could I not know?"

Heather bent over the maps. "What?"

"I remember Sikyatsi."

Heather looked from the picture to Charlie.

He set the glass down but held the picture. "I don't know how I missed the resemblance. I'm getting old and forgetful, I guess. But you have her eyes."

"Whose eyes?" Heather demanded.

"Ester. The only woman besides our sainted Abigail that I ever loved."

Heather stared at him.

"Barrett's wife," he said.

"Poppy had a wife?"

"And what a woman she was. You are so much like her. How could I have not figured it out?"

Heather stared at him.

"You asked about Sikyatsi earlier but I forgot." He pointed to the picture. "This is Soowi."

Heather leaned in to look.

Charlie's wistful voice croaked in the quiet. "She was your mother."

Heather's knees buckled and she caught herself on the edge of the desk. She grabbed the picture.

"You are Barrett's granddaughter." Charlie stood and walked to Heather. He held her face cradled in his one good and one bandaged hand. "I feared we'd lost you, too."

Heather barely breathed the words. "My grandfather?"

Charlie stood back and let Heather process. She finally looked at him. "He had a wife. And kids?"

"A boy and a girl."

"Where are they?"

"Ah, angel," Charlie said, his voice thick with sympathy.

Barrett as a young family man. Nora had a hard time with the concept. "You better tell us the whole story," Nora said.

Charlie rubbed his hand along his grizzled jaw. "I thought Mac was a true believer. It was him who helped me with that logger's office. I took the heat so he could stay with Ester and the babies. He settled onto the rez and lived the good life."

Heather stared at him with dry eyes. "He lived on the rez? Which one?"

"Ester was Hopi through and through. She wanted good things for her people—your people. She worked hard to keep the old ways and fought to stop the rapers and extractors from tearing out the heart and lungs of The Mother."

Nora cringed at Charlie using the same vernacular as Big Elk.

"Barrett was a little less peaceful. More like me. But we needed to make people aware. It wasn't like now, with Al Gore making movies and everyone wanting to be green. Back then, it was all greed and exploitation."

Heather's voice sounded like a mouse. "What made Poppy leave the rez?"

"Choices, man. Bad choices." Charlie shook his head. "Blood is thicker and all that." Charlie inhaled slowly. "Barrett McCreary the Second, your great grandfather, had a heart attack. Bam. Dead. And just like that, Mac turned coat and became The Man. He left the rez and Ester and those babies. And he made a fortune gouging the vitals of The Mother, throwing away everything we'd worked for."

When Charlie stopped and Heather couldn't form words, Nora stepped in. "What happened to his family?"

Charlie stared at the beer while seconds ticked. Finally, he looked in Heather's eyes. "He broke her. Ester took the baby and went to the land for solace. Or maybe she just couldn't do anything else. She lived on the desert for months, eating in the old Hopi way, drinking from springs and seeps."

The story wasn't over but Charlie stopped as if going on would be too hard.

Finally, he inhaled and started again. "She and Mac had been working against the mining companies, trying to force them to cleanup. She knew about the uranium leaks and contamination. But she drank from the springs anyway. And she nursed that baby."

Nora's stomach twisted.

"When she came back there really wasn't anything we could do for them except watch them die. The baby went first. Even if Ester hadn't been so sick, his loss would have killed her. I was with her at the last." His breathing sounded heavy and labored. "She suffered." He drew in a shaky breath. "So much."

Heather didn't move.

Charlie sank to the desk chair. "And Mac wasn't there to see. He was making money."

"My grandmother and uncle died. What happened to the little girl? My mother. Did Poppy raise her?"

"The tribe hid her. They wouldn't let Barrett near her. But it was a hard life for the little darling. I kept in contact with her for a long time. But she..." Tears filled his eyes and he swallowed. "Lost soul. The drink got her."

Heather stopped breathing.

"Alcoholism?" Nora asked.

He nodded. "Found her in Gallup in an old wash."

"My mother."

"If the tribe hid Heather and her mother from Barrett, how did he end up adopting her?"

Charlie stared at the desktop. His voice didn't rise above a whisper. "I heard Soowi sold the baby."

Aside from a deathly pallor, Heather showed no signs she'd heard Charlie. "Wouldn't be hard for someone with Mac's resources to have bogus adoption papers drawn up."

Nora hugged Heather but the girl didn't soften. "He's a monster. We have to stop him."

The only way to help Heather was to finish this business. Nora studied the map and dialed Cole.

When he picked up she said, "If the uranium is building in the aquifer, does that mean it will get in the Hopi water wells?"

His phone went dead.

"Cole?" Nora slapped the phone closed and redialed. It immediately shifted to voicemail. Something was wrong.

She turned to Heather and Charlie. "I've got to get to the hospital. Now."

43

"What do you mean Charlie Podanski isn't here?" Barrett worried his heart would explode as his father's had.

The middle-aged woman with bags under her eyes lowered her voice even more. "Please keep it down. It's late."

Later than this old bat knew. Barrett wanted Charlie out of the way. "How could he be released? He was in a bad accident."

She eyed him like a confidante. "He wasn't really released. There was some hubbub here today with the police and everything. Two women kidnapped him."

"What?"

She warmed to her gossip. "Well, one was a girl. That woman from the ski place, had this girl and they just took him. They say the girl is a McCreary. No one seems to know why they did it."

God damn it. Abigail would know what's going on. He headed for the elevators.

The woman behind the front desk stopped him. "Wait. Visiting hours are long over. You can't go up there."

He lowered his eyes. "Please understand. I want to say good night to my wife. I would have been here earlier but I had to keep the grandbabies until our daughter got done with her shift at the restaurant."

"I thought you came to see Charlie Podanski."

Meddling hag. "Oh, no. He's an old friend. I wanted to check on him while I was here. I came to see my wife on the third floor."

She would cave; she had that look. After a moment she said, "Okay. But please make it quick. I could get in a lot of trouble."

Nora had Heather, Charlie, and Scott's logs. Barrett only had Abigail.

But that was enough.

As Barrett approached Abigail's room he heard Cole's voice murmuring. Barrett snuck closer and peered into the room. Abigail appeared to be sleeping.

Cole stood looking out the window, phone to his ear. "Those wells are in Hopiland."

Barrett knew what wells Cole referred to. He could guess who listened on the other end of the line and he even had a pretty good idea where they were.

Everything he'd worked for was unraveling. Cole held sway over the Congressional committee. Now he knew the secret of the wells. The Hopi would never give their permission to mine once they found out he hadn't cleaned up the uranium as he said. It was lost. Over.

Barrett stood in the hallway feeling his heart expand with the panic. He labored for breath. Fucking Cole had ruined everything.

What if Cole disappeared? Barrett had already gotten away with Scott, Maureen, Big Elk and Alex. One more. Then he'd be home free. Once Cole was out of the way, Abigail would be Barrett's ticket to everything he'd ever dreamed of for Heather.

Barrett slipped into a room across the hall with a sleeping patient. He cast about for something. Anything. A phone lay on the bedside table, the charging cord stretched to the outlet. Barrett snatched it, pulled the cord free and spun around.

Cole still stared out the window, his back to the door.

Maybe he couldn't be quite as silent as his paid killer, but Barrett moved quietly enough. Cole was so shocked when the cord flew over his head and around his neck it took him too long to react.

Barrett threw Cole face first on the ground and planted his knee in Cole's back. With all his bulk, Barrett pulled the cord and twisted it to cut off Cole's air.

Cole kicked and struggled but he was no match for Barrett's weight. It sounded like a riot to Barrett but certainly less conspicuous than a gunshot.

Barrett hated what he was doing. Feeling the life seep from a body hurt his spirit, stole a bit of his own soul. God damn these people for making him do this.

It seemed like hours. Yet Barrett knew it couldn't have been more than minutes or even seconds. Cole quit moving but Barrett wasn't sure he was dead.

"Barrett?" Abigail leaned up on an elbow and starred at him.

He didn't move.

Her eyes widened. "Oh my god! Help!"

Dead or not, Barrett couldn't wait. He abandoned Cole and launched himself on Abigail.

44

"We have to go to the hospital. Something is wrong."

Charlie and Heather stared at Nora as if they couldn't understand what she said. A sudden telephone ring ripped through the room. Nora yelped and Heather lurched toward the sound. It rang again and Nora located it on the corner of the desk.

Heather grabbed it and punched it on. She listened for a second. "Where are you?" Hatred snapped in her dark eyes and she looked at the stand, punched speaker and set the phone back in the cradle.

"Can you hear me now?" Barrett's low voice snaked from the phone.

Heather dripped malice. "What do you want?"

"I'm glad you finally made it home. Is everyone safe? How is ol' Charlie holding up?"

Charlie raised his eyebrows. "Fine, Mac. Thanks for asking."

"Good to hear it. You have the cops concerned. They're trying to figure out how you're involved in all this."

"Look, Barrett," Nora said. "We know Scott was working for you and you killed him and Maureen to hide the increase in uranium in the ground water."

He laughed. "Very good."

"We're going to the cops."

"I don't think you want to do that." Barrett said.

"You mean you don't want me to do that. Too bad."

"Here's what you're going to do. You and Charlie load up that box of Scott's things, including the well logs and meet me up on the Peak. I'll be at the springs."

He paused. "Heather?"

Rage clouded her voice. "What?"

"You stay home."

She didn't answer.

"Give me another chance, Heather. When this is over, we'll take a world tour."

"Fuck you."

Silence sat for a moment. "Nora," Barrett said. "You have your instructions."

"Sure. Shall we bring wine or just the cops?"

"I think you'll want to do exactly as I say."

"Or what?"

"Or your mother might have an accident."

Bile burned in Nora's gut. "Mother?"

Charlie jumped to his feet. He leaned toward the phone.

Barrett sounded as if he enjoyed the conversation. "Well, you know how she is about the great outdoors. But she's holding up fine. Except, she might trip and fall out here in the dark and some of these cliffs can be treacherous. I don't have to tell you that."

"Please don't hurt her." Nora could barely breathe.

"Bring the papers. If you don't, I'm sure the cops won't have a problem believing you are a very sick woman—a bad seed."

"Let me hear her. I need to know she's okay."

A shuffling sound came through the phone, then Abigail's voice, strong and angry. "Nora. He strangled Cole. Don't come out here. We do not negotiate with terrorists. Do you h---"

Barrett's voice came back. "Bring the box to the spring, Nora. And bring Charlie. It's been a long time since we've partied together, man."

He hung up.

Nora immediately reconnected.

Charlie's hand shot out and grabbed the phone. "What are you doing?"

"I'm calling the cops."

"You can't do that."

"I don't care if they throw me in jail for the rest of my life. We have to save my mother."

"One hint of cops and Abigail is a goner. We have to do this by ourselves."

Tears pushed at Nora's eyes. "He's going to kill us, isn't he? All of us."

Charlie's face sharpened. "I imagine he'll try."

"Oh god, what about Cole?" Another person dead because of her.

Charlie straightened his shoulders, setting himself for battle. "Cole's a tough one, honey."

She could only save one person at a time. Right now, it had to be Abigail. Nora started for the door. She stopped and looked around. "Where's Heather?"

"Didn't hear her leave."

Heather had more courage and ingenuity than either of them. They needed her. "We've got to go without her."

Charlie reached back into the desk drawer and brought out a pistol. "We might need this, then."

45

Heather's car was gone and Nora lost precious time running to the barn to find a pickup. Lucky for them, Barrett's belief in his invincibility extended to his vehicles because the keys dangled from the ignition. Nora skirted town on the Interstate and turned off on a dark road heading to Kachina Ski. At this time of night, there wasn't much traffic and thankfully, they didn't run into any cops.

The chill of the mountain air swept across her face when she stepped from the pickup. She slid the box across the seat and threw the gun on top.

Charlie snatched the gun with his undamaged hand. "Better let me hold on to this. You've never used one before."

Her heart raced and she didn't want to waste time talking. "You have?"

He looked grim. "'Nam, remember?"

"I'm not afraid to use it on Barrett if I need to."

Charlie shook his head. "She's important to me, too."

Nora couldn't stay here and argue with him. She picked up the box and took off on a run up the mountain to the spring.

Several feet from the clearing she stopped and tried to still the panic pounding in her chest. A dull light issued from a battery powered lantern set on the rock.

Barrett's voice drifted to her. "Come on out, Nora. We're waiting."

Nora stepped forward. The moon cast enough light onto the forest to reveal Barrett in the clearing.

"I'm sure you'll understand that I had to muzzle your mother. Her tongue can get sharp." He moved toward a boulder on which Abigail perched with her hands tied behind her back. Barrett bent over and pulled duct tape from around Abigail's mouth. He worked with one hand because his other held a gun.

Abigail gasped at the sting of the tape ripped from her mouth. "Nora, get away from here. He's insane."

Nora walked into the clearing and set the box down. "Here it is. Now let her go."

Barrett eyed the box, his gun dangling at his side. "You weren't stupid enough to make copies?"

The pristine spring at the base of the rocks looked like a virgin waiting for sacrifice. "This is it. All the evidence of increased uranium heading to the Hopi wells. If you keep quiet about this, you can go ahead and kill off the whole tribe and save Heather from ever living on the rez."

Abigail stirred on her rock. "Get out of here, Nora!"

Barrett ignored her. He addressed Nora. "You've got it wrong. I'm going to save the Hopi. There's no need to reveal the uranium because I'm going to make it all go away. I'm here to protect them."

"You can't clean it up if you don't admit it's there."

Barrett smiled, his teeth white in the night. "That's where you come in. Or more precisely, where snowmaking comes in."

Abigail stood, tottered and dropped onto the boulder again. "You're a lunatic and I demand you release us this instant."

Barrett looked into the forest behind Nora. "Where is Charlie?"

The sound of a twig snapping to Nora's left was the only indication of movement. Charlie stepped into the clearing. "Right here, Mac."

Barrett didn't seem startled by Charlie's sudden appearance.

Abigail let out a sigh of irritation. "You couldn't go to the cops, just this once? I suppose it's your communist leanings that keep you from doing the smart thing."

Charlie turned toward Abigail and smiled at her. "Your spirit is as full of fire as always."

"Okay, Casanova," Barrett said. "As with everything else, you don't know when to quit. You couldn't abandon the hippy, tree-hugging life when it became clear the old methods weren't working."

"Not like you, Mac. For some of us, the battle to save Earth has real meaning. It isn't just something to pass the time while we wait to inherit our fortunes."

Barrett shook his head. "You poor, deluded fool. What has all your protests, petitions, demonstrations on the tops of flagpoles and wires strung across the trails accomplished?"

"It brought awareness, man. Changing the world I touch."

"The world I touch covers the globe. Man." Barrett's voice carried contempt. "With my money and influence I've built clinics and cleaned up the rez."

Charlie interrupted, nodding. "Yep. Built clinics for people and took away their faith in their medicine men. Cleaned up the mess that wouldn't have been there but for your greed. A real hero. But what about the messes you didn't clean up? What about the uranium tainted water on its way to Hopiland?"

Barrett toyed with the gun in his hand. "You read the logs, then?"

"What's uranium in the groundwater on Hopi have to do with snow-making, Mac?" Charlie asked.

Nora took a step in Abigail's direction. Barrett didn't look at her.

"See, Charlie, you're always thinking in local terms. Saving this trail or that Spotted Owl. You've got to look at the big picture."

Charlie's gun nestled in his waistband in the middle of his back. "What big picture is that?"

Nora moved a step at a time toward Abigail. Charlie's eyes, so often unfocused, were like lasers trained on Barrett.

"You think I only know about making money. That I'm only concerned with how to get what I can from the earth and leave it in any shape as long as I turn a profit. But you're wrong."

"Is that so, Mac? What else do you care about?"

Charlie distracted Barrett with conversation and Nora didn't waste the opportunity. She was only a few steps away from Abigail.

Barrett held the gun toward Charlie. "You've seen my Heather. She's beautiful and smart and will inherit what all three generations of McCreary's have built. Everything I do, I do for her."

Charlie put his hands on his hips, the bandaged hand as well as the good one, inching closer to the gun tucked beneath his waistband. "I see. But Heather won't be happy with you when she finds out about the uranium killing off her people."

Barrett waved his hand. "The Hopi aren't her people. McCreary's are her people. Even so, I'm not going to let the uranium hit the well."

"What are you going to do with it? Suck it out?" Charlie's hand slid toward his back and the gun.

"Something like that. Even Scott had to agree I have a clever plan."

Mention of Scott made Nora's stomach flip. On the verge of shouting at Barrett and calling him murderer, she swallowed her rage. Another step and she'd be at Abigail's side.

"Tell me about this clever plan," Charlie said.

Barrett beamed. "Diversion. If I pump water from the aquifer here, under this peak, the water that would have hit Hopi wells will flow this way."

"What happens when that uranium contaminated water gets to this well?" Charlie asked, his voice sounding dry.

Nora inched to Abigail's side and with movements as slight as the setting sun, reached for the knots at her wrists.

Barrett shrugged. "It's a mountain. Uranium is a natural element. People aren't going to be drinking the snow."

Charlie didn't say anything for a moment. "You're going to pump uranium on the sacred peak and you think the kachinas will stand for it?"

Barrett let out a disgusted breath. "Kachinas. You don't still believe in those old myths, do you?"

"You used to believe, Mac. What happened?"

"I grew up. My family, supposedly protected by the kachinas, died a horrible death, no one told me until years afterward. They kept my daughter from me, told me she died with Ester and Manangya, and they slowly killed her, too."

"They didn't kill her," Charlie said.

"What do you call raising her in such poverty and despair she turned to the bottle? If they'd have let me have her, she would be alive."

Charlie's fingers closed on the gun behind his back. "What makes you think you'd have done any better? Your record with relationships isn't that great. Seems you thought if you left the rez, Ester would follow you."

Barrett winced. "She was a hypocrite."

"I might call her stubborn, smart, bull-headed, beautiful and devoted to her people, but never thought of her as a hypocrite."

Barrett's mouth twisted in bitterness. "What do you call it when she talked about her family and duty and sacrifice for her people. But when it came to me doing for my people, she wouldn't listen."

Barrett had more skill with knots than Heather and Nora struggled to loosen the ties on Abigail's hands.

Charlie took a tiny step forward. "She saw your abandonment for what it was: a chance for you to get back to the easy life."

Barrett bellowed as a bear in pain. "What do you know how she saw anything? She knew how much I loved her, cherished her and our children. She was punishing me for not living life her way."

Charlie shook his head. "Some punishment. She's dead. Your son is buried beside her. And you're amassing a fortune, living in a mansion, and allowing enough uranium to seep into Hopi wells to wipe out the whole tribe."

"Ester wouldn't listen when I told her about all the good we could do on the rez with McCreary money. If she hadn't run away she'd have seen the food deliveries that started immediately, the visiting doctors, and then the clinic and school."

With the slightest movement, Charlie pulled the gun from his waistband. "She didn't want white doctors and water lines and electricity. She wanted the freedom to preserve the old ways. She believed in the Hopi way of life and their responsibility to the world."

Barrett waved the hand holding the gun. Words burst like bullets from his mouth. "Her bullshit religion and the kachinas and nature and balance. That's what killed her. She took my son, went out the desert to pray and it killed them."

"The uranium contamination in the wells killed her," Charlie said simply.

The rope fell away from Abigail's hands.

"If she'd have moved to town with me her water would have been filtered and clean. She'd be alive. My son would be alive."

Charlie shook his head. "The blame doesn't rest with a woman who was living as her ancestors lived."

Barrett focused on Charlie. "But I have Heather. She'll make up for her grandmother's stupid choices."

Charlie shook his head. "Sorry, Mac. I don't think Heather's going to want anything to do with you from now on."

Barrett shook his head. "She's a teenager. She'll go through her rebellion but she'll come around. She'll claim her heritage."

"I think she's more inclined to Ester's side of the family."

"She'll never know about that weak bloodline."

"She knows who she is. And she knows about the uranium in the wells."

A twig snapped in the forest opposite the clearing from Nora. Barrett turned his head.

The conversation ended.

Charlie pulled his gun.

Nora wrapped an arm around Abigail and threw them both to the ground, landing on top of Abigail to protect her.

A gunshot erupted in the clearing.

46

Silence fell on the clearing as if the whole world paused. Who would have thought blurry, alcohol-sodden Charlie could be so razor sharp. He'd distracted Barrett and rattled him enough to get the upper hand. He was their hero.

Nora rolled off Abigail, anxious to see Barrett incapacitated and get Abigail back to the hospital.

Barrett stood by the rock, the gun pointed outward.

No! Charlie lay on his back. He let out a moan.

Abigail sat up and before Nora could grab her, jumped to her feet. "Charlie!" She ran across the clearing, flinging herself at Charlie's side, sobbing real tears.

No words of adoration from Charlie, just a weak grunt. A dark stain spread from a spot under Charlie's left shoulder.

"Oh, Charlie. He's bleeding!"

Barrett stared at the scene. "They usually do when they get shot."

Abigail sat on her knees and placed her hand onto the wound. "Get me something to dress this. I need to keep pressure on it."

Barrett sounded almost light-hearted. "Don't lose your head over it Abigail. None of you are going to make it out of here alive."

Barrett swung the gun toward Nora. "They think you're crazy. They'll find you out here, your mother and Charlie murdered and a bullet through your brain, a tragic suicide."

In a surprisingly sprite move for the big man, Barrett jumped toward Nora.

She froze, like a fainting goat, then suddenly darted to one side, out of his way.

Barrett swung an arm out and it brushed against her side as she twisted away.

Panting, he stopped and pointed his gun toward Abigail. "I can take care of your mother first."

"No!" Nora charged him, intending to knock the gun away.

Barrett wrapped an iron arm around her, pulling her close enough to smell his sour sweat. He put the gun to her head. "Got to make sure the angle is right for suicide."

Failure! She'd tried so hard but Barrett outsmarted, out-planned, out-everything. She was no match. Why hadn't she gone to the cops? She couldn't save herself, Abigail or Charlie. She'd done nothing for Scott. Cole probably lay somewhere in a pool of blood. She'd doomed the mountain to wither beneath the uranium snow.

Nora fought. She twisted her torso, kicked at the tree trunks that were Barrett's legs. If she moved at all, it was only centimeters, not enough to dislodge the cold muzzle from her temple.

Wait. Something moved in the forest.

It couldn't be the cops. Maybe the Hopi or Big Elk's people waited out there, chortling over Barrett putting an end to Nora.

There is was again.

Leaves rustled in the forest and a branch snapped. A flash of blue shone in the lantern's half-light. Suddenly a hulking figure burst into the clearing. Abbey trotted behind, tail wagging in welcome.

Barrett jerked his head toward the intruder and crushed Nora even closer to his side.

After a second of confusion, Nora finally identified the oddly shaped figure. He wore a kachina mask and full regalia of feathers and costume. He carried a hatchet adorned with ribbons and feathers. Usually frightening in its foreign aspects, the mask looked terrifying in the midnight forest.

Even in the sketchy light, she saw the turquoise of the mask, its plug mouth and slits for eyes, long pheasant tail feathers rising behind.

The kachina rushed across the clearing toward Barrett and Nora with his raised hatchet. Abbey barked and raced with the kachina.

Though the kachina was much shorter than Nora originally thought, he swung his hatchet and hit Barrett in the throat with the dull edge.

Barrett grunted, his grip loosening on Nora.

She pulled away and Abbey lunged in.

Barrett jerked Nora close again and smacked Abby on the head with his gun. Abbey yelped.

"Bastard!" She squirmed to get free and he tightened his arm around her.

The kachina darted in again, striking at Barrett's gun arm, ripping the shirt on Barrett's bicep.

Barrett swung Nora as he turned and tried to get a bead on the dancing kachina. Nora's feet slid along the ground and she lost her balance. Barrett's arm pinned her to his side and kept her from falling.

The kachina retreated across the clearing to Abigail and Charlie. He didn't slow his zigzagged dance but the masked face turned toward them, as if checking on them.

Barrett raised his arm and sighted in on the kachina.

Abbey snarled and bared his teeth.

Nora regained her balance and braced on the ground. She watched Barrett's finger and sprang against him when she saw it start to flex.

His shot hammered her ears but the bullet whizzed into the forest.

Something hit Barrett in the chest and fell to the ground. A rock.

One hand still pushing on Charlie's chest, Abigail reached for another rock. She pulled her arm back and let it fly. Maybe years of golf lessons finally paid off in perfect aim.

Barrett ducked his head but the rock thudded into his temple.

The kachina circled back, hatchet raised.

"You crone! I wanted to marry you. Give you everything." Barrett aimed his gun at Abigail.

Nora pitched and writhed and kicked, screaming in Barrett's ear.

With incredible force, he flung Nora toward the rock where Abigail had perched. The back of her head cracked on the granite and she flopped to the ground. Her knee struck a rock and her leg went numb.

Abigail launched another rock. *Stubborn, stupid, Abigail.* Nora struggled to get to her feet but her leg wouldn't move. "Run, Mother!"

Barrett took a step toward Abigail, the gun came up. He couldn't miss. At that range, he'd rip a hole into Abigail that would tear her in two.

Nora dragged herself, fighting to stop Barrett.

Suddenly, the kachina flew from the forest straight at Barrett.

Barrett didn't alter his aim at Abigail. The third shot exploded from Barrett's gun.

A woman screamed.

47

Abigail screamed. And screamed again. The shrill ate into Barrett's brain like an ice pick.

Barrett had shot her. She should be lying on top of Charlie, her blood gushing onto the forest floor. Why wasn't she dead?

Abigail focused on a point behind him.

What was happening? Had he shot Nora instead? He swung his head around. No. Nora scrambled on the ground next to the boulder. He'd let go of her to aim at Abigail.

But Abigail was still alive.

Then he remembered. The kachina had darted from the forest. The fucking kachina. He'd ruined Barrett's plan.

Abigail sobbed, her hand still pressing Charlie's wound.

The kachina had flung himself in front of the bullet intended for Abigail. Barrett must have shot him.

Barrett looked at the spring. A pile of feathers, leather, and bright blue cloth soaked in the water.

Nora rose to her feet taking a shaky step toward the spring. She started to shake her head, tears coursing down her cheeks. "No. Oh god, no."

Barrett's skin turned to ice. He didn't want to but couldn't stop himself from taking a step toward the kachina.

His shot had blown the kachina backward to splash in the spring. It lay on its back.

Nora's knees buckled and she fell to the ground. A primal scream erupted from her core like the death throes of the Mother.

Please. No. No. Barrett pleaded with the spirits of the mountain. He couldn't look. He didn't want to know. But his feet carried him the few steps to the spring.

The kachina mask floated from the face. Glassy eyes stared from under an inch of water. Heather lay in the spring, blood washing away from the bullet hole in her heart.

EPILOGUE

Snow fell in fat white splats on top of Nora's Jeep. She hefted Abigail's tapestry suitcase into the back and slammed the tailgate closed. Abbey sat in the passenger seat staring out the windshield. He may not know where they were going but he'd go with Nora anywhere.

Abigail stood behind her, arms folded as if the cold mountain air could penetrate her white down jacket. "I don't know why you don't get rid of this clunker and get a car more suitable to an executive."

Abigail could be blown up and shot at and still, she kept her edge. *What a woman.* "No one will pay attention to what I drive, especially since I intend to ride my bike everywhere."

Abigail sniffed. "Always the fanatic."

"It's Boulder, Mother. I'll fit right in."

Abigail wouldn't concede. "I thought your tree-hugging days were over. You should drive a sporty, sexy car. You know what they say, 'Dress for the job you want, not the one you have.'"

Nora bent over and kissed Abigail's cheek. "I don't want that kind of job."

Charlie stepped close behind Abigail and put his arms around her, drawing her into him. "That's the spirit, darlin'. You keep a foot in the mountains and don't let the city corrupt you."

The tied-dyed rusted heap of Benny's pickup rumbled into the parking lot. They watched while he climbed out and walked to them. "Heard you're heading north."

Nora grinned. "I suppose Nakwaiyamtewa told you."

He shrugged, a hint of smile around his eyes. "Did I tell you he is my grandfather?"

Made perfect sense. Nora took hold of his hand. "I'm glad you came to say good bye. I want to thank you or apologize or, I don't know."

"You've said that before."

Charlie kissed the top of Abigail's head. "Are you warm enough?"

Abigail stepped out of his embrace. "Don't be ridiculous. It's only October. If I can't handle the weather now, how do you suppose I'll survive January?"

Good question. How would Abigail fare in Charlie's little cabin on the edge of the forest with the nearest fashion mall 120 miles away in Phoenix, no luncheons to hostess or Junior League meetings to preside over?

Charlie shook his head. "Fire and vinegar. That's my Abbie"

Abigail fought the smile that crept to her face. She gave in and patted Charlie's cheek. "Queen Abbie, to you."

"As always, my dear."

Benny pulled a small cloth pouch from his jeans pocket and gave it to Nora. "I have something I want you to do." He placed the pouch in her hand. "When you get to Colorado, plant these corn seeds. Sing to them. If you do this one small thing, it will help me."

"How will that help you?"

He nearly grinned, big emotion for him. "It will help the whole world but I like to think of you doing this to help balance me."

"Don't you grow enough corn for your own balance?"

He nodded. "But I have been given responsibility to spend a large pot of money the Gray Hair followers of Big Elk gave to Hopi. It's guilt from the harm Big Elk did. We'll use it to clean up the uranium in the water."

Nora squeezed the seeds and already felt protective of them. She hugged Benny and watched as he drove away.

Nora gazed at the mountain visible from the road in front of Charlie's cabin. Snow accumulated in the pine boughs, the ground already blanketed in white.

Charlie followed her gaze. "One good thing came of all this. The mountain can be herself again."

Tears threatened. Scott's ashes lay on the ground of that mountain. Heather's blood soaked into the soil. "But what cost?"

Charlie put an arm around her shoulders. "You sure you don't want that money, honey?"

Nora shook her head throat too tight for words. While Barrett sat in jail without bond, speaking to no one, without the heart or life to even assist his attorneys with a viable defense, he sent Nora a complicated plan for her approval.

If she sold her interests in Kachina Ski to an environmental trust at an inflated price, the trust would secure protection for the mountain to remain undeveloped. It would be available to the tribes who held it sacred and would be forever named the Heather McCreary Wilderness. McCreary Energy set it up to fund the trust in perpetuity.

Nora agreed immediately, hoping Heather would have been pleased. She signed the money over to Abigail.

Of course Abigail protested. But Nora reasoned that since Abigail's husband gave Kachina Ski to Nora, the proceeds after her debt should go back to Abigail. Her mother retained her pride and Nora cut all ties with the mountain that had taken so much from her.

"Cole called to ask about you this morning," Abigail said. The woman was nothing if not relentless.

"That's nice." *Keep it short. Get in the car. Drive away before the litany begins.*

Too late. "I wish you'd give him a chance to explain."

Nora clenched her jaw. "He kept secrets from me. I don't need someone like that in my life."

Charlie shook his head. "I lied to you too, sugar."

"And I'm not done being mad at you, either." She kissed him on the top of the head, anyway. "But you're in my life and I already love you. Aside from you and Abigail, I want to forget everything about Kachina Peak. That includes Cole."

Abigail acted like a pushy sales person. "You're being stubborn, Nora. He started out trying to nail Barrett for bribing Congress."

Nora turned her back and stepped toward the driver's door. "You've said all this before. I need to get on the road."

Abigail grabbed her hand. "But he was only trying to protect you. When he suspected Barrett was involved in Scott's murder, well, he..."

Nora wrenched open the Jeep door. "Not listening, Abigail."

Her mother sniffed. "So now it's not 'Mother' anymore."

Nora kissed Charlie's cheek. "Take care of her," she said.

Charlie reached into his pocket and pulled out a beer. He started to pull the tab and glanced at Abigail. Her slight frown made him redeposit the can in his pocket, unopened. "I believe we'll be taking care of each other."

Nora hugged her mother. "I love you." She climbed into the Jeep, set the wipers in motion and pulled away.

Giving in to the urge, she let her eyes wander to the rearview mirror, certain of what she'd see.

It was no surprise the kachina man stood in the trees watching her leave.

—

SKIES OF FIRE

A NORA ABBOTT MYSTERY

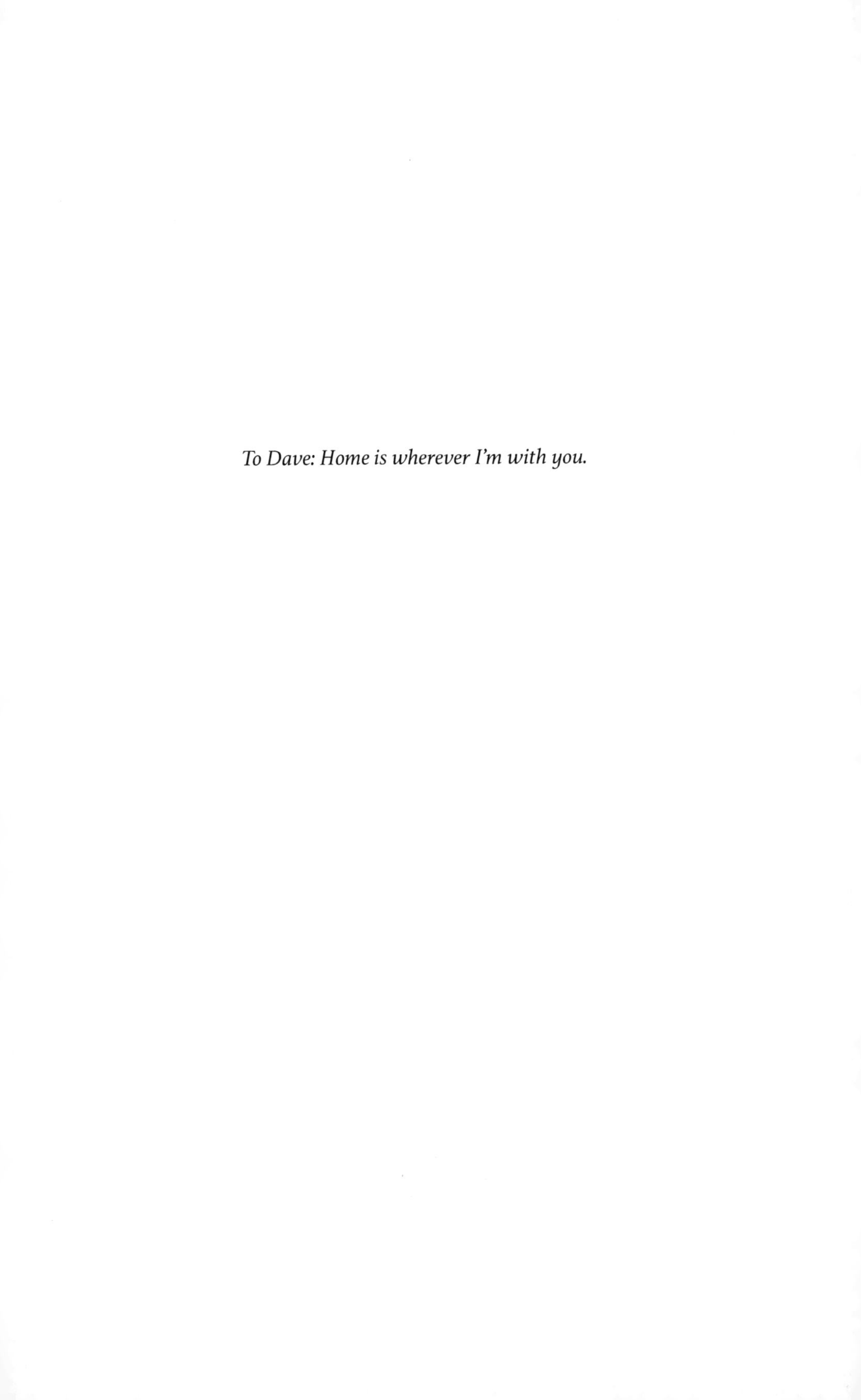

To Dave: Home is wherever I'm with you.

1

Sylvia LaFever simply had to have it. *If the Trust won't give me an advance, I'll force Eduardo to pay for it. I'm going to make him the wealthiest man on the planet.*

But of course, he wouldn't want anyone to know that.

Sylvia stared at the photo of the Chihuly chandelier on her laptop. She'd never have another chance at something so perfect for her dining room. At $90,000 it was a steal. The Trust could cough up the money. *They owed it to me.*

A squeaky voice broke into Sylvia's thoughts. "I've finished the initial calculations on the refractory angle but it seems like we're way off."

Sylvia slammed the top of her computer closed. "Nice work, Petal."

Petal stood in front of Sylvia, a mass of dreadlocks on a too-skinny body. As usual, layers of gauze and hand-knitted rags swathed Petal. She mumbled, "When the plume excites the ionosphere, are we monitoring the disturbances in the 100 km range to see if this leads to short term climatic alterations?"

Questions, chatter, like a million needles into her brain. Sylvia bestowed a patient smile on Petal. "It's complicated and I don't have time to explain it to you. If you earn your PhD we can have a more meaningful conversation about the principles behind ELF and short term climate fluctuations."

For god's sake, Petal's eyes teared up. She swallowed. "I just wondered because the coordinates bounce the beam to South America."

Sylvia rolled her chair away from her desk, the wheels rickety on the plastic carpet guard. *I deserve better than this drafty space tacked on to the aging farmhouse that Loving Earth Trust is so proud to call headquarters.* The slapped-up dry wall and builder-grade windows are bad enough but they'd simply laid industrial carpet atop a concrete floor with minimal padding.

Rust-colored carpet. *Disgusting.*

Maybe the sparse computer equipment covered the Trust's simplistic climate change modeling project, but for the magic Eduardo demanded, she needed more sophisticated hardware.

Sylvia stopped short of patting Petal on the arm, never sure when Petal showered last. "If you do as I tell you and watch and learn, you'll gain more knowledge than asking me questions all the time."

Petal nodded and wiped her nose with her sleeve. "Will we need to change the angle of the tower?"

Sylvia pressed a finger up to her mouth to silence Petal.

Petal retreated to her particle-board desk shoved into the corner of the room amid the used file cabinets the Trust provided for Sylvia. Dented metal with chipped beige paint, they maintained the same thrift store style of the rest of this dump.

I should still be in Alaska running the HAARP facility. I wish I could see their faces when they understand their mistake in firing me. Thank god Eduardo understands my genius.

The October chill filtered into the office but Sylvia forgot the temperature while she opened her laptop and emailed the art broker to secure the Chihuly. A knock on the thin door of her office disturbed the glow of acquisition. Sylvia glanced at the time on her computer. Ten-thirty.

The door opened without an invitation and a frowsy woman poked her head inside.

Sylvia sounded more welcoming than she felt. "Darla. What are you doing working so late?" The Financial Director of Loving Earth Trust didn't often stick around after four o'clock. No one at the Trust did.

Sylvia, on the other hand, worked long hours. As expected of a creative genius.

Darla stepped further into the suite, as Sylvia called the 30 square foot addition to give it more class than it deserved.

Darla stood just inside the door and gawked at the maps tacked to the walls. Sylvia changed them periodically so the office appeared dynamic. Darla's dumpy jeans and scuffed clogs fit right in with her hair —the color of spoiled hamburger, hanging in shapeless strands to her shoulders. The woman had no style. But then, those environmental types seldom worried about fashion.

Darla twisted her hands over her heavy, udder-like breasts. "We need to talk about your project."

Actually, Darla coming here saved Sylvia the trouble of going to her. "Absolutely. I've made some necessary equipment upgrades. I'll turn in an expense report tomorrow and expect reimbursement right away." How much could she get the Trust to pay her?

Darla cocked her head as if she hadn't understood.

A rustle of clothes reminded Sylvia that Petal sat at her desk. Sylvia brushed her hand through the air. "You can go now, Petal."

Petal slipped almost silently toward the door. Darla and Petal exchanged looks as if Sylvia couldn't see them. Underlings always hung together, driving home the truth: It's lonely at the top.

As soon as the door closed behind Petal, Sylvia addressed Darla. "I can give you a trend analysis of the climate change with respect to beetle kill so you can answer questions at the board meeting."

Darla smelled ripe, like a true naturalist. *God, why couldn't these people shower regularly?*

Darla's bushy eyebrows drew down in a frown.

"I found the missing money."

Sylvia didn't care about Darla's petty bookkeeping problems. "That's nice."

Color rose in the accountant's face. "I don't know how you got the money out of your restricted funds without the passwords but you need to return it."

Minions. Always bothering her with their problems. Sylvia wouldn't let Darla weasel out of paying her. "If Mark approves the funds for equipment, which I assure you, he will, you need to cut me a check."

Darla shifted from foot to foot. She peered at the ceiling and the floor. "I don't know what's going on, but money is missing. Big amounts."

Was she suggesting Sylvia somehow caused *her* bookkeeping errors? Sylvia strove to sound maternal. "I'm not the accountant but I know you're good at what you do. You'll just have to find it."

"The auditors will see it right away even if the board doesn't discover it." Darla's voice broke.

Just because Darla was a terrible accountant didn't make it Sylvia's problem. "Sometimes when I have a particularly vexing problem, I sleep on it and things are better in the morning."

Darla's porcine eyes sparked with fear. "You stole $400,000." She trembled.

Sylvia stood. "You're crazy."

"You're not doing any work on climate change here. Everyone knows it. But you're doing something. I'm going to the board and tell them."

Pathetic Darla, so jealous. She needed to learn her place.

Sylvia slid her desk drawer out. With a voice like cotton candy, Sylvia said, "Go home. Sleep on it. I'm sure you'll feel differently in the morning." Sylvia straightened and pulled her arm up.

Darla gasped.

Sylvia loved the feel of the Smith and Wesson 638 Airweight revolver. The grip caressed her palm and at slightly less than a pound, even her delicate wrists could hold it steady. The gold plating on the barrel coordinated pleasingly with the pearl grip.

When she'd bought it, she thought it might be an extravagance. So elegant and deadly—just like Sylvia—and she'd had to have it. Now it proved an expedient tool for chasing off fools.

Darla backed into a file cabinet and inched toward the door. "You wouldn't shoot me."

Sylvia raised her eyebrows and smirked, holding the gun steady on Darla, loving her feeling of command. Only a few people had Sylvia's audacity. She was truly extraordinary.

Like a quail in the brush, Darla panicked, turned tail and raced toward the office door.

Sylvia couldn't resist and followed her down the short hallway to the kitchen. She laughed to watch Darla tugging on the kitchen door and stumbling down the steps to the dark backyard.

Still laughing, Sylvia pointed the gun into the night and fired. How could she not? It would be like holding potato chips in your hand and not eating them. Besides, frightening Darla provided extra insurance that the nitwit would write that big check tomorrow.

In Sylvia's life, insurance was a good thing.

Chuckling, she locked the kitchen door.

2

Sylvia LaFever simply had to have it. *If the Trust won't give me an advance, I'll force Eduardo to pay for it. I'm going to make him the wealthiest man on the planet.*

But of course, he wouldn't want anyone to know that.

Sylvia stared at the photo of the Chihuly chandelier on her laptop. She'd never have another chance at something so perfect for her dining room. At $90,000 it was a steal. The Trust could cough up the money. *They owed it to me.*

A squeaky voice broke into Sylvia's thoughts. "I've finished the initial calculations on the refractory angle but it seems like we're way off."

Sylvia slammed the top of her computer closed. "Nice work, Petal."

Petal stood in front of Sylvia, a mass of dreadlocks on a too-skinny body. As usual, layers of gauze and hand-knitted rags swathed Petal. She mumbled, "When the plume excites the ionosphere, are we monitoring the disturbances in the 100 km range to see if this leads to short term climatic alterations?"

Questions, chatter, like a million needles into her brain. Sylvia bestowed a patient smile on Petal. "It's complicated and I don't have time to explain it to you. If you earn your PhD we can have a more meaningful conversation about the principles behind ELF and short term climate fluctuations."

For god's sake, Petal's eyes teared up. She swallowed. "I just wondered because the coordinates bounce the beam to South America."

Sylvia rolled her chair away from her desk, the wheels rickety on the plastic carpet guard. *I deserve better than this drafty space tacked on to the aging farmhouse that Loving Earth Trust is so proud to call headquarters.* The slapped-up dry wall and builder-grade windows are bad enough but they'd simply laid industrial carpet atop a concrete floor with minimal padding.

Rust-colored carpet. *Disgusting.*

Maybe the sparse computer equipment covered the Trust's simplistic climate change modeling project, but for the magic Eduardo demanded, she needed more sophisticated hardware.

Sylvia stopped short of patting Petal on the arm, never sure when Petal showered last. "If you do as I tell you and watch and learn, you'll gain more knowledge than asking me questions all the time."

Petal nodded and wiped her nose with her sleeve. "Will we need to change the angle of the tower?"

Sylvia pressed a finger up to her mouth to silence Petal.

Petal retreated to her particle-board desk shoved into the corner of the room amid the used file cabinets the Trust provided for Sylvia. Dented metal with chipped beige paint, they maintained the same thrift store style of the rest of this dump.

I should still be in Alaska running the HAARP facility. I wish I could see their faces when they understand their mistake in firing me. Thank god Eduardo understands my genius.

The October chill filtered into the office but Sylvia forgot the temperature while she opened her laptop and emailed the art broker to secure the Chihuly. A knock on the thin door of her office disturbed the glow of acquisition. Sylvia glanced at the time on her computer. Ten-thirty.

The door opened without an invitation and a frowsy woman poked her head inside.

Sylvia sounded more welcoming than she felt. "Darla. What are you doing working so late?" The Financial Director of Loving Earth Trust didn't often stick around after four o'clock. No one at the Trust did.

Sylvia, on the other hand, worked long hours. As expected of a creative genius.

Darla stepped further into the suite, as Sylvia called the 30 square foot addition to give it more class than it deserved.

Darla stood just inside the door and gawked at the maps tacked to the walls. Sylvia changed them periodically so the office appeared dynamic. Darla's dumpy jeans and scuffed clogs fit right in with her hair—the color of spoiled hamburger, hanging in shapeless strands to her shoulders. The woman had no style. But then, those environmental types seldom worried about fashion.

Darla twisted her hands over her heavy, udder-like breasts. "We need to talk about your project."

Actually, Darla coming here saved Sylvia the trouble of going to her. "Absolutely. I've made some necessary equipment upgrades. I'll turn in an expense report tomorrow and expect reimbursement right away." How much could she get the Trust to pay her?

Darla cocked her head as if she hadn't understood.

A rustle of clothes reminded Sylvia that Petal sat at her desk. Sylvia brushed her hand through the air. "You can go now, Petal."

Petal slipped almost silently toward the door. Darla and Petal exchanged looks as if Sylvia couldn't see them. Underlings always hung together, driving home the truth: It's lonely at the top.

As soon as the door closed behind Petal, Sylvia addressed Darla. "I can give you a trend analysis of the climate change with respect to beetle kill so you can answer questions at the board meeting."

Darla smelled ripe, like a true naturalist. *God, why couldn't these people shower regularly?*

Darla's bushy eyebrows drew down in a frown.

"I found the missing money."

Sylvia didn't care about Darla's petty bookkeeping problems. "That's nice."

Color rose in the accountant's face. "I don't know how you got the money out of your restricted funds without the passwords but you need to return it."

Minions. Always bothering her with their problems. Sylvia wouldn't let Darla weasel out of paying her. "If Mark approves the funds for equipment, which I assure you, he will, you need to cut me a check."

Darla shifted from foot to foot. She peered at the ceiling and the floor. "I don't know what's going on, but money is missing. Big amounts."

Was she suggesting Sylvia somehow caused *her* bookkeeping errors? Sylvia strove to sound maternal. "I'm not the accountant but I know you're good at what you do. You'll just have to find it."

"The auditors will see it right away even if the board doesn't discover it." Darla's voice broke.

Just because Darla was a terrible accountant didn't make it Sylvia's problem. "Sometimes when I have a particularly vexing problem, I sleep on it and things are better in the morning."

Darla's porcine eyes sparked with fear. "You stole $400,000." She trembled.

Sylvia stood. "You're crazy."

"You're not doing any work on climate change here. Everyone knows it. But you're doing something. I'm going to the board and tell them."

Pathetic Darla, so jealous. She needed to learn her place.

Sylvia slid her desk drawer out. With a voice like cotton candy, Sylvia said, "Go home. Sleep on it. I'm sure you'll feel differently in the morning." Sylvia straightened and pulled her arm up.

Darla gasped.

Sylvia loved the feel of the Smith and Wesson 638 Airweight revolver. The grip caressed her palm and at slightly less than a pound, even her delicate wrists could hold it steady. The gold plating on the barrel coordinated pleasingly with the pearl grip.

When she'd bought it, she thought it might be an extravagance. So elegant and deadly—just like Sylvia—and she'd had to have it. Now it proved an expedient tool for chasing off fools.

Darla backed into a file cabinet and inched toward the door. "You wouldn't shoot me."

Sylvia raised her eyebrows and smirked, holding the gun steady on Darla, loving her feeling of command. Only a few people had Sylvia's audacity. She was truly extraordinary.

Like a quail in the brush, Darla panicked, turned tail and raced toward the office door.

Sylvia couldn't resist and followed her down the short hallway to the kitchen. She laughed to watch Darla tugging on the kitchen door and stumbling down the steps to the dark backyard.

Still laughing, Sylvia pointed the gun into the night and fired. How could she not? It would be like holding potato chips in your hand and not eating them. Besides, frightening Darla provided extra insurance that the nitwit would write that big check tomorrow.

In Sylvia's life, insurance was a good thing.

Chuckling, she locked the kitchen door.

3

A cyclone roared in Nora Abbott's ears. Her gloved fingers clung to the cold stone and she fought rising nausea. She forced herself to scan the horizon, to broaden her view and take in the vast expanse opening below her.

The sharp rocks at the mountain's summit seemed like teeth about to shred Nora. The thin, cold wind tugged strands of hair from her ponytail as Nora concentrated on the big picture. Maybe gravity anchored her to the rock, but she felt as if she'd fly off any moment and kite into the impossible openness of sky. Then she'd fall. Down the expansive sweep of the cliff face, through the struggling brush at the tree line so far below her. She'd crash into the pines and rocks as the air grew thicker. Finally, she'd lie in a heap of bones and torn flesh.

Like Scott. Her husband. Forever gone.

No.

Far away, across the vast sky, peaks met her gaze, smattered with snow left from last winter. As far as she could see there was nothing but the Rockies, strong, solid, never-changing. No houses, office buildings, cars or people. The early morning clouds hung low and Nora wished for the bright Colorado sunshine to burn away her fear.

Okay, enough of the dramatics.

Today. Now. This is the day she'd overcome her dread.

No more of this craziness. She'd reclaim her lost love of the mountains and the sky.

Nora made herself come up here today after hearing a prediction of the first snow of the season for next week. After that, they'd close the road and she'd spend another winter cowering in town.

Up here on Mount Evans, the most accessible of Colorado's fourteen-thousand-foot-high peaks, the world opened before her. It was as if she balanced on a pinnacle between space and earth, held by only a brush with the stone.

Normally the summit would be packed with tourists, since they could drive to a parking lot a quarter mile down and take the narrow, rock-strewn, switchbacks to the summit. But this early, only a dozen people in twos and threes scrambled over the boulders, inching toward the edges to admire the colossal views. Nora occupied a perch alone, tucked as close to the mountain as possible, afraid to slide her foot an inch toward the edge.

Even if you didn't have to strap on a pack and climb for days to enjoy the grandeur of the view, the short hike and the precarious footing at the summit required some level of fitness. Not one square yard of the top area lay level. Boulders and rocks perched at odd angles that necessitated scrambling just to get from one dangerous visage to another.

She inhaled.

So far, so good.

Maybe she wasn't the Fear-Conquering Goddess, but she was working it.

Despite the jagged rocks and uneven footing she *would* overcome her fear. At thirty-two, her health good, her balance as steady as ever, she wasn't likely to sail off the side.

Except.

Scott had been in awesome shape. And yet he'd gone over the side on the mountain in Flagstaff. But he hadn't fallen. He'd been pushed.

Her breath caught in her throat.

Don't think about that.

And Heather. She couldn't save Heather, either.

Apparently, her flight from Arizona to Colorado hadn't been far enough to shield her from the memories of their deaths.

Nora started to tremble. A fissure opened somewhere inside her right temple. It spread downward and branched off, racing across her skin, splintering her control.

Stop it!

Falling apart would not bring back the people she loved.

Nora clenched her fists and imagined her insides of jelly hardening into steel. Her heart slowed slightly. The crashing hurricane of blood eased enough she heard the screech of a hawk. The world stretched below her—endless mountains, their tips white against an impossibly blue sky. The crisp air brushed against her cheeks.

Feeling more stable, Nora eased forward, leaning away from the mountain and toward the future. Any day, any moment, her life could change. She might soar, like that hawk. Any moment.

With one more gaze across the limitless mountain range, Nora shuffled across the boulders and scree, making her way to the trailhead down to the parking lot.

That's when she saw it.

At first, it was a flash of blue against the rocks. This far above tree line, she didn't expect much color aside from the tiny flowers hiding in cracks.

She gritted her teeth. Probably a bandana or cap left by a tourist.

But it got worse.

He stood in front of her. Hatchet in one hand, feathers in another. His fierce mask with its plug mouth faced her.

"No. Oh no. Go away."

Nora slid to her knees.

A figment of her imagination. Of course the kachina in front of her wasn't real. Kachinas were Hopi. They belonged in Northern Arizona, not the heart of the Rocky Mountains in Colorado.

That is, if kachinas really existed. Which they didn't.

She squeezed her eyes shut. *You don't exist. You're not real.*

The black blanket appeared at the edge of her inner vision, creeping toward her brain. She couldn't breathe, could only feel the wild thump of her heart trying to burst from her rib cage. She refused to open her eyes and let them lie to her again.

Paralyzed by panic, Nora curled into herself.

"Are you okay?" A little girl's voice cut through the thunder of fear.

Nora fought back from the blackness. With Olympic force of will, she opened her eyes.

Of course the kachina had disappeared. Nora sucked in the cold, thin air in relief. He never stuck around for any other witnesses. It made no sense that he chose to show himself to Nora, a white girl with red hair. As if it made sense for anyone to see the phantom kachina at all.

A cartoon of gauze and yarn swirling in color stood before Nora. The girl— or woman— Nora couldn't tell, hovered in layers of skirts, sweaters, leggings and scarves, topped with a wild growth of dreadlocks bunched on top of her head and twining around her face like Medusa's snakes.

Her appearance seemed as bizarre as the kachina, but her slight build with her small face and tiny hands didn't harbor much threat. More than that, she her timid gaze behind a pair of John Lennon—pink sunglasses, disarmed Nora.

"Are you okay?" she asked again.

Nora inhaled good air. Like a child in the throes of a nightmare, she felt relief in the presence of another person. "Yes. I'm fine."

The girl eyed her skeptically. "Having trouble with the altitude? If you aren't acclimated, you can get disoriented this high."

Of course. That explained it all. Nora could have kissed this strange mountain imp for giving her an excuse. Nora considered the parking lot several switchbacks below them. Just a small journey to safety.

The girl helped Nora stand. "I'll walk you to the parking lot. You'll feel better as soon as you get lower."

I'll feel better as soon as Hopi spirits quit popping out at me. But Nora smiled as best she could, for now satisfied the kachina had retreated to the depths of her very sick mind.

"I'm Petal," the girl said.

The name fit. "I'm Nora."

Nora ought to be embarrassed but she welcomed the steady hand on her arm. Far from an easy stroll, the trail was nothing but a pile of rocks that required concentration to navigate. Though traveled by countless tourists every summer, the trail could be easily lost. The switchbacks angled back on themselves in unexpected places and it was easy to find yourself off-trail, going around the side of the mountain with nothing below to stop a fall.

Someday Nora would be agile and fearless again. She had climbed the backside of Mount Evans in high school; today she'd driven. Driving to the top of a fourteener was nothing short of cheating. You should have to work to be rewarded with the view from the top of the world. But today was her test. If the kachina hadn't swept in, she would have passed.

Petal walked Nora to her Jeep. She waited while Nora dug into her jeans pocket for a key. "Your first fourteener?"

Nora unlocked the door and Abbey, her aging golden retriever opened his eyes. He sat up from napping on the driver's seat. "No. I've lived in Boulder most of my life. But I haven't been climbing recently. What about you? Did you hike the whole mountain?"

Petal shook her head. Her voice sounded frail, as if she'd rather not speak at all. "No. I caught a ride up."

Abbey eased from the Jeep and nosed the tire. He lifted his leg. Abbey finished and walked back to sit by Nora. "Thanks again for helping me down."

Petal nodded and stood still.

"Where is your ride?" Nora asked, mainly because Petal seemed to expect the conversation to continue. Nora motioned for Abbey to get in the Jeep.

Petal shrugged.

That's what Nora suspected. "You hitched?"

Petal nodded again, solemn.

Nora leaned into the Jeep. She pulled a backpack and a couple of paperback books from the bench seat in back to the floor. She picked up an extra ski cap and gloves from the passenger side floor and tossed them on top of the books and waved Abbey into the back seat. "If you don't mind riding in a muddy old Jeep, climb in."

Petal shook her head, her dreads bouncing. "Oh no. You don't have to do that. I'll get a ride."

"I know I don't have to. Where are you going?"

Petal studied her Chacos sandals and thick wool socks. "Boulder."

"Me, too. Let's go." Nora felt almost cheerful at being able to help someone.

Petal seemed to argue with herself for a moment then her thin lips turned up in a tiny smile. "Okay. Thanks."

She clambered into the Jeep and Nora backed out, already feeling better. Nora cranked on the heater in the rumbling Jeep, the smell of dog hair mingling with Petal's organic odor.

Petal turned in the seat and scratched Abbey's ears. "Your dog is nice. Her name is Abbey?"

"His. Named after Edward Abbey. One of the earliest conservationists." Nora braked and eased to the inside of the narrow road as they met an SUV. She'd rather hike than drive this strip of pavement carved along the mountainside.

Petal nodded. "I know."

That surprised Nora. So many people had no idea about Edward Abbey. "What do you do for a living?" Oops. From Petal's appearance, she might not be making a living. Nora cursed her rusty social skills.

Petal didn't seem offended. "I work at Loving Earth Trust."

Nora knew the name. "That's great. They, you, have done some good work, especially with open space in Boulder."

Petal turned from Abbey and pulled her feet under her. "What do you do?"

Nora maneuvered the Jeep around a tight corner, holding her breath and avoiding glancing at the edge of the road that slid into oblivion. "I'd love to work for an environmental group."

"Really? Why?"

Why. The answer involved so much history, so many regrets. "Redemption."

Petal's soft voice sounded shocked. "You're such a nice person, I can't believe you've done something you need to atone for."

"I'm not that nice, believe me."

Petal shook her head, sending the dreads waving again. "I can read auras. They don't lie, and yours tells me how good you are."

Nora smiled at her. Clouds scuttled across the sun and the Jeep felt chilly even with the heater blasting.

"No. I mean it," Petal said. "Yours is deep red. That means you're grounded and realistic and a survivor."

Not too long ago Petal's words would have made Nora scoff, not in someone's face, but inside, at least. Now dead Hopi leaders visited her on mountain tops and spoke to her in dreams. Who was she to judge?

Petal regarded her. "What is a kachina?"

Nora's hands tightened on the wheel. "Why do you ask?"

Petal cast her eyes down at the floor. "You said something about a kachina when you were on the mountain."

Raving. Super. They ought to lock me up.

"A kachina is a Hopi spiritual being of sorts. Hopi are a tribe in Northern Arizona. The kachinas are not really gods, but they're not human, either. There's about three-hundred of them and they can represent things in nature or—" she forced her voice to remain neutral—"they can be spirits of ancestors."

Petal accepted the explanation as if Nora had described an interesting recipe. "Oh."

They rode in silence for a while, Nora holding her breath at every tight switchback. It seemed like walking down would not only be safer, it would be quicker. Finally, Petal asked. "What do you think you should do for your redemption?"

Nora shrugged. "I'm not sure. I'm an accountant and I've been applying at environmental places all over town with no luck. I hate to give up and go corporate. But I need a job."

Petal's face lit up. At least, it seemed to from what Nora could tell behind the rose glasses and that bird's nest of hair. "Accountant?"

"Business manager, MBA, accountant—all that left brain stuff."

Petal squirmed like an excited child. "I knew there was a reason I met you up there. The universe introduced us to each other."

Nora raised her eyebrows at Petal.

Petal clapped her hands. "I think we have an opening for a financial director."

Nora wanted to feel optimism and excitement at an opportunity but she held back. "I already applied to them a month ago."

"It's a new opening," Petal said but the delight evaporated from her face. "Our Financial Director disappeared a few days ago and no one knows where she went."

"She just disappeared?" Like the kachina on the trail?

Petal hung her head. "I think it might have been my fault."

"I'm sorry," Nora said and meant it.

Petal sat upright. "But this is like *my* redemption. Darla left, but you're here and I found you."

Nora tried not to get her hopes up. "That's nice of you to say, but the Trust wouldn't be hiring already, with your director only being gone for a couple of days, would they?"

Petal's mouth turned down. "They were getting ready to fire her. Maybe that's why she left. Anyway, her taking off without a word to anyone was the last straw. They already have an ad set to run in this week's paper."

Nora didn't wish the old director ill, but this opportunity gave new meaning to *serendipity*. "Thank you for the head's up. Will you do the hiring?"

Petal's eyes sparkled. "Not really. But sometimes, I can suggest things."

The girl's excitement penetrated Nora. Maybe fate had jumped in and rescued her. "I'd love if you could get me an interview."

Petal smiled. She resembled a playful elf. "Done."

4

For the first time in too long, Nora joined the morning masses on their way to jobs the following Monday. Constructive, worthwhile, paycheck-producing jobs. Nora needed to work, had worked since she was sixteen, even while earning top grades in college and grad school. The last year of unemployment had depleted more than her cash reserves.

But no more. Look at her: A job! Loving Earth Trust wasn't just a job, either. It was a dream position. She'd called the Executive Director as soon as she'd returned from Mount Evans. He remembered her resume, called her in for an interview the next morning and hired her that afternoon. Two days after her failure on the mountaintop, her wheels gained traction.

Sunshine blazed from the east, sparkling on the morning. Nora turned from her apartment parking lot onto Arapahoe Street, happy to see the students with book bags strapped to their backs making their way toward campus for their first classes. There was something about people heading out for productive days, fresh from the shower, hair and clothes spiffed. Ready, expectant.

Finance Director with Loving Earth Trust. Score!

While not as well-known as The Sierra Club or The Nature Conservancy, Loving Earth Trust had earned a reputation in Colorado for getting results. Founded in the early seventies to spearhead open space in Boulder, they'd done good environmental and restoration work through the years. More than raising money and wringing hands, the Trust produced science to influence lawmakers to protect wild places. They sent volunteers out in the field for trail maintenance and landscape restoration. Now she was their financial director.

"And you get to come with me," she said to Abbey, stroking his silky head as he sat in the passenger seat keeping a keen eye on traffic.

Boulder's Flatirons rose to the west and Nora felt like saluting them. Flaming maples shouted good morning with their deep scarlet leaves contrasting to the golds and oranges of the less showy trees. She loved her town in all its outdoorsy quirkiness. The People's Republic of Boulder. The land of bicycle commuters, hippies, audacious entrepreneurs. Liberal, green, often down-right weird. Right where she belonged.

Nora's phone vibrated and she flipped it open.

"How are you?" Abigail. Again. Loving or smothering were the same in Abigail's world. It didn't help that Nora and Abigail were as alike as a Birkin Bag and a North Face backpack. In Nora's case, the backpack tended to be smattered with mud and repaired with duct tape.

"I'm the same as I was fifteen minutes ago, just a little closer to work." Nora waited at a stop light on Broadway in downtown Boulder and watched a young woman and man in business suits in earnest conversation. They cross the street in front of her, followed by a scuzzy gray-haired guy whose canvas pants barely stayed on his skinny hips. Behind them, two young women pedaled across in spandex biking shorts, colorful jackets and helmets.

"What did you decide to wear? Did you pack a lunch? You're wearing make-up, right?" Despite living in the woods in Flagstaff, Arizona for the last year, Abigail hadn't lost her high esteem for appearance. A magician, Abigail managed to look nearly perfect at all times.

Nora waited at the light. "Turquoise velour sweat suit. Sauerkraut and sausage. The darkest, skankiest Goth I could shovel on." Although Nora wore her copper-colored hair straight around her shoulders, she'd earlier told Abigail she wore a ponytail just to irritate her.

Abigail exhaled. "No need to get snippy. I'm only concerned."

Nora rolled her window down a few inches to smell the fresh morning. "Sorry. I'm nervous. I'm wearing jeans and, sorry to say, not much in the make-up department. As for lunch, Abbey and I will probably take a walk." Although Nora admired Edward Abbey, he also served as a good excuse to use a name that would forever irritate Abigail Podanski. Her mother would prefer she call her dog Fido.

"Jeans! You brought your dog to work? Oh, Nora." Abigail couldn't sound any more disappointed if Nora wore a bathing suit to a cocktail party.

"It's an environmental trust. I'll be hanging at the office with enviros, not power-lunching with the rich and famous." She rubbed a pinch of Abbey's soft hair between her fingers before pulling her hand away to shift gears. "And Abbey will probably sleep all day on my office floor."

Abigail's voice sounded distracted. "I know you were desperate for a job but that place is not up to your standards."

Nora pulled the hatched closed on her emotional cellar. She refused to let Abigail irritate her. "I wasn't desperate."

"If you say so. I've told you a hundred times you should have kept more of that money from the Kachina Ski sale instead of setting up that trust for me. In fact, you shouldn't have set up that trust at all."

The money Nora received when she sold the ski resort should be enough to keep Abigail in a decent living standard for the rest of her life. The problem was that Abigail enjoyed a higher-than-decent standard and if Nora hadn't locked it down and kept herself as executer, Abigail might run through it too fast. It had happened before.

For her part, Nora didn't keep much of what felt to her like blood money. She'd figured with her resume and business skills, even if she insisted on working in the environmental sector, she'd land a good job in no time. She hadn't planned on a wrecked economy.

"This job is perfect for me, Mother."

"But the salary is so low."

"Sadly, I'll have to forego the spa weekends and month-long cruises with you."

The sun dazzled the flower beds and brick pavers of downtown. Nora drove past the offices and shops, beyond the county buildings and library and out of town on Canyon Boulevard, along Boulder Creek

Abigail probably thought Nora was serious. "If you'd get a real job you wouldn't have to make those sacrifices."

The paved bike trail along the creek gave way to a gravel path as the highway narrowed in the canyon. The creek rushed along, as happy as Nora to be going someplace.

"I'm almost there. Let me talk to Charlie." At least he was proud of Nora working for the Trust. Charlie had been Nora's buddy long before he ended up as Abigail's fourth husband. A situation more bizarre than anything Nora had experienced—and she'd been in a vortex of bizarre.

"Charlie's not..." Abigail trailed off. "Charlie's not here."

Nora nodded. He probably headed out early for his day of relatively harmless eco-terrorism. After his stint in Vietnam, Charlie had returned to his cabin outside of Flagstaff and did his bit for the environment by blocking forest trails with logs and rocks to keep dirt bikes and quads from shredding the forest.

"Tell him hi for me." Nora's stomach churned, like a kid on the first day of school. Where would this new adventure take her?

"Okay." Abigail sounded unsure. "Nora, I probably should tell you..."

A voice interrupted Abigail. It sounded like, "Can I take your order?" Since Abigail usually didn't venture from the cabin before her lengthy morning beauty regimen, it must be the television.

Just outside of the bustle of town heading into the canyon, a graveled clearing off to the side of the road supplied parking next to a bus stop. One person stood under the bus stop sign. Nora considered him. A shrunken old man, swallowed by a canvas work coat, he stared down the road as if watching for the bus...

The canyon walls disappeared and ice raced through her.

"I have a kachina for you." She stood in a crowd in the Flagstaff courthouse lobby.

He touched her arm. A withered slip of a Native American, he wore a long, threadbare tunic, leggings and moccasins that reached to his knees. Deep wrinkles lined his face like wadded parchment and skin sagged around his eyes.

"I have a kachina," he repeated in that soft voice cracked with age.

"I don't want to buy a kachina," she said.

"Not to buy." He reached into a canvas bag and pulled out a doll carved from cottonwood root. "For you." The doll had a scary mask with slit eyes and a plug mouth. A bright blue sash fastened across his shoulder...

Her two right wheels dropped off the pavement and Nora jerked the steering wheel to pull the Jeep back on the road. It fishtailed but righted itself.

"Nora?" Abigail's voice squawked from the phone in Nora's lap.

Nora grabbed the dropped phone. "Had some traffic."

"Where are you now?"

Nora spotted a road side. "A couple miles past Settler's Park. About to the Trust."

Nora braked and turned left. She rumbled across a wood-planked bridge over the creek. Loving Earth Trust occupied a rambling old house in Boulder Canyon, butted up to the mountain side. Gables and windows, extensions and extra rooms jutted out at weird angles giving the place a disjointed feel. The picturesque front porch descended to a sparsely grassed front yard with a rail fence separating it from the packed dirt parking area. Only three other vehicles sat there. Beyond the lot, a one-lane road ran along the creek bank, but it petered out after a couple hundred yards. A large wood barn stood behind the house. Towering mountains and pines assured that the house stayed in shadow most of the time. It was beautiful, of course, but a chill goosed Nora's flesh.

"Here we are," Nora said. "Gotta go."

"Have a good day, dear. We'll talk soon."

Too soon, no doubt. That wasn't fair. Abigail had been supportive and encouraging since Nora had moved from Flagstaff a year ago. At times, Abigail had been Nora's only human contact.

Now it was time to start over. Be normal. Have a job. Friends. Maybe a social life. "Hold on, Cowgirl. Just start with a job, okay?"

If that went well, maybe she'd stop talking to herself.

She ran her fingers through Abbey's fur. Good thing first days of work didn't last forever. Too bad second days and then the first week, and month, full of anxiety and nerves followed. In no time, say a millennium or two, Nora would feel right at home.

She filled her lungs, imagining the air had magical powers to make her appear confident and smart. "Let's go," she said, pretending she talked to Abbey.

Abbey jumped out as if he'd been coming to work here every day for years. Nora leaned into the back of the Jeep and hefted out a bushy potted plant. She rested the terra cotta pot on her hip and steadied it with her arm. She had larger and heavier pots at home but thought this would work in an office. The long, wide, deeply green leaves rose from the pot and cascaded, leaving her room enough to peek over the top. She slammed the Jeep door shut.

5

Nora and Abbey crunched along the frost-skimmed dirt of the parking lot and up the old wooden stairs. The wide porch creaked as they crossed. Nora balanced the plant on her hip and opened the door, letting Abbey take the first step into their new digs.

Although Nora had bosses and structure in jobs before, this was her first Real Job. She'd gone from her undergrad to business school and right into running the ski resort in Arizona without the entry-level introduction to her career. Now she held a management position and answered to the Executive Director and the board. Gulp. But she needed to act like that was no big deal to her.

They stood in what appeared to be a large living room, complete with a stone fireplace on one end, window seats on the front porch side, a flight of stairs off the other, and some Mission style padded chairs scattered about. Whoever built this around the turn of the century must have had means to make it so spacious. As it was, the cost of this sucker, with the size and location along the creek outside of Boulder, could probably save the earth and a few other planets.

Mark Monstain, Executive Director, walked into the room carrying a take-out cup with a Mr. Green Beans logo. Nora gave him the benefit of the doubt and assumed the green in Green Beans meant the cup was recyclable. He stood about five eight, all rounded edges, with a belly in the early stage of drooping over his belt. He wore the same ensemble as he had at her interview, a white, short-sleeved shirt, tucked sloppily into black dress pants. Despite thinning hair at the crown of his head, he had to be about Nora's age. Not the typical build and dress of an outdoorsman and rugged environmentalist. More like a grocery store clerk without the apron.

"Good. Right on time." He punctuated the unfunny remark with a giggle. Nora noticed in the interview he tended to insert an annoying high-pitched giggle into nearly every sentence. She'd teach herself to ignore it. For this job, she'd ignore a roaring grizzly bear.

"I see you've brought a plant to liven up your office."

Thank you, Mr. Obvious.

"And your dog."

He'd told her bringing Abbey would be fine. "Did you say my office was upstairs?" The plant bit into her hip and she felt awkward standing in the lobby/living room with both hands full.

He didn't move. "You don't remember me after all, do you?"

Uh-oh. Awkward Alert. She hugged the plant. "I'm sorry."

"From Earth Club at Boulder High?"

"Oh, of course." *Mark Monstain?* She had no clue.

She wracked her brain to recall the flabby lips and chubby cheeks. Earth Club was little more than a group of idealists handing out flyers on weekends and railing against what they thought of as humankind's war on the environment.

"I'm not surprised you don't remember me. You were a senior when I was a freshman." He giggled.

At the interview she'd felt a vague sense of familiarity, similar to the way she felt about anchovies. She'd tasted them once as a child, had a lingering memory of nausea and never wanted to try them again.

The pocket of Nora's jacket vibrated. It had to be Abigail calling back. Even if her hands weren't wrapped around her plant, she wouldn't answer.

He sipped his coffee and began as if she'd asked. "I went to CU after Boulder High and graduated in environmental engineering. I started here as head volunteer coordinator and worked my way up. I've been here longer than anyone else."

"You're doing a great job." What else could she say?

He nodded. "Well, let me show you your office, then." He led the way up the stairs.

A sunny mezzanine opened on her right with a shared area and several offices lining it.

"This is where the volunteer program lives." Giggle, snort. "They log about four thousand man hours a year on our various projects from trail maintenance and open space restoration to range research and of course, the beetle kill problem. They're all out in the field this week taking advantage of the weather before the snow flies."

The plant tugged at Nora's arms, a heavy accessory to drag around on a house tour. Abbey followed, not acting impressed.

They wound around a hallway that opened into an office area with a large desk. A copier and other office machines sat on a counter. "This is the copy room. This computer has a graphics and design program to make fliers and whatnot."

If this tour lasted much longer Nora's arms would give out and the plant would crash in a heap of terra cotta and roots.

A narrow servant's stairway opened to her left. "The kitchen is down there. Three years ago we added a sweet addition for Sylvia LaFever. You've heard of her, I'm sure."

Nora hadn't. A faint odor of burnt toast wafted from the stairwell.

"She used to work for the government at the HAARP facility in Alaska. You know, doing all sorts of research on the ionosphere and weather and things." He rushed along as if Nora understood what he talked about. She had heard of HAARP, of course. But didn't know much about it.

Mark rubbed his hands together. "We're lucky to have her. She's doing landscape modeling in regard to beetle kill and climate change. Real cutting-edge research."

Nora didn't know how cutting edge since she'd read studies showing the slight increase in temperatures facilitated an extra breeding cycle each year for the deadly beetles. If Nora knew about it, it couldn't be all that new. Maybe Sylvia LaFever's research dug deeper.

Mark pointed but kept them on the winding maze of odd-shaped offices. The old floor groaned as they wandered down the hall. The rooms probably served as bedrooms once but now walls cut them into tiny offices. "This place is enormous."

"But you can't beat the location." Snort. "Sometimes when things get hectic I go out on the front porch and watch the creek. We've had this building about five years now. A donor left it to us in her will."

Mark stopped at an open door. Finally, she'd be able to set the plant down and see her office.

"This is Thomas. He works on air quality." Mark lifted his arm to indicate a tall man with bushy dark curls and hairy legs leaning back in his chair reading. A bike propped on the wall in the corner. His orange Life Is Good t-shirt, cargo shorts and stocking feet indicted a casual dress code. His office smelled of the oatmeal he scraped from the bowl resting on his chest. "Thomas, this is Nora, our new director of finance."

Thomas peered at them over his reading glasses. "Welcome."

Mark pointed across the hall. "This is Bill's office, but he's at meetings today. He's our litigator." More offices opened up along the foyer creating a labyrinth. "Fay, She's in charge of Open Space." Another thirty-something with blonde hair smashed into a nest at the back of her head and wisps spilling down her back. Braless in an olive green t-shirt and hiking pants, her firm muscles showed regular physical activity.

Fay turned from her computer and spoke in a creaky voice. "Nice dog!" Abbey responded by trotting in and allowing Fay to pet him.

Panic swelled in Nora. She'd never remember the names and faces and jobs. She swallowed and forced calm.

First day. Don't be overwhelmed.

Eventually she'd figure this out and make friends. It wasn't life or death in one day.

Despite the at least four people and a dog, the house felt empty. Maybe it was too early in the day for environmentalists. They wouldn't necessarily keep the same hours as corporate drones. "Seems like lots of space."

Mark giggled. "Most of the staff comes and goes a lot. Our work takes us to the field and meetings. It's not unusual for the admin staff to be here alone."

More pocket vibrations. Tenacity, thy name is Abigail.

"Just a minute." Mark poked his head in Thomas's office and spoke about meetings and legislation.

The plant dragged on Nora's arms. A window offered a narrow ledge and she stepped to it and rested the pot. Below, a jumble of flowing fabric bounced into the parking lot on a rusted bike. If the window was open, no doubt she'd have heard the clank and rattle of a chain needing oil. The mass of dreadlocks hid Petal's face. Plastic flowers wove through the old bike's front basket and streamers hung from the handlebars. The whole affair resembled more of a circus act than another day at the office.

Petal jumped off the bike, her flowered skirt fluttering around her ankles. She grabbed a satchel from the basket, flung the strap over her shoulder, and sprinted to the front porch.

"That's our Petal," Mark said from behind her. He scowled and checked his watch. "She works for Sylvia."

"Seems like there are a lot of different activities going on here."

He grinned and motioned for her to continue down the hall. "We're proud we're involved in all kinds of matters affecting the environment. We've got a great board and lots of funding."

Nora heaved the plant back up to her hip, switching sides. "Must be complicated accounting to keep so many programs and funds straight."

A shadow darkened Mark's face. "Darla wasn't up to the job. You'll get it in top shape in no time. From what I remember, you're super-smart and a great organizer."

That's a lot of confidence based on her presidency in a high school club. But Nora knew numbers. She understood accounting and could retreat into the safety of spreadsheets, where mistakes could be corrected and everything made sense.

"Do you mind me asking why the last Finance Director left so abruptly?"

They approached the end of the hall. Her office had to be close. Mark reached into his pocket and brought out a jangling set of keys. "Frankly, Darla was a flake. I'm not surprised she bugged out."

No one checked up to see why? That seemed strange.

Mark inserted a key into a heavy wood door that was probably original with the house. He giggled as he pushed the door open and stood back for her to enter. He opened his arm with a flourish. "Ta da."

Nora inhaled and stepped into the office. The long walk, talk of a disappearing Financial Director and locked doors had her expecting some kind of *Exorcist* moment with papers swirling through the air, maniacal laughter, darkness and debris filling a sulfuric atmosphere.

No overactive imagination there.

Windows lined this large corner office. Lavender paint with mint green trim brightened the walls. Plants sat on the window sills that accented a view down Boulder Canyon. A wicker chair with a chintz seat pad was tucked into a corner next to a cute patio table with a reading lamp. A large cabinet sat in the corner with the doors open. One side held shelves full of office supplies, and the other side was a coat closet. The desk and work space filled up one wall. File folders, papers, notebooks, and documents jumbled across the sizable countertop workspace. After Nora straightened and filed and got the rhythm, the office would be comfortable and pleasant.

Her pocket vibrated again. Never say die. Abigail.

Mark worked her office key off his ring and handed it to her. He pulled a crumpled notebook page from the pocket of his white shirt. "Here are the system passwords. If you change them, let me know. Make yourself at home. I've got to run." He sped away.

"Well, what do you think?" she asked Abbey.

He responded by plopping down next to a filing cabinet and watching her.

"Go ahead and act exhausted, I'm the one lugging this plant around." She eased the plant onto the corner of the counter, shoving papers aside.

"So you're going to replace Darla? Didn't take Mark long to write her off."

Nora whirled around to see Fay leaning against the door jamb. See? Normal colleague chatter. Not a threat. Remember casual conversation? "How long has she been gone?"

Fay shrugged. "Less than a week. Maybe Mark knows something we don't."

Nora surveyed the room. Two painted white wooden shelves above the work surface held porcelain figurines of bunnies and kittens painted in pastels. A snapshot showed a grinning woman, presumably Darla, shrouded in winter gear next to a Pawnee Pass sign on the Continental Divide. Several framed posters with inspirational sayings and landscapes peppered the walls. "Looks like she planned on coming back," Nora said. "She left a lot of personal things."

Fay walked into the office and peeked into the coat closet. She picked up a book from a shelf above the rod. Her voice had a cracked quality, as if she'd been yelling at a soccer match for two hours. "I don't know Darla very well. She kept to herself." She returned the book and picked up another. "Really, I thought she was weird."

Nora shrugged out of her coat. She didn't want to gossip. "How long have you been at the Trust?"

Fay wandered over to the decorative shelf and plucked Darla's picture off the shelf. "I didn't know she was a hiker." She set it back down. "I've been here about five years. I'm wondering how long I'll last."

Nora studied a bulletin board mounted behind the computer. It was strewn with multicolored sticky notes. "Why is that?"

Fay retreated to the door jamb and leaned against it, crossing her arms. Her voice croaked. "You'll see. Used to be all the projects were important. But now days, we've got one star and that's all Mark can see."

Nora leaned her backside on the work counter. She wanted to dive into the mounds of paper. "If the board doesn't like the job Mark's doing as executive director, they can replace him."

Fay's laugh sounded like a rusty door hinge. "Right. Mark isn't ED because he's so brilliant. His daddy is on the board. Mark's not going anywhere."

That answered the question of why someone so...icky... could have such an impressive job.

"So if any of us want to actually do any good, we're gonna have to make an exit."

An uncomfortable silence dropped into the office.

Fay gave that creaky laugh again. "Sorry. I've never learned the art of subtlety. I'll let you settle in. Maybe we can do a hike next week or something." She walked away with a groan of the floor.

A hike sounded way better than dipping down in the dregs of bad attitude. A hike sounded pretty good, actually.

Her phone jumped again. Might as well answer it, Abigail wouldn't stop until she did. "Mother."

"So how's it going? Did they seem to mind you wearing jeans? What about this Mark Monstain?"

Nora kept her voice down. "I'll call this evening and tell you all the details."

"Well, that's what I wanted to talk to you about."

Oh no. That tone. It meant trouble for Nora. "Not now, Mother."

"Nora." Mark appeared as if from magic. "I'd like you to meet our star here at the Trust."

Busted talking to her mother on the first day. "I have to go," she said into the phone.

"What I was saying is that you don't need to call me later."

Nora smiled at Mark and the attractive, petite woman standing next to him. An expensive black business suit draped perfectly over her compact frame, complete with four-inch pumps. Her dark hair curled around an ageless face. She looked like money all dressed up.

"Good bye." Nora tried to balance the pleasant face for her new boss and the firm voice for Abigail.

"Okay. But I wanted to tell you I'm on my way to Boulder. I should be there soon. Surprise!"

An anvil dropped, squishing Nora like Wile E. Coyote in a desert canyon.

6

Nora set the phone on her desk, resisting the urge to stuff it in the soil of her potted plant.

Mark's wet lips turned down in a frowned at Nora, then he gave the same arm flourish he'd used to present her office. He was either profoundly proud of everything at the Trust or liked the gesture. "This is Sylvia LaFever. She's working on the landscape modeling project I told you about."

Nora shook Sylvia's hand. "Mark mentioned climate change and beetle kill?"

While not exactly beautiful, Sylvia's magnetism pulled energy toward her. Dark eyes snapped and her smile commanded attention. "Don't worry about understanding my program yet. It's your first day. How unfortunate to be thrust into a financial maelstrom on the eve of the board meeting."

Board meeting! Mark hadn't mentioned an impending trial by fire. He squirmed and snorted.

A cloud of subtle scent wafted around Sylvia like million dollar molecules of heaven. Abigail would appreciate that. Sylvia clasped Nora's hand. "Was that your mother on the phone?"

If Nora could get through this day without throwing up, she'd be happy. "She's excited about my position here and wants all the details."

Sylvia gave a sympathetic nod of her head, her black curls bouncing just enough to seem alive but not so much as to muss her do. "Family is important but, as I know, they can be trying."

"Tell me about the beetle kill work," Nora said. Maybe she should offer them a chair instead of having them stand in the middle of her office.

Mark inserted himself into the conversation. "Sylvia's work is groundbreaking. She's using some of the science she developed—" his flabby lips formed these words with care to emphasize their import—"at the HAARP facility in Alaska."

Nora raised her eyebrows hoping she appeared impressed.

Mark seemed satisfied with her reaction. "Sylvia was a Senior Project Manager. The modeling she's doing for the Trust uses ionosphere measurements to gauge UA and UV waves and their correlation to the temperatures. She takes all this and overlays it with models of beetle kill. We have our field techs out gathering data on that." As usual, he followed up with a snicker. "When this is published, people will be begging to donate to us."

Optimistic, considering about ten people read scientific papers. "Sounds interesting," Nora said.

"Interesting? Sylvia is a scientific rock star and we've got her here." Although he wasn't actually slobbering he teetered on the verge. "And she's got a killer sense of style." His obvious hero-worship felt creepy.

"Now, Mark." Sylvia bowed her head graciously. "It's all due to Daniel Cubrero's fund raising. His family foundation donates generously."

The name didn't sound familiar to Nora but she didn't hobnob with the super-wealthy types that tended to sit on non-profit boards of directors.

Sylvia's dark eyes rested on Mark with indulgence before she addressed Nora. "It's exciting research. HARRP started as a government program. High Frequency Active Aurora Iononspheric Research Program."

Nora spied a stack of file folders under the desk. She'd love to dig into the work. "I don't know much about it."

No one seemed inclined to sit or at the least, leave her office.

Again, Sylvia showed a patient smile. "The technology is just as complicated as it sounds. Not many people can grasp the concept. Much of it is based on the early discoveries of Nikola Tesla and unfortunately, the bulk of his research was lost when he died in the forties. The program began as a study of the ionosphere to enhance surveillance and communication, mostly for military use. But where it interests the Trust and others concerned about our planet, is how the technology might be used to study the effects of climate change. The Colorado mountain pine beetle kill is one dramatic area to gather research."

"Fascinating," Nora's mind raced beyond Sylvia's words to the haystack of papers on the work surface. The documents and files seemed to split like protozoa, creating new stacks for sorting, identifying and filing.

"That's an interesting plant." Sylvia stepped around Mark to the pot. She ran a red fingernail along one wide leaf. "What is it?"

Nora had a sudden urge to slap Sylvia's hand away. "It's corn."

Sylvia eyed her with skepticism.

"Hopi corn," Nora said. "It's different than what we're used to." *And that's all I'm going to say about that.*

"And the pot designs? Are those Hopi, too?"

Nora had etched the designs into the clay. "Oh, they're just designs. Not significant."

"I don't know anything about the Hopi tribe." Boredom tinged Sylvia's words.

Such an ancient culture, so rich and intricate. And for some reason, Nora didn't want to share it with Sylvia. "They're a tiny tribe in northern Arizona in the middle of the Navajo reservation. They revere peace and natural harmony."

Sylvia stared at the corn for a moment then focused on Nora. "I know you're busy on your first day and I won't take up any more of your time. Why don't we have lunch next week?"

"That would be great."

"If you'll cut my check, I'll be on my way."

Wait. Check?

Nora didn't know what financial software Loving Earth Trust used. Where did they keep the checks? Did they have one general bank account or did each program have its own restricted account? What bank or banks? So much she didn't know, check writing was a definite no-go. "Um." She turned a desperate face to Mark, hoping he'd explain.

He met her with an expectant uplift of eyebrows.

This didn't bode well for a great working relationship. Nora braced herself. "I'm sorry, Sylvia. I need to get acquainted with several things before I spend any money. I'm not even a signatory yet."

Sylvia's full lips turned down in a slight frown. "I understand, of course. But the funding is there. I wrote a sizable check from my personal funds and Darla was supposed to have paid me last week. I hate to disparage her, especially since she's gone, but she was really falling apart lately."

Nora retreated behind professional formality. "As fiscal agent of the Trust, I'm responsible for the finances. I don't feel comfortable writing checks until I have a chance to see what's going on."

Mark frowned. "I can sign the check. Our dysfunction shouldn't be Sylvia's problem."

Flames engulfed Nora as she debated what to do. Her face burned. Should she play nice and make friends or be responsible, buck her boss and probably lose her job on the first day?

Sylvia never lost her expression of expectation. This was a woman used to getting her way.

Tick, tick, tick.

In the kitchen, which sat at the bottom of the servant's stairs at the end of the maze from Nora's office, someone's cell phone jingled, followed by the murmur of a woman's voice.

Did a new stack of papers materialize on the desk?

She shouldn't write a check. She really shouldn't.

Sweat slimed her underarms.

Tick, tick, tick.

Sylvia's foot started to tap. Those had to be incredibly expensive shoes.

Something crashed in the kitchen. A howl like the death throes of a rabbit rent the air, soaring from the kitchen, down the hall, into Nora's office, strangling her.

The sound of death.

7

Sylvia froze. Her mind vibrated with suppressed panic. The scream snaked up the stairs into the base of Sylvia's spine, slithering through her heart. Survival instincts honed in her dangerous childhood told her to run.

Nora leapt past Sylvia and Mark, sprinting through the hall and flying down the narrow servants' stairs. Was she an athlete? She acted like some kind of super hero out to save the day.

Sylvia knew better than to involve herself with others' crisis. She spent three seconds regaining her control.

Mark gave her an exasperated expression. "It's Petal. I suppose we should go see what it is this time."

Sylvia brushed past him. "I'm very busy, Mark. You can handle this."

He whined. "She works for you. I think it's best if you help her."

She instantly calculated her best options. Cooperation. "Of course."

Her beatific smile would do Mother Teresa proud. Great power and gifts had the annoying flipside of great responsibility. Someone always needed her wise counsel or her attention in some way.

Honestly, Sylvia's time would be better spent using her formidable mind solving the problem at which she alone could succeed. But a leader needed to help the little people from time to time. It kept Sylvia humble and human.

When they reached the kitchen, Nora knelt on the floor next to a puddle of gauze and bird's nest of hair. Nora patted Petal's back and cooed soothing words.

As if this nothing of an accountant could possibly give comfort.

Mark crossed his arms and sounded annoyed. "Petal, please try to pull yourself together. We can't help if you don't tell us what's wrong."

Sylvia stepped up. Coddling Petal would only encourage her drama. "Enough of this, Petal. Either tell us what upset you or stop the histrionics and let's see if we can get some work done today."

Nora appeared shocked. She probably thought they should perform a group hug and talk about their feelings. This bleeding-heart attitude, so common among the non-profit do-gooders, demonstrated why Nora slaved as a simple accountant and why Sylvia rubbed elbows with the world's elite.

Sylvia placed her hands on her hips and distanced herself from Petal's current meltdown. She hated this kitchen. It stretched twenty feet end to end and was little more than an extra-wide hallway. The sink and old-time cupboards of thick, white-painted wood ran the length of one wall. A window with a cheap aluminum frame opened above the sink. The counter top was pre-Formica, the floor spread with some kind of linoleum. It peeled away at the corners, reminding Sylvia too much of the house where she grew up.

There was no stove, a toaster oven and microwave filled the bill. Sylvia wished they'd get rid of those, too, since it seemed no one here could fix a snack without burning it. A refrigerator constantly full of moldering leftovers and forgotten lunches bookended the counter. A wooden booth sat in a nook between the front lobby and the kitchen. Sylvia had never seen anyone use it.

The door to the backyard opened along the other wall. The whole room acted as a corridor to connect Sylvia's suite with the rest of the ramshackle building. From the window above the sink she could see the parking lot and road. The window in the back door showed an open space of scruffy lawn ending at a border of pines and shrubs. It could be nice with landscaping and a gazebo, maybe a built-in fireplace and grill. But the staff at the Trust lacked vision.

Petal continued her sobbing. Nora kept treating her like a dog injured in traffic.

Mark's face glow red with anger. "Okay, enough of this," he said. "Stop wailing and tell us what's going on."

Face wet with tears and nose snotty and red, Petal slowly sat up from where she burrowed into Nora's lap. She hiccupped and drew in a shaky breath. She opened her mouth, presumably to explain the calamity, but let out another sob and dropped into Nora's lap again.

Nora patted her back, searching Mark's, then Sylvia's face for help. To be fair, Nora didn't know Petal's normal instability. But on her first day, she shouldn't interfere when she had no clue.

"Darla, Darla, Darla." Petal gasped between sobs.

Sylvia's stomach twisted. From Petal's first scream she'd felt a terrible foreboding.

Mark squatted in front of Petal, impatience written on his face. "What about Darla?"

Petal sat up again. This time she forced words. "She's dead." Petal blathered away, all her feelings and pain splattering everyone in hearing range.

What did this mean for Sylvia?

It didn't change anything. Whether Darla walked off in her Birkenstocks or whether she died, it didn't make much difference to Sylvia.

She needed to focus on Nora. Sure, she had a moment of hesitation about writing Sylvia a check. With Mark's urging—and Mark would do anything for Sylvia—Nora would be toeing the line in short order.

It had to happen immediately, though. The art dealer annoyingly demanded a down payment before she'd ship the Chihuly.

Petal's voice gained some strength, enough for Sylvia to understand. "Darla was just found in the trees by the road. They said she was shot close to the Trust and tried to make it to the highway for help."

The vision of the colorful glass vanished.

"She'd been there since Sunday night."

Sylvia stopped breathing. A flash flood of blood roared in her ears.

No. That couldn't be. Even her brain, that wonderful and extraordinary tool, ground to a near halt.

That night. The night Sylvia found the glass. The night Darla threatened her.

"She was shot in the back. Who would want to shoot Darla?" Petal wailed again.

Sylvia's chest crushed with the weight of realization. Shot outside the Trust on Sunday night.

One shot fired out the door into the darkness last Sunday night.

8

Nora stood at her office window, heart pounding and her breath catching in her chest. She gently rubbed a smooth corn leaf between her thumb and forefinger. There was something definitely wonky about this place. Murder. *Murder!*

She squatted down and scratched Abbey behind the ears, letting his warmth calm her. Petal's pain had seeped through Nora's clothes and into her skin. Worse yet were Mark's and Sylvia's reactions to the news that someone they worked with had been shot. They hadn't seemed at all concerned and actually more annoyed that Petal disrupted the quiet morning.

"What sort of place is this?"

Abbey didn't answer her. He lay with his eyes half closed, wallowing in the attention.

The piles of paper and chaos of the office swamped her. "We ought to book it out of here."

Abbey rested his head on his paws.

"I'm not up for more murder."

He closed his eyes and let out a deep sigh of contentment.

"On the other hand, since you're the only one I talk to these days, maybe I ought to hang around for human contact."

He wasn't going to give her any advice; that much was plain.

A light knock on her door jamb startled her.

Fay stood in the doorway, her eyes wide in her round face. Her voice crackled softly. "So what happened? I heard Petal say Darla was killed."

Nora leaned back on her work surface. "I don't know."

Another head appeared over Fay's shoulder. The hairy guy working on air quality. Thomas. Score one for Nora remembering his name. "Did you get any details?"

Fay turned to him with her creaky voice. "I'll bet it was Mark."

Thomas shook his head. "Naw. He hired her. I think he liked her because he could control her."

Fay shook her head. "I can't believe she's dead. And that she was *shot.*"

Thomas nodded. "Yeah. Right here." He scrutinized Nora's office and shuddered as if Darla had been shot in the room.

"Maybe it was Sylvia. She hated Darla. She hates everyone." Fay nodded at Thomas for confirmation.

"Freaky." Without any warning, they both wandered away.

Freaky, indeed.

Nora surveyed the paper orgy strewn across the work space. *A journey of a thousand miles begins with... filing.* She shuffled the pages into unruly stacks.

Interspersed among the spreadsheets, invoices and financial statements, Nora came across pages from a yellow legal pad. Like a child's scribbling on a blackboard as punishment, each page was filled with one line over and over. One page repeated, "I am smart." on all twenty-eight lines. Another said, "I will succeed." "I am beautiful." "I can do it." "I am rich." Nora's throat constricted with sympathy when she found the last one: "They DO like me." Over and over.

Nora picked up the picture of Darla and studied it. If Darla were thin or fat, cheerful or dour, the outwear concealed it all. One thing Nora knew for sure: Darla was not happy.

Nora replaced the photo and trudged along with the paperwork.

Well past lunch time, Mark stuck his head in her office. "Wow. You've made some headway." Snort. "Darla wasn't very organized."

He spoke casually, as if Darla—someone he'd worked with every day —hadn't just been found dead on a mountain. What a jerk.

Nora had slogged through much of the accounting fall-out on the desk. The documents consisted mostly of payroll spreadsheets and copies of paychecks, invoices—both paid and pending financial reports, and Post-it notes.

She'd found the reason for all the scribbled pages. Several self-help books occupied the closet shelf and a dog-eared self-esteem manual declared success through written affirmations. Darla was struggling to change.

Nora picked up a pile of handwritten accounting worksheets "I think Darla tracked grants and restricted donations by hand and allocated them monthly, then backed the totals out of the general fund."

He blanked.

"You can do it this way but it's a lot of work and there is a lag so that if checks were written early in the month, the actual fund allocation won't show up for a few weeks in the project budget."

He obviously had no idea what she was talking about. That gave her leeway to set up her own, more efficient system. "How's Petal?"

He waved his hand. "She's overly dramatic. I'm sorry you had to see one of her episodes on your first day."

Her friend and coworker was murdered. Nora knew what it felt like when someone you love is murdered. You can't get overly dramatic about that.

Mark's face reddened. He must have read Nora's expression. "It's terrible, of course. Unexpected and upsetting."

He stayed at the office door gazing at Nora. Not awkward at all.

To fill the void, Nora chatted. "I'll check to make sure all these invoices are entered and get them filed. I'll see about bank balances and check A/P."

Abruptly, he said, "Write Sylvia's check but everything else can wait until next week." Snort.

"Shouldn't she submit a reimbursement request and receipts?"

Mark waved that away. "She's a star scientist not an accounting clerk. She shouldn't waste her time with this trivia."

"The auditors..."

"Do it," he interrupted, and then seemed to catch himself. "Please."

She didn't commit. "I'm hoping to get this bookkeeping stuff out of the way by the end of the week so I can settle in and work on the funds and project worksheets and reports. I need to figure out how all this is organized."

Mark's eyebrows drew down and he snuffled, an even more nervous sound than his usual laugh. "That will come. But right now you need to pull some financials together for tomorrow's board meeting."

A mace, complete with spiked ball, swung straight from his hand with no wind up. It smacked into the side of her head. "A board meeting *tomorrow*?"

"Don't worry. I've got the financials Darla submitted two weeks ago for the board preview. You can just add a few expenses and a little income and they'll be good to go. I emailed them to you." His assurance felt as slimy as his dismissal of Darla's murder.

"It won't be accurate."

"No one expects them to be penny perfect. They only want an update from what they had previously. Just get through tomorrow and you'll have time to study everything in depth."

She doubted the board wanted or needed sketchy information. She didn't answer.

His face reddened as he became defensive. "We can't cancel the meeting. Daniel Cubrero fit it into his schedule. Bryson Bradshaw is over the Atlantic now and a few others won't want to cancel their flights and reschedule. These meetings are hell to arrange."

When she still didn't answer he said, "Do your best. But remember, we don't want to upset the board needlessly." He spun around and scurried away before she could respond.

She addressed Abbey. "Not a good situation." The Trust was an accounting nightmare. If someone didn't set it right, and soon, they wouldn't be able to continue to repair trails and maintain crucial habitats. The beetle kill research would take a hit.

Nora's guilt over almost spraying uranium-tainted water on the sacred peaks in Flagstaff drove her on a strange apologetic quest. She didn't make snow as she'd set out to do and the slopes were protected now, but she still felt she had a debt to pay. Maybe accounting wouldn't end global warming or save the whales, but straightening up this office could be her contribution.

Sour stew boiled in Nora's gut. How would she pull together financials to present to a board of directors when she had no notion of the organization?

9

The afternoon sun sent an uncertain ray through her window and Abbey lay in its weak beam in the middle of the room. Someone had overcooked popcorn in the microwave and the smell added to Nora's nausea.

An electronic beep sounded, startling Nora. A tinny voice invaded the room. "Nora?"

An old-school interoffice page. Must be coming from a phone. Nora raised her voice. "Hi. I'm here. Just let me find the phone." Nora pushed papers aside and finally found a beige Titanic of technology. She picked up the receiver. "Okay. I've got it."

"This is Sylvia. You haven't had a chance to tour my office suite. Why not you come down? I'm at a good break point."

Nothing like a summons from the queen. "Sure."

"I'm sending Petal to get you."

The queen and even a lady in waiting—rather, a Rasta-girl-in-waiting. A rustle caused Nora to turn to the door. Petal stood like a rag doll, all floppy and boneless, her eyes red-rimmed. Apparently, Sylvia had little doubt Nora would accept the command. "Here she is." Nora tried to sound pleased as she spoke to the intercom.

Sylvia must have already hung up.

"How are you?" Nora asked.

Petal shrugged. "Darla was my friend." Her voice sounded like a drop of water on a still lake.

"I'm sorry. Do you think you should go home?"

Petal shook her head, sending her dreads into a frantic dance. "Sylvia has work for me to do."

Nora couldn't say what she wanted to say, which was, "*Screw Sylvia.*" Could this really be her first few hours of her first day at the first shot of a job in a year?

"Well, let's go see the office, then."

Petal led the way down the narrow stairs through the kitchen. Someone had propped the back door open and a breeze blew away the scorched popcorn odor. Past the door, a few feet beyond the kitchen and an open storage area, Petal stopped in front of a closed door. She opened it and stepped back.

Nora hesitated before entering. The room was by far the largest in the building. It accommodated what appeared to be an antique banquet table in the center of the space, scattered with maps.

"Welcome!" Sylvia swept from behind a desk, graceful as a supermodel in her high heels. "What do you think?" She stepped back and displayed her kingdom as if she were a hostess at the White House.

"Impressive," Nora said, not lying.

Sylvia waved that away. "The Trust was too cheap to give me a separate office but I've adjusted to the constraints." She led Nora from the door, around the center table to the far side of the room.

The area Sylvia chose as her personal office occupied a whole corner. Her massive cherry wood desk nestled in the space created from two walls of the suite and one wall pieced together with file cabinets.

"I spent quite some time scrounging in antiques stores to find this bookcase." She indicated an ornate wood bookshelf occupying the wall behind her desk. A Tiffany lamp on her desk cast a glow to reflect off the polished wood furniture. The bookshelf held her framed diplomas, a bronze of a nude, and volumes of expensive-looking hardcover books.

"But this is my real treasure." She swept her arm in front of her to showcase the antique dining table taking up the center of the room. Maps sprawled across the table. "I'm quite proud of that table. It was an amazing deal I found at a shop in Aspen. Darla questioned the expense and said a fifty dollar table from Costco would work just as well, but Mark backed me up."

Petal slinked away to another corner and folded herself into a chair. She rolled it close to a desk more like the humble discount office store kind the rest of the Trust staffers used. A small lamp sat on her desk, draped in a pink scarf. She hunched over a keyboard and began to type.

The addition felt tacked-on, without the charm of the turn-of-the-century farmhouse. Nora pointed to a stack of computer processing units. These weren't typical CPU towers to power a regular PC. Next to the tower stood a giant, high-tech scanner, almost as large as the antique table. "What is all this for?"

Sylvia seemed pleased to be asked. "The Cubrero Family Foundation paid for sophisticated modeling software and sufficient power to run it. We needed to have the tools so I could create the maps." Sylvia indicated the scanner. "This machine prints with the necessary detail and size."

Nora studied the 3X4 foot color maps tacked on the walls.

Sylvia spoke as though conducting a grade school field trip. "Mountain pine beetle is infecting the forests at a rate ten times any previous infestation. It's at about three point two million acres in Colorado and Wyoming alone. Common wisdom says the large beetle population is the result of climate change. But I'm suspecting the beetle is actually altering local weather patterns and air quality. There's a big difference between the effect of a living forest and a dead one on the environment. I'm studying the age old question: what comes first, the chicken or the egg." She laughed at her own cleverness

Nora stepped to the table and bent to the maps.

"You know," Sylvia explained. "Is the climate driving the beetles or are the beetles driving the climate?"

Tappity-tap, tap, tap. Petal worked away.

Nora lifted the corner of one of the maps and leaned on the table to scrutinize it.

Sylvia slid the map from Nora and thrust a finger on it. "You see?

These overlay colors and shading indicate not only temperature and cloud cover but times and trends, followed by these stills." She pulled out another map from underneath and spread it on top of the first. "These indicate the spread of beetle kill. When I combine them in an animated digital process, I can illustrate the actual correlation between climatic factors and beetle spread."

"That's amazing. And you created this technology?"

Sylvia laughed. "Oh, not all of it. I used some of what I developed with my team at HAARP facility in Alaska."

"Isn't HAARP something like an array of towers that shoot energy into the atmosphere? People think it's some sort of weather altering thing or mind control or doomsday weapon?"

Sylvia laughed. "There are a hundred and eighty towers and they send out a ping but the energy used is much less than any sun burst. What happens is that the towers send a billion watts of energy into the atmosphere. That's about a hundred times a thunderbolt. It excites the ionosphere and creates a plume and then bounces back to the surface."

"What is the point of the research?"

Petal quit typing. She sat still as if listening.

"What does it matter? All major scientific breakthroughs have come about with research for pure knowledge sake. We don't know what we'll discover that will create real good. For instance, there is hope that some of the HAARP technology will actually facilitate ozone repair."

"You get information from HAARP for the beetle kill research?"

"Oh no. I've developed a tower using similar HAARP technologies. It's an advance on the work of Nikola Tesla. I've developed the technology to use only one small installation on Mount Evans, not far from here."

Oh. Where Nora met Petal.

Petal started tapping on the keyboard again.

"It's one of Colorado's tallest peaks. The highest electron density is on tall mountains because the negative charge is reaching for the positive charge in the atmosphere. My tower sends extremely low frequency waves, ELF, and the waves that bounce back create the raw data I use in the modeling software I created."

Didn't she say earlier she'd bought the software with donor funds? Maybe she worked with Al Gore when he invented the Internet, too.

"So it's a matter of tweaking the tower's angle of refraction to gather the matrices to compile the complicated 3D images."

Nora pulled another map from the bottom of the pile and slid it on top. A red Sharpie circle marked a map of South America. "Are you researching Ecuador?"

Sylvia shoved another map over the South America one. "No. Of course not."

Petal typed away, not appearing to pay any attention to their conversation.

Sylvia eyed Petal and placed a hand on Nora's arm. "It's a lovely fall day. Let me show you the friendship garden. A garden club donates their time to give us a place for reflection by the creek."

They walked through the kitchen, out the back door and into the yard. The brown grass crunched underfoot. "How are you settling in?"

My office looks like a volcano of paper erupted in it. The previous Finance Director was murdered. The star scientist is a prima donna. The Executive Director is a creepy loser from high school. The sanest person here is a dread-lock-wearing woman of indeterminate age.

"As well as can be expected for a first day," Nora said.

"That's good." Again, no mention of Darla. Sylvia stopped well short of the promised garden. "I'll need that check today."

Now we get to the point of the welcome tour.

"I won't be able to do that until next week." Firm. Competent. No nonsense. And if she kept her jaw clenched and hands clasped behind her back, Sylvia wouldn't notice how shaky she felt.

Sylvia's nostrils flared. "I don't need the entire amount right away. Just fifty thousand."

Just? Nora squinted into the sun. The soft breeze sending the scent of pine didn't make her feel as happy as it usually did. "The problem is I don't know if we have fifty thousand pennies, let alone fifty thousand dollars."

"My work is funded through the entire year."

Sure, make me feel unreasonable.

A voice traveled from the side of the house. "Yoo hoo!"

As if she heard the scream of an incoming bomb, Nora had the urge to dive for cover in the shrubs next to the house.

Sylvia gazed past Nora's head.

Nora held her breath and turned. "Mother. What are you doing here?"

Other people's mothers provided stability and support and the familiar comfort of home. Not so much with Abigail. When she dropped in unexpectedly, it usually meant drama. Lots of it.

Abigail waltzed toward them. A twelve hour drive from Flagstaff would mean she left at two in the morning, and yet, here she stood, after hours of being folded into her car, as fresh as if she'd just returned from a fund-raising luncheon. Her slacks weren't even wrinkled.

She held out her arms for a dramatic embrace. "Nora! How is your first day?"

Nora didn't fall into the maternal hug. "I'm kind of busy, as you can imagine."

Abigail dropped her arms. "It's your first day, dear. You've barely started."

Says the woman who has never worked. "How did you even find this place?"

Abigail held up a phone. "This is my new toy. Isn't it fantastic? It has GPS and the Google and weather. It even has apps for shopping."

"Nice." Nora wanted to program the phone to send Abigail back to Flagstaff.

Abigail turned to Sylvia and extended her hand. What a pair of matching fabulousness they were. "I'm Abigail, Nora's mother."

Sylvia placed her manicured hand in Abigail's. "Sylvia LaFever. I'm a scientist here."

Abigail nodded in appreciation. "A scientist. How lovely. Do you live here in Boulder?"

Sylvia hesitated. "Temporarily."

"No denying Boulder is charming in its unique way. But a woman of your obvious sophistication must find the whole casual, hippie atmosphere somewhat provincial."

Pretentious much, Abigail?

Sylvia preened, obviously enjoying Abigail's keen perception. "I'm working hard for the Trust so I don't have time to miss the luxuries lacking here. But when I wrap this up, I'll be on a fast plane to Europe."

Abigail latched on to the conversation. She might disparage Boulder's outdoorsy attitude, but it beat the glamour of Abigail's life in the mountain cabin outside Flagstaff. "What's your favorite city?"

Nora let them bond over memories of escargot and wineries in the French countryside. Compared to Sylvia's suit practically cut from dollar bills, anyone might appear dumpy. But Abigail glittered like a gold brick, holding her own on the magnificence scale.

Nora needed to get back to her office. She'd scan the documents Mark said he'd emailed her. Then she'd boot up the Trust software and see what those financials revealed.

Now she had a plan, standing here in the afternoon sunshine made her skin itch. She started to back away from the delightful duo. Her feet crunched on the fall-withered grass. She stopped.

She blinked.

No. I don't see anything.

The flash of blue to the side of the farm house stole Nora's breath.

No. Not now. Not ever.

She had left Flagstaff. Fled the mountain with its real or imagined spirits. They wouldn't follow her here. But he had followed her, at least to Mount Evans, hadn't he? Unless she was crazy. And of course, Nora was crazy. Still, she was an ignorant white woman lacking in any spiritual quality that might appeal to a kachina.

"What is it you and Nora were talking about?" Abigail didn't seem to mind prying into Trust business.

Sylvia responded as if it were a simple request. "I need her to cut me a check."

I can hear you, Nora wanted to say.

"Good luck with that," Abigail said and they both laughed. They'd only known each other for a few minutes and already worked in tandem to torque off Nora. "She can be so tight-fisted and serious."

If by tight-fisted you mean set up a generous budget that doesn't include world cruises every six months, then yes, I'm a tightwad.

Sylvia seemed quite taken with Abigail. "I'm glad to know it's not just me."

"Oh heavens, no. She's been like this since she was a toddler. When she was six she begged me to get her a cash register. Not a toy, mind you. She settled for an adding machine. She spent days writing figures in columns and adding them up. It was cute, then."

Nora forced herself to stare at the side of the house where she'd imagined the kachina. Maybe a staffer was taking a smoke break and wore a blue shirt. Of course there was no kachina. Kachinas didn't exist.

"At least she's had lots of practice," Sylvia said. More of their instant-bestie twittering.

"We should have lunch soon," Abigail said.

Sylvia headed back to the house. "It's been delightful meeting you."

Nora faced her mother with a stern expression, folding her arms.

Abigail raised her eyebrows. "What? I just stopped by to get the key to your apartment. I'll go there and wait for you. I know you couldn't possibly take time from your first day to spend with your mother."

Nora dug in her jeans for her keys and started to pull off the apartment key. "How long are you staying?"

Abigail shrugged. "That depends, dear."

A hard fist formed in Nora's chest. She half-considered refusing to give her key to Abigail and insisting she turn the car around and head home.

She saw it again. The blue. It appeared, then disappeared. Damn it.

Abigail plucked the key from Nora's limp hand. "You don't look well, Nora. You need to take better care of yourself."

Nora watched as Abigail strode across the brown grass. Just as Abigail disappeared along the path to the parking lot, the kachina stepped around the side of the house, heading toward Nora.

Nope. I don't see you. You don't exist.

Nora fought the wave of panic cresting behind her eyes. She must hang on to reality. Besides, if she blinked the kachina would disappear.

So blink.

Damn! When she opened her eyes the vision remained. But the kachina, with his plug mouth and feathers, clutching the hatchet and wearing a bright blue sash, wasn't advancing on her. Instead, a slightly built Native American closed the last few feet to stand in front of her.

He wore a plaid shirt and jeans jacket. His jet black hair combed neatly and cut short, he could be a regular guy in a regular yard.

"Hi, Nora."

Part of her wanted to throw her arms around his neck and hug him as an old friend. Part of her wanted to turn tail and run. She pushed back the silly fear. "Benny!"

His serious face broke into a slight grin. For him, that was like bursting into song. "You are well."

She hugged him. He was shorter than Nora and small-framed, but his answering hug felt strong. "What are you doing here?" she asked.

He stepped back and tilted his head to scrutinize the huge farm house. For as long as he studied it, he might have been memorizing the architecture.

Nora waited out his sloth pace. Impatience jangled her nerves.

It was Benny's faith and loyalty to his friends that had saved Nora's life in Flagstaff. She'd been forced to his home on the Hopi rez and he'd given her refuge and wisdom, both at the speed of melting snow.

"Do you like it here?" He asked by way of response.

Good question. She liked being employed. Not only was she about to start sharing Alpo with Abbey, her isolation was grinding her to a nub of insecurity and craziness. Hadn't she been seeing the kachina and those damned blue flashes?

Blue flashes and now Benny.

His steady gaze seemed to read her doubts.

"I think I'm going to like it fine. Loving Earth Trust does some great environmental work."

He nodded but didn't act convinced. "What sort of work will you do?"

Why did he get to ask all the questions? He showed up out of the blue—literally. "What brings you from Hopiland to Boulder?"

"You." He said it simply.

Not weird at all. A little Hopi farmer, aged anywhere from thirty to fifty, who hated to leave the Mesas and his corn, traveling eight hundred miles to see someone he didn't know all that well was perfectly normal.

This was going to be trouble.

"How did you find me?" She dreaded the answer.

His eyes twinkled with humor. "It wasn't hard."

Whew. She feared he'd say something far worse—.

"Nakwaiyamtewa told me."

—like that.

She swiveled on her heels and ran to the back door of the house.

10

Nora pulled into the well-lit parking lot of her apartment complex long after sunset. She located a spot between a beat-up Honda and a rusted pickup.

The complex had the ambience of a dormitory. Several buildings snugged together in a maze of two-story units with worn shingle siding. A wrought-iron railing lined a balcony that ran along the second story with the apartments' front doors opening onto the concrete walkway. Each apartment had a deck on back and many held bikes and cheap grills. Cars and motorcycles drove in and out at all hours.

Two twenty-something girls with heavy backpacks carried giant Jamba Juice cups as they chatted on their way to a first floor unit. A young man whizzed behind them on a bike. He called to the girls and they hollered back.

Nora sat in her Jeep staring up at the porch light in front of her apartment. The Stress-O-Meter didn't go high enough to measure her first day of work and now she must face Abigail and try to be pleasant.

Fall's night time temperatures brought enough chill Nora's fingers and cheeks tingled as she clumped up the metal outside steps to the second floor. Abbey followed acting as if this were any ordinary trip home and not one sending them into a wasps' nest.

"With any luck, Abigail will be tucked into the spare bed." Abbey gazed at her but, as usual, didn't answer.

Earlier, the staffers of the Trust checked out one by one, Nora stayed glued to her computer screen, studying, searching, printing documents and trying to understand the different projects and their fund details. Each discovery made Nora's stomach churn more until it felt like a bucket of acid.

The third-quarter financials Mark sent her bore little resemblance to the numbers on her computer. The climate-modeling program headed by Sylvia LaFever showed the largest discrepancy. Its deficit tilted the entire organization into red.

No wonder Mark wanted Nora to present the financials he sent, since they showed a much rosier view of the Trust. But Nora couldn't lie. And when she told the board the truth, Mark would fire he.

She'd balanced up as much as possible, printed and collated the copies for the board, and said good bye to her office. Nora already calculated the salary she'd receive for just one day—and it would barely buy a bag of dog food.

She sent a fervid prayer to the universe that Abigail would not be in one of her nitpicky moods. Or one of her nagging moods.

Or, just please don't let her harp on me about what I wore today, and what food is in the apartment, my furniture, housecleaning ability, and just for tonight, let us not discuss her budget and why, as trustee of her accounts, I refuse to open up the checkbook and let her bleed it dry.

The board meeting started at the Bolderado Hotel at eight in the morning. She must present herself as professional and competent and a lover of the environment. Normally, none of this would be a stretch. Tonight, after a fourteen hour day, it all seemed impossible.

She tiptoed the last few feet to her doorstep. Abbey waited behind her. With a fortifying breath she turned the knob and stepped into the overheated apartment.

Abigail stood in the middle of the living room, fully visible from the front door. She held her cell phone to her ear. She'd changed into black yoga pants and stylish tunic. Far from being ready for bed, her short blonde bob and makeup looked good enough for an evening out. "Oh, never mind. She just walked in." She punched the screen and set the phone down. "Where have you been?"

Like everything in the complex, the apartment was nothing more than a glorified dorm room. Just two bedrooms in what served mainly as student housing for the University of Colorado, it suited her purposes. The main room consisted of a galley kitchen separated from the dining space by a counter bar. The living room continued about fifteen feet from the dining area and ended with a sliding door. The balcony had an excellent view of Devil's Thumb hitching its way off the Flatirons. The whole unit weighed in at less than 700 square feet. A kingdom fit for Nora's command.

The weekend parties and late-night noise reassured Nora. After the frightening summer on the isolated mountain in northern Arizona, she liked knowing other people surrounded her. Though furnished mostly from Ikea, everything in the apartment was new.

"Hi, Abigail." Nora hung her bag and coat on hooks she'd installed next to the front door. She stepped into the kitchen and opened the cabinet under the sink and scooped out dog food.

Wow. You know you're hungry when the smell of dog food makes your stomach growl. She poured it into Abbey's dish, sandwiched between the dishwasher on one side and a micro-pantry on the other.

Abigail watched her. "If you had a phone like mine I could have texted you. Or even sent you a picture. Why do you have that antique?"

"I like my phone." Nora felt no need for a smart phone to keep her plugged in.

"You're young and should be hip. It isn't right to have that rusty technology."

New topic. "Was that Charlie on the phone?" Charlie was one of Nora's best friends. That he was also her mother's most recent husband disturbed and delighted her in equal measure

"Yes. He was worried about you."

Good. Keep Abigail off the Nora Improvement tack. "Why didn't Charlie come with you? Are you fighting again?"

Abigail's face hardened. "Don't try to change the subject. Do you really think it's wise to stay out late on your first day of work?"

"Nine o'clock isn't late."

"Those circles under your eyes show you're exhausted."

Abbey crunched happily on his food.

Nora always felt like her apartment offered sanctuary. With Abigail here, it felt crowded. Although Nora liked the low, flat sofa in bright red and the contrasting deep green chair, Abigail would hate the bright colors and think them garish. She might approve of the no nonsense coffee table and TV stand. A smallish flat screen monitor faced the sofa.

It all reflected Nora's effort at a fresh start. With this job, the transition into the New and Improved Nora should be complete. Why then, did she still feel like the old, insecure, scared woman who left Flagstaff a year ago?

She'd be doing fine and then at random moments, like now, the memories would crash in on her. Nora's drive to save her marriage and business had led her to push for man-made snow on peaks sacred to the Hopi tribe. By the time she'd discovered the extent of the harm she'd bring to her mountain, it was too late. In the end, she'd managed to save the mountain but she held herself responsible for the death of her unfaithful husband, Scott, and that of Heather, a vibrant and passionate young girl.

Abigail stared at Nora as if expecting an answer. Oh yeah, work. "It's okay."

Abigail frowned. "That's all you have to say?"

Nora opened the refrigerator with the insane hope food had materialized since morning. "I'm hungry."

Abigail pursed her lips. "There's not much we can do about that. This pantry is nearly empty. Not even a can of soup."

"I think there's cereal."

Abigail frowned. "No milk."

Nora opened a cupboard and pulled out a box full of creamers in tiny plastic tubs. It was her one indulgence on camping and backpacking trips. "Voilá!" She picked up the cereal box and creamers.

"Don't neglect the pantry of your life and leave it barren as a looted grocery store."

Nora stated at Abigail. What?

Abigail stopped as if reviewing what she'd said. She pulled a small notebook from the pocket of her tunic and slid out a matching miniature pen. She scribbled on the pad and caught Nora's scrutiny. "I'm taking an online poetry class."

Nora congratulated herself on keeping a straight face.

Abigail dropped the notebook and pen back into her pocket and found a bowl and spoon and they retreated around the counter bar to the small dining room table. It consumed slightly more space than a card table but was big enough to hold a basket for Nora's mail and bills. Bright, Mexican woven placemats covered most of the pine top.

After setting the dishes on the table, Abigail pointed to the sliding glass door that opened onto the tiny deck. "What is with the plants?"

Nora tried not to wince. "Nothing. I like green things. The photosynthesis purifies the air."

Abigail raised an eyebrow in skepticism. "Houseplants are all well and good, but this goes beyond a little color."

Abigail was right, of course. Most people didn't have a dozen big pots of bushy plants in their living room. Like the smaller version Nora had dragged to work, these corn plants grew in terra cotta pots decorated with Hopi designs. Six of the largest plants lined the glass slider, leaving space for one person to slip through the door to the balcony. Smaller pots formed another row inching into the living room. Nora shrugged, a response more appropriate to a teenager being asked why she didn't turn in her homework.

"They have to do with the Hopi thing, don't they?" Abigail asked.

"Why would you say that?"

Abigail's hands rested on her hips. "Because I saw Benny give you a bunch of seeds when you left Flagstaff and ask you to plant them to help him out."

Busted. "Okay. Yes. They are Hopi corn. But I think they're pretty and Abbey and I like the outdoor feel." Except maybe growing the plants created a connection with more than nature. Maybe *that's* why Benny showed up at the Trust. That was a ridiculous notion, of course.

Here came that slow drip of guilt down the back of her throat. In all probability, Benny had saved her life in Flagstaff and now she repaid him by running from him. She'd buried herself in work trying to forget all about him. If he was smart, he'd give up on her and head home. Maybe he was already on his way. She hoped he understood why she couldn't see him.

Heck, why would he? She didn't understand it herself.

Abigail lowered herself to a chair opposite Nora. Abbey retreated to his bed tucked between the corn plants.

Nora peeled the tops from the little creamers and lined them up on the table. "How are you, Abigail?"

"Tell me what's going on with you. You aren't yourself and you've taken this job, which is obviously beneath you."

Abigail normally loved talking about herself why wasn't she jumping at the chance?

"I had a panic attack." Whoa. That popped out of nowhere.

"What do you mean?" Abigail opened a creamer.

Nora dumped the little cream buckets over her cereal. "Never mind. It's no big deal."

"While you were in the mountains?" Abigail sounded on the verge of an attack herself.

Nora shoveled Cheerios into her mouth. Stupid to bring it up.

"You could have been hurt. Why do you insist on these dangerous sports?"

Nora swallowed. "Abbey and I love to hike."

Abbey raised his head and flopped his tail against the floor.

Abigail leaned in, her eyes sharp. "What triggered it?"

The kachina sightings were like drug flashbacks from the worst time in her life, and she didn't want to talk about it. But Abigail pulled the confession from her as if she were five years old again and had picked all the tulips in the garden. "I keep seeing a flash of blue, like I did in Flagstaff during all that snow-making business. Then I thought I saw the kachina and all of it came flooding back. I thought of Scott and then—" her throat closed and she had to wait a beat to let it clear—"Heather. Then I sort of shut down."

It was easier to keep things to herself in phone conversations than when her mother sat in front of her.

Abigail sat back, a frown of concentration on her face.

Nora kept eating. When she swallowed, she felt a little more control.

"Have you had a panic attack before?" Abigail asked.

Nora shook her head.

"My friend, Charlotte—you know, she and her husband used to go on cruises with Beryl and me? But her husband, what a bore. He smoked these awful cigars and the smoke always drifted to our balcony. Surprising how even the sea air didn't—."

"Mother!"

Abigail startled. "Oh, well. Charlotte had these panic attacks. Not that anything terrible ever happened. She had a weak disposition—."

Nora raised her eyebrows in warning.

Abigail huffed. "Anyhoo, she said that once you have one attack, you're prone to have more. It's like one episode introduces the behavior to your brain and it knows it can do it again."

"Great."

Abigail picked up the cereal box and poured more in Nora's bowl. She started peeling tops off creamers. "You need to do something about it."

Nora peeled a few creamers. "I'm taking Tae Kwan Do classes."

Abigail started pouring the creamers on the cereal. "What for?"

Nora shoveled in a bite and talked around it. "Self-confidence."

Abigail studied Nora. "You're spending too much time alone. You should get in touch with Cole Huntsman. You two would make a great couple."

Nora choked on Cheerios. Why would Abigail mention him? Nora hadn't seen him in a year, if she didn't count ill-advised day dreams and a fantasy or two. Cole definitely did not belong in her life now. Maybe never. "I have Abbey."

"Solitude is fine. I know I'm steeped in it on that crazy mountain. But you need people to talk to, dear."

"Is that why you're here? Too much solitude? What's up with Charlie, anyway?"

Abigail's eyes widened and she tightened her lips.

Nora sat up straight. "What's wrong?"

"Nothing."

Nora leaned forward. "Tell me."

Abigail studied her for a moment, her eyes teared up. "I'm leaving Charlie."

Smack her in the head with a two-by-four. "What? Why?"

"He's having an affair."

11

Nora dropped her spoon into her bowl with a clink.

Kachinas dancing on mountaintops made more sense than Charlie having an affair. "But he *adores* you."

"Apparently, he adores someone else more."

"You need to explain..."

A soft tap at the front door made them both turn. Abbey let out a woof. Nora pushed back from the table and started for the door. "This conversation is not over."

"You aren't going to open that without seeing who's out there?"

Nora shook her head and reached for the knob. "It's a big apartment complex, no one is going to stand out there and gun us down."

She pulled the door open to a shivering Petal, wrapped in various layers of knit and gauze.

Petal? At her front door? Why? How did she even know where Nora lived? Weird ringed this girl like a wobbly Hoola Hoop.

Nora pulled her inside. "Come in. It's cold out there."

Petal huddled by the front door. Abbey sniffed her hand, accepted the distracted pat and retreated to his bed. He plopped down with a grunt.

While Nora waited for the strangeness of Petal to explain itself, she carried on with regular old politeness. "Abigail, this is Petal, a coworker. Petal, this is my mother."

Abigail hurried over. "Petal, how nice to meet you."

Petal's eyes showed panic. "I'm sorry. I didn't know you'd have company."

Abigail tried to draw her into the living room. "Nonsense. Come in and sit down."

There goes any chance of getting the Charlie story from Abigail tonight. Nora had a big meeting tomorrow, and couldn't stay up late. She'd never outlast whatever avoidance plan Abigail cooked up.

Petal allowed herself to be seated on the couch, still wrapped in all of her layers. "Can we get you some coffee? Or a beer? It's all Nora has in the house or I'd offer you something to eat."

Petal shook her head. "I just came over to, you know, see how you are and to talk or whatever."

Doesn't anyone think about sleep?

Abigail retreated to the kitchen and made coffee.

Petal curled up in one corner of the couch. She pulled off her Chacos and slipped her feet underneath her.

Nora sat beside her. "What's going on?" *And why am I the one you want to talk to, at my house, at night, when I want to get rested for a big day, and not play hostess?*

Petal drew her fingers inside the sleeves of her sweater. "I miss Darla so much." Her voice was little more than a squeak.

Abigail stepped around the counter from the kitchen. The coffee maker hummed behind her. "Was Darla your dog? I've had dogs before and losing them can tear your heart in two. I had an adorable Bischon named Fluffer—"

"Mother." Nora slammed the brakes on that run away train. "Darla was the Financial Director before me."

"Oh." There was a moment of silence Abigail probably couldn't stand. "People move on, dear. I'm sure she saw career advancement and is in a better place. I suppose the Trust is a temporary stop for anyone with any ambition. There doesn't seem to be a lot of growth potential."

Petal sniffed and rubbed her sleeve across her nose.

Nora kneaded the growing pain in her temple. "Darla was found shot to death. Is the coffee done?"

Abigail made a choking sound and a beat of silence followed. "Oh, my. I'm sorry, dear. There's nothing more painful than losing a loved one. I, myself, have buried three husbands."

Nora glared at her. "The coffee, Mother."

"Of course." Abigail retreated to the kitchen.

"Did you and Darla spend a lot of time together?" Nora asked.

Petal nodded while tears dribbled out the sides of her eyes. "We were roommates. I can't be in our space today. I see Darla everywhere."

Nora steeled herself from feeling Petal's pain. She slid an arm around Petal, smelling the wet wool of her wraps and let her cry. "I'm sorry."

Abigail returned with a coffee mug. Petal's hands were still mittened inside her sweater. Abigail lifted one hand and pressed the mug into it until Petal brought the other hand up and clamped the mug between them. "Here, dear. Drink this. It will warm you up."

Abigail sat on the other side of Petal. She seemed oblivious that her turquoise and orange print tunic clashed with the red fabric of the couch.

Petal dropped her head onto Abigail's shoulder. "Darla was special. She invited me in when I didn't have anywhere to go. She was friends with everyone, even Fay, who can be a terrible gossip. She was even nice to Mark when he was so mean to her."

Abigail patted Petal's back. "Let it out, dear. 'Grief is a bucket of pig slop to be splashed across the mire of life.'" Abigail slipped her notebook from her pocket and jotted in it.

Petal's description of Darla didn't match up with Fay's opinion of a weird accountant. "How was Mark mean to Darla?"

Petal hiccuped. "He forced her to make up reports for the board. Like he's tried to do with you. But you aren't afraid of him like Darla was. She did what he asked but she hated it. She wanted to quit and was going to. And then she died."

This sounded fishy. "How do you know Mark wanted me to falsify reports to the board?"

Petal dropped her head. "I'm sorry, Nora. I miss Darla."

"You said that."

Abigail flashed her that I-will-paddle-you–if-you-don't-shape-up expression she'd perfected when Nora was little. "Nora! Quit badgering Petal."

Petal set her mug on the coffee table. She stared at the corn plants and maybe through the plate glass door into the darkness. "No, that's all right. I didn't mean to spy, really. I used to hang out in Darla's office. She's got all those windows and it's warm. Darla said I could be there anytime I wanted."

Nora didn't mind people in her office but she'd like to know about it.

"The day she died I didn't know what to do or where to go. So I went to your office while you were in the bathroom. I hid in the coat closet. I heard Mark tell you to make good report."

This girl was a strange ranger. "Why would you hide in the coat closet?"

Petal curled into an even tighter ball. "I used to hide there from Sylvia."

"You hid from your boss in a coat closet?" Nora asked.

Abigail nodded, making the connection. "Sylvia is your boss. She has a wonderful sense of style and smells so nice."

Petal shrank into herself. "Yes. But when she's mad she yells at me and throws things. Sometimes I can't take it and then I hide in Darla's office. I mean, your office."

Abigail collected her and held her close. "You poor thing. You should tell the Executive Director."

Petal sent her dreds in a flurry. "Oh no. I couldn't tell Mark. Sylvia would fire me.

Abigail huffed. "It's not right."

Petal peeked out from Abigail's embrace. "No. It's okay. She is under a lot of pressure."

Nora felt drained by all the drama.

Petal jumped up. "I'm sorry. I know you're tired and you have the board meeting tomorrow. I wanted to come over and warn you." She faded out.

Nora bit. "Warn me?"

"Darla found something in the books. I don't know what it is. But she was really worried about it. Maybe that's why she died."

Nora stood, feeling crowded amid her sparse belongings. "You should probably tell the police."

Petal shook her head. "I shouldn't know about it. If someone killed her because of that and they find out I know, they might kill me, too."

Kill her? Petal's imagination might be even more active than Nora's. "What do you think Darla found?"

Petal shrugged and clamped her mouth shut. After a moment of silence, she scurried to the door. "I need to get back to the Trust. Sylvia is working late and expects me to be there."

Abigail sounded aghast. "It's nine-thirty!"

Petal pulled her wraps tighter. "She works really hard."

Nora and Abigail eased around the coffee table and walked Petal to the door. They watched as she hurried along the balcony and down the stairs, disappearing into the night.

Nora shut the door and Abigail slid the chain on to lock it.

Nora turned to Abigail. "Okay, what's going on with you and Charlie?"

"We'll talk about it later. We need to concentrate on you. What are you going to wear tomorrow?"

Abigail's topic-hopping could give anyone whiplash but Nora had grown up with it. She wouldn't get any more information from Abigail tonight. They walked back to Nora's bedroom and stood in front of the closet.

Nora stared at her clothes.

Abigail whisked hangers across the rod assessing the clothes. "Wear the black Tahari suit. It shows off your fitness and is professional."

"I don't think the meeting is that formal."

"Not for the board meeting."

Nora rubbed the spot of fatigue eating at her forehead. *Just let me get some sleep.*

Abigail pulled out the suit. "I set up an interview for you tomorrow."

Nora spun from the closet. "What?"

"United Amalgamated Financial."

Nora couldn't think of anything to say.

"Pearl Street Mall. That cute coffee shop with the weird name. It'll be a quick meeting and you can give him your resume. I'm sure he'll have you meet the other partners later in the week."

Little hammers of annoyance picked in her brain. "He who? Wait. No. I *have* a job."

"I won't let you trod on the shining crystal of new life."

Argh! "Stop writing poetry about my life."

"Adam Thompson. He's my dear friend Marilyn's son. I pulled some strings and he's very excited for you to join the firm. You'll be perfect."

12

Sylvia paced from Petal's junky desk and circled the antique table, running her fingers along the polished wood. She held the phone to her ear, fuming at Eduardo's rudeness in making her wait.

How odd that Darla was found murdered on the same night she'd confronted Sylvia. The gunshot must have drawn attention and someone found Darla out there alone and killed her. Life was full of strange coincidences.

Finally Eduardo came back on the line.

"I don't appreciate being on hold." Sylvia didn't care how important Eduardo thought he was, she would not be treated as a common solicitor.

"I am a busy man, *carina*, what is it you wish to discuss?" He might think his soft voice and Ecuadoran accent would spread her knees, but it didn't work on Sylvia. When she'd let him sample her honey, it had been on her terms.

"It's not a question of want, it's a matter of deserve. There's a mix-up at the Trust. Darla's gone missing and the nitwit Mark hired won't pay me. I need you to deposit fifty thousand into my Cayman account immediately." Sylvia collapsed in her office chair. She pulled her laptop in front of the PC monitor and opened it.

"First of all," he paused in that false lazy attitude of a Latin lover. "You haven't shown progress to warrant a bonus. Secondly, World Petro is under extreme scrutiny and I can't make unexplained expenditures."

"You expect me to continue working for nothing?" The Chihuly glimmered from her laptop screen.

He chuckled. "You must appeal to the board of directors."

She bristled at his insulting tone. "In the interim I'd appreciate something to bridge the gap."

His sigh sounded as though he was reasoning with a petulant child. "That is impossible at this time."

How dare he patronize her? She slammed the lid on her laptop and jumped up, striding around her desk. "Don't say *impossible* to me. Remember what I'm doing for you."

"A business transaction. Which is overdue and over budget."

Neither of which should bother him much. She tried a sweeter tact. He wouldn't resist her if she reminded him of her other benefits. "I know what a—creative—person you are. You're clever enough and rich enough to get cash to me."

Again the pause and sigh. "The board meeting is tomorrow. Use your considerable skills to make love to them."

She wouldn't go begging like some match girl freezing on the streets. "Tell your son to sway the board."

Eduardo's voice hardened like cooling lava. "Daniel is not to know about our understanding. To you, he is a board member and nothing else."

Sylvia's skin tingled with her rebellion. Nothing more than a board member? If Eduardo only knew. "Fine. But you used your influence with him to get me hired, you could use it again to get me paid."

"Danielcito is not your concern."

"My money is my concern," Sylvia insisted. She checked the thermostat on the wall. This damned office stayed perpetually cold.

"*Mi corazon*, wouldn't you say securing more funds would be easier if you had some success to show for the time and money you've spent so far?"

Whatever happened to deferred gratification? "I'm not Walmart churning out commodities made in China."

"I must go, *carina*." He hung up.

Eduardo hung up! How dare he try to scare her. Who did he think he was?

She hurled the iPhone and it banged against the office wall. She wouldn't be threatened. He didn't scare her. He. Didn't. Scare. Her.

The office around her faded and there she was, six year-old Sylvia huddled next to her older sister, Margery, on the cracked linoleum of the mold-infused shack.

Her stomach gnawed on emptiness as they sat sweating in the liquid air of Bucktown in New Orleans.

"I'm starving," she said.

Margery hugged her. At ten years-old, she took care of Sylvia. "They'll be home soon. They promised."

But soon turned out to be the next day when her parents crawled in smelling of booze and cigarettes.

Margery stood in front of her father, twisting her grungy t-shirt in her fist. "Did you bring us anything to eat?"

Her mother stumbled past them down the dark hallway toward the bedroom. She'd probably throw herself onto the unmade bed still in her shorts and halter top. Maybe she'd get up later today, maybe tomorrow.

Her father ignored Margery and trudged after her mother.

Margery considered Sylvia who had begun to cry.

"Please," Sylvia mouthed.

Margery tugged on her father's arm. "Do you have some money? I can get hamburger and cook it."

His glazed eyes flitted over Margery and with a flick of his arm, he sent her flying into the wall.

Sylvia ran to Margery and they clung to each other in silence until snores shook the shack. They crawled to the bedroom. Margery rifled the discarded trousers and purse for enough change to buy a jar of peanut butter.

In the quiet of her office, Sylvia spoke aloud. "No one will make me feel that helpless again."

She paced the office in her Manolos. The thud of the heels gradually brought her out of the red zone and she glanced down to see the perfection of leather on her delicate feet. She let her gaze travel up her shapely ankles to her well-formed legs. The Versace suit fit her perfectly. She was a fine woman. So much more than anyone had dreamed she'd be. Amazing, really, she'd achieved all that she had.

Beethoven's Fifth sounded from the floor between two file cabinets. Sylvia's phone.

Maybe Eduardo had second thoughts about treating her so abysmally.

Sylvia stalked to the phone, disappointed to see the name on the caller ID. She composed herself before answering. "Hello, Margery." She punched the speaker option and set the phone on her desk.

Margery's weak voice trickled through the phone. "I haven't heard from you in a long time and wanted to say hello."

Likely story. While Margery droned on about the weather and the other residents at the care facility, Sylvia drew a tree chart. She labeled the circles in her chart for her various credit cards and private donors who'd funded her research in the past. If she transferred her balances from these two cards to....

"I know it's a lot to ask but if you could help me out, I'd appreciate it."

So Margery wound down to the reason for the call. Money. It always came down to that.

Sylvia opened her laptop and gazed at the screen. "What did the doctor say?"

Margery sniffed. That annoying, constantly runny nose. "He said having it removed would be a good idea."

Of course he thought it would be a good idea. It's money in his pocket. Margery's gullibility always cost Sylvia.

Unless Sylvia got firm, this would never end. "I paid an extra thousand last month. I wish I could help but I can't afford any more."

"Oh." The peep of a response barely made it through the speaker.

A razor of anger sliced into her brain. "Last month the flu ran through the home and you needed a vaccine that insurance wouldn't pay for. And before that he recommended some experimental drug."

Sniff. "I'm sorry. You've done so much. I shouldn't have asked."

But she did ask. Every month. Over and over. Always trying to apply the scalding compress of guilt. Sylvia had never asked Margery to work three jobs to pay for Sylvia's tuition at Tulane. It certainly wasn't Sylvia's fault Margery got knocked up by a low-life trucker that never paid a dime of child support.

Enough was enough. Sylvia had bankrolled Margery far too long. She'd paid her debt.

The Chihuly stretched her thin enough. She shouldn't have to give it up. "I'm sorry. I just can't do it."

13

Despite Abigail's apoplectic fit, Nora opted for the black silk shirt and black jeans with cowboy boots. She'd parked several blocks from the Bolderado Hotel on the other end of the Pearl Street Mall in the hopes that the walk in the crisp fall morning would calm her nerves.

Pearl Street was closed to traffic for a few blocks to create an open-air mall. Interesting shops from designer clothing stores to outdoor gear, free-trade stores to tourist joints, and art galleries lined the street along with eateries of all kinds. The center space of the mall contained sculptures suitable for climbing and touching and raised flower beds that changed varieties along with the seasons. Right now, bright yellow chrysanthemums blasted their cheer in the brisk mountain air.

This early, Nora passed a few joggers and walkers. Later, when the stores opened, the place would buzz with Boulder's energy. Buskers would perform everything from magic and juggling to amazing feats of yoga or memory on all but the coldest days. With Boulder's eclectic mix of business people, affluent retirees and young families, students, street people, Rastafarians, and mystics, if the mall wasn't the best people-watching venue in the world, it ranked in the top ten.

Nora inhaled the fresh morning air. *Get through today. That's all. Present to the board and move on.*

Her phone rang. Of course. Abigail burst from the line. "You left early. I wanted to talk to you."

Slipping out before Abigail got up was no accident. "It's a big day."

"I see you didn't wear the Tahari."

When Nora didn't respond she continued. "I've been thinking about Petal. She's obviously a disturbed girl. This friend of hers, the accountant, you need to find out what happened to her so Petal can find closure."

The accountant. Darla. The girl had a name and a life, and Petal seemed like the only person who cared. Nora stepped back emotionally. "The cops will investigate. I can't help Petal with this."

Bulldog Abigail. "Her coming here supposedly to warn you is an obvious cry for help."

Nora turned north off the mall and glanced up. One block away the Boulderado loomed. Tall trees surrounded the historic hotel and their bright fall leaves accented the walk. Inviting smells of coffee and cinnamon baked goods wafted from the hotel's coffee shop. "Just because Scott was murdered doesn't mean I know anything about murder investigations."

She pictured Abigail leaning forward, getting serious. "It's not just for Petal. She's got a crazy notion that Sylvia is somehow involved and we know that's just not true."

Nora laughed. "And how do we know that?"

Abigail let out a puff of air. "Look at her! She's refined and intelligent and has taste. She's got no need to commit crimes."

No fighting Abigail logic. "I'm not investigating. I've got enough to do learning a new job."

"You're making excuses."

Absolutely. She couldn't face more death now. The thought of it spun her mind back over a year ago.

In the chill of the dark forest, Nora's nostrils filled the smell of Barrett McCreary's sweat as he crushed her to his side with an iron arm. She struggled to break his hold.

Charlie lay dying on the forest floor. With one hand pressed to his gushing gunshot wound, Abigail threw rocks at Barrett.

Someone crashed from the forest into the clearing.

Barrett jerked his head toward the intruder and crushed Nora even closer to his side.

The intruder wore a kachina mask and full costume. He carried a hatchet adorned with ribbons and feathers.

With his hatchet raised, the kachina rushed across the clearing toward Barrett and Nora. He swung his hatchet and hit Barrett in the throat with the dull edge. Barrett grunted.

The kachina darted in again, striking at Barrett's gun arm, ripping the shirt on Barrett's bicep.

Barrett swung Nora as he turned and tried to get a bead on the dancing kachina. Nora's feet slid along the ground and she lost her balance. Barrett's arm pinned her to his side and kept her from falling.

The kachina retreated across the clearing to Abigail and Charlie. He didn't slow his zigzagged dance but the masked face turned toward them, as if checking on them.

Barrett raised his arm and sighted in on Abigail.

The kachina circled back, hatchet raised.

Nora pitched and writhed and kicked, screaming in Barrett's ear.

With incredible force, he flung Nora toward the rock. The back of her head cracked on the granite and she flopped to the ground. Her knee struck a rock and her leg went numb.

Barrett stepped toward Abigail. He couldn't miss. At that range, he'd rip a hole into Abigail that would tear her in two.

Nora dragged herself, fighting to stop Barrett.

Suddenly, the kachina flew from the forest straight at Barrett.

Barrett didn't alter his aim at Abigail. The third shot exploded from Barrett's gun.

And seventeen year-old Heather lay dead.

The courageous girl had saved Abigail's life by dressing up as a kachina.

Abigail's chatter grounded Nora in front of the Boulderado. "The clues are in the bookkeeping. I suspect once you dig into the finances of the

Trust you'll find it's not the place for you. You will be helping clear Sylvia, give Petal closure, and get your career on track. Win, win, win."

A jogger in black spandex tights, warm-up jacket and headphones plodded past, chugging white puffs of breath.

Nora slowed as she neared the hotel. She inhaled to give herself courage.

"Do it for Petal if not for yourself. She's not like you. You're confident and smart and beautiful."

That's right, Abigail, lay it on nice and thick.

"She's a fragile wisp of a soul searching for an anchor in a world of storms."

"Poetry?"

"I think that's a good line, don't you?"

Dog tags clinked behind Nora and a woman in a ski coat passed her with two Westies on leashes.

Nora inhaled competence and professionalism. She hoped. "I've got to go."

"See you at three. At Laughing Goat Cafe."

Nora forced herself to step up to the hotel door.

"Next to the book store."

She shut her phone off and dropped it in her bag.

In the likely event Mark fired her after her report, agreeing to attend Abigail's bizarre job interview might not be such a stupid thing.

14

Nora pulled her shoulders back, raised her head, and entered the Boulderado. Victorian elegance steeped the lobby with its dark polished wood and opulent furnishings. A stained glass copula completed the rich mood. A series of balconies viewed the lobby from two separate levels.

The meeting rooms were on the second floor. Nora climbed the thickly carpeted stairs, located the conference room and stepped through the double doors.

The conference room echoed the elegance of the lobby but with a business feel. Carpeted with a pattern of red squares and pink swirls, moldings painted tasteful beige. Striped wallpaper in more beige shades covered the walls. The twenty foot ceilings and elongated windows gave the room the feel of a historic, upper-class venue.

A breakfast buffet spread out on a couple of tables along the far wall. White draped tables in a u-shape filled the center of the room. Several chairs lined the wall.

Mark balanced a plate of pastries and chatted with a tall, thin man in jeans and corduroy blazer. Mark shoved in a bite and flakes of pastry stuck to his soft lips.

Fay sat at the conference table with a middle-aged woman, eating fruit and yogurt. They seemed in the throes of an earnest conversation.

A few knots of two or three people milled around or sat at the table to bring the total to about a dozen attendees.

Nora had read the board bios and knew the group consisted of an interesting and illustrious collection of investment bankers, trust-funders, attorneys, and college professors. Ten people in all, but she didn't know how many would attend today's meeting.

She tried to appear casual as she studied them. Which one was Mark's father?

Nora set her folder containing copies of the financials for the board on a chair along the wall. She placed the messenger bag she used for a purse on top and, with her back to the room, gazed out the high-reaching windows at the sun shining on the Flatirons. A wisp of clouds flirted with the sheer rock face.

"Good morning" a man's voice spoke behind her.

She twisted her neck to greet him. How she'd missed him when she walked in was a mystery. Gorgeous. Tall, chiseled-featured, dark-skinned, lean and Hollywood handsome. She managed not to gasp in admiration and introduced herself. "Nora Abbott, the new Finance Director."

He smiled with even, white teeth. "Daniel Cubrero. Mere board member."

There was nothing "mere" about this man.

"Daniel!" Mark inserted himself between Nora and Daniel. "How was your flight?"

Daniel barely noticed Mark. "Unremarkable. Now tell me, Nora." His Latino accent sounded like satin sheets. "How long have you been at the Trust?"

Mark snorted. "We'll get to introductions at the meeting. Right now, I need to speak with Nora, so if you'll excuse us."

"Oh, no," Daniel linked Nora's arm and headed her toward the buffet. "She has not eaten. Come, Nora, you must try the pastries."

Whew. The last thing Nora wanted to do was talk to Mark. He'd ask her for her report and she'd never get a chance to present to the board.

Mark's strangled expression converted to a wet smile instead.

They left him and headed for the food. Daniel reached for a coffee cup and filled it at the silver urn. "Have you been in Boulder long?" Nora picked up a plate and plopped a scone on it.

Before she could answer, a man about sixty years-old with a pot belly and a white beard and hair like Santa Claus approached and started talking to Daniel. "Did you see that report estimating the oil reserves in Ecuador? Now I know your father..."

Nora stepped away but when she peeked up, Mark bore down on her. She switched directions and nearly bumped into a thin Native American woman in a business suit. Straight black hair hung down her back and turquoise jewelry accented the formal business attire.

The woman held out her hand to steady Nora. "I was on my way over to say hello. I'm Alberta Standing Bear. Fay says you're replacing Darla. Welcome to the Trust."

Nora felt as though she ought to offer condolences to Alberta for the loss but had no idea what to say. "Thank you." For the welcome and for saving her from Mark.

"Maybe we can visit at lunch. Excuse me." Alberta scooted off to talk to Daniel.

Fay marched toward Nora with a heaping plate of fruit. She stuffed a strawberry into her mouth and spoke in her creaky voice. "Sylvia did it. I know she did."

Thomas appeared behind Fay. He'd covered his hairy legs in khakis but still wore a Life Is Good t-shirt, this time blue. "I think it's Mark. He embezzled and Darla found out."

A short, balding man in faded jeans, blue Oxford cloth button-down, and Chacos joined them. Fay tilted her head to Nora then to the man. "Bill, this is Nora. Nora, Bill's our resident asshole," she croaked.

Bill shook her hand. "Attorney." He glared at Fay. "*I* think it's Petal."

Thomas and Fay laughed. He joined them. "Don't you know it's always the last person you'd suspect."

Where was the grief for a dead colleague? Nora's heart twisted at the thought of the yellow pages: *I am smart. I will succeed. They DO like me.*

Fay poked Nora's arm. "Don't be so shocked. We're joking."

Thomas's eyes suddenly watered. "Darla was a loner but she was okay. I can't imagine why anyone would kill her."

Bill shook his bald head. "A random act. Some wingnut with a violent streak found a lone woman at night and BAM, it's all over."

A hand on her arm made Nora jump.

Mark whispered. "I need to talk to you. Outside."

A woman on the downhill side of fifty, with thinning gray hair and a body twice her healthy size boomed a command. "Let's get started. We've got a lot to cover." This must be Etta Jackson who served as chairman. She'd inherited a fortune her father made in banking. Her trust fund allowed her to contribute a couple of million dollars a year to causes in which she believed.

A moan of frustration escaped from Mark. He straightened his shoulders and a fake smile appeared on his face. While everyone settled in he spoke. "Welcome to Boulder dear, dear friends of the Trust."

The staffers arranged themselves on the row of chairs along the wall while the board members sat at their places at the conference table. Nora sat next to Fay.

Fay leaned close and whispered. "I saw you talking to him, isn't he one big ball of hotness?"

Nora acted innocent. "Who?"

Fay laughed.

She whispered to Fay. "Which one is Mark's father?"

The room quieted. "Stepfather." Fay's voice dropped to a breath. "He never comes. I think he can't stand Mark and avoids him."

Nora didn't blame him. "Where is the rest of the staff?" she whispered.

Fay shrugged. "They say they're out in the field. Anyone's guess where they really are. Sylvia will blow in for her personal appearance. That's about it."

From where Nora sat she had a full-face view of Daniel, Alberta, the Santa man, a Birkenstock-clad woman with long, curly gray hair and Etta Jackson. From the bios she knew a college professor of ecology who'd written several important books, two attorneys, a man retired from the auto industry, a retired advertising exec, and professional do-gooders also sat on the board. She might spend the rest of the meeting playing match with the faces and the bios.

Mark held his hands up. "We're lucky to have this golden Colorado weather to greet you here. You never know with October in the Rockies. It might have been a blizzard." He laughed and most everyone responded with polite tolerance.

"As you can see by your agendas," Mark said, "we'll start with open space and Fay. Thomas will update his air quality work, followed by Bill with his report on litigation. In the interest of time, we aren't hearing from everyone today. We'll have the financial spotlight right before lunch. We've ordered an amazing buffet downstairs. When we reconvene, Sylvia LeFever will give us her exciting update about her climate change modeling work." He stepped back. "Etta, would you like to conduct the meeting?"

Through the first two hours of the meeting, Mark groveled before the board, nearly kowtowing to them, giggling nervously, and belittling the staffers.

As the seconds ticked into minutes and hours, Nora tried to pay attention and learn about the Trust. Instead, she silently rehearsed the disaster report she'd deliver soon. The agenda called for her next, right before they broke for lunch. If her job security teetered on the brink yesterday, she headed for a real swan dive in a few minutes.

"Thank you, Bill." Etta said. "I think I speak for the board when I say we're impressed with the work you've done. Your ability to juggle our various interests is truly amazing."

Mark nodded and grinned. "Bill's been out on the front line, that's for sure. He spent Tuesday in the Colorado legislature talking to our reps about legislation to fund Sylvia LaFever's amazing study of climate change with regard to the beetle kill."

Fay leaned in. "Get a plug in for your little pet. Disgusting."

Etta kept her eyes on her agenda, crossing off items with a pen. "Yes. As Bill said. Thank you, Mark."

"It's cutting edge." His eyes glittered as if placing a delectable feast in front of the board. "We're incredibly fortunate to have her at the Trust."

Etta didn't respond.

Fay stood up. "Excuse me. If there's nothing else you need from us, Bill, Thomas and I will head back to work."

"By all means." Mark dismissed them.

Etta pushed back from the table. She and Fay embraced and agreed to meet at seven the following morning.

Amid thanks and good byes, the three walked out, abandoning Nora.

Nora's heart jumped into her throat. One more moment to remain employed before she landed back on the streets.

"Excuse me, Etta," Daniel Cubrero said.

They all turned to him.

"If I might, I'd like to bring up a topic not on the agenda but one that is dearest to my heart."

Not a woman alive could say no to that man. Etta was no exception. "Of course."

He paused and surveyed the board members in turn. "*El Oriente,* or the Amazon basin in Ecuador, as you know it." He smiled at them. "It is under attack. The region of tropical rain forest is home to the most diverse collections of plant and animals in the world. A half-million indigenous peoples live there."

No one moved. His voice caressed them and they loved it. Nora included.

"The big oil companies have discovered that the world's last great oil field lies underneath this crucial environmental area. I would like the Trust to consider joining a coalition to save the rainforest from these marauders."

The way he said *marauders* made Nora want to be overrun.

The Birkenstock woman, obviously the trust-funder named Marion Dempsey, interrupted. "Didn't the UN pay Ecuador billions to stop development of the rainforest?"

Daniel nodded. "Yes. But it isn't enough. What if there is a disaster in Ecuador? If suddenly they have tragedy like Haiti after the earthquake there in 2009? The government will acquiesce and allow the oil companies to drill and the rainforest will suffer."

One of the back of heads—Nora guessed it belonged to the advertising exec, Bryson Bradshaw—said, "Doesn't your family own World Petro? What do they think of you working on this initiative?"

Daniel's smile would bring even a serious man like a banker to his knees. "We have held very...lively...discussions about this. But my father ultimately agrees that this area must remain pristine. He is willing to donate one million dollars to set up a foundation for the rainforest protection."

Etta must be a woman of steel because she sounded as if she might turn Daniel down. "We're more of a local operation. Getting involved in Ecuador seems out of our league."

He conceded. "Perhaps."

The Santa man—he must be the college prof named Willard Been—said, "If your father is donating a million dollars, why do we need to join?"

"Mostly to add prestige to the group. The more organizations joining the coalition, the more who will want to be a part of it. It can create a snowball, yes?"

Mark held up his hand, smiling like a stray dog in the pound, hoping someone would love him. "We're running a little late. Why don't we break for lunch before the finance report and come back refreshed?"

Etta cast a slight frown in his direction. She addressed the group. "What do you say? Shall we add this to the agenda for the next meeting?"

The guy in the corduroy blazer—he was either an attorney or a philanthropist, Martin or Stanzio—consulted his watch. "I'd agree to that. What about a working lunch?"

Marion Dempsey said, "I need to catch a flight so I'd like to keep forging ahead."

Etta leaned back in her chair. "I'm going up to Silverthorne to do some hiking tomorrow and wouldn't mind wrapping up early, as well."

Daniel Cubrero addressed Mark. "Perhaps you could ask the kitchen to bring our food in here for a working lunch." Not only did Nora like his idea of sending Mark out of the room while she spoke, she nearly melted at his South American accent.

Mark dipped his head, never losing his grin. "I'm not sure they'll do that. They're planning for us downstairs."

Professor Santa's voice sounded like a mallet. "We'd appreciate it if you'd do what you can. Cancel the lunch and bring us deli sandwiches if you need to."

Mark jumped up as if hit with an electric prod. "Of course. I'll take care of it."

Daniel Cubrero nodded, satisfied. "*Bueno.* Now, let's see how our finances are sitting." He smiled at Nora and her legs went wobbly.

Mark pushed back from the table. He walked past Nora on the way out of the room and when his back was to the board, he widened his eyes in what she assumed was a warning.

Etta cleared her throat. "We're deeply sorry to hear about Darla Barrows. She served as Finance Director competently and thoroughly for three years. She was always willing to help and ready to answer our questions. She'll be missed." Etta leaned over and pulled a tissue from a canvas bag. She honked her nose in tribute.

Bradshaw cleared his throat. "Is there any news on the investigation?"

Etta shook her head. "As I understand it, there are no leads and the detectives will be questioning staff."

"Perhaps we should hire a private investigator?" Daniel said.

Marion Dempsey shook her gray hair. "We're here to save the environment, not track down murderers."

At least they had their priorities straight.

Etta allowed the minute or two of murmurings about the sadness and waste of Darla's murder and then cleared her throat. "At this time, I'd like to welcome Nora Abbott. Yesterday was her first day so we'll muddle through this together as best we can."

The members turned pages in their board reports to settle on the financials. Nora stood and hefted her stack of pages. "I studied the financials in the board packet. Unfortunately, they don't match up to what is currently in our system, so I prepared another P&L. I'm sorry I haven't had time to work up a cash flow, but I printed out a balance sheet."

She handed out the reports and gave the board a second to digest the new information. These were professional board members and business people used to cruising financial statements like NASCAR drivers ran a track.

Corduroy guy, Martin/Stanzio, frowned. "What happened to the cash balance in the general fund?"

Bradshaw frowned. "The long-term investment asset balance is substantially down, too."

After they'd mumbled among themselves for several minutes, Nora spoke. "As you can see, there are some differences from the previous report and generally, they show the Trust is in a worse financial position. I assume December will bring an influx of donations, but until then we're in for a dry spell as far as cash flow."

Etta's double chin wobbled. "Can you give us a quick overview?"

Nora skimmed through, surprised her voice sounded strong and confident because inside, she was a sickening swamp of anxiety. Somewhere in the middle of the report, where Nora kept reminding herself to breathe and speak clearly instead of racing along and mumbling, the door behind her opened and closed. It had to be Mark. If he had an ax in his hand, he'd swing and her head would roll onto the plush hotel carpeting, blood clashing with the tasteful reds.

When Nora paused, Etta spoke. "What I'm hearing is that the open space and air quality are on budget, forest restoration and trail maintenance are slightly over, but climate modeling has already surpassed the entire budget for the year."

Nora nodded.

"If this is accurate," Professor Santa said, "We won't have the funds to fight oil exploration in the Amazon basin."

Daniel Cubrero frowned. "We can't allow that situation to continue in Ecuador. We must do something to protect the delicate eco-system."

While Nora stood with her face burning—her palms a puddle of sweat and her heart banging in her chest—the board erupted in concern over the careless oil companies denuding the rainforest. It was a topic that concerned Nora as well, but hardly relevant to this meeting.

Etta raised her arms to quiet the table. "First things first. We obviously need to deal with these disturbing financials." She waved a come-in motion to the person behind Nora. "Can you explain this, Mark?"

He walked past her, the smell of nervous sweat wafting from him. Of course he began with a laugh. "Obviously Nora hasn't had time to get to know our system." Mark lasered such murderous intent at Nora she almost dove for the carpet.

Etta drew in a deep breath. "Mark, Nora, would you mind stepping out for a few minutes while we discuss this among ourselves?"

"Of course." Nora walked past Mark on her way to the door. She was pretty sure she could outrun him once the conference room doors closed.

"Lunch is on its way. They'll bring it any second." Mark's shrill voice rose.

Etta sounded strained. "Thank you."

As the door clicked closed behind Nora, Mark said something else. It probably irritated them that Mark didn't leave as instructed but it suited Nora fine to have a few minutes to escape.

She strode down the hall, heading for sanctuary in the rest room.

A light touch on her arm set her off like a rocket "Agggh!"

Benny stood beside her. He'd made no sound when he approached, like his mysterious ancestor that haunted Nora's imagination.

"Maybe you should cut back on the coffee," he said, his face expressionless.

It was too much to hope that he'd returned to Arizona. Tenacious little guy. If she didn't listen to what he had to say he'd never leave. She glanced down the hall and saw no sign of Mark. She slipped into an empty conference room and pulled Benny after her. "What are you doing here?"

"I came to talk to you."

He had all the time in the world. After all, the Hopi had been promised over a thousand years ago they'd be the longest surviving tribe of all. Nora didn't have time to spare. In a matter of minutes she'd have to face Mark. "What is going on, Benny?"

He paused. "I was sent to warn you."

15

If she thought it would stop her from hearing she'd ram her fingers in her ears. Warnings, threats, messages from long-dead Native Americans. She'd left Flagstaff to get away from this.

She stood in the darkened conference room. The red patterned carpet, tall windows and striped wallpaper decorated this room but with the lights off and no tables or refreshments set up, it felt cold and dead. "Go away, Benny. I don't want to hear it."

"You need to stay watchful and do what you can to protect the Mother." His unfathomable eyes watched her in endless serenity.

"You know this message is going to make me crazy, right? I want to ask you what is going to happen and what to watch for and what I'm supposed to do. But you'd only tell me the balance depends on me and you can't tell me what to do because that's not the Hopi way."

Her words brought the ghost of a smile. "You can learn. That's good."

She thought back to the time she'd spent with him at his shack on the mesa in northern Arizona. Hopiland. She'd been sent there by Cole. *Kidnapped* was the technical term.

Cole...

. . .

The heat of the Arizona summer that morning seared the top of her head. Benny walked between bushy corn plants in the blazing desert sun below Second Mesa. He caressed their leaves. "Hopi have a respect for life and trust in the Creator."

"Seems like you could grow more corn if you used a tractor or irrigation sprinkler. Why would your spirits want you to do everything the hard way?" Nora asked.

Benny straightened and brushed his hands together. "Making things hard prepares us for what may happen. Like a runner practices every day, building strength and endurance so he can run the marathon, we Hopi live a meager and hard life so we're ready to survive when the time comes."

He handed her a stick about a foot long and thick as a broom handle. He reached into his pocket and brought out a small plastic bag of corn seeds. "You stay here and plant these seeds over there." He pointed to a sandy spot next to the outer corn plants.

Planting corn was a stupid idea and she didn't want to do it. She squatted down and thrust the stick into the ground. She dropped in a few seeds and packed the earth around them.

She straightened and stepped sideways, falling on her knees to dig a new hole, dropped in the seeds and scooped dirt.

After a while, Nora rose from the ground, feeling deep connection with the seeds. The earth gave life to the corn which nourished the people here in Hopi-land. It was this way all over the world. Abigail had given life to Nora and loved her, teaching her and protecting her. And if she were lucky, someday Nora would be able to do the same with a child of her own.

Words wouldn't form but rhythm and sound grew naturally, boiling up her throat and erupting from her mouth in a song. She danced, tears falling from her face, her voice loud and deep with love for the corn and the earth that would nurture it.

Now, she felt her boots firmly rooted on the conference room carpet. She focused on the Hopi man in front of her. He believed his tribe held responsibility to keep the entire planet in balance. If they didn't perform their ceremonies in the ancient way, the two brothers who sat on the serpent on the Earth's poles, would let the serpent lose.

It had happened before. The Hopi said it was when the Third World ended due to man's wickedness and the good people had climbed to this world, the Fourth.

Modern scientists had an explanation that sounded similar. They speculated the earth had shifted on its axis maybe sending the dinosaurs into extinction. Some said it could happen again.

Nora knew this and more but she didn't want to let Benny know how many hours she'd spent online reading about Hopi, studying their thousand year-old prophesies, trying to follow the instructions for living a simple life. If she believed everything she read, she'd be crazy. She found it interesting, that's all.

Nora ran a hand through her hair. "I suppose Nakwaiyamtewa" —she stumbled over the pronunciation— "thinks that me working for the Trust positions me to protect or restore something. Maybe he's worried about the Amazon rainforest. But I'm having a hard time believing a chief from the 1800s—."

"*Kikmongwi,*" Benny interrupted.

"Okay, what you said." Nakwaiyamtewa was a *kikmongwi* who lived on the rez nearly a hundred and fifty years ago. When Nora had been stressed to the breaking point because enviros tried to kill her, she'd imagined she saw him in the form of a helpful little man. Again, if she believed that, she'd be crazy.

Not believing, not crazy. "Anyway, I'm a white woman and I don't understand Hopi so Nakwaiyamtewa can choose one of you spiritual Native Americans to work for him."

Benny shrugged. "I can't answer for him. I only know what he told me."

"And he didn't tell you much."

He shook his head. "He never does."

"I've had about enough of kachinas coming and going in my life. He shows up, tells me I've got to do something then disappears without helping. In the meantime people die. Heather died."

Benny lowered his head, the sorrow evident.

"Why me? Is it because I planted the corn you gave me? Or that I've read a little about the Hopi Instructions and I'm trying to live a more balanced life?"

His face remained inscrutable. "The Hopi life is for Hopi. It's not for everyone."

"Right. So that means, since I'm not Hopi, you and your *kikmongwi* can leave me alone."

"The hardest thing in the world is to be Hopi. We must constantly be vigilant. I see things. Signs the Fourth World is coming to an end and we will enter the Fifth World."

Every religion thought the end was near, pal. "I don't believe that, Benny."

He spoke with his usual speed of a snail on sedatives. "The prophesies call for us to act, to lessen the violence of the end of the Fourth World."

Mark stomped past the open door without glancing in. He hunted her.

"What I have been told to tell you is this: 'the whole world will shake and turn red and turn against those hindering the Hopi.'"

Nora could make a run for it, get out of the building before Mark found her. "I'm sorry, Benny. I don't understand this."

He inhaled and waited. "You will learn things moment to moment as you need to understand."

She calculated the distance to the stairs.

"The message I have to give you says the prophesy is being fulfilled and if you stop it, all will be well. If not...." Again he shrugged.

"You need to conference with Nakwaiyamtewa. Let him know I'm not up for the role of Enviro Girl."

Mark pounded by the other way and this time, his head swiveled toward her and he stopped dead. "Are you hiding from me?"

Nora shook her head. "No. I saw an old friend we wanted to catch up."

Mark's eyebrows shot up. "Really? And where is she?"

Startled, Nora spun around. She hadn't noticed a door on the other side of the room. Apparently, Benny had. He must have slipped through it before Mark saw him. "I'm not sure where he went. I'd better go find him."

Nora whipped from the dark conference room into the hallway.

"Stop." Mark caught up to her and stood too close. His stomach must be a boiling mass of anxiety because it came out in sour breath. "What did you tell them?"

Gulp. "Just that the finances aren't as rosy as their last reports indicate."

He sucked in his flabby lips. "We've got money coming in any day now that will make those reports accurate. God, what a mess."

Nora almost felt sorry for him. "We could create a projected revenue report for the board."

His face looked like an angry tomato. "You didn't tell them that Sylvia's work is over budget?"

The overhead glare of the hallway lights felt like a heat lamp. "They need to know the truth."

"Sylvia is brilliant. She's amazing. If you've done anything to hurt her..."

The hallway was closing in on Nora.

Mark held his hands to his head. He seemed to be talking to himself. "I need to think. How can I save her? We can't let her go."

"Maybe we—."

"You did this." You don't understand. Don't know how special she is."

"If we—."

"No." He shook his head. "You can't be here. You're fired."

16

Even though Christmas was a few months away, they resembled a human candy cane standing in the hallway outside the conference room. Mark's bright red face contrasted with Nora's pasty complexion.

Sylvia expected to see Nora Abbott in a business suit, not a jeans and cowboy boots. Such an interesting choice to wear something so earthy to the board meeting. Nora had that annoyingly fresh and healthy appearance. Her copper hair bounced around a face alive with interest and blue eyes that seemed ready to smile. That easy beauty and confidence annoyed Sylvia, who'd had to fight for every ounce of her own sophistication.

Someone should tell Mark to tuck his shirt in. Actually, someone should tell Mark to quit dressing like a Mormon boy on mission.

Mark sputtered in Nora's face. Another crises he obviously couldn't handle. Sylvia would talk him down from this one, as usual. She sighed and considered the diamond-encrusted watch on her slender wrist. She'd hoped to get to the board meeting early enough to schmooze them over lunch.

Damn Eduardo. She shouldn't have to do any of this.

She approached Mark and Nora. "What is the problem here?" Her voice sounded like cool spring water.

Mark jumped as if swatted from behind. He verged on tears. "She told the board your project is over budget. That all of the Trust is running in the red."

Damn.

Sylvia smiled warmly. "I wasn't aware of any overages. But the board understands the importance of the work. It'll be all right."

"All right?" His voice raised two octaves. "She ruined everything."

Despite her bloodless appearance, Nora managed dignity and calm amid Mark's breakdown.

Sylvia forced herself to touch Mark's shoulder, knowing contact with her would soothe him. "Stay calm. I'll take care of this. Etta is a dear friend, and Bryson Bradshaw and I attended a world environmental conference together last year. Over lunch I'll explain the situation and why it's taking time. They'll approve the increased budget."

Mark shook his head as a sweat rained from his temple toward his pudgy chin. "They're taking a working lunch." He pointed to the closed conference room doors. "The caterers just delivered their food and we aren't allowed in. Even to eat."

Why was everything going against her? "I'm on the agenda right after lunch. I'll work my magic and we'll be running smoothly again. Please don't worry."

"I'm sorry, Sylvia," Mark said, his voice cracking slightly. "I thought she'd be good. At least grateful for a job in this economy. I didn't know she'd turn on us. But she's gone. I swear. I fired her."

Still, Nora didn't say a word. She could pass for a marble statue, all chalky and cold.

Sylvia displayed the exact amount of disappointment and sympathy in her beatific smile. If she weren't such a brilliant scientist, she could have been another Julia Roberts because inside, she flared with anger. "Let's not over-react Mark. She's new and hasn't learned how to manage the board." Sylvia addressed Nora. "They don't want to be alarmed with hiccups in cash flow. They're busy and important. Your job is to ease their minds. Unless, of course, there is real cause for concern. But there isn't, so you see, you've worried them needlessly."

Nora opened her mouth but Mark rushed ahead. "I told her that. I told Nora we're getting a donation next week that will right everything."

Sylvia nodded. "See? It's all okay. I'll make it good with the board."

"She's still fired." Mark set his moist lips in a pout.

"You're the executive director. Do what you think is right."

The door of the conference room swung open. Daniel Cubrero leaned out. What a perfect specimen of male sexuality. "We're ready for the next agenda item. Has Sylvia LeFever arrived?"

Mark swallowed, obviously grappling for control.

Glad she opted for the four-and-a-half-inch heels and the shorter skirt, Sylvia imagined the glow of her skin and her inviting full lips. She stepped forward and extended her hand as if she didn't know Daniel as intimately as she did. "How good to see you again, Daniel."

He wrapped his hand around hers, with his long, tapered fingers. "Ah, Sylvia. I did not see you there."

A shiver of anticipation ran through Sylvia. Sometimes the old cliché about men's fingers held true. At least in Daniel's case it did. She had no qualms about mixing business and pleasure.

Later, though. Now it was show time.

As Sylvia strode into the room, taking command of the situation, Daniel said, "Mark, please join us. You, too, Nora."

How annoying. Really though, what did it matter to Sylvia who sat in the meeting? As usual, she would have them begging to do her bidding. She sat opposite Etta. Amid the scattered detritus of lunch, Sylvia would shimmer like a diamond. She smiled at Etta. "How are you, dear?"

"Thanks for joining us. Can you give us a brief update?" Etta must be ignoring their friendship in an effort to be professional.

Nora sat to the side of the room in one of a dozen chairs along the wall. Mark plopped next to Etta.

"Most of you are familiar with my research but I'll brush over the basics to remind you." Ordinary people needed a refresher on this complicated science. "HAARP stands for High Frequency Active Aurora Ionospheric Research Program. This is the government's program located in Alaska that includes dozens of aluminum dipole antennae towers that send out high frequency signals."

The board members stared like drugged bunnies.

Sylvia chuckled. "It's technology difficult to discuss with non-scientists."

Again, Etta must be struggling to mask her affection for Sylvia and said with a straight face, "You're no longer with HAARP so we don't need to know this."

The old bag. "I developed much of the HAARP technology and am using the principles in my modeling work here at the Trust."

Etta frowned. "We'd appreciate it if you could be brief."

"Of course." Sylvia nodded in Daniel's direction, letting her eyes connect in a subtle, seductive signal. "Before I left HAARP, I worked on developing a tower that uses ELF, extremely-low-frequency, waves and I've taken the technology further to create a single tower that sends concentrated beams of particles into the atmosphere."

Etta frowned at her, probably because she was too dull-witted to understand.

Sylvia tried to dummy it down. "The key Tesla discovery was that the earth reverberates with a pulsing electrical current in the low ELF range. I discovered the exact frequency at which the earth normally pulsates. Of course, HAARP takes credit for that breakthrough."

Bryson Bradshaw interrupted. "Isn't what you're talking about—the ELF waves and ionosphere and all that—isn't that linked with weapons of mass destruction?"

Sylvia shrugged. "HAARP is a government program. It's not inconceivable a classified study works on weaponry."

Marion Dempsey gasped. "You're not working on weapons, are you?"

"Of course not. The tower I've installed is for climate study only."

Bryson Bradshaw leaned forward. "How does that work?"

"Extremely-low-frequency waves are much shorter than short waves." She paused to let them digest that. "ELF waves are focused into the ionosphere to a specific location, creating a bulge in the atmosphere. The waves are then bounced back and can be sent beyond the horizon."

She surveyed the board, her kingdom of the moment. They appeared dull-eyed, probably struggling to absorb the simplistic explanation of a concept far more complicated than their normal minds could grasp.

Etta waved to indicate Sylvia should continue. "You're using those waves to gather data for climate-change modeling. You've told us this already."

Although Sylvia enjoyed imparting some of her vast knowledge to the uneducated, they didn't want to learn. "Exactly. We know that warming temperatures have allowed the pine beetle an extra breeding cycle each year, but what we don't know is how their destructive habits might be affecting the climate and perhaps exacerbating temperature increases. By using ELF waves in the ionosphere I'll be able to chart that and create models predicting future trends."

Silence fell on the room. Once again, Sylvia had wowed them with her brilliance. Most of the board studied their papers or stared at Etta.

Etta cleared her throat. "Your progress report is nearly verbatim from our last meeting four months ago. Is it that you didn't take the time to write a new report or has there been no progress?"

Progress? She'd solved a particularly difficult question regarding wave intensity and direction. She'd pinpointed several possible locations for targeting the waves to achieve Eduardo's goal. She'd researched long-term weather patterns and was far into a computer modeling program the likes of which the world had never seen. But none of it had a thing to do with the mountain pine beetle. "Much of my time in the last months was spent struggling with insufficient software. Too much of the data needs manual input and my assistant, Petal, and I can only work so many hours. As you can see, I've added upgrades into my budget for next year."

Again, silence. A few members shuffled papers, perhaps considering the budget. Then Etta spoke, "You're proposing an increase of four hundred thousand dollars."

Sylvia eyed Daniel. A mere pittance for his family, especially when she delivered on her promise. "That's correct. I realize this is a non-profit organization run with donations and I'm operating on a shoestring."

"I see," Etta said.

Alberta raised her finger. "I have a question. I've heard that with HAARP technology it will be possible to alter the weather. Is that true?"

Etta interrupted. "Sylvia isn't working on HAARP."

"But I want to make sure her tower can't do any damage to the mountains," Alberta said.

Finally, they were moving away from money. But the direction wasn't much better. Sylvia laughed. "Conspiracy alarmists are out there cruising the Internet for anything to feed their paranoid minds. HAARP is located in the Alaskan wilderness because it is an auroral region but they see it as 'hidden' and shrouded in secrecy. The technology is difficult to understand and therefore, scary. Ronald Regan funded it as part of his Star Wars defense and suddenly nefarious intent is suspected."

Face cold as stone, Alberta said, "So, can it alter weather?"

Who was Alberta to ask for a follow up when Sylvia had given her all she needed to know? "The HAARP facility will not affect the weather. Transmitted energy in the frequency ranges used by HAARP is not absorbed in either the troposphere or the stratosphere—the two levels of the atmosphere that produce the Earth's weather. No association between natural ionospheric variability and surface weather has been found, even at the extraordinarily high levels of ionospheric turbulence that the sun can produce. If the ionospheric storms caused by the sun don't affect the surface weather, there is no chance that HAARP can do so either."

There, you simpleton.

Etta didn't have anything to say, she must acknowledge Sylvia's superiority. "Okay."

Still Alberta wouldn't quit. She shuffled papers. "I found this quote from a Russian journalist about HAARP." She read from the paper. "Ionospheric testing can trigger a cascade of electrons that could flip the Earth's magnetic poles."

Sylvia laughed. "Preposterous. This is what I mean by crazy theories."

Etta bowed her head briefly toward Alberta to politely end the tangent. She didn't give Sylvia the same respectful expression. "We understand that despite your efforts at economy, you're way over budget."

Sylvia avoided Nora. "The financials might technically show a deficit. But there is obviously a mistake. Our new Finance Director is top-notch but she only joined the Trust yesterday. Darla had a great deal more insight."

Etta stiffened as if bracing to eat a plate of worms. "We started funding your research three years ago with high hopes for achieving important and lasting environmental restoration. We're not a large organization and can't afford this kind of fiscal drain. This" —Etta picked up a packet of stapled pages that must be Nora's financial reports— "drives the nails in the coffin."

I'll pound some nails in a coffin and it won't belong to my project. The Chihuly chandelier retreated from her grasp. She wouldn't let that happen, even if this two-bit board pulled her funding.

"We're asking you to wrap up your research and do a final report by the end of the year."

Sylvia had the power to smile like a queen. She inclined her head in grace.

The door behind her opened and the entire board suddenly became more alert as if threatened by attack.

Sylvia spun around.

A hotel employee, in her company blazer and polyester slacks stood just inside the doors, a strained expression lining her young face. Behind her, two uniformed police officers walked into the room. Their waists weighted down with guns, handcuffs and who knew what sort of hardware, their clothes crisp, black shoes sturdy. One officer stood several inches taller than his partner. The shorter, darker man stood akimbo. They both surveyed the room with serious expressions.

Etta stood. "May I help you?"

The taller of the two addressed Etta while the other focused on Sylvia. "We're here to see Sylvia LaFever."

What?

The room fell silent and all eyes rested on Sylvia.

The cops zeroed in on her. "You're Ms. LaFever?"

Sylvia forced a smile. "Yes. What can I do for you?"

"We'd like you to come down to the station for questioning in the death of Darla Barrows."

Cool, collected, Sylvia chuckled. They didn't know anything. "Don't be ridiculous."

The taller one with blond hair spoke again. "I'd advise you to get a lawyer before saying anything else."

She allowed her indignation to surface and stepped close enough to scrutinize their name tags. She addressed the tall one, A. Langston. "What's this all about?"

"We understand you own a Smith and Wesson 638 Airweight

Revolver," Langston said.

Everyone stared at her.

Ice picks bit into Sylvia's skin, yet her voice remained calm. "It's a popular model."

The shorter officer, B. Kirby, smirked. "It happens to be the caliber that killed Darla Barrows."

"Not a hundred yards from your office," Langston said.

Sylvia sounded unconcerned. "I haven't even seen my gun in ages. It's probably on a shelf in my bedroom closet."

Kirby's smirk deepened. "Actually, it's in evidence at the station" Pause. "Seized from your office." Pause. "Showing a shot was fired recently. We're having it tested for rifling right now."

Her gun! "How dare you go to my office. That's breaking and entering. What gives you the right?"

"A search warrant," Kirby said.

"Issued on the strong suspicion from a tip," Langston said.

"Whoever gave you that tip lied."

Kirby held his palms up. "And yet, we found the gun just where they suggested it would be."

Every eye in the overheated conference room focused on Sylvia. She must show them her steel. "It was planted. It's not my gun."

Kirby raised his eyebrows. "It's covered with your fingerprints."

Langston studied her. "We understand you have a trip planned to South America. We'd like to have you cancel that and stick around."

What were they talking about? Her silk blouse acted like a greenhouse to direct scorching heat on her skin. "I have no trip planned."

They exchanged smirks and Kirby said, "You didn't book a flight on your credit card this morning?"

"I suppose the same person who planted the gun and put your fingerprints all over it charged the ticket to your credit card." Langston laughed.

Even her scalp felt on fire. "You have no proof."

Langston nodded agreement. "Not until the test fire results come back, anyway."

Kirby raised his arm to indicate the people watching. "Wouldn't you like to come down to the station to discuss this?"

17

The thrill of victory and the agony of defeat in less than forty-eight hours. Okay, maybe she hadn't been so thrilled with Loving Earth Trust on the first day, but the agony of finding a new job felt crushing. Maybe getting free of the cornucopia of dysfunction at the Trust might be a good thing. Oh well, as Charlie would say, she was looking for a job when this one came along.

Nora trudged down the stairs of the Hotel Boulderado, glad she hadn't bothered to dress up. She strode across the Victorian lobby toward the outside doors. Laughter erupted from Q's, the bar on the ground floor. Maybe an unhappy pre-happy hour cocktail would ease the sting. Or maybe not.

Nora peeked in the door of Q's and wasn't surprised to see Thomas, Bill, and Fay. No doubt they saw Sylvia escorted out by the police.

Sylvia might be the only person who had a worse day than Nora. Being accused of murder trumped getting fired. No matter how awful Sylvia seemed, she couldn't really be a murderer. No one liked Sylvia but did anyone hate her enough to set her up?

Nora stepped into the brilliant sunshine. The morning's chill turned to a perfect fall afternoon. She'd need to walk several blocks to meet Abigail at the coffee shop on the Pearl Street mall. All old brick interior with a menu featuring organic and healthy food, it opened the busy pedestrian mall. Maybe the sunshine, the beautiful, rugged surface of the Flatirons, and the dazzling air would work their magic and Nora's mood would bounce back.

Nora fell in behind two young mothers pushing strollers and herding a toddler. She wasn't in a big hurry. Yes, she needed a job. Yes, an investment firm might be a great job. No, she didn't covet corporate games and daily dress-up.

Her boots found their way onto Pearl Street, now bustling with Boulder's eclectic population mix. The pizzeria's aromas faded into the burger joint and then Thai as Nora made her way with heavy steps toward the coffee shop. She stopped to gaze at rock climbing gear in a women's-specific sporting goods store window. Next year, she vowed, she'd overcome her fear of the mountains and start rock climbing again.

It was possible. She could do it. She could make her life new and exciting. She would. Yes.

In fact, tomorrow she'd take Abbey back up to Mount Evans and try again. The kachina could go take a hike—not the hike she planned, but one somewhere in Arizona.

Nora noticed her watch. What kind of supernatural powers did Abigail possess? She'd scheduled the meeting with Adam for three o'clock. She didn't know when Nora would present to the board, let alone plan for the hoopla that ensued and she certainly didn't predict Sylvia being led away by two cops. Yet, if Nora hurried, she'd make it to the coffee shop just in time.

"Nora." Her name spoken in a hushed but commanding voice paralyzed her. She knew who owned that voice. Waves of warring emotions crashed inside her. Happy, apprehensive, fearful, excited—one rolled into the next in a powerful tsunami.

Cole. Ah, damn. Cole.

She froze and lowered her head, closing her eyes.

Cole's hiking boots made no sound on the concrete as he walked around to stand before her. How could she isolate the feel of him amid the group of college kids, shoppers and the few homeless hanging out on the mall?

Nora struggled to appear unrattled. She might have turned tail and run but her limbs refused to move. So she forced open her eyes and straightened her neck.

He hadn't changed in the year since she'd last seen him on the mountain in Flagstaff. He still had the soft, sandy hair falling across his forehead, the deep blue eyes, the long legs lanky frame. He wore a flannel shirt with rolled sleeves, jeans, and hiking boots. But instead of the warm smile she remembered, he looked nervous.

"Hi, Nora."

She forced words. "What do you want?" It sounded mean. Too late to take it back.

He studied the ground in front of them then caught her eye. "I was hoping… I thought maybe…Oh hell. How are you?"

Finally the shell hardened around her heart. She stepped around him. "Best day of my life. See ya."

His hand shot out as if to grab her but thought better of it. He let it drop. "Wait. Please."

She stopped. Couldn't help it.

He strode around and faced her again. "I know this is a shock and not exactly the way I wanted to make contact again. But…"

"But what?" She didn't want to hear him speak… She wanted to hear everything he had to say… She wanted to run away… She wanted to step into his arms.

What had he been doing for the last year? Did he think about her? Did he care about her now as much as he had in Flagstaff? Should she have cut him out of her life before they even had a chance to know each other?

Pink tinged Cole's ears. That happened when he was embarrassed. Gaa! Nora didn't want to know these details about him. She spun away and bumped into a white-haired man wheeling a cart full of silly hats.

Cole steadied her. "Abigail called."

She should have known. "Holy mother of dog. What did she tell you?"

A high school-aged-boy and girl approached with clipboards. One said, "We're with Greenpeace and wondered if you'd sign this petition."

Nora snatched the clipboard and scribbled her name. She must seem like a lunatic because as soon as she handed it back to them, they scurried away.

"Are you okay?" Cole asked.

Okay? For a year she'd struggled to get solid footing. Cole had a way of slicing her heart open and she couldn't risk that exposure now. "I'm fine."

He squinted at her. "Abigail didn't say much but she said you needed help."

Cole liked to show up when she needed saving. If she had any idea of being whole and sound again, she needed to work out her own life. "I don't know why she'd say that. I have an appointment so I've got to go."

He smiled tentatively. "Maybe we can get together later? I'm in town and I'd love to catch up."

Catch up on a whole lifetime of not knowing each other, punctuated by a few weeks together in mortal danger? "I'm not interested." She started to walk away again.

He fell in beside her. A mom-and-dad-visiting-their-college-daughter group separated Nora and Cole. After they passed he closed the gap between them. "Benny called too."

Her jaw tightened. "Are you and Benny planning to kidnap me again?"

Cole ran a hand through his hair. "We've been through this before. It kept you alive, didn't it?"

"I don't know what Benny is doing in Boulder. He's got ideas about the Fourth World ending, or maybe wants to ease the transition into the Fifth. Whatever. Why don't you and Benny have a night on the town and leave me alone? In fact, invite Abigail." She sounded angry. But she wasn't angry. Cole scared her in a completely different way than the kachina did.

"Benny's already on his way back to the mesas. You know he hates leaving the rez."

She stomped down the mall, weaving in and out of meandering shoppers and gawkers. A breeze rustled the dying leaves on the trees and it sounded like they whispered, telling her run.

His hand closed on her arm. "Can't we just go someplace and talk?"

"I have legitimate reasons for not going out with you." Because she found him attractive and had from the beginning? Because she craved his strength even as she fought against it? Or because she felt too fragile to allow herself to be vulnerable? "The first of which is that you remind me of a terrible time in my life I'd like to forget. Second, I don't trust you. And third—maybe most important—my *mother* thinks you're a hot fudge sundae with a cherry on top."

"Maybe you should listen to Abigail. She was right about your first husband."

Silence grew between them. "Oh, you must mean the dead one." She glared at him, daring him to make light of the situation.

He bent his head again. "I'm sorry. I'm really nervous and I'm not saying anything right. Will you have dinner with me? Or drinks? Or even coffee?"

She shook her head.

His face almost glowed red. "You know I was raised on a ranch in Wyoming?"

She nodded. "So?"

"So, spilling my feelings doesn't come naturally to me. It's been bred out of us macho rancher types."

"You wear hiking boots and eat tofu. You're no rancher."

"It's hard to overcome your raising."

Arguing with Cole on the Pearl Street Mall while leaves sifted to the ground in the brilliant afternoon sunshine felt almost natural. Time to stop it. "I've had a terrible day so far. You aren't making it any better."

"I'm sorry. The truth is, Abigail and Benny aren't the reason I'm here."

His tone was way too serious. "I've got to go."

She peeled off from him and skirted around a raised flower bed, rushing down the mall.

The coffee shop nestled between a headshop and a new age bookstore. Several café tables sat in front filled with normal folks enjoying a normal break. Abigail must be inside. Nora stopped several feet from the shop to pull herself together. Beyond the windows Abigail sat across from a dapper young man with thinning hair. She had that absorbed expression she usually wore when she wanted to impress someone. Dear Abigail was doing all she could to help Nora.

Here I go, girding my loins or whatever it is women warriors do. I'll make a hella investment banker. Abigail will be so proud.

Nora stepped toward the shop and noticed pile of garbage in the niche between the coffee shop and a display for tarot cards and crystals. Wait. Not garbage.

Petal curled into the crevice, not more than a pale face amid a jumble of fabric and dreds.

Nora hurried over and held her hand out to pull Petal up. "What are you doing here?"

Petal didn't meet her eyes. "Waiting for Abigail."

"Does she know you're here?"

Petal focused on the ground. "No. Everyone at the Trust was at the board meeting and I got scared and didn't want to be alone. I went to see Abigail and she said she was meeting you here."

"Nora!" Her shouted name startled her. Daniel Cubrero jogged down the mall, dodging people.

She patted Petal's arm. "Wait here." She stepped toward Daniel.

"I'm glad I found you," he said, catching his breath from the short run. His white shirt must be tailored to cling to his muscular chest and arms in just the right way without looking too tight. His short dark curls absorbed the sunshine and his brown face glistened slightly from exertion.

Over Daniel's shoulder, Nora spotted Cole. He watched the scene as he made slow progress behind a family of shoppers.

It seemed extreme that a board member would make such an effort into wishing a fired staffer well, but maybe Ecuadorans were ultra-polite. Besides, whatever Daniel Cubrero had to say, Nora would listen, just to watch his gorgeous face and hear that liquid accent.

Nora pulled out the professional persona, the one who graduated top of her class in business school and was offered enviable positions with New York's best financial institutions. She didn't need Loving Earth's measly finance director position.

Well, maybe she did, but she wouldn't let Daniel Cubrero know that.

"It was good meeting you today," she said.

His Latin accent sounded like melted chocolate. "The board is impressed with you, Nora Abbott." His brown eyes warmed her as she fought to be professionally cool.

"I'm not sure the board liked what I had to say. I know several project directors at the Trust won't be happy."

"The board did not have much faith in the previous Finance Director. We suspected the picture wasn't so rosy as Darla painted. We discussed hiring an auditor."

Interesting, but not her problem. "I hope you can find someone to help figure it all out."

He gave her a puzzled expression. "You think we should hire an auditor to help you?"

From a short distance Cole stopped and studied them. Petal watched them from beneath her dreds.

"You might not need an auditor if you can find a competent accountant for your Finance Director," Nora said.

Daniel shrugged and held his arms out. The flamboyant gesture suited him. "What do you mean? We have a Finance Director. Surely our meeting didn't scare you off? We were tough, admittedly, but we are concerned for the Trust and you were giving us information that has been lacking in recent years."

"I'm not scared," Nora said. "I was fired."

Daniel laughed. Oh my, if she thought his accent, his dark handsomeness, and smoldering masculinity were intoxicating, this cheerful abandon nearly did her in. "You are definitely not fired. The board begs you to stay."

They wanted her? But did she want them? "I don't know. I'm not sure I'm such a good fit at the Trust."

He considered that. "I understand the atmosphere around there might not be, shall we say, warm and fuzzy. But stay, please. We are serious about getting the Trust back on track. Our first priority is the finances."

Nora studied the sophisticated and, no doubt wealthy, investment banker sitting with Abigail.

Petal's eyes pleaded with her.

Daniel murmured, "Please join us, Nora Abbott. I am begging you. You will have total autonomy and report directly to the board, to me."

Talk about employment benefits. She still hesitated.

"May I be frank with you?" Daniel said. He seemed earnest and his eyes focused on hers.

She nodded.

"I am a wealthy man."

No surprise.

"It is family money. I am ashamed to say I have not always been responsible and wise. But it is time for me to grow up. I chose to serve on the board of the Trust and to raise money for them because I am passionate about this planet. But my father?" When American's shrug it's usually a simple movement of the shoulders. Daniel's shrug seemed to come from his whole body. "My father indulges me because he thinks I am a child. I want to show him I chose a good organization and I can make it successful. "

Nora peeked into the coffee shop. Abigail hadn't spotted her, yet. "The Trust's work on open space is a model for cities all over the country. That's got to say something for the Trust."

Daniel agreed. "But that was before my time. I am eager to see the work move ahead in the Ecuador rainforest."

Nora tried to inch out of Abigail's sight line. "Sylvia's research has potential to be very press-worthy."

He shifted uncomfortably. "However, when my father discovered I was on the Trust board, he used his influence and money to bring Sylvia here. He did it out of goodness, to prove to the board I could bring in world class scientists. I did not ask him to do this."

Cole watched them from several yards away. Yes, Nora knew what it felt like to have someone else always saving you.

Abigail spotted Nora. She waved.

Nora pretended not to see her. "What do you have in mind?"

"I will work here with you and together we will find the financial discrepancies and grow the Trust into an international environmental protector."

Petal shivered even though the afternoon felt warm to Nora.

Abigail rose as if to hurry out to get Nora.

Nora looked from Petal to Abigail and back again.

18

Sylvia sat on a hard plastic chair in a tacky lobby. The drafty space with muted colors and linoleum smelled of commercial room freshener punctuated by the odor of the unwashed as they came through the doors. Body odor, cheap perfume, clothes steeped in grease from fast food restaurants—low class.

A uniformed woman cop, nothing more than a clerk, stood behind the counter tapping on a computer screen and pretending to ignore Sylvia. A few other uninteresting drones worked away on their dull jobs sitting behind their metal desks. Boulder's police station wasn't like the gritty TV shows where cops dragged in perps, and hookers and pimps wandered around. This was just a hard office with Sylvia endlessly waiting.

Sylvia had been here for hours at the mercy of these imbeciles. She had refused to talk to them, of course. She insisted they wait for her attorney and they'd allowed her a phone call. She contacted Daniel, who had dispatched a lawyer.

The Cubreros always had connections and this lawyer was some whip-smart savant from Denver who wasted no time freeing Sylvia from custody, if not suspicion. Without the results from the test fire to match the bullet rifling, they had no hard evidence. In their fear Sylvia was a flight risk, they'd overplayed their hand. The hard-nosed young woman Daniel sent had no trouble springing Sylvia from their clutches. The attorney had double-timed it back to Denver leaving Sylvia waiting for Daniel to pick her up from the station.

Finally, Daniel sauntered into the station. As usual, he created a ripple of admiration when he appeared in the station. The clerk behind the counter perked up and smiled eagerly. At forty-five, Sylvia had a few years on Daniel but she was every bit his equal. Together they were a couple worth noting.

Sylvia jumped up and hurried to him, her heels clacking on the cheesy linoleum. She met him halfway through the lobby, fuming. "How nice of you to grace me with your presence."

He lifted her hand and kissed it. "At your service."

She scurried to the door and waited for him to open it for her. "You should have been here twenty minutes ago."

"*Carina*, I arrived as soon as I could. Did the attorney not get here in good time?"

Daniel and his father used the same endearments for her. If only they each knew where the other had whispered those names.

She pushed the glass lobby doors open herself and stomped to the parking lot, only to slow down for Daniel to show her where he parked. She'd been waiting so long that the afternoon had drifted into evening and the sun dropped below the Flatirons. She scanned the lot filled with Subarus, economy cars, rugged SUVs , and the collection of various sedans and minivans. She didn't see a sports car she'd expect of Daniel. She glared at him, waiting for his direction. "The attorney made it here from Denver."

He strode down a row of cars with easy elegance. "She's very good, I'm told."

"She made it to the Boulder Police Department before you could drag yourself away from whatever consumed you." Sylvia's short legs worked double time to keep up with his saunter.

That smile of unconcern burned her. "Your charms are difficult to resist, *carina,* but I have other business to attend to. See? You are not so injured. Let me take you home and we will see what can be done to erase your troubles."

Did he think to appease her with a roll in the hay? If Daniel knew the riches she was about to provide for him, he'd treat her with more respect.

At least Eduardo knew her value. She hoped he wouldn't find out about her being accused of murder. Still if this hotshot attorney didn't get her off, Nora would have to call Eduardo. He'd take care of it because he needed Sylvia.

David pulled a key from his pocket and hit a button. The taillights on the car in front of her lit up.

She laughed. "A Prius? Taking this environmentalist image a little too far, aren't you?"

He raised his eyebrows and gave her an amused smile. He pressed another button on his key and the door unlocked. She waited for him to open it and she slid inside. With the smoothness of a jaguar—the brand of car he should be driving—Daniel eased himself into his own seat.

Sylvia anticipated their tryst in a few minutes between the silky sheets of her exquisite antique bed.

"So," he said, as if starting a casual conversation. "Why did you feel it necessary to kill our little Darla?"

"Don't be ridiculous." *I couldn't have killed Darla. A shot in the dark couldn't be that lucky—or unlucky.*

She folded her arms and viewed the city park outside her window. As usual, grungy college students and leftovers from the hippie days of Boulder's glory sprawled on the grass. The cops should be out rounding them up and carting them off the streets instead of chasing Sylvia.

Sylvia tried to calm down and think of something pleasant. She would wear the new lace bustier with the black garter belt and the spiked leopard print sling-backs Daniel favored.

Daniel switched lanes and turned right on Broadway. "A charge of murder is serious. Even if you did not kill Darla, you will have to devote much time and expense to defend yourself."

A flare of panic flashed inside her before she thought about it. No. Eduardo wouldn't let her go to prison. "My work is very important. Perhaps the Trust can pay for my legal defense."

They drove in silence and Daniel hummed tunelessly while maneuvering through traffic. After several minutes he pulled into her exclusive neighborhood directly underneath the Flatirons and stopped in front of her house. The 5,500-square-foot home with its cathedral ceilings, thick pile carpets and polished wood floors and, what the realtor described as "spectacular Flatirons view" always made Sylvia cringe. It seemed so pedestrian and ordinary. But she didn't have the time to devote to building something more suitable. When she finished her work here, she'd pick the perfect location—maybe several locations—and build something more fitting. For now, she could tolerate this, as long as she obtained the Chihuly.

Daniel's gaze flitted to the cement porch. It really should be much larger with a few columns. Stone lions might be too much.

"I did not know you were an animal lover."

Sylvia spun around to see the scruffy calico cat on her porch. "I'll need to call the HOA again. She turns up every few days and begs for food. Someone in the neighborhood must feed her."

Daniel raised his eyebrows in dismissal. He waited a moment. "And how do you propose the Trust find the money for your defense?"

She thought he'd dropped the subject.

"You haven't given the board much progress to make them inclined to pay for expensive lawyers."

What had gotten into everyone all of the sudden? The board and Eduardo, all of them thought she did nothing all day except dance to their tune.

Only her dignity kept her from slapping him. "What about your family foundation? Can't you get it from your father?"

Daniel eyed her as if gauging her mood.

Sylvia opened her car door and a rush of cold air invaded them. "Are you saying you won't support me in this?"

His eyes focused on her cleavage in obvious desire. "I did not mean to upset you. I am only wanting you to think about the problems you've created for the Trust and my family."

His family. As if Daniel had the slightest clue what his father felt about anything. "Ask Eduardo. He'll make sure I don't go to prison."

Daniel's eyebrows jumped up. "How is it you and my father met?"

In her anger she'd made a wrong step. Eduardo wouldn't want his name brought up to Daniel. "He admires my work. That's why he brought me to the Trust."

Daniel digested that. "He brought you to the Trust, where I sit on the board, so your groundbreaking study would reflect well on the organization. And he so generously allows the family trust to donate to your research."

Careful now. She ran a fingernail along the base of his throat and watched the goose bumps rise. "Eduardo wants you to be happy."

He caught her hand and pulled it away from his neck. "Is that why he sent you? Because I can't find my own importance in the world? Because I can't find my own women?"

"You couldn't be suggesting Eduardo is pimping me out to you, either personally or professionally?"

Daniel studied her. "Did he?"

How dare he? She flew out of the car. "Eduardo doesn't control my research or who I sleep with."

He narrowed his eyes. "Are you on his payroll to keep an eye on me?"

Intolerable. She slammed the door and started up the walk.

The damned calico cat twined herself between Sylvia's legs nearly bringing her to the pavement. She kicked it into the grass. The cat yowled and sped away.

19

The old farmhouse creaked every few minutes. Nora thought ghosts probably wandered the dark hallways and empty offices. If they didn't, they should. This building seemed strange enough in the daytime but at night, when she was the only one here, it felt like the House of Dracula.

Darkness filled her window, casting a reflection on her office and the light she'd turned on to dispel the creeps. *Thank dog no wind howled down Boulder Canyon to rattle the window and shriek against the siding or I wouldn't have been able to stay here this long.*

After her escape from Pearl Street and Abigail's dreams of a corporate career, Nora had hurried home to get Abbey. Then she met Daniel at the Trust. They'd tried to sift through the various activities and funds, bank statements and grants. Daniel said he had something to do and left for about an hour, then came back and insisted he take her to dinner.

They'd eaten at a Mediterranean place downtown. He was as charming as he was handsome, and the food was delicious. They'd chatted about childhood and exchanged details of colleges and highlights of their lives. Nora passed over her marriage, the snow-making scheme in Flagstaff, and the drama associated with it.

She'd been fascinated by Daniel's self-deprecating humor as he told of growing up in excess. He'd spent his youth chasing excitement from skiing in the Alps to scuba diving on the Barrier Reef to misadventures in Europe and the Middle East. Nora was sure he had enough stories to keep talking for months. But after all that running around, he said he finally understood his wealth could be used for something besides his own pleasure and he planned to spend it protecting the Ecuadoran rainforest.

Nora felt an urge to get back to the office and he'd obliged. He tried to talk her into going home but she wanted to get a few things organized before she called it quits for the night.

She'd been building the mother of all spreadsheets. Tomorrow she'd populate the columns and rows with the data from bank statements and financial statements and then she'd be able to analyze where the money came from and where it went.

Her eyes burned and she leaned back for a break. "That's enough for tonight," she said to Abbey.

He opened his eyes and thumped his tail.

Nora's eye caught the empty box she'd used to bring some of her personal things to the Trust. "She's not coming back." This time Abbey didn't bother to open his eyes. Nora stood and stacked the self-help books into the box and placed the porcelain animals on top. She carried the stack of Darla's affirmations she'd collected and added them to the box. Finally, she picked up Darla's picture.

A heavy blanket of sadness fell on Nora. She couldn't imagine someone so overlooked in life would be remembered long after death. It seemed a terrible waste.

She placed the picture in the box and contemplated the top yellow sheet. "I will confront Sylvia." It was copied the length of the page. Nora picked up the stack of sheets and paged through until she found what she searched for. "I am strong enough to stand up to her." Nora assumed the *her* was Sylvia.

"What do you suppose she wanted to confront her about?" Abbey lifted his head and yawned. The other staffers and now the police suspected Sylvia of killing Darla. Maybe Sylvia had something to do with whatever it was Darla supposedly found in the books. And maybe the moon is made of green cheese, as Abigail used to say whenever Nora's imagination got the best of her—which happened often.

Nora winked at Abbey. "I agree. Time to call it a night." She donned her coat and picked up her bag. Abbey followed her as they descended the narrow stairs to the kitchen. They turned toward the lobby and Nora stopped.

She hesitated. "It wouldn't hurt to check it out."

Abbey didn't protest as Nora tiptoed through the kitchen to Sylvia's office. The kitchen floor creaked and Abbey's toenails clicked on the linoleum. Nora slowed as she approached Sylvia's office door. She shouldn't snoop.

She whispered to Abbey. "I won't touch anything. Just look around a little. No going through drawers or anything like that." She pushed open the door, the sound like thunder in the quiet house. Nora stepped into the room and felt for the light. She flicked it on.

Someone screamed.

Nora screamed.

Abbey barked.

Nora jumped back, ready to retreat.

Her eyes finally focused. She clamped a hand to her chest and sucked in air. "Petal! What are you doing here?"

Petal sat in a nest of her own clothes close to her desk. The pink glow of her scarf-draped lamp faded in the overhead light. She blinked in the sudden brightness. "I'm—uh—I'm—sometimes Sylvia can't sleep and works at night. I thought maybe she'd be up tonight because of the, uh, the—because of the trouble."

"This is crazy," Nora said. Abbey sat in the doorway.

Petal rose and pulled out her desk chair. She huddled into it. "She doesn't ask me to do it. It's okay."

With Darla gone Petal had no one to go home to, no one to keep tabs on her.

Even if Abigail was furious about Nora's no-show earlier, at least she knew her mother loved her and would care if she never came home. "I think I saw some hot chocolate mix in the kitchen cupboard. Why don't I make us some?"

Petal jumped up with a grin on her face. "I can do it." She scurried from the office and Nora heard banging in the kitchen.

She tilted her head at Abbey. "As long as we're here..." She wandered casually to Sylvia's desk. A 24 inch monitor dominated the desk and a laptop sat on the edge. The wood gleamed with only one lone sheet of notebook paper shoved half under the laptop.

The microwave hummed in the kitchen. Nora gingerly slid the sheet of paper from under the laptop. A tree graph with several circles showed a confusing jumble. It looked like Darla's idea of fund accounting. In other words, chaos. Nora bent closer. Credit card and bank names labeled the circles along with various names of people. Dollar amounts in the thousands were inked on arrows going from circle to circle.

What a financial juggling act. Sylvia was either a genius or heading for a big crash.

The ding of the microwave warned of Petal's return. Nora shoved the paper back and headed for the kitchen.

"That smells good," Nora said when Petal handed her a chipped mug of hot chocolate. Actually, it smelled sickening sweet. "Let's sit at the booth."

Petal acted surprised. "Okay. I don't think I've ever sat there before."

They settled themselves in the booth with the glow of an overhead light casting their reflection in the darkened window.

"Can I ask you something?" Petal said. "What's your mother's story?"

"Her story?" Nora thought a moment. "Well, she grew up in Nebraska and went to school here in Boulder at CU. I guess she met my father there, but he apparently left us when I was a baby."

"Where does he live?" Petal asked.

Nora shrugged. "I don't know and don't care. He didn't want us, so why should I want him?"

Petal frowned and sipped her hot chocolate. "What happened to your mother after he left?"

Nora held her palm over the steaming cup. "She married Berl when I was about five. He had a lot of money and that suited her."

Petal sipped and set her mug down. "I thought so."

"What do you mean?" The hot chocolate tasted too sweet for Nora.

"Well, she's got all this high society class and taste and stuff, but she's too nice to have been raised with money."

Nora wrapped her hands around her warm mug. "I hadn't thought about it but maybe Abigail's coming full circle. She started out humble, lived large for a while and now she's back to humble."

"With Charlie?" The pinks and oranges of Petal's layers became flowers in the window's reflection.

"Well, there was another husband between Berl and Charlie, but he died of a heart attack when they'd only been married a couple of years."

Petal finished her hot chocolate and curled her feet under her. "Do you like Charlie?"

The house had been growing steadily colder since the heater's timer set it on nighttime temperature.

Nora couldn't stop her grin. "Charlie's my best friend. Or he was when I lived in Flagstaff. He's a real character. Vietnam vet, true environmentalist. Loyal and completely devoted to Abigail." No matter what she said about an alleged affair.

Petal sighed.

"What about you? Where is your mother?" Nora asked.

Petal swirled her cup. "Oh. My mother lives in New Orleans. She's got some medical problems. That's why I need this job. I help her out."

A boom sounded from the front door. Nora and Petal both jumped and Petal let out a squeak of alarm. Abbey lifted his head and woofed.

The building sighed as the front door opened.

Nora's heart nearly burst. Petal flew out of the booth and raced toward Sylvia's office.

"Boulder County Police," a low-pitched woman's voice called.

Nora rose on shaky legs and stepped around the kitchen wall into the lobby. Abbey followed her.

A uniformed police officer stood by the door, her belt weighing her down with all manner of tools or weapons. She held a flashlight but hadn't turned it on.

Nora hurried to her. "I'm Nora Abbott. Can I help you?"

The officer studied her. "Officer Garcia." She introduced herself. "Do you work here?"

"I just started yesterday." Nora's heart still thudded.

Officer Garcia surveyed the room and let her gaze travel up the stairs. "Are you here alone?"

Nora pointed toward the kitchen. "My colleague is here."

Garcia nodded. "Working late?"

"Yes. Trying to catch up." Nora adopted the spare speaking style of the officer.

Garcia's voice bordered on masculine and she sounded almost angry. "You know a woman was murdered out here a few days ago."

Fear spiked Nora's flesh. If Garcia were here to reassure Nora, she failed.

"I'd suggest you wrap up your work for tonight and head home."

"I was just leaving."

"Good. I'll wait in the parking lot and follow you out." Garcia swept her gaze over the lobby and she walked out the door.

Petal crept around the corner. "Is she gone?"

Nora watched Garcia out the front window. "Guess she's checking up on us. Probably a good thing."

Petal hung her head and retreated to the kitchen.

Nora followed feeling suddenly felt exhausted. "Can I give you a ride?"

Petal shook her head. "No. I've got my bike."

Nora carried their cups to the sink. Petal scuttled to Sylvia's office.

Nora shrugged into her coat. She hollered to Petal. "I'll wait for you and lock up."

Petal stuck her head out of the office. "Go ahead. I'm going to leave Sylvia a note in case she comes in."

Nora held the door open for Abbey and closed it after he stepped out on the porch. Cold mountain air chilled Nora's fingers and nose. The deep silence closed around her.

Darla died on a night like this. Not a hundred yards from where Nora stood.

Someone killed her.

On a night like this.

20

The furnace rumbled to life in the drafty farmhouse. Nora reached under her desk and turned off the ceramic heater that had made her office tolerable for the past two hours. She scoped out at the clock on her computer. Seven o'clock. Weak light sneaked from her western-facing window announcing another day.

She'd been here late last night with Petal; late enough that Abigail had given up waiting for her and gone to bed. Nora returned hours before dawn, cutting her night short. Whenever something creaked or bumped—which happened often in the rambling old building, Nora had to talk herself into staying calm and ignoring her urge to leave.

As creepy as the Trust was, it seemed a good alternative to facing Abigail's wrath. She'd endured one raging phone call about missing the interview yesterday and would probably be in for a few more. But if she could delay it, Abigail might lose steam. She could hope, anyway.

She scratched Abbey behind his ears and he didn't bother to open his eyes. "Another hour before anyone comes to work." At least, Mark said they were supposed to show up at eight.

Her green banker's lamp illuminated the work space around her computer and she hadn't bothered turning on any other lights. She'd focused organizing and familiarizing herself with the inner workings of the Trust. The $4 million budget divided into eight distinct projects with their own budgets, each funded with grants and donations, some shared, some specific with restricted and unrestricted funds coming in and going out of five different bank accounts and tied to several investment accounts. She'd need to simplify the system. No one could monitor of this financial maze. Tracking the grants alone might be a full time job.

Nora could usually drill into a problem and block out any distractions. It's how she'd been so successful in school and able to run a ski resort on her own. But this morning, her brain was like a kindergartener with ADHD.

One moment she thought about Cole standing amid the colorful fall leaves on the mall yesterday. The Cole slideshow flipped to him on her ski mountain in Flagstaff, defending her at Scott's funeral. Next slide: Cole fighting off an attacker who tried to strangle Nora to keep her from making snow on the sacred peaks. Flip: Cole grinning and catching her in his arms when she'd discovered he hadn't been killed. He'd risked his life to save hers.

Stop this!

As soon as she forced her mind from Cole, it bounced back to Benny and worse still, Nakwaiyamtewa. She was never sure if he and the kachina were one and the same. The kachina wore colorful clothes and feathers, his mask fierce and frightening.

Nakwaiyamtewa stood no taller than five feet and appeared and disappeared like Whac-a-Mole. Nora had only seen him a few times in quiet moments. He was a man of few words and those were usually some kind of annoying riddle.

Turns out, Nakwaiyamtewa died in the 1880s. His descendent, Benny, carried on the Hopi traditions. No doubt they had coffee together every morning and discussed the local corn harvest and state of the world they claimed responsibility for.

Another reason Nora had climbed from her bed so early was the dreaming. The kachina had crashed through the forest every time she drifted off last night. He chased someone, maybe her, she couldn't tell in the dream. The fear bursting through her sleep into her bedroom left her panting and unwilling to go back to sleep. Now a low grade headache banged behind her eyes.

Focus.

The Trust staffers should be showing up soon. Would they find out she'd spilled her guts to the board and revealed whose work was in the red or black? If so, they might treat her like a squealer. Good bye to the notion of friends.

Mark must hate her. Thinking about him gave her the creeps.

Footsteps on the stairs made Nora stiffen. She couldn't hear the front door from here and someone was already on their way up.

"Don't think you can avoid me forever." It wasn't what she expected.

"Good morning, Abigail."

Anger wafted from Abigail in waves but it didn't affect her appearance. She wore wool slacks, turtleneck and boots, all coordinated with a car coat that carried the chilly fall morning into Nora's office. "Don't 'good morning' me. I set up an appointment with a very busy man on your behalf and you embarrassed me in front of him. I can't imagine what he'll tell his mother."

"I'm sorry." She'd repeat it as often as necessary. It would do no good to shut Abigail down. Might as well let her spew.

With the Abigail white noise, Nora was finally able to concentrate. She stared at the screen. What was this? Wasn't the balance of Sylvia's restricted account much higher in August than the balance the computer showed for September?

Abigail slapped the desktop. "Are you listening to me?"

Nora pulled her gaze from the screen. Ignoring Abigail wouldn't work. She noted the time and gave Abigail ten minutes to rant. The headache gained momentum.

"'Casting away radiance in pursuit of mediocrity in a flight of fear.'" Abigail reached into her slender leather handbag and pulled out a tiny notepad. It sparkled with gold glitter adorning Michelangelo's cherubs and had a matching, miniature pen. She paused and slid the pad back into the bag. "Something not right about that. I'll work on it."

The morning lightened enough Nora snapped off her desk lamp. "Poetry aside, Abigail, I'm trying to work. Can we talk at home?"

Undaunted, Abigail continued. "You're making a big mistake. Even Cole agrees with me on that."

Nora sat back in her chair with a creak of springs. "You discussed me with Cole?"

Abigail's tone softened, as it always did when she talked about Cole. "He's concerned about you working at the Trust and frankly, after hearing what he had to say, so am I."

"What, do you have him on speed dial?" She rubbed at a knot on her neck, hoping to ease the knocking in her brain. Maybe she needed coffee.

And here it came again. The speech Abigail worked herself into every time Cole's name came up. "Why do you have such a problem with that man? He's strong and capable, certainly not hard on the eyes. And he cares about you."

Easy lob to Nora's court. "Let's talk about you and Charlie."

Abigail stiffened. "Nothing to talk about."

"You don't really think he's having an affair?"

Abigail clamped her lips and spun toward the door.

Victory! Sometime soon she'd have to dig into the details of the Charlie mess, but not now.

Abigail walked back in. Drat. She'd called the match too soon. "I saw it with my own two eyes. Some woman your age."

Nora's eyes wandered to the screen but she swiveled her chair to give Abigail her full attention. "Did you ask Charlie about it?"

Abigail set her bag on the desk and slipped out of her coat, dashing Nora's hopes for her hasty departure. "Why would I give him the opportunity to make up a lie? I won't allow myself to be mocked and humiliated."

Nora wanted to rush Abigail to the finish line. She definitely needed caffeine to battle the headache. "Charlie's a good man. There's probably an explanation."

Abigail perched on the edge of the wicker chair. The burnt orange and browns of her fall ensemble clashed with the lavender and mint motif. "I wasn't surprised when I caught him. All the signs were there."

"What kind of signs?"

Abigail straightened her shoulders in sturdy dignity. "He started cleaning up and wearing nice clothes every day. Or rather, what he considers nice clothes. He refused to wear the chinos and golf shirts I bought him. I know they'd be more comfortable than his old button-down flannel shirts and Nora, his jeans were a nightmare of faded and frayed."

Coffee might save Nora's life. The rickety heater chugged warm air through the floor vents pushing aside the abandon feel of the night.

"He left the house every day, as usual, but he wasn't going into the woods."

"How do you know?"

Abigail's despairing expression stabbed at Nora. "I can't believe I sank so low. I actually sniffed his clothes. They didn't smell the same as when he wandered the trails with the fresh air and pines."

Nora stood and stretched. "Why didn't you talk to him instead of building resentment?"

"That's the most telling part. His personality changed. With me, anyway." Abigail's gaze traveled toward the window. "You know how charming and solicitous he usually is with me."

Abigail always appreciated goddess worship.

"He became moody. Sometimes he ignored me. And once, he even snapped at me."

Abigail made Nora want to snap like a feral Chihuahua, but Charlie had endless patience.

"The real clue though, is that he wasn't interested in," she lowered her voice, "the bedroom."

"Really, Abigail? This is what you want to tell your daughter?"

"It's natural. Do you think your desire goes away when you hit forty?"

"I don't want to think about it." Nora paced to the door and scanned the hallway to see if anyone else had made it to work.

"Well, it doesn't. I'm a healthy woman with healthy needs like any other woman. I notice when my lover loses interest."

"Stop talking now."

Abigail sat back. "You can't hide from the realities of life, dear."

Nora wandered back to her desk and propped against the work surface. "We're going to have to talk about this later. I've got a raging headache. Probably because I haven't been sleeping."

Abigail hurried over to Nora and placed a cold hand on Nora's forehead. "Are you sick? Why haven't you been sleeping?"

Nora brushed Abigail's hand away. "I'm fine. Just having dreams."

"Nightmares?"

Maybe it would help exorcise them if Nora talked about it. "Kachina dreams. It's probably new job stress."

Abigail acted overly concerned about Nora's lack of sleep.

Nora rubbed her forehead. "From what I know, kachinas are supposed to stay on the sacred mountain in Flagstaff or on the mesas in Hopiland. They don't travel all over the place like goblins with frequent flyer miles."

Abigail frowned and stared out the window.

"I know that November starts a new season for the kachinas. So they leave the mesa where they've spent the summer and go back to the mountain for the winter. Maybe Nakwaiyamtewa thinks a visit to Colorado would be nice before he goes home."

Abigail put on her coat. "You're over-thinking things. It's just a dream."

"Maybe it is just a dream about Hopis. But I saw the kachina on Mount Evans and then Benny showed up here. Why?" Nora waited for her mother's dismissal of kachina sightings as signs of Nora's overactive imagination.

Abigail seemed distracted and in a hurry to leave. "Why wouldn't Benny visit? He likes you."

Nora shook her head. "No, it's more than that. He hates leaving the mesa for anything." Nora leaned back and mused. "What is my connection to Hopi?"

Abigail grabbed her bag and scurried to the door.

This didn't seem right. "Mother?"

"I've got to go, dear. Talk to you later."

Nora's radar kicked in. "Hang on, Abigail. What are you hiding. You've got that secretive look on your face."

Abigail's smiled looked strained. "I don't know what you're talking about."

The hairs on Nora's neck jumped to attention. "What?"

"I try to live in the present. I don't like to dwell on unpleasant things in the past," Abigail stammered.

As much as it sounded like more of Abigail's bad poetry, Nora thought she might be serious. This wouldn't be good. "You're going to tell me something you should have told me a long time ago, aren't you?"

Abigail huffed. "You don't need to know everything about me. I'm entitled to a few secrets."

It only got worse. "But this secret involves me, doesn't it?"

"Maybe." Abigail's eyes traveled from the coat closet up to the ceiling, over to the shelves and to the window. Then she focused on Nora's lightweight hiking boots.

"Spill it, Mother."

Abigail glanced down the empty hall and stepped back into the office. "Did you ever wonder how I met Berle?"

Berle was Abigail's second husband. The man who raised Nora.

We're going to take the long way. "This train has a caboose, right? And when we get there it's going to tell me something I need to know, right?"

Abigail sat in the wicker chair. "I met Berle in Flagstaff. He was there on business with Kachina Ski."

Nora's stepfather had given her the ski resort in Flagstaff as insurance for Abigail. He was afraid if he died before Abigail, she'd run through his money. Which is what happened. Nora promised him she'd take care of Abigail. Which she did.

Nora would die of old age or frustration before Abigail made her point.

"I never told you the reason I was in Flagstaff. It had to do with your father."

"My biological father?" Nora didn't remember Abigail ever voluntarily mentioning him.

"Yes."

Nora plopped into her chair.

"Your father was from the Flagstaff area. He grew up there. Had a bunch of family."

Abigail paused. Nora wanted to scream at her. *More. More!*

"He didn't really run away from us, you know." Abigail said it softly. "He died. And I took him home and let him be buried by his family."

Nora's throat felt too dry to speak. "My father died? Why didn't you tell me?"

Abigail stared ahead, her eyes misty with tears. "I thought if I told you he died, you'd go looking for his family but if I told you he abandoned us, you'd hate him and not ever try to contact him."

"That makes no sense."

Abigail raised her eyebrows. "It worked, didn't it?"

"Yeah, but I've spent my whole life angry at a man who didn't deserve it."

Abigail considered that and then went on. "We were so young. We met in college and married within a month. Neither of us ever finished. So in love. We didn't have any money and we didn't care. Oh, I know you won't believe me when I say that. But your father was... he was special."

Nora couldn't speak; she struggled to breathe.

"It was a car wreck. The sort of thing that happens to other people. And suddenly... our dream ended. He was gone and I was a few weeks pregnant."

"I'm sorry." Nora wanted to cry for her mother's loss. "Why didn't you tell me this?"

A father and family she didn't know. How could her mother not tell her? When could she meet them and begin to understand her past? Thoughts flew at her like hailstones battering against a window.

Abigail fought tears. "I wanted what was best for you. Maybe I was wrong. I don't know. You turned out so well and you're successful and educated. But it's coming full circle."

Chills snaked through Nora.

Abigail's eyes pleaded for understanding. "Your father was Hopi."

After so much tension, Nora laughed. "He was not. I've got red hair."

Instant anger burn Abigail's words. "He most certainly was Hopi. Maybe there was an indiscretion in his ancestry. There's also red hair in my family."

Could that be true? Maybe that's why she could see Nakwaiyamtewa. "Am I related to Benny?"

Abigail waved her hand. "I imagine so."

"Does he know?"

"I don't know. He seems to know a lot of things."

Hopi heritage. This wasn't true. It couldn't be true.

Nora rubbed her forehead. "Why didn't you tell me my father was dead?"

The fire went out of Abigail. "I was afraid. I was young and alone with a baby. The Hopi have very strong family attachments and I thought they might take you from me. I would have shared you with them but I didn't know them and I didn't trust they would give you back."

"And they're destitute. You couldn't stand the thought of me not having all those cute Urban Outfitters clothes and going on spring break."

"I am not a monster!" Abigail sounded hurt. "I wanted the best for you. And you got the best."

Nora tilted her head to stretch her neck. "I'm sorry. Can you..." She couldn't think what she wanted to ask.

Abigail stood and backed toward the door. "You need some time to think about this."

The world faded, leaving her isolated on her desk chair, floating in dense fog. Nora nodded. "Yes."

Nora sat still. If she moved, she might crumble.

Hopi.

She had family.

21

Nora sat at her desk, struggling with the idea of a father. A Hopi father. Did he love peaches and hate liver as she did? Was he a Rolling Stones fan or did he tend more toward Elvis. Or maybe he didn't like music at all.

"Good morning."

Nora gasped at the greeting. Mark stood at her doorway. "Sorry. I didn't mean to startle you."

Nora brought herself back to reality. Bright light shone from her window.

Last time she saw Mark he had fired her. Now he stood in her doorway. She scanned his hands for the giant butcher knife he probably brought to ram into her ribs. Instead, she saw two tall compostable paper cups with a Mr. Green Beans logo. "Hi, Mark." She tried for casual but it came out a croak.

He held out one of the cups. "I saw your Jeep out front so I turned around and went back for coffee."

She accepted the cup. This would help with her colossal headache. "Thanks."

"I got you a double shot skinny latte. Next time, you can tell me your favorite." He sniggered.

Mark's one-eighty in attitude made her more than a little jumpy. Abbey stood, stretched and wagged his tail as he ambled to Mark. When Mark didn't pet him, Abbey plopped down. Mornings exhausted him.

Nora sipped. Yuck. Mr. Green Beans over-roasted their beans or grew their own in the back yard. The coffee had a sickening, super-bitter taste. She smiled. "That's really nice of you."

He sipped his own coffee. "I need to apologize for my behavior yesterday. I'm only glad the board prevailed with their calmer heads." He snorted.

What a freak. "It's okay. I understand how stressful a board meeting can be. Sort of like a college final when your whole grade depends on one essay question." What had her father studied in college?

"I want us to be friends. We're on the same team—Team Earth." He raised a fist.

Everything he needed to know about life he learned in kindergarten and he must have been absent for half the lesson. "Thanks, Mark. I'm really happy to be a part of the Trust." Was her father short, like a lot of Hopis?

Mark studied her office as if he'd like to know what each carefully stacked pile of papers signified. "Have you been here long this morning?" He sounded more probing than friendly.

Long enough for my whole life to get tipped over.

Time to compartmentalize. She shook off her shattering news and concentrated on Mark. New job. Loving Earth Trust. Here. Now. "I wanted to get an early start. It's a complicated system and the sooner I get it conquered, the sooner I can write checks and pay bills."

The friendly slipped from his face. "The sooner the better. Sylvia needs that money."

Would it be poor form to ask about Sylvia and the police?

He pointed to her coffee. "How do you like the latte?" He seemed to expect her to drink more.

She took another awful sip and swallowed down the nasty brew. "It's great."

He nodded and watched her closely. *Again: freak.* "Okay, then. I'll let you get back to work."

She sipped just to be a good sport. "Thanks for the coffee."

He scrutinized her once more and left.

Nora set the coffee down and typed in the August dates on Sylvia's restricted account. The fund showed $1,295,672.56. She entered the dates for September. $895,672.56.

$400,000 difference. Exactly. Where did it go? It shouldn't be hard to spot.

Fay poked her head in Nora's office. She wore jeans and a fleece pullover, her thin blonde hair tangled down her back. Her voice crackled. "Some drama yesterday, huh?"

Abbey stood and offered himself for a pat from the newcomer.

Fay obliged. She spoke in comforting baby-talk. "What a sweetie you are."

Nora braced for harsh words. After all, she'd announced to the board that several projects at the Trust were over budget. That would probably mean cuts and someone might even lose a job to save money.

Receiving his fair share of welcome, Abbey made his way back to lie at Nora's feet.

Fay stepped into the office holding a Mr. Green Beans travel mug. She lowered her voice. "Did you get a chance to tell the board about Sylvia? They ought to know she doesn't do anything."

Nora didn't know what to say to that. "I only reported the financial situation." Which just worsened with a $400,000 disappearance.

Bill stopped outside her door. He hadn't shaved since yesterday and his shirt had more wrinkles than Harrison Ford's face. He also sipped from a Mr. Green Beans mug. He gave her a thumbs up and said, "Did you turn Sylvia in for embezzling?"

"What?" Nora gulped. "No. I..."

Bill grinned. "Just joking. They think she killed Darla."

Fay cackled. "Why would they think that?"

His tone dripped sarcasm. "Ballistic evidence? Flight risk? I wouldn't know."

Bill winked at Fay and they laughed.

Had they set Sylvia up? *Yes, they probably did and they're going to take her Ferrari and run away to Mexico. Sheesh, Nora.*

Darla's murder probably had more to do with the missing $400,000.

But maybe it wasn't really missing. Nora needed to check out all the statements before she assumed it was stolen.

Fay nodded sagely. "I have no doubt she killed Darla."

"If she killed Darla, who do you think is next on her list?" Thomas walked up behind Fay. He unzipped his parka and gulped his coffee from Mr. Green Beans. The Trust ought to get a volume discount.

They stood in her doorway discussing motives and future victims of Sylvia's murder spree.

How could they joke about this? Further, how could they stand that coffee? Thinking about hers, Nora's stomach gave a twist.

"Petal and Darla, they're both strange if you ask me," Bill said.

The three of them carried on their gossip fest without including Nora. She didn't know how to shoo them out of her office without being rude.

"I don't know how she can work for Sylvia. Do you know how many grad students I could get into the field on that bitch's budget?" Thomas said.

"Maybe you'll get your chance now that she's going to prison on murder charges." Fay said.

An unmistakable Latino accent floated over Bill's shoulder. "I do not think Sylvia is going to prison." Whatever Daniel Cubrero said sounded like silk on skin.

Bill flushed. Thomas disappeared. Guilt settled on Fay's features.

"A police officer is downstairs now ready to conduct interviews. Perhaps you should make yourselves available to him." Daniel spoke to Fay and Bill as he slipped into Nora's office and removed the black sport coat he wore over a white shirt. His jeans snugged to his body like they were custom tailored. It occurred to Nora that they might be. That must be the finest Italian leather on his feet, the shoes probably felt more comfortable than her slippers and cost more than her Jeep.

Fay's eyes glazed slightly and her jaw slackened. Nora knew how she felt.

Daniel raised Nora's hand to his lips. Kissing her hand? Nora could never remember anyone kissing her hand before. Such an affectation and yet, it seemed natural for Daniel. "How are you this morning, *mi bonitacita*?"

Bill's eyes widened.

In an effort to appear more grounded than the gapers in the doorway, Nora pulled her hand from Daniel's and gestured to the wide work counter full of neat stacks. "I'm making progress." Nora didn't think she allowed herself to be undone by total handsomeness, but her stomach roiled and bile rose in her throat. Maybe the milk in the latte was spoiled.

"Point me in a direction and I will do your bidding."

His accent sent a little shiver through her. Or was it the nausea from the latte? She burped a little, the taste of the bitter coffee revisited made her feel sicker.

Daniel turned toward Fay and Bill. "The officer downstairs?"

"Oh, certainly," Bill said.

"Nice of you to get so involved." Fay blushed and blinked rapidly. "I hope we'll see you again."

"*Bueno.*" He turned back to Nora leaving the others to slink away.

"I'm not really sure what we're searching for. I'm starting with the most recent bank statements and working backward." Oh. Her stomach whooshed up and turned over. She held a hand to her mouth.

"Are you feeling okay?"

Nora waited for the wave of nausea to pass. "I think so." Another wave hit her.

Daniel grasped her arm. "You must sit down."

She let him lead her to the desk. She leaned against it and spotted a swirl of pinks and oranges outside her door. The fact it wasn't blue made her want to sing. But it might be Petal, alone and afraid, wanting to hang out in a safe office or maybe hide in her closet.

Nora plopped into her chair. She opened her mouth to call Petal into her office but what came gushing out wasn't words. Nora didn't have time to feel aghast at the stream of vomit coating the fine Italian leather of Daniel's shoes.

She swayed to one side of her chair, slid off and passed out on the floor.

22

The emergency room beyond Nora's curtained cubicle bustled with activity. The ER didn't smell quite as hospital-ly as she'd expect, but enough antiseptic and chemical lingered to remind Nora where she was. Wheels, feet, voices, clanking, urgency—it all seeped under the drape to add to Nora's anxiety.

Nora watched the IV drip into the tubing attached to the back of her hand. It looked pale resting on the white thermal blanket. She got up enough nerve to peek at Daniel. "I'm so sorry."

He grinned, showing white, even teeth and inviting lips. "You've already apologized."

She'd emptied her guts and wasn't sure her hair was always out of the way. She had sweated and then chilled. She must be gorgeous.

Nora wanted to hide under the blanket and yet she had to make conversation after she'd puked on his shoes. "Thank you for bringing me here." She had a sudden thought. "What about Abbey?"

Daniel raised an eyebrow. "Abbey?"

"My dog. I left him at the office."

The curtain around her bed swiped back. Cole burst in wearing his typical flannel shirt and jeans topped off with a navy blue down vest. He pushed his hair from his forehead and scanned her from head to feet

"Abbey's in my pickup. Are you okay? What happened? Are you sick? Did you break anything?"

Daniel's eyebrows popped up in surprise. "Nora, you did not tell me you were married."

"I'm not." To Cole she said, "Why do you have Abbey?"

Daniel's mouth formed a slight smirk. "My mistake."

Cole scowled at Daniel. "I didn't think you'd want him shut up in your office when you weren't there. What happened?"

"I got sick. Threw up. I'm feeling better."

A doctor with a lab coat over a simple brown paisley wrap dress stepped into the curtained space. She held a tablet computer in one hand and planted her other on her hip, staring down the two men. "One person allowed at a time. One of you will have to leave." She shook Nora's hand. "I'm Dr. Taylor."

Could Nora get a prescription for that attitude? Dr. Taylor had no trouble asserting her control.

Cole glared at Daniel.

Daniel raised one eyebrow in response and spoke to Nora. "If your... friend... will see you home, I need to attend to a few chores." Daniel bent over and kissed Nora's forehead. Maybe he did it to annoy Cole in some testosterone standoff. But his familiarity startled Nora. They might slobber all over each other in Ecuador but Nora preferred her nice, roomy American personal space. Especially since she suspected she might smell a little "off."

Cole frowned.

Dr. Taylor snapped the IV drip with her thumb and forefinger. "How are you feeling?"

"Much better."

Dr. Taylor studied her. "The nausea gone?"

Nora nodded. "It didn't last long."

"I'd guess you got it out of your system with all that vomiting."

Cole butted in, as if it were any of his business. "What made her sick?"

Dr. Taylor swiped her finger across her computer screen. "Could be any number of things. Her symptoms suggest food poisoning."

"Can you run some test? Is this normal?" He sounded insistent.

Dr. Taylor glanced from the screen. "We could. Yes. We could spend a lot of time and money and not come up with anything definitive. Nora is feeling better."

"When can I go home?" Nora asked.

Dr. Taylor tapped the drip again. "This is your second bag?"

Nora nodded.

"As soon as you empty this—unless you feel the nausea returning. If that happens," she turned to Cole, "bring her back immediately and we'll run those tests."

With that, she spun on her toes and zipped away.

Nora stared at the bag, three fourths drained into her veins. "You can go. I'll call Abigail to come get me."

"Call Abigail if you want but I'm not going anywhere."

"What are you even doing here?" Not that she cared what Cole thought but she'd rather he didn't see her this vulnerable.

"I stopped by the Trust to talk you and they told me you'd gone to the emergency room."

Could she poke a hole in the bag and make it drain quicker? "We don't have anything to talk about."

"Benny called and..."

Would that be Benny, her long lost cousin? She dropped her head on the pillow. "I don't care what Benny said. He's just a guy living out on a mesa in the desert having delusional episodes."

Cole's mouth tipped up in a half smile and his eyes danced. "Keep telling yourself that. You know better. You've seen it."

A year ago the kachina had directed her to the save the mountain, but he hadn't helped her save Heather. Nora saw the headstrong, passionate sixteen-year-old flipping her blue-back hair over her shoulder, courageous and foolish in her fight for her Hopi heritage.

Did Nora blame the kachina or herself more?

Nora felt tempted to tell Cole about her new-found heritage. She had the strangest urge to know what he thought of it. But she wanted to get used to it before she shared it.

Nora tried to reach up to tap the bag and force it to empty. Her efforts failed. If Cole would just leave she could relax and let her body rehydrate. "How is it you can just show up? Don't you have a life?"

He paused. "I've been in Wyoming on my family's ranch. It's slow season so they can spare me for a few days."

"I don't need you to babysit me. Go home."

His ears turned red. "There are more pleasant things to do than be rejected by you."

"Okay then. We agree. You need to go home."

"I can't do that."

"Why not?"

He shook his head as if it were obvious. "Because you need someone to protect you."

Now he was really dancing on her nerves. "And since you think you saved my life once you have the responsibility to keep saving me."

"It's not a case of responsibility," he said quietly.

Time to stop the conversation before he said something she didn't want to hear. She turned her head away.

He didn't leave. "You need to get away from the Trust."

She whipped her head around. "Why would I do that?"

"Because someone tried to kill you."

"I got food poisoning."

"What did you eat this morning?"

Nothing. When she got to the apartment last night she'd eaten handfuls of Cheerios from the box. The thought of Abigail's annoyance almost made her smile. That was the last food she'd had.

Until the coffee Mark brought.

The coffee she couldn't stand even though Fay and Thomas guzzled theirs.

23

Sylvia stood with her arms crossed assessing her dining room. The expensive original oil paintings and the thick hand-woven rug over the shining rosewood floor pleased her. The chandelier glittered, throwing sparkles into the dark cathedral windows. An ordinary person would think it adequate, maybe even like it. But it didn't suit Sylvia in the least.

The Chihuly should hang directly over the wrought iron and glass dining table she'd commissioned from an artist in Jackson Hole last year. A hard knot of frustration hit her gut as Sylvia adjusted one of the dining chairs. Until she had her glass, the room would be incomplete.

Sylvia's heels sank into the deep pile of the rug and the folds of her negligee swished softly against her legs as she paraded down the hall. She paused in front of a full-length mirror, the designer frame setting off her image. Daniel would appreciate the view. Too bad they'd had that spat after the police station yesterday. She'd expected him all day but he hadn't shown up. Sooner or later he would return to her.

The doorbell rang. The grandfather clock showed it was after nine. It could be Daniel, or maybe not. Her heart thudded against her ribs.

She descended two stairs to the foyer and tiptoed to the door to peek out the side window.

Daniel stood under the porch light. He oozed sex in his black blazer and jeans. He held a bottle of Courvoisier.

Sylvia smiled in satisfaction. She adjusted the neckline on the slinky black negligee, patted her hair, then unlocked the door and swung it wide.

"*Buenos noches.*" So much like his father; but he replaced the confidence of the mature man with the raw sexuality of a younger man.

"Please come in." She stepped back and her vision dropped to his shapely backside as he walked past her.

A splash of fur zipped by her, hurtling into the foyer. The damned calico cat slowed to a trot and wound around Daniel's legs.

"Oh, that pest!" Sylvia lunged for it.

Daniel bent down and picked it up. He handed the bottle to Sylvia. He stroked the cat's fur as he walked back to the door. "*Mi gato bonito.*" He murmured as if he actually liked the fur ball. He set it on the porch and gave it a gentle shove then stepped back inside.

His focus slid around the oversized vases with their exotic dried grasses that had cost Sylvia a fortune. He looked up the stairs. "Very nice." Whether he meant the house or her didn't much matter. He wasn't here for words.

Clever Sylvia hadn't wasted any time seducing Daniel three years earlier when she started at the Trust. The complicated twists of who used whom—between Daniel and his environmental sensibilities, Eduardo with his eyes on a most lucrative venture, and Sylvia with the expertise to pull it off—landed Sylvia at the Trust with a multi-million dollar budget funded almost entirely by the Cubrero fortune.

Daniel believed she researched climate change and he'd convinced his father to donate enormous funds. Eduardo knew he was paying for something entirely different than global warming research and that Sylvia and Daniel were colleagues, nothing more. Sylvia played one side against the other, hedging bets with her body and her brain. Why not? She had the skills.

Catering to Daniel's desires had more benefits than as simply life insurance against Eduardo. "I have a fire in the living room. Why don't we enjoy our drinks in there?"

He inclined his head, willing to let the evening unfold as it would. He chose a sofa in the glow of the fire. Sylvia would look irresistible in the dim light.

After she'd poured the cognac into the snifters and settled next to him on the imported white leather sofa, she said, "I regret our harsh words yesterday. I know you provided me with the lawyer and you did your best. Please, can we forget our tiff?"

He reached out and trailed a long, slender finger along her jaw. "I do not wish to fight you."

She made her eyes smolder with desire. "We fit together so well. It's as if we recognize that spark that makes us different from other people."

He leaned closer and the scent of warm skin and subtle spice of his cologne wafted around her, spreading moisture between her thighs. "Let me show you how we fit together."

She unfolded herself from the sofa and held her hand out to him. He took it and stood. She led him from the room. "Let's discuss this upstairs."

"Excellent idea."

He stepped close behind and slipped his arm around her, cupping a breast beneath the silk of her negligee. "We have found another area of agreement, no?"

She swayed her hips climbing the stairs, giving him a preview of what would follow. They ambled down the long hall to her bedroom. It might be her favorite room in the house, decorated in black and white with splashes of red. The duvet highlighted the room with massive scarlet orchids covering the white satin.

She pushed him gently onto the bed and stepped back. His body settled on the giant four poster she'd found at a Southerby's auction. She slipped her feet from the delicate mules. One spaghetti strap slid from her shoulders as she stared into his hungry eyes.

He rose and pulled the other strap down, letting the silky fabric puddle around her ankles. He paused for only a moment. She found men loved to gaze on her exquisite beauty. He pulled her to him, bending to kiss and nip at her breasts.

Like most men she'd allowed to touch her, he relished her physical artistry and she enjoyed his worship. It didn't take him but a moment to shed his clothes and lay her back on the bed. Sylvia went into her routine. What man could resist her?

She let him climb on her, wild in his desire. She'd learned to moan in the right places and move beneath him in a way that excited him. After an appropriate interval, she increased the volume and frequency and raw tones of her moans, faked her orgasm, and let him finish his own journey.

It wasn't that she didn't enjoy sex. All the foreplay and excitement of watching her partner get aroused created a deep pleasure in her. But the final act, the sweating body and heaving need, the squirt—all seemed sordid. There was a point when men quit seeing her as a priceless work of art and sought their own release that made it impossible for her to climax. She'd take care of that later, alone in her masterpiece of a bed.

Daniel rolled off. "You were right, *querida*. We have a special connection."

She watched as his fingers traced her areola.

She toyed with the black hair on his chest, enjoying the steady beat of his heart beneath well-formed pecs. It thrilled her that she'd had both father and son as lovers. "What kept you busy all day?"

He raised his jet black eyebrows. "I was at the Trust being a dutiful trustee and keeping an eye on Nora Abbott."

Sylvia didn't like the idea of him spending time anywhere near that troublemaker. "Isn't a non-profit trust beneath your talents?"

"I'm helping out temporarily. The finances are not what they should be. The budget is over projections. You don't happen to know anything about that, do you?"

The warmth of their lovemaking dissipated. "I haven't done anything. Nora said I exceeded my budget but it shouldn't be. Darla must have made a mistake."

He nodded, a quirk of a smile on his face. "Nora will find out, assuredly."

He obviously suspected Sylvia stole money from the Trust, just as Darla had accused her. She could tell by his smirk. "Why are you the one to keep an eye on her, anyway? Mark is there."

"I find her fascinating. And, as it turns out," he pulled his head back and studied her, "Nora might need protecting. She ended up in the ER this morning."

So what? Apparently she didn't die. "That girl can take of herself, believe me."

He lifted her hand from his chest and sat up. "Perhaps. At any rate I did not come here to discuss Nora."

She ran the tip of her tongue around his lips with the slightest touch. "I didn't think you came to discuss anything."

He grabbed her, kissing her with desire, thrusting his tongue past her lips. He let her go. "I have enjoyed you very much and now I must go." He rose.

She let the sheet fall just below her satiny breast. "Do you have to leave so soon?"

He dressed quickly, almost as if he couldn't wait to leave.

Of course she was being sensitive. He'd just made love to her and obviously couldn't resist the sexual spell she had over him. Maybe he wanted to give her time to recover from her awful experience with the police.

He didn't turn back before he sauntered out the door and down the stairs.

She waited until the front door clicked shut. Then she rose and showered. She padded down the stairs to finish her glass of cognac in front of the fire.

Her cell phone chirped and she considered not answering. She recognized the number and changed her mind. "How lovely to hear from you, Eduardo. Have you made my deposit?"

He didn't take the time to hear what she said. "You have murdered the accountant? For money? Are you insane?"

She stood in front of the fire but it wasn't responsible for the sweat that broke out under her negligee. "I didn't—."

"The police arrested you."

How did he find out? Did Daniel tell him? "They brought me in for questioning."

"And you have involved Danielcito, as I asked you not to do."

She trembled at the rage in his voice. "I was set up. It was Nora Abbott's fault. That conniving little climber."

"She was not at the Trust when this happened."

"I can't explain it. She's jealous." Sylvia paced away from the fire. "It's like at HAARP". Someone always tried to stand in Sylvia's path to greatness. "Bruce Franklin wanted my job and he spread lies about me. He stole the credit for my work." Of course she delegated the more tedious aspects of her job. That didn't mean she wasn't responsible for the work her department accomplished. He'd gone behind her back and got her fired.

"Enough of your jabber, *carina*." The endearment sounded like a curse. "I grow impatient."

"I need more time. And money. If you deposit—."

"No more money. But in case you need incentive to work, I've sent Juan to watch over you. Time is running out."

"Juan—." He severed the connection.

Sylvia ran to the control panel and slapped off the great room lights. She tiptoed to the dining room and snaked her arm around the corner to douse the chandelier. Then she ran up the stairs to her bedroom in the dark and slipped to the window facing the street.

A Lincoln Town Car sat on the opposite side of her street one house down, facing her way. She couldn't see inside the car so could only assume someone named Juan sat there watching her house.

Her hands shook as she dressed in black leggings and turtleneck. She pulled on the black riding boots she'd bought last week.

She wouldn't tolerate Eduardo's bullying. She didn't know where she would go but her Ferrari 430 could outrun a Town Car and she'd lose Juan in a hurry. That would show Eduardo she couldn't be intimidated.

Sylvia hurried down the stairs, through the kitchen to the garage. Who did he think he was treating her like some kind of minion?

She stomped to the Ferrari and slid inside. With one hand she hit the garage door opener and the other she pressed the start button.

She twisted to view over her shoulder. An unusual lump at the passenger window startled her and she caught her breath. Her eyes focused on it.

Snakes of fear slithered across her skin. A scream of terror built in her gut and exploded with echoes in the small car.

Her foot slipped off the clutch. Her hands flew in spastic flutters and she kept screaming.

The calico cat struggled against the passenger side window. Its head was trapped inside, the window rolled up just to where it trapped the cat, the body dangling outside, claws scrabbling to free itself. Its mouth gaped in a ghastly snarl, the sharp teeth bared and white, while it wheezed in a scant air supply. The cat hung with her neck suspended between the top of the window and door.

Sylvia's shaking fingers barely found the window toggle and she didn't wait to see if the cat survived after it fell from the side of her car.

24

The key twisted in the ignition and Nora's old Jeep fell silent.

Thankfully Abigail had been out somewhere when Nora and Abbey returned home in the early afternoon. Cole had driven her to the Trust to get her Jeep and made her promise she'd stay home all afternoon. But after a shower she'd headed back to the office.

Now she scanned her apartment, dreading another round with Abigail. She wasn't ready to discuss her father. She needed time and solitude. Instead, she had Abigail.

What a day. The Trust was a crazy place and Nora weighed whether saving the earth was worth sorting through the problems. Okay, maybe working as Finance Director didn't rise to the status of saving the earth.

She didn't hold with Cole's conviction Mark had tried to kill her. For all her wild imagination and despite the events in Flagstaff, she believed murder and mayhem occurred in movies and novels, not in real life.

Not usually.

Cold seeped into the Jeep. Much as she'd like to start it up and drive away and not have to deal with Abigail tonight, she could use a bucket of Abbey-love.

A group of students walked by chatting and laughing. They passed under the parking lot light and continued into the night. Nora smiled remembering the feeling of a new fall semester with all the hope and possibilities and freedom of youth. She climbed out of the Jeep and headed to the stairs.

Without warning, her mind flashed to an image of Cole at the hospital this afternoon. Maybe she'd thought of him more than she'd like to admit in the last year. It didn't matter that sometimes when she saw couples walking hand in hand along Boulder Creek, she'd imagined what it would be like to walk with Cole. But she'd trained herself to shove those sorts of thoughts far away.

She inhaled the crisp fall air. With every step she drilled more determination into her brain. She would not discuss her father with Abigail tonight. Nora was bound to say something hurtful. She needed to process it on her time, whenever that might be.

I will be nice to Abigail.

She opened the door and stepped from the chill into a cozy apartment. In that tuned-in way of dogs, Abbey already stood by the door, tail wagging, tongue lolling, smile ready. Of course, in the micro-apartment, Abbey would only have to hear her hand on the door knob to get up from his bed under the corn plants and meet her at the front door.

Nora dropped her bag and squatted next to him, burying her face in his fur. "How're you doin'?"

Abigail's voice cut through Nora's closed eyes and the haze of comfort coming from Abbey. She stood in the galley kitchen, which opened into the four-foot square entry area. "I'm so glad you didn't work any later. Dinner would have been spoiled."

Nora realized she'd been inhaling a savory aroma, just like a real dinner. Meat with onions and garlic undertones and bread. Bread? Man, it smelled wonderful

Who thought she'd be hungry after her terrible morning in the ER, but her stomach growled. Guess she was emptied out pretty thoroughly. "You cooked dinner? That's great. I'm starving."

Nora surveyed the small dining room table. Instead of the colorful Mexican placemats and bright Fiestaware Nora furnished for herself, a white lace cloth draped over the table. Two places set with china sporting a sweet rose pattern. Wine glasses and candles added to the decidedly un-Nora table.

Forcing her lips into what she hoped passed for a smile of pleased surprise, Nora said, "Very nice, Mother. You really went all out."

Abigail picked up Nora's bag and thrust it onto a hook. "You only have those garish dishes. I thought you needed something more formal so I bought you a set of china and some stemware."

Abigail couldn't afford this. Neither could Nora. "I don't do much entertaining. Maybe we can box it up before we use it and take it back."

Abigail frowned. "You'll thank me. Believe me, you'll use these more than you think. Besides, I didn't spend a fortune. I bought all of this at the outlet mall. Of course it's not Wedgewood."

Hold the snark. She's only trying to be nice.

Abigail threw back her shoulders and lifted her chin. "Life is made more full by the simple joy of beauty. The red of the rose, the kiss of a lover."

Nora struggled with a response "Is that something you wrote?"

Abigail pulled the cherub notebook from her pocket. "I just thought of it. When you tune your subconscious to poetry, it springs forth." She paused. "Oh, that's good, too."

Poetry and spending. Her mother's talents never ceased. *Be nice, be nice, be nice.* "So what's for dinner?"

Abigail beamed. "We'll start with a butternut squash soup. The entrée is pork tenderloin medallions with garlic mashed potatoes and steamed green beans almandine, followed by apple pie."

Nora noted the clean kitchen. "You slaved all day on this?"

Abigail laughed. "That wonderful deli just off Broadway closed since I lived here. But I Googled around on my phone and found a great new place. I sampled them at lunch yesterday and they're excellent."

Dollar figures rolled in front of Nora's eyes like cherries and oranges on a slot machine. New dishes, stemware, and now a catered dinner for two. Nora bit down on the lecture forcing itself from her lips. Tomorrow. She'd sit Abigail down and explain about budgets and frugality and of living within her means—again.

With a nod of satisfaction, Abigail stepped back. "It's been a long day and I've got a novel I'm dying to sink into." She yawned. "I'll see you tomorrow."

"Wait. What?"

"Good night."

Nora spun around, fighting the rising horror of what she suspected.

Yep. Cole opened the sliding door and stepped into her mini-living room from the balcony.

"Mother!"

Abigail's back retreated down the hall. "It's like the china, Nora. You'll thank me."

Molten lava of indignation erupted in Nora. "This is asinine. My life is not some clichéd romance novel."

Abigail paused outside her bedroom door. "The pages of the novel that is life bursts with the genres of the soul." She reached into her pocket. "Oh, that's good."

"That doesn't even make sense," Nora shouted after the closing door. In the game of stubborn, Abigail had the upper hand. Nora studied Cole standing awkwardly in her apartment. "Hiding on the deck, huh? The Queen of Darkness pulled you into her black web of deceit." Gaa! Now Nora was creating awful poetry, too.

Cole's eyes twinkled. "I wasn't hiding, just planning an entrance. Abigail tricked me, too. She said you asked her to call me because you lost your phone."

"You weren't suspicious?" Nora's stomach growled. She pulled out a dining chair and sat. The simple cotton napkin revealed another of Abigail's penny-pinching ways. In the old days, the napkin would have been brocaded linen with a monogram.

"Of course I didn't believe her." He bent to rub Abbey's ears. "But when I found out you went back to work after you promised you wouldn't, I decided to come over. I knew it would annoy you as much as you annoyed me."

"Very funny."

He grinned. "You'd never lose your phone."

"What's that mean?" She tore off a piece of dinner roll and popped it into her mouth. Warm and buttery with just enough sweet to set off the yeast. Abigail knew her caterers.

Cole walked to the front door and reached for his down jacket on the hooks. Why hadn't she noticed it hanging there when she came in?

"Come on, Nora. When was the last time you lost anything? I'll wager you've never even had a sock go missing in the dryer. It wouldn't dare."

She fought a smile. "Are you saying I'm controlling?"

He stood at the front door, about fifteen feet from Nora. "Well, if Abigail is the Atlantic Ocean, you're Lake Superior."

She lifted an eyebrow in question.

"You're land locked; only want to control your own shores."

She piled mashed potatoes on her plate, the garlic tickling her nose. "Abigail's tides are epic."

He watched her. "I never picked you for a cruel woman."

She spooned out green beans and slivered almonds. "Huh?"

Cole hadn't donned his jacket. "I've been sitting here for a half hour smelling this gourmet meal and you're helping yourself while sending a starving man into the wilderness to pick up a greasy burger and fries at the nearest drive-through."

She served herself some tenderloin and gravy. "I didn't concoct this romantic farce, but I'm going to end up paying for it. You're on your own, buddy."

He addressed Abbey. "Heartless."

Nora forked in pork and rolled her eyes at the savory goodness. "Let this be a lesson: Don't trust Abigail."

He surveyed the table. "That's an awful lot of food."

She regarded Cole and the table and imagined her empty apartment after he left. But it wouldn't be empty. Abigail would swoop out of her room and harangue Nora.

Cole might make a good Abigail buffer. "Fine. Come enjoy the bounty of Abigail's non-existent fortune. But no talking about... anything I don't want to talk about."

He tossed his jacket back on the hook. "Agreed. So, nice plants. Is that Benny's corn?"

"I don't want to talk about it."

He nodded. "Is that wine I see?"

Nora poured while he seated himself. "This will probably be a bad idea."

He flapped out his napkin and placed it on his lap, reached for his glass and sipped Cabernet. "Why is that?"

"Because I like you. But I don't trust you. So the best thing is for me to steer clear of you. I've had enough of untrustworthy men in my life."

He heaped food onto his plate. "Just let me have my last meal. Abigail went to so much trouble."

"I don't know why she's obsessed with you."

He shrugged. "I think Charlie's behind it. He's in love with me. Always has been."

She laughed and the weight of the day slid off, crashing to the floor and disappearing into dust.

Tomorrow she'd deal with The Abigail Ocean of Control and all the mess at the Trust. For just this one dinner, she'd let herself relax. No Lake Superior, just a free flowing Boulder Creek.

25

Sylvia whipped the Ferrari onto the turnoff, across the rickety wood bridge, and into the Trust parking lot. She shut the lights off and held her breath.

Headlights passed the turn and continued up Boulder Canyon. She sat another five minutes watching the highway. No one followed her.

After she'd calmed down enough from the cat prank, Sylvia had released the creature from her window and sped off from her neighborhood. She'd zipped through town and out Highway 36 to Denver. It hadn't taken her long to lose Juan in Denver's streets and then she'd backtracked to the Trust.

Sylvia slipped into the old farmhouse and locked the door after herself. She hurried to her office and snapped on the lights.

Fear fluttered like bats' wings in Sylvia's belly. Damn Nora, damn Eduardo. Damn them all! They didn't understand the way genius worked. She couldn't be forced to a timeline like an hourly drone. But if she didn't deliver something, Eduardo might just cut off his nose to spite that aristocratic face.

Alone, she paced the office. All the common people were home with their droll spouses and their stupid children, watching reality TV and eating cheap dinners. She could have been just like them. Even that would have been a step up from her childhood.

Sylvia sank into her office chair and gripped the side of her cherry wood desk as the office faded.

"Come and get your supper." She smelled her father before she saw his bare feet with the thick, yellowed toenails and dirt caked in black crescents. He stood on the linoleum in front of the torn and faded sofa with one of the legs replaced by a cinder block.

Margery lay next to her, eyes wide, breath only the merest whisper. If he found them under the sofa it would be bad. Her sister grabbed Sylvia's hand and squeezed.

"I slaved over this meal so you git your ass out here and eat it." He shuffled away, shouting into the room. He was leaving. In a few minutes he'd drink another glass of whiskey and he'd forget.

Suddenly the heavy plate, something his mother had stolen from the last diner where she'd worked, crashed against the wall. Two slabs of the plate hit the floor amid the mush of canned tuna fish, white bread and mayonnaise.

The crusty feet lurched across the room and he was on his knees, reaching under the sofa.

Sylvia screamed. She and her sister scrunched as far back as possible but his meaty fist stabbed after them. His hand closed around Sylvia's arm.

"No!" She cried and fought but her skinny little girl's body was no match for him, even if he was on his knees. Margery clamped onto Sylvia's ankle as their father yanked her from safety.

"You little shit! I made you supper and you're goddamned gonna eat it!" He pulled her with him as he stood up, dangling her by her arm, wrenching it from the socket.

She screamed again. And again. And kept screaming as his fist full of the tuna he'd scooped off the floor rammed into her face.

Suddenly he dropped her. She hit the floor on her tailbone and scuttled like a crab to the corner.

Margery hit him again in the arm with her small fist.

Her father clamped his hand on Margery's shoulder and drew his arm back.

"No. Oh, please." She couldn't say anything else as she watched her father slam his fists into her sister's face.

Sylvia jumped up from her desk to halt the images. She'd successfully blocked them from her mind for decades. With all this stress they were coming back.

The door of the lab squeaked open and Petal peeked in.

Sylvia motioned her in. She wanted to scream at Petal for taking so long to get here. "Hurry. You're letting out the heat."

Petal slunk in like a stray dog, a mess of hair atop a rag basket. She rubbed her hands against the cold. "It feels like a front is coming in."

What did Sylvia care about the weather in Boulder tonight?

She stomped around the map table to a wall of filing cabinets. "I don't know why you've been dragging your feet. We need to have the tower positioned to refract the ELF wave. Let's get that done tonight."

Petal showed all the reaction of an office chair.

Sylvia's hand shook when she raised it to push her hair from her forehead. "Why are you standing there? You haven't given me the angle of refraction. Why not? Are you too busy making friends with Nora Abbott?"

Petal flushed and stared at the floor in front of Sylvia. "It's Mother. She's been ill and I've been trying to get Medicaid figured out. They say her treatments aren't covered."

Such mundane matters. Sylvia opened a file drawer and slammed it closed. "Are you blackmailing me into giving you money?"

Petal's voice cracked. "No! It's the truth. She's sick."

"Tell you what, if all goes well here I'll give you a bonus and you can help your mother out."

Petal's eyes glimmered with gratitude. "Thank you."

So Eduardo sent Juan to watch her. Would he order Juan to kill her if she didn't deliver? Sylvia paced around the opposite side of the map table and stopped at her desk chair. "I need that angle measurement tonight. I don't care if you stay here all night. The beam will go out tomorrow."

Instead of running to her desk to start working, Petal gazed at her from under the disaster on top of her head. "I can help you. But the coordinates you've given me don't make sense. Why Ecuador? I thought we needed to measure the soil and air temperatures in sector 43. That's where the field crew is monitoring beetle kill."

She wanted to slap Petal. Of course she didn't do that. She inhaled and composed herself. Sylvia chuckled to show she was a good sport. "You give me the details I ask for and I'll do the strategic thinking."

Why had she let herself get so upset? She'd handled the situation, as she always did. Petal should have delivered the refractory angle earlier, but Sylvia hadn't stayed on top of her flakey assistant. All Sylvia had to do was be a good manager. After Petal provided the corrections, Sylvia would adjust the tower's angle and she'd send the beam tomorrow night.

Sylvia waited until Petal hunched over her computer then she left her office and hurried through the kitchen. She paused at a sink window to survey the Trust parking lot.

Petal's silly bike leaned against the front steps and Sylvia's Ferrari sat close to the front door.

A Lincoln Town Car sat at the side of the road, just across the wood bridge.

26

Nora opened her eyes to the dark bedroom. She should get up and head to work. But she rolled onto her back and stretched, enjoying one moment to think about last night. Because as soon as her feet hit the floor she'd grab hold of reality and force Cole out of her thoughts. She knew better than to spend time with him. It was sort of like going to the Humane Society and saying you were only going to look. Pretty soon, your heart mutinied and you ended up with a dog.

Abigail would say Nora should take a risk on love. But Nora already had her fragile heart and ego out there with this new job. And the whole suddenly-you-have-a-Hopi-father thing she would have to examine.

After a year of isolation, she needed to pace herself on total life immersion

Nora threw back the covers and planted her feet on the rug. She showered and dressed as stealthily as possible so as not to wake Abigail. She didn't want to discuss her dinner with Cole and she definitely didn't want to get into daddy issues.

"I will be nice to Abigail," she said to herself in the mirror. "And maybe I'll work on not talking to myself."

Nora tiptoed out of her bedroom and down the hall. She whispered to Abbey and grabbed her coat and a plastic bag and slipped out to take him for his morning routine.

Fifteen minutes later, she snuck back inside and slid his leash over a hook.

"Good morning!" Abigail chirped from the kitchen.

Drat. "Morning." The smell of fresh brewed coffee hung in the air.

Abigail set a mug on the counter bar. She wore a white robe with embroidered pink roses on the lapels and pink slippers. "I made coffee. It's that hazelnut kind with the nonfat creamer."

Don't tell her you hate flavored coffee. Keep your mouth shut about artificial creamers. "I'm kind of in a hurry to get to work. Thanks anyway."

"Oh nonsense." Abigail filled her own cup. "I want you to sit down and tell me everything about last night."

Nora pulled her messenger bag from the coat hooks. "Dinner was delicious. Thanks."

Abigail patted the table to invite Nora. "You hit it off with Cole, didn't you? You two are perfect for each other."

"Yeah. I've got to go."

"Don't be silly. Come over here and have a cup of coffee."

Don't do it. Walk out the door. Really, DO NOT DO IT. "Can you leave me alone? Please just back off."

Abigail's face fell.

Damn it. What happened to that resolve to be nice to her? "I'm sorry. I didn't mean to hurt your feelings. The best thing I can do is to go to work."

"Oh, honey. You didn't hurt my feelings." That martyr tone always guilted Nora. "I'm only concerned for you."

"I really should get to work."

"It's not even six o'clock."

"I have a lot to do."

Abigail set her coffee on the table, and reached for Nora's bag. She hung it up. "I'm serious, dear. You need to talk about your father."

"I'm not ready."

"Ready or not—."

A soft thump on the front door stopped Abigail. They stared at the door. The noise came again but this time it sounded like a light tapping.

Nora walked past Abigail and unlocked the door.

"Wait!" Abigail whispered. "It's not safe. We need a weapon."

Nora rolled her eyes as Abigail searched for something dangerous. She opened the door.

Petal huddled on the welcome mat, shrouded with layers of wraps, probably from some sweatshop-less, free-trade market. Heavy hiking socks covered feet stuffed in her Chaco sandals. Her breath puffed from a cloud of dreds.

"Come in." Nora reached out, pulled her inside and shut the door. "What are you doing here—and so early?"

Petal shivered by the entryway. "I don't know where else to go."

Blurgh. Nora didn't need any more trouble. If she had any brains in her head, she'd shove Petal back outside and slam the door. Instead, she helped unwrap the first layer, a blanket it seemed, from Petal's shoulders and draped it on the coat hooks.

Abigail grasped Petal's frozen fingers. "Why, you're an ice cube. Let me get you some coffee."

Petal curled up in the same couch corner she'd sat in before.

Nora sat beside her. "What's going on?"

Petal's puffy eyes implored Abigail. "I can't go home. Darla is everywhere."

Abigail pushed dreds back from Petal's face. "I know, honey. It hurts."

Petal hiccupped. "I open a cupboard and see the coffee mug I bought her with the happy face on it. I tried to move on, but when I reached for the tea it was the special blend of coconut and white tea she loved."

Abigail nodded. "I know."

"So I went to lie down and the pillows smell like her."

Nora wanted to help but Petal's words brought sharp images slicing through her. The empty spot next to her in bed after Scott died. Cleaning out his closet, touching his bike gloves, knowing his fingers would never fill them again.

Abigail patted Petal's hand. "It's okay. You can stay here today. I'll bet you haven't slept. We can make you a bed on the couch."

Sure, Abigail invited Petal to camp out on Nora's sofa, but when Scott died, she'd insisted they go shopping. Petal could whimper and cry; Nora had to get on with life.

"Thank you so much, Abigail." Petal turned hopeful eyes to Nora. "You don't mind, do you? It won't be for long. Maybe just until after the funeral today?."

In the olden days—72 hours ago—Nora's small apartment felt like a quiet haven she shared with Abbey. They took walks and Nora read or watched TV or searched for jobs while Abbey napped in his warm bed. Suddenly her apartment transformed into a circus with Abigail as ring master.

"Sure. Let me round up some sheets." That was another problem. Nora owned the sheets on her bed and a second set on the guest room bed. She never imagined she'd need more than that. Maybe she could take the top sheet from her own bed. She mulled over the unacceptable possibilities on the short walk down the hall. At least she had a sleeping bag Petal could use. Nora pulled open the flimsy linen closet door to retrieve the sleeping bag she stored on the bottom shelf.

Abigail kept cheerful patter going in the living room. No doubt distracting Petal from her grief. Either that or numbing her into a false calm.

What?

Nora faced two shelves of new housewares. A set of sheets bordered with delicate eyelet embroidery and several fluffy pink towels stacked neatly next to an electric roaster pan and—what was that? A fondue pot?

"Mother?"

Abigail's chatter stopped. "Yes, Nora."

"Could you come here, please?"

Abigail swept down the short hall in her robe and slippers.

Nora indicated the closet. "What is all this and where did it come from?"

Abigail checked the closet. "Oh, that. Honey, a woman needs to have things to feather her nest. If you don't have beauty and comfort to surround you, you'll feel prickly."

"I hate pink. I've always hated pink. I like my home the way it is."

"You say that now, but you'll be surprised at how much comfort a little luxury and a well-supplied home can give you."

The evil Abigail troll climbed behind Nora's eyes, pulled herself on her little trampoline, and jumped, throwing her body against the inside of Nora's forehead. "I don't want towels and china, with matching stemware. I'd rather strap on my backpack, whistle for Abbey, and go to the mountains."

Abigail raised her eyebrows. "You won't be able to do that forever. You aren't getting younger."

Nora bit back a retort. "And what is this?" She pointed to the roaster pan.

"You don't have one, do you?" Abigail sounded concerned.

"Why would I have something that would feed a dormitory? It's only me and Abbey here."

Abigail placed her hands on her hips. "You have no vision for the future. Every woman should have an electric roaster. Someday you'll have children and they'll bring their baseball team over for sloppy joes or you'll need to supply chili for the gymnastics fund raiser, and then you'll thank me."

"How do you even know these words? When did you ever cook for my friends or volunteer at any of my functions?"

Abigail sucked in her lips and held her breath as if holding back tears. "There you go again, heaping blame on me for not being the perfect mother. I tried, Nora. I was a single mother focusing all my energy on keeping food on the table and clothes on your back."

"What alternative universe did you live in?" Nora managed not the fling the towels from the shelves. "We lived in a four-thousand-square-foot house with a crystal chandelier in the entryway. You hosted catered cocktail parties on a regular basis."

Fire lit Abigail's eyes. "I'm sorry, dear. I didn't have the luxury of going to college and business school. When I married your father we had no money and I worked at a department store. When I married Berle, my job was being his wife. You enjoyed the nice things and a wonderful education because I kept Berle happy."

Nora exploded. "I don't know anything about your life with my father. You told me he abandoned me!"

Abigail grew still. "Now we're getting to the real problem. You hate me for protecting you."

Nora pulled the one-thousand-thread count sheets from the closet and marched down the hallway. "I don't hate you."

Abigail jerked the pillow from the closet and followed her. "There you go, running away from the truth like you always do."

The hallway wasn't long enough. Nora had to pull up or she'd be in the living room with Petal. "Stop trying to run my life."

Abigail stood too close. "Someone has to because you're creating a disaster."

"And now we're talking about Cole again, right?"

"If you weren't so stubborn you'd see I'm right."

"If you weren't so controlling you'd see I can manage my own life."

They walked into the living room to find Petal dissolved in tears. She curled into the couch, head in her arms, sobbing silently.

Abigail hurried to sit next to Petal and gathered her in her arms. "Now, now. It's going to be okay."

"I can't do it." Petal choked out the words.

"Do what, honey?"

Nora deposited the sheets on the couch and stood above Abigail and Petal. Hard fingers of sympathy squeezed her heart; she knew what it felt like when someone close was murdered. If only she could lift Petal's pain and toss it into the chilly morning. But part of her, a large part, wanted Petal to take her drama and all the memories it stirred up and find another friend. Nora had only known Petal a few days, why did she have to hold the unraveling ball of nerves together?

Nora sat on the arm of the couch and patted Petal's back. Why, indeed? The least she could do was let Petal cry.

"The funeral," Petal squeaked.

"What about the funeral?" Abigail had to draw every word from Petal.

"It's later this morning. I can't go."

"Of course you can go, dear."

Petal pushed herself up and swiped a sleeve across her nose again. "Whoever killed Darla will be there."

Abigail gave Nora a helpless expression. "You don't know that."

Tears continued to run down Petal's face. "If they killed Darla they might kill me."

"Oh, posh." It appeared Abigail would only cotton to so much drama, even from Petal. "No one wants to hurt you."

Petal sobbed again and dropped her head onto Abigail's lap.

Abigail patted Petal's shoulders. "I think you're being paranoid but if you'd like, Nora and I will go to the funeral with you."

Funeral? No way. Nora didn't do funerals any more. Heather's funeral following so closely after Scott's had cured Nora from going to another funeral. Ever. She hadn't even known Darla. Abigail could go. She could hold Petal's hand and feel needed and like a hero for rescuing an unfortunate waif.

Not Nora. Uh-uh. Nope.

27

Cold, dry air sent shivers down Nora's arms and raised goose bumps on her legs as she hurried along the sidewalk with Petal and Abigail. The church occupied a whole city block just south of the Pearl Street Mall in downtown Boulder. Because snow threatened, they'd parked in a covered public garage several blocks away and now suffered the winds of the cold front as they hurried toward the church. The heavy clouds snuffed out the sight of the Flatirons. Nora could have used a sunny day and mountain view to balance the dread of the funeral.

Despite the foul weather, cyclists buzzed by on the streets and an occasional runner dodged them. Students bundled in ski coats and Uggs hurried by with their heads down.

In the cozy warmth of her apartment, her mother's disapproval of pants versus a dress didn't seem important. Today, she should have worn the slacks and let Abigail stew. Abigail appeared regal in her appropriate black pencil skirt, pumps and wool coat. At least Nora wore boots and a long skirt against the gusts coming off the mountains.

In their traditional and tasteful funeral wear, Nora and Abigail flanked Petal, dreds a wild mass flowing around her shoulders, her eyes and nose tomato-red and puffy. Petal huddled under layers of everything from yoga pants, an unhemmed denim skirt and the perennial gauze, t-shirts, sweaters, scarves and wraps. Abigail didn't seem fazed at accompanying Petal in her disheveled homeless fashion.

A tall, black metal fence outlined the church property. The red-brick structure loomed ahead of them, with a bricked courtyard in front, a well-equipped playground to the side, and what was probably a school, attached to the create a block-long building. They crossed the courtyard and headed for the massive double doors of the chapel. Nora fought the urge to run. So far, Darla's death felt more like a movie or novel. Attending a funeral made it as real as Scott's murder. As horrific as Heather's violent passing.

You can't hide from death forever. Now is the time to face it down.

Her hands closed on the cold metal handle and she pulled the door open. They entered a posh narthex. Carpeted in muted rust and browns, spotless and perfect in the way of affluence, the room could accommodate a crowd of Sunday worshippers on their way from the chapel. Nora inhaled the heat and underlying candle wax and furniture polish, relieved to be out of the coming storm. "It doesn't seem like anyone is here. Are you sure this is the right place?" she asked Petal.

Petal swiped a sleeve across her nose and sniffed. "Darla didn't have much family. She didn't have many friends. Just me."

Abigail marched across the narthex to more double doors that must lead to the chapel. These stood open. She poked her head inside and hurried back to them. She whispered, "I think this is the place."

Petal threaded her arm through Nora's and attached herself to Nora's side. They made awkward progress through the doors and several steps down the aisle. An older woman sat behind an organ at the back of the altar. She played what sounded like a succession of chords but was probably a standard hymn, the elevator music of a conservative church.

Petal raised her head and must have caught her first sight of the simple casket on the altar. She froze, her mouth open in silent despair.

The light wood of the closed casket blended with the pulpit and altar railings. It looked lonely with few flowers surrounding it. Petal trembled and sucked closer to Nora.

Together they followed Abigail down the aisle. "Do you want to view the casket, dear?" Abigail whispered to Petal.

She answered with a whimper.

A handful of people spread out in the pews about five rows down from the front. Abigail headed toward the altar. Petal reached out and grabbed Abigail's arm to stop her. Her hand gripped a back pew. As usual, Petal tried to be invisible.

Nora slid into the pew and Abigail let Petal in next to sandwich her.

Nora shrugged out of her coat and surveyed the sparse crowd. She recognized Fay's blonde tangle next to Bill's slightly balding pate. Three others sat between Bill and Thomas, with his bushy brown hair. They must be staffers she hadn't met.

Daniel sat in a middle pew across from Nora. He glanced back and tipped his head in greeting, then sat straight. Nora wouldn't think he'd be required to attend the funeral of a staffer, but it showed a certain decency.

The organ music droned into the chapel. A couple of people picked away on their phones. Apparently, they weren't close with Darla.

With a jolt, Nora realized she had more than passing familiarity with one of heads two rows back and to the outside of Daniel. She knew the sandy hair and laugh lines around the side of the mouth visible to her.

Cole. What was he doing here?

Nora glared at Abigail. It must be more of her mischief.

A ruckus at the back of the chapel caused several heads to turn. Mark and Sylvia entered amid a flurry of urgent whispers. Their argument stopped when they realized people watched them. Sylvia straightened her spine. Her high-heeled black boots and long coat gave her the sleek appearance of a panther, despite her petite frame.

Petal squeaked and sank into herself.

Mark guided Sylvia to a front pew and they sat, staring ahead.

Finally a middle-aged woman in a dark suit, thick calves and grandma-style pumps appeared from one of the doors off the side of the altar. "Good morning. Today we're gathered to celebrate the life of Darla Barrows."

Nora's throat closed up. She struggled for air. The chapel disappeared and all around her stood tall Ponderosas. The casket turned into a pine box full of her husband's ashes. Death. Everywhere.

Nora could almost feel Charlie's arm circling her for support and

Abbey sitting at her feet. Scott's friends paid tribute, giving tale after tale of Scott's crazy antics. Nora's insides felt scraped raw and hollow.

She'd been sure she'd never feel happy again.

Two weeks later she'd huddled between Abigail and Cole on a pew in a Flagstaff church. The casket on the altar contained Heather's body. Nora squeezed her eyes closed and fought for control. Heather was young, so alive. Nora couldn't hold all her grief.

Of course, today she sat in a church in downtown Boulder, Colorado, but it couldn't convince that panic-prone mush serving as her mind. She thrust herself out of the pew and stumbled over Petal and Abigail to rush down the aisle to the narthex. Cold sweat filmed her body as she cast about for someplace to hide. Tears threatened her throat and eyes. She didn't want to explain her flight from the funeral to her new co-workers.

A stairway to the side of the narthex offered escape. She gripped the rail and lurched up, focused on slowing her racing heart and steadying her breathing. The stairway led to a choir loft, giving her full view of the altar and the casket. She whirled around and exited, plopping herself on the top stair.

Damn. Another panic attack. Did this herald the end to sanity? Soon she'd lock herself inside her apartment amid a maze of old newspapers and magazines, with food delivered to her door, afraid of the sunshine. She'd hold endless conversations with a long-dead Hopi *kikmongwi*.

Get a grip.

Cole shot from the chapel. He scanned the lobby and his eyes locked on the stairs. His gaze followed it up and he spotted Nora slumped at the top. He bounded the stairs two at a time.

Ugh. Why did he have to be here?

He sat next to her. "What's the matter? Are you okay?" he whispered.

She swallowed. Maybe Cole showing up was the best thing for a panic attack. It got her torqued up and helped her focus. "What are you doing here? Following me to a funeral is really low." She matched his whisper.

He opened his mouth to speak. The outside doors opened and the two police officers entered. Nora recognized them from the board meeting. She searched her brain for their names. Langston and Kirby. They wandered to the chapel and slipped inside.

The organ music swelled and weak strains of attendees' singing filtered up to them.

Cole blushed. "I thought you might have a hard time going to another funeral."

"Did Abigail call you?"

He studied his hands. "She's concerned about you."

"She's trying to set us up."

"Ya think?"

Nora felt the tingle of a smile.

"She was right, though. It's tough on you and I thought you could use a friend"

Was he her friend? Did she want him to be?

A man in jeans and work shirt trudged into the narthex from an entryway across from the choir loft stairs where they sat. It must be a basement. He taped a computer printed sign to the wall and disappeared downstairs again.

Nora needed to shift from her memories. "Okay. If you're my friend, help me figure out who killed Darla."

His jaw dropped. "You're kidding, right? That's the cops' job."

She waved that off. "I found some money missing from Sylvia's accounts. A lot of it."

His whisper grew stronger. "The cops already have enough evidence to suspect her. Let them know about this and be done. Get out of there."

The man appeared from downstairs carrying a long folding table. He glared at Nora and Cole before setting up the table and heading down the stairs.

She shook her head and lowered her voice. "It's a little too clean, don't you think? They find a gun in Sylvia's office. Someone tells the cops Sylvia has plane tickets and plans to flee the country—which she denies. Suddenly money goes missing in Sylvia's accounts?"

"Sounds like Sylvia killed Darla."

Nora thought about it. "Sounds more like she was set up. She's too smart to leave all those clues."

The man popped up from downstairs carrying a giant coffee urn he placed on the table.

Always the reasonable one, Cole said, "Tell the cops about the missing money and let them deal with it."

"I haven't gone through all the accounts yet. It could have been transferred somewhere or in an account I don't know about. I'm going to ask Mark."

Cole's eyebrows drew down and shielded his eyes in doubt. "Stay away from him."

She waved that off. "He's harmless. Just creepy and Sylvia-obsessed."

"He probably tried to kill you. I don't suppose you told the cops about that, either."

Two well-dressed woman stepped from downstairs carrying trays of cookies and coffee cups. They must be volunteers from the church to help with services. They eyed Nora and Cole with distaste before returning to the stairs.

He sounded impatient. "Would you let the cops do their job? This isn't a game, Nora. Darla was murdered."

Nora went cold. "Wouldn't it be stupid to murder two Finance Directors within a week? I think I'm safe."

The service must be over. People started to filter out of the chapel. A few coworkers formed a solemn knot in the middle of the lobby. Fay wiped at tears and Bill hugged her.

The small crowd milled around the coffee and cookies.

Nora stood. "I'm going to take Petal and Abigail home before I go back to work."

They walked down the stairs. "Let me get you some coffee." Cole headed toward the refreshments.

Nora stood at the foot of the stairs apart from the smattering of people. She watched the chapel doors for Abigail and Petal. The sooner they got out of here the better.

Sylvia swooped out from the chapel and Mark followed. He grasped her elbow and turned her toward the coffee. She pulled her arm away, surveyed the table and started toward the front door.

Fay glared at Sylvia, as did several of the other staffers. Sylvia smirked at them.

Daniel walked out of the chapel with the grace of a tiger. He burned three degrees hotter than handsome in his Armani suit. Sylvia's eyes focused on him.

Mark said something and Sylvia nodded. He scurried to the coffee with a stupid grin on his face. Abigail and Petal finally made it from the chapel. Abigail propped Petal against a wall next to the chapel doors and headed for the coffee. Her eyes scanned the lobby, probably trying to locate Nora.

Nora should try to be sociable but she didn't feel up to mingling and making small talk to people she didn't know, about a dead person she'd never met. Instead, she watched.

The group of half a dozen staffers congregated at one end of the refreshment table. Three or four other people held foam cups and spoke in hushed tones. Maybe they were family. The two church volunteers chatted with the basement guy, helping themselves to the cookies. Petal leaned against the chapel entrance like a lost puppy. Sylvia stood in the middle of the narthex. The minister and Daniel seemed deep in conversation with the Langston and Kirby by the basement stairs.

Cole filled two cups. He might be annoying but having him with her did help quell her panic. Mark handed Sylvia a cup and Nora watched him giggle, thankful she didn't have to hear it.

Cole returned with the coffee. It tasted better than Mark's Mr. Green Beans but still reminded her of acid. "Thanks."

"So what do you know about Daniel Cubrero?" Cole asked.

"Aside from being handsome and rich?"

Cole rolled his eyes.

"His big concern is fighting oil mining in the Amazon basin so I'm not sure why he's on the Trust board. He's from Ecuador and his family has money." She didn't have to tell Cole she'd had a nice dinner with Daniel recently and found him interesting.

Cole considered her. "Against mining in the Amazon basin? His family made their fortune in oil. A substantial fortune, by the way."

"And you know this how?"

He shook his head. "Do you think I research everyone you've come in contact with?"

"Sounds paranoid when you say it."

He laughed. "Did you forget I spent the bulk of my career in mining?

I know who the biggest players are. And Cubreros are the biggest of the big."

The cops moved from Daniel and the minister to the knot of staffers.

Daniel spotted Nora and started across the lobby to her. When he arrived, he clasped Nora's hand and brushed it with his lips. "Did you feel ill during the service? Not quite over the food poisoning?"

Self-conscious at the hand-kissing silliness, Nora sounded more brusque than she intended. "I'm fine. Just needed some air."

Cole frowned at Daniel and didn't say anything.

Abigail butted next to Cole, dragging Petal with her. "There you are, dear," she said to Nora, all the while eying Daniel as if might be there to eat Nora.

Before Nora could introduce Daniel to her mother, Sylvia slinked next to him. "Well, hello." Her voice dropped low. "How nice of you to come to Darla's service when we know how important and busy you are."

Puke. Food poisoning might be better than listening Sylvia's gushing. "Well, I'd better get back to the office. Ready to go?" Nora said to Abigail and Petal.

Mark appeared, hovering behind Sylvia like a broken satellite.

"Oh, Petal," Sylvia said, her voice losing the pseudo-sexy lilt. "I need you to run out to the tower this afternoon. I checked the angle measurements you submitted and they're accurate. We just need to make sure the tower is functioning."

Petal lowered her eyes and nodded.

Sylvia beamed at Daniel. "You can report to the board that we're working. We'll be sending an ELF wave to gather the latest data associated with this cold front."

Petal shivered noticeably.

Abigail slid an arm around her. "Where is this tower? Is it far?"

Sylvia puffed up. "It's on Mount Evans."

Abigail saw Sylvia's ego-puff and raised her a her regal head-tilt. "You shouldn't go up there alone when they're predicting snow. Nora will go with you."

Wait. What?

Nora didn't want to go to Mount Evans this afternoon. But there didn't seem to be a gracious way out. *Thank you, Abigail.* Nora ignored Sylvia's glare. "Sure. Yeah. I've got some stuff to do first and we can go."

Cole's tone didn't invite argument. "I'm going, too."

Abigail smiled with satisfaction. "Thank you."

Nora focused over Sylvia's shoulder at Mark. "If you're going to be around I'd like to talk to you about something when I get to the Trust."

He barely made eye contact. His attention shifted between Sylvia and Daniel. "What do you want to talk about?"

Just four-hundred grand that's gone missing that I think has something to do with a murder. "I have a couple of questions, that's all."

Obviously irritated, he grabbed her arm and pulled her to a corner of the narthex. "What is it?"

She caught Cole zeroed in on her. He scowled. "I'm not sure if it's anything or not, but I found $400,000 missing from Sylvia's restricted account."

He threw back his head and let out a shrill cackle. "That's crazy. There's a mistake, obviously. We'll check into it, of course. Of course." *Snort.*

Freak. "Okay. Can we get together later today?"

His attention slid to Sylvia. "Yes. I'll be at the Trust soon."

Nora nodded and walked away, unsettled by his overwhelming strangeness.

Nora, Abigail, and Petal donned their coats and wraps and braced themselves before opening the church doors. Cold air blasted them as they stepped from the church and hurried toward the parking garage.

Abigail bent her head to Petal. "Do you think the killer was there?"

Petal kept her head down.

Abigail continued. "If he was, he wouldn't dare do anything suspicious with those cops. But he'll make a move sometime, don't you think?"

Nora caught Abigail's eye and whipped her finger across her throat to tell Abigail to drop it.

Abigail tilted her head. "I'm glad Cole is going with you this afternoon."

Maybe they could go back to talking about murder.

Petal peeked out from her dreds. "He's really hot. And his aura is orange. That means he's detailed and scientific and has a good soul."

"I don't want to talk about it." The fact is, being with Cole did feel good.

"You can't keep saying you don't want to talk about it whenever someone brings up a touchy topic. What color is my aura?" Abigail asked.

Petal smiled shyly. "Yours is pink. It means you're creative and sensitive. You're loving and tender."

Abigail beamed.

They stepped from the curb to cross to the parking lot. A gust of icy wind, bringing a smattering of dry snow, hit Nora full in the face. The three of them drew together, lowering their heads against the onslaught.

Abigail's voice floated out from her tightly-wrapped pashmina. "Cole is more than a good soul, Nora. He's got integrity and is a commanding presence."

The overcast sky blended with the gray of the street. Nora kept her head down to avoid the wind. "He's not rich, you know that, right?"

Abigail huffed. "I'm not that shallow. You're perfectly capable of earning your own living."

Damn right. Maybe Abigail was evolving.

"Besides, his family owns one of the largest ranches in Wyoming. There's money there."

And then again, maybe not. They crossed the street, huddled together as the pedestrian light blinked a warning.

The roar of an engine cut through the icy air. Startled, Nora instinctively reached for Petal.

A shiny black widow of a sports car careened toward them in the far right lane. The crazy driver must not see them. He accelerated.

Petal froze in the sights of the deadly bullet.

Good thing Abigail and Nora had her by either arm. They weren't willing to be smashed on the pavement by some careless driver. Both of them lurched for the curb, dragging Petal with them.

At the last minute the car veered from them and screeched around the corner. Nora's hair blew back from her face in the rush of wind from the retreating car.

Her heart thundered in her ears.

Abigail caught her eye over the wild tangle of Petal's dreds. "Was that...?"

"Sylvia." Nora finished the sentence for her.

Petal's red-rimmed eyes traveled from Abigail to Nora. "She doesn't like me."

28

Sylvia hummed as she lay back and savored the beauty of her bedroom. She'd had Petal set the beam to send into the ionosphere in a few hours. The fruits of years of study and sacrifice would culminate in this monumental success. It was only a sample, but Eduardo would understand her genius. Then the money would flow.

What a perfect way to wrap up a morning. The snowy Egyptian cotton sheets with a weave so tight it felt like silk, made her skin glow, and the color contrasted nicely with her dark hair. She resembled Cleopatra in all her royal splendor.

Her broad-shouldered Latin lover, lay next to her, caching his breath from his final passion. She'd provided the kind of lovemaking he could only dream about with younger, less experienced women.

The day hadn't started out well. She'd had a fight with Mark. He wanted her to wait for any money until the heat died down from the board. She'd had to attend that tacky funeral, nothing more than a waste of time. Then there was that nasty episode with Nora trying to hone in on Daniel.

Sylvia teased Daniel's nipple. "It's pathetic the way Nora Abbott throws herself at you. I suppose it's to be expected. You are a Cubrero."

Sylvia had succumbed to that silly moment of jealousy. The pressure of her genius sometimes needed to blow off steam. She wouldn't really have plowed into Petal and Nora and her pretentious mother. But it made Sylvia chuckle to think of them scrambling to the curb.

"Nora is not an ordinary woman and she isn't throwing herself at me." He sounded bored. As he should be with someone as common as Nora.

Sylvia needed to be subtle. "She doesn't like me much. I think she senses you and I are... close and she's jealous. You know, I think she's the one who set me up with the police."

He studied her. "You were set up?"

"Of course I was, darling. Someone told the police about my gun and stole my credit card number to make plane reservations. I'm positive Nora did it."

"It is your gun, then? So, if it is your gun, did you kill Darla?"

Sylvia laughed. "I couldn't kill anyone." She didn't kill Darla any more than she'd run down Nora. It was all just releasing the pressure valve.

He didn't say anything as he enjoyed the feel of her hands on his chest.

She scooted close to Daniel and traced his mouth with the tip of her tongue. He jerked his head away and she laughed. "Did I tickle you?"

He stared at the ceiling, ignoring her.

She knew what he wanted and it wasn't conversation. She'd give it to him, slow and excruciatingly delicious. She swirled her tongue along the skin of his belly, tantalizing him as she worked her way lower. A young man like him wouldn't be done with one blast. She'd make him explode with desire for her. Then he'd protect her from Eduardo, if needed. To keep her in his life, in his bed, he'd do anything.

He definitely rose to her bait. Her mouth closed around him, teasing him with her tongue.

Her phone blared. Daniel pushed her head away.

She smiled at him. "I'll call them back." She leaned over him again.

"Answer it. I've got to get back to the Trust anyway." The sheets bunched around the bottom of the bed and the duvet spilled to the side, splashing scarlet orchids on the white carpet.

The Trust and Nora.

Stupid ignorant people always calling, always needing something from her. They wouldn't leave her alone for a minute.

She reached for the phone. Every great leader dealt with idiots. "Yes," she said, sounding powerful and competent.

"Sylvia, it's Adrianne."

She couldn't place the name or voice.

"Your attorney?"

"Yes. What is it?"

"We need to go over your deposition as soon as possible. Can you meet me at my office in two hours?"

Sylvia laid a perfectly manicured hand on Daniel's chest. Taking the phone from her face she whispered, "Stay. This won't take a second."

He sat up and her hand fell away. He didn't say anything as he stood and reached for his pants.

Adrianne ruined everything. "Your office is in Denver. With the traffic, I'd have to leave now. That won't work for me."

Daniel pulled a cobalt blue shirt on and worked at the buttons. He didn't pay any attention to Sylvia. Damn Adrianne for destroying her perfect afternoon.

"You realize you're being indicted for murder? This isn't a picnic, Sylvia. It's your top priority."

Sylvia employed Adrianne, not the other way around and she needed to realize that. "I can't drop everything and run up there. Just because some idiot police want to accuse me of killing someone doesn't make my work any less important. We'll have to schedule something later and it must be in Boulder."

Daniel sat at the edge of the bed to pull on his shoes and socks. Sylvia ran her nails lightly down his back. He arched away from her, stood and tucked his shirt in.

"Maybe you don't understand the serious nature of the charges," Adrianne said.

Daniel zipped his jeans and buckled his belt. He walked out the bedroom door.

"I understand that I have important work to do. This is your job and you're being paid a fortune." Sylvia punched the call off and wound up her arm, ready to fling the phone at the wall to watch it splinter. She lowered her arm.

Dignity. Control. Poise.

Then she threw the phone anyway.

She climbed out of bed and considered herself in the full wall of mirrors attached to the closet doors. Daniel must have important business to leave this.

Sylvia pulled a silk kimono from the closet.

A shower would restore her composure, and she'd scurry back to the Trust to make sure all was ready for tonight's launch of the ELF beam.

She hummed as she turned on the shower sauna to let it warm. She'd be more energetic and productive after relaxing for a bit. Maybe a glass of wine would help her unwind as she let the heat soak into her skin.

29

Nora leaned back in her desk chair and rubbed her eyes. After she'd taken Petal and Abigail home and made plans for going to Mount Evans later, Nora changed into her hiking boots and jeans and hurried back to the Trust. Abbey settled in his now-usual place by the coat closet and Nora pulled her chair up to her desk.

For two hours she'd been waiting for her meeting with Mark and going through the financial statements and monthly project reports. She'd discovered the $400,000 had been withdrawn from a long-term investment account over a year ago, though the Trust's accounting program didn't reflect that. She guessed Darla didn't actually reconcile savings and investment statements often. If they weren't used for general transactions, they shouldn't change and maybe Darla counted on that. If someone else had passwords and could transfer and if the financial director didn't pay attention, $400,000 could go missing.

Who would have those passwords besides Darla?

Mark.

The initial transfer was deposited in a short term savings account one month. It had been moved from one account to another over the course of several months, sometimes in a lump sum but more often in two or three transactions. If you weren't zoned in on that sum, and you weren't a particularly good accountant—or lazy—you'd never notice it.

Last month, the money had been transferred to Sylvia's restricted account and soon after, an ACH payment went out to an unnamed bank account.

"Excuse me, Ms. Abbott?" The authoritative voice belonged to a thin man in his mid-fifties standing at her office door. He combed his gray-streaked hair neatly from his head and smelled of Old Spice. He wore khakis and a navy blue blazer. "I'm Detective Ross from the Sheriff's office. Can I ask you a few questions?"

She stood and shook his hand and indicated the wicker chair. "Have a seat." She wheeled her desk chair over.

Detective Ross sat and pulled a small notebook from his blazer pocket. "I was supposed to meet with Mark Monstain but he's out. Do you know when he'll be back?"

Guess she wasn't the only one Mark had stood up today. She shook her head. "Sorry."

He flipped open the notebook. "That's okay. Can you answer some questions?"

"I'll try."

He clicked his pen. "Did you know Darla Barrows?"

She shook her head. "No. I was hired to replace her." She indicated a box on the floor near the door. "That's all the personal stuff I found here. I didn't know who might want it."

He gazed at the box. "No one's come to claim it?"

Nora studied the framed picture of Abbey on her desk, her iPod dock, a silly figurine of a polar bear and her Tree Hugger mug. If Nora disappeared suddenly, Abigail would collect her things. Darla's remained unclaimed.

He studied her. "I understand you were here when they were notified about Darla."

The thought of that scream sent a chill over her skin. "Petal found out. She was a friend of Darla's. I think the police called her."

"Petal. I see. What's her last name?"

Good question. Part of Nora's duties involved payroll and some HR. Nora fished in a desk drawer and produced the file cabinet key. She unlocked the employee file drawer. She flipped through searching for Petal's file. She finally found it and pulled it out. "Petal Rainbow."

The detective didn't crack a smile. He flipped open his notebook. "Address?"

Nora scanned the papers inside the folder. "62 Canyon Boulevard."

He started to write and stopped. "That's Loving Earth's address."

That was stupid. "You're right." She paged through the rest of the forms. "They all have the same address."

"Do you have a phone number for Petal?"

Nora snatched a staff contract printout off a bulletin board next to the desk. She ran her finger down the list. "I guess not."

He closed his notebook and stuffed it into the chest pocket of his shirt. "One last question. Do you have any theories why someone would want to kill Darla Barrows?"

She really needed to talk to Mark about the missing money before going to the police. Maybe he had a perfectly good explanation. If she didn't meet with him by the end of the day, she'd go the cops with her financials tomorrow. "Sorry," she said again.

He picked up Darla's things and walked to the door. "Thanks for talking to me."

Nora wanted to dive back into the books. Why had Abigail volunteered her to go with Petal to Mount Evans? She needed to investigate the missing money.

Bright blue flashed in the corner of her eye and she jumped and gasped.

Daniel stood in the doorway wearing a deep blue shirt. "Sorry I couldn't get here any sooner."

His jeans hugged his long legs and all his shapely... shape. The top buttons of his shirt were undone, showing a bit of black hair. Man, oh man. "No problem. I need to go to the mountains with Petal in a few minutes, anyway."

"And Cole, no?" He stepped into her office and rolled up his sleeves. Like a strip tease, his fingers played with the fabric. Dark hair lay soft against his forearms. Who knew arms could be so sexy?

"Where would you like me to start today, boss?" His lips formed a smile but Nora imagined those lips kissing someone. Okay, kissing her.

She grabbed a handful of files and set them on the work surface. "These are invoices and payments. I've been going through them for this fiscal year, sort of hunting for..."

A light touch on her shoulder startled her. She paused and saw Daniel's dark eyes fixed on her face. She straightened.

His hand traced down her arm, his fingers light. "You are beautiful."

How did her legs continue to support her weight when her knees felt like peanut butter? Breathing was out of the question. "Um." That was witty conversation.

His hand traveled up to her cheek, his touch like satin. "Not only beautiful but brilliant. Do you have any idea how sexy you are?"

Tongue-tied would be super compared to how she felt. Good thing he didn't seem to expect a response.

Daniel leaned into her. His lips captured hers with the same gentle touch of his fingers on her skin. He kissed her slowly, and even if it sounded like a bodice-ripper novel, he kissed her thoroughly. Her knees weren't the only body part melting.

He drew away slightly and gazed at her with intensity from his bottomless, fire-lit eyes.

He kissed her again. Sweet, with deep undertones and a hint of restrained passion. For dog's sake, she sounded like she described a glass of wine. Really good wine. Like the five-hundred-dollar a bottle kind. The sort of wine she couldn't afford.

Right. She didn't drink wine like that because, well, because. It would end up making her throw up in the morning... or something like that. What she meant was that she didn't really want him.

Nora stepped back. "Okay. Well. So."

He laughed. "Nora. You can take a little pleasure, no?"

She reached for her coat. "I think I ought to go find Petal."

He leaned back on the counter with a cat-chomping-canary smile on those full, warm lips. "You looked radiant this morning. You should wear a dress more often. Your legs are exquisite."

If only he weren't so gorgeous. She zipped her coat. "Knock it off."

"Life is short, *mi amor*. Why not enjoy each other?"

"I'm an accountant. We don't enjoy things." She unzipped her coat.

He laughed. "You are ripe for pleasure."

Her face could not burn any hotter. She zipped up again.

A vibration in Daniel's pocket—not the kind he'd been hinting about—thankfully ended the talk of juicy fruit.

Daniel's face clouded with annoyance as he listened to the phone call. He slid the phone back in his pocket. "Sadly, we will finish this conversation at another time. I must go."

He hurried away and Nora plopped into her desk chair. It took a few moments for her vital signs to return to normal.

"'You should wear a dress more often. Your legs are exquisite.'" Cole's mocking voice made her jump. He leaned against the door frame.

"You were spying on me!" She flamed in embarrassment.

He walked into the room grinning. "Petal's waiting in the pickup. Are you ready to go?"

How long had he been there? Had he seen Daniel kiss her?

Nora followed him out the door, wondering why she cared what he thought.

30

The doorbell rang as Sylvia opened the shower sauna door. She set her wine glass on the bathroom counter and tightened the kimono. Had she ordered anything and forgot about a delivery?

Sylvia padded down the stairs and peered out the window at the side of the door. The irritating stray cat would be a more welcome sight than what stood on her porch. What was Mark doing here? She unlocked the door and opened it. A whoosh of cold air followed him in, making the kimono feel like a sheet of ice. A few flakes swirled outside. "I'm in a hurry to get back to the Trust. What do you want?"

That supercilious grin begged for a slap. "Sorry. I need to talk to you."

She left him in the foyer and started up the stairs. "Can we schedule a meeting? How about sometime tomorrow?"

He seemed to be trying for coy. "Oh, I think you'll want to talk to me."

"What is it?" The sauna would be warming up nicely by now.

He stayed just inside the door. "Nora Abbott and Daniel Cubrero are combing through everything."

She stopped and gave him a frosty stare. "So what? I have nothing to hide."

He licked his fat lips. "We know better, don't we?"

"What are you talking about?"

His eyes had a weird gleam. "It can be our secret. We take care of each other, isn't that right? We're special friends."

What would get him out of here the quickest? "Yes, Mark. We're good friends. But I don't think I need to be protected."

His voice rose in a hysterical giggle. "They could find the four hundred thousand dollars you stole last month."

More ways to waste her time. "Don't be ridiculous. I didn't take any money."

He sniggered. "You don't need to play stupid with me anymore. I know you have it. Darla made the approval and the money disappeared in an electronic transaction. No record."

All the oxygen suddenly left the room. Someone took her money. "Where did it go?"

He shrugged. "Only you and Darla know that. And Darla turned up dead. Do you suppose the cops will suspect you had a motive?"

She stared at him.

"I won't tell. That is, if you show me what good friends we are."

She didn't have time for this. She stomped up the stairs in search of her phone. Eduardo needed to know her money was stolen. It proved Nora set her up. Sylvia didn't know how Nora could have done it when she didn't work at the Trust until a few days ago, but she'd figure it out.

Her toes sank into the deep pile of her white carpet as she hurried down the hallway.

Mark's heavy breathing startled her. He'd followed her. "Oh, I know that with someone like Daniel Cubrero around no one notices me. But, Sylvia, I promise you, whatever Daniel has to offer, I can do better."

She couldn't concentrate on what his words meant.

Mark followed her into the bedroom.

Sylvia strode to her black lacquered dresser but the phone didn't sit in its usual place. She hurried to the bedside table but it wasn't there. She spun around scanning the spacious room and her gaze found it. Her phone lay in a heap at the base of the wall by the bathroom.

Mark minced his way across the room and stepped close to her, his fetid breath warm on her neck. "You're a beautiful woman."

She skirted him and walked to the end of the bed. "Where would Darla have hidden the money?"

Mark brushed his hand against his crotch. "You won't be disappointed."

She glared at him. "I'm trying to save your butt. If four-hundred-thousand dollars is missing, it'll be your fault. If you don't go to prison, at the very least, the board will fire you."

He closed the space between them. "I can make you feel like a woman."

"Are you sure the money is missing?"

His hand snaked out and brushed her waist. "We've denied our desire for three years. Here we are. Your bedroom. Now is the perfect time for us. I'm more than you would suspect."

The hiss of the shower sauna filled the silence while Sylvia stared at him in disgust. The faint odor of stale coffee and sweat seeped from him.

He reached out and stroked her breast through the silk of the kimono.

She sprang back. "What is the matter with you?"

His eyes glazed and his moist lips slackened as he stared at her breast. "You think I'm stupid, don't you?" He spoke with a whine, like a four year-old.

What a hideous man. She backed up.

He stepped toward her. "I've treated you like a goddess. I left you alone so you could work on your oh-so-important research."

"You're way over the line. Leave now."

Sweat glistened on his face. "But now you need me even more. You don't want me to tell the cops about the money, do you?"

He wouldn't have the *cojones* to go against her.

He stepped toward her again. "You're not really working on climate change and beetle kill, are you? You never were. Where are the reports, Sylvia? Where is all that money going? Who are you really working for?"

She laid a hand on his sweaty chest and shoved him back. "You're crazy. I'm calling the cops."

His shrill laughter sent a chill up her spine. "The cops? When they get here let's tell them about the night Darla died."

Sylvia didn't kill Darla. Of that, she was certain. "What do you know about that?"

He crowded her against a cabinet and slid his fingers under the kimono belt. "I know she came to see you. You argued. She left and I heard shots fired. Next thing we know, Darla is a goner."

Her mind reeled. She needed to shut him up.

The kimono slipped open and Mark slobbered on his fat lips. His gaze traveled to her face. "Do you want to know what I was doing there?"

Think Sylvia. How can you shut him up?

He touched her nipple and moaned. "I've waited for you for a long time. And I've watched. I know your favorite coffee shop. I know where you buy your lingerie." He panted. "I'm good for you, Sylvia. And I can make you feel so good. Even Daniel Cubrero can't do what I can."

"You need help," she said, letting her contempt drip from her voice in a hiss like the sauna. She jerked her kimono closed and strode to the other side of the bed. "You're a disgusting little man."

"I would kill for you. In fact, if Nora hadn't thrown up all the drugs I gave her, I would have been successful. As it is, I destroyed all the bank statements for the climate mapping account. That will slow her down."

"Get out."

He followed her. "You don't need to fight it, Sylvia. I've loved you and protected you. Now let me pleasure you as only I can."

She pointed to the door and shouted. "GET OUT!"

He ignored her demand. "I know you were here. With him."

Sylvia curled her lip. "Leave."

He stalked her around the bed. "Not until I get what I came for. Only I can protect you."

She laughed, a cruel sound meant to emasculate him. "You think I'd sleep with you? You really are crazy."

"I'm not planning to sleep."

He grabbed her wrist, leveraging her to toss her onto the bed.

Sylvia wrenched her wrist free and whirled around to the bedside table. Her fingers clasped the handle and jerked open the drawer. Keeping her eyes on Mark, she felt around for the plain Smith and Wesson Airweight she kept there. It didn't have the sex appeal of her gold-plated model, but it was as deadly.

He only had a nanosecond to register his surprise before she slipped off the safety, buried the small barrel in the soft flesh of his chin, and pulled the trigger.

31

Nora drove her Jeep and Cole sat in the passenger side. Petal huddled in back with Abbey's head on her knee. They headed south out of Boulder in the light early afternoon traffic. Clouds still hung heavy and low, blocking their view of the front range of the Rockies. The air carried the smell of snow and a few dry flakes swirled in the wind.

The Jeep rumbled along with its noisy cadence and they barely spoke. Petal's occasional sniffs and quiet tears wrenched Nora's heart. Cole seemed lost in his own thoughts, now and then glancing at Nora as if he'd like to start a conversation, then deciding against it.

They worked their way through a few stop lights in the foothills town of Golden then up I-70 into the mountains. Too early for commuters and few people out to play in the middle of the week left the six-lane Interstate feeling empty. The green slopes with scattered houses turned into sheer rock faces hidden in shadow.

After forty-five minutes of driving, Nora pulled off the Interstate onto the road leading to Mount Evans. She hated this treacherous drive and to have to face it so soon after her last climbing attempt stretched her courage. Familiarity ought to ease her tension but she dreaded the narrow road winding up above timberline.

"What's your ranch in Wyoming like?" She wanted to distract herself from the anxiety building inside her.

Cole seemed startled to have a question directed his way. "It's up by Sheridan. A hundred thousand acres."

"You grew up there?" Keep him talking.

He seemed to understand her need for distraction and launched into a monologue. "My great-grandfather homesteaded it. My father inherited it from his father and they both added land to it. My younger brother runs it now. I've been working there since I left Flagstaff last year. It's about time for me to move on, though. I'm weighing my options."

She quizzed him and he answered, telling her anecdotes about growing up on the range. Wild horses, wild cows and two wild boys.

It helped, and they eventually pulled into the parking lot at the top of the mountain. Nora held the front seat up for Petal and Abbey to exit.

The wind tugged at Nora's hair and battered her cheeks. She reached into the glove box and pulled out an elastic band to gather her hair back. Technically, Abbey wasn't allowed on the trail up to the top but since the Jeep was the only vehicle in the lot, Nora broke the leash law and let him go.

They headed toward the trail and the series of five switchbacks that led them to the top. Cold, brittle air felt so thin Nora was soon puffing to fill her lungs. The snow still struggled and miniscule drifts accumulated in rocky crags along the trail. When they reached the top, low clouds hid the view.

Petal pointed to the east. "It's around that outcropping there. It's hidden behind two sharp ledges so no one will mess with it."

"I can't believe the Trust let her install a tower someplace so dangerous to get to," Nora said, her stomach lurching at the thought of scrambling over the rocks to find it.

Petal climbed toward the outcropping. "I don't think they know. Sylvia told Mark it's up here and he never checked. She had me take a picture for the board and it doesn't show how remote it is."

"If you can climb out there," Cole said. "What keeps vandals away?"

Petal dug in a pocket of her skirt and brandished a key. "There's a fence and padlock. But Sylvia needs me to check it every once in a while to make sure it's okay."

The summit was long and flat, but boulders and rocks piled in a jumble across the surface to create precarious footing to climb from one smooth surface to the next. Petal clambered with the surety of a mountain goat and soon disappeared around a bend in the east.

Nora and Cole followed Petal up the rocky pile to the bend. Abbey explored on his own, pausing occasionally to keep Nora in sight.

Nora's heart thundered against her ribs. She glanced at Cole. Did he see her fighting with the panic?

He squinted against the wind and snow and watched Petal climb on all fours around another bend.

Nora gritted her teeth and focused on the forest green of Cole's down jacket in front of her. She'd follow him and it would be okay. No reason for panic.

Cole stopped and waited for her to catch up. He lowered his head, suddenly serious. "Can I ask you something?"

She tried to still her heavy breathing. Fourteen thousand feet in elevation left little air for her lungs. "Sure."

The flush of his skin didn't come from the wind. "Is there something going on between you and Daniel?"

"What?" She laughed.

"I'd like to know."

One thing about Cole, he didn't play games. "No. Absolutely not."

Well, one kiss—but it wasn't her idea and she had no plans of repeating it.

He eyed her, and then seemed to accept her answer. He turned and followed Petal's course.

The wind howled with a menacing sound. They scrambled up a boulder in time to see Petal disappear again. They had to be getting to the edge of the summit. How many more crags, boulders, or bends could there be before they reached the eastern side of the mountain?

She stumbled up a smooth, cold rock to see Petal just one bend away.

Panting and using her hands to maneuver up a slick rock Nora spotted the tower. Similar to any number of weather stations she'd seen, one metal rod extended about twenty feet into the air. The rod had a twelve-inch circumference with a four-foot dome at the top. Smaller legs extended from the dome to the ground in a tripod configuration, probably for stability. The stem must be anchored deep into the stone of the mountain to hold it steady in the high altitude storms. A chain-link fence about five feet high encircled it. Someone could climb the fence, but only a fool would try because the whole fixture perched on an overhang. Only a few inches of rock bordered the fence before solid ground ended. From there, a sheer drop of several hundred feet would mean certain death.

A gust buffeted Nora from behind and she stumbled. "Ah!" Despite herself, she screamed.

Cole whipped around and grabbed her arm. "Are you okay?"

She started to nod then shook her head, not trusting her voice.

"Here. Sit." He helped her off the boulder to a crag, out of the wind.

She dropped to the rock and leaned back. "Thanks."

"Abigail said you have panic attacks in the mountains."

The cold stone radiated through her jeans. She glared at him. "That's why you offered to come up here. To protect me again, right?"

He nodded. "What are you going to do about them?"

Time to change the subject. "So, I've been thinking about Benny coming to Boulder and wondering what he meant about the prophecies."

Cole gave his head a slight shake as if acknowledging her conversational duck and weave. "End of the world stuff?"

"That seems extreme. But Benny is worried." Should she tell Cole that Benny worried because Nakwaiyamtewa him some warning? "Maybe there's something in the prophecies we should think about."

Cole chuckled. "Hopi corn and now prophecies? Doesn't sound like the skeptical Nora I know."

"And the Hopi Instructions. I've been studying those, too."

His eyes registered surprise. "Since when?"

She played with a pebble while the wind whistled above them. "Since I left Flagstaff."

"Benny got to you, didn't he?" Cole grinned at her.

Nakwaiyamtewa had the real powers of persuasion. "I guess. And then..."

He tilted his head and waited.

She swallowed and viewed the gray sky. "Turns out I'm half Hopi."

He slapped his hand over his heart in exaggerated surprise.

It took Nora a beat to understand. "Abigail told you."

He nodded.

"You guys are a regular best-friends club."

Abbey bounded over the ridge above them and bumped Nora's side. He sat and panted in her face.

Cole reached over to pet Abbey. "So what about the prophecies?"

Nora ticked off the list in her head. "Okay, these all came to the Hopi over a thousand years ago. They say there will be roads in the sky. There will be moving houses of iron and horseless carriages. People will have the ability to speak through cobwebs and to speak through space. Women will take on men's clothing and wear skirts above the knee which devalues the sacred female body. Apparently that demonstrates how low society sinks."

"Not much to go on there." Cole said.

She agreed. "There are more. People of the cross will lead Hopi away from the Great Creator. Short hairs of the Hopi will join the *pahana* government and dilute Hopi beliefs." She paused and explained to Cole. "*Pahana* is the white man"

Cole narrowed his eyes. "I know that much."

She thought about the list of prophecies, trying to remember. "Do not bring anything home from the moon or it will lead to weather disturbances..."

Cole interrupted. "Now we're getting somewhere. Weather disturbances. Sylvia is working on climate-change modeling isn't she? That's disturbed weather."

"I don't know. That seems like a stretch. Prophecies can mean anything. There's one that talks about inverted gourds of ashes that will boil rivers and cause disease no medicine can cure." A lump formed in Nora's throat when she remembered Heather's excitement to tell her about the prophesies and that the one about the inverted gourd that referred to nuclear weapons.

"Maybe we should try to get Benny back to Boulder," Cole said.

They'd never be able to figure out what these obscure predictions meant. "There's one about the Earth turning four times and then mankind will crawl on all fours and only the brother and sister will survive to recycle the Earth."

"There you go. Recycling. Definitely your bailiwick."

Didn't a board member wonder if the HAARP research would flip the Earth on its axis?

Petal appeared at the top of the boulder above them. "It's fine. Sylvia can run her procedure now."

Cole helped Nora up.

Nora's shoulders tensed but she felt in control enough she didn't think the panic would return. She shouted above the wind. "Is that safe up here?"

Petal nodded. "It's sturdy. If someone punctured the tower the energy would leak out, sort of like if you drove a copper nail into a tree and the energy leaks out and the tree dies. But it would be hard to do that."

The wind changed directions. Nora said, "That's the only way someone can ruin it?"

Petal spoke matter-of-factly. "Well, you could take the tunable inductor out of the tower. It's just two PVC pipes with wire coiled around them. When you tune the capacitor just right, it oscillates with the ionosphere. So if that's removed, the energy won't transfer through the spark gap."

Riiight.

Petal stared at the tower. "This is a simple concept for creating energy and the world should know about it. They could shut down the coal and the nuclear plants. This is natural and how we are meant to power our planet. It's the resonance we can all connect to. We can align our chakras with the power. We should build more of these towers on every mountain and they should become places of worship. Because it's a place of creativity."

Nora didn't know what to say. Her eyes met Cole's and she realized he was at a loss, too. "I guess we'd better head back," Nora said.

They scrambled over the ridge toward the trail. "If Sylvia is sending out beams to bounce off the ionosphere, wouldn't that require a lot of energy? I don't see bills that would show that?"

They made it to the switchbacks. Abbey trotted ahead.

Petal stopped beside the cliff wall, out of the wind. "Tesla came up with all sorts of discoveries but they were stolen by the government and kept secret. They use them at HAARP. One study they did is an expansion of the Tesla Coil and it's what we've adapted here. That's an electrical resonant transformer used to produce high-voltage, low-current, high-frequency alternating-current electricity."

Nora gaped at Petal.

Petal wore a shy smile. "It's like this: the tower here uses electricity from the atmosphere. Like in a thunderstorm with a lot of lightening. You know that impressive energy? That energy is the most dominant outward factor in all kinds of storms. So the energy at just the right ELF frequency can create the power of storms."

They walked down the trail in single file. Petal first, then Cole and Nora last. Nora studied her feet to choose each step on the rocky path. She had to project her voice over the wind and with her shortness of breath, her sentences came out in two-to-three word bursts. "So she gets all this energy and she's going to shoot out a beam to collect climate data and she's figured out how to aim it down here, in the Rockies?"

Petal stumbled. Cole jumped forward to help her up.

"And you just checked to make sure it's all functional but she sets it where she wants it to go with her equipment at the Trust?"

Petal mumbled and kept her head down.

"I'm sorry," Nora shouted. "I didn't hear you."

Petal stopped and faced Nora. "She's going to run it tonight."

32

Sylvia paced the foyer, her heels pounding. She'd chosen three-inch pumps tonight because of the solemn occasion. It wouldn't be appropriate to dress flamboyantly with a dead body in her bedroom.

She'd left Eduardo a message on his voicemail over an hour ago. Why didn't he call her back? She told him she needed to speak to him immediately. There was nothing to do but wait.

Eduardo must have a fixer who handled situations like this. Maybe Juan.

The sheer volume of blood surprised Sylvia. It splattered the white walls and carpet and ruined the black lacquered furniture. It soaked her silk duvet clashing with the scarlet orchids. All of that would be ruined.

Maybe she'd change it up now. Go contemporary with splashes of primary colors. On second thought, she'd avoid red.

The phone distracted her from redecorating plans. She punched it on. "Eduardo. Oh, thank god."

He didn't greet her. "Juan says there's problem."

How did Juan know? "He came at me. He wanted to kill me."

Silence met her outburst. "Are you talking about the Director?"

"Mark. Yes. Mark. It was awful."

"Why did Mark Monstain want to kill you?"

His voice made her think of her father's yellowed toenails. "I don't know. He was crazy." She broke off and swallowed horrified tears.

"So you shot him?"

"He was going to rape me! He would have exposed our plans. I protected you!" Sylvia stomped up the foyer stairs and pounded down the hallway. She paced back.

Again, the dead-sounding voice. "Do you know the problem you've created?"

Why wasn't he outraged? He should have wanted to kill Mark himself for attacking Sylvia. "I didn't ask Mark to defile me."

Despite his velvety accent, Eduardo's voice drove ice into her veins. "First you kill Darla and now Mark."

"I didn't kill Darla!" What was that odor drifting down the stairs? Death smelled like a rotten forest.

"And you did not take thousands of dollars from the Trust?"

He was turning on her. She dropped down the two steps into the great room and stared at the foothills outside her windows. "I've been set up. Nora Abbott is behind all this."

"If you've not taken money from them, how do you afford the Ferrari? The crystal? The leather, furs—my god—the shoes?" He paused. "And the Chihuly? Do not worry about that. Your order was cancelled."

Her glass? "That was mine!"

"Where did the money come from for all your indulgences if it did not come from the Trust?"

How did they know all of this? Eduardo was out to get her. But he didn't know everything. He thought she got money from the Trust. He didn't know of her masterful system of borrowing from one card and another and juggling money from friends willing to donate to a brilliant scientist.

"You're a liability."

Icicles pierced her heart. Damn him for upsetting her like this. She needed to play it cool. "I've done it, Eduardo. I've given you a taste of what I can do. Watch the news tonight."

"Have you really accomplished our task?" Eduardo asked, a little perk to his voice.

"Yes. And I need you to clean this mess." She thought of the blood splattered across her bedroom.

"We'll see." Eduardo said.

"The police might come here. I'm still under suspicion for Darla's murder. If you don't take care of Mark it will all be over. You won't get what you want."

"How about this, Sylvia." His tone was slow and deliberate. "You give me what I want and we'll see about cleaning up your mess."

He hung up.

She stood at the foot of the stairs staring up, the coppery stench of blood filling her nostrils.

33

Another day done. In the glow of the eternal parking lot lights, Nora trudged up the stairs to her apartment. The air smelled of snow and wood burning in someone's fireplace. A door below her opened and loud music momentarily disturbed the night and then the door closed again.

They'd returned from the mountain at dusk. Cole left in his pickup and Petal disappeared to Sylvia's office. Nora had spent the next few hours creating a spreadsheet to trace the missing money's journey. She waited for Mark. She wanted to show it to him before taking it to the police. She eventually gave up, resolved to take the spreadsheet to the police in the morning and headed home exhausted.

Maybe Abigail had a delicious dinner cooked and waiting. More likely, she had reservations for some fancy restaurant Nora couldn't afford. What else were credit cards for if not to overspend on her mother one month and live on cheap noodles the next?

First things first. She'd take Abbey for a long walk. She'd convince Abigail to come along. They'd stop and get a few groceries for dinner and instead of going out, prepare it together. And maybe, just maybe, she and Abigail could enjoy each other's company.

She slipped the key in the lock and opened the apartment door. Abbey trotted in and Nora unzipped her jacket.

A burst of laughter drew Nora's attention to the living room. She blinked at what she saw.

Abigail sat on the floor in yoga pants and tunic, legs spread out. She bent from the waist to grasp her bare feet. She let out another bout of giggles.

Petal sat across from her in a similar pose. Her bare feet stuck out from black leggings that disappeared under three layers of skirts. "You need to breathe, Abigail. That's the essence of yoga."

Abigail swung her head around to the doorway, tears of hilarity shining in her eyes. "Oh, Nora. I didn't hear you come in."

Nora pulled off her jacket. "How did you not notice me? The door is right here."

Petal giggled. "I guess we were preoccupied."

Abigail burst out laughing. She covered her mouth with her hand. "We were concentrating."

The both cracked up. Abigail fell back, her chest and belly rising and falling with her howls. Petal fell to her side with her head resting on Abigail's stomach. She snorted and laughed all the harder.

Nora addressed Abbey. "What's up with them?" She inspected the galley kitchen, hoping for some kind of dinner. Instead, chip bags and a package of Oreos littered the counter.

Nora stepped into the living room and her nose itched with the telltale smell. She stared at the giggling women on the floor. "You've been smoking pot!"

Abigail sobered. She lifted Petal's head off her belly and sat up. She grew serious for five seconds and then cracked up. "I told Petal you'd know."

Fear clouded Petal's eyes. "I'm sorry."

Abigail stoned? With Petal? The whole scenario twisted so far from reality Nora could only stand mute and watch as Abigail and Petal fell back into giggles.

Nora reached for her jacket and the leash. "I'm taking Abbey for his walk. We'll discuss this when I get back."

The labyrinth of paved paths running through Boulder intersected with the parking lot in her apartment complex. Students used these trails as bicycle highways to campus. Runners trod up and down at all hours and the general, outdoor-loving Boulder population found them necessary to their lifestyle. Access to the trail system was one of the big advantages to Nora's apartment.

Nora and Abbey tromped along the Boulder Creek trail. The creek babbled and leaves rustled in the brisk wind. For the first fifteen minutes Nora railed in her head about Petal. How dare she get Abigail stoned? The next ten minutes involved blaming Abigail. After that came the question of why Abigail would experiment with pot. And just before they returned to the apartment, Nora started to chuckle at the idea of her mother, Abigail the Perfect, sprawled on the floor experimenting with yoga. Smoking a little pot might not be such a bad thing for someone as uptight at her mother.

By the time Nora and Abbey stepped from the cold into the apartment, Petal and Abigail had cleaned the kitchen. They sat in the living room with steaming mugs, watching the evening news.

It seemed strange to have the television on. Nora rarely watched it.

Abigail stood. "Can I get you a cup of tea?"

Nora motioned her to sit. "I'll get it. Are there any more of those cookies?"

Abigail smiled sheepishly. "A few. In the cupboard." She leaned against the counter bar.

Nora fixed her tea and found the cookies. "You didn't drive to get your snacks, did you?"

Abigail regarded her tea mug. "I.... I rode Petal's bike."

Nora stopped steeping her tea and gaped at Abigail.

The only sound was a commercial chirping in the living room.

They held each other's gaze for a heartbeat and Nora lost it, nearly spewing cookie crumbs at Abigail. "I wish I'd seen that."

Abigail smiled. "I'm glad you didn't."

Nora carried her tea into the living room and sank into the green chair while Abigail settled herself on the couch next to Petal.

Petal hadn't said anything, just watched Nora with big, fearful eyes.

Why was it that Petal could get stoned with Abigail, laugh and carry on, yet she seemed afraid of Nora? Furthermore, how old was Petal? It was impossible to tell under all that hair. "You know," Nora said to her, "I'm not mad."

"'Let not anger snuff out the youthful delight of new life.'" Abigail considered the line and wisely shook her head rejecting it.

Petal twisted her hands in her lap. "You're not?"

"I was at first. It's not every day I discover my mother is a pot head."

"Nora!" Abigail exploded in indignation. "One shared joint does not make me a pot head."

Nora struggled to keep a straight face. "I think you should be able to cut loose once in a while. In fact, why don't we do it together? Have you got any more, Petal? We could make brownies."

Petal looked from Nora to Abigail and back again. She didn't say anything and kept wringing her hands.

"So why are you smoking pot, Mother?"

"I wanted to see what all the hoopla is about. Is there anything wrong with that?"

Nora sipped her tea. "The 'hoopla' has been going on for decades."

Petal's voice squeaked from the end of the couch. "It's not her fault. I invited her. I was feeling so sad about Darla and I asked if she'd mind if I smoked a little, just to take my mind off Darla for a while."

"So Abigail joined in to be supportive?"

Petal stared at her hands.

"This has something to do with Charlie, doesn't it?"

Abigail pursed her lips. "Charlie is out of my life. I don't even think about him anymore."

Might as well talk about this now. "There's no way Charlie had an affair."

"Of course you'd defend him."

A low moan escaped from Petal. Abigail and Nora both turned to her.

Even paler than usual, Petal's eyes formed giant dark circles in her face. Her mouth gaped and she seemed drawn into the television.

The news announcer's voice spoke over the image of what might have once been a meadow but now appeared to be a field of mud. The wide-angle shot showed an open area ringed by trees with fall leaves. As the view closed in the trees faded and ground came more into focus.

Petal dropped to her knees in front of the screen. "No. No. No." She covered her mouth with her thin hands.

Abigail grabbed the remote and punched up the volume.

While the camera narrowed in on the ground, showing mounds of black feathers, the announcer said, "Hundreds of thousands of blackbirds fell from the sky in an unexplained rain of death." The image on the screen showed piles of dead birds. "Apparently the kill happened sometime in the late afternoon when the birds dropped onto this Georgia meadow. No explanation is forthcoming although Timothy Peterson, Professor of Ornithology at the University of Georgia had this to say."

The screen switched to a tall man standing outside a collegiate-looking brick building. "It could be the result of a washing machine-type thunderstorm extremely high in the atmosphere. This type of storm would agitate and create a vortex, suddenly appearing and sucking the red-winged blackbirds into its midst and spitting them back onto the ground."

Petal rocked back and forth. "How could she?"

The announcer, a blonde woman with skin like rosy plastic and eyes so rimmed in makeup they might have been painted on, held the microphone to her full-lipped mouth. She stood at the edge of the meadow with a view of the carnage behind her. "Of course, there are other explanations for the bizarre phenomenon."

The camera drew back to reveal a bony woman with gray hair down to the middle of her back. Her face burned with intensity. "This is obviously a government conspiracy. It's the result of a doomsday weapon experiment. Wake up, America!"

Behind her, a small group carried signs and chanted. The scene reminded Nora of the activists who hounded her about manmade snow on the peaks. Her stomach churned.

The announcer smiled knowingly. "According to conspiracy theorists, there is such a doomsday weapon in development since the 1970s. The HAARP facility in Gakona, Alaska is home to what was once touted as Star Wars Defense." The screen flipped from the announcer's face to a photograph of a group standing in front of an array of towers.

Petal gasped. She pointed. "Sylvia," she whispered.

Nora leaned forward. It was difficult to tell with the grainy shot, but a petite woman with curly black hair stood in the front row. It could be Sylvia.

The announcer continued. "The government and private contractors insist they are performing ionospheric research for better communications. But some, including former Minnesota Governor, Jesse Ventura, say HAARP is creating weapons of mass destruction." The screen flashed a video of Jesse Ventura at the gates of a government facility, presumably HAARP, being pushed back and refused entry.

Back to the announcer. "Midnight thunderstorms, government weapons testing, or signs that the world is coming to an end? Whatever the reason, residents of Harris County will be cleaning up for some time." The plastic-faced reporter signed off on her segment of the day's bizarre stories from around the country.

The program cut to a commercial and Petal collapsed into sobs. "I did this. It's my fault!"

34

Petal fell to the floor in a heap and Abigail patted her back. "You had nothing to do with this, dear."

Nora's first instinct was to console and protect Petal's total vulnerability. That's the thing, though. You can't protect people from the world.

Abigail jabbed the Off button and huddled over Petal. "I know it's hard to see all that death." With her facial gyrations, Abigail signaled Nora for help.

Petal pulled away and rolled into a ball, sobbing. "She promised. Never again. She promised. She promised."

Abigail sent Nora a puzzled expression. Maybe Mark and Sylvia were right about Petal: Don't feed the drama.

Abbey whined. He sniffed at Petal and came to Nora, thrusting his nose into her hand.

"Who promised? What did they promise?" Abigail asked.

Petal inhabited her own world. "No more death. She said it. No more."

Abigail and Nora half-lifted Petal and plopped her on the couch. Abigail snugged in beside her and Nora knelt in front. "Calm down, Petal. Tell us what you mean."

Petal swiped her sleeve across her eyes and nose. "First it was the fish kill in Missouri. And now this." Sob, sob, sob. "They were innocent birds. They didn't need to die." Even more sobbing. "She lied. She *lied.*"

Maybe Nora should call an ambulance to take Petal to the nearest psych ward. "You're going to have to start at the beginning if you want us to understand."

Petal hiccupped and turned her red-rimmed eyes to Nora. "Sylvia."

No surprise there. "Sylvia what?"

Petal sniffed. "She killed those birds."

While Abigail rubbed Petal's back, she opened her eyes wide, tilted her head, and dropped her jaw. She either had a sudden stroke or she tried to communicate silently with Nora. If Nora had to guess, Abigail was saying Petal was one enchilada short of a combination plate.

Her silent message delivered, Abigail concentrated on Petal. "How could Sylvia have anything to do with those birds? She was here in Boulder at the funeral this morning."

Petal shook her head, eyes watering again. "She can do it all from here. She did it."

Nora had nothing to say.

In between intense eye roll signals to Nora, Abigail said to Petal, "When you calm down you'll see you're not making sense."

Nora tried to fit the bits of Petal's scattered thoughts into some shape. "Does this have to do with the tower? Is it linked to the HAARP research?"

Petal grew still, like a frightened kitten hiding in a corner. "Yes," she squeaked.

"What is *harp*?" Abigail asked, impatience fraying her words.

Nora answered for Petal. "Sylvia worked there before she came to the Trust."

"What does that have to do with birds dying?" Abigail asked.

Nora answered Abigail. "I don't know. She said she researched sending a beam up to bounce in the ionosphere. She's using that technology to gather data on climate and beetle kill. What do you know, Petal?"

Irritation colored Abigail's voice. "You're speaking Greek."

Petal sniffed. "It's more than that. The HAARP facility is in Alaska because it's close to the atmospheric conditions like the aurora borealis. It's all really secure with government soldiers and things."

"I still don't see where this has anything to do with birds," Abigail said.

Nora understood that Petal needed to wind down the path of her brain to get to any meaningful destination. Abigail might as well slow her pace.

"Tell us everything," Nora said.

Petal inhaled a shaky breath. "When we worked for the private contractor who worked for the government, we studied communication systems based on bouncing lasers off the ionosphere. But we also worked secretly on weapons research."

Abigail opened her mouth, probably to hurry Petal along.

Nora jumped in. "You worked with Sylvia before?"

Tears seeped from Petal's eyes. "I've been with her for seven years."

That was one clue to Petal's age. "Go on."

Petal searched Nora's face as if to test her worthiness. "While we were with HAARP, we found Nikola Tesla's secret studies and they showed the exact frequencies needed for incredible power. The technology we discovered can be used to alter the weather."

Right. And Santa Claus kept a list with Nora perpetually in the wrong column.

"So Sylvia learned to alter the weather. Why did she quit HAARP?" Nora said.

"She didn't quit. She was fired." Petal swiped her nose with her sleeve.

"Why?" Abigail asked.

"She wasn't doing any of the work but taking credit for it and they finally figured it out."

"Why didn't she publish her findings?" Nora asked gently.

"They made her sign a document about government secrets and that she wouldn't continue her research."

"But she has?" Abigail crossed the room and grabbed another tissue from a box on the counter bar. She handed it to Petal.

Petal wiped her eyes and nodded. "Besides, if Sylvia tried to publish her work there's a good chance someone would kill her."

Abigail's eyes narrowed in offense. "From our government? That's preposterous."

It sounded more like a spy novel than real life. Maybe that's where Petal came up the plot.

"Now all those innocent birds are dead." Her voice faded into sobs.

Abigail did some weird eye roll thing that Nora thought meant Petal was not just crazy but a full-out Looney Tunes.

Nora tried to ground Petal. "But changing weather doesn't have anything to do with thousands of dead birds."

Changing weather. One of the prophecies had to do with weather.

Petal gulped. "It's the freak thunderstorm like the ornithologist said."

"But he said there was no record of the phenomenon," Abigail said.

"That's because it happened so far up in the atmosphere the only indication was the impact it had on the birds."

The pieces didn't fit together any better than Petal's outfit. "Even if this is what happened and Sylvia is behind it, why would she do it?"

Petal looked from Abigail to Nora. She lowered her voice. "Because she's really not working for the Trust. That's just her cover."

"Cover for what?"

"She's continuing to work on controlling the weather."

Abigail stood. "I think we need coffee. Nora, can you help me find the beans you like?"

Even a flake like Petal could see through that obvious ploy. Nora rose and followed Abigail into the kitchen. Abigail opened and shut cupboards, all the time keeping an eye on Petal over the breakfast bar. "If it were me, I'd keep them here." She nearly yelled and banged a cupboard door closed.

She leaned close to Nora and whispered. "Do you think we should call a doctor?"

They should call somebody skilled with delusional hippies but Nora had no idea who that would be. "Let's just—."

"Nope, not here, either," Abigail yelled and opened and slammed a door.

"—see if we can talk some sense into her."

Abigail opened and closed a door and whisper. "Do you think that will work? She's really nuts."

"Make her some hot milk and maybe we can get her to sleep." They kept their eyes on Petal.

Petal hugged herself and rocked on the couch.

"She can smoke some more pot," Abigail said.

"Petal has a flimsy enough grasp of reality. She doesn't need that kind of encouragement from us." Nora slid a canister of coffee from its spot on the counter and stopped it in front of Abigail. She walked back to the living room.

The doorbell rang and Petal sprang from the couch and sprinted down the hall toward the bedrooms. Abigail patted Nora's arm. "You get the door. I'll go see about Petal."

"No illegal drugs, Mother."

35

Nora pulled open the front door to see Cole standing there with a pizza box balanced on his outstretched hand

It smelled like cheesy, spicy wonderfulness. Now it made sense that Abigail hadn't cautioned Nora to take a weapon with her when she answered the doorbell. "Let me guess," she said, grinning and stepping back to let him in. "Abigail and Petal called and asked you to bring this."

He stepped inside. "How did you know?"

She closed the door against the increased wind. "Lucky guess."

He set the box on the kitchen counter. "I thought it might be another of her tricks to get us together."

She laughed. "You're becoming as skeptical as me."

"But she swore it wasn't." He unzipped his green down jacket. "And she sounded so desperate I couldn't say no."

The cold clung to his coat as Nora hung it up. She was strangely glad to see him. Cole carried assurance as comforting as a warm sleeping bag.

That sounded like Abigail's poetry.

She reminded herself how unpredictable Cole could be. If he thought she was in danger, he might chain her up in a basement.

He folded his arms and leaned back on a kitchen counter. "In the interest of full disclosure, I should tell you I didn't believe her."

She walked to the hallway and shouted to the closed bedroom door. "It's safe. It's only Cole and pizza."

He shook his head. "*Only* me."

"Hey, you got top billing over the pizza." She grinned.

Abigail appeared with her arm around Petal. "Let's get something in your stomach. You'll feel better." They stood beside the table.

"You mean something besides Oreos and Doritos?" Nora headed into the kitchen.

Cole set the pizza on the dining table and opened the box. The spicy aroma of sausage and cheese made Nora's mouth water.

Petal paled as if no blood circulated in her veins. She wouldn't make eye contact with Cole. "Where did you get it?"

Abigail only cringed slightly at Petal's rudeness.

Cole carried the plates and spatula Nora handed him to the table. He slid a piece of pizza on a plate and held it out to Petal. "That place down the street."

Petal waved it away. "No. I can't eat that. They use pork sausage and cow's milk cheese."

Right. "Vegan," Nora explained to Cole.

He offered the plate to Abigail.

She waved it away, too. "It seemed like a good idea at the time but I'm not hungry anymore."

Nora accepted a plate. "Munchies all satisfied?" Petal had eaten the chips and Oreos. Did dietary restrictions take second place to THC cravings?

Cole piled a couple of slices on his plate. He raised a questioning eyebrow at Nora. "I guess pizza *was* another of Abigail's matchmaking tricks."

Abigail sniffed. "It was no trick. We were very hungry. Now we're not."

Abigail led Petal into the living room and settled her on the couch.

Nora opened the refrigerator and found two beers hanging out with the leftovers from last night's arranged dinner. She handed one to Cole.

Nora hiked herself to sit on the kitchen counter and Cole leaned back across from her.

Nora gulped the cold beer. "Petal and Abigail spent the afternoon taking the edge off their problems in a haze of smoke."

Cole's eyes widened. Around a mouthful of pizza he said, "I thought I smelled something and chocked it up to residue on Petal's clothes." He swallowed. "Abigail stoned. What led to that apocalyptic event?"

Nora hated the reference to End of the World, even in jest. All that Hopi Fourth World-ending stuff didn't seem like a joke to her.

"She claims Charlie had an affair and she's leaving him." The pizza tasted as good as it smelled.

Cole nearly spit out his mouthful of beer. "You better invest in long underwear because hell is freezing over."

She finished her pizza and hopped down. She reached for his plate and piled pizza onto both and returned. "Speaking of the end of the world, a bunch of birds fell from the sky in Georgia and sent Petal into a meltdown. We've been teetering on the edge of reason ever since."

Nora gave Cole the skinny on the escalating events leading up to the pizza delivery. The warm, gooey pie might be the single best thing that happened to Nora all day. Having a rational person to provide and share it with didn't feel too awful, either.

They left their plates in the sink and Nora set the beer bottles on the counter for recycling. Cole leaned on the counter and watched her. "What are you going to do?"

"Bring this all back to reality." She walked into the living room where Abigail and Petal sat on the couch talking quietly. They seemed calm, Petal's hysterics a thing of the past. Perching on the edge of a chair, she addressed Petal. "If what you say is true, we need to go to the police."

Petal jumped from the couch and screamed as if Nora poked her with a torch. Abbey leaped up and let out a few barks.

Crazy was back in fashion.

"No, no, no. I can't." Petal folded herself into the corner between two pots of corn.

Now would be a good time to call the folks with the white jackets.

Cole stood by the kitchen table watching it all with a blank face.

Abigail squatted in the corner with Petal. "It's okay, honey. Why don't you want us to call the police?"

"She'll kill me, too." Petal whimpered and drew even tighter into the corner.

Abbey sat by Nora, welcoming her fingers in his fur. Why couldn't everyone in her life be like him? He didn't need expensive trappings, stayed calm most of the time, gave her affection and comfort, and having an affair amounted to sniffing another dog's rear end. All this in exchange for a daily walk and a full food dish.

She regarded Cole. Actually, he didn't require much, either. And he showed up with his own food.

"Sylvia's not a killer." Abigail sounded reasonable

Petal shook her head. "No. You don't understand."

"What don't we understand, honey?" Abigail drew Petal from the corner.

"She killed Darla and if she finds out I know, she'll kill me, too."

Abigail and Nora exchanged helpless expressions. What would they do with Petal?

Petal gazed from one to the other. "Sylvia stole a bunch of money from the Trust. Made it look like Darla took it and then she killed her."

Using only her eyes, Nora asked Abigail what to do.

Petal saw their silent exchange. "You don't believe me. But it's true. I saw her kill Darla. I was there."

"Oh, my," Abigail said.

Petal continued in a halting voice. "I was with Darla that night when she went to ask Sylvia about the missing money. I waited in Darla's office and I heard her run outside. I watched out the window to the backyard and I heard a gunshot. Darla fell. I didn't know what to do so I hid. And then Darla died."

"But she was found closer to the road," Nora said.

Petal sobbed and they waited until she could talk. "I carried her out there."

Aside from Petal being too weak to carry a dead cat, it seemed strange. "Why?"

"To protect Sylvia." The weirdness compounded the longer she spoke.

Nora said, "You have to go to the cops."

"I can't. If the cops arrest Sylvia she won't be able to do her work and if she can't, they'll find someone else."

"'They' who, dear?" Abigail asked.

Petal sniffed. "And if they don't arrest her, Sylvia or the people she works for will kill me." Petal gulped air. "If she kills me, who will stop her?"

"Stop her from what?" Nora asked.

Petal's eyes acquired a desperate gleam. "I don't know. But something awful."

Abigail sat back in disbelief.

Nothing about Petal's story sounded the least bit sane. Still, it made Nora's heart pound with dread for Petal. "It's too dangerous for you to do this alone. You have to go to the police."

Petal squeezed Nora's hands with more strength than Nora thought possible. "Please, please. Not tonight. I'll go tomorrow. Please, let me just stay here and rest tonight."

True or not, Petal was terrified. Nora didn't have the heart to rip her from the slight comfort of Abigail's mothering.

36

Sylvia's Ferrari squealed off the road and across the bridge and into the Trust's lot. The parking lot light was out again. She was sick of this rinky-dink facility and their slip-shod maintenance. It was wrong. Everything was wrong tonight. She slammed on the brakes and skidded on the gravel. The few flakes falling hadn't started to accumulate.

Birds! Goddamn birds. How did this happen? Petal had calculated the angle, and Sylvia trusted her. Petal should have known. How could Petal make this mistake?

Eduardo would have been watching the news anticipating his victory. What would happen when he saw a sea of dead birds instead?

Brittle flakes of snow whirled through the frigid air. Clouds threatened to drop more before the storm moved on. Sylvia climbed from her car and hugged her fox-lined jacket close, thankful for the fur-topped, snow boots with the rubber tipped-heels. She may have to live in an inhospitable climate but at least she could maintain some style. Not like Alaska where she'd had to wear clothes straight out of survival catalogues.

Sylvia hurried across the front porch and unlocked the front door. She didn't bother turning on lights and ran through the kitchen to her office suite.

Where was Petal? Sylvia needed her to recalculate the refractory angles of the tower and reset the beam.

But no, she couldn't trust Petal. Sylvia should have known that girl didn't have the brain power to accomplish something so delicate. Why hadn't she checked Petal's calculations?

Because Mark had shown up and ruined it all.

Think, Sylvia! But her mind chased itself. Dead cats, Daniel's body in her bed, blood on her carpet, the black Town Car, her fur-topped boots, Daniel's naked body, Mark's bloody body, Mark, Daniel. Stupid, stupid Petal.

She leaned against the door jamb and held her hands to her head trying to push the random thoughts into order.

Sylvia snapped on the light and ran across her office. She flung her bag onto her desk and booted up her computer. She'd checked the coordinates Petal calculated. They should have been correct.

Sylvia entered her passwords and navigated beyond the firewalls. In a matter of minutes she understood Petal's mistake. The moron had transposed two numbers. Perspiration lined her body as she reset the program. Her fingers shook and her nails kept hitting the wrong keys.

Finally she sat back, her insides a molten stew of acid, her skin chilled from sweat. She'd done it. As only she could do.

Sylvia rummaged inside her bag for her phone before she remembered where it lay—hurled against the wall after Eduardo's last call—broken on the floor of her bedroom, spattered with Mark's brains.

She grabbed the headset of the ancient landline phone on her desk. Her fingernail tapped the buttons and she dialed the country code, area code, and private number. She waited while it ran.

Finally he answered. "Ah, Sylvia, *carina*."

"Eduardo. Listen, I can explain."

His robust laugh sounded cheerful. "No need. Truly."

She didn't trust his good cheer. "It was an error. I'm fixing it right now. I can send another ELF wave at dawn. You'll see. I'll do it for you, Eduardo."

"Yes. Yes. That will be excellent. Good bye, Sylvia."

"Wait! Don't—"

He hung up on her. Again.

Thud.

What was that? Sylvia ran across the room and slapped off her office light. She couldn't stop her rapid breathing as she snuck into the dark kitchen. She stood on tiptoe to see out of the window above the sink. In the unlit parking lot she made out the Lincoln Town Car sitting next to her Ferrari.

The knob on the front door rattled and she felt the pressure in her ears as it opened.

Sylvia tiptoed to the back door and stealthily turned the lock. She grabbed the knob, twisted, yanked. She didn't bother to shut the door, knowing that Juan—or whoever it was Eduardo sent to kill her—would already be chasing her.

She sprinted across the icy lawn, slipping. *Is this what Darla felt like just before the bullet ripped into her back?*

37

Abigail had coaxed Petal into Nora's bedroom, convincing her to lie down. Petal would only relax if Abigail stayed with her. Both were sleeping when Nora checked on them a half hour ago. Cole hadn't made any move to leave and Nora hadn't asked him to. They'd been sitting on the couch ever since, staring at the television.

After the Petal drama and the exhausting day, Nora didn't know what to do. Tomorrow morning she'd take Petal and the spreadsheets to the police. Tonight, she felt helpless. She plopped down on the sofa and turned on a daily news satire show. Uninvited, Cole sat next to her. She didn't complain. The host reported on the day's events with pithy political commentary. Cole stared at the screen without any reaction and Nora assumed he heard as little of the show as she did.

Too bad Nora didn't have any more beer. She could use another cold one.

Too many questions banged around her brain to concentrate on television. What if what Petal said was true? Did Sylvia really possess the means to alter the weather and kill birds? If so, did that mean Petal's life was in danger?

Abbey lay in his bed under the corn plants, snoring softly.

Cole stirred. "What was Petal saying about Tesla?"

Nora sat up. "I don't have any idea. I thought Tesla was a car. I didn't know it was a person."

Cole scanned the apartment. "Do you have a computer?"

Nora hurried to a small desk in the corner of the room. She shoved the leaves of a corn plant out of the way and grabbed her laptop. She booted up. "Okay. We've got weather and Tesla and HAARP." She typed them all into the search engine and hit enter.

Cole leaned into her and read the screen. "Might want to narrow that down."

She grinned at him as results appeared and she clicked on one. She scanned it then read to Cole. *Tesla was also reportedly working on resonance machines, or devices whereby he could shake one or many large city buildings from some distance away.*

This capability has now blossomed into the ability to create earthquakes in any desired location on earth, of the desired magnitude, and desired depth. HAARP can create such earthquakes.

Cole lifted the computer, settled it on his lap and kept reading. *Tesla's experiments in Colorado produced powerful artificial lightning, in the millions of volts. Producing this lightening was one of the earliest examples of Tesla being able to create weather phenomenon. A mushroom-shaped radio tower was instrumental in Tesla fine-tuning his ability to create all manner of weather. As he beamed radio waves at the exact ELF frequency by which earth's weather is naturally created, Tesla discovered he could alter the weather.*

A chill spiked up her neck. "Syliva is going to create an earthquake."

Cole's eyebrows shot up. "Not jumping to conclusions, are you?"

"Well, maybe. It could be."

Cole laughed. "You're sounding like Petal. Just because the first site you randomly hit spouts crazy conspiracy theories, it doesn't mean it's true."

Maybe she was getting carried away. She shot him a sheepish grin.

Instead of teasing, as she'd expected, he grew serious and his eyes darkened.

She caught her breath. She tried to tell herself she didn't know him well, but she understood his expression. He leaned into her, sliding his warm fingers along the back of her neck. With the gentlest touch, he drew her toward him.

"Is it okay if I kiss you?" he whispered.

She nodded, not trusting her voice.

They'd only kissed once before and yet his touch felt natural and familiar. She closed her eyes and blood rushed through her ears. His lips moved with soft pressure against hers and suddenly her arms and legs felt like pudding. She smoldered against him.

Cole stopped long enough for Nora to set the computer on the floor.

His arms encircled her, pulling her against him as his heat matched hers. They paused for breath and Nora sank into his eyes, dark with passion. Without thinking, she allowed herself to fall into another kiss. And another.

How many years since she'd made out on a couch with her mother asleep in another room? It was as exciting and erotic now as it had been at seventeen. The bad tension eased from her shoulders, replaced with the good kind—the tingly kind that accelerated her pulse and made her warm all over, some places downright steamy. She could go on like this forever. No guilt, no expectations, no past or future.

She was so far gone she didn't hear anything until Abbey woofed and focused on the door. That's when she realized the pounding came from fists on the door and not the blood in her ears.

"Oh." She stood up and yanked at her shirt that had twisted around her belly. She walked to the door on shaky legs, rubbing her mouth and struggling to regain some dignity.

In the year Nora lived in the apartment, she could count visitors at her door in the single digits. They'd all been trying to sell her wrapping paper or hoping she'd help fund a grade school field trip or wanting her to buy magazine subscriptions to help an inner-city delinquent on the road to better himself. Maybe this time the cops waited on the other side. They might have found out Petal witnessed Darla's murder and needed to question her. Or it could be the bad guys that Sylvia supposedly worked for, come to pop a cap in Petal's brain. In which case, they'd kill everyone in the apartment.

Not overreacting or anything.

Nora slipped the chain on the door and opened it to peek outside.

What waited outside trumped whatever fantasy she concocted. She slammed the door, unhooked the chain and swung it open again. She threw herself into waiting arms. "Charlie!"

He hugged her hard, his grizzled face roughing her cheek. "You are sunshine and light and give me reason to live."

The snow fell in giant white flakes, swirling in the gusts. She drew Charlie inside, out of the storm. She'd missed his forest smell, the gravelly voice, and his strange way of speaking as though he were in a soap opera.

Abbey wagged his whole body in delight to see his old hiking buddy and Cole grinned.

Charlie scratched Abbey's ears. "You're a fine fellow. Fine fellow." He straightened and surveyed the apartment. "Nice crop of corn."

She hugged him again.

He grinned at her. "In a world of sorrow and pain you are a bright angel of joy."

Cole grasped Charlie's hand. "Good to see you, man."

Charlie's bright eyes traveled from Cole to Nora. "Awfully good to see you here."

Nora grasped his cold hand in both of hers. "Why didn't you call and let me know you were coming?"

His face grew serious. "A wise soldier relies on the element of surprise." Charlie didn't often speak in war metaphors. His eyes drooped with weariness.

"Take your coat off and tell me what's the matter."

"Element of surprise, is it?" They all whirled around to see Abigail standing in the dining area. Her hair smashed against one side of her head and a dark rim of mascara smudged under one eye. Only a life-threatening emergency would bring Abigail out in in such disarray. "Don't you mean ambush?"

"Now, Abbie..."

Nora tugged at the neck of Charlie's army jacket as he shrugged to shed it.

"Don't you 'now Abbie' me." She pointed at Nora. "Don't take his jacket. He's leaving." Abigail made a chameleon seem consistent. She could go from pothead to Florence Nightingale to a panther all in the course of a few hours.

Charlie gazed at Abigail with sad eyes. “I’ve come to take you home.”

“I’m not going anywhere with you. My home is here now, with my daughter.”

Whoa! Cole and Nora watched like spectators in the Thunderdome.

Charlie stepped toward Abigail. “You are my very breath. My home and my bed are cold and empty without you.”

Nora cringed.

Abigail held her hand up to stop him. “You’ve destroyed whatever home we had together. And as for your bed...”

“Okay, okay.” Nora stepped between the two. She had to stop this talk before she was scarred for life. “I’ll make some tea and we can sit down and discuss this like adults.”

Abigail’s voice rose an octave or three. “He won’t drink anything but beer so unless you have a twelve pack on hand, don’t bother.”

“Hey,” Nora said. “You knew he drank beer when you married him.” Everyone knew Charlie drank beer. He kept the pockets of his army jacket well supplied. Come to think of it, she hadn’t felt any cans when she’d hugged him. Maybe he wisely didn’t drink and drive.

“‘The heady party of our love has faded to the painful pounding of a hangover.’” Abigail cast about, probably for paper to record her poetry. The universe would be forever grateful to lose that particular verse. Abigail turned her attention on Nora. Her eyes glistened with tears. “I won’t sit down with you and Charlie together. You always take his side.”

Nora stammered. “What side?”

Abigail ignored her and shot back at Charlie. “Are you so immune to your effect on women?”

Charlie? He didn’t stand more than five feet, eight. He smelled of pine forest and beer and wore baggy-butted jeans and a faded plaid shirt. He had a kind and gentle nature like a benevolent dwarf in a Disney movie. He was Nora’s dear friend but she’d never thought of him as romantic. Using the word sexy in the same sentence as Charlie would be a stretch.

“Can’t we talk about it?” Charlie asked.

"No. No. And no. You ruined our wonderful love with your thoughtless, selfish ways."

Nora knew Charlie to be one of the most caring and considerate people in the world. "Come on, let Charlie explain."

With all four of them standing in the apartment it felt as crowded as a Japanese commuter train at rush hour. And at least as uncomfortable.

Abigail tossed her head back. "You!" She shot a finger at Nora. "I would think after what you went through with that philandering husband of yours, you'd understand."

Nora tried again. "Charlie wouldn't cheat on you."

"See? I told you. You're taking his side and you haven't even heard the facts. Fine."

Charlie started, "I'm not—"

Abigail whirled around. "As far as I'm concerned, you deserve each other. I'm through with both of you." Abigail stomped down the hallway and into her room. It surprised Nora that Abigail didn't slam the door. She probably did that out of consideration for Petal.

Nora exhaled and said to Charlie. "I have to ask. Did you have an affair?"

Sorrow wafted around him like flies on a corpse. "No."

Nora pulled out a chair at the table and sank into it. Cole and Charlie followed her. "Then what is she talking about?"

Abbey sat next to Charlie and rested his muzzle on Charlie's lap.

Charlie stared down the hall and petted Abbey. His face grew rigid. "I would walk across hot coals for your mother. I would chase the great white whale to please her. I would rope the wind, cage the man in the moon. I would..."

Nora rested a hand on his. "Okay. But what did you do?"

He focused on Nora. "I gave up beer."

Those were the last words she expected from Charlie.

Cole's chair creaked as he sat back acting as astonished as Nora felt. "That's a pretty big deal."

Charlie nodded. "I thought she wanted me to."

"What does giving up beer have to do with you having an affair?" The connection didn't seem obvious to Nora.

Charlie went back to staring down the hallway. "I had a little trouble giving it up cold turkey so I went to someone the VA paid for."

"A therapist?" Cole asked.

"Yep. A pretty young thing about your age." Charlie propped his elbow on the table and leaned his face against his hand.

Nora stood and slipped around to the kitchen. She spoke over the counter bar. "Good for you. Did she help you?" Nora filled her tea kettle and set it on a burner.

Charlie lifted his head to answer her. "Oh, sure. She helped me a whole lot. But she had me start going to meetings."

Cole nodded. "AA meetings." A gust rattled the patio slider.

Abbey placed a paw on Charlie's knee as if commiserating. "And they helped. So I went to them every day. And I quit."

"That's great. Was Abigail happy?"

He turned his sad eyes to Nora. "If she noticed she never said a word."

Nora leaned over the counter. "Ouch. Did you ask her about it?"

Charlie stroked Abbey's paw. "She had other things on her mind. She wanted to know where I went every day. I lied and told her I went to the forest, like I always do."

"Why didn't you tell her the truth?" She pulled out three heavy mugs.

"I was ashamed I couldn't quit on my own."

Nora grabbed a few boxes of tea bags from her cupboard. She caught Cole's eye and started tossing them to him. "So you kept going to meetings and lying, and she knew you were lying."

He shrugged. "I guess so. She followed me."

She brought the mugs around and placed them on the table. "And she saw you went to a meeting right? So why does she think you were having an affair?"

Abbey dropped his paw and closed his eyes, still leaning into Charlie. "Because the day she followed me was a big test day. I met my therapist at a bar downtown and she ordered a beer. I had a club soda, which is a poor substitute, by the way. We stayed there for a few rounds so I could get a feel for what it was like to say no."

"And Abigail saw you," Cole said.

"That would be my guess."

Nora brought the kettle from the kitchen. "You didn't talk to her?"

Charlie's chin fell to his chest. "I didn't know she was there. When I got home, her bags were packed and she was gone."

"So tell her now." Nora picked an Earl Gray tea bag for Charlie, dropped it in his cup and poured the water.

He wrapped a hand around the mug. "Nope."

Oh no. Charlie needed to make up to Abigail, and the sooner the better. If not, Nora would be stuck living with her in perpetuity. "You have to talk to her, tell her the truth."

Cole chose orange flavored black tea and steeped it in his mug.

Charlie stared at his tea. "Don't you see, sweet child? If she doesn't have faith in me, there's really nothing for us."

Cole stared down the hall. "Does it feel cold to you?"

Nora noticed the chill. She stood and started down the hallway to investigate a draft. Cole followed.

She opened her bedroom door expecting to find Petal curled up on her bed. Instead, the bed held nothing but a pile of rumpled blankets. The curtains billowed with the storm blowing in the open window.

38

Nora raced to the window and scanned the balcony that ran along the second floor of the building. Most of the well-lit parking lot was visible from that vantage point. Snow accumulated where it caught in ridges and tiny drifts. The wind grabbed the bent screen and banged against the building. Nora slammed the window closed.

"Is she out there?" Cole asked.

Charlie appeared uncharacteristically rattled. "She ran from me? Why would she have to steal into the frigid night to escape from me. My Abigail angel."

Abigail answered from behind him. "I haven't gone anywhere, you old fool. It's Petal who's jumped ship."

"Thank the morning star you're safe," Charlie said. "Who is Petal?"

Abigail now wore one of her velour jogging suits with matching jacket. She'd repaired her hair and makeup. "How long has she been gone? What did you do to her?"

Nora snapped on a bedside lamp but it did little to illuminate the room. She made her way around the rustic log footboard of the bed and squeezed past Abigail to check the closet. "I didn't do anything. Last I knew, you were napping together."

"Humph." Abigail watched Nora as she closed the closet door and scanned the small space between the matching log night stand and the wall, then turned and focused on the corner by the dresser. "You need a bigger bedroom. Or smaller furniture. Or both, would be my opinion. That rustic decor is..."

Nora glared at her.

Abigail sounded disdainful. "I suppose you think Petal running off is my fault, as you think everything is my fault."

Nora held back a retort. She wished she had more light in the dim room.

Cole squinted out the window. "Why would she take off?" He pulled down the mini blinds.

Now that she looked at her room through others' eyes, it did feel over furnished and generic. She'd only hung a couple of prints she'd found at Target and the comforter and curtains were a solid shade of light blue. All of it serviceable because, she admitted, not much exciting happened in her bedroom these days. Her eyes strayed to Cole and she blushed.

Abigail knew where to place the blame. "She's scared to death Sylvia or someone else is going to kill her. And along comes Charlie. He storms into our home. I'm sure she heard his angry voice and fled for her life."

They all stared at Abigail for a moment then Cole said quietly, "Charlie didn't sound threatening to me."

Nora ran a hand through her hair. "Doesn't matter what set her off. She's gone."

"Who is Petal?" Charlie asked again.

Cole started for the door. "Come on. I'll explain while we'll search outside."

Charlie reluctantly followed Cole out the door, his eyes still pleading with Abigail.

Abigail slammed her hands on her hips. "We should go after Petal. She's had very rough life."

Nora didn't want to get involved with Petal. It was okay to let her stay the night, to feed her and listen to stories and to tuck her into bed. But Nora wasn't responsible for every stray that wandered into her path. "What did Petal tell you?"

"She grew up poor and her mother is ill. She has an aunt who, apparently, is well off. But she won't help with Petal's mother. I think she has some resentment issues with the aunt and she ought to see a therapist. If you don't take care of these negative feelings they can fester—"

"Mother!"

Abigail smoothed her jacket. "For heaven's sake, Nora, she worships you because she thinks you've been so kind to her and frankly, you barely notice her."

"Notice her? She's living in my home!"

"At *my* invitation."

"Thank you for finally giving me the sister I always wanted. Maybe we can play Monopoly and read *Teen* magazine together."

Abigail lasered a withering shot at Nora, creating instant guilt. "What's happened to you? You used to be generous and kind and giving. Now you're locked up like a clam, holding back all your love lest it wither in the salty waves of life." She pulled her notebook from her pocket, uncapped her special pen, and scribbled.

Out of nervous energy, Nora pulled the comforter up and straightened the bed. "You're nuts."

"Is that so? I remember a little girl who always included the most forlorn and ostracized child on the playground."

"That was only because no one else would play with me." Nora plumped a pillow and tossed it onto the bed.

Abigail tsked. "That's not true. You were always the leader and the most popular."

"Whatever." Nora didn't like this conversation.

"This's why you're so unhappy these days." Abigail was rolling on the Nora-improvement wagon and there was no stopping her.

Nora walked out of the bedroom. "I'm not unhappy."

Abigail followed. "Of course you are. You can't hide it from me."

"How could I hide anything from you? You're living in my back pocket." Nora stopped in the middle of the living room, not knowing what to do. She stomped to the kitchen and leaned on the counter.

"I know you're refusing to let yourself care about Petal because of what happened to Heather." Abigail paused in the kitchen doorway.

Nora froze. They said time would heal but after a year, it still felt like an open wound.

Abigail took out her chisel and hammered away on Nora's heart. "You push Cole away with both hands. Just because Scott betrayed you."

"Enough!" Nora brushed past Abigail.

Abigail watched Nora pace into the living room again. "You need Petal as much as she needs you."

Nora walked to a corn plant and held a broad leaf. She wanted to be left alone to take care of Abbey and herself.

Snow swirled outside the window. Petal didn't have a coat. Nora spun around and searched the side of the couch where Petal had curled up. Petal's Chacos peeked from beneath the blanket. No shoes, either. Damn it.

Abigail nudged her. "It's a nasty night out there."

"I don't know where she would have gone."

Abigail considered. "She talked about wanting to stop Sylvia."

"Do you think she'd go to the Trust?"

Abigail shook her head. "I think she'd go to Sylvia's house."

"I wonder where that is."

Abigail grinned. "I know."

"How do you know?"

Abigail rolled her eyes. "There's this thing called the Google. You might have heard of it."

"Why...?"

"I was curious." Abigail defended herself. "It's a swanky neighborhood. When Berle and I lived here it wasn't much but since then, they've scraped off most of the older homes and built new. It's where the people with money live. We'll GPS it."

Abigail grabbed her phone from the corner of the counter bar. "Got it. Let's go." She opened the coat closet by the front door. "I didn't bring a causal cold-weather coat." Abigail slipped into Nora's newest, warmest down coat. Of course Abigail would commandeer that coat and leave Nora digging in the closet for a lighter-weight, beat-up version.

They headed out the door to Nora's Jeep. Abbey bounded toward them across the parking lot enjoying the snowy evening. Abigail opened her door and before she could climb in Abbey scrambled into the passenger seat. Abigail waved him into the back.

"Nora, wait." Cole jogged from the end of the parking lot.

Nora walked to her side of the Jeep and watched him approach.

"Where're you going?" His breath puffed in a white stream.

"To find Petal." Her fingers tingled in the cold.

He stood motionless between her and the car door.

"So, we'll see you later." She reached behind him for the door handle.

He placed a hand over hers. He gazed down at her, the struggle for words visible in his eyes. Finally he said, "I know you've had a rough year and I've stayed away because I wanted to give you space, or whatever."

Nora studied Abbey in the Jeep. He sat in back, staring out the windshield, unaware of her thudding heart and rushing blood.

Cole let out a breath. "Here's the deal. I understand you're afraid of commitment because Scott had an affair and you don't know if you can trust anyone. And you think I kidnapped you and—"

"You did kidnap me."

He flared. "That was becau—never mind. What I want to say is this. I like you, Nora. I mean, probably more than like you."

She wanted him to stop talking but he kept going.

"The timing might not be ideal for you but I can't put my life on hold waiting for you any longer."

She turned to get in the Jeep.

Again, he tugged her hand so she'd face him. "I'm not asking you to move away with me. I just want to know if there's a chance for us."

Why did he force this on her? "I don't know."

"What about tonight? I thought maybe you felt..."

She jerked her hand away. Jobs, mothers, runaways, discovered fathers, weather manipulation. She couldn't bring anything else into her life. "I'm going to find Petal. If you want me to confess undying love and fidelity to you, forget it. I'm not ready for this. With you or anyone."

Nora slid onto the icy car seat and started the engine. She refused to make eye contact with Cole, didn't want to know if he still stood there or if he'd walked away.

Abigail rubbed her arms. "Get that heater going."

Nora eyed Abigail's coat with envy. She shivered inside her second-best coat. And Petal was loose out there somewhere with no coat at all.

Abigail punched her phone. "Go east from the parking lot."

Nora started the wipers. Snow stuck in small patches to the pavement.

"What did Cole have to say?" Abigail pointed to the left and Nora turned.

"Private conversation."

"He told you he loves you, didn't he?" She clapped her gloved hands together. "That's romantic. He could have chosen a more intimate moment but men don't always think things through."

Either Abigail was blind to body language or she hadn't been watching the exchange. Nora maneuvered down Arapahoe Street, thankful for light traffic.

Abigail's giddy planning bubbled along. "You're going to start slowly, right? Dinner, outings, that sort of thing. Will he move to Boulder? He's not suited to that ranch anyway. Turn right at the next light."

The Jeep slid at the turn and Nora slowed. The wipers flapped at accumulating flakes. "Cole and I aren't an item. Let's drop it. Where next?"

"You should have a smart phone like mine instead of that ancient model you have. It's as bad as Charlie's. Turn here."

Nora did. "Charlie has a cell phone?"

Abigail stared out the window. "Of course."

They hit a puddle and the water splashed on the windshield. By morning it would be ice. "That doesn't seem like something Charlie would care about."

Abigail spun toward her. "I suppose you two are simpatico on this subject too."

Let's jump off one tangent and onto another. "Don't know what you're talking about."

"The two of you. Always judging me about how I live. Abusing Mother Earth. He wouldn't get a cell phone because he said it made him too dependent on others. He wanted to commune with nature and rely on his wits. Of course, he didn't care that I worried day and night he'd get hurt in the wilderness, lying on the ground, dying alone. I finally bought him a phone and insisted he carry it." Abigail pointed.

Nora turned right onto Table Mesa Road. They were heading in a giant circle. Way to go, smart phone. "Good. Did he?"

Abigail's voice faltered. "He said he only did it to humor me. But he never called me and the minutes usage went up."

Nora squinted against the barrage of flakes in the headlights. "Who was he calling?"

Abigail's voice hardened. "I did a little research and found out he was calling that woman."

"What woman?"

"That woman from the bar. Beth Ann Troutman."

Nora flopped her hand against her thigh in frustration. "Are we anywhere close to Sylvia's house?"

Abigail exhaled in frustration. "We're discussing my marriage, my life. Why must it always be about you?"

"You drag me out to save Petal and you're upset because I won't tell you that Charlie isn't having an affair."

Abigail folded her arms in a huff. "Oh, what do you know?" She pulled one arm loose and pointed a right turn into a neighborhood with two elephant-sized sandstone slabs as neighborhood signs.

Nora slowed and drove through the dark neighborhood, the splash of her wheels on the wet pavement accompanying the wipers. Nora had hit her limit for games.

"He wanted to quit drinking because he thinks it will make you happy and all you can do is ride him and accuse him of things that if you really knew him, you'd know he wouldn't do."

Abigail's jaw went slack. "He's quitting?"

"Yes, Mother. And you haven't noticed. That woman, Beth Ann, is his therapist."

Abigail sat motionless for a moment and Nora peeked at her phone. It indicated another left so she headed that way.

Abigail's eyes went soft as she thought. "You're right. I haven't seen him with an open beer for a long time." She came back to the present. "He said he's doing this for me?"

Nora nodded. "Can we get back to the drama at hand?"

Abigail kept her satisfied smile. She checked the phone. "The next house."

Abigail had the expression of a twitterpated teenager. "Why didn't he tell me? I would have supported him."

Nora slowed.

Abigail pointed to a house. "This is the place." She gave it the once over. "A bit gouch."

Nora eased the Jeep to the curve in front of a huge house. The lawn, now smooth and white under the accumulated snow, yawned in a ridiculous expanse that would need watered and mowed—the opposite of sustainable. The foothills rose from behind the multi-gabled McMansion with its covered portico and two-story front windows that must accent a great room with the mother of all vaulted ceilings. No direct lights shone through the great room windows, only a glow cast by another room. A window inside the massive stone entryway framed a crystal chandelier.

Abigail started punching numbers into the phone. "I have to call him. Tell him I was wrong."

A minuscule sliver of light escaped from the front door and sliced the front porch.

The door was open.

Abigail held the phone to her ear.

Nora slid from the Jeep and started up the walk.

39

The snow eased off but the wind continued to howl through the trees behind the Trust farmhouse. Bright moonlight reflected off the white ground, leaving Sylvia's footprints visible.

Sylvia huddled at the edge of the backyard under an evergreen shrub. Her feet felt damp in her fur-topped boots. She'd broken a heel in her flight down the back porch stairs.

She strained to see though the darkened windows inside the house. Where was Juan? He must be hunting for her. He'd be skulking around the dark building, stopping to listen.

The rumble of boards on the creek bridge sounded like machine gun fire. She barely heard the purr of a car engine but seconds later a car door slammed. More of Eduardo's thugs?

Sylvia slithered from under the branches, feeling them claw at her smooth cheeks. She limped across the yard, staying close to the outer edge along the trees. With a burst, she scurried toward the farmhouse and hugged the wall, where no one inside could see her from a window.

She peeked around the edge of the house to the parking lot. The Town Car still sat in the lot with a smattering of snow on the roof. Daniel's Prius was parked next to it. Sylvia's Ferrari was hidden on the far side of the Town Car. She couldn't get to it without running in full sight.

Pounding and what sounded like a scuffle erupted on the front porch out of Sylvia's view. Male voices rose in anger. Juan slid out from the front of the house on the slick grass as if he'd been pushed. He fell to his knees.

Daniel strode after him. He fired off a rapid string of Spanish and advanced on Juan.

Juan scrambled to his feet and hurried to his Town Car. He turned and shouted at Daniel, throwing up his hands. He yanked open the door of his car and jumped inside. In a matter of seconds he gunned the engine and spun out of the parking lot. He fishtailed and banged a back fender on the bridge before he accelerated down the highway.

Sylvia ran from hiding. "Daniel!"

He watched her.

When she grew close enough, she launched herself into his arms. "You've saved me. I knew you'd come."

He grabbed her hand and pulled her up the stairs and across the front porch. He shoved her inside and slammed the door. "Tell me now, Sylvia. What are you doing? Why did my father send Juan?"

Why was he being so rough? She settled herself and brushed her fingers through her hair. She sidled to him and ran her hand on his chest under the leather of his jacket. "Don't be grouchy. You're going to love me when I tell you."

He pushed her hand away. "Tell me."

She rose on her toes and slipped her tongue around his cold lips. "I did it for you."

"For god's sake, Sylvia. Get away from me."

Why was he acting like this? "I set it in motion, Daniel. Like you wanted me to. Like Eduardo demanded."

His face froze. "What did you do?"

She smiled and reached for his hand. "Come here, I'll show you."

40

This is not a good idea.

In fact, it could be one of her worst. That didn't stop Nora from climbing the stone steps on the front porch and approaching the open door. Wind whipped her hair and stung her ears and her hiking boots left waffles in the snow on the walk.

Abbey stayed close on her heels. She should probably have left him in the car with Abigail but she didn't mind the four-legged dose of courage at her side.

Nora rang the doorbell. She didn't expect anyone to answer and they didn't.

She pushed the door open and stood outside. "Hello!"

Silence.

She should call the cops. Tell them Petal had gone missing. And that Sylvia was involved in a mysterious and deadly venture involving Tesla towers and dead birds, and the powerful people Sylvia worked for would kill Petal if the police didn't intervene.

They'd have no trouble believing that.

Abbey trotted in front of her, leaving muddy paw prints on the marble foyer.

A wide staircase to the right of the entryway swept to the second floor. The curved wood railing shone with polish in the light from the foyer. Splashes of bright oranges, blues, and reds blazed from abstract oil paintings on the wall.

Abbey's claws clicked on the marble and his breath sounded like an elephant snuffle as he sniffed the floor.

"Hello?" she said again. Silence in a house this size was a big silence.

Directly in front of them, the marble of the foyer gave way to a white-carpeted sitting room. A baby grand piano left room for two white upholstered chairs. The night darkened on the other side of a floor-to-ceiling window.

Nora chose to head left down a short hallway. It opened onto the great room facing away from the street.

She stepped around a stone pillar and Nora nearly gasped at the expanse and opulence. Down three steps that ran the length of the room and across the wide space covered with the impossibly thick white carpet, floor--o cathedral ceiling windows faced the Flatirons. In the daytime, the view would be breathtaking. Tonight, with snow swirling outside, was merely spectacular. A huge stone fireplace occupied one whole wall and several white couches and chairs made up a couple of conversation areas. It resembled the lobby of a posh hotel more than a real person's living room.

How often did Sylvia entertain? Nora couldn't imagine one person wanting to spend time with Sylvia, let alone a team large enough to make this room practical.

"She's not much for color."

Nora gasped and whirled around at the sound.

Snap. The room burst into light and Abigail adjusted the dimmer from spotlight to natural. She stepped from behind a pillar and surveyed the room from the top stair, hands on her hips.

"My god, Mother, you scared me. I thought you were in the Jeep talking to Charlie."

Abigail waved her hand. "A phone only works when you turn it on. I can't make him understand that. I left some voicemails but I don't think he knows how to retrieve them."

Nora gazed out the tall windows at the swirling snow. Petal might be out there.

"Did you see that chandelier in the entryway?" Abigail asked, disgust ringing her words.

The fireplace gaped at Nora as if waiting for a sacrifice. "I didn't pay any attention."

Abigail loved to tour houses. She wasn't shy about giving her decorating opinions. "It's ostentatious. The entryway calls for something smaller and more tasteful. This place reeks of new money."

As if Abigail came from a long line of aristocrats. She'd grown up in Nebraska and only later, married money. Lots of it. Mostly gone now.

Nora started for the stairs. "We shouldn't be here. I think it's breaking and entering."

Abigail scrutinized the room. "Nonsense. The door was wide open. As friends we're obligated to check things out and make sure Sylvia is all right."

"Friends?"

"Small detail," Abigail said and descended the stairs. "The carpet is a nice weave but the white is much too risky if you want to actually live in your home."

"This is a bad idea," Nora said to Abbey.

"It's too stark with all this white. Although I do appreciate the natural elements of the stone. And, oh Nora, look at those beams. Those are very nice. I can't identify the wood. Not pine."

Who cared? Nora gave up the sane notion of high-tailing it out of there and advanced on a bookshelf inset into the wall opposite the fireplace. Framed photos sat amid glass sculptures. Compared to the sharp angles and abstract contemporary art on the walls, the frames twisted in ornate gold gilt.

Abigail stood in front of one of the furniture groupings assessing the accent pillows. Abbey plopped down and rested his head on his paws.

The photos mostly showed professional studio shots of Sylvia. From the headshots at various angles and the posed casuals, it seemed Sylvia loved playing fashion model. There were a few photos not done with the intent of making Sylvia gorgeous.

Abigail abruptly walked from the furniture to the fireplace. "This room is a mosh-posh of mixed styles. Most unsettling."

"Shhhh." Nora cocked her head. "Do you hear anything?"

Abigail paused a moment. "No. You're letting your imagine loose again."

Nora turned back to the photos and Abigail walked over to peer over her shoulder.

Abigail pointed to a picture. "What about this?" Sylvia stood next to a dark-haired, older and more-worn version of herself. An awkward girl of about thirteen stood in front of the two women, shooting a cheesy grin at the camera. From the style of clothes, the picture must have been taken twenty years ago.

Nora studied the picture. "Must be family. At least it proves she didn't rise from a lagoon on a dark, stormy night."

Abigail picked it up and stared at it. "That little girl is Petal."

Nora focused on another interesting shot. "Right. Now who's imagination is running wild?"

Abigail thrust the frame under Nora's nose. "Look at it."

Nora hadn't seen Petal's impish side as much as Abigail had, but the little face did bear a resemblance to Petal in her rare happy moments. "I can see how you'd think that. But it's a coincidence."

Abigail pursed her lips and set the photo on the shelf.

Nora picked up the frame she'd been studying. "Whoa." She handed Abigail the snapshot of Sylvia arm in arm, gazing adoringly at someone.

Abigail gasped. "It's Daniel!"

Nora pointed at the picture. "See in the background? They're standing in front of World Petro."

Abigail shrugged and handed it back. "She's having an affair with that Latin lover. I knew there was something fishy about him."

"World Petro is his father's company." Nora stared at the picture. "Supposedly, Daniel is trying to stop them and others from drilling for oil in the Amazon basin."

Abigail trod across the room and up the steps. "It's shocking that a woman Sylvia's age would cavort with someone like Daniel but it happens."

"Cavort?" Nora set the picture down and followed Abigail.

They continued down the hall toward what appeared to be the kitchen. "You know what I mean," Abigail said.

Nora noticed the muddy paw prints Abbey left on the white carpet.

Sylvia wasn't going to be pleased. "If Daniel and Sylvia are having an affair, why are they keeping it a secret?"

Abigail felt around on the wall of the dark kitchen. "It isn't good policy for a board member to be sleeping with the hired help."

If the dark, silent house weren't so creepy, and if they weren't breaking the law, and if she didn't think that Petal might be in some kind of danger, she might find the idea of Sylvia being called hired help amusing.

Abigail slapped on the light to reveal a kitchen fit for the Iron Chef himself. Copper cookware hung from a rack above a center island covered with gleaming granite big enough to dance a tango on. The cook top had more burners than the Octomom had babies. Two ovens, two refrigerators, miles of counter space and gadgets Nora could only guess at. If anything had been used, Nora couldn't tell.

Abigail didn't sound impressed. "It's all for show. She clearly doesn't cook."

"Daniel's been helping me to sort out the financials. If he and Sylvia are together, why would he do that?"

Abigail slapped off the light and brushed past Nora. "Maybe he's trying to keep you from finding something that incriminates her."

Could he be protecting Sylvia? But if he loved her, why didn't he just give her $400,000? For someone with his resources, that wouldn't be much.

Next up was the dining room. Abigail found a dimmer switch and turned it up. "Oh my. My, oh my."

The dining room table was a mass of wrought iron and glass. The chairs twisted in bizarre shapes like torture devices. Dinner in this room would be about as much fun as an evening in the dungeons of the Spanish Inquisition.

Abigail tsked. "I suppose Sylvia thinks this passes for art. She's obviously trying too hard."

"Petal said Sylvia worked for someone powerful. With World Petro behind him, Daniel is certainly powerful."

Abigail stared at the dining table as if considering how to destroy it. "The only thing worth keeping in this room is the chandelier. That's quite lovely, actually."

She brushed her hands as if to get rid of the room and strode down the hall. "Let's check upstairs."

"No," Nora said. "This has gone too far already."

Abigail waved her off. "We need to make sure Petal isn't hiding up there. Besides, I want to see the bedrooms."

"Big mistake," Nora grumbled to Abbey. He sat in the foyer watching her.

Abigail trotted up the stairs, scowling at the abstract oil paintings and shaking her head. She reached the landing halfway up and her phone jangled.

Abigail held it up and frowned. "Why is Cole calling me?" She answered and her face lit up like Rockefeller Center on Christmas Eve. She pulled the phone away and said to Nora, "My knight in shining armor. His battery died but he was dying to talk to me." She turned her back on Nora and spoke into the phone. "I'm so sorry!"

Nora stopped several steps down. Abbey hadn't moved.

"Just a minute, dear." Abigail pulled the phone from her ear. "I need to take this in privacy. You check upstairs and I'll wait for you in the Jeep."

"I'll come with you."

Abigail lowered her eyebrows. "Private conversation, Nora." She skipped down the stairs, knocking Nora to the wall.

Nora watched Abigail hurry outside. Abbey sat at the base of the stairs. Once more Nora eyed the front door and escape. "Did I mention what a mistake this is?" She said to Abbey. The golden retriever wisely kept his own counsel. She climbed the stairs, feeling the weight of the silence grow more dense with each step. "Abbey, come."

Abbey gave her the I-don't-wanna attitude.

"Stop being lazy," Nora said. "Come."

Reluctantly, he got to his feet and climbed after her.

A strange odor crept into her nostrils like a hairy caterpillar. Was Sylvia's toilet clogged? But no, it didn't smell like bad sewer. Whatever it was, it stunk.

The hallway ran the length of the foyer, looking down on the chandelier—now that Nora noticed, it really was gaudy. To the right a few doors opened onto dark rooms.

The slightly worn path in the thick pile led to the left. Must be the master bedroom.

Nora leaned down and scratched Abbey's head. *Stupid, stupid, stupid.* And yet, her feet carried her down the hall, however slowly.

The stench was like thick Yuck Chowder.

Nora glanced behind her to make sure Abbey followed close behind.

She snaked her hand around the wall to the dark room and felt for the light.

41

At first the muted light of the bedroom didn't reveal much. Sylvia must keep the lights dim in here to set the mood. The bedroom was only slightly smaller than the great room. The section closest to the door contained a sitting area with a fireplace. A television the size of a child's wading pool hung on the wall.

The massive four-poster bed jutted from the far corner of the room and black dressers accented the room. Even with all the furniture, someone could still perform a gymnastics floor routine. Who needed this much space?

The covers bunched at the foot of bed and spilled onto the floor. The carpet seemed to have a splotchy pattern in a dark color by the bathroom door. Odd.

A nightlight cast a glow from the bathroom across the room. Sylvia was not the neatest person because she'd left shoes and clothes strewn on the floor.

Abbey whined. He'd retreated to the stairs.

Nora found the light switch and toggled it up. The wall sconces brightened, as did the chandelier. How many crystal chandeliers does it take to please Sylvia?

Nora stepped tentatively into the room.

Dear god.

Nora gasped and stepped back, running into the doorjamb.

She wanted to run but couldn't make her feet move.

What she'd thought was a pattern on the rug so obviously wasn't.

Blood. So much blood. Crimson splashes on the wall by the bathroom. Deep ruby on the white carpet. The smell. It made horrible sense.

Scuffed black men's shoes with thick leather soles, black socks and the bottom of black trousers made up what she'd thought was a pile of Sylvia's clothes.

Nora gagged. The walls and white sheet of the bed resembled a macabre Jackson Pollock interpretation of red, with enough lighter colored chunks to add texture and depth.

Nora spun and raced down the hallway. Abbey barked. Nora lunged into the closest bathroom and made it in time to vomit into the toilet. Shaking and slimed with cold sweat, she braced herself on the counter and turned on the tap. She rinsed her mouth, her legs trembling and threatening to give out.

She had to go back. The shoes and pants gave Nora an awful sense of recognition.

Nora knelt and buried her face in Abbey's fur. She hesitated a moment to calm down enough to force herself return to the room. She pulled herself up and step by awful step, made her way back to the bedroom. She stopped in the doorway, staring at the black shoes.

Nora needed to see around the foot of the bed. She swallowed but her mouth felt like a desert.

Step. Step. Bit by bit the body came into view. Dress pants covered the legs. A white shirt pulled out of the waistband over a soft, pudgy belly.

One more step revealed the entire body.

Nora held her hand over her mouth. "Oh, no." The head had been blown away. Bits of it stuck to the wall and the side of the bed. White pieces of skull with wisps of black hair clumped amid globs of bloody brain.

Nora backed away. Tears ran down her face and she gagged again. There was no face, but she'd seen enough to know it was Mark Monstain.

A voice squeaked from the dark corner of the room next to a tall armoire. "Nora?"

She whirled around, heart in her throat.

The wad of fabric and hair wedged between a dresser and the corner of the room mewled. "Oh Nora."

Nora rushed to Petal. "What happened? Are you all right?"

Scarlet slashes marked Petal's cheeks, matching the rings around her eyes. Tears streamed down her face. "Sylvia and Daniel. They were here."

Nora kept her face turned away from the gruesomeness at the other end of the bedroom. Waves of toxic fear sloshed inside her. She reached for Petal and tugged at her to stand. Together they lumbered to the hallway. "Did Daniel do this? Is he still here?"

Petal shook her head. "I don't know. Mark was dead when I got here."

Nora kept her arm around Petal as they moved toward the stairs. "Where did they go?"

Petal trembled against Nora as they descended one stair at a time. "They went to the Trust. Sylvia wanted to set the coordinates. They're going to send a beam at dawn."

Abbey squeezed around them and plodded down the stairs to the foyer.

"Sylvia's not gathering data on climate change, is she"

Petal shook her head.

They made it to the foyer and both sat on the bottom step, huddled together. "Tell me what's going on."

Petal swiped her sleeve across her nose. "The beam is set at a refractory angle to strike in Ecuador."

Now it made sense. "Daniel isn't really trying to protect the rainforest. Why are they targeting Ecuador?"

Petal shivered despite all her layers. "The beam will start an earthquake. That will trigger the volcanoes and they'll erupt. They'll wipe out whole cities. After that happens, the government will sell the oil rights so the companies will pump money into the country and they can rebuild."

Heat surged over Nora's body and her ears rang. "They're staging a massive natural disaster so World Petro can get richer? They can't do that."

Petal stared at her with round, watery eyes. "They can."

Nora jerked her to her feet and noticed she wore damp wool socks and no shoes. "We have to stop them!"

She pulled Petal to the door and reached for the knob. A movement through the side windows stopped her.

She caught her breath and watched through the window as a Lincoln Town Car stopped at the curb and shut off its lights. The driver's side door opened and a tall man dressed in black started up the front walk.

42

Nora dropped to the marble floor, pulling Petal down. "Someone's coming," she whispered.

"No." Petal's cry sounded plaintive.

Nora crawled toward the hallway. "This way. I think there's a door in the kitchen."

Abbey plodded after Nora, unconcerned with her strange behavior.

As soon as Nora was far enough into the hall she couldn't be seen through the foyer windows, she jumped to her feet and sprinted toward the kitchen.

Petal ran after her, small moans escaping with each step.

Nora pushed the kitchen door open and halted in the darkness, remembering the layout. Island, stove, sub-zero freezer, more counters. Her mind found escape just as her eyes adjusted to the dark.

They heard the front door open. Why hadn't they locked it? It snicked closed.

She grabbed Petal's hand and patted her thigh to bring Abbey closer.

"Here." They skirted the kitchen island, heading for the garage door. All three of them hurried through the door.

If they had the time, they could have had a barn dance in the garage. With no windows, it was even darker than the kitchen. Nora's feet clattered on the textured concrete floor as she dragged Petal toward the back where she hoped she'd find escape.

She fumbled beside the large overhead garage door, desperate to find a regular door knob. If they used the automatic door it would sound like buffalo stampede and they'd lose any chance of sneaking away.

She couldn't find a door. Frantic, Nora stopped and searched the dark garage. A small light by the kitchen showed the overhead door control. They might be able to escape if the man in black had started upstairs in his search.

At any rate, they had no choice.

Nora ran back to the kitchen door and punched the control.

The motor roared with the sound of a freight train. The overhead light burst on.

Nora sprinted for the opening, grabbing Petal's hand on the way. "Come, Abbey!"

The garage door rose with the speed of a frozen river.

The kitchen door swung outward. "Hey!" The man shouted at them.

Nora dove and rolled under the door.

Petal copied her.

Abbey ran after them.

"Stop!" The man yelled.

"Run!" Nora leapt to her feet, heading toward the Jeep.

A gunshot exploded from the garage, shattering the wood of the door.

Petal screamed.

43

Nora skidded on the snow in the driveway. "Petal!" Had she been shot?

She'd barely turned when Petal plowed into her, knocking her on her tailbone.

Another shot pegged the driveway next to them.

Nora must have jumped to her feet and dashed across the driveway and street to open the Jeep door, but she didn't remember it. Now she held the door open for Abbey and Petal to dive into the back seat.

Abigail gasped. "Whatever is—?"

Nora vaulted into the driver's seat. "Hang on." She cranked the key and jammed it into gear.

"Hurry!" Petal screamed form the backseat.

Nora peeled away from the curb, the back end slipping in the slush.

She caught a glimpse of Sylvia's house in the rearview mirror. The man stood in the light from the garage watching them.

"What's happening?" Abigail asked.

Nora pointed at the phone. "Is that Charlie?"

"Well, yes it's Cole's phone because he didn't char—"

Nora careened around a corner and gunned it. "Tell him to meet us at Baseline and Foothills. In the Safeway parking lot."

Abigail swiveled in her sit and gasped. "Who is that man?"

"Mother! Tell Charlie."

Abigail repeated the instructions into the phone.

Nora slid around the next corner and ran a red light.

Abigail pulled the phone away from her ear. "He doesn't know where that is."

Another light at the intersection on Broadway turned from yellow to red. Nora glanced left and right, saw headlights, and slammed on the brakes. Abbey crashed into the back of her seat. "Cole can get him there."

Nora waited for the sparse traffic to pass in front of her, and then crossed the intersection despite the red.

Abigail spoke into the phone and ended the call. She twisted to see into the back seat. "Petal, are you all right?"

Nora didn't hear any response. She concentrated on the street. The pavement ran with melted snow and slush. If you headed to the grocery store for milk, it would be a matter of slowing down to be safe. If you were running for your lives, it meant some sliding turns.

Abigail braced her arms against the dash. "You're going to kill us."

Nora whipped into the Safeway parking lot and slid to a stop behind a bank building.

"Now, will you tell me what's going on?" Abigail folded her arms, the slick fabric of Nora's best ski jacket whizzing in the silence.

"Sylvia and Daniel killed Mark."

"Oh my god!"

"They plan to send out a beam to cause an earthquake in Ecuador."

Abigail's lips turned down in skepticism. "Well, that's just silly."

Nora didn't have time to convince Abigail. "I've got to stop them. So you and Petal have to stay with Charlie."

Abigail held up her phone. "We need to go to the police. I don't know who that man at Sylvia's house was, but he shot at you and that's against the law."

"No!" Petal came to life in the back seat.

Nora and Abigail wrenched around.

Petal placed her hands on the back of their seats. "I need to go up to the tower. It's the only way to stop this. I can disable it."

"Can't we stop the beam from the office?" Nora asked.

"Yes" Petal squeaked. "But it's very secure and Sylvia is the only one who knows the codes to get in and cancel the launch. If she's got it set there's nothing we can do."

Nora straightened and stared ahead. The Town Car sat at a red light on Baseline.

Duck! Hide! Run! But all she could do was pray he didn't see them.

If the shooter twisted in his seat and surveyed the parking lot, he could spot them parked behind the bank.

Abigail's no-nonsense tone set the course. "The police can take you there."

Petal trembled. "They won't believe me. They'll waste time and the beam will go off before we can get there."

The light turned green and the Town Car eased across Foothills Highway, heading east.

People live in Ecuador. Cities lie at the base of several volcanoes. An eruption or a high magnitude earthquake would kill... Nora had no idea how many people. Not to mention the devastation to the rainforest and what long term, world-wide environmental problems that would create.

She addressed Petal. "Cole will take you to Mount Evans. I'll go to the office and see if I can cancel the launch."

"What am I going to do?" Abigail asked.

Nora rubbed her forehead. "You stay with Charlie and Abbey. I don't want to worry about you."

Abigail reached for her handbag on the floor of the Jeep. She unzipped a pouch on the bottom of the bag Nora had never noticed and pulled out a small pistol. She held it out to Nora. "You'd better take this."

What the—? "Mother, why are you carrying a gun? Is it loaded?"

Abigail wore a satisfied smile. "The gun isn't real, dear. I saw it in SkyMall. It's an authentic replica designed to scare muggers. You pull that out and they run away."

"And this will do me what kind of good?"

"You didn't know it was fake. How do you expect Sylvia to know the difference? Wave it around, demand she cancel the death beam, call the cops, save Petal, easy as pie."

Nora doubted it would be that easy.

Headlights appeared around the west corner of the bank. Cole eased his pickup beside them. Charlie's door opened and he raced around the front of the Jeep toward Abigail's door.

Cole climbed from the driver's side.

Nora scanned the intersection of Baseline and Foothills for the Town Car's return. All clear. She jumped out of the Jeep and stepped in a puddle. She met Cole by the bed of his pickup. "You need to take Petal to Mount Evans."

He scowled. "You want me to do you a favor?"

"It's not for me. It's—" She couldn't explain it all again. There was no time. "Please. Just trust me."

He folded his arms. "I'll do this for you. But this is it. No more."

"What do you mean?"

He ran a hand through his hair, now damp with falling snow. "I need to get on with my life. Right now, that means going back to the ranch in Wyoming."

She didn't want him to leave. But did that mean she wanted him to stay? She couldn't deal with this now. "Do what you need to do." It sounded more harsh than she intended.

Nora sped back to the Jeep and helped Petal from the back seat. She'd removed the wet socks and was now barefoot. Nora settled her into the passenger side of Cole's pickup. The heater made it cozy away from the wintery wind. "Be careful. Cole will help you."

Petal reached out and hugged Nora. Her voice choked. "Thank you. You're a good friend."

Charlie and Abigail huddled together under the portico of the bank. Their heads bent together in quiet conversation. Abbey sat at their feet.

When Nora ran to them, Abigail pulled out her phone. "I already called a taxi. Get going."

Nora gave her a quick hug. "Take care of her," she said to Charlie.

"She is my galaxy," he said. Crazy old Charlie.

Nora followed Cole's pickup out of the parking lot and west on Baseline. At Broadway he turned south toward the mountains and she turned north.

Toward...

She didn't know.

44

Despite the broken boot heel and the snow-dampened hair, Sylvia knew she carried herself with class as she led Daniel through the darkened kitchen to her office suite.

There, she laid out the maps of Ecuador showing the Cotopaxi volcano and the oil fields in the rainforest. He was suitably impressed by her brilliance.

At first he acted angry. She assumed that was because he felt inferior to her genius as he struggled to understand the difficult principles behind the plan.

He studied the maps on the banquet table in front of him. "If you actually make the volcano erupt..."

She kissed the back of his neck. "Oh, it will."

He ducked away from her kiss. "You will kill thousands of people."

They weren't the kind of people who mattered. It was far better to accentuate the positive. "But the Cubrero family will be rich. We can have whatever we want, whenever we want it."

He walked to her desk where her monitor showed a diagram of the tower on Mount Evans and the angle of refraction of the beam that would send it directly into the volcano. "When will this event occur?"

She ran her hands through her hair pulling her arm back to give him a view of her breast outlined through her cashmere sweater. She sauntered to where he leaned over the monitor and hiked a hip on the desk. "It's scheduled to activate at dawn. About three hours from now."

He stepped back from the screen and paced across the office. "And you are the only one who knows of this?"

He was starting to understand how special she was. "I designed it. I set it in motion. Yes, my love, it is all mine."

"My father paid for all of this and yet does not know about the dawn launch?"

She sprang to her feet. "Eduardo! He's so unreasonable. I tried to tell him but he hung up on me. Hung up!"

"And sent Juan."

She purred. "But you saved me."

Daniel frowned. "If you're doing my fahter's bidding, why does he want you dead?"

She couldn't stay still and strode across the office. Her skin suddenly felt too small. "He's irrational. He thinks I killed Darla and Mark and that I stole Trust money. And when last night's launch misdirected and killed birds, he wouldn't listen to me."

His face froze and he stared at her. "You killed Mark? And you are behind the birds dying?"

She hurried to him and slid an arm around his neck. She snuggled her cheek into the warm spot where she felt his heart beating. "But you can talk to him. You can tell him about our love and how I am doing what he wants."

"Can you stop this beam or whatever it is?" He lifted her hand from his neck and stepped back.

"Of course I can, but why would I?" She couldn't stop it, though.

He ran a hand back from his forehead across his short, black curls. "What if someone tampers with the tower?"

She waved her hand toward the window. "It's snowing. Petal was up there earlier today and it's working correctly. Believe me, it's safe."

"Does Petal know of your plan?"

She tickled his chest just above the button of his shirt. "She might suspect something but she's not bright enough to figure it out."

"But she could be out there now."

A warning flashed in Sylvia's brain. "Petal. You're right. She hates me. She and Nora are out to get me."

Daniel grabbed her arms. "Why does Petal hate you?"

"Because I won't give her mother unlimited money. Because she thinks I stole her ideas. She thinks *she* deserves the credit at HAARP for taking Tesla's technology forward. But she worked for me. She couldn't have done it if I hadn't nurtured her. If I hadn't given her the opportunity."

He glared at her. "Petal developed this?"

No. He would *not* dismiss her the same way they did at HARRP. "No. *I* did it. *I'm* the one."

He spun toward the door and strode into the kitchen. "I've got to stop her."

Sylvia ran after him, tripping on her broken heel. "Yes. Go. Don't let her destroy my tower."

She hurried after him from the kitchen to the dark lobby. She bumped into his back. "What?"

Daniel stood motionless.

Sylvia shoved him to send him to the mountain. But he wouldn't move.

Sylvia stepped around him to pull him forward and she suddenly understood what stopped him.

Nora Abbott stood just inside the front door, pointing a gun at them.

45

Great. Now that Nora pointed Abigail's gun at Daniel she didn't know what to do. Fake gun, fake bullets, fake courage. "You aren't going anywhere." She sounded a lot tougher than she felt.

Sylvia whirled around and raced through the kitchen.

Daniel backed up, keeping his eyes on Nora. "Why are you here?"

Good question. "To stop you."

Daniel held his palms out. "You don't understand, Nora. I'm not the bad guy."

Was Sylvia getting a gun? A butcher knife? Nora was outnumbered, out-experienced, and—wielding a SkyMall Special—out-gunned. With Sylvia probably on her way back with a Katyusha rocket—or just a real gun—Nora had to come up with something.

Nora spotted the old-school landline on a side table. She walked to it, keeping the gun pointed at Daniel. She picked it up and pushed 9, heading for the 1. She took her eyes off Daniel for the splittest of seconds.

He charged. With all of his sexy muscle he rammed into her, sending her flying several feet.

She cracked a hip and her elbow when she landed against the fireplace and slid to the floor. Blood filled her mouth where she bit her tongue on impact. Amazingly, she still gripped the gun.

He came at her again and she raised it as if taking aim. "I'll shoot!"

It didn't faze him. Maybe he suspected she'd never fire on him. Or maybe he wasn't afraid of a toy gun.

He dove on top of her and clawed for the gun. She raised it above her head and he boosted himself across her with his knees to reach for it.

"Uff." It felt as though his knees pushed all her organs out of the way and ground her spine into the floor. His hand closed on the wrist that held the gun.

Nora twisted beneath him. She pushed off with one foot and kicked the knee of her other leg. She knocked him in the back, causing him to lose balance and tip to the side, slipping off her.

She rose to her hands and knees and scrambled to get away.

He grabbed her ankle and fell on her again.

This time he grabbed her gun hand with both of his. He slammed her hand onto the ground and wrested the gun from her grip. Pain shot through her forefinger as though he'd snapped it from her hand.

He sprang to his feet, waving the gun at her. Abigail's fake-out fooled him.

What did it matter if the gun could kill her or not? Even without a weapon Daniel was bigger, stronger, and more lethal than Nora.

He stood above her, hesitating. Nora readied herself to jump up, grab his ankles, tackle him to the floor. And then?

She might bring him down but Sylvia would show up to kill her any minute. Nora anticipated the bullet ripping into her, shredding her kidneys, mangling her guts. Blood would splatter across the fireplace and soak into the carpet.

The sound of a gunshot tore open the night.

Bullets didn't shred Nora.

Abigail said it was a fake gun but that was a real gunshot. Nora rolled to the right before Daniel could fire again.

But the shot hadn't come from Daniel's gun. She realized the sound hadn't come from this room.

Daniel's head jerked toward the kitchen. He hesitated only a second then he sprinted to the front door, yanked it open, and dashed into the night.

The old farmhouse fell silent. Nora lay still, straining to hear Sylvia rushing from the kitchen ready to fire off more shots. This time, the bullets would find Nora.

Nothing.

46

Nora got to her knees and pushed herself up. Someone had stolen her femurs and her legs wobbled. She considered following Daniel out the door and heading directly to the police station.

Instead, she tiptoed to the kitchen. The back door stood open allowing flakes to blow into the narrow passage. The brisk air washed away the smell of burnt toast.

With careful steps she snuck past the door heading toward the light spilling from Sylvia's office. Her footsteps caused the old floors to creak. She inched closer to the lighted office. She didn't want to see inside.

But she had to.

A smell like spent firecrackers and hot oil hung in the air and Nora froze. She listened to the nothingness around her.

Bang, whoosh, groan. She jerked and catch her breath. The heater kicked to life in answer to the open kitchen door.

Nora focused on the office door hoping to hear something, anything, moving inside. She slid her foot forward and leaned toward the door. She eased around the door jamb and surveyed the room.

The office appeared empty. The overhead light glared, reflecting on the maps spread on the table. The computer monitor on Sylvia's desk cast a faint glow as if she'd been working. Petal's chair snugged up to her desk and the lamp with the pink silk scarf was off. The papers stacked neatly on Petal's desk. Nora stepped into the room and moved tentatively toward the desk. Something creeping along the floor caught her eye. She narrowed her gaze to the floor in front of Sylvia's desk.

Not creeping. Leaking. Deep crimson, it spread like gruesome syrup, dripping from the edge of the plastic chair runner and soaking into the thin carpet.

A low moan escaped from Nora's throat. She held her breath to silence herself. Fighting every step, she advanced until she saw the whole scene.

Nora fell back against the wall. Part of her fought to deny the image while the other part struggled to understand it. She gagged on the smell of death.

Sylvia sat wedged in the far corner under the desk. Mascara smeared under her eyes and her black curls flopped in wild disarray. Her eyes stared sightlessly at Nora.

A river of blood flowed from the mangled flesh that had been Sylvia's chest.

47

Nora staggered out of the office. The kitchen door still stood ajar and freezing night air blew in. She slid down from the sink and sat in front of the blast.

Earthquakes of revulsion and fear cracked her surface. She couldn't do this. She shivered and stared into the backyard.

Get control. Think.

Sylvia was dead. But Daniel, the man who stood to profit from the rainforest's destruction, was on his way to the mountain to stop Petal from dismantling the tower.

Cole.

He was on the other end of Daniel's deadly quest. Nora had sent him there. And Charlie had Cole's phone so she couldn't warn him.

She shot to her feet and clattered through the kitchen and foyer, out the front door, and across the porch. She lurched down the stairs two at a time, slipping on the last one and crashing a knee on the ground. The snow had tapered off and the temperatures weren't at their winter worst. The wet snow stuck to the grass in clumps and would be gone before lunch. She bounded to her feet and sprinted toward the Jeep.

The Town Car sat next to hers.

She dove to the ground and rolled under a shrub. Not the smartest move she'd made. If he'd been in the car he'd have already killed her. Now she was wet and muddy.

The Town Car Guy had killed Sylvia and he wouldn't think twice about doing Nora the same. She pulled her feet under her and crouched next to the shrub. Obviously he'd used the kitchen door to the back yard. Where was he now? At the edge of the house waiting to gun her down?

She had no choice.

Nora dashed to the Jeep. The roar of a pistol did not shatter the silence. The bullets didn't burn into her exposed body. In fact, she made it to the Jeep without incident even if she couldn't breathe from terror. She jerked open the door, dove inside and turned the ignition key, seemingly at the same time.

Hunched over the wheel to make as small a target as possible, Nora punched the gas and sped away. She studied her rearview mirror. Nothing moved at the Trust farmhouse. The black rectangle where the front door stood open gaped back at her.

Since it was a weeknight—technically a week morning now—it was too late for people to be out and too early for them to be up. She raced through Boulder heedless of the stoplights. The snow had melted on the pavement leaving the streets wet but not icy.

Nora punched on the heat and let it blast from the vents. Her damp jeans and coat made a comforting wet-Abbey smell in the Jeep.

She climbed out of town south on Highway 93 toward Golden. As soon as she dipped over a hill the lights of town disappeared. Starless night closed around her. The Jeep's heater tried, but in the drafty vehicle it couldn't keep up with the winter chill. Shivers ran through Nora at irregular intervals, nerves and cold vying for credit.

Two glowing pinpricks at the side of the road alerted her to deer. She tapped her brakes in response. The steering wheel jerked from her hand and the back end of the Jeep swerved to the right. Black ice.

Heart pumping, she counter-steered. The back end slid the other way, gaining momentum like a deadly pendulum. She yanked the wheel back. This time, the Jeep responded with a *swoosh* to the right that kept going. And going. The Jeep spun across the road like a drunk ice skater. It finally stopped with two wheels off the pavement, facing back toward Boulder.

The engine idled. The headlights shone crazily across the center line. She wanted to break into tears and sit still to gather herself. She needed to take the time to stop her shaking. She felt like tearing the seat belt off and jumping out to walk off the adrenaline pumping through her.

There was only one thing she could do. Nora locked her jaws tight, rammed the Jeep into gear and pulled onto the highway. At least the wild ride warmed her but the sweat would chill her.

She made it through Golden and onto to I-70 heading into the mountains. It seemed to take ten years to find the exit from I-70. The whole time she expected death to arrive in any number of ways. She could slide across the median and into oncoming traffic; Town Car guy could catch up to her; she could keel over from fear alone. Or she might arrive too late to save Cole and Petal.

Nora exited the Interstate and began her long climb up Mount Evans.

Another mountain. Another fight for life. Why did it always happen on mountains? Why did it have to happen at all?

White, fluffy flakes started falling again. "Of course," she said aloud.

Shutters covered the windows of the Park Service toll house and a bar blocked access to the road. Nora eased the Jeep off the road and around the barrier. Shoulders hunched up high enough to be ear muffs, she gripped the wheel.

In daylight, the harrowing road pushed Nora to the limit. At night, the switchbacks, narrow ledges, darkness, and ice became a nightmare.

She inched her way along the cliff-side road. Snow accumulated over packed ruts. Cole's pickup probably made those, followed by Daniel's Prius. She shifted up and down around each precarious switchback. Her headlights revealed a frustratingly small section of the mountain. She knew the edge dropped forever down the mountain but she couldn't see it. She stayed in the middle of the road, praying her tires would grip the snow.

What was happening on the dark summit? Her progress seemed like swimming through quicksand. Every time she tried to gain speed she fishtailed. But every second she lost gave Daniel more time to kill.

She pictured Cole smiling at her on the Pearl Street Mall. The fall leaves a swirl of golds and reds. He had been shy and uncertain about her but he'd been happy to see her.

"You were happy to see him, too." She scowled at the shadowy road. "Quit talking to yourself."

Was she happy to see him? What about earlier tonight, in her apartment? Didn't that feel right?

She'd spent the last year wrapped in a cocoon, gluing herself back together.

How long are you going to stay shrouded in self-pity? See, you don't even need Abigail around to harass you with her sloppy poetry.

She slipped the lever into first gear and pulled around a steep U-turn.

What if she died tonight? Or worse, what if Cole died? What would all the protecting and taking time to repair her heart get her? She didn't want to waste any more time shielding herself from life for fear that something might hurt again.

She wanted Cole.

Nora turned the last switchback into the parking lot. She ought to slap her headlights off for stealth but she wouldn't be able to see. Besides, anyone up here would have heard the Jeep's engine.

Four inches of snow sat atop Cole's pickup. Daniel's Prius still dripped melted snow from the warm engine.

Nora pulled next to Cole's pickup, cut the motor, and climbed out. The dry, cold air caused her nostrils to stick. The air burned into her lungs and out again in puffs.

The trailhead to the summit should be at the corner of the lot but in the darkness and covered with snow, Nora couldn't make it out. In a matter of seconds her fingers grew numb and her ears ached. She ducked back into the Jeep. A knitted purple ski cap with bright braids peeked from under the back seat. She yanked it on her head and found a cheap pair of thin knit gloves she kept in the Jeep to protect her from a chilly steering wheel. They wouldn't keep her hands warm, but they'd help a little. Her headlamp rested in the glove box and she pulled it over the ski cap and snapped it on.

The weak beam from the headlamp held the darkness at bay a few feet in front of her. She shuffled toward the trailhead, swinging her neck back and forth to sweep the area for footprints. The fluffy flakes had erased even Daniel's tracks.

Though not easy to make out, she found the start of the trail by locating a flat area about three feet wide between two boulders covered with snow. Feeling for each foot step along the bumpy, rock strewn path, Nora started toward the summit.

The headlamp provided a faded glow and snow plunked in her eyes. Her feet slid along under several inches of fluff, stubbing into rocks. She leaned as close to the cliff face as possible, using it to catch her when she slipped.

After two switchbacks she found the terrain becoming increasingly rugged as she headed around the side of the mountain. She must have missed the spot where the trail turned back up. The somewhat level path she'd been following became a jumble of snow covered rocks edging away from the cliff face. She soaked her gloves scrambling over a mound of stones. Her jeans wicked melted snow from the hem and her knees where she'd had to climb on all fours.

Shivering and panting in the thin air, she swung her head to the side. Her headlamp disappeared into nothing. She hung on the very edge of the mountain. Nora swung the beam back to where she suspected she lost the trail. She tilted her neck up, gauging whether it would be better to bushwhack up the side or try to find the trail.

Uneven and full of rocks, the trail wasn't an easy way to go. Backtracking to find it would eat up valuable time. She held her breathe, listening for voices or sounds of a struggle.

Nothing.

She reached her hand upward to feel under the snow for a solid hold. Her frozen fingers felt like clubs. She searched for a platform for her numb feet and pushed upward.

One movement and pause for a breath. Still, she panted. Despite frozen fingers and toes, sweat slicked her body, creating an even deeper chill. She could only see as far as her next hand hold.

She pushed off again. Her sole slid off the rock and she careened to the side.

No!

She flailed at the snow-covered rocks trying to find something to grab. Her fingers wouldn't grip. Her arms splayed out and her chin whacked the boulder under a pile of cold snow, sending a shower of lights behind her eyes. She cried out.

Desperate to keep upright, she scrabbled, but her fingers only raked the icy surface of the rock.

Nora couldn't get her balance. Her other foot twisted and she toppled to her right. She crashed to her knee and momentarily paralyzed her leg.

Her body sailed onto her side, kicking and fighting, she managed only to skid around so her head pointed downhill. Nora started to slide.

She threw her arms out trying to wedge them against any rocks. She gathered speed like a luge. If she didn't arrest herself she'd go over the side. She'd land in a pile of broken bones. Dead. Like Scott. Like Heather.

Like Cole.

Her forehead crashed into a boulder. Her body accordioned into her neck like a train hitting a brick wall. She stopped in a burst of white hot pain.

She lay with her head slammed against the boulder, her body in a heap uphill. Snow accumulated all around her, freezing her neck and cheek. At least she wouldn't fall all the way to her death at the bottom of a fourteener.

But she might never walk again.

Nora couldn't feel anything below her neck.

They'd pull her out of here, prop her in a wheelchair in front of a TV for the rest of her life. Over and over again she'd have to relive her failures and mourn the loss of Heather. Of Petal. Of Cole.

No more negative talk. She couldn't quit. Nora rolled onto her stomach and pushed herself up. Her hands ached with the cold and wet. "Ow!"

Her neck was nothing but frozen pain. But her arm—gave new meaning to *agony*. Excruciating molten bone somewhere just below her elbow. She wanted to scream. Or curl into the snow and wait for help.

She had to keep going. What choice did she have?

Slowly she maneuvered her legs and feet to push herself to stand. Okay, she wasn't a quadriplegic...yet.

She surveyed the side of the mountain where she'd slid. The rock strewn slope would be a challenge to scale in the best of circumstances. With a broken arm, it might be impossible.

She tucked her damaged arm close. With shaking legs, shivering and gasping for air, she climbed.

Find solid footing, brace your numb hand against a rock, push off. Repeat.

She gritted her teeth against shrieks of pain but nothing could stop her grunting and yes, even a moan or two.

She searched for handholds with her good hand and fell to her knees, pushing off with her feet. She slid, banging her chin again and sort of hopped by shoving with her feet. She gained a few inches.

Her foot slipped and she landed on her arm. "Ah!" She humped herself another few inches.

Cole. Petal. Rainforest.

Slipping and sliding and earning a foot to losing six inches, she finally made it to a spot where the trail reversed direction for the last climb to the summit.

She pulled herself over the side and lay on her back, resting for just a moment to ease her broken arm. At least the climb would be easier now. She dug in her feet and pushed to roll over.

A brilliant beam of light lit up the snow two feet to her right. It swerved to illuminate her. Snow puffed and metal skidded on rock.

The sound of the gunshot ricocheted in the darkness.

48

Nora rolled to the side of the trail and tucked into the cliff face. She turned off her headlamp. Daniel wouldn't be able to hit her now without climbing down the trail. The cliff provided shelter for the time being.

But she couldn't stay there.

A slight gray appeared on the eastern horizon. While it afforded Nora enough light to make out large objects, it reminded her that time was running out. Dawn was near and the beam would go off soon.

A boulder sat ten feet up the trail. She lurched for it and slid behind it, out of line of fire from the summit. Snow blew into her eyes. No gunshots.

She made another dash up the trail to the cliff face. She gulped in air. Again, no shots.

He must be busy with Cole and Petal.

Nora cantered up the trail watching her feet carefully. Each step jogged her bad arm, firing pain through her, but the thought of Cole in danger kept her moving forward. She pushed herself until black dots formed around the edges of her vision and she had to stop to fill herself with oxygen and windmill her arm to force blood into her fingers.

She hadn't gone too far before tracks appeared in the snow. They led up a rocky side and disappeared around an outcropping of stone. The summit lay ten feet straight up or another hundred feet if she stayed on the safer and more level trail. Even knowing the last time she'd bushwhacked she'd ended up with a broken arm, Nora couldn't opt for easy. She leaned into the cliff and planted her frozen hand in the snow, searching for leverage. She lurched up.

A noise made her freeze and she fought against her loud panting, trying to hear around the pounding of blood in her temples. The voices came as a relief. At least Petal was still alive.

On her hand and knees, she crawled the last few feet to peer over a rock to the summit.

Petal held a flashlight toward the ground and the light cast large shadows.

Daniel stood with his back to Nora, facing Petal. He wore a black down jacket with a cap pulled over his head. Somewhere he'd acquired a much larger gun. A real one. He held it in his hand, ready to pull it up and shoot Petal.

Petal stood swallowed in a barn coat, obviously one of Cole's. Her various skirts flowed in the gusts. She wore cowboy boots too large for her and they made her appear even more loopy than usual. They must also have been borrowed from Cole too.

Nora pushed with her feet and pulled with her hand to slide over the top of the cliff. She lay on her belly, the snow soaking through her jeans, seeping under her coat to her stomach. She shivered uncontrollably.

"Why are you doing this?" Daniel asked. His voice didn't sound nearly as sexy to Nora as it used to. It carried the sour note of threat.

Petal wasn't crying. Her mouth turned down in a fierce scowl. "You know why. Sylvia cheated me out of what was mine and I want what I deserve."

Where was Cole? Was he okay? He must be injured. If not, he'd be standing in front of Petal, protecting her. But he could be out at the tower now. He'd climb the fence and somehow destroy the tower.

Despite dawn threatening, darkness made it difficult to see much outside the circle of Petal's flashlight.

Even though he didn't have his normal bedroom voice, Daniel seemed to gentle his tone. "You know you needed her."

Petal shrieked, frightening in its sudden intensity. "That's not true. It was Sylvia who needed me."

"Now she's gone and she won't hurt you anymore."

Petal started to cry. "I'm glad she's dead. She deserved to die. She stole my science like she stole my mother's life."

Daniel didn't argue. He slid in another step closer.

He was getting ready to attack and all Petal did was rattle on in her disjointed sobs.

Daniel sounded soothing. "I know you were instrumental in her research. You should be rewarded. We could get you a position back with HAARP if you want."

Petal backed up and when she shifted her weight a pile of gear appeared behind her in the gloom.

Another step and Daniel was within striking distance of Petal. "This is not the way."

Petal pleaded with him. "It's the only way."

Nora squinted in the ashy light. The lump of gear moved.

No. Oh no.

It wasn't gear. That was Cole's green coat. She couldn't detect any blood but her vantage point wasn't good. Daniel must have shot him!

Nora cast around for a weapon. She crawled a few feet to a pile of rocks under the snow. Moving with as much stealth as possible, Nora pushed herself up. With her broken arm hugged to her side, she bent down and picked the biggest rock she could hold. It would have to do.

Ten minutes ago she'd have been hidden in darkness. Now she crept forward in half light. She faced Petal and Daniel in slow motion, praying that she wouldn't give her away when she noticed.

Petal's eyes flicked to Nora and widened slightly. She refocused on Daniel, who thankfully, seemed clueless.

Nora slid another foot forward, arm raised, ready to lunge in and smash the rock on Daniel's head. It wouldn't be enough to knock him out but it should throw him off balance and Nora could tackle him to the ground.

She couldn't fight him at the Trust with two good arms so she'd need a miracle to stop him now. It all rested on Petal. With any luck, Petal would come to her senses and help. Once they had Daniel contained,

Nora could hold the gun on him and see to Cole, while Petal disabled Sylvia's doomsday machine.

It was a plan. Not a good one, but a plan.

One more step. She tensed, ready to spring.

Whether he noticed the slight change in Petal or heard Nora's movement, Daniel's instincts kicked in. He glanced over his shoulder.

Nora didn't hesitate. She yelled and jumped forward, bringing the rock down with all her strength.

The blow landed squarely on Daniel's head, bounced off his ski cap, hit his shoulder of well-padded down, rebounded up and skidded off his arm. It caused no more damage than if she'd spit at him.

"What?" he demanded before Nora plowed into him. She screamed at the jolt of fire in her arm.

He outweighed her and was a whole lot stronger, but she couldn't back down. Everything depended on her. She crashed into him. They tumbled backward and landed in the snow. The gun sailed behind them.

Despite ending up beneath her, Daniel gained the advantage. He grabbed her arms and she howled in pain. He held her arms and looked up at her. Desperation lined his face. "Stop. You don't understand."

"You want to destroy the rainforest and kill thousands of people." She struggled for release, wishing her arm would fall off and stop the torture.

He held her arms in an iron grip. He bucked her off never losing his hold. He flipped her and planted her on the ground. "You have it wrong."

They struggled in the snow, the rocks bruising and scraping her.

"Petal!" Nora yelled. The girl needed to help her.

As long as Daniel had hold of her arms, he couldn't reach for the gun. This might be their only chance. "Petal. Get the gun!"

Daniel shook his head, panic in his eyes. Obviously he didn't like it when the tables were turned and he might be hurt. "No. You're wrong."

From the corner of Nora's eye she saw Petal dive for the gun. The cowboy boots slid on the snow and rocks as Petal scrambled to help.

"You have to stop her," Daniel said.

In the high altitude and with Daniel on top, Nora could barely breathe, let alone give a good fight. *Hurry, Petal.*

It seemed Petal didn't feel the urgency but finally she stood over

Daniel's shoulder. Thank god it wasn't too late. Nora waited for Petal's warning for Daniel to stop.

Daniel knew Petal stood behind him and he tried to swivel around while keeping Nora under control. Nora might be able to take advantage of his distraction and wrench free.

She threw herself backward and bucked against Daniel.

"No. Don't." He sounded frantic.

Please, just let Petal do something effective. We might get out of here alive.

Nora expected Petal to knock Daniel in the head with the gun but she leaned down slowly. She reached toward his back.

Daniel pulled away. "NO! Nora, stop her!" He started to get to his feet, knocking into Petal and sending her off balance. She stumbled backward.

He whirled around, ready to lunge for the gun. It wouldn't be hard for Daniel to overpower Petal. Then he'd shoot them both.

Petal brought the gun up with both hands. Daniel surged forward.

The bang of the gunshot exploded in Nora's ears as Daniel's his arms flew out. Down puffed from the blackened hole in his chest, just above his heart. He was airborne momentarily then his full weight crashed onto Nora, knocking the wind out of her.

The echo of the shot faded and Nora realized the sound ringing in her ears was her own screaming.

Daniel sprawled on top of her. His head slipped off her shoulder into the snow. Blood gushed from the gaping hole in his left shoulder blade. Petal had aimed for his heart and missed. He groaned.

Maybe he wanted to kill them both the way he'd murdered Mark, but this was horrible. Beyond horrible.

"Stop screaming," Petal said, deadly calm.

It might have been Petal's uncharacteristic chill that shocked Nora to silence.

Nora squeezed out from underneath Daniel, her arm numb from the pain and cold. His blood gushed over her coat and jeans, leaving a sticky, warm mess.

Nora's hands shook as she leaned over Daniel. "We need an ambulance." She searched for something to use to apply pressure. There was so much blood.

She wanted to help him but she needed to be with Cole.

The fresh scent of the mountain and the snow couldn't wash away the stench of Daniel's blood. She wanted to vomit to rid herself of the sight, the smell, the memory. Mark, Sylvia, Daniel.

Heather.

Petal remained motionless, the gun weighing down her arm. She watched Nora with no expression.

Nora ran to Cole. He lay on his side, trembling in the snow. She managed to roll him onto his back.

He opened his eyes, cloudy with shock. "Nora."

The jeans covering his right calf were dark and soaked with blood. It stained the snow, so much like the carpet in Sylvia's bedroom covered in Mark's blood. "He shot you?"

Cole shook his head. "Petal..."

Petal. The tower. Nora twisted to locate Petal watching the point on the horizon where the sun would appear. She shouted at Petal. "Did you dismantle the tower, yet?"

Petal shook her head.

"We don't have much time." Nora yelled.

Still Petal didn't move.

Nora bent toward Cole. "Hang on. I have to go."

Cole's hand shot out and grabbed her wrist. "No."

She pulled from his weak grasp. "I'll be right back."

Nora stumbled and slid over the rocks. She fell to her knees and fought to keep moving. Over the first ridge.

Petal finally came to life and followed her.

Nora slipped going down the second ridge and landed on her tailbone. She had to wait until her legs would move again. Petal caught up to her.

It surprised Nora that Petal still held the gun. She must be more shocked than Nora thought.

"Go to the tower," Nora said. "I've got to help Cole. Daniel shot him."

"Daniel didn't shoot Cole." Petal's voice held a flat calm that sounded eerie.

Nora started back to Cole, only paying slight attention to Petal.

"I did."

49

Relief flooded Nora. "You did? You dismantled the tower? Before Daniel got here? Good. Let's go." She grabbed Petal's arm.

Petal shook her off. "No," Petal said, again with the strange flat voice. Her face didn't have the typical Petal vulnerability. Instead, her eyes glittered with lethal intent. "I shot Cole."

Nora couldn't comprehend Petal's words. "What?"

"I shot Cole and if Daniel hadn't attacked me I would have shot him, too. Then I would have killed you." Petal raised the gun and pointed it at Nora.

"Petal, no!" Nora didn't understand.

Petal's face contorted in rage. "What a condescending, arrogant bitch you are. You have to take care of helpless Petal. Be big and strong for her, make sure no one hurts her feelings. Do you know how I laughed while I manipulated you to do exactly what I planned?"

The sky lightened. How long until dawn? Minutes? Seconds? "I thought we were friends."

"I needed you to turn Sylvia in for embezzlement and the project would have been mine. As it should have been. Once the missing money was discovered it wouldn't be hard to pin Darla's murder on Sylvia."

"You stole the money? Sylvia didn't kill Darla?" She focused on Petal's gun.

"Don't you dare think I enjoyed shooting Darla. It was terrible. But I had to do it. For my mother."

Keep her talking. "Does your mother know what you've done?"

Petal's face reflected a frightening combination of tears and pride. "I'm protecting her. Like she protected Sylvia."

How would Nora get to the tower before Petal shot her? "It sounds complicated."

"What's complicated is creating a technology and setting it up to cause a volcanic eruption." Her voice rose to a shriek and she wiped her sleeve across her runny nose.

"So you killed Mark?"

Petal's eyebrows angled into angry slashes. Her lips drew back in a sneer. "Sylvia did that. I told you, I don't like killing."

"But you're about to kill thousands and thousands."

"I have no choice." Where the old Petal would have been sobbing, this new monster twisted her mouth into a grimace of hate.

Nora calculated the distance to Petal. "There's always a choice." One more step.

Petal shoved the gun at Nora. "You can't stop me."

Oh yeah? Nora jumped to the right and zigzagged to fling herself at Petal.

Petal fired. The bullet struck the rock where Nora had been standing. Petal couldn't aim again before Nora smashed into her.

"Uft." Petal fell back on her butt.

Nora splayed on top of Petal, driving her into the snow. Petal's arm flung out but she still gripped the gun. Nora reached for it. How was it that petite Petal had the arms of an ape and Nora couldn't reach her hand?

Petal screeched and bucked against Nora, bringing a knee up to smash into Nora's groin. It might have been an effective move if Nora had alternative anatomy. It hurt, sure, but it didn't stop Nora from scooting on top of Petal and grabbing the gun.

She should have been able to pull it easily from Petal's grasp, but Nora's fingers cramped with cold. Petal held on.

Nora took hold of Petal's wrist, yanked her arm in the air and smashed it down on the hard ground. Petal's grip loosened and she dropped the gun.

Nora struggled to her feet and scooped up the gun and ran to the outcropping of rocks, desperate to reach the tower. The gun made it hard for her to scramble across the boulders on her hand and feet. She ratcheted her arm back and snapped it forward, sending the gun end over end into the abyss. Slipping and sliding, she finally made it to the top of the rock and located the tower. She would have to climb on the narrow ledge to the fenced enclosure and scale the chain link.

Her control slipped. A black veil threatened at the edge of her mind. She couldn't do it. Impossible to force herself to dangle on the lip of the mountain like that.

Nora dropped to her knees. Her heart threatened to rip through her chest. Her vision blurred. She gulped and choked.

And there he was. A flash of bright blue in the gray light.

The kachina.

He balanced on the ledge next to the fence. Enemy or friend?

Nora glanced over her shoulder. Petal raced toward her. But she wore Cole's too-big boots so Nora could outrun her.

The rocky surface covered with eight inches of new snow threw hidden obstacles in Nora's path. She stubbed her toes, fell to her knees, and her arm went from excruciating to debilitating. She kept her focus on the kachina.

He raised his hatchet with one hand. The other held a fistful of feathers. The blue accent of his sash flashed with brilliance. His fierce mask with the slit eyes and plug nose, the face in her nightmares, seemed to encourage her.

With the oversized coat and boots, Petal should be falling behind but she gained on Nora.

Just a few more feet.

Nora launched herself on the five-foot fence. She hoped to start high enough that she'd be able to throw her good arm around the top on the second lunge.

The toes of her boost were too wide for the narrow chain link openings. She fell back. Without hesitating she jumped to her feet to try again. This time, she worked with her momentum and kicked against the fence as soon as she touched it.

It worked. With the second lurch up, she threw her arm over the top of the fence, knocking the snow from the rail. Her feet kicked and she pulled and finally fell down the other side.

"AH!" She screamed at the jarring of her arm.

The fence clanked as Petal jumped onto it.

The enclosure left only the barest room to maneuver between the tower and the fence. Nora stared at the tower. How could she destroy it?

Petal crashed over the fence. She scrambled to her feet. "Stop. Don't touch it!"

The thingy. The conductor/transducer/transmitter/inductor. What had Petal had called it? The tunable whatever made of two PVC pipes with wire. She needed to find it and pull it out.

Petal launched herself at Nora. They careened into the fence. It stretched and swayed over the edge of the mountain. The posts at either corner loosened in their anchors.

Nora shoved back and they rolled to the ground. Petal ended up on top. The heel of Petal's hand caught Nora on the chin and pressed upward, driving Nora's head back. With her one arm, Nora knocked Petal's hand away.

Petal was little more than fragile bones wrapped in twenty layers of fabric topped with Cole's coat. Nora shoved Petal off and stood. She lunged toward the tower and bent under the structural supports. She felt along the stem. There it was! Her numb fingers fumbled with a device about the size of brick, made of two plastic pipes.

Petal collided with her. She pushed Nora toward the loose fence. Nora's boots slid on the slick rock and she lurched backward.

Petal shoved her.

Nora hit the fence. It creaked.

One corner post popped from its anchor and tipped outward. Nora screamed. The bend of the wire created a lip in the chain link that would pour her over the side. Her fingers clawed into the openings and she held on. She pushed and pulled herself back to safety.

Petal stood above her waiting for Nora to climb to the rock so she could push her over the side.

Petal's mouth turned down as if she bit into something sour. Her eyes widened. Her arms flew out just before Nora heard a shot fired.

Petal screamed. A gaping hole blew through Petal's chest. Warm blood and tissue smacked Nora's face and spattered against her coat. Petal crumpled to the ground.

Nora scurried off the fence a few feet through the snow. She stayed on her belly and turned toward the gunshot.

The man from the Town Car stared through a scope in a rifle pointed at her. He stood on the tip of a rock pile jutting over the ledge.

Twenty yards behind the man, Cole advanced, dragging his wounded leg. The fool was trying to save her.

The Town Car guy would shoot Nora, turn and plant a bullet in Cole.

Nora backed up and squatted on the far edge of the enclosure. She had to get to the tower, giving Town Car Guy an easy target.

To the east, the outline of Gray's Peak blackened against the imminent sunrise.

Nora had one chance. She'd have to spring up and grab the tunable whatever from the tower before Town Car Guy could squeeze off a round and kill her.

Impossible.

Nora closed her eyes. She exhaled, opened her eyes, and sprang up.

A shot pinged the fence, hit a rock and ricocheted a hair's width from Nora.

She dove for the tower, hitting hard rock under the snow. She lay at the base of the tower. Above her, the device sat in the stem. She'd need to grasp it immediately and when Town Car's bullet ripped into her and she flew backward, her dead fingers would clutch the bundle and dislodge it.

One more breath in this life. She jumped up. Her fingers closed on the device.

The metal of the tower rang next to her ear and she heard Town Car's gun. He missed.

She jerked on the device and looked over her shoulder.

Cole had closed the gap but he wouldn't make it to stop the next shot.

The gunman held his rifle up, sighting into the scope.

Nora caught her breath. She tugged on the device and it inched from its slot. One more pull and it fell to the snow. She knew Town Car Guy's next shot would kill her.

But it never came. She jerked her head to see him shoot.

The kachina appeared behind Town Car Guy. He held his hatchet high.

The kachina brought it down on the gunman's back. The shot fired into the air and the man lost his footing. He fought to regain his balance but he slipped to one side. His foot flew in front of him and he fell forward. He hit one boulder and slid off.

His scream echoed in the morning air.

EPILOGUE

The smell of burnt toast wafted up from the kitchen. The *tick-tick-tick* of wheels sounded as Thomas brought his bike into his office. Fay's creaky voice greeting him and Bill joined in the morning murmur of voices down the hall from Nora's office.

Creak, thump. Creak, thump. Creak, thump.

Nora smiled at the sound and continued typing the staff memo. Abbey stood and stretched. He wagged his tail while he walked to the door of Nora's office.

Creak, thump. Creak, thump. First the rubber tips of the crutches and then Cole appeared in her doorway. He grinned. "Too bad your office isn't on the first floor."

She pecked her name on the keys of her computer with her one good hand. "And too bad I don't have voice recognition software."

He bent over his crutches and scratched Abbey's ears. "We're in pretty sorry shape."

Nora pressed Send. "But happy to be alive."

Cole shook his head and eyed Nora. "I can't get over how a gust of wind could have knocked him over the side like that."

It wasn't the first time Cole seemed skeptical. He never saw the kachina, of course, but didn't quite buy a freak gust. Oh well, he could blame his fuzziness on the concussion he got when Petal shot him and he banged his head on a rock when he fell. She switched topics. "I stopped in to see Daniel this morning."

He leaned on his crutches. "Just came from there, myself."

"Any change?" She hoped Cole had good news but she didn't expect it.

"Still in a coma."

Neither one spoke of a moment. Nora sent a silent prayer into the universe and wondered if Cole did too.

Cole lumbered to one of the wicker chairs and sank down. "I thought about bringing you coffee but didn't have enough hands for all of that."

She shook her head. "I'm off the coffee for a while. I'm afraid there might be more than cream added to it."

Fay poked her head into Nora's office and croaked. "What do I need to know before you leave?"

Nora pointed to her corn plant. "He needs to be watered every few days. He likes it if you'll sing to him."

Fay questioned with her eyes.

"Okay, just talk to him when you give him water." Nora had turned into one of those eccentric plant ladies. Next thing you know she'd be wearing purple hats and talking to herself. She caught sight of the purple ski cap she'd worn that morning. At least she had dogs and plants to talk to.

And Cole. She had him to talk to.

"Anything else?" Fay asked.

"The bills are paid, payroll is set to hit at the end of next week. I'll be back in time for the staff meeting on the tenth."

Fay nodded.

"I'll check in every couple of days by cell."

"Gotcha. Have a good time." Fay waved and left.

A good time wasn't necessarily what Nora sought.

Cole studied her. "You sound like a real live Executive Director."

"I am a real live Executive Director."

"Does it feel good to be in charge again?"

She laughed. "Again? When have I ever been in charge of anything?"

Cole grew serious. "So you're leaving for the rez today?"

She turned her computer off. "Abigail is supposed to pick me up any minute. Charlie's been bugging her for the last three weeks to get home."

"How long will you be gone?"

The anxiety surged and she stood to shake it off. "Two weeks. I'll stay with Benny's cousin. Well my cousin, I guess."

"Total Hopi immersion. I won't know you."

Ask. Do it. She braced herself. "Will you be here when I get back?"

His ears turned red. "Do you want me to be?"

She trembled and a tornado roared in her brain. Commitment. Saying yes sunk her deeper. It was a bigger deal than even caring for Abbey.

What a drama queen!

If she could face down her fear of the mountain and embrace the strangeness of Hopi, maybe she could take this one more step. "I'd like that."

His grin widened. "Do you promise I won't get shot again?"

She shook her head. "With as much certainty as you can guarantee you won't break my heart."

He pulled himself up. *Creak, thump. Creak, thump.*

Nora waited. Her skin tingled with anticipation; her heart stuttered a giddy cadence. Wait a minute. That didn't feel like fear. It didn't smell of panic. She remembered happy and this felt strangely like that.

Creak, thump.

He finally stood close enough she felt the heat of him through his flannel shirt. His smile faded and his eyes turned that deep blue she recognized. He leaned forward and brushed his lips softly against hers. "Nora Abbott," he whispered. "you are dangerous."

She closed her eyes and inhaled the warmth of him. She stepped even closer and wound her good arm around his neck. Even in the city he smelled of outdoors, fresh air, pines, a breeze.

His crutches banged on the floor as he gently slid his arms around her, careful of her broken arm.

He bent his head to hers and kissed her in a way that promised more. "I guess you're worth a bullet or two."

CANYON OF LIES

A NORA ABBOTT MYSTERY

To Janet Fogg
My hero.

1

Warren Evans felt the hand of God wrap around him, holding him straight and strong. Others might panic or lose their temper, but with God's help, Warren waited for the chaos in his head to subside.

He picked up his phone and resumed the conversation. "I see." Barely controlled rage strangled his nephew's voice. "She figured it out. I don't know how. But she was going to expose us."

Warren leaned back, and the well-oiled springs of his chair whispered in his spacious office. He gazed out the window overlooking Central Park, the trees a mass of green. But his thoughts were in the canyon lands of his childhood.

The Promised Land.

The impossible red rock formations rising in majestic splendor under the vast sky, a blue never visible in New York City. He imagined the circling hawk and heard its cry echoing off God's canvas. He longed to see the hoodoos—the tall rock spires that marched across the high deserts of southern Utah—defending the castles of stone carved by wind and water, to feel the searing sun on his skin and taste the pure air.

Instead, he addressed his nephew in clipped tones. "Did you get the footage she's completed?"

"I'm working on it." Anger ebbed from his nephew's voice.

Warren clenched his fist, resisting the urge to pound it on the distressed surface of his antique oak desk. He stared at his hand, commanding his fingers to relax, then spoke with his characteristic authority. "That means you aren't sure she has it on tape."

His nephew swallowed. "She told Rachel she'd been to Fiery Furnace. We couldn't take the chance."

Fiery Furnace. Mention of the name sent a wave of longing through Warren. He should be in Moab instead of his corner office high above Manhattan's streets. With the end so near, they needed a steady hand, and he needed the strength and comfort of the land. The first lights announcing evening flicked on in countless other offices, but Warren sat in the growing gloom, straining to see the sky.

"I've done what needed to be done," his nephew said. "For you." Bile burned Warren's throat. "For us. For mankind."

Pause. That hesitation of a nonbeliever. "And you'll lead us."

Those words hit like knives. Leading his flock had sustained him for years. But it would soon be over for him. Like Moses and even Martin Luther King, Jr.—though Warren hated to compare himself to a black man—Warren wouldn't enter the land of milk and honey with his people. God had told him that much.

But God hadn't told him who would lead in Warren's place.

Time was running out, and Warren needed to decide which of his nephews would inherit the mantel.

2

Nora Abbott shut her eyes against the onslaught of icy water. She gasped in shock at the fury of the wave as it slapped at her face and knocked her against the back of the raft. Her feet slipped from the rubber strap that anchored her to the boat. Disoriented, she scrambled to her knees. The raft bucked and lurched, tossing her from side to side. She clutched the rigging threaded around the raft and braced herself to face downstream.

The raft crested the top of a swell and the canyon narrowed. Nothing but foam, frigid waves, and rocks ahead. The raft tilted to the right, banged against a boulder, and pitched forward, careening through another wave. It smashed into the canyon wall.

Nora popped from the waffling bottom. Her feet flew over her head. She clawed for the rope, but her fingers only scratched at slick rubber. A somersault catapulted her from the raft and she splashed into the freezing river, cracking her tailbone on rock.

Fighting for her breath in the glacial water, she succeeded in flipping onto her back with her feet pointed downstream. The life vest offered neck support and her wetsuit and splash jacket kept her from instant hypothermia. She cooperated with the current until the canyon walls widened and the water calmed. She navigated to the bank, struggled for solid footing, and crawled out of the river moments before the raft crashed into the bank.

Cole jumped from the raft, nearly flattening her. He yanked on the rigging and the raft slid out of the water, coming to rest on the grassy bank. He spun around, breathless, his eyes wild, and focused on Nora, surveying her from head to toe. Apparently satisfied that she had indeed survived, he relaxed as his face split into a grin. "Whoo-hoo!"

Nora whooped in response, releasing tension. "I've never seen this river so full."

They'd pulled out in a small meadow—green grass lit by bright Colorado sunshine, edged in by pines and a few elms. The Rocky Mountains rose on either side of the Poudre River, where a heavy spring runoff raged. The rapids roared upstream, but peace reigned here.

They shrugged out of their life vests. Cole settled to the ground, pulling off Neoprene socks and wiggling his water-wrinkled toes. His sandy-colored hair dripped, and he pushed it back on his forehead.

Nora stripped off the splash jacket to let the sun warm her. She yanked the elastic from her ponytail and squeezed her shoulder- length hair, wringing out the river water. Stretching into the raft, she unbuckled the water bottle securely fastened to the rigging. She flopped down on the grass next to Cole and handed him the bottle. The sun kissed her and she tilted her head to catch its heat while the breeze teased a few strands of her drying, copper-colored hair into her face. "Whose great idea was it to play hooky today?"

He leaned back with easy grace. "You needed to get out of the office."

He was right. Probably. "What if Lisa needs something?" "She'll figure it out." A mountain wren twittered, answered by more sweet birdsong.

Nora ignored the knot trying to form in her belly. "She called yesterday while I was Skyping with the board about forest restoration. I figured she'd call back if there was an emergency."

Cole's eyebrows raised in surprise. "That doesn't sound like you." "It's killing me, but I'm trying to learn to delegate more."

He kissed her. "And you're making fine progress."

They watched the river race past. She stole a glance at Cole and found him smiling, his blue eyes twinkling. "What?" she asked.

He shrugged. "Nothing."

She landed a playful punch on his arm. "Talk to me."

He laughed. "I'm from Wyoming. Men aren't big on sharing feelings there."

"Says the man who insists I tell him everything like he's a therapist. Come on. It can't be bad—you're smiling."

He let his gaze rest on her and his smile faded. The blue of his eyes deepened. "I was thinking how damned lucky I am to have found someone who fits me so well."

His simple words took her breath with as much force as the icy river. "Me too," she whispered and kissed him.

They took a moment together, making out on the bank like teenagers. It was a perfect day—too perfect. At that thought, worry flooded in and Nora sat back.

"The film deadline is tomorrow. Lisa says she's almost done, but I haven't seen it." Reminding herself of the timeline sapped her of the exhilaration from the rapids and from her day with Cole. So much rested on the success of the film.

This was Nora's first big project as executive director of Living Earth Trust. She'd hired her college friend, Lisa Taylor, to create a feature film documenting Canyonlands National Park in Utah and the threats it faced. They were scheduled to screen the film for a committee of congressmen to advocate for expansion of the park's boundaries.

A flash of blue in the trees behind Cole made Nora gasp. Cole twisted to look. He turned back to her. "What?"

She inspected the tree where she thought she'd seen the blue, then plastered on a smile. "Nothing."

"Is he there?" He studied her.

So much for brushing it off. Cole knew about her kachina. "No. I haven't seen him in months."

A blue jay squawked and fluttered onto a pine bough behind Cole, as if mocking her.

"That's good, right?" Cole asked.

Nora didn't miss him, exactly. "It's great. Who needs a visit from an ancient Hopi spirit? It's scary, and he always gets me into trouble anyway."

Cole didn't look convinced. "Except you'd like to see him."

There was no hiding from Cole. He knew her better than anyone and, surprisingly, still wanted to be with her. She'd struck a gold mine in him. "He made me feel like ..." She struggled for the words. "Like maybe I really am Hopi and, well ... " Exposing herself like this, even to Cole, made her hesitate. "Like I might belong."

"Belong to what?"

He actually seemed to take her doubts seriously. Once again, he proved she could trust that he really cared. "I don't look Hopi. I've got no evidence. But as long as a kachina shows up every now and then, I don't feel like a poseur."

Cole threw an arm around her shoulder. "You worry too much." "I used to dream about him. And even though I've been dreaming about Hopi stuff, he's not appearing. And then I wake up nervous."

"I think you're dropping off to sleep nervous, fretting about Lisa's film."

She rested her head on his shoulder. "Probably. But these dreams are vivid. I'm standing in front of a petroglyph panel in the desert. There's this big design with concentric circles, like a bull's- eye, and lines shoot out from it."

"Like a sunburst?" Cole lowered to rest on his back, moving slowly so Nora lowered down, too.

She'd dreamed about it so often that she could see the petroglyph in detail. "Kind of, but not really. Instead of rays all around the circle, there are two parallel lines spaced evenly around it. Anyway, in my dream, I'm looking at it and feeling all this angst."

His voice vibrated in her head. "That's it?"

The sound of a telephone interrupted them. It was muffled, but Nora's ears pricked. She jumped up and raced for the raft. It rang again while she fumbled to unbuckle the dry sack from the rigging. She unrolled the top of the sack, but by the time she dug through the towels and lunch to find her phone, it had stopped.

Cole stayed on the ground with his hands behind his head. "You brought your phone along on your day off?"

Nora glanced at the caller ID. "I thought it might be Lisa." "And?"

"It's Abigail."

"You don't want to talk to your mother?"

Nora switched the alert to vibrate and set the phone on the raft. She gathered up the sandwiches and apples and settled next to Cole. "She only wants to tell me about a new skin product or alert me to an executive position opening up in some bank. Besides, I said I'd take the day off to spend with you, and that's what I'm going to do. Sorry I weakened."

Her phone vibrated. Cole raised his eyebrows. Nora opened a plastic container and pulled out half a ham sandwich. "Abigail's nothing if not determined."

"You don't think it's Lisa?"

With determination, Nora said, "I'm taking the day off."

Cole sank his teeth into an apple. A muted Mexican tune played from the raft.

Nora listened in surprise, then grinned. "You brought your phone, too?"

Cole shrugged. He stood and hurried to the raft. "Guess it's my turn now."

He found it easily in the near-empty bag, swiped it on, and held it to his ear.

Nora took another bite of the sandwich, enjoying the salty ham after the exertion of their morning on the river. Slowly, Cole's influence had pulled her from her driven, make-every-moment-productive lifestyle to one where she took the time to enjoy what she loved: Cole and being outside.

She realized she hadn't heard Cole speak. She twisted toward him. His face seemed to melt as it went from happy to serious to alarm.

Her phone vibrated again, and she debated. No. She and Cole still had a day off together, and she'd cling to that.

It only took seconds for Cole's shocked expression to harden with control. He had formed a plan and was ready for action. He lowered the phone and stared at a spot above her head, obviously working out details in his mind.

When she couldn't wait any longer, she asked, "What's wrong?" "That was Mom. Dad had a stroke a couple of days ago and..."

He gathered up the sandwich container and started stuffing things in the dry bag.

Nora followed, once again ignoring her phone when it started buzzing. "A couple of days ago and she's just calling you now?"

He didn't address that. "My brother is causing some trouble and I need to get up there and see what's going on." He picked up his life vest and shrugged into it.

"Your younger brother?" "My only brother, Derek."

She retrieved her life vest. "What kind of trouble could he be causing?"

For the first time since Nora had known him, he snapped at her. "I don't want to talk about it. I've got to go home."

"Home? As in Wyoming?"

He inspected the raft to make sure it hadn't been damaged in the rapids. "Yes. I don't know much, but I need to get up to the ranch and see what's happening."

He secured the water bottle. Nora rolled the top of the dry sack. He strode away from her, crashing into the forest. "Pit stop."

Nora moved to buckle the dry sack when her phone went off again. Their day together had taken a bad turn; she might as well answer. She checked the ID. At least it wasn't Lisa with a problem. "Hello, Mother."

"Nora! Thank god. I've been trying to call you. Don't you ever check your phone? I've left you a million messages since early this morning." Abigail sounded distraught, but that could mean anything from suffering a paper cut to losing her house in an earthquake.

Damn. Maybe that's why she hadn't heard from Lisa. "This stupid phone drops messages sometimes. I don't know why."

"You need a decent plan with a legitimate company. Not that one you got for Trust employees because it's the greenest."

"Okay, whatever." Nora began with the usual questions. "Is something wrong? Is Charlie okay?" Abigail's fourth husband, Charlie, traipsed off into the mountains outside of their Flagstaff cabin nearly every day. So many accidents lurked in the wilderness.

"We're fine, dear. But ... "

Something in Abigail's voice made Nora hold her breath. "What?"

"Sit down. Is Cole with you?"

"Just tell me, Mother."

"I don't know how to say this." "Mother!"

"Okay, okay." Nora pictured Abigail waving her arms. She waited impatiently while Abigail drew in a deep breath. "Rachel called me."

"Rachel? Lisa's wife? Why would she call you?" *Because Lisa couldn't.*

"Nora, please; you're not making this any easier."

Part of Nora wanted to scream at Abigail to spit it out. Another part wanted to end the call and turn the phone off.

"Nora, I'm so sorry, but Lisa had an accident."

Nora's breath caught in her throat. "What kind of accident? Is she okay?" How soon could Nora get home and pack her car for the six-hour drive to Moab? How many days would this put the film behind schedule? Nora would have to take over and do whatever Lisa needed her to do. Together they'd meet the deadline. They had to.

Abigail made a clicking noise as if her throat refused to form the words. Nora tapped on the warm rubber of the raft, hating Abigail's struggle. "Is she injured? How bad is it?"

Finally Abigail's voice found the words. It sounded like they had traveled through a tunnel from the center of the world. They rang in Nora's brain, refusing to make sense.

"Nora, honey. Lisa's dead."

3

Warren Evans pushed himself to sit up. His weak fingers clasped the protein drink, and he raised it. The can's metal cooled his lips. The vanilla-flavored concoction touched his tongue, and he lowered his shaky hand to set the can in a shaft of sunlight on the desk. A drop of white splashed against the oak.

Nausea overwhelmed him, and he waited for it to pass.

He concentrated on the blueprints spread across his desk that detailed the masterpiece he'd created. With God's help, of course.

His calculations satisfied him that he'd provided perfectly. Three more groups planned to arrive in Moab today. He needed to contact his nephew to make sure everything was in place.

He paused and fought his stomach for control. And won. At least he'd already lost his hair and it wasn't coming out in handfuls everywhere. His new toupee pleased him. It had cost him more than his first house, but it looked natural. He assumed the housekeeper or one of her workers had vacuumed up the evidence of his weakness.

He knew for certain Christine wouldn't. She barely spoke to him these days.

Trying not to think about his wife of nearly thirty years, he sighed and reached for his phone.

Christine only wanted him for what he gave her in this life. She loved his wealth. She'd smiled and kissed him at every charity ball and political fundraiser from here to Hollywood, but she hadn't shared his bed for a decade. And when she'd learned of his illness, she'd only grown more distant.

She was a great public and business asset, but she'd provided him with no heir and gave him little comfort as he neared his end. Still, with the trust fund she'd handed over for his use after they were married, she'd been a fortuitous initial down payment on his fortune.

Now, with time dwindling, he needed to make sure nothing was left undone. Warren pushed speed dial and waited.

"Uncle Warren. How's New York?"

Warren lied, "I only have a moment. We're about to hit the back nine." Warren lowered his head and closed his eyes, willing himself not to vomit. His heirs didn't need to know about his illness.

"Weather must be good there." His nephew's voice held the slightest edge of resentment.

Warren forced a good-natured chuckle. "I know you're working hard. It's the curse of the young."

"Enjoy your rest. You've earned it."

Warren said, "I just learned another group will join the other two today. You need to meet them for initiation rites and instructions."

"I've already been in touch with them, and it's all arranged."

Warren liked the way his nephew took charge. Did he have the faith to lead the chosen? "And the film?"

His nephew paused. "I'm making some progress." Warren clenched his teeth. "What about Rachel?"

More uncomfortable silence. "She's planning the funeral."

Acting as if she were a widow. When did homosexuality become so respectable? "She's vulnerable. Now is the time to approach her."

"I'll see her tomorrow at the service. I'll talk to her then."

Warren sat back. The chair used to fit like a power suit, with the soft leather caressing him like a lover. Now he felt dwarfed in its massive expanse and the leather chafed his skin. "Find the camera, too. Her last images could be damaging."

"I'll find them. What's going on in Washington?"

He couldn't blame his nephew for asking. Warren hadn't told anyone the timeline, and they didn't know the end would come sooner than they expected. "The debate is close. Stanley insists expanding Canyonlands will devastate the local economy. Ruben waves the letter from the Outdoor Industry Association defending expansion. Right now the congressmen on the energy corporation's payroll probably hold a slight lead."

His nephew sounded worried. "They can't see the propaganda on that film or we'll lose the homestead."

Warren's jaw ached from grinding his teeth. "I'm glad you see the importance of getting that film."

"You know you can count on me."

4

Nora pulled up in front of the Days Inn in Moab. She'd risen before dawn to drive the six hours from Boulder to arrive in plenty of time for Lisa's funeral. She climbed from the Jeep into the bright sunshine and let Abbey, her aging Golden Retriever, hobble out and water a tire.

The sun lit the red rocks around her, chasing off the morning chill. Light air tickled Nora's senses, tingling with new-day freshness. Moab hadn't awakened yet, so voices and bustles didn't disturb the town as it stretched and yawned and readied itself for another day.

Lisa loved mornings like this. A thousand phone conversations had started with Lisa's breathless account of a sunrise bursting over the jagged purple La Sals or of the play of light on the red canyon walls. Lisa couldn't wait to be out in the majestic beauty of the towering red rocks.

Only three days ago—maybe a warm day, just like this—Lisa had gone for another shot of petroglyphs at the Moonflower campground. At dusk, the light faded, and she'd have put her camera away. Why had she climbed the ancient log scaffolding deep in the crevice? The prehistoric site was restricted, and Lisa respected that kind of protection, especially the antiquities she cherished. It made no sense for her to cross the barrier and wedge herself in the incredibly narrow space where the Anasazi had set logs zig-zagging up the straight walls. They'd cut slices out of the logs, worn smooth by countless feet and centuries of weather, to create a ladder to the top of the deep canyon.

It seemed unbelievable that Lisa, mountain goat that she was, would lose her footing and fall. Even more unlikely was that the fall would snap her neck so cleanly, killing her instantly.

A stone stuck in Nora's throat. Instantly killed, like Scott. Only her husband's death hadn't been an accident. Nora pushed the thought away.

So many hikes, so many miles they'd covered together—Nora couldn't believe they'd never share another adventure again. Her throat tightened. How could Lisa be gone?

Nora stretched the kinks from her back and walked into the hotel. She approached the front desk and the young man behind it.

"I need a room for tonight."

He shook his head slowly. Any quick movement of his body might have caused his khaki chinos to slide the last half inch off his narrow hips and puddle on the floor at his feet. The company tie didn't quite cover a dark stain on his wrinkled Oxford shirt. "I'm really sorry, ma'am," he said. "This bike race's eaten up all the rooms. There's nothin' left anywhere around Moab."

Nora leaned on the chest-high counter in the cool, tastefully decorated hotel lobby. A teenaged girl clanked dishes while she straightened up what was left of the breakfast buffet in an alcove off the lobby. Just one more problem. But one that would have to wait. She had a half-hour to get to Lisa's funeral, and though she'd hiked the trail with Lisa before, she didn't remember the exact location of the trailhead and how far up the creek the mourners would gather.

She left the air-conditioned lobby and walked into the hotel parking lot, the summer sun blazing overhead. Memory stalled her—her last conversation with Lisa, just days ago. She'd been updating her on all of the Trust's projects.

Nora had munched on her deli turkey sandwich and caught up with Lisa via Skype.

Lisa's eyes twinkled, even through the blur of the screen. She sat in front of her laptop in her renovated cabin in Castle Valley. She'd chosen Castle Valley because it was an enclave of like- minded liberals twenty miles outside of Moab. "This is an unbelievable experience. I'm learning so much! Not only about the land but about the history and about making a film."

Nora couldn't fault Lisa for lack of passion and energy. She swallowed the chipotle-laced turkey. "What about results? Is the film ready?"

Lisa laughed with the carefree delight Nora always envied. "You're so you —always cutting away the bullshit and going for the kill."

Nora slurped her coffee. "What about it? You're at deadline and thirty grand over budget."

Lisa looked startled. "That much? Wow. This is so worth it, Nor. This place —god, this place is gorgeous. You've got the funding, right?"

"Not millions, but enough for the proposed budget you just exceeded. That's not the point. I need something to show the board. Even more important, are you ready to take it to Washington?" The hard knot of worry balled in her belly, and she wadded up the remainder of her sandwich in the paper wrapper.

"I know the goal, Nor." Lisa ran a hand through her long mass of dark waves. She licked her full lips, chapped by days in the sun. "And I'll get it done. I sent you some footage."

"And it's as amazing as you've said. But you're spending a ton of money, and I haven't seen the whole thing."

Lisa rolled her eyes. "You'll be impressed by the dawn images, Fat Bottom-Line Girl. It's probably the shot that will seal the whole deal. How could anybody deny the park expansion after seeing it?"

"I know you're going all George Lucas out there, but you've got to wrap it up. Time is running out."

"Da, da, da ..." Lisa sang the doomsday notes and grinned at Nora, the sunlight streaming in through her home office windows and highlighting her own glow. "Lighten up, chica."

Nora shoved the coffee away, suspecting it contributed to the sour burn in her belly. "Maybe I'll get Cole and we'll come to Moab next week. You can show it to me then."

"Speaking of Cole and gorgeous, how's that hunk o' burning love of yours?"

The air surrounding Nora brightened, and an irresistible smile replaced her responsible executive director face. "Cole is great."

"And he's still treating you like a queen?"

Movement behind Lisa captured Nora's attention. Rachel bent over a table and shuffled through a pile of papers. "Hey, Rachel," Nora teased. "Would you keep Lisa on task and get me that film?"

Lisa hunched her shoulders as if taking cover.

Rachel whipped her head toward the computer screen. She glared at Nora across the miles. "You're the boss. You do it."

Rachel spared one scathing look for Lisa and whirled around. Footsteps stomped and a door squeaked open, then slammed closed.

Nora raised her eyebrows and waited for Lisa.

Lisa shrugged and showed a toothy grin tinged with discomfort. "She's cycling. You know how emotional women get." Rachel and Lisa had been together for three years. Last year, Nora had met them in Minnesota for their wedding. Same-sex marriage hadn't been legal in Utah at the time, but Minnesota had seemed like such a random pick. As far as Nora could tell, they were the perfect couple. "What's going on?"

Lisa's false cheer slipped. "She's had enough of the film, I guess."

Lisa glanced toward the door, then leaned closer to the screen and lowered her voice. "You gotta understand. Rachel's family has been out here forever. She's, like, fourth-generation Mormon. Obviously she's evolved, but it's not easy for her." Lisa's eyes twinkled as she teased. "Out here, everyone is on one side or the other. The hip, smart folks, like me, are for expansion, and the Neanderthals are on the other side."

"So Rachel doesn't believe in park expansion?"

Lisa was quick to respond. "Oh, she's on board. But it's causing her some grief, okay?"

"Her family is harassing her?"

Lisa shrugged again. "A little more than that."

Alarms jangled Nora's nerves. She tried to squelch the reaction—okay, overreaction. "Explain."

"The brakes went out of my old Toyota pickup last week. Rachel thinks someone tampered with them. But they were shot and needed to be replaced."

"Lisa!"

Lisa tossed her hair. "See? You and Rachel are more alike than you know. In fact, if you didn't have that strange preference for men, you and I might be married now."

Maybe for people with normal lives, no one tampered with brakes or plotted murder. But in Nora's world, these bizarre and dangerous things happened. "Be careful." But what she wanted to say was "Run!"

Lisa looked over her shoulder again. "Listen. I probably shouldn't say anything, and I promised myself I wouldn't until I get more information. But you know me, I can't keep a secret."

That wasn't entirely true. She'd kept her gayness from her family for over twenty years.

"But this is important. I was out at Fiery Furnace and I found this petroglyph—"

The door squeaked in the background.

Lisa jerked her head around. She turned back to the screen and the conspiratorial tone vanished. "Okay. Have a great week."

"Lisa, wait."

Lisa blew a kiss at the computer screen. "Love you, babe." She severed the connection.

Nora climbed into her dilapidated Jeep. Abbey wagged his tail and slapped his tongue in Nora's direction. She scratched behind his ears. "You're a good boy," Nora said, more to practice a solid voice than anything else.

Nora drove east out of town for several miles. The road ran along the Colorado River, which was usually wide and smooth here, a serene glide. Today, though, red silt raged, probably the result of a heavy rain upstream, swelling the banks. At least the water had a channel to travel here. In the open desert, it would cascade down any indentation and create dangerous flash floods.

She needn't have worried about locating the Moonflower trailhead. Cars and pickups and bikes spilled from the dirt parking lot to line the road.

Lisa had taken Nora on this trail before. It was one of her favorites. It wound next to a creek, along a valley of willows and cottonwoods. Then the trail climbed out on top of slick rock and, after a couple miles, dipped back into a box canyon with the sweetest swimming hole, complete with a rock slide. Nora and Lisa had spent a few lazy afternoons sunning on the rocks, swimming and talking about life.

They'd discovered the spot together on their first backpacking trip to

Canyonlands. They later learned it was a favorite spot for locals. Nora remembered one sunny day when she'd had an epiphany about her life.

Nora had sat up on the warm rock. "I know what I'm going to be when I grow up," she said to a dozing Lisa.

"The first woman president of the New York Stock Exchange?" "That," Nora agreed, "and an advocate for the environment. I want to do business and conservation."

Lisa rolled over and propped her head on her elbow. "You're not as confused as you think you are."

Nora would miss Lisa's way of clarifying her life.

Nora and Abbey climbed out and followed a group of three down the road, into the lot, and onto the one-track dirt trail. Watching the group ahead stung her. They were dressed in what Lisa referred to with rolled eyes as "Moab chic." One woman wore a short black skirt and leggings with Chacos on her feet. Another woman wore a green broomstick skirt and covered her head with a battered straw cowboy hat. The guy with them sported dreds that hung down to the middle of his back and were gathered in a tie-dyed bandana. He wore baggy shorts and a wrinkled T-shirt.

Deep drifts of fine, red sand covered the grass, burying smaller shrubs and piling around the willows. The destruction of a flash flood showed in the narrow canyon. It must have been a wild hour or so as the water screamed through, drowning anything unfortunate enough to be trapped on the canyon floor. Now the sand piled in drifts, still damp from yesterday's afternoon shower, and the clump grass and white flowers of the bindweed and evening primrose poked through the surface.

Vertical walls of sandstone rose high on either side, creating a slot canyon. Their variegated layers blended from yellows to reds with blackened surfaces near the top. The leaves of the cottonwoods rattled in the soft breeze with sweeping arms creating cover from the sun.

Nora and Abbey plodded after the others. She longed to feel the strength of Cole beside her, but he had his own problems to deal with in Wyoming. He'd been tight-lipped about that on the phone the last couple of days.

The day warmed enough that Nora removed her light jacket and tied it around her hips. It slapped against the back of her shorts as she trudged up the trail. Sand squeaked under her hiking boots with every step. She'd briefly considered dressing more formally but rejected the idea, knowing Lisa would think it pretentious. The burbling creek felt too cheerful for Nora's heavy heart. Even the air betrayed Nora's mood, smelling green and moist and full of summer's growth.

The three people ahead of Nora slowed behind an elderly couple making their way up the trail. Behind her, hushed voices of more people broke the silence. Bushes closed in on the hikers, and trees shaded the path. In a few moments Nora and the others entered a large clearing created by several slick red rocks. The creek, now back to normal after the flash flood some time ago, bubbled happily as it wound around the rocks and bumped against the cliff wall.

About fifty people crowded together under the willows and elms.

Rachel stood next to the creek. Her blond hair hung straight down her back. Her pale skin only highlighted her red-rimmed eyes and nose. Nora wanted to hug her, to tell her that it would be all right— but it wasn't all right. Rachel might love again. She might build a life full of exciting and fun challenges, might go on to be successful, and each day might radiate with happiness. But as Nora knew from her own experience after her husband's death two years ago, the pain would strike at odd moments. It would rush in like a black tide and wipe out the carefully constructed levy around her heart.

Not overly dramatic, huh, Nora? Okay, well, maybe that was all flowery and nostalgic. Nora and Scott had been headed for divorce, and it's likely that after they split, Nora would have felt a measure of the loss she felt now when she thought of Scott. But he hadn't had the chance to divorce Nora. He'd been murdered.

And Nora had stood on a mountaintop in Flagstaff, in very much the same way Rachel stood here.

Nora found a place at the back of the crowd so that Abbey could lie in the shade and not be stepped on. He settled under a bush, lowered his head to his paws, and dozed.

The crowd mostly consisted of outdoors types of various ages— from twenty-somethings all the way to gray-hairs. All wore hiking or casual clothes. Nora didn't spot any of Lisa's family, and she hadn't expected to.

They'd turned their backs on Lisa when she'd come out her sophomore year, and as far as Nora knew, Lisa hadn't wasted any time trying to bring them back into her life.

A man about Nora's age in faded Wranglers and cowboy boots stood by himself. He held a black felt cowboy hat that left a ring around his light brown hair. His lips flattened in a look of irritation and he glared at Rachel. Another, more handsome man stood behind Rachel, close enough to touch her. Nora wondered if he was her brother, though with his dark wavy hair, trim and fit body, and alert expression, he looked like her opposite.

Rachel cleared her throat. "I'm happy to see all of you here. Moonflower was Lisa's favorite place."

Rachel's composure impressed Nora. She'd barely been able to tie her shoes after Scott's death.

"There is nothing Lisa would have loved more than all of you gathered here in the sunshine."

Nora stared at the rock under her feet and fought the lump lodged in her throat. Someone sniffled. An older man put his arm around a gray-haired woman and pulled her close.

Rachel held her shoulders erect, her head high. "What I loved most about Lisa was her one hundred percent devotion to whatever she believed in."

Nora lost her fight for control and let the tears spill down her face. A smile threatened Rachel's pale lips. "She'd spend hours watching the giant white flowers of datura open in the evening, delighted with the hawk moths that came to pollinate it."

Rachel swallowed and continued. "After hiking trails all over the world and covering almost every foot of her beloved southern Utah wilderness, Lisa died from a freak accident. How did the land she loved so well betray her?"

Rachel's voice wavered and she pulled her shoulders back. "When we backpacked together, I always headed out on a mission. I'd pop out of the sleeping bag ready to hit the trail, putting miles under my feet. Lisa loved to linger. She'd sit quietly with one more cup of coffee and watch the sun slide over rocks, shadows changing slowly. She'd pause on the trail to watch a toothpick-size lizard perform pushups or just to listen to the stillness of the desert." Rachel swallowed a hiccup. "I loved to spend time outdoors with Lisa because she forced me to stop and appreciate what I might otherwise zoom past."

Rachel swiped at tears. "Thirty-three years weren't enough for someone so vital and passionate. She should have had a lifetime to savor, more time to help the land she devoted herself to. And I needed more years to love the woman who brought me so much happiness."

A sob sounded from somewhere to the right.

Rachel's voice hardened and rang clear in the morning sun. "It was her passion for this place, southern Utah, that killed her."

The anger in her tone made Nora lift her head.

Rachel's eyes burned into her. "I loved Lisa. But she could be stubborn." This message seemed aimed at Nora. A subdued chuckle of agreement sounded from those gathered.

"She couldn't leave well enough alone." Rachel's glare was so fierce a few people turned to look at Nora.

Rachel started to shake. All at once, her knees buckled. The man behind her leaped forward and closed his arms around her. She leaned into him and buried her head on his shoulder. He spoke in a clear, strong voice. "Rachel would be pleased if you'd join us for a reception at Read Rock Bookstore on Main Street."

Rachel's eyes looked vacant in her pale face, as if she'd used up every bit of emotional strength she possessed. She dropped her head, and the man took hold of her hand, and led her toward the trail.

Nora glanced up and met the malevolent stare of the man with the black cowboy hat. His dark eyes bored a hole through Nora's forehead. He slammed his hat on his head, pulled it low over his eyes, and stomped away.

He must have picked up on whatever ill will Rachel had directed her way.

A small group of people spoke quietly, several of them with wet eyes, some sniffing. "Obsessed with the film." "Probably exhausted." "Wonder what will happen with the film?"

Most people dribbled away from the clearing with heads down.

If they spoke at all, their words were too quiet for Nora to hear.

Eventually the mourners disappeared, leaving Nora shaken. She lowered herself to the ground, and Abbey rose from his spot under the tree. He sauntered over to her and accepted her caress.

Before Rachel faded, she'd been angry with Nora. Did she think Nora was responsible for Lisa's death? Lisa had begged Nora to fund the film. Had Lisa jumped in over her head, making her careless?

The sun danced through the branches. Humidity from a recent rain weighted the air and brought out the spice of sage and muted scent of damp sand. Life continued in an almost insulting way.

Nora wouldn't have been able to stop Lisa even if she hadn't funded the film. Lisa would have found another way.

Still, Nora's being here stabbed Rachel like a splintered arrow. Nora didn't want to cause her any more pain. She decided to quietly head back to Boulder.

She stood and brushed the dirt from her hiking shorts. A flash of blue caught her eye. Her heart jumped to her mouth, and she went numb.

Maybe her kachina was here in the sacred lands of the Southwest. With a growing hope that mingled with dread, Nora faced the spot where she'd seen the color. She stared in the bushes at the edge of the clearing and exhaled. No kachina. Her heart sank just a little.

But the blue hadn't been her imagination.

A wooden box with a beautiful inlaid band of blue sat on a rock by the creek. Nora approached it, Abbey at her heels. It sat alone, oddly at home in the natural setting. Sunlight danced along the inlay. Rachel had been so lost, she must have forgotten this.

Nora placed a hand on the sun-warmed surface of the box and sank to her knees.

It was Lisa.

5

The weight of Abbey's head rested comfortingly in her lap. Tiny wrens and warblers chirped and flitted amid the branches. The sun warmed the crown of Nora's head. The willows swayed gently, their wispy green leaves contrasting with the deeper green of the new grass peeking out from the sand. The creek chattered along the bend. To the life in the clearing, it was just another day.

The kindest thing for Rachel would be for Nora to skip the gathering at the bookstore and head back to Boulder. But Nora couldn't leave Lisa out here. She tightened her lips.

Nora shifted to stand, disturbing Abbey. He pulled himself up and shook, starting at his head and vibrating all the way to his tail.

"Guess we're going to Moab," she told him.

Nora picked up the polished wood box. Its heavy weight surprised her. The beauty of the intricate Native American inlaid border in blue and black suited Lisa's taste. It seemed impossible that Lisa's vibrancy and energy had been reduced to this.

Nora trudged up the path to the empty parking lot at the trailhead. The Jeep sat alone on the side of the road. Nora let Abbey in, placed Lisa's box on the floor of the passenger side, and climbed behind the wheel. She glanced up the quiet road and twisted to see the area behind her. Two lanes stretched in both directions, empty. About a quarter of a mile to the south, the road curved east. A slight rise to the north blocked the view after several yards. Nora hadn't seen any traffic on her walk from the trailhead. Like much of the area around Moab, this was a lonely stretch of road.

It was the emptiness Lisa had found so compelling. The vast swathes of rugged spires and canyons and stunning red rock formations resulting from millions of years of wind, ancient oceans, and the hands of the gods spoke to Lisa. She felt compelled to protect them from the modern world. Lisa raved about the archaeological sites with their petroglyphs and pottery shards much like other women might babble about their babies.

Nora inserted her key into the Jeep, and as she turned it, a squawking noise startled her. For a moment she thought she had a problem with her engine, then realized it was her phone. Fay, one of the staffers at the Trust, had programmed Nora's phone with bird calls. This one sounded like an angry raven. She reached into her pack in the back seat and pulled it out.

Along with the announcement for the incoming call, Nora noticed six new voicemails. She punched a button to answer.

"Etta here." The no-nonsense blast from the chairwoman of the Board for Living Earth Trust sent the usual ball of snakes into Nora's gut. "I've been thinking about Lisa Taylor and this situation."

Did Etta think the Trust should make a tribute? A grant in Lisa's name or tree-planting event would be nice. Maybe gather money from the staff for a memorial. "What situation?"

"The film, of course. We've invested well over a hundred thousand dollars so far. The committee vote is in three weeks, so they need to see this film tomorrow, if not yesterday."

Nora's grief left little space to worry about the film. "The screening is scheduled in two weeks. I'll be back in the office on Monday. Can I call you then?"

Etta exhaled. "Today is Thursday. I don't feel we have days to waste. How close was Lisa to completing the film?"

Nora stared out her windshield at the yellow wild asters and tried to sound like a smart and savvy executive director. She failed with her first uh. "I haven't seen much of the footage. Lisa wanted to edit it and show it to me when it was done so I'd get the full impact."

"Oh," Etta said and paused. "I would have thought you'd be in on the whole project."

Nora lowered her voice to sound more confident. "Lisa was close to being done."

"Good. Bring it back to Boulder. I'll meet you on Monday, and we'll see what we need to do from there."

The last thing Nora wanted to do was to confront Rachel and ask for Lisa's work. "I'm not sure I can do it that soon."

Etta's long-suffering sigh wafted from the phone. "I'll get an early flight from DC and be at the office Monday." Etta didn't wait for Nora's reply. The phone went dead.

Nora tugged on Abbey's ear. "You don't think it would be awkward to ask Rachel for the film on the day of her wife's funeral, do you?" Abbey's eyes drooped at the massage.

Nora tapped at the voicemail retrieval and entered her password. "Hey, Nor," began the first message. Her heart stopped, and her hand holding the phone turned to ice.

Lisa.

When had she called? And how had Nora missed it?

Lisa's voice sounded strained. "I really need to talk to you. You know those petroglyphs I told you about? In Fiery Furnace?"

Nora couldn't focus on the words. Lisa's voice sounded so alive.

Nora's eyes came to rest on the box of ashes.

"The Mormons are—well, it's at the Tokpela Ranch. There's this—oh, shit. I've got to go."

There was some fumbling on the other end, then a breathless continuation. "I taped it all just in case. You'll know where the camera is. You know ... if I can't call."

Nora listened to the silence for a few seconds before the automated voice invited her to delete the message or save it to the archives. She pressed the archive number before it disconnected.

She replayed it again and again, noting the call had come in the evening before Lisa's accident. She checked the other five messages. All were from Abigail the morning after Lisa's accident. Nora was so changing her phone plan as soon as she got home.

"She sounded scared," Nora told Abbey. He opened his mouth to pant in the warm Jeep.

Fiery Furnace was a labyrinth of rock fins and canyons in Arches National Park. While Canyonlands encompassed a huge tract of land south of Moab, Arches was a smaller, if no less dramatic, park just a couple of miles north of town. Lisa had mentioned Fiery Furnace a few days ago. What about Tokpela Ranch?

She started the Jeep and turned the wheel to make a U-turn across the lanes and head to Moab. What should she do about Lisa's call?

Just as the Jeep moved into the middle of the road, a white pickup popped over the western hill. Instead of slowing, the pickup seemed to gain speed. The driver laid on the horn.

Electricity sparked in Nora. Her mind blanked.

The truck sped toward her like a flash flood in a slot canyon, arrowed at the very spot where she sat frozen, hands on the wheel.

She stomped on the gas and shot across the road, straight into the sandy shoulder. She slammed on the brakes before crashing into a stand of willows. Abbey tumbled from the seat to the floor, coming to rest on top of the box of ashes.

Still leaning on the horn, the pickup sped past her bumper, close enough to shake the Jeep. Nora turned in her seat, spotting the black cowboy hat of the driver as the pickup slowed, eased into the right lane, and continued around the curve and out of sight.

Not nearly as shaken as Nora, Abbey scrambled back on the seat. He wagged his tail and licked at Nora's face. She managed to avoid his tongue as she sucked in a breath.

Blood that had froze in those milliseconds of panic now thinned and surged. She concentrated on breathing. After a few seconds, Nora leaned over and righted Lisa's box. Thank goodness the lid was still nailed shut. She couldn't have faced her best friend's spilled ashes.

Nora put the Jeep into reverse. It revved. The tires spun in the sand; the Jeep didn't budge. She shoved it into first and hoped to rock it to gain momentum. More spinning.

"All this rock around here and I have to find a sand pile," she grumbled. Abbey didn't care.

Nora climbed out and located the shovel she kept in the back. She went to work. The six-hour drive, the exertion, and the sun stole any crispness that had remained from her shower a million years ago at her apartment in Boulder.

She dug a trench behind the wheels, found a few large stones to line it, and reversed the Jeep. It popped out onto the road and Nora and Abbey were back in business, sweaty, irritated, and craving a cool drink.

By the time they made it to the Read Rock Bookstore and circled around the block to find parking in the back, not many cars remained.

An alley ran between the bookstore and another building that led to Main Street.

Easing the Jeep into a spot shaded by the building that would catch enough cool breeze to keep Abbey comfortable, Nora frowned at her disheveled appearance. She rummaged in her overnight bag, found a brush to run through her hair, and scrubbed the dried sweat from her face with a hand wipe from a container she kept in her glove box. It was the best she could do for now.

She pulled Abbey's collapsible dish from the back, filled it with water from the jug she always carried in the Jeep, and waited while he lapped it up.

Moab was a small town of about five thousand that spread across the valley floor. Settled by Mormons, it had served as a rural supply center for the nearby ranchers. The population expanded with a uranium mining boom in the 1950s, then contracted again when it burst. Years later, its reputation as a recreationist's dream spread. Mountain bikers and four-wheel enthusiasts gathered, followed closely by the enviros and hippie types. Trust funders and wealthy retirees building second homes wandered in, drawn by the amazing scenery. Now it had a mismatched feel. Eclectic shops featuring sweat-shop-free items comingled with farm and ranch supply stores, tourist shops, outdoor gear, vegan restaurants, and old-time diners. If the population of the area mimicked the town structures, this was one schizophrenic community.

Nora picked up the box. "Be good," she ordered Abbey before cranking down the windows for the cross breeze and leaving him to nap.

Most of the vehicles in the lot were covered with the red dust of Moab. The luxury cars and expensive SUVs probably belonged to the moneyed people who had moved here for the gorgeous views and then tried to protect them from the traditional uses of the people who had lived here for generations. The old beaters most likely carried the more earthy types, those with master's degrees in biology and environmental studies who worked for peanuts for conservation nonprofits. She made her way through the alley to the front of the store and scanned the street. She nearly dropped the box.

A white pickup. THE white pickup. It sat empty along the street. Nora changed direction and approached it. She placed her hand on the hood. Warm.

With new purpose, she strode to the bookstore and wrenched open the door.

Bookshelves had been shoved to the side of the cozy shop to make room for the reception. The dark wood that lined the walls was filled with hardcover, trade paperback, and mass market titles. It wasn't a big shop, but the inventory filled the room. An old-fashioned sales counter angled next to the front door, its surface cluttered with crocks full of pens and other bookish notions. Dreamcatchers, sand art, pottery, and other Native American art decorated the walls and shelves. Nora quickly scanned the space for kachinas but didn't find any. The relative dimness of the store felt cool and welcoming, inviting people to stay and browse.

The wood-planked floor creaked with the movement of Lisa's friends as they mingled. White plastic tablecloths covered two five- foot tables in the center of the shop. Remains of a cake, sandwiches, and chips lined one table. The other table held a basket for sympathy cards and the used plates, cups, and forks from the funeral refreshments. It wasn't fancy, but Lisa had never cared about finery. If she were here, Lisa would have a few words to say about the wastefulness of the plastic dinnerware.

No one turned to greet Nora. She walked into the hushed store.

Nora spotted a guy holding a black cowboy hat. He was the same one with the hate-filled gaze at the clearing. He stood with the man who'd led Rachel from the service.

Both appeared to be in their mid-thirties. Where White Pickup Guy looked about as old-school cowboy as Gene Autry, the other man looked more boardroom suave. He wore black suit pants, cut and draped to show a well-toned lower half. His fresh-from-the-laundry blue shirt fit his broad shoulders perfectly. The conservative cut of his wavy dark hair and the tie knotted neatly at his neck gave him a professional air.

Their conversation didn't appear friendly. The dapper guy spoke, and his handsome face drew down in a frown. The cowboy looked at him dismissively. With one more muttered word, the clean-cut guy strode away.

Nora stomped over to White Pickup Guy. "Did I do something to make you mad?"

The cowboy's thin mouth turned up in a smirk. He stood several inches taller than Nora's five-foot-seven frame and looked as ropey and tough as a dried stalk of corn. Nora suspected the deep tan on his face and neck ended where the V of his shirt hit his chest. Not one gleam of friendly showed in his eyes. "Don't know what you're talking about."

Nora's heart banged away and heat radiated from inside out. "At Moonflower, you nearly killed me."

He spoke in a low, slow voice, reminding her of Cole—except Cole had never sent goose bumps over her flesh. Not the scary kind, anyway. "I didn't see anyone out there. Rachel sent me back for the ashes, but they were gone." He nodded at the box Nora held.

She hugged the box to her. "You ran me off the road and I had to dig out. You never saw me?"

His dark eyes bored into her. "Tourists, such as yourself, don't understand the local ways. They tend to get in the way and sometimes end up getting hurt." His words came straight out of a spaghetti western, but the threat behind them felt real.

Unnerved, Nora answered with bravado. "Next time, I'll call the cops."

He threw back his head and let out a guffaw. "You do that." He stuffed his hat on his head and sauntered away, cowboy boots thudding on the wood floor of the Read Rock.

Anyone watching wouldn't see her tremors. Probably. Why had she thought going head-to-head with a stranger would be a good thing?

The well-dressed guy appeared at her elbow. He raised an eyebrow in humor. "Wow. Not many people stand up to Lee like that."

She watched the cowboy's broad back. "Lee who?" "Evans. A long-time local family."

The door closed behind Evans.

A well-established family who wouldn't want Canyonlands' borders expanded? "Does he have a ranch?"

The man at her elbow nodded and held out his hand. "I'm Darrell Burke." He said it as though they were having a casual conversation at a cocktail party.

That's when she realized she still held the box containing Lisa. Nora's face burned even more. "I'm, uh, I'm Nora Abbott."

His face opened into a warm smile. "That's obvious. You're not from Moab, and since Lisa's family disowned her, you have to be her best friend, the famous Nora Abbott."

She opened her mouth to say something but had no response.

Even though he was a stranger, he made her feel comfortable.

He laughed quietly. "Lisa told me a lot about you."

Had he said his name? Nora's brain tilted on overload. Between losing Lisa, the voicemail, and the lunatic cowboy, she wasn't at the top of her game.

Lisa's box weighed heavy in her hands. She stepped over to the plastic-covered table littered with used plates and cups to set it down, hesitating. It seemed disrespectful to plop it down next to red Solo cups with dregs of lemonade and plates holding half-eaten ham sandwiches, but she didn't know what else to do with it. The sun-drenched clearing by the creek felt more appropriate. Maybe she should have left Lisa there after all. She hugged the box harder, glad she hadn't left Lisa for Lee Evans to find.

The nice guy didn't comment on the box but kept his eyes on her. "So Lee ran you off the road?"

"Right into a ditch." She set the box on the table.

"Lee has a temper. Most folks avoid provoking it. Lisa didn't." He looked pointedly at the box.

Nora asked the obvious. "If Lee didn't like Lisa, what's he doing at her funeral?"

He lifted his chin, indicating something behind Nora. "He and Rachel used to be close."

Nora turned to see Rachel standing across the room. She was speaking to a blonde woman in a silk summer suit, her back to Nora. Rachel crumpled and fell into the woman's arms. The sight brought Nora to tears.

Nora knew how Rachel felt and almost wished she could fall into comforting arms, too. In fact, if she couldn't feel Cole's arms around her, the woman holding Rachel might make a good substitute.

The handsome man followed Nora's gaze. "This is going to be a hard time for Rachel."

Nora nodded, not trusting her voice.

They watched the pair, and he spoke. "I thought I knew just about everyone in Moab, but I don't recognize that woman."

"She's not from around here," Nora said. "You know her?"

"That," Nora started across the room, "is my mother, Abigail Podanski."

6

Abigail stood a trim five foot six with a soft blonde bob—the perfect shade and cut to make her appear fashionable and age appropriate. She wore a beige silk suit and scuff-free heels. She and the man talking to Nora—what was his name?—would fit right in at a luncheon on Capitol Hill but were too formal for Moab.

Nora's natural inclination would be to take off in the opposite direction. But for one of the few times in her life, she actually felt happy to see her mother. After an uneasy relationship that often bordered on outright war, Nora and Abigail were forging a new bond. Well, working at it, anyway—a few ignored calls notwithstanding.

Rachel sobbed silently against Abigail's shoulder.

Nora inched around to stand in front of Abigail. "Mother?"

Abigail made eye contact with Nora. She continued to pat Rachel's back and murmur to her, "I know, dear. I've lost three husbands. I understand." In between all of this, she managed a smile of acknowledgement to Nora.

Rachel pulled away from Abigail. "Lisa thought of you as her mother."

Nora didn't know whether to wait for Abigail to break from Rachel or wander away and give them space. She backed up and into a warm body. "Excuse me."

The nice guy took hold of her elbow to steady her. "I can't even imagine her loss." His eyes filled with compassion.

Nora stepped away from him. "You must be a good friend of Rachel's."

He studied Rachel. "It's hard to get to know someone as guarded and private as Rachel. I knew Lisa better. We worked together on some land-swap issues over the years and now on this film project." A light clicked on inside her brain. "Oh, Darrell Burke—congressman. I'm sorry I didn't recognize you earlier." He brushed it aside. "I'm not here campaigning."

"You were helping set up distribution of the film to the congressional committee. Lisa told me you made a lot of progress."

His eyes rested on the box halfway across the room. "It was a passion Lisa and I shared. This land needs someone to protect it from over-grazing and mining, and even from too many tourists. I just wish I could have protected Lisa with the same effectiveness."

What a strange thing to say. "Did Lisa say anything to you about needing or wanting protection?"

He laughed in that sad way people do at funerals. "As if she'd allow anyone to take care of her, except maybe Rachel. She was a real force for the environment. I don't know that there's anyone who can take her place around here."

Lisa was irreplaceable, but they had to do something. "You've arranged for the committee to screen the film?"

He inhaled. "I hate the thought of cancelling it."

"Don't. We can make it. Lisa's work shouldn't be lost."

Darrell sounded sad. "As I understand it, the film isn't finished."

Nora ignored the spike of panic in her heart. "The film can make the difference in the vote."

"Still," Darrell said. "There's no one to finish it, edit it, and get it out in time."

"Don't cancel that screening." Nora watched Rachel and Abigail, wondering how and when to ask Rachel for a copy.

Darrell continued. "Obviously, I'll still lobby for the park expansion.

I've got some favors to call in. We're not out of fuel yet." Nora liked the warm way his attention seemed totally focused on her, as if this problem were his only concern. She'd heard certain politicians had the ability to make everyone feel unique, and despite knowing that, she still felt a little special.

Her phone vibrated in her pocket. She glanced up at Abigail, who was the one usually calling. But Abigail still had her arms around Rachel. Nora pulled out the phone and glanced at it. A little thrill raced through her, as it usually did. "Excuse me," she said to Darrell. "I've got to take this."

She spun away and headed for the door. She punched the answer button and stepped into the sunshine, letting the door close behind her. "Cole." She exhaled his name with a mingle of sorrow, hope, and longing.

She felt his support through the phone. "You sound stressed."

She found a spot of shade under the store awning and leaned against the stucco wall. "I wish you were here."

"I'm sorry. I know this is tough. How are you?"

Nora watched an ant scurry along the sidewalk. "I'm okay. Abigail is here."

"That's good." A long pause followed.

When Cole didn't continue, she asked, "How's your father?" "He's in the hospital in Sheridan. He's not doing well."

Another brick piled on their load. "How about your mother and brother and the ranch?"

Silence fell as the little ant darted on its erratic path. Finally Cole spoke. "When do you think you'll be home?"

Nice nonanswer to her question. Things must not be going well. "That's hard to say. I need to get Lisa's film. I'm hoping to do that this afternoon and head out later. There're no hotel rooms here so I'll probably stay in Grand Junction overnight."

"Isn't the film digital—on the cloud or something?"

Nora nodded as though he could see her. "Probably. But I don't know where. I need to talk to Rachel about it." Nora sighed. "It's bad timing to bug her today."

"Then don't. Come home. I can get away from here for a day or so and meet you there."

She craved being next to him. "I'd love to. But I really need to get that film."

"It can't wait a few days?"

The ant wound back around. He didn't seem to be making any progress. "Etta called and jumped all over me. This is a big deal."

"That woman doesn't have any compassion for people—just the environment." Cole knew about Etta from Nora's conversations.

Nora nodded again. "I pushed for this film. I guaranteed the board that spending a hundred thousand dollars would give Canyonlands its best shot at Congress. I've got to see it through."

"Maybe you can do a scaled-back version. You ought to let Rachel have a day at least." He sounded like Darrell.

"You're right. But ... " She wanted to suck that last word back. "But what?"

Might as well tell him. "I had a voicemail on my phone that I didn't get until today. It was from Lisa."

"When did she send it? Why didn't you get it before now?"

Another ant joined the first. "Don't know. Abigail's probably right about the service I contracted."

"What did Lisa say?"

"It wasn't so much what she said, it was how she said it. She sounded scared. Then she hung up abruptly."

He sounded concerned. "Scared? What about?"

One ant scurried away, leaving the other on its own. "She said she taped whatever she had to say, so I guess I can get the camera and find out."

There was no smile in his voice. "If you think it seems fishy, take it to the cops and let them deal with it."

Again, the pause felt uncomfortable. Good thing they didn't have to carry on a long-distance relationship because they both were bad on the phone.

The door of the Read Rock opened, and a group of people came out and headed for the parking lot.

"I'd better go," Nora said. "I'll call you when I know more." "Right."

"Well, bye."

A slight pause. "Nora?" "Yes?"

"I love you." He hung up.

Nora stood in the shade of the building. The ant must have dashed from her sight when she wasn't looking. A chill ran across her skin. While it was always nice to hear those words, Cole didn't use them often. Like, maybe once before.

This meant something. But what?

7

The sun shone bright on Central Park and streamed across the thick carpeting in the office, but Warren stuffed his arms into his cashmere cardigan and shuffled to the thermostat on the wall. He pictured healthy cells decked out like gladiators swinging their broadswords to cut down the pale cancer cells.

The image didn't hold up. He hated to admit the warriors had dwindled to only a few holdouts backed onto the cliff face. The cancer army stood poised to run them through. *I only need a few more days.* Maybe God would listen to his plea.

His desk seemed miles away across the expanse of his office. The plush carpet felt like deep sand under his feet as he focused on the leather chair behind his desk. He loved this office. He'd chosen everything in it to fit his needs and desires. Christine and her platoons of decorators ruled over the rest of the penthouse, but no professional decorators had set foot inside his office. He allowed the cleaning lady in and, reluctantly, Christine.

He succeeded in making it to his desk. The beat-up oak monstrosity had belonged to his grandfather. It had sat in the corner of the sitting room for half a century until Granddad passed over. By then, Warren could have afforded any world-renowned artist to customize his desk.

But he wanted this reminder of his roots in Utah. It helped him to remember that possessions were only vanity, and in the end, they didn't matter. His grandfather was a righteous man, dedicated to both the church and his many children, grandchildren, and great-grandchildren. Warren had no doubt Granddad waited for him on the other side. But like everyone who had come before him, Granddad depended on Warren to complete the task God had set before him.

Warren dropped his head and leaned heavily on the desk. His focus strayed to the architectural drawings spread on the rough surface. He pictured the actual structures the lines represented with satisfaction.

No one else could have done what Warren had accomplished. Why would God call him home before he saw it through to completion?

The answer was obvious.

Humility. God fulfilled his promise through Warren. Together, they'd done the impossible. Warren would be rewarded, along with all his ancestors. He just wouldn't lead the final exodus.

Who would?

Warren had it narrowed down to two of his nephews. Neither of them had Warren's strength or his brain. Why hadn't God provided a successor for such an important job?

"My goodness, it's like an oven in here!" Christine swept into the room, pulling Warren from his plans.

The heels of her pumps left mini craters in the carpet as she swished across the room in her flowing black pants and jacket like a queen strutting around her chambers. She adjusted the thermostat.

Warren straightened and strode to the chair, costing himself too much in an effort to appear strong. "I thought you were having lunch with Amanda Reynolds."

Christine folded her arms, her back to him as she studied a framed five-by-seven-foot artist's rendering of the solar system. "That was hours ago." She tilted her head one way, then the other. "I don't understand why you have this here."

Of course Christine wouldn't appreciate Warren's fascination. "Reminds me of our place in the universe."

She spun toward him. Warren wished he could capture the energy she wasted on her quick movements. "It seems out of place here."

"Can I help you with something?" On a good day he could indulge in chatter. This wasn't a good day. Christine didn't enter his sanctuary often, so she must have a reason.

She ignored his question and wandered over to an amateur's painting of an old-fashioned white barn with red rocks in the background. "Has Bourne Financial weathered the recession?"

Money. She wanted to know if the giant financial conglomerate Warren had created would keep her in style. "Yes."

She left the painting, crossed to the far side of the room, and stood in front of a slab of sandstone he'd had extracted from a Utah cliff. Unknown hands had etched designs into the rock more than a thousand years ago. "How much do you think this petroglyph panel is worth?"

Heat rose to his face and his heart beat faster. "It's not worth much since I can't sell it on the open market."

She kept her back to him. Christine had a head for numbers. She had come to his office to appraise his treasures and see what she might expect in a payoff when the cancer finally won. "It came from your family's ranch, didn't it?"

He wanted to rise from his chair and pull her away from the panel. Her calculating eyes felt sacrilegious—especially as she focused on the figure of a person in what appeared to be a boat. "Doesn't matter if it was private land. You can't cut into a petroglyph panel and remove it from the rock. It's a violation of the Antiquities Act."

"So you having this here is illegal?"

He didn't answer her. She knew this. Maybe she wanted to drive home the point that she knew his secrets. That brought a smirk to his face.

"So why did you want this petroglyph? It just looks like a bunch of stick people with big heads. It's not nearly as remarkable as the drawings of horses or deer."

An electric shock of pain made a circuit up Warren's spine to the base of his skull. He closed his eyes against it and waited for the worst to pass. "What's on your mind, Christine?"

With practiced nonchalance, she started toward him. Her voice sounded young and lilting. "My goodness. You have such an interesting mix in here. I don't know much about decorating"—he scowled at her blatant lie—"but I think they would tell you to pick a theme. You have this barn picture that looks like a first-year art student with little talent painted it, then kachina dolls and pottery on shelves and the strange mix of astronomy and rock art."

"I'm not interested in what a decorator thinks." It came out as a short-tempered growl. "What is it you want?"

Her lower lip protruded. "I haven't seen you much lately. I thought maybe we could catch up."

Clouds brushed across the sun and the shafts of light on the carpet disappeared, as if God was toying with a dimmer switch. "Actually, I'm glad you're here." Her practiced grin made her face sparkle as if she delighted in this news, when Warren knew it was nothing more than the effort of a consummate actress. "We're going to Moab Saturday."

Her well-shaped eyebrows shot up. "I can't make it. I've got two committee meetings."

"You'll have to reschedule. Darrell Burke is running a close race, and we need to throw our weight behind him."

She shifted into a sympathetic tone. "It's Utah, dear. Darrell is Mormon. I can't see there's a crisis."

Bile rose in Warren's throat, and he waited it out. "Darrell isn't traditional and can't count on the Mormon vote. He's going to need our help."

"You should concentrate on you now. The chemo's made you weak, and you shouldn't be running around the country." She paused for effect. "Darrell needs your money, not your personal testimony."

He didn't have the strength or the will to parry with her. "Tell me why you're here."

Her lips tightened and her dark eyes lasered in on him. She lowered herself to a leather-covered client's chair opposite his desk and stared at him. "I don't know how to bring this up," she began.

He watched her struggle for the right words that wouldn't make her sound like a vulture. Maybe he held a modicum of responsibility for what she'd become. Thirty years ago she'd been a vibrant, loving young woman. She'd grown up in New York in wealth and privilege. She hadn't even finished her undergraduate degree at Columbia, something she was certainly smart enough to complete, when they met at one of her father's cocktail parties.

By that time, Warren had already accumulated his first million. But he'd divvied up those profits into investments and needed a cash flow so he wouldn't miss out on the opportunities opening before him. More than that, he needed a wife. Back then he had considered a career in politics, and that required a bright, well-connected, impeccably raised woman by his side.

That was before he'd found his true aptitude lay in creating huge wealth. That kind of money could buy whatever politics he wanted without him having to suffer public scrutiny.

Warren had only loved one other woman. Puppy love, really. Christine, with her fine breeding, dark beauty, and social ambition was a completely different species than the naïve, simple blonde of his college days.

Christine and her trust fund entered his life at the right time. He gave her value for her money, though. She wanted an ambitious man, one who would provide for her, not only financially but give her the kind of notoriety and status even money couldn't assure.

It sounded cold in retrospect, but he'd loved her. He thought she'd loved him. Through the years of toil, when he'd spent eighteen to twenty hours a day amassing a fortune whose dimensions only he knew, the disappointment of no children and the demands of great wealth had evaporated their affection, leaving only a functioning business arrangement.

Finally, Christine spoke. "What has the doctor told you?" He leaned back in his chair. "I've got cancer."

She tilted her head in annoyance. "Yes, I know that much. But you won't allow me to accompany you to your appointments or consultations with your medical team. I have no idea what's going on."

"You mean, you don't know how long you have to wait for me to die."

Her shoulders slumped the tiniest bit. "I've upset you." "No. This disease upsets me."

She pushed herself from the chair. "I'll go."

He waved her down. "You want to know how much money you'll have when I'm gone. Is that it?"

A flush rose to her cheeks, but she remained where she was and nodded. "I don't like talking about this, but I'm ignorant of our holdings. I'd hate for the estate to wither from neglect after you've gone."

She made it sound as though her concern was for his legacy. "Don't worry. I had Darrell draw up papers for a generous fund for you. The rest is not your concern." He'd left her more than enough to last into her dotage.

Her face tightened. "That's generous of you to take care of me, but what about your businesses and investments?"

"It's all down to one holding. And the rest will go to the church."

He didn't need to wonder how this news struck her. The pale face and wide eyes revealed shock. "One holding? How is that possible?"

He smiled at her. "I've invested in an important project." The most important since Noah's nautical venture.

"What project?" Her voice sounded strangled.

He pushed his chair from his desk with shaky arms. "It's time for my medication. Please excuse me."

He envied her quick jump to her feet. Her flushed face indicated the panic that must be raging inside. "It's not fair that you don't share the details of the estate with me."

"I've left you a hundred million dollars. If you live frugally, it should last. The houses, of course, are in both our names, as well as the yacht, art, plane, and cars."

She nodded, cool as January snow. "And the bulk of the estate?"

"Invested in the family ranch." He watched her, fascinated by her self-control.

She drew in a long breath. "Your entire fortune is invested in a cattle ranch?"

He grinned. "It's a very nice ranch."

8

The little bell above the door tinkled and the wooden floor creaked as Nora walked into the Read Rock. The musty smell of old books lingered in the cool air, making the shop feel comforting after the blazing sun outside.

Nora realized she'd been holding her breath. She let it out and inhaled. She'd never heard such heaviness in Cole's voice. He had to be hurting about his father, but he didn't want to talk about it. She'd give him time before she pushed. Maybe he knew how much Lisa's death pained her and wanted to give her support. She wanted nothing more than to hurry back to him and feel his arms around her. But first, she needed to get a copy of Lisa's film. According to Lisa, she'd completed everything except one video session and the final edits.

Darrell stood in front of her, all warm sympathy again. "You're frowning. Are you worried about the presentation to the committee? Don't be. Even without Lisa's film, I'll make a great case for expanding Canyonlands' borders."

No simple presentation would pack the wallop that viewing the iconic landscapes would. Lisa had created time-lapse footage with stars and sun trading places and views of pristine sunrises juxtaposed with damage from tar sands mining.

If there was no film, Nora might as well start sending out her résumé again. Just the thought of leaving the Trust hurt. Nora's position at Living Earth Trust was so much more than a paycheck, even a much-needed one. For twenty-five years, the Trust had done good work for the environment. But recently, it had been tainted with scandal and murder and corrupt leadership. In the last few months as executive director, Nora had worked endless hours repairing its reputation. She'd flown from coast to coast meeting with past and potential donors. She'd staked her personal integrity, taking responsibility for the programs and policies coming out of the Trust. Another disruption could finish the Trust, and all the good work would stop. Nora would lose the anchor of a job that gave her life meaning.

Darrell's voice brought her out of her funk. "It'll be okay. I can be very convincing. You can come with me, and together we'll make the committee understand the importance of preserving this area."

Maybe Darrell was right. Probably he wasn't. "I'll get a backup of the film and figure out how to edit it," Nora told him.

Darrell looked skeptical.

The door opened again. The sunshine outlined a slightly stooped, thin man with a halo of unruly hair.

Nora grinned. "Excuse me," she mumbled to Darrell, leaping around him and running the two steps to fling herself at the grizzled old man. "Charlie!"

His arms circled her in a bear hug. "You are a vision of loveliness." She loved the way he always spoke, as if acting in a melodrama.

"I didn't know you were here, too!"

He patted her arm. "It's tough when your friends leave this world.

Your mother and I thought you'd need us with you." Nora squeezed his hand. "I'm glad you're here." He scrutinized her. "How're you holdin' up?"

Why did he have to ask? Her throat closed up, and she fought tears.

"Nora. Dear." Abigail spoke from behind Nora.

Nora didn't anticipate her reaction when she turned to see her mother. She stepped into Abigail's comforting embrace, probably surprising them both.

Abigail patted her back. "There, there." Her soft words lasted only seconds. She took Nora by the shoulders and held her at arm's length. Abigail reached up with a tissue that had magically appeared in her hands and dabbed at the tears streaming down Nora's face. "Since you don't wear makeup, at least you don't have black streaks." Yep, typical Abigail. Thank goodness some things didn't change.

Abigail lowered her voice. "You have to be strong for Rachel. She's going to need you now." Then she turned to Charlie. She placed her white hands on either side of his Velcro face and planted a solid kiss on his lips. "Thank you for parking the car, dear."

Charlie glowed in his worship of Abigail.

Darrell approached them. He held out his hand to Abigail. "Hi.

I'm Darrell Burke."

Abigail slipped her hand into his and smiled. "Abigail Podanski. This is my husband, Charles."

Charles? Nora raised her eyebrows at Charlie. He had been one of her closest friends for years. But once he'd laid eyes on Abigail, he'd been a goner. No one, ever, in a million years, would think of him as Charles. No one, that is, except her mother.

Charlie locked eyes with Nora, shrugged, and gave her a little grin. Darrell shook Charlie's hand. "Were you friends with Lisa?"

Abigail's mouth tightened. "What a lively spirit. I can't believe it's been snuffed out. How did you know Lisa?"

Nora tuned out while Darrell explained. She looked around the bookstore. All the guests had disappeared, leaving only their little group and Rachel.

Charlie nudged Nora and tilted his head toward Rachel. Rachel stood alone, her eyes unfocused.

She should go speak to Rachel. Nora understood how confused and alone a person felt, how you quit thinking and doing ordinary things when your spouse dies. When Scott died, Charlie and Abigail had helped Nora.

Nora took a tentative step toward Rachel, then another, and soon stood directly in front of her. She opened her mouth to ask about the film but couldn't do it. "Can I drive you home?"

Rachel's head snapped up and her eyes focused. The sorrow turned hard. "You..."

Abigail appeared and took Rachel's hand. "It looks like everyone has gone. Charles is bringing the car around. We'll take you home."

Rachel gave Abigail a tired smile. "Thank you."

Abigail linked her arm with Rachel's and they started for the door. Abigail looked back at Nora. She raised her eyebrows, indicated the box on the table and Nora, and gave her head a "come-on" wag. Translation: Bring the box to Rachel's house.

Great idea. It sounded like Rachel blamed Nora for Lisa's death. The last thing she needed was for Nora to traipse into her home uninvited.

And yet, there sat Lisa. Since Nora had brought her from the creek, it seemed like her responsibility to look out for her the way Lisa had always looked out for everyone.

Nora remembered the first week of their freshman year at CU. She'd been in the communal bathroom on their dorm floor, brushing her teeth. Someone was taking a shower. A pale girl from several doors down crept into the bathroom. She slipped into a stall. Within seconds, the sound of sobbing wafted over the stall walls.

Nora didn't know what to do. She couldn't pretend she hadn't heard the poor girl's misery, but knocking on the stall door seemed inappropriate. She stood, paralyzed by indecision.

Water turned off in the shower and the curtain swished aside. A petite girl with dark hair that curled despite the weight of the water drenching it wrapped a towel around herself. She strode to the closed stall door. "My name is Lisa. What is it, honey?"

"Please. Go away." The girl's voice barely carried in the echo chamber of the tiled bathroom.

It was as if Lisa broke a barrier and Nora was able to act. She joined Lisa at the stall door. Together they talked the girl out of the stall and coaxed her to talk.

Charlotte came from rural southern Colorado and trusted everyone. The attention of an older guy thrilled and flattered her. Until the creep got himself invited to her dorm room, didn't understand the word no, and nearly raped her.

As soon as Lisa got the story, she stomped from the bathroom, not bothering to dress. Nora bounded after her, and they burst into Charlotte's room in time to confront the weasel.

It still tickled Nora remembering Lisa, with the towel barely covering her, giving the shocked creep what-for.

Nora and Lisa had been friends ever since.

Curtains concealing a passage at the back of the bookstore parted and a tall woman peered out. She scanned the store, eyes resting briefly on Nora and dismissing her. She flowed out of the back room and into the store. She appeared to be around fifty and had the face of someone used to being outdoors: weathered and wrinkled, browned by the sun. Her gray hair was shorn short enough that it spiked at the top of her head, and the large hooped earrings she wore dangled nearly to her shoulders. She wore a long skirt and blouse in the deep reds, oranges, and golds of a desert. She appeared solid and strong under the rich fabric.

She moved with purpose but didn't hurry as she reached under the counter and pulled out a trash bag. She started at the refreshment table, tossing the disposable dishes into the bag.

Nora felt she should say something. "Can I give you a hand cleaning up?"

The woman didn't look up. She wound the plastic table covering, careful to keep the crumbs from spilling out. "I can do it."

"You must be Marlene," Nora said.

The woman stopped moving. She raised her eyes to Nora. They were dark and full of suspicion. "That's right."

Nora tried to look harmless. She didn't know why Marlene should be worried. "I'm Nora Abbott. A friend of Lisa's."

Marlene studied her. "The one who gave her the funding for the film."

Nora nodded. "She loved this bookstore. She told me she spent a lot of time here."

Marlene turned pale. A moment passed, and she started to breathe again. "I'm going to miss her."

She moved on to the next table. Nora met her there and picked up empty plates and cups. She stuffed them in Marlene's trash bag. "She told me this place was her office away from home. She liked to come here when she felt stymied."

Marlene's mask of control slipped. Her smile looked heavy, like sand after the tide. "She was so smart. So quick-witted. She had that sort of energy people envied." Marlene stuffed the table covering into the bag. "You knew her a long time, didn't you?"

Nora nodded. "Since freshman year. Sometimes we wouldn't see each other for a while, but every time we talked, it was like picking up the conversation mid-sentence."

Marlene nodded and tied the bag. "She was special."

Nora followed Marlene to the sales counter. "It was really great that we could work together on this film."

Marlene stared out the front window. "She was committed to it.

Maybe more than she should have been." "What do you mean?"

Marlene turned her focus to Nora. It felt as though her dark gaze seeped inside of Nora, exploring her worthiness. After a moment she spoke slowly. "It caused problems between her and Rachel."

That landed heavy on Nora. "She didn't say anything to me about it, but I had suspicions."

Marlene raised one eyebrow. "It's hard to overcome your upbringing."

Lisa had said the same thing.

Marlene moved out from behind the counter and flipped one of the tables over. Nora worked at folding up the table legs. "Because she's from here?"

Marlene hefted the table and set it against the wall. "Rachel loved Lisa. The Mormons aren't so big on lesbians. Until Lisa showed up, no one knew Rachel was gay. But suddenly, here is Lisa with all these liberal notions of protecting land that's been in their hands for generations, and she scoops up one of the local girls."

"People around here didn't like Lisa, is that what you're saying?"

"No, what I'm saying is that people around here hated Lisa."

"But so many people came to the funeral."

Marlene smiled. "The people who loved Lisa aren't locals. They're the transplants, the newbies, the outsiders. They aren't Mormon. They love this land just as an art aficionado loves Rembrandt. The old-time Mormons love it as a member of the family."

Nora gave Marlene a questioning look.

"It's this way: The environmentalists want to preserve it. Tread gently on the trails, gaze at the arches and hoodoos. Sit quietly and contemplate its beauty. The Mormons want to live on it, work it. Fight with it to give them sustenance, care for it so it stays healthy and productive. Do you see the difference?"

Nora summed it up. "Conservationists want to put it in the parlor and cover it in plastic, and locals want to sit on it and watch TV?"

Marlene laughed. It changed her whole appearance. She went from stern and formidable to friendly and accessible, and Nora could see why Lisa had found refuge in this place and with this woman. "Not exactly how I would put it, but you get the idea."

They moved to the next folding table, the one that held Lisa's ashes. Marlene clenched her fists, her face suddenly pasty.

Nora reached for the box and transferred it to the counter next to the cash register. "You weren't out at the creek, and you didn't come out of the back room while everyone was here."

Marlene busied herself with clearing the table. "I'll say goodbye to Lisa in my own way."

Fair enough. Marlene seemed a curious mixture between stern and loving, restrained and straightforward. "Did you and Lisa talk about the film?"

Marlene brought her eyes slowly to Nora's. "She talked about it to everyone. You know Lisa—whatever churned in her head frothed out her mouth."

"She said she only had one more shooting session and she would wrap it up."

Marlene dumped the table over and Nora hurried over to help fold up its legs.

Marlene straightened and stared out the window again. Maybe she waited out waves of pain to keep from breaking down. "Everything she did was the most important thing. The next moment, there would be a new most important thing. She leaped from peak to peak." Marlene hefted the table across the room.

Maybe Nora wouldn't have to bother Rachel. "She didn't happen to leave a backup here, or do you know where she stored them?"

Marlene slammed the table on the floor and spun around. "How should I know? If I felt like chatting about Lisa and her life and her work,

I'd have joined the gathering at the creek or at least come out of the back room. I lost my friend, and I don't feel like being social." Nora's face burned. Her whole body felt on fire from Marlene's anger. She hurried across the room to retrieve the box. "I'm sorry.

I'll go."

Marlene geared up. "You all come in here with your tears and sorrow. You tote around her ashes as if they were a gym bag or yoga mat. You'll go home to your lives, doing what you were doing before this incident disrupted you. But I'll be here. Missing her every day."

Nora didn't want to spook the majestic Marlene during her meltdown.

"She's not going to fly through those doors, nearly sending the bell sailing across the room. She won't open new shipments of books and oooh and aahhh with me, falling in love with every title. No more sharing tea in the mornings or a bottle of wine on a winter evening." The hot tears Marlene refused to shed coursed down Nora's face.

Marlene's shoulders never sagged; her backbone remained straight, chin raised. "You didn't see her eyes light up and hear her words tumble out faster than she could keep up when she came in after a day of shooting or scouting locations. You don't know what I'm going to miss. Every. Single. Day. For the rest of my life."

Nora's voice filled the silence. "She loved you, too."

Marlene broke. Like an avalanche on a rocky mountain, first one boulder broke loose, followed by a few more, gaining momentum and power. Marlene folded over and gasped, massive sobs shaking her.

Nora placed a hand on Marlene's heaving back, keeping watch while the big woman mourned. After several minutes, the sobs tapered off and Marlene straightened, only slightly less regal.

Nora strode to the sales desk and found a box of tissues. She pulled out several and hurried back. Marlene accepted them and wiped her eyes.

If it were anyone else, Nora might lead her to the oak library table and sit her down, pat her hand, or rub her shoulders. Instead, she stood silently and waited.

Marlene focused out the window again. Tourists meandered outside the door. She inhaled deeply. "Lisa was right. You're a good person."

Nora allowed a smile. "You know, she was my best friend." Marlene nodded.

"And at least a dozen other people who showed up today called her their best friend, too," Nora said.

Marlene dabbed the last of her tears. "She was that way, wasn't she?"

"I need to go out to Rachel's. Are you going to be okay?"

Marlene tilted her head and gave Nora an are-you-kidding-me look. "Leave that door open on your way out. I've got books to sell." Nora understood drawing all that pain and anxiety deep inside to form an impenetrable ball of strength. "Sure. I hope you don't mind if I call you."

Marlene frowned at her. "Why?"

Nora traced the bright blue band on the box. "You might have some insight into what Lisa had planned. I've got to finish the film."

Marlene came around the sales counter to face Nora. "That's a bad idea."

"Sort of like someone taking Hemingway's unfinished novel and publishing it. I know I won't get it the way Lisa would have wanted, and heaven knows it won't be as good. But I need to finish it."

Marlene's weak moment had definitely passed. "Are you some kind of idiot?"

Nora was lots of kinds of idiot but didn't know which kind Marlene meant.

"Do you honestly think Lisa slipped and fell? Use your brain. Someone didn't want her to finish that film, and they found the most effective way to silence her."

9

The spotless Bentley eased to the curb and Warren braced to step out, knowing his neuropathy would shoot pain into his feet. "I won't be long, so circle around."

Ben nodded. "Sure thing, Mr. Evans."

Ben's easy manner and friendliness saddened Warren. He'd always liked Ben, ever since he'd brought him here from Salt Lake City thirteen years ago. Back then, Ben had been a homeless runaway, just one of the countless others Warren had given a hand up.

Warren pulled himself out and patted the top of the car to send it off. He pushed aside the stinging in his feet and strode through the bustling crowd to the glass doors and into the plush office building. He rode the elevator twenty-one stories up and exited to one of his shell corporation's headquarters. The attractive receptionist, who had no idea what business was transacted there, greeted him. "They are in the conference room waiting."

Warren liked to personally greet the new immigrants whenever possible. A good leader took the time to know his followers, and even though Warren wouldn't go forward with them, giving them individual attention would create a more cohesive group.

He entered the window-lined conference room with a grin. "Welcome to America. How was your flight?"

The straight-backed man looked exhausted. From the carefully vetted application and extensive Skype interviews, Warren knew Hans had made a respectable fortune in construction in Germany. At forty-five, he'd never had any serious health issues, left behind no siblings, and his parents were deceased. His wife, Katrina, likewise had no extended family. They had brought their four children with them.

Katrina and the children looked equally worn out by the overnight flight from Germany. Two boys, ages six and eight, sat together in one leather chair. The oldest, a girl of thirteen, blinked bleary eyes at Warren. Katrina leaned back in another chair with their youngest, a cherub with pink cheeks and dark ringlets who stretched across her lap, sleeping.

Hans jumped to his feet and shook Warren's hand with enthusiasm. "Mr. Evans. I'm honored. I had no idea you would meet us personally." His English, though precise, was heavily accented and halting. Warren insisted all the immigrants speak English.

At the sound of voices, the little girl opened her eyes. She flashed an immediate smile and sat up, rubbing a hand across her nose. With that minor transition between sleep and play, she slid off her mother's lap and hopped to the two boys. Her little tennis shoes twinkled with lights in the heels.

Hans glanced at her but didn't give her his complete attention. He seemed oblivious to the precious gift of his daughter. Abundance bred thoughtlessness. If he could, Warren would have scooped her up just to hear her giggle. He'd tousle those soft curls, tell her a story, grant her every wish.

Hans's eager eyes sought Warren. "You are a man of true vision. I can see that God speaks through you." His voice sounded sincere even if his words felt prepared.

Warren tried to deflect adoration. "God speaks to us all if we listen. As scripture tells us, we all have the capability to become brothers to Jesus Christ."

Hans nodded eagerly. "Yes. Yes. I believe and that's why we've come to join you."

Katrina's worried smile showed a little less enthusiasm, but joining her husband demonstrated obedience, a trait lacking in most modern women.

Warren's feet throbbed and he needed to return to the penthouse to rest. "You'll be met at the airport in Denver and given keys to a vehicle big enough for your family and luggage. Maps to Moab will be inside."

"Thank you, Mr. Evans," Hans said.

"It's best if you go straight to the compound. But if you get lost, my nephew's phone number is included with the maps."

Katrina stood and thanked Warren with a more fluid English than Hans. "I have studied the scriptures, taking special interest in those you pointed out. I see how the timing is perfect, how this is what God asks of us. I appreciate you allowing us, our children, for inclusion."

The praise the immigrants heaped on him made him uncomfortable. "There are still a couple of days until the solstice, so enjoy the beautiful scenery. The compound is isolated, but be vigilant and stay out of sight."

They thanked him again and Warren turned to leave.

Before he pulled the door open, he gave in to his desire. Even though it cost him the pain of several extra steps, he went to the little girl and placed his hand on her head. To Hans and Katrina, it probably looked like Warren was blessing her. In reality, the feel of the soft curls and skin still warm from sleep blessed him.

10

Despite the blazing mid-day sun, Nora felt chilled. Clutching Lisa's ashes, she trudged around the bookstore to the parking lot. Local antagonism over the feds snatching more land ran high. Lisa had been accosted in restaurants and lambasted in the local paper. But would the locals feel threatened enough to kill her?

Marlene's ominous insinuation had to be the fallout from grief and anger.

Still, Lisa had sounded scared in that voicemail.

Nora shivered in the shade as she stood in the alley next to the bookstore. She glanced up to see if clouds had moved in for an afternoon monsoon rain. A flash of blue in her peripheral vision made her freeze.

Someone had scribbled graffiti on the side of the bookstore, too high to reach on foot. In blue spray paint they'd imitated countless rock art figures throughout the Southwest. This collection of drawings consisted of big-headed figures with antennae, the profile of a saucer-shaped boat with a person sitting in it, and some giant human-type figures holding goats or antelope in their hands. Toward the bottom the symbol from her dream jumped out at her. Three concentric circles, sort of like a target, with six sets of two parallel lines radiating out-ward. It looked like a weird sunburst. Goose bumps rose on her arms.

Oh, for heaven's sake. Her imagination was up to its usual mischief. Shaking her head, she crossed the lot to the Jeep. She balanced the box on her hip, pulled the Jeep key from her pocket, and unlocked the door. Abbey uncurled himself from where he'd slept in the passenger seat and stood. He delicately stepped over the gear shift, wagging his tail in greeting. He stuck his nose toward Nora for a hello pat and jumped from the Jeep.

Darrell popped around the corner of the bookstore. His face lit up when he saw Nora. "Hi again."

Nora couldn't help but notice Darrell's good looks. If he hadn't gone into politics, he would have made a terrific movie star. Even his saunter spoke of assurance laced with an animal sensuality. A comparison to John F. Kennedy hit her. Women voted for Kennedy in droves because of the same qualities she observed heading toward her across the broken blacktop of the parking lot.

Abbey lifted his head at Darrell and stepped up to greet him. Darrell bent down and offered Abbey the back of his hand to sniff, then rubbed him behind the ears. "This your dog? He's a handsome old guy."

Nora glowed with affection for him. "Abbey's like any gentleman—the gray around the muzzle only adds to his distinction."

Darrell laughed. "I'll remember to resist the Grecian formula when my time comes. Abbey? But he's a male?"

Unbidden, Nora's mind flashed to an older Darrell with a smidgeon of salt to go with his pepper-dark hair.

Cole. She loved Cole. An immediate rush of warmth surged through her again. Strong, capable, kind, and funny Cole. She missed him even though it had only been a few days since they'd gone in different directions. No wonder he'd said he loved her on the phone. He was feeling that tug, too. "He's named after Edward Abbey."

Darrell considered that with a tilt of his head. "The conservationist. That makes sense. Are you staying in Moab tonight?"

Nora motioned for Abbey to climb into the Jeep. "I've got to go to Castle Valley. Abigail and Charlie took Rachel home, and I'm still on Lisa duty." She indicated the box.

Sadness fell on Darrell's face. "I can't wrap my head around Lisa being gone."

Nora placed the box on the floor in the back seat and wedged a backpack and fleece pullover around it. "I'll get in touch when I find the film."

He stepped to her door after she climbed in and said, leaning over her window, "I'm available for whatever you need."

"Thanks." She turned the key. A weak sound like the final movement of a wind-up toy rose from the engine and faded. She twisted the key again, and this time a click greeted her. One more twist resulted in the same click.

Darrell raised his eyebrows. "Sounds like you've got trouble."

She tried once more. Nothing. Drat—and lots of other words she didn't want to blurt out. Slamming the steering wheel wouldn't solve her problem and would only make her look like a spoiled brat in front of Darrell, so she clenched her fists in her lap. She reached for her pack to find her phone. "I'll call Abigail and Charlie."

Darrell put a hand on hers to stop her from dialing. "Don't do that. I'll take you to Rachel's."

"But it's twenty miles."

He chuckled. "Yeah, I know where it is."

Of course he did. This was his district. She hated to impose on him but couldn't stand the thought of prolonging Rachel's ride by making Abigail return for her. "Okay, thanks. That would be great. I saw a Conoco station a couple of blocks up the street. Can we stop there and see if they can work on it?"

He opened her door and she slid out.

He pulled his phone from his back pocket. "That place will gouge you. They feed off tourists. I know a better place." He dialed and arranged for a tow while Nora let Abbey out and grabbed her pack that contained an extra change of clothes and the barest of necessities. If Abigail was true to form, she might have scored a suite somewhere in town where Nora could crash on the sofa for the night.

Darrell slid his phone into his pocket. "All arranged. Ready?" He led them to a shiny dark blue Toyota 4Runner.

"I'm sorry about Abbey," Nora said. "You probably aren't used to hauling dogs around in your backseat."

Darrell grinned at the dog. "I live in Moab. Keeping a vehicle clean is a challenge I deal with regularly." He pointed a key fob at the back window and it slid down. He reached in and pulled out an old blanket.

Nora set Lisa's box in the back and tossed her pack beside it. Darrell spread the blanket in the backseat, let Abbey jump in, and he and Nora settled in the front seat.

The 4Runner sported leather seats and a black interior. It felt like riding on a cloud compared to Nora's geriatric Jeep.

Darrell glanced at her. "So tell me about Nora Abbott."

She gave him a sideways glance. "Going all politician on me?" He tilted his head back and laughed. "Got me."

"Why don't you tell me about you instead?"

He shifted his eyes toward her. "That's a boring story." "We've got a half-hour. Bore me."

11

Nora admired the beauty of massive red and black cliffs as they rose on either side of the highway that wound along the Colorado River east out of Moab. She inhaled the heated afternoon air that blew in the open window. Willows, Russian olives, and tamarisk lined the banks and whipped in the afternoon wind. At this point in its journey, the Colorado hadn't gained the power and wildness that was its trademark as it made its way through the Grand Canyon. But it ran high enough to accommodate adventurers in their colorful rafts bouncing in the waves.

Rain clouds built in the distance to fuel the over-active monsoon rains of this season.

"That's a big sigh," Darrell said.

Nora dug for a smile. "I was thinking about all the river trips Lisa and I took together."

Darrell laughed. "I joined her on a trip last year. We were having trouble getting funding for the Canyonlands film, and she decided to invite a few potential donors for a river trip."

"Since she ended up coming to the Trust for money, I'm assuming the trip didn't go well," Nora commented.

He gave her an irresistible grin that promised whatever adventure he cooked up was sure to be fun. "It started off great. We had sunshine and a light breeze to keep the bugs at bay. But things went downhill pretty fast when one of the older gentlemen kept ordering Lisa around like she was a waitress."

"Uh-oh."

"You know how everyone takes turns with chores on a river trip? This guy didn't do anything. Two nights before we pulled out of the river, we were sitting around the campfire after dinner. Lisa and I had just finished cleaning up the dishes and settled in with the group when this old duffer raised his empty glass and nodded at Lisa to get him a refill of wine."

"Did she toss him into the river or just his sleeping bag?" "Actually, Lisa smiled as sweetly as I've ever seen and took his cup.

I thought maybe she would sacrifice her pride for the good of the film."

Nora laughed.

"Yeah, I didn't know her very well then." "So what did she do?"

"She walked back with the last two bottles of expensive cab he'd brought along. When I saw the look on her face I jumped up, but I was too late. She lifted the bottles and poured them on the rocks of the fire ring."

Nora could envision Lisa's fiery eyes. "He was lucky."

"Classic Lisa." Darrell laughed. "It took all of my people skills to keep him from decking her. I'm not sure he ever understood what he'd done wrong."

"Lisa was okay with you defending her?"

The twinkle in his eyes showed his shrewdness. "She didn't know about it and I wasn't going to tell her. As far as she knew, he realized his error and donated much less than she'd hoped."

"I see why you're a successful politician."

"Ouch." He grew serious. "I didn't do it for a vote. I'm pretty sure I lost that one. I did it because we needed the cash for the film. It's important work."

"Yes. But politicians tend to do what's expedient for their careers, not necessarily what's right."

Red cliffs blackened by unrelenting sun rose in majestic splendor on

Nora's right. Rows of tourist cabins nestled in a grassy meadow that led to the river on the left.

Darrell glanced at her, then back to the road. "You're right, of course. And I'll admit to a little hedging here and there. Quid pro quo. But not on something this serious."

"A sincere politician?" The resignation in his eyes made her regret she'd teased him.

"People never trust my integrity. But I was raised to do what I believe is right. We lived on a ranch and worked hard. I learned that if you ever want to gain a person's trust, you've got to do what you say. There's no faking true belief."

"You've never taken a stand you didn't believe in just to get the votes?"

His dark eyes, full of good humor, flicked to her again. "Not on the big issues. And Canyonlands is huge. If we destroy the land, it can't be replaced. And the cultural sites, the rock art, and archaeological treasures are beyond value. I can't compromise on that."

"What makes you so committed to this place?"

"It's in my blood," he said. "My family is from around here. I believe in my legacy as a son of Utah."

She tried to gauge his sincerity.

One eyebrow cocked up in humor. "You're doubting me." "How could I question you?" she teased. "You're our voice of Canyonlands. Single-handedly, you're carrying our message to Congress."

He waved his hand in a come-on motion. "And I'm ruggedly handsome and completely irresistible."

No denying Darrell was attractive, but he couldn't compete with Cole for her heart.

He grew serious. "I was born here. But what most people don't know is that my mother was one of three wives."

"Polygamists?" She couldn't hide the surprise in her voice.

He nodded with a sad smile. "It's not in my official bio, so this is between you and me. When I was fourteen, my father kicked me off the ranch. He'd picked my half-brother as successor and didn't want any other men around the place."

"Fourteen?"

"It's pretty young. But I got some help to get to Salt Lake City and I managed to finish school. That's when I met Warren Evans."

"THE Warren Evans? Bourne Enterprises Warren Evans?" Darrell grinned.

"With a friend like that, I'll bet you don't have to set up many campaign fundraisers."

A slight frown creased Darrell's face, then disappeared. "Warren may be wealthy, but he's frugal. Probably has to do with his Mormon upbringing. He didn't give me cash outright, but he buried my embarrassing past so deep no one will find it. Now my bio simply says I was raised by a single mother." He eyed her. "Again, this is not for public consumption."

"Why are you trusting me with this? We just met."

He chuckled. "I'm an amazing judge of character. That, and you're Lisa's best friend. That's good enough for me."

She frowned at him.

"Okay. I feel like maybe you understand what it's like to not always fit in."

How did he know this? She squirmed, not comfortable with confessions. "Maybe I've never really felt like I belong, but my upbringing wasn't nearly as traumatic as yours. I'm sorry you had to go through that."

He shrugged. "Makes me stronger. Why did you feel like an outsider?"

He had a way of making her want to talk, which was unusual for her. "Sounds cliché, but I didn't have a father. I didn't fit with the geeks, even though I got good grades. I didn't fit with the druggies, and I wasn't an athlete."

"What happened to your father?"

Her father. Now that was a mystery. What was he like? If he'd had the chance, would he have loved Nora, nurtured and raised her? "My mother manufactured a tale about a young man who fell out of love and left. She wanted me to dislike him so I'd never search out my roots."

"Why would she do that? Is he a celebrity?"

Nora shook her head. "I've never been able to decipher Abigail's thought process." The truth turned out to be more complicated than the fiction. "My father was a Hopi. Don't ask me where my red hair comes from; that might be a mystery I never solve."

He considered the news. "Did it bother you to find out you're Hopi?"

"No. It's strange, though. In the last couple of months I've been able to spend a few weeks on the mesas in northern Arizona. My new cousin, Benny, has been trying to teach me the responsibility of being Hopi."

"As I understand it, Hopi are pretty secretive."

"They've been really nice to me on the rez, but they won't tell me about their secret ceremonies." She watched the clouds building for an afternoon monsoon storm. "I try not to worry about it too much. I have a job that fits me and a boyfriend I love."

Darrell lifted an eyebrow. "What inspired you to be an environmentalist, and what brought you to the Trust?"

"It certainly wasn't the way I was raised." Darrell nodded. "Abigail? She seems lovely."

"She's not the fire-breathing harpy I saw her as while I was growing up. And I could do a lot worse. But we've had our difficulties. Right now, I'm trying to be a grown-up and appreciate all the good things about her."

"That's enlightened."

Nora couldn't claim success. "It's progress."

He laughed. "So Abigail isn't a conservationist. What happened to you?"

"I grew up in Boulder, so me being an environmentalist is sort of like a baby beluga knowing how to swim."

He accepted that and kept probing. "But you're more on the business side than the science side."

"I owned a ski resort in Flagstaff and decided the best way to turn a profit was to make snow." She didn't see any reason to address the whole Hopi-kachina-visiting-her-and-choosing-her-to-protect-the- sacred-mountain issue.

"After realizing my misguided ways could have led to disaster, I decided to work for an environmental protection organization."

He gave her a sideways glance. "You wanted to use your powers for good."

"Exactly." She paused. "Or to be honest, to make reparations for the damage I almost did."

"Guilt."

She hesitated. "Maybe. But I'm proud of the work we do at the Trust. We're making strides on the pine beetle problem in the mountains and we've done a lot of research on cattle grazing impacting the way ranchers are using their lands."

"And Canyonlands," he prompted.

"Yes, Canyonlands. This is my first big program for the Trust. All the other projects were in place when I became executive director. But Lisa's film and the campaign to enlarge the park is on me."

He kept grilling her. "So you need to make it succeed or your career is toast."

"No. I need to make it succeed because it's important." "And your career has nothing to do with it?"

She realized the trap she'd fallen in and laughed. "You're good." That charming twinkle hit his eyes. "I know."

He flipped on the signal and turned right, skirting along a rock ridge. The black face of the rock absorbed the afternoon sun.

"So now you're back to guilt," he said. "What are you talking about?"

His eyebrow shot up again as if he questioned her declaration of innocence. "You facilitated Lisa in her dream of creating this film and saving Canyonlands. She died trying to fulfill the quest, and now you feel you need to complete it for her to make her death meaningful."

Maybe Darrell was a politician because he was so insightful or maybe he was insightful because he was a politician. Whatever chicken-or-egg scenario, he dug too deep inside Nora for her comfort.

His mentioning Lisa dying in association with the film brought back Marlene's hint that Lisa's death wasn't an accident. The message Lisa left on her phone seemed ominous, too.

He glanced at her. "I didn't mean to upset you."

She felt her scowl and lightened her expression. "I was thinking about a voicemail Lisa left me that I didn't get until this morning." He turned off the highway onto a steep one-lane road into Castle Valley. "That must be bittersweet to hear her."

The massive hoodoos called Preacher and Nuns that marked the edge of Castle Valley glowered down on them. "She said some things that don't make sense."

Darrell slowed in anticipation of turning off the highway. "Can I hear Lisa's voicemail?"

Nora cued it up, and he listened while they wound through the sleepy enclave of Castle Valley.

Castle Rock, the reason for the settlement's name, towered above them on the left. It looked like a fortress built to defend the community from the outside. Castle Valley, a small community of houses, filled the grassy valley. The original settlement snuggled in a green expanse shaded by old growth elms, cottonwoods, and willows. The rest of the houses were scattered along the scrubby valley floor between towering canyon walls.

Large tracks of undeveloped high desert terrain separated the houses, isolating them with scrub oak and juniper shrubs. The residents ranged from the very wealthy—retired or living on trust funds —to aging hippies who had accumulated enough to afford a modest home to the young people keeping close to the land with little more than a sleeping bag and camp stove. But the people who lived in Castle Valley were Moab's outsiders. They didn't own cattle or raise crops. They didn't run the gas stations or the hometown grocery store.

Darrell handed the phone back to her. "She sounds upset. She said she'd hide the camera. Do you know where?"

"I don't have a clue. Lisa could be so dramatic." Darrell agreed. "She could overreact. That's for sure."

"If I had any insight to Lisa's brain, I could find the film and camera myself. I hate asking Rachel to get me the film."

They turned onto a gravel lane and continued for a mile.

"Give her a little time. If there are copies, she'll come around eventually."

Eventually. The word dropped like lead in Nora's stomach.

Darrell pulled into Lisa's winding driveway. The cabin hid behind trees and shrubs, not fully visible from the top of the dirt driveway with its deep ruts. After several yards, they rounded a slight curve. Abigail's champagne-colored Buick sat close to the front porch. Lisa's rusting black Toyota pickup was parked in the weeds next to the cabin, and Rachel's Passat snugged behind it.

Several other vehicles lined the side of the dirt driveway heading to the road. Didn't this funeral ever end?

Nora's phone rang, and she answered. The garage mechanic explained the damage was a minor problem with her starter, but they needed a part that couldn't be delivered until late that afternoon. She hung up. "Damn."

Darrell raised an eyebrow. "Trouble with your Jeep?"

She shook her head. "Not really. I'll have to stay overnight, though." "You need a ride back to town?"

No crisis, just annoying. "No, I'll get my mother to take me." "Okay." Darrell eyed the vehicles parked on the road. He pulled the key from the ignition. "At least Rachel didn't have to come home to an empty house."

No one stood on the front porch so they all must be inside. "I suppose they're Rachel's family."

Darrell opened his door and climbed out. "I doubt that. They're not exactly supportive of her lifestyle."

"You'd think the outside world of the rich and artists and all those left-leaning people moving into Moab in the last twenty years would have desensitized the locals to lesbians. But I guess it's hard for old timers to change."

"It's not just her marrying Lisa."

Nora picked up the box and climbed from the 4Runner. She let Abbey out to trot off. "They're mad about expanding Canyonlands?"

He swung the door closed and came around the vehicle to walk with her. "To them, it feels like she's trying to steal their land."

Lisa's cabin was not one of the tonier houses in Castle Valley, but Nora had loved it from the moment she saw it ten years ago. Made of native logs, the front porch ran the length of the cabin, raised from the front yard by three steps. The railing around the porch made it look like a set piece in a spaghetti western.

Lisa had given her heart to the old place, renovating it room by room. She still needed to do some work on the foundation and replace some windows, but she'd succeeded in creating a perfect home for her and Rachel.

Lisa had placed four Adirondack chairs on the porch. Before Rachel and her artistic talent, an ordinary forest green paint covered the chairs. Now they bore bright images of nature scenes and animals, sort of like useful totem poles.

Darrell's kind eyes touched her. "Are you going to be okay?" No. "Yes."

"If you're sure, I'll head back to town. I have to make some arrangements for a community meeting in Moab on Saturday afternoon. If you're in town, why don't you stop by?"

Life continues. "Of course. Thank you so much for bringing me out here."

Darrell's smile warmed her like a cozy fire. "I'm glad we met. I'm looking forward to working with you." He placed a hand briefly on her arm.

She watched him climb back into the 4Runner and reverse down the rutted driveway.

A pair of hiking boots with dried mud caked on their soles sat next to the door. Nora caught her breath at the sight. She knew they were Lisa's by the size. For a short woman, Lisa had unusually big feet. They'd been the subject of many jokes over the years. Nora stood on the grass, unable to move.

The front screen door squeaked open. Charlie appeared. "Nora?" She forced her eyes away from the boots. "Yep. Coming."

Charlie stepped onto the porch and waited for Nora to climb the stairs with the box. She nodded toward the door. "Is everything okay?"

Charlie rubbed his grizzled chin. He spoke in a falsetto. "There's not a stitch of food in the house. And it's inconceivable the neighbors haven't brought casseroles and cookies. And not even any coffee."

His Abigail imitation made her laugh.

"And," he continued in the same voice, "there's only one roll of toilet paper."

"Sounds like Abigail will get it set straight. It's her superpower."

Charlie nodded. "The only good thing is that everyone will have to up and leave soon and let poor Rachel have some peace."

Nora stared into the darkness on the other side of the screen and heard a murmur of voices. "Maybe she doesn't want peace. It's tough to be alone."

Charlie followed her gaze.

The weight of Lisa's box pressed into Nora. Maybe asking for Lisa's film would actually be good for Rachel—help take her mind off her grief.

That was a stupid thought. Rachel didn't want to think about the film.

"I'm being sent back to town with this." He held a long list written in Abigail's perfect penmanship.

Maybe Nora should help Charlie with his mission. "Nora," Abigail called from inside the house. "I need you."

No escaping now. Nora raised her eyebrows to Charlie. "I've been summoned."

"We live to serve," he said. For Charlie, that was true. The moment he'd seen Abigail when she stood in the parking lot of Nora's ski resort in Flagstaff, he'd handed over his heart.

She watched Charlie take the steps and hurry to the Buick on legs kept spry by his daily forest ramblings. He climbed into the car, looking as out of place as a can of Pabst Blue Ribbon at a champagne brunch.

Nora scanned the yard and spotted Abbey investigating the pines on the other side of the driveway.

Nora missed Lisa. The girl she'd stayed up all night with, watching old movies and talking about how they'd change the world. Lisa always felt comfortable in her own skin. She knew herself and felt confident about her place in life. Lisa might not have told her parents she was a lesbian until her sophomore year at CU, but she'd never hidden it from them. It hurt Lisa that her parents couldn't accept her, but she understood, even at that young age, everyone lives their own life.

It angered Nora that Lisa's parents had turned away. Lisa didn't have time for anger. She had things to do. Nora admired Lisa's confidence.

Spring break their sophomore year Lisa had planned a backpack trip in Canyonlands. It would be her first time visiting southern Utah and she'd been talking about it for a month.

Nora sat on Lisa's bed in the tiny dorm room while Lisa laid out her supplies and gear on the other bed. "Come with me, Nor. We'll have a blast."

Nora's feet itched to be laced into her hiking boots. "I can't. My mother and Berle have an Easter brunch planned, and Abigail commanded I attend."

Lisa put her hands on her ample hips. "That's Abigail's deal.

What would you rather do?"

Nora could almost feel the chill of dawn and the first burst of sun over the horizon. "You know I'd rather go backpacking."

Lisa flipped her dark waves over her shoulder. "Then get your pack. We leave first thing in the morning."

"Abigail would have a fit. I'd pay for this for the rest of my life."

Lisa clicked her headlamp on to check the battery. "Only if you allow it."

Nora leaned forward, feeling the inkling of possibility. She sat back. "You don't know Abigail the Terrible."

Lisa shook the canister of fuel for the camp stove. "It's your life, chica. Abigail has her own."

Nora stood, jumpy at the thought of outright rebellion. "Yeah. But I should—"

Lisa spun around. "Should? Do you want to live your life for everyone else? Who are you?" It wasn't rhetorical. Lisa stared her down, waiting for an answer.

Nora's face burned. If she backed down now, she'd look like a weenie. She could defy Abigail and go backpacking. "Okay. I'll do it."

Lisa didn't budge, didn't smile. "Nope. You're not invited anymore."

"What?"

Lisa shook her head. She picked up a packet of dehydrated beef stew. "You're only going because I bullied you into it."

Tongues of frustration licked at Nora. "I love backpacking." "So why does it take me badgering you to go?"

"I'm going now. That's good enough."

Lisa turned back to her gear. "Of course you can come with me. I'm super excited to have you, and we're going to love it. But you really ought to figure yourself out, chica."

The clatter of dishes sounded from inside the cabin, and Abigail's voice wafted through the open screen. "Why don't you lie down, dear? You've been through so much today." From the volume and tone,

Abigail was sending a message to people that it was time for them to leave.

Rachel mumbled something.

Nora addressed the boots silently. "I'm still trying to figure out who I am."

Abigail opened the screen door and stepped out on the deck. "Come in here. Rachel needs you."

Rachel probably had tons of friends she'd rather talk to than Nora, a woman she barely knew and had never really connected with. Still, if Abigail thought Nora could help Rachel, she ought to give it her best shot. Maybe she'd be able to gently ask about the film. Abigail met her on the porch. She lowered her voice in conspiracy. "Try to get rid of those people. Rachel needs to rest." "Who are they?"

Abigail threw a disgusted glance at the screen and the low voices inside. "Environmental activists, from what I can tell. They're discussing their next meeting and protest with no consideration of Rachel."

"Where are you going?" Nora asked.

Abigail descended a step. "I can't send Charles to the store on his own. He gets the store brand or organic or local or who knows how he decides. It's rarely on quality and taste."

"So I'm supposed to clear the house and wait for you to get back?" Abigail hurried down the remaining three stairs. "That and comfort Rachel."

Nora balanced the box against her belly, opened the screen door, and stepped inside.

Nora hadn't been to the cabin since Lisa and Rachel married. Significant differences from when she'd been here last jarred Nora, but once she thought about it, she realized the changes were normal. As Lisa and Rachel twined their lives together, their house would morph from simply being Lisa's to theirs. And now, just Rachel's.

The screen door opened into a sunny great room. Hardwood floors stretched out, bright Navajo rugs spread at odd angles. Heavy leather furniture added to the lodge theme. Frameless canvases of desert flowers, much like Georgia O'Keeffe paintings, hung on the walls. As was evident with the porch chairs, Rachel's painting style here was unmistakable.

The kitchen sat off to the left, a breakfast bar separating it from the great room. French doors framed an office at the far end of the room. Lisa's massive pine desk, reclaimed from an old government office and refinished by Lisa's determined hand, sat littered with papers and file folders. Her laptop rested amid the debris, the top up as if Lisa had momentarily walked away.

Stairs led off the left of the doorway, heading up to the three bedrooms on the second floor. Even though Lisa had bought a four bedroom, she'd ripped out a wall, installed another bathroom, added a balcony, and created a romantic master bedroom with an incredible view of Castle Rock as a wedding gift for Rachel.

Rachel stood in the kitchen, hands on the breakfast bar, staring across the great room at a window between two of the giant flower paintings. Her eyes didn't seem to focus on the mountains in the distance.

Two thirty-something women flanked her. They seemed focused on their conversation with the two men standing in front of the mantel of the fireplace. A gray-haired woman and man sat on the leather couch.

A lively discussion filled the room. "I think we need posters showing tar sands damage and we don't make a sound."

"Yes! Like those pro-life posters of half-aborted babies. Demonstrate the evil. A picture is worth a thousand words."

"That's stupid. We should do like PETA. Remember when they splashed blood on women wearing fur?"

"It was paint. And that won't work."

The arguments flew around the room with everyone stepping on each other's sentences.

Nora crossed the room, the floor creaking as she passed Rachel's line of sight. "I'm going to set this in Lisa's office."

Rachel's eyes slowly focused on Nora, and she gave a short nod. "Why bother with a protest around here, anyway? These people have their minds made up."

"Besides, they aren't the people voting."

"Heath's got a point. We should go to D.C. and picket on the Capitol steps."

"Not everyone is a trust funder and can fly all over the place."

Nora entered the office. To the right, another set of French doors opened out onto a low redwood deck without rails. Abbey lay on the warm wood, dozing in the sun. He acted as though he'd been here dozens of times and knew his way around, which, of course, he had—just not in the last couple of years.

The deck was one of the first things Lisa had refinished after buying the cabin over ten years ago. The plumbing hadn't been up to snuff, and smelly carpet had covered the floors. The windows were tiny and leaked with the slightest breeze, but Lisa installed the French doors and built the deck because she needed contact with the land and sky. She loved the view of the La Sal Mountains and, most days, wasn't content to see them from behind the doors.

Her desk faced the doors, which she kept open in all but the worst weather. She loved watching the jagged peaks, purple in the morning, turn green and brown and black as the sun played against them. She said their grandeur reminded her to be humble.

Like the sculptor who finds the image hidden in stone, Lisa had discovered the beauty of the cabin. But Nora had to admit Rachel's art and decorating touches made the home bright and comfortable. More than once Lisa had raved about how Rachel had improved her life: "I had no idea how much I needed a wife!"

A wood-burning stove nestled in the corner opposite the deck. An antique pine cabinet sat along the wall, its surface scattered with piles of papers. Nora pushed several file folders out of the way and set the box on the desk. Lisa couldn't look at the view anymore, but somehow, placing her ashes there made Nora feel better.

Voices rose, reminding Nora of Abigail's orders. She spun around and returned to the living room. Rachel no longer leaned on the counter between the two women. Nora glanced around the room and out the screen door. Rachel sat on one of the Adirondack chairs, leaning forward, her face to the mountains.

Nora held her hand up. "Thanks for being here for Rachel. I know she appreciates your concern. But it's been a long day. Please call and visit again."

A couple of the people looked confused. Some seemed to take Nora's words at face value and got ready to leave. At least one woman scanned the room for Rachel, and when she realized Rachel was no longer with them, looked stricken and ashamed.

Nora ushered them out the front door. The storm clouds blotted out the sun and a few drops plopped onto the porch roof. While they said their goodbyes and offered to help Rachel in any way, lingering on the porch, Nora returned to the office.

She stood in the center of the room, feet planted on a blood-red Navajo rug. Her eyes scanned the surface of the desk and the shelves, traveling to the cupboard doors and across to a pine filing cabinet. Where would Lisa keep copies of the film?

Soft raindrops pattered on the deck. Nora hesitated. Lisa still lingered in this house, in the office, and Lisa hated anyone messing with her stuff.

Lisa and Nora had shared an apartment the last two years of undergrad in Boulder. It drove Nora crazy the way Lisa cluttered the tiny space with her books and papers, socks, sweaters, shoes—everything. Nora would gather all of Lisa's things from the common space and deposit them in Lisa's bedroom. That led to a major confrontation and a compromise. Nora wouldn't mess with Lisa's stuff if Lisa would try not to clutter the living room.

"This office is like you, Lisa—messy, beautiful, and bright." Nora wrapped her arms around herself.

Outside, Abbey stood and shook. The rain didn't appear too serious so Nora left him to enjoy it.

She ran her fingertips along the edge of the desk while her eyes took in the chaos of papers on top. Lisa worked in a whirlwind, often losing items or forgetting appointments. Rachel's hand kept order in the rest of the house, but this office belonged to Lisa.

Nora slipped around to the desk chair and sat in front of the opened laptop. "Where did you put the film?" she spoke, even if Lisa couldn't hear.

Abbey stretched, circled around twice, and flopped down again. Without the film, Nora's best option would be to collect photos and write narration for Darrell. That seemed like a poor solution. Even with the amazing landscapes, a slideshow seemed stagnant. To stir the committee's passion, they needed movement, light, breathtaking sights, and ugly images to demonstrate the threat.

Nora slid her finger on the laptop's touchpad and waited for it to wake up. She surveyed the pinion and juniper outside. The sun broke out, highlighting individual raindrops. The tangy smell of sage drifted through an open window.

The sound of car engines indicated the activists must be on their way.

Nora glanced through the file icons on the computer's desktop. Nothing indicated a film project. She found the directory and looked through that, too. She opened a few files that might have contained some portion of the project. Nothing. No notes for narrative, no digital pictures, and certainly no film.

Abbey no longer sprawled on the deck. Nora pulled herself from behind the desk and crossed the room, peering out the doors in search of him.

She located him by the movement of ginger hair against the scrub and sand. He trotted toward the front of the house. Maybe Charlie and Abigail had returned. If so, they hadn't been gone long.

Nora popped open the doors. She stepped out on the deck polka-dotted by drying raindrops. It took her a moment to recognize what she heard.

Rachel's voice sounded irritated. A man responded, matching her heat. Nora jumped to the edge of the deck, ready to dash to the front of the cabin if necessary.

The sight of Lee's white pickup stopped her. She inched a ways before she spotted Rachel and Lee standing in front of the hood of the pickup. Lee held Rachel's hand and only a couple of feet separated them. Lee's head bent and Rachel's raised face was only inches from his. Nora couldn't see their expressions, only their profiles. Their anger dropped away and they stood, motionless. They communicated without words. These were not the movements of strangers.

Nora backed up and retreated to Lisa's office. She clicked the door closed and stood in front of it, staring into nothing, trying to understand what she'd seen. Her eyes slowly focused on the Navajo rug. She lifted her gaze to the bookshelves next to the wood stove.

She already suspected Lisa's death might not have been an accident. Maybe Lee killed Lisa so he and Rachel could be together, Nora thought wildly. Right. That made sense because people always killed someone instead of just asking for a divorce. Sheesh, Nora. Jump to conclusions much?

Her eyes came to rest on the jumble of loose pages and books, pamphlets, and magazines scattered on the bottom shelf. Wait. What was that? There, thrust between stacks of papers, she caught sight of a DVD case, the slim black edges barely visible.

Nora rushed across the room and squatted down. She snatched the case, excited to see the DVD nestled inside. Lisa's bold handwriting dated it May 28. No year. But if it was this year, this DVD was only three weeks old. If it was a backup, it would only be missing images from a couple of shoots.

Hope swelled in her chest. This might save the day.

Nora lunged for the laptop, fingers running along the sides, looking for a disc drive. Damn. The newer machine didn't have a one. Desperate, she jumped from the desk and rummaged through the debris scattered across its surface.

She yanked out a drawer. The wood stuck. Nothing but files and notebooks. She shoved against it and tried another drawer. This time she hit pay dirt. An external drive sat amid discarded phones and charger cords.

Nora pulled it out, sweeping her hand through the dead and dying electronics. She came up with a USB cord and quickly attached the driver to the computer and inserted the DVD.

This was it: Lisa's work. Something for Nora to hold on to.

Nothing but a whirr of digital and black screen. Nora's heart shriveled.

The screen flashed bright and suddenly sprang to life with a broad view of the cliffs. Time-lapse photography took the scene from dawn to midnight in a matter of seconds. Stars shone bright, then faded as the sun swept across the sky and reemerged. The image faded to a creek, the same spot Lisa's box had rested just that morning. Again, the images on the screen shifted to show a trampled, barren creek bed eroding away and leaving desolation behind. A gushing black flood of tainted water showed the uglier side of tar sands mining.

Lisa's film. Edited but without narration. Nora and Darrell could finish it. No one with a heart could turn down the chance to protect this iconic landscape. Lisa had done it!

"What are you doing?" Rachel's ragged voice demanded as she stood in the doorway between the living room and kitchen.

Nora jerked and sucked in air. "You scared me." "This is Lisa's office. She'd hate for you to be in here."

Nora couldn't point out that someone, sometime would have to be in here and pack up Lisa's life. Maybe sharing the news that Lisa's work would go on might help Rachel. "I found it."

Rachel's face blackened like a storm cloud. "Found what?" Nora spun the laptop around to face Rachel. "The film. I suppose it's missing the last bits, but we can totally use this." "Where did that come from? There were no backups." Nora pointed toward the bookshelf. "I found it, buried."

"No! No more. Leave it alone." She leaped forward. Before Nora could stop her, Rachel grabbed the computer and jerked it off the desk. The attached player dangled from the upraised computer. Rachel brought the laptop down on the side of the desk with all the rage of an abandoned wife. "I won't have it!"

She raised her arms and smashed it again and again.

Nora kept her eye on the external drive that swung back and forth, occasionally smashing against the side of the desk. As long as Rachel's temper tantrum focused on the laptop and left the player alone, the film would survive.

Rachel grabbed the cord of the player. She yanked it from the computer and threw the laptop with enough force that it crashed against the bookshelf and fell to the floor, separating the screen from the keyboard. She held on to the drive and ejected the DVD.

"No!" Nora cried as she lunged across the desk.

Rachel gritted her teeth and, using both hands, brought the disc down on the corner of the desk and leaned her weight on it. It bent slightly, then snapped with a popping that might as well have been a BB to Nora's heart.

12

Rachel stood in front of Nora, panting with spent rage. Her flashing eyes dared Nora to challenge her.

Heat surged through Nora, her hands clenched in their urge to throttle Rachel. The film. The only copy she knew existed. All Lisa's work—her passion, her talent—destroyed in a tantrum. She stifled the frustrated scream, fighting to understand Rachel's grief but really wanting to smack her.

"Why did you do that?" Nora barely restrained her temper. Tears glistened in Rachel's eyes. "Forget about the film." "But it was Lisa's dream!"

Rachel flung her arm in the air. "If you'd never given her funding, she'd have had to give it up. She'd be alive now."

There it was, the familiar guilt drenching her. Nora fought to keep from drowning in it again. "Her death was an accident."

Rachel spit her words at Nora. "You keep believing that."

Marlene had said it, now Rachel. Nora kept her voice slow and even. "I understand how you feel."

Contempt dripped from Rachel's words. "You don't know anything about how I feel."

Sadly, Nora probably understood more about it than either liked to admit. She knew because her husband had been murdered. It had felt like her heart had been ripped out, leaving a raw, bloody hole. She'd barely been able to breathe, let alone believe she'd ever smile or laugh again.

Nora stepped toward her, intending to reach for Rachel's hand or put an arm around her.

Rachel stepped back. "I won't have anything to do with that film." Nora nodded. "Okay. I ... " She was going to say she understood but stopped herself. "Saving Canyonlands meant so much to Lisa. She believed, and I do, too, that her film would make all the difference with the committee. I'd like to finish it for her."

"It's not safe to continue." Rachel's thin lips disappeared in her anger.

"What do you mean?"

Rachel skirted Nora and stomped into the living room. "You have no clue what it's like around here. The Mormons—my family and everyone I grew up with—believe they own this land. And why not? They came here when it was empty. Nothing."

Sure, empty—except the indigenous people scratching out their existence, migrating and living off the land. The first people to live around here were the Anasazi, and the Hopi believed they were descended from the Anasazi. That would make them Nora's ancestors. The Anasazi wrote their history on the rocks everywhere throughout this place. They built shrines across the land.

Rachel spewed in her rage. "My ancestors were persecuted. They were chased from New York to Illinois and Nebraska. They only wanted to live their lives in peace. They sacrificed every luxury to move west and settle here. It was a hard life, but they survived. And now you do-gooders, who think you know what's best, are trying to steal their sanctuary."

Nora kept her voice calm. "Protect it, not take it away. We're only trying to keep it alive and safe for future generations."

Rachel glared at her and let out a bitter laugh. "Sure. Because the Mormons are stupid and haven't been good stewards for the last hundred and seventy years."

Nora didn't mention the riparian areas ravaged by tromping hooves. Overgrazed, arid pastures that blew sand, creating such severe dust storms that highways had to be closed down. "Things can't stay the same way they've been. The land won't last."

"The Mormons believe in stewardship. Joseph Smith wrote about taking care of the land and the animals so we'd have abundance."

"We're trying to use science to conserve the land," Nora explained.

"From what you call over-grazing. What they call making a living," Rachel countered.

"Grazing cattle out there is inhumane. There's not enough for them to eat."

"These people, my family, only want to raise their children the way they were raised."

"Expansion of Canyonlands can't destroy a livelihood that doesn't exist because the land has been exhausted."

Rachel's hands shook and tears glistened. "It's their land, and people who don't understand their way of life are trying to steal it. Do you know what that's like? It'd be like social services barging into your home and taking your child because they don't agree with your religion."

A kinder person would not say anything. "Is that why someone killed Lisa?"

Rachel's eyes widened until Nora thought they'd pop like water balloons. "Don't say that."

"Lisa climbed like Spider-Man. She wouldn't have fallen from that ladder."

Rachel dropped to a brightly padded Morris recliner and buried her face in her hands. Nora sat on the sturdy pine coffee table in front of Rachel and tried to peer into her face. "You said as much yourself." Rachel lowered her hands and stared at Nora with dead eyes. "Leave it alone. You can't bring Lisa back. If you keep after this, you might have an accident, too."

"So you're just going to ignore that someone might have killed Lisa?"

Rachel glared at her.

Nora stood. "I'm going to the cops."

Rachel jumped to her feet. She took two steps toward the galley kitchen and spun around. "Don't do that."

"Why not?"

"Because the law around here is Mormon. They'll take care of their own, but if you go telling them what to do, you'll only get in trouble. And I mean big trouble."

"I can't just leave it alone."

"I'm begging you! Go back to Boulder and the Trust and find another project. The planet is a mess—surely you can find another way to spend your time and money."

"If I could find a copy of Lisa's film, I'd be out of here right now." "There is no copy. I destroyed them all."

"They weren't yours to destroy! They belong to the Trust." Nora wanted to hit something. She placed her palm on her forehead, trying to think. "Did she put anything in a safe deposit box, maybe? Or store it in the cloud?"

Rachel lowered her eyebrows. "It's not like home videos of a birthday party. This stuff can't be put in the cloud. And believe me, I've thought of every place Lisa might have stored a backup. I've destroyed them all. Every one."

"There was that one on the bookshelf." "You won't find another. Go home." "But if Lisa was murdered..."

"She wasn't!"

"Who wasn't what?" Abigail interrupted, opening the screen door on the front porch.

Rachel startled and spun toward Abigail. "You're back."

Abigail's sandals clicked on the wood floor, then thudded on a Navajo rug, then clicked again. Charlie dogged her, balancing several grocery sacks. "Put them on the counter, dear."

Charlie obliged and retreated to gaze out the window.

Abigail pulled gourmet coffee from one of the bags, followed by a bottle of white wine. "You said 'she wasn't' and sounded all worked up. I asked who she was and what she wasn't."

Rachel shrugged. "Nora thought Lisa planned on going to D.C. to screen the film and represent the Trust, and I said she wasn't."

Abigail bustled about the kitchen putting the groceries away. It looked like she'd bought all the basics. It's true that Abigail's presence often turned Nora into a raving lunatic, but sometimes she knew just what to do. In this case, it was making sure Rachel's kitchen was stocked. "I have to agree with Rachel. Lisa, while I adored her, would never have been good presenting her case to Congress."

Abigail set a bag of pasta in a cupboard. "Nora, you can be very cool, almost standoffish. You should be the one to make a professional presentation, and Darrell can supply the charm."

Nora ignored the insult nestled in there. Rachel's lie had slipped out so easily. She must have plenty of experience with them. She could be lying about more backups.

Charlie spoke softly. "Don't see your Jeep anywhere."

A stab of annoyance flashed. "It's not going to be fixed until tomorrow. Can you give me a ride back to town?" Nora asked.

Abigail inserted a corkscrew into a bottle of Chardonnay. "We can drop you on our way home tomorrow."

Rachel sat on a barstool made from pine and covered with a woven cushion similar to the Navajo rugs. She rested her cheek on her hand and watched Abigail.

"I need to go tonight."

"Why tonight?" Abigail asked. The cork extricated from the bottle with a cute little pop. "Your Jeep won't be done until tomorrow."

"I need to get a hotel room."

Rachel pointed to a stemware rack above the sink. Abigail slid three glasses off and placed them on the counter. "All the rooms are booked. There's a big bike race or somesuch and not a room to be had."

"Then I'll get my camping gear from the Jeep and sleep outside."

Abigail poured the wine and handed a glass to Rachel. She picked up the other two and walked around the counter to hand one to Nora. "That's silly. Rachel has kindly offered to let us stay here. You know, Lisa always said since I gave her the loan for this place, I could stay anytime I wanted. Rachel won't mind if you take the other room, will you, Rachel? And I'm sure Lisa would want us to be here."

Rachel took a sip of wine and lowered her glass. She glared at Nora. "Feel free to stay as long as you like."

13

The chill of early morning pricked Nora's nose. She sat huddled on the front porch in a soft throw she'd found on the couch. The glow over the tips of the La Sals hinted at the sun's arrival. She drew the throw, with its earth tones and gentle pattern, closer around her. Abbey sniffed and explored the yard, stopping to pee on an Apache plume shrub beyond Abigail's Buick. Nora tucked her feet under her in the Adirondack chair. She'd chosen the chair painted with mountains and dancing yellows and blues of swirling Van Gogh skies. Small birds flitted from the gnarled branches of the scrub oaks and the meadowlarks had just let out their first blast of song.

Nora's mind had been spinning in circles all night. She'd fought the blankets and finally cried uncle. She'd plodded down the stairs, intending to go through Lisa's office again. She'd no sooner clicked on the desk lamp when Rachel had appeared and stood in the doorway with her arms crossed until Nora retreated to the front porch. Rachel had gone back upstairs but Nora didn't want to upset her any further, so she left the office alone.

She'd been sitting on the deck for the past few hours. Cole would be stretched out in his family's house in Wyoming, no doubt flat on his back, sleeping that deep sleep he fell into almost every night. She longed to cuddle next to him.

Her brain switched to Etta and her threats. She loved her job but hated the dance to keep the Board of Directors happy. After that, she felt the weight of Lisa's death. Had someone killed her to keep her from finishing and distributing her film? Rachel said local law enforcement wouldn't help. Nora had no proof and only a vague suspicion, so taking it to another agency, like the FBI, wouldn't do any good. Wrapped in frustration and helplessness, she tried to distract herself by trouble-shooting an upcoming public education event the Trust planned to sponsor next month in Boulder.

But an image of her kachina popped into her head. His absence felt like rejection. Maybe she'd been fooling herself into thinking she could be a part of the tribe when really, she'd never be anything more than a tourist.

Unable to stay still for another second, she threw off the blanket and scurried into the house. Trying to be as silent as possible, she leaped up the stairs and ran to her room. With growing urgency, she rummaged in her backpack until her fingers finally closed on the small leather pouch. She pulled it from the pack and raced back to the porch.

Her hand shook as she reached into the pouch, pinched at the corn dust inside, and brought it out. She faced the mountains and held her breath.

Three ... two ... one.

The sun flared over the peak. Nora inhaled and tossed the corn dust into the air.

A real Hopi would sing out loud. She'd express her gratitude to the spirits for creating the world and pledge herself to protecting it.

Nora gazed at the sun over the mountains, inhaled the fresh morning air, and kept her mouth shut.

"What are you doing?" Abigail's voice preceded the squeak of the screen door opening.

Nora jumped and spun around. Heat rushed to her cheeks. "I couldn't sleep so I got up early."

Abigail stood on the porch in one of her velour workout suits, this one a brilliant turquoise. She held two thick pottery mugs with swirling browns and deep reds adorning the sides. She must have been brewing coffee in the kitchen when Nora raced upstairs. Nora had been so wrapped up in her own angst she hadn't even smelled it. Abigail narrowed her eyes. "Did you just toss corn into the air?"

Nora shoved the pouch into her shorts pocket. She sauntered back to the chair and picked up the throw. "Is that coffee I smell?" she said.

Abigail handed her a mug. The warmth of the coffee penetrated Nora's palm and the moisture from the aromatic steam greeted her. "Thanks."

Abigail lowered herself into a chair painted with a red armadillo, purple javelina, and yellow ground squirrels. She sat on the edge and clutched her mug. "You and that old fool, Charles."

Nora raised her eyebrows. "What about Charlie?"

Abigail waved her hand in dismissal. "He was up hours ago. He said he couldn't sleep and went trudging off like he does."

Nora scanned the yard. "I didn't see him."

Abigail sipped her coffee and stared ahead. "He wouldn't disturb your vigil. He's like that."

Nora nodded. "Abbey must have gone with him."

They sat in silence for a while until Abigail said in a tight voice, "I don't suppose there's anything wrong with saying thank you for this sunrise."

Nora sat in her mountain chair, careful not to spill the coffee. "This porch is the reason Lisa bought this place."

Abigail spoke quietly. "I remember that first summer she lived here. No running water, the stairs threatening to cave in. I believe a family of skunks lived under the porch."

The coffee tasted a little like heaven, though not a big chunk of heaven because Abigail had made her usual anemic brew. Still, it was good enough that Nora felt a pang for enjoying it, knowing Lisa would never drink another cup.

That kind of maudlin attitude wouldn't help anyone and certainly didn't honor the spirit of her friend. "It was really nice of you to loan her the money for this place."

"I was happy to do it."

That wasn't exactly how Nora remembered it. To Lisa's face, Abigail was all generosity and graciousness, but to Nora, Abigail complained about the foolishness of buying a dilapidated shack and fixing it up herself. She argued that the house sat on a flood plain, although no one living could remember a flash flood so violent it would rush though this wide valley. Abigail had told Nora one reason she lent Lisa the money was to distract her from the ridiculous notion of being a lesbian. If she focused on something else, she'd get over it and find a man, her mother reasoned. Abigail had progressed a long way since then.

Nora closed her eyes to the sun's warmth. "She loved it here." "I've never liked Moab."

Nora watched Abigail's tense face. "I didn't know that. Why?" "Bad juju." Abigail twisted her mouth in distaste.

"What do you mean?"

"The vibes. I just don't like it."

It surprised Nora that Abigail noticed anything beyond the retail experience of a place. "I didn't know you spent any time here."

"A little."

"When?"

"What is this? Twenty questions?" Abigail snapped. Nora sat back, puzzled at Abigail's reaction. "Sorry."

After a pause, Abigail said, "Your father and I visited once." Nora sat up. Abigail didn't offer up much about Nora's father.

"When?"

Abigail gazed at the mountains. "Not long after we met. He loved it here and wanted to show it to me. We backpacked in Arches and spent some time in Canyonlands."

Nora nearly choked on the coffee. "You ... " She couldn't picture it. "You backpacked?"

Abigail frowned at her. "I wasn't born being your mother. I was young once, too."

In principle, that made sense. Nora could see Abigail as a high school girl in Nebraska, being head cheerleader and dating the football captain. She could imagine her in college giggling with the girls on her dorm floor. What she couldn't fit into her brain was her mother sweating under a pack and sleeping on the ground, covered in the red dust of the Southwest.

"So you and my father came up here? What did he show you?" Nora grabbed hold of any knowledge about her father. She longed to know more about him, and these rare snippets from her mother were all she had.

Abigail waved her hand. "Oh, I don't know. We hiked around and it all looked pretty much the same to me. I was young and just happy to be with him."

"Did he tell you anything about the landscapes or traditions? This isn't typical Hopi land, so I wonder why he brought you here and not the mesas."

Abigail clucked her teeth. "You've been to the mesas. They aren't much to look at. I suspect your father felt reluctant to introduce me to his family. They weren't likely to approve of me."

Nora waited. There had to be more.

"He did what you just did, though. Every morning he would get up ridiculously early and say prayers to the sunrise and throw corn dust into the air." Abigail shook her head. "I'm glad you don't grunt and moan like he did."

"Singing, Mother. They call that singing."

Abigail waved it away. "Yes, I know what they call it. What I call singing is the Beatles or Neil Diamond. And throwing corn is odd." "You and Berle used to go to church every Sunday. What's the difference?" Berle was Abigail's second husband, the man she'd been married to the longest—unless she and Charlie stayed together for another twenty years.

Abigail gave her an incredulous look. "How can you even compare the two? Sunday services at Boulder Presbyterian were conducted at reasonable times on the day of rest. Not at sunrise, except for one day of the year, of course."

Maybe Abigail wasn't as progressive as Nora hoped. Nora reached across to Abigail's chair and took her hand. "Thanks for coming. It's good to see you and Charlie."

Abigail looked startled by Nora's affection. She eyed Nora closer, as if checking for fever. "Lisa was special to me."

They sat, silent for a moment, probably as long as Abigail could stand. "But this whole thing she was doing, this film. I don't understand what it's about."

Nora sipped her cooling coffee. "She was making a film to screen for the people at the Department of the Interior and to Congress to show them how important and fragile Canyonlands Park is and how desperately we need to enlarge the park boundaries."

Abigail sat up, as if spoiling for a fight. "That's silly. You've got Arches Park," she pointed behind them, toward Moab. "There's Escalante and then Canyonlands. The whole darned state of Utah is practically a giant park."

Who knew Abigail harbored such resentment for conservationists? "Actually, Mother, there's one point four million acres of public lands surrounding Canyonlands National Park that need protection." Nora heard the edge in her own voice. It was the defensive hue that colored her words since she'd first berated her mother for crimes against the rainforest when Nora was in fourth grade.

Now, Nora and Abigail were grown women. They could be friends. The kind of people who respected each other and could engage in civil discussions.

Nora started again. "The original proposal for Canyonlands, way back in 1936, was for one million acres."

Abigail's mouth set in disapproval.

"But it was whittled down to 338,000 acres before Congress voted. That's about a third of its original size."

"Even if it's desert wasteland, you can't restrict such huge portions of land."

"So many cultural resources and relics lay just outside the park with no protection."

Abigail waved her hand in the air again and made a dismissive noise with her lips. "Do you really believe there aren't enough petroglyphs and pot shards protected already?"

With clenched teeth, Nora said, "Do you really believe we need to preserve *Romeo and Juliet* since we already have *Henry the VIII*?" "That's not at all the same thing." Abigail stood up and reached for Nora's empty coffee cup. She retreated into the house.

Nora watched the light play on the mountain range, the shadows deep on Castle Rock. She leaned her head back on the chair and closed her eyes. The bird chorus erupted in full sunrise crescendo. Even the flies and other insects buzzed in their morning busyness.

The screen opened again and Nora smelled coffee. Abigail must be back with a second cup. "I'm going to stay," Nora said, more to herself than to Abigail.

"Good idea. Enjoy the sunrise and have another cup of coffee. I'll start breakfast." Abigail set the coffee cup on the wide arm of the chair.

Nora sat up, eyes on the changing light of the mountains. "No, I mean I'm going to stay here in Moab."

"Now what's the point in that? As I understand it, there are no copies of Lisa's film so there's no reason for you to be here."

"I have to do something about this," Nora replied. "About what, the film?"

"Find it, yes. But ... " "What?"

Nora wanted to take back the "but" she'd uttered. Abigail didn't need to know Nora suspected Lisa's death wasn't an accident. If the local police wouldn't help, she'd have to do it on her own.

Abigail frowned, "This isn't ... "

Nora jumped up, letting the blanket fall to the porch. "Where is Lisa's camera? She said I'd know. They might have destroyed the film but not the camera."

"They who?"

Nora grabbed Abigail and coffee splashed from the mug. She pulled her mother close and squeezed. "I'm going to finish this for Lisa."

She jumped toward the door, ready to get started.

Rachel stood just inside the screen, coffee cup suspended halfway to her mouth. She glared at Nora for half a second, and then whirled around.

14

Fueled by determination, Nora hurried from the porch. The screen banged closed behind her, then opened and tapped closed to let Abigail in.

Nora rushed into the office and stood in the middle of the room, the wool of the Navajo rug warm under her feet. She placed a hand on the cool wood of Lisa's box. "What were you trying to tell me?"

If Lisa were murdered, the logical suspect was a local landowner with a grudge against environmentalists. While Nora didn't know many people who fit that description, one face popped to mind.

Lee Evans. Those hate-filled dark eyes focused on her at the funeral. He ran her off the road and pretended it was an accident. Was he trying to scare her and make her go home? Had he done the same to Lisa? When she wouldn't back down, had he created an accident?

He'd been out at the cabin yesterday having a serious conversation with Rachel. Rachel wanted Nora to drop the film project and go home. Was she protecting Lee? If so, why?

A cold wind blew across Nora's brain—an affair! Both Marlene and Lisa mentioned Rachel's upbringing and how hard it was for her to give up her old life. Maybe she was trying to go back to it.

Lisa's message said she'd recorded something on film. Her voice had sounded terrified. Whatever she wanted to tell Nora was on that camera, and Nora needed to find it soon.

She glanced quickly around the office, but didn't see a camera sitting anywhere. She hadn't expected it to be in plain sight. She shook her head at the pile of papers on the desk and lowered herself to sit. The bottom left-hand drawer squeaked as Nora tugged on it. Inside, a mass of file folders, envelopes, and odd bits of articles torn from newspapers and magazines tumbled in an orgy of clutter. She shoved it closed and tried for the drawer on the other side.

The stairs creaked and seconds later Abigail appeared in the doorway. She'd traded her velour running suit for beige slacks, a T-shirt with all sorts of shiny bling attached, and flats. For Abigail, even a few days away from home required an extensive wardrobe. Even if Nora had expected to stay longer than overnight, she wouldn't have packed much more than a change of clothes. As it was, she was reduced to wearing the same shorts but had donned a clean T-shirt and underwear. "Would you like more coffee?"

"Yes, please." She looked around for her cup, couldn't remember where she'd left it, and shrugged at Abigail. She returned her attention to the desk and started arranging the piles of papers. None of them had to do with household expenses. Rachel must handle all that. Lisa's papers mostly dealt with environmental issues. Articles about climate change and the benefits and challenges of sustainable energy tangled with maps of Utah in various iterations. Topo maps, park boundary maps, historic renderings. Black Sharpie circles pointed out various locations. Next to many of these, Lisa had scribbled dates and times.

A few articles about Mormon history and beliefs were scattered amid the environmental information clutter, although it really didn't fit Lisa's MO. Maybe she was studying the local culture to better deal with the opposition. Or maybe she wanted to understand Rachel better.

A raven squawked in Nora's pocket. It startled her and she reached for her phone, checking the ID and hoping it was Cole. Disappointed, she answered. "Hi, Fay. You're up early."

Fay directed the open space programs for the Trust. "Weed Warriors. We were going to do this on Saturday, but a few people couldn't make it so we bumped it back a day. I've got a ten-person crew to pull Russian thistle along the road, and we wanted to get it done before it gets hot."

Nora knew that but had forgotten.

"Sorry to bother you. But I checked the Trust voicemail, and Etta Jackson left a long message about being here at eight on Monday morning and bringing a couple other board members."

A giant sour ball burned in Nora's stomach. She'd known about Etta's trip but not about her bringing a brigade. "Thanks for letting me know." After hanging up, Nora clenched her fists and stared at the La Sals. That left her three days.

Abigail walked into the office and placed a steaming cup of coffee on a spot Nora had just cleared.

Nora picked up her cup. "Thanks." She took a sip and, with effort, kept from making a face.

"I used that hazelnut creamer you like," Abigail said. "When did I tell you I like flavored creamer?"

Abigail walked over to a bookcase and gazed at an owl's wing. She must not have realized it was a real wing and not an artist's rendition. "Oh, maybe that wasn't you. It wouldn't make sense that you'd like flavoring. You only want that whole grain, tasteless stuff, vegetarian and quinoa."

"Pronounced *keen-wa*, Mother. Not like the city in Portugal. And I'm not a vegetarian. I just prefer food that wasn't manufactured in a lab." Nora eyed the coffee, gauging whether she could stomach the sweet to get at the caffeine. She decided not to risk it.

Abigail spun around and sashayed to the French doors. "How long do you think you'll stay in Utah?"

Nora eyed the mess on the desk. "Not sure."

Lisa might not be the most organized person, but she would have at least stashed a copy off-site. The work had consumed her for years. And the camera—where would she have hidden that?

"Can't you work from Boulder? Load up Lisa's files and take them with you." Abigail swayed as if listening to calming music. Her air of casualness was entirely too practiced.

"When are you going home?" Nora stacked the maps on one corner of the desk, the random articles on another, the Mormon stuff, unrelated pictures, and ads in yet another pile behind Lisa's box.

"This morning. As soon as Charles gets back from his walkabout. We'll drop you off to pick up your Jeep." Abigail sipped her coffee and hugged herself with the arm not holding the cup.

Nora studied a photo of a rock art panel. It showed the typical snake squiggles, running antelope, and big-headed people with spears. An ancient hand had carved the weird sunburst image into the corner of the panel. Nora tossed the photo into a pile with several other pictures of rock art panels.

Abigail rocked on her heels. "What about Cole? Doesn't he miss you? You shouldn't leave him alone too long."

Nora sat back in her chair. "Have you talked to him lately?" Abigail and Cole had a whole relationship separate from Nora. They'd conspired last year to get Nora together with Cole.

Abigail frowned. "No. Why? Is something wrong?"

Nora shook her head. "He's in Wyoming. His father's health is failing and there's something going on with his family."

"There's something else, isn't there? What is it?" Abigail advanced on her.

"Nothing." Nora picked up a map of northern Arizona and dropped it on the map pile. "It's just..."

"Just what?"

Nora sipped her coffee and nearly gagged. She'd forgotten about the creamer. "He sounded funny on the phone. And he said..." Nora trailed off, knowing it was going to sound silly.

"He said what?" Abigail's impatience surfaced. Nora pushed her hair back. "He said he loved me." Abigail stared at her.

"I know, you think that's good, but it's not like him. It's weird. To me, it sounded like one of those things like, 'I'll always love you, but it's over.'"

Abigail brightened. "Don't be stupid. Cole telling you he loves you obviously means he's going to ask you to marry him."

Wait. What? Marry him? Nora shook her head. "No. He's probably upset about his father."

"Nora." Abigail sounded exasperated. "It means a proposal. I have experience with these things and I just know."

It isn't as if she hadn't thought about it. "No. It's too soon. Besides, if he wanted to marry me, he'd discuss it with me." Nora went back to sorting Lisa's papers.

Abigail might be all giddy and excited about a wedding, but not Nora. Something was up with Cole, and Nora braced for the worst. When it hit, having her mother around wouldn't be a bad thing. "What's the big rush to go to back to Flagstaff?" Nora said without looking up. "I haven't seen you for a while."

Abigail spoke into the French doors. "Don't you need to get back to work? Charles and I can come up to Boulder in a few weeks, after things settle down."

This jumble of papers seemed daunting. Nora's battered emotions clenched again when she thought of all the note-taking systems she'd offered Lisa over the years. She'd sent her day planners, lovely little notebooks, custom-made sticky notes, yellow legal pads, anything to help Lisa organize her life. As far as she knew, Lisa burned it all at summer solstice and danced around the bonfire naked.

Rachel wouldn't help her with this mess. Maybe Marlene could give her some insight. Nora glanced at the clock. She calculated. If she left here in fifteen minutes, she could get to town when the Read Rock opened.

"I'd think you'd work much better at your own office instead of this foreign environment."

Nora noticed the tension in Abigail's voice. "Why do you want me to leave?"

Abigail whirled around, a too-bright smile on her face. "Oh, it's not that. Not that at all."

This behavior seemed odd, even for Abigail, who often baffled Nora. "You're itching to get out of here and are trying to get me to leave, too. Why?"

Abigail kept her false cheer and opened her mouth as if to deny it. Nora narrowed her eyes. "Tell me."

Abigail bit her lower lip. Not a good sign. She set her cup on the edge of the desk, inhaled, then exhaled and folded her arms in front of her. "I just don't like being here. It reminds me too much of Dan."

Dan. Nora's heart jumped. Abigail hardly ever used her father's name. "How long were you here with him?"

Abigail's eyes lost focus, as if she watched her past. "Not more than a week. But the air feels charged with him. It makes me miss Dan, and that feels like cheating on Charles."

If Nora moved, it might stop Abigail mid-story. "Charlie understands he isn't your first love. He had a whole life before he met you, too," Nora assured her.

Abigail brought her focus back to the room, all business. "Of course he did."

Nora paused to let the last sentence drop. "Maybe you need to remember it all. Live it and embrace it, and then you can let it go."

Abigail tilted her head and narrowed her eyes. "What are you up to?"

Nora stirred. "Stay here with me. Let's spend some one-on-one time together. We'll drive through Arches Park and you can tell me about my father." Arches—where the rock formation Fiery Furnace stretched across the mesa.

Abigail shook her head. "Oh, no." "Why not?"

"I don't want to remember. There's no good to come from dwelling on sad things. I don't like being here."

Nora stood and squeezed around the desk to stand in front of her mother. "Don't you think you owe me something? Shouldn't I know my father just a little?"

"I barely knew your father. We weren't together more than two years. I've got nothing much to tell you."

"Tell me what you remember," Nora begged. "Please stay."

Abigail studied Nora for a long time, but Nora doubted Abigail saw her. Eventually her eyes focused and she said, "No."

15

When Charlie hadn't shown up from his morning march, Nora had begged Abigail to drive her to Moab. She'd picked up her Jeep and drove through the quiet town to the parking lot behind the Read Rock, making sure Abbey would be cool and leaving the Jeep's windows down. As she turned off the street, movement ahead caught her eye and she drew in a sharp breath. A battered stock trailer disappeared around a corner a few blocks away. The vehicle pulling it eased behind a building but before it did, Nora was sure she identified a white pickup.

So what? There were probably twenty white pickups in Moab. It didn't mean Lee Evans was in town. Even if Lee was, what difference did it make? Just because he was sinister and opposed to everything Nora strove for, and he'd run her off the road yesterday, didn't mean he was dangerous. Okay, it might mean that. She wondered just how violent his temper could be.

The sun already blasted down even though it was still too early for shoppers to line the streets. A dented, dusty late-model black Suburban was the only other vehicle in the lot.

Nora hurried through the alley, eyeing the graffiti rock art. She thought about taking a picture to give to Lisa for her collection before remembering Lisa was gone.

The sign in the front window of the Read Rock said they opened at nine, but when Nora tried the door at 9:10, it didn't budge. Marlene didn't seem like the type to open late. Nora peeked through the window.

The curtain to the back room rippled. Marlene probably worked in the back and didn't realize the time. Nora banged on the door to alert her. A moment passed and Nora banged again.

After another few seconds, the curtain swept aside. Marlene burst through, glanced over her shoulder at the back room, then hurried to the front door. She unlocked it and frowned at Nora. "What do you want?"

Surprised at the abrupt greeting, Nora stammered. "I, uh, wanted to talk." What a stupid thing to say. She'd meant to start off on a more friendly note and ease into the topic of the film project, even though Marlene made it clear yesterday she didn't think Nora should pursue it.

Marlene didn't step aside to let Nora inside. She tilted her head, as though fighting not to look behind her. "Sure. There's a café down about two blocks. I haven't had breakfast. I'll meet you there."

She shut the door and locked it again. Nora leaned toward the glass and watched Marlene hurry to the back room.

Nora was still puzzling over Marlene's strange behavior ten minutes later as she sipped an iced chai and sat in the dappled sunshine on the patio of a funky little vegetarian café. Flat sandstone slabs created an uneven surface and the tables and chairs rocked with movement. A koi pond gurgled behind her and busy black scavenger birds perched on chair backs awaiting the slightest ebb in vigilance when they'd swoop in and steal crumbs from tables and plates.

Nora gazed out at the red cliffs to the west that created one side of the deep canyon that housed Moab. The fresh morning air brightened the patio that overflowed with white tea roses, fragrant honeysuckle, bright purple irises, and brilliant blue cornflowers.

Most of the customers seemed to be regulars—not the old-time cowboy contingent but the rock climbers, bike riders, and Earth savers. Lots of rumpled, free trade clothes to go with the free trade coffee and vegetarian entrees. Nora had eaten here several times with Lisa. They could make a mean tempeh BLT and had a pretty tasty quiche of the day. This morning, Nora picked at a soyrizzo breakfast burrito and waited.

The café sat on the highway that ran through Moab and served as one of its main commerce streets. Four lanes and a wide median made the road an ordeal to cross on foot. Cars and SUVs whizzed by, the day heating up with tourist activity. There a big race in town and everyone seemed to buzz with excitement.

A table of what appeared to be affluent retirees chatted over steel-cut organic oatmeal and vegan scones. They looked fit and wore spotless outdoor gear adorned with the labels of the most expensive outfitters. A group of twenty-somethings who looked and smelled as if they'd been living in the desert for a week grabbed a table on the patio.

One of the women from the table of well-dressed couples stood and approached the youngsters. She gave them a sincere, concerned face. "Good morning. Are you here for the bike race?"

One of the young women, her brown hair in a wispy pony tail, smiled up at her. "We've been here all week. It's a great event."

The dark-haired woman nodded. "I'm sure you've noticed some of the unauthorized HOV trails cutting through the fragile landscapes." She sounded like a public service announcement. Two girls and one guy near the end of the table nodded and gave her their attention while the other people in the group carried on with their own animated conversation.

She continued as if lecturing her children. "We're trying to place restrictions on people running all over the place with their ATVs. The locals don't seem to understand the land is delicate. They abuse it as if it is worthless."

The young people looked trapped and uncomfortable. One of the girls shifted away and joined her friends' conversation. The other two looked trapped.

"These old ranchers don't even know about global warming." The two young people exchanged a look of desperation.

Marlene shot down the sidewalk. She wore a deep red flowing skirt with vibrant embroidery along the hem. Her sleeveless shirt dipped in a low V in front, hid by a filmy turquoise print scarf.

The finely coiffed woman continued her practiced speech. "They over-graze the sparse prairie lands that have no chance to recuperate, thinking the weather patterns of their ancestors will hold today. But they don't realize their forefathers stripped the land and it needs to rejuvenate without the hooves and teeth of cows."

The girl nodded and stood. "Did you want us to sign a petition or something?"

The woman seemed encouraged by the question. She snapped her fingers at the table where her cohorts sat. One of the men jumped up, grabbing a spiral notebook and pen. He hurried over.

The woman snatched it from him and flipped it open. "If you'll give me your e-mail addresses, I'll put you on our action alert list. We'll contact you when we need you to write your lawmakers and advocate for this special place."

Marlene strode to the front door of the café and caught Nora's attention. "I'll order and be right out," she called. The white pickup pulling the stock trailer slowed and parked on the curb across the street as the two well-dressed couples stared. They leaned across the table and began to talk excitedly. Nerves twanged the first bar of Dueling Banjos in Nora's chest as she recognized the black cowboy hat.

A raven squawked on the table and Nora jumped for her phone, happy to see Cole's ID. "Hi!" she answered.

After a few seconds of hellos and where are yous, Cole said, "When are you going home?"

"I need to stick around here for a day or two." She kept her eyes on the white pickup.

"Abigail just called. She's worried." He didn't sound happy.

Lee Evans stepped from his pickup. He hurried up the sidewalk and inside a river raft outfitter's office. Why would a cowboy like Lee go into a river raft outfitters? "About what?"

"She said you're not accepting Lisa's death and she's afraid you'll get hurt like Lisa did," Cole explained.

She couldn't tell Cole her suspicions about Lisa's death. "I need to find Lisa's camera. I think she might have hidden it. I'll be careful."

Frustration darkened his voice. "Why would she hide her camera?" As the conversation continued, Nora noticed a yacht of an SUV pull up and park along the street in front of Lee's pickup. A blond man and woman climbed out, followed by four kids. A little girl of about five, with fine dark ringlets haloing her head, trotted up the street, the lights adorning the bottoms of her sneakers twinkling. The adults wore worried frowns and scanned the street. The mother called to the little girl and herded all the children inside the outfitter's office.

She knew someone wanted to kill her and put information on the camera she hid. She thought I'd know where to look. Nora watered it down for him. "She was scared of something."

He sighed. "You got all that from her voicemail? Please, just come home. Ever since I've met you, trouble finds you. So far I've been around to protect you, but I can't now."

Her jaw hardened. "I don't need you to protect me."

"Hey! No! Wait!" Cole shouted away from the phone. He came back on the line. "We're branding some calves, and I've gotta go. Do me a favor. Just head back to Boulder."

"Is that an order?"

"Damn it, Nora." He'd never taken an angry tone with her, and he sounded as shocked as she felt. He sighed. "Do whatever you want." He must have thought he hung up, but she heard the phone clunk as if dropped on the pickup seat. Cole hollered in the distance. She was about to hang up when a woman spoke into the phone. "Who is this?"

The voice took Nora by surprise. "This is Cole's phone." She thought maybe the woman didn't know.

"Yes. And you are?" The woman definitely sounded annoyed.

"I'm Cole's friend," Nora answered, trying to sound bolder than she felt. "Who are you?"

"His wife."

16

Nora punched her phone off and stared at it. She couldn't move.

Breathe, she ordered herself and sucked in air. Married? Cole's wife. Wife! This couldn't be.

"I thought you'd be on your way back to Boulder by now." Marlene sat down at the table with a plate of eggs and soy sausage along with a cup of coffee.

Nora's attention jolted back to the café patio. Sunshine, flowers, people milling around her. Marlene sitting down. She shoved the woman—Cole's wife—to the back of her mind and tried focusing on Marlene. Right now, Lisa took precedence.

Nora waited until Marlene settled in and took a sip of her coffee. "Can you think of where Lisa might have hidden her camera or where she might have stored a copy of the footage?"

Marlene glared at her and slowly speared a piece of sausage and put it in her mouth. She chewed longer than necessary and swallowed. "You asked me that already. Let me repeat: You need to forget this nonsense and leave town." The older activists pushed back from their table, their chairs scraping against the stone patio.

Nora leaned across the table. "You think Lisa was murdered."

Marlene's fork dropped to her plate with a clang. "I didn't say that, but if it's true, it's the best reason I know for you to leave."

Another boat of a vehicle cruised down the road and pulled in front of the outfitter's. "That seems strange," Nora commented.

Marlene twisted in her chair to watch seven people climb from the vehicle and head into the office. "What?"

"First Lee Evans pulled up and went in. Then a family, and now this group."

Marlene whipped back around. "So?" She sounded uninterested, but she frowned anyway.

"So, none of them are dressed in outdoor gear. They're in jeans or slacks. You don't go down a river dressed like that."

Marlene turned and studied the people entering the shop. "They're tourists. Probably didn't plan on a river trip today."

Maybe, but something seemed odd. She dismissed it, turning back to Lisa and her camera. "Aside from the Canyonlands thing, can you think of any other reason someone would want to kill Lisa?"

Marlene picked up her fork with a shaking hand and poked at her scrambled eggs. "Why?"

Argh. Couldn't she simply answer a question without probing for Nora's hidden agenda? "Lisa had all this information about Mormons and women in the church. Maybe a religious fanatic hurt her." The color drained from Marlene's face.

Interesting, Nora thought. "Maybe something to do with Lisa marrying Rachel?" she continued.

Just then, Darrell rounded the corner, scowling at Lee's pickup across the street. He took a few steps toward the street, then looked back at the café. He spotted Nora, pasted on a smile, and started toward her. Several heads turned in his direction and a few people whispered. Darrell stopped at a couple of tables as he headed toward Nora, shaking hands and throwing out greetings. He stepped over to Nora. "Just the person I wanted to see."

He wore Levi's that seemed to fit him perfectly, deliberately faded to look worn and casual without seeming old. His white shirt, the buttons at his throat open and the sleeves rolled gave a Saturday morning feel, giving him a studied, attractive look. His perfection rivaled Abigail's and felt just as contrived.

Darrell smiled too warmly, felt way too familiar. "Since time is limited, I think we ought to get busy putting together a presentation with some of the stills Lisa sent us."

She wanted to get back to her conversation with Marlene. The woman knew something she wasn't telling Nora. "We've already decided the stills won't have the impact of the film," she reminded him.

Something in the road caught Nora's attention. "What the...?" It took her a couple of seconds to understand the looming catastrophe. She jumped up, her chair overturning on the patio, and took off in a run, brushing past Darrell.

The doors of the stock trailer stood wide open. One rangy Hereford cow nosed the back end of the trailer, looking as though she wanted to jump out.

Nora raced to the street, dodging vehicles on her way across the busy road. The cow dropped her two front hooves onto the pavement. Nora yelled to try to scare her back in. If the cow got loose in the road, it would cause trouble and someone—the cow, drivers, pedestrians— could be hurt.

The trailer door swung inward. The cow spooked and backed up. The door closed with the metallic clank of metal banging on metal. Lee threw his weight against it and slammed the latch shut.

Nora panted, hands on her hips. "Thank god. That would have been bad."

Lee towered over her, fury surging from him. "What were you thinking?"

"Wha—?"

He tilted his head down the street toward the older activists, now lurking in the shade of a shop that rented four-wheel drives. "You and your buddies thought it would be funny to turn my cows loose to prove how bad they are? Did you think someone might be hurt? Did you even think about safety of the cows?"

"I didn't—"

Darrell joined them. "Hey, let's calm down. Nora was at the café with me."

Lee turned on Darrell. "You're involved in this?" He took a step toward Darrell and lowered his face so they were nose to nose.

"Now isn't the time," Darrell threatened.

"When then? You're gonna have to answer for all this. For bringing these meddlers here," Lee shot back.

Marlene stood on the far side of the road, watching with full attention. Her focus wasn't on the men by the stock trailer, though. Nora followed her line of sight. The family with the four kids were climbing into their SUV, the doors slamming one by one.

Lee whirled, facing Nora. "Meddlers like you and your friend."

"Leave her alone," Darrell warned.

Lee, full of menace, leaned toward Nora. "Only you lost this round. That film Lisa was making is gone, along with all the money you spent on it."

How did he get his information? It had to be from Rachel. Nora egged him on, defiant. "Lisa told me where she left her camera. I'll finish that film."

He folded his arms. "That so?"

Coupled with the disturbing phone conversation, Nora bristled with stupid bravado. "When we show it to the committee, they'll vote to expand the borders and there's nothing you can do about it."

Lee smirked at her. "Yep. Seems I heard that before."

17

Warren studied the rock art panel under the glass and let the hand of the ancients pull at him. His feet nestled in the plush of his carpet as he stood in the climate-controlled comfort of his office, but his mind soared over the high desert outside Moab. He felt the crunch of rough sand under his boots, squinting in the blazing sun. His strong, young body climbed the twists in the trail, winding through the spires of Fiery Furnace. The weathered rocks formed a forest of jutting hoodoos that created a maze so dense, hikers weren't allowed to enter without a permit and guide. A hawk sailed overhead. Warren saw it all as if he were actually drawing breath in Utah.

Heat radiated from the rocks that baked in the sun, but between the spires, shadows cooled the sand. Orange globemallow and pinkish milkweed bobbed in the constant wind sweeping across the open desert. Warren traveled deeper into the rocks that stood more dense than the towers that lined Wall Street.

He tilted his head back and lifted his gaze to the revelation some twenty-five feet from the sandy floor. Warren remembered the day his destiny was revealed to him.

The ancients wrote it on the rock for him to discover. His uncle had told him about the sacred drawings located here, but only after Warren had already discovered the messages written on the rocks at the ranch. It had taken Warren days of searching Fiery Furnace to find the rock that told him all he needed to know.

He stared up at the rock and drifted between the past and future. The torment of the Third World's end melded with the coming destruction. Warren saw it all, just as the ancients intended. He alone knew what was coming and had prepared for it.

As they'd done that day over thirty years ago, the couple wandered into his view, interrupting his vision. He knew their meeting was not coincidence. The man, only slightly older than Warren, was obviously Native American. He had to be Hopi, sent to instruct Warren. It was no mystery why the ancients brought them together.

Even now, all these years later, Warren's heart still clutched when he thought of the woman. He'd never felt that way about anyone, before or since. He'd been consumed with her at first glance. Surely God had created her for him, and Warren thought she'd been sent to be his helpmate. But time proved God had only sent her to tempt Warren and harden his will while teaching him self-discipline.

Warren's phone rang and he whiplashed back to his weak body. He took a step toward his desk and his feet shrieked in pain, the neuropathy from the chemo plaguing him.

He picked up the phone and dropped into his office chair, his eyes focusing on the rock art panel, hoping to hold on to the power of the ancients.

"I think we've got a problem." His nephew, always full of dire warnings.

"I trust you can manage it."

"It's that Nora Abbott woman. She's nosing around. What if she finds out about Lisa Taylor's death?"

A minor annoyance at this stage, thought Warren.

His nephew sounded distressed. "She was at the pick-up site today."

He clenched his fist. "Did she see anything?"

Warren heard the worry in his nephew's voice. "Don't know. But she threw attention our way and that bookstore owner sure looked interested."

"Can't Rachel get her to leave?" He'd hoped Rachel would join them.

She'd had so many opportunities to destroy them, yet she'd kept her own counsel. But now that her friend—Warren couldn't stomach the disgust he felt at the real definition of their relationship—was dead by his nephew's hand, they'd need to keep her much closer. This was a critical time for Rachel. She'd either become one with them or turn against them.

His nephew didn't sound convinced. "I can try." "I would prefer you don't kill her."

Shock found its way to his nephew's voice. "Rachel?"

"Either of them." They'd all known the far too independent Rachel since she was born and Warren preferred to keep her alive.

The excitability that often led his nephew to bad decisions flowed in the voice on the phone. "I won't if I don't have to."

Warren crossed his leg over his knee and rubbed his foot, barely biting back a moan of pain. His doctors wanted him to take it easy— no travel, no stress. That wasn't going to happen.

"I'll be there tomorrow."

18

Amid a cloud of dirt and flying pebbles, Nora jammed on her brakes and jumped from the Jeep. Abbey clambered after her.

Married.

She'd tried to ignore the news from Wyoming, to let it sit until she had time to talk to Cole. But it flooded into her head until everything else washed away.

His wife? When did this happen? Not more than a week ago they'd been talking about their future together. He'd told her how lucky he felt to be with her. Nora finally trusted the relationship, trusted him.

Damn it! Were all men pigs or did she have unusually bad luck? First Scott, handsome and mischievous. He'd been faithful for about ten minutes. The only reason she'd been open to loving again was because Cole had been so patient and kind.

She'd pushed him away and yet he'd wormed his way back to her. She'd treated him pretty rotten and still, he'd stayed by her side through some terrible times. He'd taken a bullet for her. He'd risked his life. And in a couple of days, he'd married someone else.

Betrayed. Again.

Abigail and Charlie stood at their Buick with the trunk open. Abigail crossed her arms over her chest and tilted her head, her mouth moving.

Charlie bent into the trunk and pulled out a large suitcase, then hefted a different one from the ground. They both spun around at the sound of the Jeep.

"Nora slammed the door closed and ran for the porch steps. She needed to focus on something other than herself. Lisa's murder. If it was a murder.

Of course it was. Rachel, Marlene, and Darrell all warned her to leave town. They lived here and they had suspicions. Add to that, Lee's arrogance and veiled threats and it made him a prime suspect.

"Nora, what's the matter?" Abigail called after her.

The screen door swung open and Rachel stood in the threshold. "I hear you're spreading it all over town that you're going to find Lisa's film." It hadn't taken Lee long to call Rachel. What a surprise—the backward cowboy had a cell phone! Okay, that was snide and unfair and a tired stereotype. Too bad.

Nora detoured to the side of the porch and climbed over the railing, dropping to the sand.

"Hey!" Rachel shouted. "What's wrong with you?"

Nora was obviously too upset to make nice with Rachel. "Nora! For heaven's sake," Abigail called again.

Nora stomped off around the back of the cabin, Abbey hot on her heels, ignoring everyone. Think about Lisa. The film. A lump the size of Castle Rock lodged in her throat. She closed her eyes and fought for control, clenching her fists and teeth.

"Nora." Abigail caught her and placed a hand on Nora's rock-hard shoulder. "Are you okay?"

Nora opened her eyes. "Yep." She drew a deep breath and focused on relaxing. "Did you call Cole and tell him I was in danger?"

"What's the matter? Did you and Cole have a fight?" Abigail asked. "I wouldn't take it too seriously, dear. We know Cole is a good man. But every man, especially young ones, can be insensitive at times."

"A fight?"

"I assumed he doesn't think you should stay here in Moab. He thinks you should go back with him to Wyoming. And you, being the independent woman you are, said no. I'm solid with that."

Nora had difficulty following Abigail's blather. "'Solid'?" Abigail straightened her shoulders. "I've been reading the Urban

Dictionary. I can Google it on my notebook and they send me a word of the day. You should try it. It would do you good to update your vocabulary and keep up with technology. That phone of yours is pathetic."

Nora rubbed her forehead, stress headache beginning to throb.

Abigail moved behind Nora and reached up to knead her shoulders. "Let Cole cool off and he'll apologize."

"He's not going to apologize." Nora lifted her chin and stepped away from Abigail's massage. She strode back toward the front of the house.

Abigail scurried after her and tucked Nora's hand in her arm. She slowed Nora's gait. "He's just miffed right now. Give him time."

Nora tugged at Abigail's arm. "He's married."

"When he cools off, he'll—" Abigail stopped. "What?" "His wife talked to me today when I was in Moab."

Abigail stood in the sand, hand on hips. "What did he say? There's got to be an explanation."

"What explanation could there possibly be? We're through."

Abigail studied Nora as if waiting for a punch line. When Nora started walking again, Abigail fell in step with her. "You can't take this lying down."

"I knew when he told me he loved me that something like this would happen."

"You need to fight for him."

Fight for a man who'd already made an irrevocable decision? "I'd say the battle was over before I even knew shots were fired."

Abigail sounded exasperated. "Marriage isn't permanent, you know."

That one stopped Nora in her tracks. Abigail shrugged. "Well, it's not."

Nora strode away, kicking sand, her backbone hardening with each step.

Abigail struggled to keep up. "What are you going to do?"

Did she mean instead of curling into a ball and waiting for the desert sands to bury her? "I'm going to figure out who killed Lisa."

"Killed? What? Now you're being silly."

Nora regretted blurting that out. "Killed as in working too hard on the film and having the accident."

"Of course. You need to be more careful what you say. People can take things the wrong way." Abigail's attention turned toward Charlie. "No. That bag needs to be up front." She hurried away.

Nora stopped in the driveway and tried to shove Cole from her mind. Focus on something else.

Lisa.

Rachel and Lee had a relationship, but just how close were they? Lee didn't want the film made. The locals didn't approve of Rachel marrying Lisa. Just before Lisa died, she'd mentioned petroglyphs and Mormons and that she'd been afraid. It certainly pointed toward Lee. But if Nora was going to get law enforcement to look into anything, she'd need some proof.

Charlie held a small picnic cooler. He spoke to Abigail. "I've packed your water and Diet Coke. There are those little cheeses you like. I didn't have room for the apples."

Abigail considered that. "I hope there's not too much cheese. I don't need the extra pounds."

Charlie patted her still-shapely rear as he ambled to the backseat of the Buick. "Extra pounds just means more of you for me to adore." Abigail swatted at him. "Oh, you." She turned her focus back to Nora, probably gearing up for a lecture about the difficulties and rewards of a committed relationship. A thought interrupted and she turned back to Charlie. "Did you remember those biscuits I bought yesterday?"

He looked puzzled.

"Biscuits," she repeated. When he still didn't get it, she said, "The cookies with the dark chocolate." Abigail could spend the rest of her life trying to pound Charlie into a pretentious dandy, but she'd never succeed. "We can stop in Monticello and get some coffee for that boring drive across the reservation."

Nora shook her head. "That boring drive is called Monument Valley."

Abigail shrugged. "I've seen it a thousand times."

Nora stepped toward Charlie and gave him a hug. He smelled of pine forest and friendship. "Come visit me in Boulder soon."

Abigail joined them. She put a palm on Nora's cheek just as she'd done when Nora was a little girl. "Go to Wyoming, dear."

A fat tear struggled to escape Nora's eye. She clenched her teeth and inhaled, willing it away. Abigail kissed Nora's forehead. "You need to decide what you want—a career or a life."

Nora pulled away. "Drive safely."

Abigail's lips tightened and she glared at Nora. The stare-down lasted several seconds before Abigail narrowed her eyes. "All right, then."

She swiveled toward Charlie and snatched the cookies from his hand. She stomped up the stairs, pausing at the screen door. Over her shoulder she said, "Charles. Will you bring my suitcases upstairs, please?"

19

A hard rain battered the deck outside the opened French doors of Lisa's office. The afternoon faded toward evening. No wonder Lisa loved this office so much. With the open door and windows, it felt like working outside, except she stayed dry. She let her fingertips outline the blue and black inlay on Lisa's box. She snapped on the desk lamp. Pictures of petroglyphs and pictographs panels covered the desk.

Nora lined them up side by side, looking for similarities. Lisa had carefully labeled the backs of the photos she'd shot with the location and date. She'd scribbled the site addresses on those she'd downloaded from the Internet. They showed the various figures Nora had seen all over—humans, animals, mazes, hand prints. The weird sunburst from Nora's dream showed up in most of the photos, along with snakes and birds and even the profile of the person in a boat.

Nora replayed Lisa's message. What was she trying to say? Nora typed Tokpela Ranch into her laptop and was rewarded with a livestock auction report. Tokpela Ranch sold six cows several days ago. A little more research revealed the location of the ranch to be about twenty miles south of Moab and that it bordered Canyonlands.

Nora's phone vibrated, startling her. She checked the ID—Cole.

Her heart leapt and she smiled automatically. Then her heart plummeted with a bruising punch as she remembered her situation. Her hand was already halfway to the phone and she hesitated.

He was married. She shouldn't answer it. Clean cut. Don't make it worse, she told herself. Against her better judgement, she picked it up and said hello. He was seven hundred miles away. How could talking to him do any harm, she rationalized, even though she knew better.

There was a slight pause and he spoke in a strained voice. "I wasn't sure you'd answer after this morning."

She pictured the blush climbing his neck and burning in his cheeks. She longed to feel his arms around her but he belonged to another woman. What she really needed was a big dose of backbone. She mouthed the words to try to make it more real. He's married. "I spoke to your wife this morning."

He exhaled. "Oh." "Oh," she repeated.

"Nora." The longing in his voice made her grab the edge of the desk. She held her breath.

"This thing that's going on. This ... marriage." She swallowed, her skin hot.

"It's ... complicated."

"Complicated? As in, my wife doesn't understand me, but you do, let's have an affair?"

He exhaled again. "No. Amber." It sounded like he choked on the words. "My w-wife. I need to be careful. She's dangerous."

"Dangerous how?"

He hesitated, then the words spewed out in a decidedly unCole- like manner. "Please, trust me for now. Don't give up on us. I love you, Nora. I know you love me. I'm going to fix this, but it'll take a little more time. Can you give me that?"

No. She should end it, like she'd already ended it in Moab this morning. Why was she talking to him on the phone anyway? She'd trusted Scott years ago when he said his affair was over. That had been a stupid mistake. She should learn from that. "Yes. I can give you time. But not forever." She smacked her forehead. Stupid, stupid, stupid. But Cole wasn't Scott. She did trust him. "How's your father?"

His tone brightened a bit. "He's holding his own. The tough ol' guy might just make it."

There was that. He asked about Charlie and Abigail and she asked about the ranch, then the conversation stalled out. “Can I call you again?” He sounded sweet and shy. That vulnerability always undid her. Her gut told her it was authentic even as her head argued.

“Yes,” she heard the longing in her own voice. She smacked her forehead again. If she didn’t start having easier relationships, she’d give herself brain damage.

She sat for a long time after he hung up, listening to the rain patter on the deck.

20

Another sunrise on Lisa's front porch. More corn dust tossed in gratitude for another day. Another appeal to the spirits of her father's clan. More silence.

Maybe the kachina only showed up when Nora faced real, physical danger or when he had something he wanted her to do. But she'd like a personal deity to wrap some support around her. She'd probably lost Cole, someone she thought she'd love for a lifetime. Would it be so much to ask she not lose her imaginary spirit as well?

When the kachina first appeared to Nora on her mountain in Flagstaff, she'd been terrified. There are hundreds of Hopi kachinas that represent everything from animals and nature to ancestors. They generally show up for ceremonies and dances or appear in clouds to rain on the desert corn. The kachina that visited Nora was an old Hopi *kikmongwi*, or chief, from the 1880s. Benny said he was her grandfather of many generations past. Benny knew this because the kachina was also his grandfather and they were in regular communication. If Nora hadn't experienced the kachina's visits, she might not believed what Benny said. Choosing to go along with Benny's explanation let her believe she wasn't a complete lunatic.

He appeared to her in Flagstaff so she would stop the manmade snow on the sacred peaks. He'd inexplicably shown up in Boulder last fall, just weeks before the strict Hopi calendar dictated all kachinas return to the three mesas in Arizona. Then he'd had another mission for her. She tried to convince herself he was only a figment of her over-active imagination.

But he'd saved her life in a very tangible way.

Despite Utah's rising sun warming her face, Nora shivered remembering the Rocky Mountain peak last fall. She'd felt the freezing air of Mount Evans in a snowstorm, seconds before dawn.

Trapped on a ledge, her arm useless from a gunshot, a terrorist dead at her feet, Nora had no choice but to step into the rifle sight of a killer. The gunman held his rifle up, sighting into the scope.

Nora caught her breath. She knew the killer's next shot would tear her apart.

But the shot never came.

The kachina appeared behind the killer. He held his hatchet high.

She'd been to the mesas, listened to Benny's stories about the Hopi and their migrations. She'd prayed with him and walked the trails where the Hopi had lived for centuries. But since that morning on Mount Evans, her kachina remained silent.

Maybe she didn't want him popping out at her all the time, but it might be nice if he'd let her know he still watched over her.

She remembered Benny's words: "When Hopi know things are wrong, they look to themselves for personal responsibility."

What had she done to chase the kachina away? She'd planted corn in pots all over her apartment and office as the Hopi instructed. She hadn't been living simply, though—not if that meant growing her own food and not using electricity or any other convenience.

Benny told her that Hopi would reach a point of confusion because the modern world clashed with the traditional one. This world was in its fourth revision. The three previous worlds had ended when the leaders were corrupted by greed and power. Hopi prophesies warned it could happen again. Was Nora too steeped in the modern world?

A cupboard door banged in the kitchen behind Nora and she was suddenly back in the bright morning on the porch. She studied the yellow bloom of the blazing star in the front yard, still looking for the flash of her kachina's blue sash. He'd abandoned her.

The siren scent of bacon called to her nose. Abigail knew Nora loved bacon and she'd be crisping slices in the microwave. The thought of her mother's care lifted her heart a little. But if she wanted the comfort of the bacon, she'd best hurry inside before Abigail pulled her usual trick and blackened it.

The screen squealed open and banged softly behind Nora as she padded on bare feet to the kitchen in time to see Rachel slide a plate of bacon from the microwave.

Rachel's stony face froze, then thawed slightly after a second. She banged the plate on the counter bar in front of Nora. "So, I hear you're single now, too."

It sounded harsh and the bacon wasn't offered with gentleness, but it showed a modicum of sympathy. Nora plopped on a barstool. "Abigail told you."

Rachel nodded.

"Single's not so bad," Nora said.

Rachel reached over and took a slice of bacon. She'd cooked it just the way Nora liked it, crisp enough to hold its shape but not charred.

"I don't like single," Rachel said.

Maybe she and Rachel could call a truce. "After my disaster of a first marriage, I can fully embrace living alone." She tried to grin, but the words tasted bitter. She truly didn't mind being single, but she hated the thought of losing Cole before ever really having him. She grabbed a piece of bacon and bit into it, tasting the salty, fatty goodness. An entire blue-ribbon pig cured and fried wouldn't be enough to take away her pain, but this mouthful wouldn't hurt.

Rachel stuffed a half a slice of bacon into her mouth, slid the last one off the plate and onto the counter in front of Nora, and reloaded the plate with raw slices. She covered it with paper towels and slapped it into the microwave to convert calories to comfort.

"I've never really been on my own," Rachel said. She stared out the window toward Castle Rock.

Nora didn't know much about Rachel. She'd come into Lisa's life a few years ago. "What did you do before you met Lisa?"

Rachel's inhale vibrated in her chest, as if she were fighting tears. She twirled around and checked the bacon through the microwave window. "I was married."

Nora didn't have to ask if Rachel was married to a man. Marlene was right; Rachel had not only stepped outside the lines, she'd leapt clear to another coloring book. Though if Rachel had been married before, it showed she had relationships with men in the past. Would it be such a stretch to think she might have another? And if so, why not an affair with Lee?

Nora tried to keep the suspicion from gaining a foothold. She needed to trust Lisa and Lisa had loved Rachel. "Will you stay here?" Nora asked.

The microwave dinged and Rachel reached in for the plate. "Where else would I go?" She didn't sound defensive, and it appeared to be a legitimate question.

After the events in Flagstaff and she'd lost her husband, her business, and her entire direction in life, Nora fled to Boulder, where she'd grown up. She'd needed to back up before she could move forward. But Rachel had nowhere to back up to. And even though Nora had pushed him away, Cole had been there for her. Who did Rachel have?

Lee's image popped into Nora's head again.

Abigail's footfalls sounded from the stairs. "What decadence do I smell?" She rounded the corner, coming to stand with her hands on her hips, surveying Nora and Rachel as though they'd broken into a bank. Abigail had sent a forlorn Charlie back to Flagstaff, insisting that she stay until Nora came to her senses.

Nora reached for the plate Rachel set on the counter and helped herself to another slice. "Ambrosia from the pork gods."

Abigail lunged for Nora's hand, but she quickly stuffed the bacon into her mouth. Abigail frowned at her. "You'll never get Cole back if you let yourself get fat."

"A few pieces of bacon aren't going to ruin me. Cole doesn't matter anyway."

Abigail leaned toward the plate. "I suppose a little bacon won't hurt." She snagged a piece and savored a bite. "But you're wrong about Cole. There's an explanation for this alleged marriage, and when we find out, you'll be sorry you were so hard on him."

"Hard on him?" Nora choked out, wanting to start a tirade but realizing the futility and letting it drop. "So, you stayed in Moab to help me cope with my broken heart?"

Abigail made her way to the kitchen and reached for the coffee. "Absolutely not. There will be no feeling sorry for yourself. I'm here to make sure you don't give up on Cole."

"Do you have a plan?"

Rachel leaned back on the counter and watched their interplay.

Abigail measured coffee into a French press. She tapped the tea kettle on the stove, found the temperature acceptable, and poured the water on top of the grounds. "Frankly, I don't know."

Nora hopped off the stool. "Good. I've got a plan, then." "And what, pray tell, would that be?"

"You can take me to some of the places you and my father visited."

"Why would you want to do that?"

"I don't know. Maybe it will make me feel closer to him. Maybe I can learn something about him." *Maybe a trip to Arches can take us to Fiery Furnace and I can figure out what Lisa wanted to tell me.*

"Well, that's just more of your woo-woo mystic lunacy." Rachel's eyes twinkled as though she watched a comedy.

She wouldn't admit that her mother might be right. So far, Nora didn't feel any real connection to her father and her Hopi ties felt shaky. If she didn't find Lisa's camera, she might lose her job. Cole was most likely a lost cause. Right now, the only things that felt solid were her connections to Abigail and the land. And her commitment to finding Lisa's killer.

"Okay, then let's just go to Arches and sightsee," she told Abigail. Abigail depressed the plunger on her coffee. "Can't we go shopping instead?"

Nora turned to Rachel. "Where were some of the last places Lisa filmed?"

Rachel pushed against the counter. Her eyes turned hard. "I don't know. Why?"

"Maybe we could hit a few of the sites. Get some idea what Lisa was thinking."

Rachel picked up the empty plate and banged it into the sink. Luckily, it didn't break. "Lisa was thinking she wanted to change the world to better suit her own whims. The world had a different notion."

Abigail opened a cupboard and plucked out a coffee cup. "It was an accident. It would have happened whether she'd been filming or picnicking."

Rachel stared into the sink, her shoulders rigid. She didn't reply.

Perhaps because she knew Lisa's death wasn't an accident?

"Let's go to Fiery Furnace. It was a special place to Lisa." Nora studied Rachel's back. Rachel gripped the edge of the sink, but didn't turn.

Abigail laced her coffee with hazelnut creamer. "I don't suppose there's a mall in Moab," she said, trying to diffuse the tension.

Rachel turned slowly and glared at Nora. "Leave it alone." "What is there you don't want me to find?" Nora said.

Abigail scoffed. "Rachel's only concerned you don't torture yourself like this, Nora. Going to Lisa's favorite places will only rub salt in the wound."

Rachel and Nora didn't move or acknowledge Abigail. Silence ticked in the kitchen. A mourning dove hoo-hoo-hooted outside.

Abigail set her cup on the counter. "Fine. If you're so set on wallowing in death and pain, we'll visit some of the spots your father and I went to. Now quit harassing Rachel."

21

An hour later Nora held the Jeep door open for Abbey to jump in the back.

Abigail walked onto the porch and called back inside through the closed screen door. "I've got my phone, dear. Text me if you decide you need anything from town." She hefted a wicker tote bag onto her shoulder and stepped down the porch. She wore khaki capris and walking shoes. Her cardigan sweater matched the pink T-shirt underneath as well as the trim on her socks and she looked like a catalogue image for tasteful outdoor-wear for older women.

"Ready?" Nora was more than anxious to get moving.

Abigail slid into the passenger seat of the Jeep and twisted around, settling her tote bag on the floor behind Nora's seat. "I've brought sunscreen, snacks, water, an extra jacket, and a first aid kit. Anything else?"

Nora flung her arm over the seat back to look behind her. She backed down the dirt driveway, concentrating on the narrow passage. "I've got most of that stuff in here. I filled my water bottles at the house."

Abigail raised her eyebrows. "I'm sure you've got all sorts of things in this vehicle. How you ever find anything is beyond me—looks like you haven't cleaned it out in years."

Nora pulled onto the road and slid the Jeep in gear. "Abbey and I spend a lot of time in the mountains. I have extra coats and gear in here for that."

"Too bad they didn't wash and detail your Jeep while it was at the shop."

Just another verse of the old "Clean Your Room" ballad. "Where would you like to go first?"

Abigail reached around and dug into her tote bag, pulling out a granola bar. She unwrapped it. "I don't care."

They turned on the highway and headed toward Moab. "Let's start at the windows arches. You and Dan hiked there, didn't you?"

"You can call him your father. You don't have to say his name." "It's just weird for me. All my life he was this guy that abandoned

us, so I didn't want to feel any affection for him. Now I know he died, that he didn't leave us voluntarily. I'd like to know him, even a little."

Abigail chewed her granola bar and watched the tamarisk and willows on the river. Finally she spoke. "It was a long time ago." She finished her granola bar and fidgeted, drumming her fingers on the seat belt buckle. If she felt as nonchalant as she claimed, she wouldn't be eating compulsively and squirming like a five-year-old at church.

"Okay, so Arches it is," Nora decided.

On the half hour drive to the park just north of Moab, Abigail talked nonstop. She commented on the rafters floating the Colorado River and complained about the loud Harleys that zoomed up behind them and passed in a roar. She remarked about the new paved bike trail running alongside the highway. She chattered about her service club in Flagstaff and how it contributed to scholarships for struggling women. Nora heard more about Abigail's efforts to reform Charlie's diet and exercise habits than she cared to know. Obviously, Abigail wanted to avoid talking about Dan Sepakuku.

Abigail's reluctance to share details about this man puzzled Nora.

What could Abigail want to hide?

They approached the park entrance—a long, sloping valley dotted with cactus, scrub, and rocks. An RV had pulled off to the right into the parking lot of the visitors' center. Several yards ahead, a kiosk squatted between the outgoing lane and the lane entering the park. The sun wasn't serious yet and the morning felt fresh.

Nora showed her National Park pass and collected the maps and park pamphlet. "Anywhere specific you and my father visited here?"

"Just the regular places. The window arches and Delicate Arch." Abigail dug out another granola bar and tore off the wrapper.

Nora drove up the long incline and maneuvered a few switchbacks. This early in the morning, they had the road to themselves.

The sky opened in an infinity of blue. No clouds marred its perfection. Nora rolled down her window and her lungs enlarged as she let the cool desert air fill her. Abbey poked his head over her shoulder and lifted his nose to the rushing wind.

The red sand and boulders of the hills popped against the sunshine and crisp air. Yellow blazing star and bright orange globemallow dotted the sparse ground along with the pinks and purples of the milkweed and Utah daisy. Sage, Mormon tea, and clump grass accented the sand, still damp from yesterday's afternoon showers.

"So many wildflowers this year. Has it been a wet spring?" Abigail seemed lost in her thoughts, so it surprised Nora she'd be so observant.

Always eager to encourage Abigail's curiosity of the natural world, Nora answered, "Unusually wet here. The ground is pretty well saturated. We'll probably be seeing some flash floods in places that haven't been flooded in years." She'd never understood how anyone could describe the desert as barren. The land sang an aria of beauty, bringing tears to Nora's eyes.

This place cradled Lisa's soul.

Spires rose in majesty like a fantastical army of aliens marching across the desert. The unbelievable power of wind and water formed these gigantic castles of stone. Awesome, in the most basic sense.

They didn't speak as Nora drove past Balanced Rock. They wound up to the parking lot and climbed out of the Jeep to view North and South Windows and Double Arch. Nora let Abbey jump down and clipped a leash to his collar. They climbed a quarter mile on smooth stone along a rock-lined trail in the red sand. Abigail stopped in the shade created from the elongated stone arch. She stared across the desert valley toward the La Sal Mountains in the distance.

Nora sat in a sunny spot and soaked up the scene. Abbey plopped down next to her and she trailed her fingers through his soft fur. The warmth of the stone radiated into her skin. The valley swept before her, an endless ocean dotted with deep green scrub against the amber ground. The soft summer felt like kisses on her bare arms and the tang of sage teased her nose.

Abigail's shoulders hitched. Nora wondered if she was sobbing. She scrambled to her feet and jogged over to Abigail, Abbey following.

Instead of tears, Abigail's face was bright with humor. She chuckled as Nora got close. "See that?" She pointed to a cluster of stunted trees on the valley floor. "We camped there the first night we arrived."

Nora waited, hoping there was more to the story.

Abigail giggled. "We'd brought a bottle of wine and some chips. I was nervous because I'd never been camping and this was the first time I'd been alone with a man. Even though I was sure Dan was The One, I'd only known him for a few weeks."

Nora fought against wanting to know more about her parents and not wanting to know too much. This could slip into the too much zone quickly.

"Sometime in the middle of the night, I woke up with a terrible stomachache. I should have scurried out of the tent to, well, do what you might have to do."

Tilting to the dark side. "You had gas?"

Abigail stared at the old camp site. "But the night was dark and the outside seemed so big and frightening. I stayed where I was and, well, let it go." She blushed and giggled in embarrassment, not noticing Nora at all.

"Oh my. It even brought tears to my eyes. But Dan's breathing never altered so I assumed he slept through it and with us being outside, I figured the tent air would be pure by the time he woke up."

Nora didn't want to think about her mother farting. Ever.

"The next morning, I was making coffee by the fire and Dan was frying bacon. He didn't look at me as he said, 'A bear came by our camp last night.' Well, you can imagine how that upset me. I dropped the coffee pot and almost couldn't speak. 'A bear? When?'"

Now Abigail laughed out loud. She caught Nora's eye. "He shrugged and said, 'Well, I didn't actually see him. But I sure smelled him.'"

Abigail laughed again. "I nearly died of embarrassment. 'I thought you were asleep!' I said. He tilted his head and said, 'I was.'" She shook her head. "I can still see that mischievous twinkle in his eye."

Nora's father had a sense of humor. Clearly he had an honest streak that was mixed with kindness. Was this too much to glean from one little story?

Abigail relaxed a little. She didn't mention Dan again, but she no longer prattled with nervous energy. They drove to a few more overlooks, commenting on the beauty of the landscapes and sharing bits and pieces of their day-to-day lives.

The sun reached its zenith. They'd eaten the balance of the granola bars and shared water with Abbey. "Do you feel like taking a short hike?" Nora asked.

Abigail shrugged. "If you promise it will be a short one. I don't want to get stuck on a forced march. And it better be on a level path." "I'd like to walk in Fiery Furnace. Then we can head back to town and I'll buy you lunch."

Nora pulled into the parking lot at the site. They climbed out and Nora waited for Abigail to slather herself with sweet-smelling sunscreen. The desert sun hit Nora's skin and she could almost hear it sizzle. She reached into the back of the Jeep for her own unscented sunscreen spray. It didn't help the heat, but it'd keep her from crisping.

A wood fence blocked the trailhead that led to a one-track path a short distance across a flat plane and wound into an impenetrable stand of fins and spires. Heat waves warped the view across the valley in the opposite direction. A sign at the trailhead warned hikers that they couldn't enter the maze of stone without a permit and a guide. Nora slipped around it and onto the trail.

"We aren't permitted in here," Abigail said, standing her ground.

Nora cast around for witnesses, saw they were alone, and waved her mother in. "If we hurry, we can get behind the stones before someone sees us."

Abigail glanced behind her. "This isn't a good idea," she protested, but hurried after Nora.

They followed the path threading through the fins of stone. The close formations caused them to squeeze between the narrow passages. Could she dislodge another anecdote from Abigail? Nora felt a greedy need for more of her father, but maybe she'd have to be content with one story, albeit one indelicate and incredibly crude by her mother's usual standards, but so telling.

They walked on, breathing in hot air, conserving their water with small sips. She unclipped Abbey from his leash and followed his plodding pace. An unusual change in rock color caught Nora's attention and she veered off the trail to wind through a few fins, hoping to find the petroglyphs Lisa had told her about. The rocks were warm under her hands as she maneuvered through tight places.

"Where are you taking us?" Abigail didn't sound pleased.

"I thought there might be a rock art panel here, but it's just weathered rock."

"Shouldn't we go back to the trail?" Abigail asked.

Nora tried to get her bearings and looked for a trail. "I'm not sure where it is."

Abigail put her hands on her hips. "I knew we shouldn't have come in here without a guide!"

Nora waved her hand. "No big deal. We'll head back toward the trailhead and get there eventually."

Abigail held up her bottle. "I hope that's not a long time. I'm nearly out of water and this heat is withering me."

"We've only been out here for a half hour or so. I'm sure you won't dehydrate."

"I'm glad you have confidence." She glared at Nora. "You take the lead. This place is a maze."

Nora sidled around Abigail in the narrow passage and Abbey struggled to get ahead of them. Nora studied the scenery, trying to put herself in Lisa's head. Where would she hike that she accidently ran into petroglyphs?

She studied the rock around her, peering into crevices as they walked. She followed Abbey's red flag of a tail, already rounding another sharp turn, and nearly smacked into a wall of stone.

Abbey disappeared into a tight passage but Nora stopped in the shade to wait for Abigail. She uncapped her water bottle and tilted her head to take a gulp of warm water, halting as something grabbed her attention.

She gasped and stepped back to get the whole impression. An amazing assortment of images were etched in the rock above her head. The panel measured about six feet wide and four feet tall and started twenty feet above the ground. Either erosion had dug a path or the artists had stood on some sort of bench. The faint designs scratched in the rock could easily be missed if a hiker wasn't paying close attention.

Nora leaned in, a sense of awe she always felt when viewing something so ancient washing over her. A person had stood here a thousand years ago or more. A real someone who loved and struggled and laughed, worried about survival or wondering about God. That person had taken the time to chisel this rock, and the images must have been filled with meaning because carving on rock deep enough to last for millennia was no idle undertaking.

This artist, or artists, had created a hodgepodge of images. Human shapes with large, almost triangular bodies and tiny stick arms and legs shared space with unmistakable images of birds and snakes. Other figures weren't as easy to place. Some looked like they might be turtles or big bugs. Goats or deer ran alongside a boxlike creature that looked sort of like ET. There was even a boat shape, like a half moon on its side, with a figure sitting inside. Big circles, like giant ears, stuck out from the head of the boatman.

Panting behind her that didn't sound like Abbey. She glanced over her shoulder to see Abigail leaning against a spire. Her eyes looked panicked in her pale face.

"What is it?" Nora put a hand to Abigail's forehead to check her temperature. It didn't seem warm enough outside for heat exhaustion. Abigail was nearing sixty but in good shape. Was it a heart attack?

Abigail waved Nora's hand off her face. "Fine. I'm fine. Let's get out of here."

Nora understood. It wasn't heat stroke or heart attack. Fear. It radiated off Abigail's skin. She followed Abigail's gaze to the rock art panel. "What scares you?"

Abigail chuckled, but it sounded more like choking. "Don't be silly. I'm not afraid."

Nora studied the rock. Humans, other animal shapes, a few strange lines. Toward the bottom of the panel she noticed something familiar.

The weird sunburst shape. The same design on the graffiti at the Read Rock and in her dream. Her heart stammered, too. "Did you come here with my father?"

Abigail shifted from foot to foot. "Yes. No. Oh, how do I know? Red rocks, sand, arches. It's all the same. Here or in Canyonlands or anywhere else."

Nora stared at the rock again. "Is this what Lisa wanted me to see?" she wondered out loud.

"What?" Abigail sounded irritated.

Nora pointed. "That symbol with the lines. It keeps popping up."

Abigail squinted at the panel. "Dan liked that. After he saw it here, he used to doodle it."

"Do you know what it means?"

Abigail waved her hand. "Who knows? Whatever you want, I suppose."

"My father never said?"

"I never asked. Let's just go."

Nora lowered her gaze to meet her mother's. "Why are you so upset?"

"I'm not upset. Rachel's right. You need to leave things alone. There are enough wilderness places around here to satisfy everyone. Come on. I'm hungry and want to get out of this heat."

Something about the rock art crawled under Abigail's skin. Nora needed to coax it out. They squeezed through the tight passage behind the fins and intersected a worn path.

Abigail tore down the trail. She seemed to have developed a whole new level of fitness, winding in and out of the rock towers and pushing Abbey to keep ahead of her. Nora thought about the symbols on the rock panel. It had something to do with her father. She was sure of it. That's the only connection Abigail would have with Native American history. Her father, the rock art, and Lisa's murder. They couldn't all be coincidence, she thought.

Abigail practically ran the last quarter mile to the Jeep. She stood by the passenger door, her arms crossed and her face tight with tension. "Where should we eat?"

Nora unlocked the door. She pulled Abbey's collapsible dish out of the back seat and filled it with the last of her water. He lapped it up. "Doesn't matter to me."

When Abbey finished his water and jumped in back, they loaded up and headed across the mesa and the switchbacks that led to the park exit.

"How many days did you and Dan spend in Arches?" Nora probed as carefully as she could.

"I don't know, three or four days," her mother responded curtly. "Did you like it here?" Nora rolled down her window. She inhaled the new growth and sunshine on the breeze. It smelled green and blue and yellow, alive with the unusually wet season.

Abigail's shoulders hiked up with tension. "I was in love. It wouldn't have mattered if we had toured the moon."

"What about Dan? There must have been a reason he brought you here." She steered around the gentle slopes, tapping the brakes in order to keep an easy speed.

"I guess. I don't know. He said it is an important place and he seemed interested in the rock art." Abigail slapped her palms on her leg. "Can we please drop it? Bringing me here makes me sad. He was a good man and he never got a chance to grow old. Like Lisa. We need to let them rest in peace."

A meadowlark's song swirled into the window and around Nora's head. She rounded a curve and headed down the mountainside. The park maintained the road and it was nothing like the narrow, twisting ribbon on the side of Mount Evans outside of Denver. Thinking about that piece of highway leading up to a fourteen thousand-foot peak made Nora break into a sweat.

She gripped the wheel. She was driving too fast. She'd miss a curve. This road descending toward the visitors' center didn't have the hairpin turns of the Mount Evans route, but there were switchbacks and Nora was going too fast to navigate around them.

"Nora, why are you pumping the brakes?" Abigail's voice cut into Nora's concentration.

"What? Oh. I'm ... " *Get a grip, Nora.*

"You're driving like a bat out of Hell." Abigail raised her voice. It brought back memories of the one time she'd taken Nora out to teach her to drive. No surprise—Nora had a heavy foot and didn't stop at the stop sign long enough and nearly got them killed in traffic. Berle had taken over driver training after that.

"I'm fine. This is a good road." Nora agreed that she should slow down, too, but reacted automatically to Abigail's complaint.

"You're scaring me!"

Nora tapped the brakes, but instead, the Jeep gained a little more speed. Nora stepped harder on the brakes, but didn't feel any resistance. The hillside out her window blurred. The speedometer needle inched further to the right.

Nora slammed on the brakes.

Nothing.

"What's going on?" Abigail clutched the dash in a panic.

Nora pumped her foot, but she met no pressure from the pedal. "The brakes aren't working!" Sweat lined her face, yet she felt cold all over.

The wind roared. The wheels sounded like a train in Nora's head. Her vision narrowed, seeing only the strip of pavement in front of her. She tried to remember the road when they'd driven up earlier.

How many turns? How sharp? She hadn't paid attention and now couldn't conjure it up.

A yellow diamond sign warned of a curve ahead. Nora automatically hit the brakes again and the action unleashed jolts of panic. She held her breath and gripped the wheel, terrified by the upcoming bend. A boulder the size of the *USS Arizona* sat on the outside of the road. If they didn't make the turn, they'd smash into the side, creating their own gruesome rock art of blood and bone.

They'd never stay upright if Nora stuck to her own lane. The narrow wheelbase of the Jeep would cause it to flip at this speed. If she crossed the center line and someone came uphill on the curve, Nora would smash into them.

She strained to see past where the road swerved. Was another vehicle coming? What should she do? The pavement started to turn. She concentrated on the double yellow line in the middle of the road. Her shoulders felt like steel with her hands welded to the steering wheel. As the curve tightened, she edged to the outside, venturing into the opposite lane.

The wind, the squeal of the tires, and Abigail's screams all combined in a mind hurricane, blocking out everything but automatic action. They rounded the corner with the grill of an ocean liner of an SUV looming a few feet ahead of them.

A screaming horn penetrated Nora's brain. Her hands jerked the wheel to the right before she could form a thought. They swerved out of the SUV's path, the protesting horn following their flight. The Jeep's right tires dropped off the pavement. Abigail screamed again. The raw cliff face loomed inches from the passenger window.

The outside mirror exploded as it tore away from the door. Nora yanked the wheel to the left. The Jeep swung back onto the road. But she'd overcorrected and now they headed for the steep shoulder drop off. Nora swung the wheel back. The Jeep lurched to the right, the tires stuttering. In that instant, she knew they were going to flip. She twisted the wheel one way, then the next, without any conscious thought. Muscle memory or luck or possibly even her kachina guided her, though he didn't show himself. In seconds or minutes or perhaps years, the Jeep settled into a straight line race down the road. With no curves in her immediate sight, Nora took a second to gather her bearings. The high rev engine shrieked. The valley stretched before them with one long slope to the visitor's center and a gradual flattening of the road as it swept toward the highway. They still careened down the hill, going way too fast for safety. If they passed the fee kiosk at this speed, they could hit a pedestrian or crash into another vehicle.

Nora considered ramming the Jeep into first or second gear, but if she disengaged the clutch now she might not be able to force it into another gear and they'd be free-wheeling.

A line of cars inched through the fee station on the left. A Cruise America RV with a cheery vacationing family painted on the rear loomed in front of them, making its way through the exit.

"We're going to hit them!" Abigail shrieked. She braced her arms on the dash.

The Jeep lost some momentum as the road leveled, but they still barreled out of control. The back end of the RV grew in the windshield.

Nora laid on the horn.

The brake lights of the RV lit up. No! She needed them to speed up, not stop! Nora held her breath and gripped the wheel. They would collide with the RV at the kiosk. The pavement widened to accommodate the traffic at the fee station.

Please stay inside the RV. If someone stepped out from the either the RV or the kiosk, she'd plow into them.

Amid Abigail's screams and the shrieking engine, Nora yanked the wheel. They shot to the right side of the RV, wheels balancing on the edge of the pavement.

Whack. They guillotined the driver's side mirror.

Nora sucked in air. They'd made it! Only a long, flat road ahead, with plenty of time for the Jeep the slow to a stop.

Then she saw it.

A group of motorcycles pulled out in front of her, leaving the visitors' center. Between the group of six or eight, they covered both lanes. They didn't know Nora couldn't slow down. She laid on her horn, but they didn't have enough time to react. She jerked the wheel to the right and the Jeep flew off the road into the sand.

It only took fifty feet or so for the Jeep to come to a complete halt. They banged across shrubs and rocks, their seat belts biting into them as they crossed the brain-rattling, rough terrain. Abbey slammed into the back of Nora's seat and yelped.

They finally stopped and Nora cut the engine.

"My god! We could have been killed!" Abigail panted and clutched her chest. Nora tried to draw in a breath, but struggled. She couldn't let go of the steering wheel.

"I told you two years ago to get a new car. But no, you didn't listen. You aren't happy unless you've got the oldest car on the road."

Oxygen finally seeped into Nora's lungs. She hoped her heart didn't split her chest.

"You're lucky this didn't happen in the mountains. I'd have had to bear the loss of my only daughter."

Nora wanted to close her eyes, but they were stuck wide open in panic mode.

"It is irresponsible of you to have held on to this antique this long. At least now you'll have to get a new car."

Nora popped her seat belt loose, flung her door open, and jumped out. Abbey hopped out after her, no worse for the terror.

Feet on solid ground, Nora leaned her hands against the hot hood and dropped her head. The shaking commenced and when her knees buckled, she sank to a squat.

22

Abigail's ranting sounded like The Chipmunks on speed. When the shaking subsided and her bones felt solid, Nora stood up. She found her phone in her backpack and called Marlene.

Marlene's voice boomed through the phone. Maybe her annoyance wasn't directed at Nora, but she sounded like she wanted to punch something. "You're at the visitors' center? The brakes? Are you okay?"

"Just hurry. Abigail's lecture is about to drill a hole in my brain." "Wait." Marlene spoke to someone. After a minute she came back on the line. "Bill Hardy is here. He said he'd come along with me." "Bill Hardy?"

Marlene spoke to the phantom Bill. "I'll lock up and meet you at the garage." The bell above the door tinkled and Marlene spoke into the phone. "Bill owns the repair shop down the street from me."

That must be the shop Darrell warned her against. "The Conoco? How do you know Bill?"

"He's a friend." Marlene sounded distracted, probably closing up the Read Rock.

"And you think he's a good mechanic? Fair?"

"What are you talking about? I just told you he's a friend. So yeah, he's fair. Would you like to call the Better Business Bureau?" The bell dinged again and a door bang closed.

Nora closed her eyes against the glare. "No, sorry. I'm not thinking."

"Of course not. We're on the way."

Marlene and Bill Hardy arrived in less than a half hour, long enough for Abigail to calm down. She had pulled out some moistened towelettes and done some sort of magical repair to her face and hair that made her look as though she'd just stepped out of the salon. The sweat drying from her shirt and a quick wipe of one of Abigail's towelettes constituted enough freshening up for Nora.

Park rangers and a few curious tourists ventured out, hoping to get the story. Nora explained the brake failure and that help was on the way. Since no one was injured and the damage was limited to the Jeep's mirrors, the authorities seemed willing to let the incident drop. Abigail sat in the Jeep with the doors opened to catch the slight breeze. Abbey stretched out in the shade under the Jeep. Nora paced, going from a three-foot Mormon tea shrub, around two rocks the size of picnic tables, and back again, her boots crunching on a crust of gravel and grit.

Marlene and Bill arrived in a tow truck that had faded to a colorless gray. Tool boxes lined the heavy truck and an assortment of tools and equipment filled the bed. Marlene spilled out of the passenger side, her red-and-yellow-striped skirt billowing in the breeze. She strode over to Nora and Abigail and stopped to inspect them. "You seem okay."

"Barely," Abigail spewed in a breathless fury. "That Jeep is done for and it nearly took us out with it."

Bill Hardy sauntered over. He might have been fifty or eighty, with deep lines etched in his face. He reached out to shake Nora's hand, his grease-stained paw bearing black half-moons under his fingernails. He wore dark blue Oshkosh overalls and a stretched and faded T- shirt. "How do."

Nora accepted his quick and crushing handshake. "The brakes went out."

"Hmm." He stepped to the Jeep and popped the hood. He hummed while he surveyed the engine. Nora turned to Marlene. "Thank you so much for coming out here," she said.

Abigail gazed up at Marlene, whose Amazonian elegance seemed fitting to the red stone and sand. "You're an angel. I just don't know what we would have done without you."

Still humming, Bill pulled back from the engine and squatted down to look under the Jeep.

Marlene watched the mechanic as he got on his hands and knees and reached behind the passenger side front wheel. "You were lucky Bill was in the shop when you called. He's a big mystery fan and comes in once a month for all the new paperbacks."

Bill came out from under the Jeep and put a hand on the fender to help himself up. "Found your problem. It's an easy fix and you'll be on your way." He ambled toward his truck.

"What happened?" Nora asked.

He rummaged in the bed of his truck and pulled out a plastic gallon container and held it up. "Out of brake fluid."

Abigail crept up behind him. "That's all?"

He walked back to the Jeep and addressed Nora. "Have you noticed the brakes getting spongy lately?"

She nodded.

"Fluid's probably been leaking out for a couple of days. When you hit the brakes coming down that slope, it squeezed the last of the fluid out and then you were done. Nice work getting her slowed down and stopped, though." He picked up his humming again.

"I've never heard of the brakes losing fluid," Abigail said.

He interrupted his humming. "I haven't seen it myself. Not like this."

"What do you mean?" Nora asked.

He twisted the cap of the brake fluid container. "Looked like the bleeder valve somehow worked loose. Then the drive sort of wiggled it even more loose. It leaked out a little at a time, until you hit them hard, then it blew the rest of the fluid out." He unscrewed a cap in the engine and poured the fluid. "I tightened the bleeder valve and I'll get this filled up. You'll be good to go."

"How would this have happened?" Nora asked.

He put the cap back on the jug and puckered his lips in consideration. "I don't know."

Abigail crossed her arms. "It happened because this Jeep is so old it's literally falling apart. I say we drive it right onto a lot in Moab and get you something decent."

Bill sauntered back to his tow truck. "Oh, this beauty has lots of life in her. I wouldn't go trading her off just yet. Especially now that she's all fixed up."

Nora braced herself. "What do I owe you?"

He placed the jug into the mess of his truck bed. He squinted his eyes and gazed down the road, calculating. "Let's see. Mileage out here both ways, plus filling the fluid." He winked at Nora. "And a little something for my expertise." Here it comes. Darrell said this guy gouged tourists. "How about twenty bucks?"

Nora waited. The first twenty for the drive one way, then another twenty for the drive back. Add a hundred or so for his expertise.

He waited. Frowned. "You think that's too much?"

Marlene hit Nora on the arm. "Twenty? For the whole thing?" she stammered.

He hardened his face. "Any lower and I'd lose money on the gas alone."

"No, no. Of course." Nora trotted back to her Jeep. She dug in her pack for her wallet, extracted a twenty and a ten. Then put the ten back and took another twenty. She hurried to Bill and handed him the cash.

He took it, then held out one of the bills. "You got a couple of them stuck together."

"That's for you. For your trouble. Buy yourself a few new paperbacks." He shrugged as though he couldn't understand her and didn't really care to. He climbed back into the truck.

Marlene and Abigail stood chatting by the passenger door to the truck. Nora hurried over. "I hate that you closed the bookstore for this. If I'd been thinking, I would have called the shop where I had it fixed earlier. But I'm really glad I didn't. Bill's great."

Marlene glanced into the cab and grinned. "And more well-read than you'd expect. Where did you have it worked on before?"

"A shop Darrell suggested."

Marlene tilted her head. "What's the name of it?"

Nora tried to remember the logo on the letterhead. "A star or planet or something."

Marlene's eyebrows drew together. "Polaris?" That didn't sound good. "What's the matter?"

"Nothing." Marlene's worried eyes didn't look like it was nothing. Abigail put her hand on Marlene's arm. "You need to tell us."

Marlene gazed up at the spires in the distance. She inhaled and looked at Nora. "Polaris is owned by one of the oldest Mormon families in Moab. They kind of keep to themselves and mostly service their own and relatives' vehicles."

"So?" Abigail was clearly running out of patience.

"Ranching around here is a hard way to make a living. Most ranchers need to supplement their income."

"And?" Abigail urged.

"Lee works for them sometimes."

If that hadn't knocked the air out of Nora, the next words out of Marlene's mouth would have.

"They serviced Lisa's truck." Marlene paused. "Right before her brakes went out."

23

Warren Evans denied the pain in his bones. The meds his physician prescribed were becoming less effective. He sat upright and plastered an enthusiastic grin on his face. All he needed to do was pull himself together for an hour, then he could return to his house and collapse, alone. He had the strength for that.

He lowered his head to pray, resisting the urge to rest his forehead on the steering wheel. He wanted to sleep, to lie back in his four-poster bed, surrounded by his children and grandchildren who would weep at the thought of his passing.

He would promise to see them again in the afterlife, when he, like his brother Jesus, would command his own planet, populated by his sons and daughters.

But he didn't have his own sons and daughters. God had withheld that blessing from him.

Christine's sharp voice cut through the silence in the Cadillac. "I don't know why you insist on putting yourself through this. You obviously don't feel up to it."

Warren pushed himself from the steering wheel to sit oak-tree tall. "We need to help Darrell. It's our duty."

Christine flipped the visor down and studied her face in the mirror.

She pulled a tube of lipstick from her purse and twisted it. The red color emerged like the disgusting penis of a dog. Before she applied it, she addressed him. "Why? Because he's Mormon and you have to stick together?"

He wanted to slap the lipstick from her hand. God made her the way He wanted her. And yet, never satisfied with His blessings, she'd pulled and tucked, dyed and plucked until she resembled a cartoon of the beauty he'd married so long ago. Maybe there had been the need for subterfuge while they courted investors and built Bourne Enterprises, but his fortune was made. He needed her to be his wife now, his helpmate—not just a cosigner on some of his bank accounts.

He unbuckled his seat belt. "I want to help him."

She ran the lipstick over her mouth, smacked her lips, and puckered for the mirror, then fluffed her raven hair. "You've earned your rest. Why would you drag us both to this godforsaken dust bin to campaign for Darrell when we could have stayed in Manhattan so you could recover from chemo?"

She didn't fool him. Christine didn't care if this trip made Warren uncomfortable. She hated Moab, always had. She preferred expensive restaurants and shopping and her work on her charitable committees. She disdained anything that reminded her of Warren's roots. He'd watched her cringe every time he'd mentioned his Utah upbringing to prospective business associates. Maybe he should have left her in New York.

But she was his wife, married before God. Not a Temple wedding, because he'd been headstrong and hadn't chosen in the faith. For that, God had punished him. Maybe she didn't comfort him and he couldn't count on her to walk hand in hand with him to the threshold, but she hadn't shirked her public responsibilities. As far as he knew, she'd been faithful to him. When her time came, he'd call her through the veil. He owed her that much.

"This is important." He opened the car door and pulled himself to stand. He'd lost weight, as well as his hair, during the chemo. The well-made toupee camouflaged his bald pate and only the most observant would detect anything out of the ordinary. His tailor had made him a few new suits. He hoped he didn't look anything worse than tired.

Warren crossed in front of the Caddy and opened the passenger door for Christine. She climbed from the car with as much grace as an actress stepping onto the red carpet. She smiled up at him, habit from years of playing generous and supportive spouse to a rich man. She never let her cover slip. He should be grateful.

They walked across the dirt parking lot and up the wooden boardwalk. He held the heavy log door open for her and she entered the restaurant. He followed and let the door close behind him.

He'd always liked this restaurant. The adobe walls, slick and whitewashed, made him feel clean and cool. The umber tones and the rustic log furniture felt far removed from the pretensions of New York and high finance. He missed this country, his roots. He wouldn't go back to New York. He had no need to acquire more on this side of the veil. Surely God would grant him peace now.

But not just yet. He still needed to decide who would carry the banner when he was called home.

The tables had been moved to the perimeter of the large dining room. Smells of roasting meat and the grease from French fries and onion rings permeated the building. The room buzzed with energy and conversation, knots of people congregating throughout the dining room.

He spotted Darrell at the far end of the room. Rage squeezed into him, but he banished it in a heartbeat. Not even Christine noticed. He kept his face relaxed as he watched Darrell raise a frosty glass of amber liquid to his mouth.

Beer! Darrell knew better than to indulge in sin like this. It showed a weakness that troubled Warren deeply.

Warren and Christine weren't in the room more than three seconds before Todd Grayson, a local sporting goods store owner, noticed them.

Todd hurried over, all grins and outstretched hand. "Warren! So good to see you. Darrell didn't say you'd be here." Warren returned a firm grip, followed by several more hearty handshakes with others. People swarmed around him as they usually did. Some wanted to bask in his celebrity, some hoped to get close enough he'd do them a favor down the road, some genuinely liked him. He didn't waste energy trying to figure out which category they landed in. He shook hands, accepted hearty pats on the back, chatted and joked. A crush of admirers swept Christine away. Hers or his fans, he didn't care.

The crowd around Warren parted and Darrell stood in front of him, an ear-to-ear grin playing on his face. The boy was good. Even Warren couldn't discern the authenticity of his smile. He grabbed Warren's hand and gave it a warm squeeze. "What a great surprise. When did you get to town?"

"Christine and I got in around two this afternoon." "Good flight?"

Inane conversation. He had more on his mind than the endlessly uncomfortable flight in his private jet. "Not bad. Looks like you've got a great crowd here." At two hundred dollars a plate, he'd better. Of course, Moab never brought in many campaign dollars. But a vote was a vote and Darrell needed them all.

Darrell surveyed the room with satisfaction. "We've got a lot of good friends here. Thanks to you."

Warren kept up his warm tone but lowered his voice a bit. "The polls have you slipping a few points."

Darrell's expression didn't falter but the light hardened in his eyes. "Nothing to worry about. We have a slump in cash flow right now so we're holding off for a media push in a couple of weeks."

Meaning, if only Warren ponied up cash, all would be well. Darrell so cleverly blamed his declining numbers on Warren.

A waitress wearing jeans and a too-small T-shirt appeared with two beading glasses of lemonade on a tray. The shirt stretched too tight across her breasts and the jeans rode too low on her hips. Sinful, thought Warren. Darrell took the glasses from her and held one out for Warren. "Thought you might be thirsty."

Warren accepted it and watched as Darrell drank nearly half of his glass. He probably hoped the lemon would mask the smell of the beer. His religion allowed no caffeine and definitely no alcohol. These might seem harsh and arbitrary rules, but the kosher restrictions of the Jews were equally as obtuse. God asked; man must comply. "We'll talk later," he said to Darrell. "You need to circulate."

Warren turned to an aging dowager, who wanted to discuss environmental issues. He did his best to focus on the woman, but nausea threatened and he felt weak. He caught a passing waitress, handed her the lemonade, and asked for ice water instead.

When he looked up, he caught sight of a black cowboy hat. The hat dangled in Lee's hands as he stood awkwardly in the back corner of the dining room. His mood brightened. Lee looked so much like Warren's dear sister Lydia, right down to the perpetually worried expression. It made them appear stern when Warren knew the opposite was true.

He disregarded the pain in his bones and strode over to Lee, hand extended. The corner of Lee's mouth ticked up. "Uncle Warren. Thought you might be here."

"It's good to see you supporting Darrell like this."

Lee chuckled. "I'm here to see you, not that blowhard."

Warren refrained from smiling. "The Lord uses everyone according to their talents."

The worry line appeared again in Lee's forehead. "I know you've been called to do great things. And I know the sacrifices you've made. Me and mine, we're grateful."

The toupee, the new suits, and the effort to appear energetic hadn't done the trick. Lee had detected his illness. Darrell probably had, too. He took the opportunity to drop into a chair next to a table that had been shoved against the wall. Lee sat down across from him.

Warren tried to lighten the boy's mood. "I wasn't fishing for compliments. And before you start in with your humility and all the proof of God's plan for you to be a steward of the land, I'm not going to lay any more burdens on you. Today." Lee looked at him in the same grateful, trusting way he used to when Warren took him fishing or hunting or they worked cattle. "But you said you came here to see me. What about?"

Lee hesitated. "A lot of people are arriving daily."

Warren glanced up to make sure they wouldn't be overheard. "Is there a problem?"

Lee positioned his chair so his back was to the room, trusting Warren to keep watch. "Lisa Taylor was close, Uncle Warren. She figured out what we're doing. If she hadn't died, we'd have been exposed."

Warren nodded. He couldn't let anyone know how shaken the incident made him feel.

Lee focused on Warren's face. "Rachel said that Trust woman thinks Lisa was murdered."

"That's why I'm here."

Lee exhaled in relief. "I hoped you'd handle it this time. With you here, it won't be as much a problem as it was with Lisa."

There. That's what Warren looked for. "You're a faithful servant, Lee."

The lines in Lee's forehead deepened. "I'm here to defend God's plan from the people who wouldn't understand."

Warren offered a gentle smile. "I'll let you know if I need you. And until then keep doing what you're doing—living a righteous life, keeping God's principles, and protecting the lands he gave us."

Lee pushed his chair back and stood. He made room for Warren to rise. Despite his effort to appear strong, Warren leaned heavily on the table. He stumbled and Lee grabbed Warren's elbows. With the strength that told of his days of physical labor, he righted Warren. As soon as Warren felt solid, Lee stepped back, deftly turning them so Warren faced away from the room and Lee looked into the room. Warren took a moment to regain his balance and wipe the strain from his face. Lee pretended not to notice. "No doubt you and Christine will want to stay here for a while. I'll send Tessa around with some fresh eggs and produce." He paused to see if Warren felt up to answering and then continued. "I know Christine has a fond spot for Tessa. And Tessa thinks the world of Christine." As he spoke, Lee's eyes traveled the room as though searching for anyone who would dare harm Warren here.

Warren willed his legs to be like thick pine branches. He demanded his queasy stomach to calm. He only needed to stay a few more minutes, then he could make excuses that Christine was tired after traveling and he could retreat home to his bed. He looked up, ready to get the ordeal over with.

Lee's face reminded Warren of the cow dog he'd had as a youngster. His eyes shone with purpose as he zeroed in on his prey. The rest of his body seemed ready to strike. Warren swiveled around to see what caught Lee's attention.

A young woman with coppery hair that swung around her face spoke with Darrell. She smiled briefly but seemed to be concerned with the business at hand. Instead of a dress or slacks, she wore khaki shorts and hiking boots. By the dust on her well-worn hiking shirt, it seemed she'd just stepped off the trail.

Lee's voice sounded like a growl. "That's her. Nora Abbott. The woman from the Trust." It did seem like the red-head had a feisty edge to her. "We've got to deal with her before she causes us trouble."

"I don't like what happened to Lisa and I'd hate for it to happen again. Let's see if I can't send Ms. Abbott on her way."

Lee's mouth clamped shut. He'd never been one to argue. Not that he gave in. Words never meant a lot to Lee.

Warren approached Darrell and Nora Abbott. She seemed agitated. "Did you know he worked there? Would he tamper with my brakes?"

Lee's mouth clamped shut. He'd never been one to argue. Darrell leaned closer, his face wreathed in concern. "Do you have any proof? The sheriff in this county is—"

"Mormon and won't help me. I know. Someone messed with Lisa's brakes, too."

Darrell's frown of distress pleased Warren. "We can't talk here.

Meet me tonight."

She obviously didn't like the brush-off, but she nodded briskly and turned. She smacked into Warren. "Excuse me."

He put out a hand as if to steady her, but it was more to keep himself from toppling. Her eyes flew open in recognition. Immediately she snapped her head to the right, then left, then over his shoulder as though looking for someone. People often wanted their friends to witness their brush with celebrity. She frowned briefly and returned her attention to him. "Mr. Evans."

He gave her his easy grin, the one investors trusted. "And you're Nora Abbott from Living Earth Trust. Darrell has told me about the accident involving that young woman making a film."

Before she had a chance to respond, Warren continued. "I'm a great supporter of expanding Canyonlands boundaries." She looked skeptical. "I've looked into Living Earth Trust and am impressed with your organization's stellar reputation. I'd like to make a sizable contribution."

Her eyes lit up. "We're always looking for additional funding." "I've got some Hollywood connections. We'll get a top-notch videographer, writers, and a director. Let me see what I can do," he said. She sighed. "That would be great, except we need the film before

Congress votes in two weeks."

Warren made sure to look disappointed and concerned. "That's not good. However, they'll vote again. This subject comes up often. Having spent a lifetime following political dog fights, my advice is that you present your strongest testimonial and not dilute it with a less than professional film. Then channel your resources on a spectacular film. I do have an in with Robert Redford." For added impact, he acted as if he'd just thought of it. "Or even Ken Burns."

She seemed to consider his pitch. Most people would have been salivating over an offer like that. He didn't need unbridled enthusiasm. He just needed her to back off—and by the time she received any word from him, it would all be over.

Darrell's grin flashed with charm. "Wow! Ken Burns. That would be perfect. Do you think you could do that?"

"But it wouldn't come up for vote again for a year at the soonest, probably later," Nora said.

"That's unfortunate. But we don't have much choice, do we? Perhaps you and Darrell can make a compelling enough statement to bring in the vote now. Just in case, let's start the ball rolling for the next round and come back swinging." Money, celebrity, promises of future success—he'd given her a golden triangle of reasons to leave town.

Darrell continued to cheerlead. "This is the best news we've had since..." His face contorted in sorrow before he went on. "Lisa would have been thrilled."

Time to close the sale. "Do you have a card? Never mind. I know I can contact you at Living Earth Trust. That's in Boulder, correct? I'll make some calls and get back to you early next week."

24

Warren stepped from the noisy, cool restaurant onto the wooden boardwalk. He let the heavy log door bump closed behind him. He'd put in his appearance, made his generous offer to Nora Abbott, and said his goodbyes.

Christine had been right behind him, but one of her fans must have sidetracked her. Christine loved her admiring public, but probably enjoyed making him wait. She knew he wanted to get back to their spacious home by the creek.

He leaned against the side of the restaurant and watched as cars and RVs zipped past on the highway. Across the valley the cliffs rose in familiar splendor. It wasn't in his destiny to lead his people to the new land but here, this harsh and rugged place, was his promised land. He thanked God for letting him come home.

He pushed himself upright and stepped across the boardwalk and down into the gravel. He held his head high, his shoulders erect. Not long ago, that posture wouldn't have required conscious thought. Careful steps carried him across a rutted parking lot. With daily monsoon showers, the dirt lot stayed damp with muddy puddles.

His eye caught sight of a petite woman with blonde hair standing beside a beat-up Jeep. His breath caught as it always did when he saw someone like this. The reaction had been his personal torture for the last thirty years. He never forgot her. Every blonde woman with that height and build shot him back in time for a split second and his heart cracked every time.

Of course, none of those women ever turned out to be her.

This woman stood with her back to him. It wasn't her, either, but seeing someone so similar in this place stole another beat of his heart. He didn't have many to spare, but he'd willingly give one to her. He started to look away just as she moved her head to give him a view of her profile.

The world stopped.

A swell of blood rose through him, rushed to his arms and legs, and surged through every cell. It couldn't be. It was impossible. And yet, she stood in front of him.

Unconsciously, he moved until he found himself by her side. He heard his own choked voice before he realized he spoke. "Abigail."

She squeaked and jerked around, her hand at her throat. Blood rushed to her face and her eyes, still crystal blue, flew open. She stepped back and flattened herself against the side of the Jeep.

Warren reached for her hand, but she pulled it away. "You are still so beautiful," he told her.

She swallowed hard. "Get away from me."

He understood her shock. They hadn't seen one another for at least thirty years. No doubt he'd aged beyond her imagination, especially as a result of the cancer. She'd probably aged as well. She had to be almost sixty. Yet to his eyes, she looked the same as she did almost every night in his dreams. "Abigail, I ... "

Christine's voice chirped from behind him. "There you are. I'm ready to go."

He couldn't turn away from Abigail, even though he knew he had to. If he closed his eyes or looked away, she might disappear forever. He'd learned to live without her for so long. But now that she stood close, now that God had put her back in his life, he couldn't let her go again.

"Warren?" Christine said.

Abigail brushed past him and hurried to the passenger side of the Jeep. She climbed inside, locked the door, and stared straight ahead.

Christine put a hand on his arm and shifted her gaze from him to Abigail and back. "Ready?"

A trickle of air leaked into his lungs and he blinked, fighting to appear normal. "Of course." He forced himself not to glance back at the woman in the Jeep as he followed Christine's elegant stride to the Caddy.

They opened their respective doors and slid inside. Christine let out a relieved breath. "Thank God you cut it short. All these people want to talk about is environmental issues and Darrell Burke's future." Warren backed out of the parking space, his breath still ragged,

his head a muddle of memories and desire.

He put the Caddy in gear.

The door of the restaurant opened and Nora Abbott walked out. She scanned the lot, then headed in the direction of the Jeep. Warren couldn't help but follow her with his eyes. She gave him an excuse to look in Abigail's direction and maybe catch sight of her again.

He expected Nora Abbott to climb into the sedan parked next to the Jeep. But she didn't. She pulled open the driver's door and plopped inside, her lips moving in conversation.

Nora Abbott and his Abigail. What was the connection?

25

Nora jumped into the driver's seat. Abigail sat in the passenger seat, her head held at an angle, staring ahead, ramrod straight like a steel statue. Abbey sat up in back, greeted Nora with a cold nose to her cheek, and turned his attention to the windshield to help Nora watch the road.

"What's the matter?" Nora asked.

Abigail appeared every bit as frightened as when the Jeep caromed down the mesa. "Nothing."

Nora exhaled in frustration. "Mother."

Abigail spied her from the corner of her eye without turning her head. "I can't stand that man."

"Which man?"

"Warren Evans. He's a scoundrel and a cheat."

Knowing how Abigail admired wealth, this news surprised her. "That sounds personal."

"It is."

"You know Warren Evans?"

Abigail folded her arms and stared straight ahead."Okay, cough it up. How do you know him and why didn't you tell me about it?"

Abigail spoke through tight lips. "Did Darrell tell you anything about Polaris or Lee Evans?"

Nora started the engine. "Don't evade the question. What about Warren Evans?"

Abigail's jaw twitched with her clenched teeth. Without turning from the windshield, she said, "We knew him in college."

"We, as in you and my father? Evans went to CU?" She didn't remember that from the bios of the tycoon she'd read while in business school. What she knew was that he was from southern Utah, had grown up poor, built a windshield repair business that he leveraged to buy another company, and had kept adding and building businesses. He eventually became a corporate raider, had more money than anyone could count, and freely donated to charities.

"Only for a year or so, then he transferred to Yale." "And you were friends?"

Abigail reddened in agitation. "I wouldn't call it that." Nora grinned. "You had a thing, didn't you?"

"Stop it!" Abigail shouted the words. They echoed in the quiet Jeep, swallowed by Nora's shock. Abigail still hadn't turned from the windshield. "Just drop it. Tell me what Darrell had to say."

Nora backed out of the parking spot, wrenched the steering wheel, and edged around the lot toward the exit. She strained to the right to make sure no one was driving through the alley.

Wait!

Her eye caught the white of Lee's pickup. She slammed on the brakes as Abbey scrambled to stay on the backseat.

"What in heaven's name?" Abigail gasped.

Nora gestured to the white pickup parked by the restaurant's back door. "Lee's pickup."

Abigail eyed the vehicle, then Nora.

"For a man that makes his living off the land, he sure spends a lot of time in town."

"Was Lee Evans at the bookstore after Lisa's funeral? Is he the sour-faced man with the black hat?" Abigail's forehead wrinkled.

"That's him," Nora affirmed.

Abigail settled back into the seat. "He seems to have anger issues. You remember Margie Bowen. Her husband went through a behavior modification course to learn to control his temper. Might do Lee Evans some good."

Nora drummed her fingers on the wheel, thinking. "Lee works part time for Polaris. Lisa's brakes went out recently, then our brakes went out. Plus, Lee ran me off the road after the funeral."

Abigail inhaled and looked at the pickup. "You think he's trying to scare you away from finding the film?"

"Or something worse." "Why would he do that?"

Did Abigail not pay attention to anything? "Maybe to keep Canyonlands' borders from expanding. Maybe because he's old school Mormon and hates that Rachel married Lisa."

Abigail huffed. "You're being ridiculous." Nora pushed the gearshift into first and rolled forward. "Where are we going?"

Nora gunned the Jeep and popped out on the highway heading south into Moab. "To try to find some answers."

Nora threaded her way through heavy traffic. Banners and signs celebrated the bike race and Moab buzzed with activity. She found a shady spot in the packed parking lot behind the Read Rock.

"Why are we here?" Abigail asked.

Nora opened her window for Abbey and scratched his ear. He loved napping in the Jeep and with a slight breeze and the shade, it didn't feel too warm. "Marlene knows more than she's telling me."

They climbed from the Jeep and walked through the alley. "About what?" her mother wondered.

"Not sure."

The bell above the door jingled as they walked in. Marlene stood at the display of local books with an elderly couple. Her gaze acknowledged them but she kept talking to her customers: "This is the best map for day hikes. Some of them are challenging, but there are some nice ones on level ground."

The man flipped through the guidebook Marlene handed him. "We liked the rim trail at the Grand Canyon. Is there something like that in Canyonlands?" Marlene pulled another book off the shelf and handed it to the woman as they continued discussing the best hiking options.

Nora and Abigail browsed the shelves, waiting for Marlene. Nora settled herself by the paperback mysteries located close to the back room. Whispers and a nervous giggle filtered through the curtain. Someone was in the back of the store.

The floor creaked as Marlene led the couple to the cash register with three books. "How long will you be in Moab?"

Marlene was busy with the customers and ringing up the sale. With only a moment of hesitation and a deep inhale to control her nerves, Nora slipped behind the curtain and into the back room.

She waited several seconds for her eyes to adjust to the darkness. Shelves and boxes cluttered the small space, which was little more than a wide corridor leading to a door that must open out into the parking lot. A secretary desk heaped with invoices, catalogues, and books was shoved against a wall.

A gasp brought her attention to the corner next to an open doorway. It must be a bathroom because a sink was visible. Two figures stood in the doorway.

Abigail practically shouted from the bookstore. "I'm not sure where she went. Maybe to the coffee shop down the street."

The curtain was whisked back and light flooded the back room.

Two teen-aged girls in ill-fitting pastel dresses huddled together. "What are you doing back here?" Marlene lunged toward Nora, her big hand clamping on Nora's arm. Marlene yanked her into the store and stood guard in front of the curtain.

Abigail pushed in front of Nora. "She had to use the restroom so I suggested she look back there."

Temper pushed around the edges of Marlene's eyes. "You said she went for coffee. I think she got nosy and went snooping where she doesn't belong."

Nora tried to put it together. "Are those girls hiding?"

Marlene lowered her eyebrows. "Not very well." She whirled around and disappeared behind the curtain. Her muffled voice sounded stern. "I told you to stay quiet and keep this door locked. What if it had been the church people?"

The girls whispered. Marlene lowered her voice. A door closed and seconds later, Marlene appeared. "Sit down." She indicated the reading nook in the corner.

When they'd settled, Abigail started in. "What girls?"

Marlene considered them a moment. "Those are runaways.

They're from Colorado City."

Abigail gasped and put a hand to her mouth. "Polygamists. I saw this on *60 Minutes*. They lock these girls away in their compounds, don't let them go to school past the sixth grade, and keep them brain- washed. When they turn fourteen or so, they marry them off to middle-aged men as second and third wives and they start having babies every year."

Nora's stomach turned. "Those girls?"

Marlene nodded. "It's criminal, but the local cops around there are all part of the church."

Abigail's face burned. "Why would a man want so many wives and children?"

Marlene's eyes hardened. "The mainstream LDS church has some strange ideas and one of them involves descendants and what happens when men die."

Nora and Abigail waited for Marlene to continue.

"Basically, if a man is righteous, when he dies he'll get his own planet. That planet will be populated with his wives and children and all their children. So the more he has here on Earth, the bigger planet and more powerful he'll be in the afterlife."

"That's nuts," Abigail said.

"That's bad enough, but there are pockets of the Mormon Church—cults—that have their own notions. The LDS church doesn't condone polygamists, but other Mormons practice it. And even among polygamists, there are decent families and then there are the Taliban types that make women slaves, like the Colorado City bunch."

Frustration and helplessness pooled in Nora. Marlene sighed. "So we help when we can." "We?" Nora asked.

Marlene frowned. "Look. This is dangerous for these girls and for us. Secrecy is vital. I can't tell you who else is involved. The girls are here today, and tonight they'll be gone. We'll move them to someplace safe and give them what help we can."

Nora couldn't imagine the terror of being so young and running from everything you've ever known. "What happens if they're found by the church?"

Marlene's hands clenched on the table. "They'll go back and be under so much control they'll never be able to break out again."

Abigail placed a hand on Marlene's. "What a brave and admirable thing you're doing."

Tears threatened in Marlene's eyes. "I have to help. I can't let them to go through what I did."

Nora braced herself. "You were raised in that?"

Marlene closed her eyes. "I ran when I was sixteen and pregnant. It was ugly and I won't talk about how I survived. When my baby was born, I gave it up. I don't even know if was a boy or a girl, but I do know it has a better life than I could have given it, either on the compound or away."

Abigail patted Marlene's hand. At least she had comforting words—Nora couldn't make her mouth work. "You did the right thing. And now you're helping those girls."

They sat quietly for a few minutes. Finally, Nora thought she ought to speak. "Lisa helped, too."

Marlene nodded.

That explained all the articles on Lisa's desk about women in the Mormon Church. Maybe Lisa's last message dealt with the underground railroad and not Canyonlands. "That's what she meant when she said the Tokpela Ranch. Is that one of the places you take the girls?"

Marlene's eyes opened wide. "When did Lisa say anything about that place?"

"Right before she died."

"It's got nothing to do with helping these girls."

Maybe, but it upset Marlene. "Why would she mention it?"

Marlene stood up and walked toward the center of the room. "I wouldn't know. But whatever it is, you need to leave it alone."

Nora followed Marlene. "The Tokpela Ranch? Why?"

Abigail made a beeline for the back room, but Marlene intercepted her. "Don't go back there."

"I only wanted to give them a hug."

Marlene stood firm. "No."

Abigail looked like she might argue, and instead, reached inside her purse. She brought out her wallet and pulled out several bills, handing them to Marlene. "Then give them this. And if you won't do that, buy them some clothes or a nice dinner."

Marlene took the money. "Thank you," she whispered.

Abigail nodded and strode toward Nora. She threaded her arm through Nora's and they walked out the door, leaving the bell tinkling behind them.

26

After giving Abbey a chance to stretch, water a tire, and get a drink, they settled back into the Jeep.

Abigail clicked her seat belt. "Those poor girls. I'm glad Marlene is helping them."

Nora vowed to get involved when she got back to Boulder. Right now she had to figure out what had spooked Lisa and if it was related to the reason someone tampered with her brakes, if all of it led to Lisa's death and why.

Nora squinted out the windshield.

Abigail scrutinized her. "What are you thinking?"

She started the Jeep and backed out of the parking place. "Want to take a drive?"

"No."

Nora grinned. "Okay." "Where are we going?"

Nora pulled onto the street, working her way west out of town. "We're going to the Tokpela Ranch."

Abigail shook her head. "Marlene said to leave it alone." Nora nodded. "That's a good enough reason to go." Abigail's voice was tight. "Bad idea."

"We'll just look around, see if we find any reason it would have concerned Lisa." Her heart picked up its pace.

Abigail sounded tense. "What could you possibly find?" Nora shrugged. "Won't know if we don't try."

Abigail put a hand on the wheel in protest. "Turn this around. We are not going snooping at someone's ranch. Especially if you suspect it might be dangerous."

"We'll pretend we're tourists that got lost. What's the harm in looking around?"

"Do you even know where it is?" "Actually, I do."

"Oh, for heaven's sake." Abigail pursed her lips and folded her arms.

They rode in silence for a while, nothing but Abbey's panting and the knocking rhythm of the wheels on the highway to keep them company.

Finally Abigail spoke. "I'm sorry I never told you about Warren. It was a long time ago. I never liked him and he's still creepy."

Nora needed to tread gently, but to say she was curious would be to call Mount Everest a bunny hill. "What was he like in school?"

Abigail's shoulders crept toward her ears with tension. "We actually met him here. He took a real liking to Dan."

Nora held her breath and waited. Abigail didn't continue. "Did a lot of people like Dan?" She corrected, "My father."

Abigail considered the question. "Not really. You have to remember in those days, being a Native American wasn't like it is now."

"What do you mean?"

Abigail considered. "That was the seventies. A time of transition and we were living in Boulder, the epicenter of change."

For Abigail, wherever she existed was the epicenter. But Boulder was probably an interesting place to experience that decade.

"The hippies and 'enlightened' people embraced the Indians and thought everything they did was superior to white people. The others, the older people and establishment types, thought of Indians as inferior and lazy. They believed the stereotypes of all Indians being drunks or on welfare."

Nora tried to study Abigail out of the corner of her eye. She couldn't imagine her mother in bell bottoms with a bandana tied around her head, John Lennon sunglasses perched on her nose. She always pictured

Abigail wearing a pink empire-waist mini dress with a white sash, carrying a white patent leather purse with matching go-go boots. Her hair would be teased in a That Girl flip.

But Abigail had fallen for Dan, a Native American. They'd back-packed and, even though it seemed more like science fiction than truth, probably slept together before marriage. Reconciling her life-long image of young Abigail with the facts might be more than Nora could assimilate in a few days.

Nora tiptoed. "Which camp did Warren fall into?"

Abigail's mouth twisted with distaste. "Warren honed his persuasive skills early. He didn't seem to belong to either category. He showed up on campus right after we'd met him in Moab. He acted like he accidently bumped into us and then sort of weaseled his way into being Dan's friend."

"What do you mean?"

Abigail paused as if remembering. "Dan kept to himself a lot. He didn't trust many people and he was serious about his classes."

Nora interrupted. "What was he studying?"

A smile of pride crept onto Abigail's face. "Physics. He wanted to go into the space program."

This bit of new information shifted her mental image of her father. That was one thing she didn't share with him. Nora's science aptitude ranked even lower than her interest in the subject. And where she inherited her accounting acumen was anyone's guess because Abigail couldn't even balance her checkbook.

Abigail readjusted herself. "Warren wanted to hang out with us and hike and drink coffee, you know, just young people things."

"So what changed?"

Nora could almost see the ice form along Abigail's spine. "He wasn't a friend to Dan. Or to me."

"What happened?"

Abigail snapped her head toward Nora. "Can we drop it, please? It doesn't matter. Warren is and was an opportunist and takes what doesn't belong to him."

"He stole from Dan?"

Abigail's eyes shot a ray of anger mixed with a hint of something else.

Revulsion? "I don't want to talk about it."

Nora turned off the highway. According to directions she'd looked up, getting to Tokpela Ranch meant driving south about twenty miles along questionable roads. The route outside of Moab twisted around what looked like industrial sites, complete with large Dumpsters overflowing with debris, broken blacktop parking lots, and giant Quonset garages with their gaping doors open and all manner of equipment and trash visible inside. Electrical wires with bright red balls crisscrossed the skyline as far as Nora could see. Despite its earth-loving, outdoors-enthusiast reputation, the area around Moab hosted pockets of environmental neglect.

The road turned south and after a few miles, the pavement gave way to gravel that pinged against the underside of the Jeep.

Abigail's voice sounded pinched. "We should not be going there." Nora didn't answer. She was more and more convinced Lee had something to do with Lisa's death and maybe she'd find some proof at

Tokpela Ranch.

The road wound along a creek in a narrow valley with oaks and elms and cottonwood trees shading sandy clearings and entrances to slot canyons. A monsoon rain could make the canyons deadly. A big storm upstream might send water flash flooding downstream where the weather was clear. With no way to climb the slick sides to safety and water roaring through them, the canyons could claim people caught unaware.

The road deteriorated even further. Washboards nearly rattled their teeth loose and grass grew thicker down here. They rumbled across a cattle guard and a wide valley spread before them. In dry weather, the valley would be a lush pasture. But in this unusually wet spring, a small lake had puddled in the low ground with tall reeds forming a circle, giving way to spongy ground.

Across the valley, a collection of buildings marked the headquarters of Tokpela Ranch. The narrow dirt road wound around the edge of the meadow, leading directly to headquarters. Nora followed the bumpy trail, closing in on the buildings. The traditionally shaped barn sat like a sentinel at the side of the road. The enormous wooden structure looked like it had been built over a hundred years ago and hadn't been painted since. It blocked the view of the rest of the compound. A pit of anxiety formed in Nora's stomach. What would they find at the Tokpela Ranch?

Nora's foot was light on the gas pedal as they crawled past the barn. Weathered wood corrals opened off the barn and a gray work- horse stood dozing in the sun. He didn't stir as they idled past. Another corral held a large, bony cow. Its white and black markings copied onto a rambunctious calf that kicked and sprinted across the enclosure. A fat, spotted pig lay on its side in the dirt of another corral.

An acre of fresh plowed ground showed evidence of soft green plants breaking through the rich, dark soil in neat rows, along with rows of bushy greens. A garden this size would feed a small village and take that many to tend it. The road curved into the center of the ranch compound, its area about a quarter of the size of a football field and the packed dirt spotted with patches of worn prairie grass. A giant structure faced the aging barn across the center yard.

Only two small windows graced the ground floor of the plain two-story building. A smattering of tiny windows lined the second story, evenly spaced, making it look like a barracks.

Off to the side of the barn, a cozy-looking stone house filled the gap between the barn and the looming building. It must have been the original homestead. A front porch faced the east and the sunrise. The chinking appeared to be falling out between the colored stones and the roof sagged with age. A lean-to jutted off to the south and a cellar door took up space to the north of the house, with a small building, no doubt an outhouse, off to the back. A kitchen garden added a bright spot of green to the front yard and a hitching post marked the transition from the rugged grass to the dirt.

Nora pulled the Jeep in front of the hitching post and shut it off. Two young blonde girls and a dark-haired girl with a purple ribbon around her ponytail squatted in the grass of the front yard. The blondes each held a small tennis shoe and were banging them on the ground to watch them light up. The blondes' pale eyes widened in their faces when they saw Nora and Abigail climb from the Jeep. "Hello!"

Nora turned to the greeting from a woman coming from the barn. "Are you lost?" The solidly built blonde woman wore jeans and a faded blue T-shirt, smeared with dirt or mud or maybe something even earthier. Her round, flat face gave off a friendliness mixed with a good dose of wariness. She looked sturdy enough to dispatch Nora and Abigail with one solid swat. Nora's chest tightened.

The woman strode across the dirt carrying a red plastic bucket. When she stopped in front of them, Nora saw the bucket contained a dozen or so brown eggs. She glanced behind the woman to a shack with a low roof in the shade of the barn. The door stood open and white hens pecked at the ground.

The woman held a hand up to shield the sun. "That curve to the highway can be easy to miss. You aren't the first one to keep going straight and end up here instead of turning back toward the highway." A stooped slip of a woman stepped onto the porch of the stone house. She wore a housedress covered by a full apron in a pastel print. Wrinkles as deep as the slot canyons ran along her face. She descended the porch steps quicker than Nora would have thought possible. She tottered over to them in a rushed gait that rocked from one foot to another. The top of her balding head barely reached Abigail's shoulder.

Abigail smiled at her. "Good afternoon. This is a lovely place." She indicated the stone house behind the woman. "When was it built?"

The little woman's face soured, as if detecting some sort of falseness in Abigail's compliment. "It's old. Like me. If you go back up the road a piece, you'll see where you turned wrong. Won't take but an extra fifteen minutes."

What was Nora going to say to the woman? Should she tell them they weren't lost tourists? What good would that do? While she debated her next move, she watched the blonde woman. Something about her looked familiar. Then it clicked.

Rachel. She looked like an older version—she had the same thin blonde hair, same blue eyes, round face, and guarded expression. She supposed that wasn't unusual. The gene pool around here might be pretty shallow and the families large. Rachel had to be related to many of them.

Abigail stepped closer to the house. "The colors of the stone are really striking, especially in the sunlight. It looks like the house was built first and all the others sort of came along as money and need dictated."

The old woman's distaste showed in her beady eyes. "You from Salt Lake City? LDS?"

Abigail was undaunted. "How many generations have lived here?

I'll bet you are descended from the first homesteaders."

The wizened woman frowned outright. "We mostly like it out here because no one bothers us."

The younger woman, who was probably ten years or so older than Nora, maybe in her mid-forties, forced a smile. "Lydia doesn't mean to be rude, but she's right—we're busy."

Nora thought the old woman did, indeed, mean to be rude. "Cassie and me got a lot to get done this time of year. Like I said, follow the road back out and you won't get lost."

The front door of the big house opened and another blonde woman emerged. From where Nora stood, about thirty yards away, she appeared much younger than the egg woman, Cassie. She resembled Rachel as well, and looked to be in the home stretch of pregnancy. A tow-headed toddler tumbled out the door after her.

Abigail appeared not to notice. She addressed Cassie. "Your garden is very impressive. I like to think of myself as an amateur horticulturist, but even if I had the space, I couldn't possibly raise a garden like that without a crew to help with the work or people to eat the produce. Do you raise other livestock, too?"

Abigail sounded too nosy for a random tourist and Cassie's expression hardened by the second. "We make organic cheese and sell it at farmer's markets."

The pregnant woman stepped off the concrete slab that served as a front porch. She held the hand of the child as he, or she, tottered into the grass. Nora looked for the little girls sitting in the old woman's yard. Sometime during the conversation they had sneaked off.

Abigail suddenly strode out, heading across the dirt toward the barn. "Was that chard I saw growing in your garden? Is it a particularly hardy hybrid to stand the cold nights this time of year? You know, I love the early vegetables. The peas and lettuces and broccoli." Cassie took off after her. Lydia scowled at Nora. "That's a chattery old fool."

The pregnant woman stretched and rubbed her lower back. She glanced over to where Nora and Lydia stood. Her head jerked to the Jeep.

She bent over, scooped up the toddler, and hurried into the house. Abigail succeeded in getting to the garden, Cassie in tow. Her perky chatter carried across the yard. Annoying at her best of times, when she put an effort into it, Abigail could make Mother Teresa snap. Although Cassie seemed nice enough, she was no saint. "We don't allow tourists in our garden."

"Oh, look at these carrots. How do you keep your rows so straight?" Abigail was doing her best to distract Cassie.

A lot of good it did Nora, with Lydia eyeing her like a hawk sizes up a mouse.

Nora struggled for something to say while trying to take in everything in the compound. "You should have seen her at the Hopi reservation. She kept looking in people's houses."

Lydia perked up, her eyes becoming lasers. "Hopi? Not LDS?"

Lydia's reaction seemed strange but then, nothing about this place was normal. Nora understood why she kept asking if they were LDS since the mainstream church didn't approve of polygamists and this place could be one of those cults Marlene spoke of. But why would mentioning Hopi set her off? "I've got friends on Second Mesa."

Lydia flicked her hands in a "scat" motion. "It's time for you to leave. Pick up that fool and get gone."

There wouldn't be any finessing this woman. Abigail crossed the yard toward Nora and Cassie stormed behind her with a stony face. They heard the rumble of an engine. Whoever was coming might mean trouble for Nora and Abigail. They should leave now. "Come on, Mother. We should go." Nora tried not to appear panicked as she hurried back to the Jeep.

Abigail slowed her pace even though Cassie seemed determined to keep her moving. "I'd love to see the inside of the barn. I'll bet it has some history. When did the Mormons settle this part of the country?"

Wheels rattled on a cattle guard, warning of an approaching vehicle. Nora tried to sound casual. "Mother? I think we've bothered these people enough. We really should be heading back."

"Perhaps we could come back another day," Abigail said, not making a move toward the Jeep.

The hood, then cab, then bed of a white pickup popped around the barn, taking the curve of the road into the yard. The silhouette of a black hat hung in its rear window. Lee.

Was the Tokpela Ranch his? If so, that doubled Nora's suspicions. Abigail finally noticed it. She spun around and skipped to the Jeep.

"Thank you much for the tour. You have a lovely spread here." Spread?

They both jumped into the Jeep and slammed the doors. Nora turned the key and shifted into reverse.

She twisted to look behind her, aware that a couple of children could be anywhere.

The white pickup loomed in her rearview mirror like a shark with open jaws.

Nora spun around, jammed the gear into first, and eased off the clutch to crawl forward. She might have to run across the yard a little, but she'd just be able to squeeze around the hitching post.

Before she moved more than an inch, though, Lee jumped in front of the Jeep and banged his fists on the hood. The clang made Abigail scream.

Nora squeezed her brakes.

He slapped the hood of the Jeep again and glared at her. Abbey barked. The noise gnawed through her control. She disengaged the gear lever.

Cassie joined Lee in front of the Jeep. Her fierce expression was even more frightening than Lee's. Lydia, probably the scariest of all, hobbled in that see-saw way toward them.

Nora grabbed the door handle and Abigail clutched at her. "Don't go out there. This is an evil cult and they'll take you into the barn for human sacrifice."

While that jibed with Nora's imaginative scenario, it seemed an exaggerated response, even in Nora-world.

She jumped out of the Jeep, slamming the door before Abbey could join her. With way more courage than she felt, Nora demanded, "Get out of the way."

Lee strode over to her. She fought the wise urge to run. He stopped within inches of her, breathing hard. "What do you want?"

Nora countered with, "Did you mess with my brakes?"

He let out air as though she'd punched his stomach. His face clouded. "Did I what?"

Nora felt a little momentum shift her way. "Like you tampered with Lisa's brakes."

He narrowed his eyes. "You're crazy, aren't you?"

Nora imagined him slipping his hands around her throat and squeezing her like a chicken. A smart woman would bolt, run for the hills. But even if Nora could leave Abigail to fend for herself, locked in the Jeep, she wouldn't get far with Cassie standing a few feet behind her. Her only weapon was her wits.

They were screwed.

"It wouldn't be a good idea to hurt us. Everyone knows we came out here. If we don't show up in town, they'll come after you." Sweat beaded on her lip and pooled under her arms.

He smirked. "Everyone? Rachel?" He chuckled.

She didn't see the little girls so she wouldn't have to worry about flattening them with the Jeep in a quick getaway. If she jumped in and gunned it, they could probably make it out of here. Lee didn't have a gun in his hand, so he'd have to get to his pickup to chase them down. "She's not the only one who knows we're here. We told Marlene. She already suspects you killed Lisa." How would he react to an accusation of murder?

He laughed. "Half the town of Moab thinks I killed Lisa. They're convinced I swallow hikers whole. They suspect I kill cyclists and sell their mountain bikes on the black market. They can't prove it any more than you can prove I messed with your Jeep."

His ridicule brought out her anger. "Did you hate Lisa because she was a lesbian or because of her work to expand the park? Or maybe it was something else." *Like her helping rescue girls from polygamist cults like yours?*

Cassie let out a huff of annoyance.

He spoke slowly. "I wasn't the one trying to change her way of life. She—and all you people—are working pretty darned hard to destroy mine."

So you killed her. She didn't say the words out loud but they must have been plain on her face.

His face looked like black thunder. “Lisa was someplace she shouldn’t have been and she had an accident.”

Cassie put a hand on her hip. “You don’t belong here, sister.”

The air felt like lead as Nora tried to steady her breath. Was this where they’d drag Nora and Abigail away and bludgeon them?

Lee’s hateful eyes bored into her. “You’d best get while you can. You’re too scrawny to do much good, but we can always use some bones for soup.”

Cassie lunged forward, as if to attack, and laughed.

Nora marched to her Jeep with as much dignity as she could muster. She pulled open the door and pushed Abbey into the back seat.

Abigail’s voice squeaked. “Could we please get out of here?”

Nora turned at the anxiety in her mother’s tone. Abigail sat straight, staring ahead, all blood drained from her face. Her hands trembled.

Lydia stood outside Abigail’s rolled-up window. Her creepy dried apple face hovered only inches away, a malevolent and toothless grin aimed at Abigail. The nightmares from that image would stay with Nora for a very long time.

Nora eased forward, the vehicle nearly brushing the hitching post. As soon as she straightened the wheel, she surveyed the area for any stray children, saw none, and gunned the engine. They sped around the curve by the garden and down the road.

Nora’s insides felt as solid as the marshy lake in the meadow. Her hands shook on the wheel. “That was straight out of a horror movie. I expected an army of zombies to come out of the barn with scythes and torches.”

Abigail reached for her handbag and rummaged inside. Her hands shook every bit as much as Nora’s. She pulled a lipstick case out and opened it, taking out the tube. She held the case open for the mirror and started to apply the lipstick. She shook too hard for precision and dropped both hands to her lap. “They lacked basic social graces.”

That was the worst Abigail could come up with? “Can you imagine tea and cookies with Granny Evil?”

Abigail shook her head. “The woman should have started a good skin regimen about eighty years ago.”

They laughed and it eased some of the strain.

Nora didn't start breathing regularly until they found the road to the highway and headed safely toward civilization. "Marlene knows they're dangerous. That's why she told me to stay away."

Abigail finished a successful attempt at her lipstick and slid the kit into her bag. Her voice shook and she clutched her hands together. "Who knew farmer's markets could be so lucrative?"

"What do you mean?"

"I assumed they'd have a couple of old tractors in that big barn. But they had three SUVs back there. One of them was an Escalade."

What?

Recognition slipped into place. The dark-haired little girl sitting on the grass reminded Nora of the little girl outside the outfitters in Moab yesterday. She wore the same purple T-shirt and light-up shoes. Wasn't she getting into an Escalade?

"Something else," Abigail said. "There's more?"

"You know those images on the petroglyphs? The symbols you were so fascinated with?"

"The symbols you said my father doodled?" "Yes. Well, that was painted on the barn."

27

Crickets chirped somewhere in the desert beyond Lisa's front porch as night closed around the cabin. The glow from a citronella candle gave the only light. Abbey stretched on the porch floor, twitching in the rabbit hunt of his dreams.

The boards on the north end of the porch squeaked again as Nora pivoted and paced back to the south. She was convinced Lee had tampered with her breaks and tried to kill her and Abigail. He'd murdered Lisa. Did he really think he could eliminate everyone advocating park expansion? He'd eventually run out of clever ways to arrange accidents and the environmentalists would keep coming. Sort of like the Indians trying to staunch the flow of white immigrants two hundred years ago. Right or wrong, Lee would lose.

But Nora didn't care about the park issues right now. Runaway girls, religious cults, and attempted murder seemed more important. Abigail had gone to ground. Actually, to her room. When they'd returned from the excursion to Tokpela, she'd marched upstairs and closed her door. She'd done her share of pacing, too, but Nora hadn't heard movement since the sun set several hours ago. Maybe she'd finally gone to sleep.

Rachel wasn't home when Nora and Abigail reached the cabin and still hadn't returned.

Aside from the crickets, the night had the volume set on mute. The perfume of the sand, sage, and other scents from the typical afternoon shower didn't do much to ease Nora's concerns. A sliver of moon barely restrained the darkness. Nora wore Lisa's old hoodie to ward off the chill.

Did whatever Lisa left on the camera reveal Lee's threats to her or the runaway girls? Where would Lisa hide it so that Nora would find it? And what about the symbol? It was in Nora's dreams, on Rachel's pictures, and now on Lee's barn.

Headlights swung from the dirt road to shine along the rutted driveway lane. Rachel must be coming home. Nora steeled herself. Rachel might be on a war path and want to engage Nora in combat. Or their truce from breakfast might hold and she'd want company.

The soft purr of an engine approached, sounding nothing like the rumble of Nora's old Jeep. When it got closer, Nora let out a breath. It wasn't Rachel's Passat. The Toyota 4Runner belonged to Darrell. He shut the engine off and climbed out.

"I'm glad you're still up," he said. "I was afraid it's too late. I got hung up in a meeting with some constituents, but I wanted to check on you and your mother."

He plodded up the steps and leaned on the porch railing. Somewhere along the day, he'd pulled his tie off, leaving the collar open on his wrinkled blue shirt. Dark whiskers dusted his chin and cheeks.

"You didn't need to come all the way out here. We're fine." "You seemed pretty upset at the fundraiser this afternoon and I felt bad about not being able to help you." He stood and held out his arms. "So here I am, even though it's nearly midnight, at your disposal."

His easy grin teased one of her own in response. "Can I get you something? A beer? Iced tea?"

He plopped into one of the Adirondack chairs and slumped down. "Mormons have some strict rules about alcohol and caffeine."

She should have known better. "Let me see what Rachel has in the kitchen."

He laughed. "I'd love a beer. But if you tell anyone, I'll call you a liar."

"I have to warn you, I crack under torture."

"I'll take my chances and hope the Mormon deacons don't get a hold of you."

She slipped into the house for the beers. The light from the refrigerator splashed across the dark kitchen. She was trying to flirt with Darrell, but it didn't feel right.

It should be Cole on the front porch. They'd sit together on the steps, laugh and tease and share a kiss or two. Maybe even stroll into the soft night hand in hand. She pictured his lanky frame in his jeans and hiking boots, goofy grin on his face, pointing out the columbines on the hillside next to the trail. "I'd pick you a bouquet but I know you'd rather I let them live," he'd say.

In the short time they'd been together, Cole seemed to understand her and know her from the inside out.

"Did you get lost?" Darrell's voice floated in from the porch.

She reached inside and grabbed two bottles of beer, then shut the door. While she opened the bottles in the scant light from the window, she reminded herself that Cole was married and though she clung to some hope he'd work it out, she had to be prepared that he wouldn't.

By the time she got back to the porch and handed Darrell his bottle, she'd found a smidgeon of equilibrium.

"Did you raise a lot of campaign money today?" She sank into a chair.

He took a long pull and sighed. "It wasn't really about the money.

We've got a lot of work to do with getting the locals on board."

"It didn't look like many ranchers or native Moab folks were there today." Except Lee.

"That's the problem. The activists and environmentalists that have retired here or moved here in the last few years have more money than the old timers. But votes are votes. We need to find a way to talk to the traditionalists and get them to understand how important it is to protect Canyonlands."

"As much as I'd like the locals on board,"—*if for no other reason than to keep them from trying to kill us*—"the decision is really out of their hands. It's up to Congress."

He gulped his beer. "Right. Did you make any progress on finding Lisa's camera?"

The beer tasted bitter and she set it aside and stood. "Since the cops won't help, I went out to Lee's ranch this afternoon."

He sat up at full attention. "You shouldn't have done that. He's dangerous."

"I didn't know he owned the Tokpela Ranch. Lisa seemed interested in it so I wanted to check it out."

He set his empty bottle on the porch floor. "What did Lisa ... ?" She interrupted him. "He's a polygamist."

Darrell stared at her. "How do you know?"

She waved him off. "There were a couple of wives and a ton of children and this creepy old lady. It's obvious. But there's something else."

He leaned back and studied her. "What?"

"I can't figure it out, but it has something to do with this symbol I saw on petroglyphs today. It's three concentric circles, like a target. Then lines run outward, like rays. Or kind of like the state symbol for New Mexico, but instead of several lines coming out from one circle in four directions, two lines shoot out in six directions. "

He laughed. "What are you talking about?"

She sounded like Abigail chattering away and realized she'd probably inherited that tendency.

"This symbol that I saw on the rock is the same one painted on the side of Lee's barn."

He tilted his head as if waiting for more. "Uh-huh?" "It means something." She pointed out the obvious.

"What does it mean?" He stood up and walked to where she'd planted herself by the rail.

She paced away. "I don't know. That's the problem."

"Maybe he likes the symbol. You know, like the coil symbol you see everywhere or the hand or kokopelli. People tack them up on their houses or jewelry because they like the design, not necessarily because of their meaning."

The coil he talked about was a Hopi symbol telling the story of their ancient migrations. After they'd climbed from the Third World into the new and improved Fourth World, they wandered for years, probably centuries, until they settled on the garden spot of the three mesas in barren, sun-scorched Northern Arizona. The more time she spent on the mesas, the more she appreciated the hidden beauty. The Hopi might have settled in the desert but they'd figured out a way to survive and knew how to grow corn and other food. Benny had taken her to spots of lush green hidden from the casual visitor.

"Everything on the Hopi reservation has a meaning. Those symbols represent something."

"Maybe they aren't Hopi." He followed her to where she'd retreated across the porch.

"They might not be. But they're ancient. The Hopi traveled all over this area centuries ago. They claim to be descendants of the Anasazi." She hesitated. "My cousin on the rez will know."

"You've talked to him?" Darrell asked.

She swallowed a gulp of beer. "He's not answering his phone. He probably let the battery die. He's got a generator for electricity, but he doesn't use it all the time."

"Why not?"

Good question. "I haven't figured out how he decides which modern conveniences to use and when. He grows most of his own food, but then also had prepackaged stuff. He has a cell phone but only uses it sometimes."

Darrell seemed to consider that. "Interesting."

It normally fascinated Nora, but not tonight. "I need to figure out what the symbol means."

Darrell seemed to have lost interest in the conversation. He studied her face. "Can I ask you a personal question?"

No. She didn't want any personal questions. She shrugged. "Sure." "Are you in a relationship?"

Yes. Cole and I should be together. We were together. Until we weren't. "Yes. No. Not anymore. I mean, it's complicated."

He waited a moment. "I'm sorry. It must be a recent breakup?" "Very recent." She didn't want to talk about it. And she didn't

want Darrell standing quite as close to her as he was. "I'm sorry." His voice softened like melting ice cream.

She stepped back. "I'm sorting through Lisa's desk drawers. I'll bet she left some clue for me about where the camera is hidden."

A small smile played on his face as if acknowledging her not-so-subtle topic change. "I'm a good politician. I can mediate disputes and persuade. I can talk to people who don't agree with me and negotiate different positions. But I'm a disaster in my personal life. As you can see from me being thirty-five and still single."

"Single is not a bad thing." Single is fine.

His confidence evaporated in an uncertain smile. "Even strong people need a partner."

Time to change the subject. "What do you know about Lee? You grew up around here, right? Did you know each other when you were younger?"

He dropped his shoulders, the long day falling on him. "I left this place when I was young. My mother and I moved to Salt Lake City. I didn't come back until I had finished law school. Don't tell anyone, but I really came back to establish residency so I could run for office here."

Nora pulled her hoodie closer to ward off the night's chill. "Lee's lived here all his life; do people like him?"

"He's kind of anti-social, don't you think? If you're right and he is a polygamist, he probably doesn't want to call attention to himself. Polygamy is still against the law, even if it is tolerated."

Nora eyed Darrell, weighing whether to tell him her suspicions. Maybe he could help. "I'm sure he messed with my brakes. And," she inhaled, "I think he killed Lisa."

Darrell grabbed her hand, startling her. "Leave him alone. Go back to Boulder, send your mother back to Flagstaff. I'll do what needs to be done here. I want you safe, Nora."

"You believe me?" Part of her hoped he'd convince her it was all coincidence.

Darrell stared into the darkness. "Lee's afraid of losing his way of life. He's desperate."

"I just need undeniable proof, then I can go to the FBI or tell someone not connected to this place."

"I won't allow it!" he hissed. It sounded like a shout in the quiet night.

The words fell to the porch floor like a bucket of cold water. They faced each other and it was hard to tell who was more surprised.

"You won't allow it?"

He rubbed his eyes. "I'm sorry. I didn't mean that. I'm beat and the thought of you getting hurt upsets me."

He may act charming and steady, but a crack here and there gave Nora the uneasy feeling he might not be so perfect.

He pulled his phone from his pocket. "Don't do anything right now. Let me make a phone call and see what I can get going."

"Now?"

He gave her a tired grin. "I know people who never sleep."

She watched him plod down the porch steps, murmuring into his phone. The screen door squealed and Nora jumped.

"What was that about?" Abigail stepped onto the darkened porch wearing her pink bathrobe and slippers. She smelled of expensive face cream and her skin sparkled in the glow of the candle. Darrell stood with his back to the porch, his voice vibrating quietly. "He's calling someone to help prove Lee is guilty of Lisa's murder."

Abigail frowned at Darrell but she didn't argue. She must be starting to accept the possibility.

"I thought you'd gone to bed," Nora said.

"I can't sleep. I came down for some warm milk. Where do you suppose Rachel's gone?"

Nora shrugged. Abigail folded her arms. "You need to call Cole. His pride won't let him call you."

Abigail had her priorities. Murder and white slavery took second place to romance. "Pride? I'd say it's more like his wife that won't let him call."

"So 'it's your party and you'll cry if you want to.'"

Nora lowered herself to sit on the front step. Abbey got to his feet and ambled over to sit next to her. He put a paw into her lap. She trailed her fingers through his fur. "This hardly seems like the time to discuss my love life."

Abigail leaned against the porch rail. "Or lack thereof."

Irritated, Nora stood, disturbing Abbey. He trotted down the porch steps. "I need to go to the rez."

Abigail furrowed her brow. "In Arizona? That seems a bit out of the blue."

"Benny's not answering his phone and I need to know what that symbol means."

"You think Benny can help?"

Nora moved close to Abigail to give her some warmth. "I don't know, but he's the best source I can think of."

Abigail wrapped an arm around Nora.

Nora studied the dark circles under her mother's eyes. "What upset you so much today?"

Abigail waved her arm in the air. "Oh, I don't know." Her voice rang with sarcasm. "Your antique car fell apart and nearly killed us, and if that wasn't enough, you drove us out to a hostile enemy camp to be harassed by polygamists. And then there's the possibility Lee Evans is a murderer."

"You got spooked when you saw the rock art, then seeing Warren Evans at the restaurant pushed you to the edge, and the symbols on the barn just about did you in. What's going on?"

Abigail swiveled and swung the screen door open. Her slippers scuffed across the wood floor toward the kitchen.

Nora followed. "Does all this remind you too much of Dan?"

The glow from the refrigerator light glistened on Abigail's greased cheeks. "Don't be ridiculous."

"Then what?" Nora tucked one leg under herself and perched on the edge of a stool.

Abigail snatched the milk carton and slammed the door closed, shutting off the light. "Then nothing."

"Lisa's brakes went out about a week ago."

Abigail thumped the milk carton on the counter. Her face paled. "Lee Evans is dangerous."

Abigail gasped as if discovering a new horror. Her fist flew to her mouth. "No."

Nora jumped up.

"Evans. It has to be." Abigail slumped against the counter and gripped the edge.

Afraid her mother might be having a stroke, Nora rounded the counter to Abigail. "What is it?"

Abigail trembled. "Evans is a common name so I didn't put it together, but it has to be."

Glad her mother hadn't fallen to the floor clutching her head, Nora said, "What?"

"Lee Evans is related to Warren."

Warren had no children. Nora remembered that from business school when she and her friends joked about getting him to adopt them. Lee must be a nephew or cousin or something.

Tears glistened in Abigail's eyes. She trembled. "I didn't see it before."

Nora led Abigail to the couch and sat her down. She clicked on a lamp, glad for the soft glow of the stained glass shade. "Didn't see what? Tell me."

Abigail's cloudy eyes cleared and she collected herself. "It's Warren Evans."

"What does Warren Evans have to do with this?"

Nora waited for Abigail to explain, fighting the urge to squirm, shake her mother, or simply crawl up the side of the wall to expel tension.

Finally, Abigail started. "I thought your father's car crash was an accident. It didn't occur to me that Warren killed him."

Whatever Nora expected, it wasn't this.

Abigail's voice shook. "His car flipped going around a curve. At the bottom of a steep hill. The brakes went out because there was no fluid in the brake line."

"What?" Nora couldn't believe what she was hearing.

Abigail swallowed, hardening her tone. "It had to be Warren." "Why do you say that?"

Abigail inhaled. "Dan and I met Warren here, in Moab. In fact, at that place where we were today. The rock art panel."

"And that's why you got upset?" Nora asked.

Abigail seemed to float back to that time. "Warren was sitting there studying the panel when we hiked out there. He had all this wild, dark hair and even wilder eyes. He was so suntanned he looked like he could have been related to your father.

"He didn't say anything at first, just watched. We'd been laughing and chatting on the hike up there, but as soon as Dan saw the petroglyphs, he became serious. It made me nervous the way he stared at them for so long."

Nora tried to picture a young Abigail holding hands and flirting with a Hopi man.

"After a time, Warren stood up and introduced himself. He started asking Dan questions about the symbols. I could tell Dan didn't want to answer." Abigail considered Nora. "Well, you know how secretive Hopi are. And the symbols seemed important to your father.

"Warren was polite and friendly. He dropped his questioning right away. See, even back then, he knew how to work people. He offered to show us around the area. Dan was reluctant but I thought Warren was fun and nice and he knew where the great hiking and camping and swimming places were. We told him all about CU and exchanged phone numbers.

"The week after we returned to Boulder, Warren showed up. He got a job and earned money so he could go to school the next semester."

None of this explained why he would kill Nora's father. She waited for Abigail to continue.

"He seemed to always be around. I thought he was one of those woo-woo types who wanted to understand the relationship Indians have with the earth and sky and all of that."

Abigail's hands wound round and round each other in her lap. "Dan didn't like to talk about his beliefs. But he was always polite and sometimes he just couldn't avoid telling Warren things."

"Warren Evans, the guy who amassed a fortune, was a Hopi wannabe?"

Abigail fluttered her hands. "I don't know what he was. Maybe it was his excuse."

"Excuse for what?"

Abigail fidgeted. Her voice sounded like someone had stretched her vocal chords. "I should have put a stop to him coming over. It seemed like he was always there. Even when Dan was at class."

Abigail rocked slightly. "I didn't think too much about it. And, I'm sorry to say, I enjoyed the company because Dan was studying so hard and not home a lot and I got lonely. And Warren was so charming."

Her rocking accelerated and her voice broke. "I probably did something to encourage him. I don't know what. I didn't mean to, I know. We just became good friends because he was there so often. At least for me, it was only friendship."

Nora put a hand on Abigail's back and her mother startled. "What happened?"

Abigail jumped up and paced to the window. "I should never have let him be there when Dan wasn't home. It gave him ideas. It must have suggested I liked him. Liked him in that way."

Nora didn't want to hear the rest, but knew not to stop Abigail from purging a secret buried so long.

"He." A sob escaped. "Warren. He. He." She covered her face with her hands. "He... took me. Right there. In our apartment. On the floor in front of our broken sofa."

A wave of ice crashed around Nora's head. She held her breath against the shock. Her paralysis broke and Nora rushed to Abigail. She pulled her close and held her while Abigail sobbed. When the worst had subsided, she led her mother to the couch and lowered her to sit.

Abigail found a tissue in her robe pocket. "I never told Dan." "And you think Warren killed my father? Why? Jealousy?"

Abigail closed her eyes. "I never considered it, honestly. But now I see the coincidence of the brakes and I add it to the... incident. And then the fight Dan and Warren had the day before the accident. It all makes sense."

"They had a fight?"

Abigail blew her nose and got up to dispose of the tissue and pluck another from the box on the kitchen counter. "I came home from class and heard shouting from our apartment. Dan never raised his voice. Dan was Hopi and believed in peace. But something had him more upset than I'd ever seen him. I opened the door and he was calling Warren stupid. Stupid! I'd never heard Dan say anything so mean. "When they saw me, Warren ran out. Dan refused to tell me anything. And the next day, he died."

Nora pictured the scene. Dan, dark skinned, black hair cut in a bowl, his eyes sharp. Actually, she pictured him looking like her cousin Benny. Warren, shoulder-length hippie hair, faded bell bottoms, calculating expression. And Abigail. Nora still fought to see her in jeans, maybe a bandana, a peasant blouse ...

Peasant blouse. Over a pregnant belly? If Dan died the next day, Abigail would have been pregnant with Nora when Warren raped her. According to Abigail, Nora had been born after her father died. Nine months after? Or six? It made a difference.

Nora's heart thudded. "How long after Dan's accident was I born?" Abigail's eyes flew open.

Nora squeezed Abigail's thigh. "How long, Mother?"

"It's not what you think," Abigail said. "Dan is your father!" "Could it have been Warren Evans? Is it possible?"

"You were born eight months after Dan died. You were not premature. I know Dan is your father."

"You don't know!" Nora's chest constricted. She struggled for the words. "Warren Evans could be my father."

Abigail shook her head, tears streaming from her eyes. A floorboard on the porch creaked.

Nora swung her head around. She'd forgotten Darrell.

He sounded normal and raised his hand in a wave. "I got the ball rolling looking into Lee. It's late so I'm going to head home."

Abigail buried her face in her hands.

Nora strode to the front door to say thanks and goodbye. She returned to a sobbing Abigail.

"He heard me, I know he did."

Nora patted her back and reassured Abigail, even if she had her own doubts. "He was on the phone in the yard. He didn't hear anything."

28

Coarse yellow sand crunched under Nora's hiking boots and echoed in the deserted dawn atop the mesa. Abbey padded next to her, probably enjoying his freedom after the five-hour drive from Moab to the mesa. As soon as Abigail had calmed down, she'd returned to bed and Nora had taken off for the rez. The sun danced suddenly from the edge of the world beyond the valley floor accompanied by the low, soft rhythm of Benny's singing.

She lifted her head and abandoned herself to the feeling of floating. At the edge of a mesa that rose from the valley, she felt like she stood on the deck of a mythical god's clipper ship as they circumnavigated the globe.

She tried to shed the heaviness she'd carried from Moab at the thought of what Abigail had endured so many years ago—rape, her husband dead, having a baby on her own. Growing up, Nora had always thought of her mother as a vapid social climber. It now made sense that Abigail clung to a wealthy husband and security. The new insight also revealed how far Abigail had come when she'd let go of the financial stability to marry Charlie.

Nora rubbed at the fatigue behind her eyes. After Abigail's confession, the only thing Nora could think to do was run to the reservation.

Even this seemed like a bad idea. It didn't matter how much her mother protested and claimed Nora resembled Dan in gestures and "that look in your eyes," Nora could be Warren Evans's daughter. If the Evans family had red hair in their lineage, it would explain a lot.

Instead of joining Benny with her own morning tribute of cornmeal, Nora stayed back and listened. If she had no Hopi ties, it didn't seem right to barge into his ceremony. Still, she didn't deny the warmth of the new sun felt welcoming and hopeful.

Lisa could no longer laugh in that deep, freeing way. Cole probably greeted the new day with a kiss for his bride. Two runaway girls huddled together in uncertainty, and Nora's future seemed iffy. But the sun still climbed its cheery path across the sky—keep it all in perspective, her Hopi training would tell her.

The Hopi way of life still had value, even if the tribal blood didn't pump through her veins.

Right?

Benny finished his song. When he backed from the edge of the mesa and turned to Nora, he already grinned, as if he knew she'd been standing there. He probably did. Not much surprised him, even someone showing up unannounced on the isolated mesa at dawn.

"It is good to see you."

Though not much of a hugger herself, she didn't let Benny off with that formal of a greeting. She threw her arms around him and welcomed his returning embrace. "I need to talk to you." Her throat crept dangerously close to shutting, but she managed those few words before tears filled her eyes.

He plodded away from the precipice down a worn path in the yellow dust. Nora fell into step beside him and they walked the fifty yards to the squalid village in silence. The sound of their feet crunching on the sand echoed through the collection of several dozen dwellings that sprawled along the mesa. They spoked from a plaza formed by four two-story structures. Their construction showed desert rock, cinder blocks, and various cheap building supplies.

Benny lived in a section of one of the buildings that made up the plaza. In a modern city, it might be an apartment or condo. Here, it was his part of the pueblo. He led her toward the far side of the plaza. "I'll make coffee and you can tell me."

Benny never told her his age but she guessed he was somewhere between forty and sixty. He spoke as if each word formed from the sands of time and baked in the sun. It would take Nora several days to acclimate to his pace before she lost the urge to dangle him by his feet and shake the words out quicker.

This morning he wore his usual dark blue jeans that hung loose on his narrow hips, plaid cotton shirt, and dusty cowboy boots. His black hair lay thick and short on his head. He stood a few inches shorter than Nora but carried an air of confidence and strength she rarely saw in others.

The yellow powder of the path trod by countless generations puffed around her boots and the silence felt like gauze around her. Not many people lived in Benny's ancient village, and if they'd been out greeting the sun in the traditional way, they'd picked their own private place on the mesa.

The first time Nora had been on the Hopi rez, about an hour's drive north of Winslow, she'd gone to a dance on another of the three mesas that made up Hopiland. She'd been disappointed by the poverty and dirt and general third-world feel. As in Benny's village, the houses were an odd collection of ancient stone and every cheap kind of repair imaginable meant to shore up dwellings that were originally built a thousand years ago. Four pueblo-like structures outlined a central plaza used for dances and ceremonies. These buildings rose two stories and lacked all but the tiniest of windows. The plaza stretched about half the length of a soccer field and had a stone floor.

After spending time up here with Benny a few months ago, Nora accepted what she'd once thought sad and desperate was a free choice to live the traditional life they cherished.

Nora enjoyed her dishwasher and microwave too much to embrace this Spartan lifestyle, but she now understood Benny's priorities didn't mirror hers.

No breeze disturbed the peace, just a gentle sun and soft air. They made their way across the plaza to Benny's house and he held the screen open for her and Abbey to enter.

The same dilapidated couch with a yellow sheet serving as a slip cover, the folding table with a couple of woven-seated camp chairs, the bare bulb dangled from the ceiling—she'd have been shocked if it had changed.

Benny stood in the kitchen and filled a coffee pot with water from a four-gallon jug. He set it on a propane stove, struck a match to the burner, and turned to Nora. "Let's sit outside."

They sat on a low wooden bench perched along the side of his house. "Tell me what is bothering you."

"He won't come to see me anymore." She blurted it out without premeditation. This wasn't what she was here to talk about.

Since Benny didn't answer—though he might be formulating words that would take another lifetime to crawl from his mouth—she rattled on. "I know it's not like he's a genie I can call on demand and I know that I haven't been all that welcoming when he's shown up in the past. But I really feel like I need him to put in a cameo appearance. Even a walk-on in a dream or something."

Benny displayed his usual poker face. "Nakwaiyamtewa?"

Slow down, inhale. Remember to think in Hopi time. "Yes. I've been in Moab and there's all this rock art that has something to do with Hopi and I can't figure it out. If I can understand what these symbols mean, I know I can figure out who killed my friend Lisa and why."

Benny's gaze drifted to the plaza as if in thought. "You are making no more sense than your mother did."

"My mother?"

He still focused into the plaza. "Yes. She sent me a long text that said you were upset about your friend's death and that you questioned your place in Hopi."

"Wait a minute. Abigail texted you that I'd be coming to see you?" He nodded.

"So you'll text with Abigail, but you won't talk to me on the phone?

I've been trying to call you all night."

"I didn't say I texted Abigail back. Besides, why talk to you on the phone when I knew you'd be here?" A twinkle sparked in his eyes.

"Did Abigail tell you I might not be Hopi after all?" "Why do you say this?"

"Have you heard of Warren Evans?"

His mouth turned up and he actually chuckled. "Every three moons I ride my pony into the white man's town, scalp a few settlers, and steal their cattle. I then take the opportunity to catch up on my investments and read the Wall Street Journal."

"Okay, fine. Sorry. But I have no idea what you keep up on and what you don't. You don't answer your phone and you hardly ever turn on your generator. What do I know?" Benny could use his cell phone when it suited him. Nora's phone never had a signal on the mesas, but Benny didn't seem to have any trouble. Nora chose not to question that fact.

He patted her hand. "Yes, Nora, I know who Warren Evans is." "He's probably my father."

One of his eyebrows arched, a sign she'd shocked him.

"He raped my mother. Nice Mormon family guy. All those years my mother lied about my father abandoning us and finally she told me about Dan Sepakuku. Now I find out the father she wasn't telling me about was really Warren Evans."

Benny let that settle. "You didn't know you were Hopi until a few months ago. Now you find out it's possible you are not Hopi and you feel betrayed?"

"Why would I have this red hair? Hopi don't have red hair." "Warren Evans does not have red hair."

"When I found out about Dan Sepakuku, for the first time in my life I felt like I belonged."

"To Hopi?"

She felt a burn in her cheeks. "Well, maybe not really, yet. I was excited to learn everything Hopi. I felt kind of special that Nakwaiyamtewa visited me. He chose me to save the sacred mountain."

Pause. "As I remember, you were not that excited at the time. 'I'm not Enviro Girl' is what you said to me."

"Okay. Yes. At the time, it seemed scary and dangerous and weird that this chief from the 1880s was visiting me with mystic messages. But why isn't he coming to see me now?"

"It could be that he's busy. We are in the summer season and the kachinas are performing their ancient duties."

The fatigue of the five-hour drive pounded in her temples. "You're right. I didn't really come here to whine."

Again, the shocked, raised eyebrow.

The smell of coffee perking wafted from Benny's house. "I came here to ask you about all these weird petroglyphs in southern Utah. I think they mean something."

"Of course they mean something."

"If I show you, can you tell me what it is?"

He shrugged. "How would I know? The people who made those images lived over a thousand years ago. I'm a modern guy, growing my corn, trying to ignore my cell phone when it rings."

"Maybe, but you have a daily coffee klatch with a guy who's been dead for over a hundred years."

"Not every day. And he doesn't know everything, either. Maybe he likes my coffee."

They filed back into Benny's house. He found a used envelope to write on and scrounged around for a pencil. While he poured the coffee, she sketched the sunburst symbol from the rock and the barn.

He handed her a chipped mug and took the envelope. They stood in the kitchen while he sipped his coffee and studied the drawing. The *Jeopardy!* theme song dinged away in the back of Nora's brain while she waited for his comment.

He set the envelope on the table and took another swig of his coffee. "These lines are a special message from the Sky People."

"What Sky People?"

"The people who come from beyond." Beyond. Great.

He placed his cup on the table. "You might call them aliens. They visit Hopi. Always have. They bring messages. These lines, they indicate places where the Sky People are welcome."

"You believe in aliens? As in, people from other planets who visit here. Flying saucers?"

"I've never met them. They come to certain people—elders, mostly."

Nora picked up Benny's cup and poured them both more coffee. He opened a cracked wood cupboard and pulled out two granola bars, his version of breakfast. It looked like a feast to Nora.

The nighttime chill evaporated as the little house absorbed the heat from the rising sun.

"You saw this on a panel? What other signs were there?"

She drew the animals and the person in a boat. "These lines are also on a barn on Tokpela Ranch."

"Tokpela?"

She nodded. "It's close to Canyonlands Park."

He gave her a puzzled look. "A white man's barn?"

"Warren Evans's nephew's barn. What do you make of that?" "Tokpela is a Hopi word."

Of course he wouldn't simply say. "What does it mean?" He tilted his head in consideration. "Sky."

"Is that significant? Sky Ranch. With the space alien symbols?" "Hmm." She wouldn't get much more out of him on that.

"Do you know what the rest of this stuff means?"

"Not much. I can tell you this," he pointed to the drawing of the person in a boat, "is a Hopi maiden in a Sky Person's ship. You see the circles on the sides of her head? That is the traditional squash blossom hair worn by Hopi maidens. The rest?" He shrugged.

She lowered herself to one of the chairs. "So here's what I know. Lisa was murdered, maybe after she filmed the panel with this on it. Abigail freaked out when she saw the line symbols on the wall. She said Warren Evans was all into the Hopi stuff and that's why he hooked up with her and my father, or rather, Dan Sepakuku."

Benny munched on his granola bar and didn't seem to have heard anything she'd said.

"Oh, and here's the other thing my mother thinks. She thinks Warren killed Dan. Because he died in a car crash when his brakes went out and the brakes in my Jeep went out the other day."

Benny leaned back. "Do you think Warren Evans tried to kill you?"

She shook her head. "No. I think his nephew did."

He considered that. "And you wonder if the Sky People have something to do with Warren Evans and his nephew and your friend?"

Sure, when he put it like that it seemed far-fetched. "Yes."

Benny threw his granola bar wrapper in the trash. He took a half dozen steps to cross the room and open the one door leading off the living room. "First you must sleep. Then we will investigate this mystery."

"I'm not tired. Let's figure it out now."

Benny held the door to the bedroom open for her and she knew arguing would do no good. She trudged into the dark room, sparsely furnished with a chipped dresser and sagging double bed. The blanket was tidy and clean. Benny picked up a blanket that had been folded at the foot of a neatly made bed. The faint smells of damp dirt, soap, and coffee lingered in the dark bedroom.

Nora took it and sat on the edge of the bed to remove her boots. Abbey plopped on the floor next to the bed, apparently agreeing with Benny. A short nap wouldn't do her any harm.

Benny stood in the doorway. "You worry that because Nakwaiyamtewa has not been to see you that you are not Hopi. Think of who you are in your heart. How many signs do you need to make you believe?"

Nora curled up on the bed, certain Benny's words would swirl in her head and prevent any sleep. But not Benny's coffee, worry, or thoughts about her identity kept her from falling into a deep sleep.

29

Warren couldn't ever remember feeling this much hope. Not even when his first IPO exceeded everyone's expectations. This time, God had given him his heart's desire.

The soft purr of the Caddy carried him down the highway to his long-awaited dream. He'd given up on this so many years ago. Like Job, he hadn't cursed God, but the pain of loss burned in his bones throughout his life. Again, like Job, God rewarded him at the end.

The early evening light on Castle Rock glowed with promise. He rolled down the window just to let the soft air blow across his face, its touch feeling like a kiss from heaven. He hadn't felt this strong in months. The desert floor bloomed with orange, purple, yellow, and green. Air perfumed with sweet clover and fresh cut hay from lush bottom land filled his lungs. He'd lived long enough to see the summer in its fullness, to smell the new life, and to know that his legacy would survive.

It had taken one phone call and less than an hour before his sources confirmed what he'd hoped. Nora Abbott, the only daughter of Abigail Podanski, was born thirty-two years ago. As soon as he was certain, he'd rushed to Castle Valley.

The driveway leading to Rachel's house needed new gravel, but his

Caddy navigated it handily. He hummed in anticipation as he eased to a stop. The bright warble of a meadowlark greeted him as he opened the door and planted his foot on the sand. He marched toward the rustic cabin, alive with the sensation of a circle closing, the perfection of God's plan flowering as surely as the wild sweet pea blooming by the porch.

The screen door squeaked opened and Rachel stepped out on the porch, her arms folded across her breast. The warm breeze lifted her thin hair and sent single strands dancing around the eyes she squinted at him. "What are you doing here?"

"I haven't come to see you." A few days ago he could barely stagger across his Manhattan office. Now he knew he'd charge through Rachel if she didn't get out of his way.

She crossed the porch to stand guard at the top of the stairs. "You're not welcome here."

He didn't need to lean on the rail as he climbed. "You were always one of my favorites, Rachel. You were smart and courageous. You had a spark your sisters lacked. I'm truly sickened by what you've become."

"My own person, you mean? Not ruled by the church or men?" He reached the top stair without slowing. He could tell she didn't know what to do. At the last minute, she stepped back instead of shoving him from the stairs.

"God intended for men and women to be together. What you're doing is unnatural."

Her thin lips turned into a hard sneer. "You're the expert on natural? How natural is it for one man to have two wives, or three, or even more?"

"There is an order to the world. Tell me you can't feel God's disapproval."

He stepped toward the screen but this time, Rachel didn't move. He bumped against her, taking a step as if she weren't there. She thrust her chest, poking her folded arms against him. "Go away."

"I'll pray you find your true path, but I'm afraid it's too late. You know the time is short. Who will call your name and draw you through the veil if you don't give up your sinful ways and ask forgiveness?"

"Screw you." The bright blue of her eyes, the same eyes of her mother and sisters, clouded with hatred. He grieved for her lost soul.

He put a hand out to shove her aside. He'd done his best to save her. Now he would do what he'd come for.

She shoved back. "Get out of here."

He stumbled and a wave hit him again, the affliction more insidious than the cancer that ate his insides. He'd thought, with God's help, he'd conquered that black rage that rose up and flooded his mind. He gritted his teeth against the urge to fling Rachel from the porch...

"Warren!" Small hands grabbed his arm and yanked him backwards.

Rachel sprawled on the porch in front of him, her eyes wide, hatred splashed in red slashes on her cheeks. He'd shoved her yet couldn't remember doing so.

Warren's eyes traveled from the delicate hands on his arm to the woman standing beside him. He'd imagined a moment like this a billion times. He'd turn in a crowd and there she would be. Her golden beauty radiated toward him. She would have thought of him over the years, missing him, imaging what their lives would have been like together.

But this was no dream.

His Abigail, standing close enough that his senses filled with her sweet scent, her touch, the life in her eyes. He saw a woman in her twenties, firm skin and muscles strong from mountain hikes. He saw the sprinkle of freckles across her nose, the swinging gold of her long ponytail. It had only been one time but he still felt her beneath him, her longing matching his own. Why had he ever let her go?

"Warren, stop it. Go away." Her words pummeled him like stones.

He focused on her now. Still beautiful. Still full of life. "Abigail. You've come back."

He hadn't meant to say that. She flinched and disgust stole the shine from her eyes. She hurried over to help Rachel to her feet. Together they faced him. Abigail laced her arm through Rachel's.

"I need to talk to you, Abigail."

"I hoped I'd never have to set eyes on you again."

He knew how she felt. Throughout his life he'd been tempted to find her. It would have been easy, given all his resources. But he knew if he did, they'd never be able to resist each other. Maybe he and Christine didn't have a loving marriage, but he'd promised her and God he'd be faithful. No other woman except Abigail would make him break that vow.

"It doesn't matter now. All the pain, all the longing. It's over and our reward is here."

"You're as deranged as you were then. The difference is that I'm not afraid of you now."

"Afraid? You have never needed to be afraid. I love you, Abigail." What a relief it was to say those words, so often resisted and never spoken out loud. He laughed like a young buck after his first kiss. "Do you hear that? I love you. I've always loved you."

Her revulsion was obvious. "What are you talking about?" Rachel's eyes opened even wider. "You know each other?" Abigail's nose turned up as though she smelled rotten garbage.

"Knew. Briefly."

The warmth of the memory filled him, loosening the tightness cancer had clamped on him. "We never had the time together we should have. That's my fault. I'm sorry I left you. But I felt God called me to a mission. Sometimes, the signs are clear and sometimes they seem murky. Now that we're together again, I know that road, no matter how hard and lonely, was the right one."

Abigail pulled herself up. "Go away."

He loved her fire. He loved the bright flash of her eyes. Everything about her stirred him in a way Christine never had. "I don't understand why you're so resistant. This is our chance, after all these years, to grab our small piece of happiness. Is it because you're married?"

She advanced on him, dropping her arm from Rachel. "It's because you raped me and you killed my husband!"

The words sat between them for several seconds. She didn't pry her eyes from his face while he studied her and tried to find a response.

"I could never hurt you. Never. How can you call what we had together rape?"

He watched the struggle for composure play across her face. Her eyes filled with tears and her voice sounded like sandpaper on rough wood. "I trusted you. I let you into our home. And you forced yourself on me."

Warren shook his head. "No. No. That's not the way it was. We loved each other. I know you felt it, too."

She spit at him like a feral cat. "I only felt sorry for a kid who seemed so lost and eager to know about Hopi."

She must have justified her infidelity over the years. Thirty years of convincing herself she'd never loved him might have turned her heart. She'd remember. "Isn't there something you need to tell me?"

"The only thing I need to tell you is to leave us alone!"

"What about our daughter?" Saying it filled him with a pounding strength.

She paled. "What?"

"Nora. The evidence of our love."

A flush of fury rose quickly to her face. "Nora is not your daughter. She's Dan's."

"There's no way God would allow Dan to be her father. He needs me to have an heir. Someone to lead the faithful."

Rachel watched the exchange of words with her mouth open in shock.

Why did Abigail fight against him?

She set her face in hard lines. "I have proof she's Dan's daughter. Something a Hopi-lover like you will appreciate."

His confidence never wavered. "You can't prove what isn't true."

"I know she's Dan's daughter because she's had Hopi signs and visitations."

He knew God had chosen him and his heirs for glory. "Tell me. What do you mean, visitations?"

She waved her hand in the air. "She won't tell me everything. I've had to piece it together from conversations between her and her cousin. Her real cousin. Benny Sepakuku, from the Hopi reservation." She pointed at him. "An old chief that talks to her. I know it's true because Benny knows everyone and everything and he is her Hopi spiritual guide because they're related."

If God had revealed all of this to him when he was younger, he might not have understood the great gift he'd received. His childhood of disgrace and rejection all made sense now. The sad pieces of his journey fit together to create a life lived for God. Now, he had an heir to complete the task.

He smiled. "You never knew about my family."

She folded her arms. "I read the 'Man of the Year' article about you. You were raised on a farm in southern Utah by hard-working Americans. You lived the American Dream, rose from poverty, made a fortune, and now you just want to protect America for future generations, blah, blah, blah."

He wished he could draw her inside his mind to share his memories so that she could know his heart. "It's true. I was raised in southern Utah by hard workers. It's just that four of those hard workers were my mothers and one was my father. My biological mother wasn't a favored wife, though. And I wasn't like the rest of my siblings. When I got old enough to be interested in girls or maybe just because he didn't like me, my father sent me away. I was fourteen and my mother came with me. She couldn't get a job so I supported us. And then I made a fortune."

Abigail pretended to be bored. "Good for you. Now go."

Hope surged through him as he went on. "Here's why I know Nora is my daughter. The reason my mother was least favorite and the reason I was so different is that she wasn't born and raised a good Mormon girl. She grew up on the reservation, a full-blooded Hopi."

He'd succeeded in shocking Abigail. Her eyes widened. "If you're Hopi, why did you need Dan to tell you about the history and prophesies?"

He itched to take her hand, to set his lips lightly against hers. "The people on the mesas happily welcomed me. They invited me to several ceremonies. But they wouldn't trust me enough to tell me what I needed to know. It would have taken me decades to learn."

"What did you need to know so badly?"

Such relief to tell her. "It's the signs. I first saw them on the ranch. My father drove me away, but he didn't know God put me there to see the signs."

"Your Mormon God? How does that mesh with Hopi?" "You're like the others. You think religions are mutually exclusive. But it's all one. God showed me that. I needed Dan to teach me about the Sky People."

She laughed in a cruel way he didn't remember from her youth. "You're absolutely insane. Completely fruit loops."

"All great leaders were considered crazy. Many thought Jesus was a lunatic."

She smirked at him. "What are these Sky People going to do?"

Her skepticism bit at him. "They're coming for the faithful. We'll be taken away and given planets of our own. This is written in the Book of Mormon as well. It all fits together."

"And you're the chosen one?"

Instead of the sorrow and frustration, a surge of joy lifted him. "God has provided an heir."

"She's not your heir, but even if she were, she's a woman. You can't believe your God would hand over the keys to a female."

"It's God's plan. Maybe she'll give birth to a great leader." Abigail's eyebrows drew down in concern.

Warren spun around. He scanned the porch and didn't see anything. "Where's Rachel?"

Abigail widened her eyes in feigned innocence. "I didn't notice she'd gone."

Warren strode across the porch and into the house. Abigail ran after him. "Leave her alone!"

Rachel stood in the kitchen with a phone to her ear. When she saw him, she set it down.

Warren's heart jumped to his throat. "Who was that? What did you say? Did you tell him?"

Rachel didn't answer.

Warren couldn't waste time. He rushed across the room and grabbed Abigail by the arms. "Where is she? Where's Nora?"

Abigail clamped her mouth closed and glared at him.

He shook her and a strand of hair stuck to the corner of her mouth.

Her eyes glittered with fear but she still didn't speak. "Tell me!" Tears threatened and her lips quivered but stayed locked.

"Rachel just told my nephew about Nora. He expects to be the leader. Now that he knows I have a true heir, he'll kill her!"

30

Nora woke, disoriented. It took several moments of that frantic, lost feeling to place the rickety furniture in the dim light of Benny's bedroom. Abbey stretched and wagged his tail. It only took Nora a few seconds to lace up her boots and shoot from the bedroom.

Benny stood at the front door gazing into the plaza. "Are you ready to go?"

"Where?"

"I have something to show you."

They walked into the quiet village in the blinding sunshine of early afternoon. Across the plaza a woman stepped from a door, probably from a home similar to Benny's. She didn't wave and offer a hello as you might expect in suburban America. Hopi respected each other and seemed to have genuine affection for their neighbors, but they didn't jump into each other's lives. Nora had been surprised to learn they didn't have a word for hello.

Late morning sun blazed in the plaza, bringing out the red of the adobe buildings. Dust settled across the stone surface. The doors of the other dwellings remained closed against the gathering heat of the day.

She followed Benny around the edge of the plaza and through winding alleys to his aging pickup. Rust covered it so completely that it reminded Nora of tie-dye. She held the door open for Abbey and he hefted himself onto the floor, then up to the bench seat to sit and eagerly stare out the windshield. Nora and Benny climbed inside and he coaxed the engine into a rough rattle.

At the speed of a dozing snail, they made their way down the steep switchbacks of the mesa and bottomed out onto the highway. Benny didn't speak so Nora spent the ten-minute drive following wormholes in her brain.

After five miles, Benny pulled off the highway onto an obscure two-track trail heading across the desert. Another six or seven miles north of the highway, they bumped down a steep arroyo and Benny followed the dry creek bed, winding around stones and the sandy banks.

After a time he idled to a stop and cut the engine. He climbed out and Nora followed.

"Where are we going?" she finally asked.

"I told you about the prophesies given to us by the one who brought us here."

"Yes." Ever logical, Nora felt uncomfortable with thousand-year-old prophesies that foretold the coming of the white men, the political splits of the tribe, the decline of Hopi. They warned about taking things from the moon and had even described the atom bomb.

He gave her one of his rare smiles. "And we talked about the instructions."

She matched his steady pace as he climbed from the creek bed and hiked toward a stand of three rocks that stood like eight-foot-high sentinels. "Live simply. Take no more than you need. Plant seeds. Recognize the creator is within us."

Benny kept walking without looking at her. "Are you living according to the instructions?"

Guilt bit at her. "I could do better."

"Hopi need to immerse ourselves in Mother Earth and blend with her to celebrate life. As we join together, a new attitude will take hold and the world will be gently transformed."

Nora thought about that while they trudged along. "I think what you're saying is that I'm focusing on what I want to happen, like having the kachina come to me, instead of focusing on what I should do for the world."

He chuckled. "Always looking for the answers."

Benny made it to the rock formation and rounded a corner to stand in the enclosure created by them. He gazed up the smooth surface of the towering rock.

Nora followed his line of sight. Before her, a series of images etched in the stone told a story. Of course, it was in a language she couldn't understand. She recognized the Hopi maiden in the space ship and the weird sunburst symbol. She turned to Benny. "Do you know what it means?"

He shrugged. "No."

She gave him an exasperated glare.

That little grin slipped onto his face. "I can tell you what I think." "Please do."

He picked up a stick and pointed at a long, diagonal line that ran from the bottom left corner to the top right corner of the scene. "This is the journey of Hopi." He sketched along vertical lines. "These three that intersect show where the people have made choices, some for good and some not so good. These three circles are world wars. You see, this last one is on the other side of the third decision."

"Does that mean if the people make a good decision we won't have another war?"

"Maybe."

Gotta love those definitive messages.

"This maiden, who represents the Sky People." Benny pointed to the image. "You see she is next to the symbol that interests you?"

"Yes."

"And it all sits above the third decision and the circle of war." "But what does it mean?"

"The Sky People have been visiting the Hopi for many years. Our elders know of them. Many of them have gone with the Sky People."

"Gone with them?"

"The prophesies tell us that Sky People will come gather the true Hopi at the end of the Fourth World and take them to the other planets."

"You never told me anything about Sky People."

"Hopi is an old tribe. There is much you don't know. This symbol," he outlined the image. "It is a sign for the Sky People. It tells them where they are welcome."

Nora's phone vibrated in her shorts pocket. She hadn't been aware she carried it on her. Habit. She pulled it out, not recognizing the number. "How is it there's a signal this far out?"

Benny's eyes twinkled. "How many times have I told you that Hopi is the center of the world?"

She rolled her eyes and answered her phone. Darrell's words tumbled out. "He's got your mother."

"What?" Alarms jangled through her. "Who? Where?"

He was breathless. "Warren Evans. I came out to the cabin and she was gone. Rachel said Warren took her."

"Oh, God." Panic shot through her veins. "I'm calling the cops." "No!"

"Why not?"

"No telling what Warren will do." He paused. "I'm sorry. I heard Abigail tell you about him last night. He might want to shut Abigail up. Or maybe he wants to claim you're his daughter."

"But he doesn't know for sure."

Darrell hesitated. "He thinks he knows. He came out here and confronted Abigail. Rachel isn't your friend. She found out about Abigail and Warren and went straight to Lee."

Nora struggled to restart her brain. "Why would she go to Lee?" Darrell hesitated. "They're in it together."

"Wait. I don't understand. In what together?"

"Lee is set to inherit Warren's estate. Warren's tried to keep it secret, but he's dying. If Warren thinks you're his heir and decides to leave his wealth to you, Lee is cut out."

She turned from the rocks. "I'm coming to Moab. I've got to find Abigail."

"Where are you?"

Her heart thundered in her chest. "I'm at the rez." "Stay there and let me handle it. Lee is dangerous."

Nora was already running to Benny's pickup. "I'm coming." Darrell sighed as if resigning himself. "Rachel is somewhere with

Lee, so meet me at the cabin and we can go after Abigail together."

31

Dark clouds, heavy with rain, blocked the sun. Thunder rumbled and occasionally cracked. A few drops, fat as bumblebees, splatted on her windshield. She slapped on her wipers and sped down the highway. She'd been driving for hours across empty Navajo land.

What kind of danger was Abigail in? Nora had to find her and get her back to Flagstaff. She'd hand Abigail over to Charlie and make him promise to never let her mother out of his sight.

Abbey resettled himself in the passenger seat, yawned, and closed his eyes again. He obviously didn't feel empathy with her anxiety.

The raven cawed. She checked the phone's caller ID. Cole. A dose of his calm would do her good. But he was married. "Don't answer," she instructed Abbey.

Her phone squawked again and she punched it on.

"It's over." Cole sounded jubilant—definitely not his usual tone. "Huh?" She'd thought those words might refer to his father, but

Cole sounded happy.

"It all worked out as I'd hoped and my marriage has been annulled. When are you coming home so we can celebrate?"

Pop, pop, pop, swish. Pop, pop, pop, swish. The rain and wipers filled the silence.

"I don't understand," she finally said.

"Sorry. Here's what happened. When I was eighteen, I thought I was in love with Amber. She was sixteen. We ran off and got married. But, of course, we headed home after a couple of days and she went back to her parents and I went to college and I figured since she was under age it wasn't a legal thing anyway. Years later, she and my brother got married."

"Your girlfriend married your brother?"

He paused. "Yeah. It caused some bad blood. Still does, I guess. I thought we'd gotten past that."

"How did it end up you were still married?"

"It was a real mess. Derek divorced Amber last year. He didn't have much, since the ranch is in my father's name. So Amber makes her living waitressing in Sheridan." She pictured his frown. "But when Dad had his stroke and it looked like he might not make it, Amber figured she could get a piece of that inheritance."

"How is your father?"

Cole rushed on. "He's starting to talk again. He's confused, but I think he's coming back."

Nora welcomed that good news. "That's great. So what happened with Amber?"

"She dragged out this license. It looks legal since her parents' signature is on it, but I know she forged it."

"Why didn't you deny it and call her a liar?"

"I didn't want it to come to a big public battle. So I sent it off to a lawyer and had him draw up a legal letter. It only took a couple of days—she's backed down and it's all over."

"You don't want to be married to her?"

He laughed. "Of course not. I want to be married to you."

She caught her breath and managed to squeak. "You do?" "Yes." It sounded strong and definite. "Whenever you're ready.

As far as I'm concerned, we could head up to the courthouse as soon as you get back to Boulder."

She blinked back a tear. "I thought you didn't want me."

He sounded exasperated. "Nora. How many signs do you need before you have some faith?"

Wham. Talk about a brick upside the head. Benny said the same thing to her. Both Lisa and Abigail told her to figure out who she was and what she wanted. In that magical confluence that almost never happens, Nora felt the truth of something she'd always believed but never completely understood: She got one life. Her life. No genetics, no expectations, no doubts or fears could define her. She could make it her own.

Great insight. It might take her the rest of her life to believe it, but she had a start. She grinned. "I'll be home soon. Then we'll take that trip to the courthouse."

"I love you, Nora."

"I love you, too." Much as she hated to, she severed the connection. Almost immediately, her rosy glow disappeared. Lee wanted her dead. Warren had Abigail. If Nora wanted to keep that date at the courthouse, she needed to find proof to lock Lee away and get Abigail from Warren's clutches.

No problem.

The pavement darkened, then shone in her headlights as the rain continued to smash against the windshield. Nora topped a hill and the smattering of lights from Moab glowed below.

"Where is your camera?" she spoke to Lisa.

Lisa probably suspected Rachel and Lee were plotting together. At the very least, Lisa was fighting with Rachel due to the film and maybe even her involvement with the underground railroad. So obviously Lisa wouldn't hide the film at home.

Think! The camera had to be someplace that had specific ties to Nora.

Nora always stayed at the cabin when she visited Moab. They hiked trails all over the area. It would take her months to check out all those places. Lisa would pick a place special to the both of them.

Almost immediately, as if Lisa's ghost had whispered the answer in her ear, Nora knew. She blinked and her mouth opened and closed. "How could I be so stupid?" She might be talking to Abbey. Probably she just talked to herself.

They popped into Moab from the south, racing along the highway. Nora gunned the Jeep and turned left in front of an oncoming Cruise America RV. It honked as she sped down the residential lane. Such an obvious hiding place and yet, Nora hadn't thought about it.

She wound through town and out west, racing through the curves and bends. Her back tires slipped on some of the sharper curves. The Jeep wouldn't go fast enough and Nora rocked in her seat with impatience.

Rain smacked the windshield between the swish of the wipers and the squeak of the dry glass. The sky hadn't opened up and dumped here, yet, and Nora hoped it would wait until she had the camera. Finally, she spotted the turnout at the trailhead and whipped off the road. She slammed on the brakes and slid ten feet on the loose dirt at Moonflower campground.

In the gathering darkness, the canyon walls loomed, creating shadows amid the cottonwoods and shrubs. Beyond her headlights, the trail wound into a void. The rain pocked the sand and dotted the rock faces as Nora climbed from the Jeep. "Stay here," she said to Abbey.

It did no good to try to avoid seeing the rock art panel and the crevice containing the ladder at the opening to the canyon. The ancient tree trunks notched to create a vertical path to safety. Nora struggled not to picture Lisa laying there, her sightless eyes staring at the sky, dark waves falling across her cheeks, her neck twisted at an impossible angle. They found her here, but that's not where she died.

Nora concentrated on the path, dodging rocks and willing herself to move quickly without stumbling. She gulped air, her lungs protesting the long and difficult run. She passed the clearing by the creek where people had gathered for Lisa's funeral.

Hiking this trail with Lisa could take a couple of hours as she'd bend to take in the tiniest rare flower or contemplate the clouds. In the looming darkness and gathering storm, Nora cut the time to twenty minutes.

The canyon narrowed so the trail climbed a steep ridge and traversed twenty feet above the creek. It wound along a ledge then opened onto a wide expanse of slick rock. She crossed the open stretch of wet rock and managed to arrive at the worn trail on the other side without slipping to the creek below.

She made it to where the trail ended at the swimming hole with its natural rock slide. If Nora and Lisa had a special place, this was it. Of course she would have hidden the camera here. But where, exactly? The swimming hole filled the bottom of a small valley roughly fifty feet in diameter.

The walls of the box canyon were made up of stone pillars and cliffs raising high in the air, hiding the area and making it feel secret. Bubbles rose in her gut and she clenched her teeth. Panic wouldn't help. She slowed her panting, exhaling long and inhaling deeply.

What would Benny do? Benny would still be on the rez thinking about getting into his pickup. She needed to act. But not irrationally. Calm down.

She studied two rocks separated by a narrow crevice, letting her eyes travel up the mystic columns. A video camera case could be wedged in any of the crags and niches along the phallic structures. Suddenly, Nora knew exactly where Lisa would hide it. She remembered that afternoon right after Lisa had moved to Moab.

They'd climbed from the pool after one last slide down the slick rock. Lisa spread her towel in a shaft of sunlight. Nora wrapped herself in her towel and chose a shady spot to protect her fair skin from sunburn.

"This is a beautiful place," Nora said.

Lisa leaned back and sighed in contentment. "I love it here." She eyed the two columns close together. "Except I'm not fond of those rocks."

Nora twisted around to inspect them. "Why?"

Lisa laughed. "Look at them! They look like two penises." "They do not. They look more like a woman the way they line up." Nora blushed a little at the thought.

Lisa grinned at them. "You're right. I'm claiming them in the name of all lesbians."

That had to be the spot.

Nora scrambled to the rock. A swollen raindrop splashed on her nose and dripped down her chin. Thunder cracked overhead.

Nora wedged herself between the two rocks and started to climb. She managed inches at a time, her back to the cold face of one rock, her knees scraping the other and her feet pushing while she searched for each hand hold to pull her up.

Rain fell in a steady patter now, chilling the top of her head and dribbling down her neck. She cursed Lisa for her natural rock climbing ability. Nora always followed Lisa on the more difficult climbs. Nora would struggle to find hand holds and have to concentrate to distribute her weight just right. It often felt counterintuitive to lean away from the rock instead of into it or to understand the three-point of contact rule. With Lisa to lead her, Nora placed her hands in the same holds.

Tonight, Nora was on her own, trying to imagine Lisa shimmying in the crevice between the rocks, somehow managing a camera case, desperation driving her on.

Nora propped her foot against the rock in front of her and pressed her back into the other. With her legs more or less parallel to the ground and her knees bent, she wedged between the two stone pillars. She paused to snatch a breath before tilting her head back and surveying the rock above her. She was nearly to the top and she imagined the corner of a black vinyl case peeking over the ledge.

Only ten more feet. She pushed with her legs and slid her back up the rock. Her T-shirt caught on a sharp nipple of rock and ripped. Nora inched her feet up and repeated the motion several more times. There. It wasn't her imagination. The camera case barely showed over the lip of the summit. Nora stretched, pushing her feet into the rock and arching her back. Her fingers brushed the case and pushed it further away from her.

She shimmied up the crevice once again. Reached and tapped at the side of the case, shoving it at an angle away from her but closer to the edge of the rock. She lunged and knocked it with her fingers, finally sending it tumbling into her lap.

Rain tapped the vinyl lid. Balancing the case on her legs and steadying it with each movement as her grip allowed, Nora scraped and slid down the crevice until she finally stood at the base.

She gripped the case and scrambled into one of the narrow, cave-like arches next to the swimming hole to escape the increasing rain. Her legs trembled. With shaking hands, she snapped open the latches and pulled the camera out of the dense padding. It took a minute to make out the labels on the dials in the fading light.

She finally gave up and through trial and error and a fair amount of cursing, found the right command to play the video.

Lisa's face came on the screen in a good imitation of a scene from *The Blair Witch Project*. "I knew you'd find this, Nora. I'm sorry it's not the film project you expected. I'm afraid all copies of that are gone. Or will be by the time you see this. Unless Rachel doesn't find the one in the bookcase. You've got to tell someone. I don't know who. The cops around here are all in on it. It's a Mormon thing. Only, not the official Mormon Church. This is a cult. And Warren Evans is their leader."

The background of the video showed hazy light and the trailhead where Nora's Jeep sat now. Lisa must have propped the camera on her old Toyota pickup. The sun was setting behind her. Lisa's face looked drawn and pale and her eyes kept darting where the road would be.

Nora wanted to reach into the camera and throw her arms around her friend. Why hadn't she taken Lisa's call that afternoon?

"I know you. You'll want to go all mother hen and take responsibility for everyone. This is not your fault. And it's not Rachel's fault, either. She was raised a certain way and it was pounded into her over and over. She tried to get away from it. But it's too deep inside her. Don't blame her."

The hitch in Nora's chest forced her breath into a tight wheeze. It sounded like Lisa knew Rachel had turned against her. Did she suspect Rachel and Lee were together? Had Rachel helped Lee murder Lisa?

"It's the rock art, Nor. The signs and the lines on Tokpela's barn are the same. They think the Sky People are coming for them. It's happening soon. I think at summer solstice. The lines tell them where to go. Marlene knows some of this. If I can't call her, tell Marlene..." Her head jerked up and she gasped. "Damn. Nora, I've got to go. Protect Rachel. She needs your help."Nora watched as Lisa jumped up and grabbed the camera but didn't turn it off as she swung it around. The view showed a sickening mishmash of sage, scrub, red dirt, gray sky, and the white of the evening primrose. Lisa grunted and the black of the camera case flitted in and out of the screen as she struggled to load the camera. A heartbeat before the screen went black and the sound died, Nora saw something, just a snatch of an image caught as Lisa swung the camera on its final arc to the case.

Nora's stomach clenched and she held her breath. She hit rewind, then play.

Oh my God.

Rewind. Play. Pause.

Her ears rang as she stared at the image. A white pickup straddled the center line of the road, heading up the last stretch to the trailhead.

She had her proof.

32

The rain fell just enough to make the trail slick and in her rush to reach the trailhead, Nora tripped and scraped her knee. Heart thundering, she sprinted past the clearing. Muddy and wet, Nora made it back to the Jeep. She wrenched open the door and jumped in. Abbey licked her face and sat in the passenger seat.

Warren had Abigail. The Evanses were all killers, and now that Nora had proof Lee had murdered Lisa, she might be able to use it to save Abigail.

Somehow.

Nora started the Jeep and backed onto the highway. She grabbed her phone and dialed Marlene.

"I found Lisa's camera," she said when Marlene answered. "She said to ask you what's going on."

Marlene hesitated. "The less you know, the better."

Nora barely restrained herself from yelling into the phone. "Warren kidnapped Abigail. I need to know everything!"

"What's he doing with Abigail?"

Nora clamped the phone to her ear using her shoulder and shifted gears. Still breathless from her run from the swimming hole, she said, "I don't have time to explain. Lisa said Warren Evans is leader of a cult.

Did he have Lee kill Lisa? It's got nothing to do with Canyonlands, does it?"

"You think Lee killed Lisa?" She sounded disbelieving.

Nora concentrated on the black road in front of her. "Is it the Underground Railroad? Did she help one of his wives escape?"

Marlene whispered. "Slow down. Lee didn't kill Lisa because of the railroad. He was helping those girls."

"Maybe he's just acting like he's helping. He's dangerous. I know it." "Okay, maybe there is something else going on," Marlene stammered. "It's not what you think. But we learned about it through the girls."

"About what?" Nora wanted to scream.

"You know all those people you saw with Lee the day the cows almost got loose?"

"Yes."

"They're immigrants to Warren's colony. They came from Germany."

"How do you know this?"

"A few months ago one of the girls we helped said her mother's family had disappeared. Before that, her mother had talked about Sky People coming for them."

Nora hit a flooded dip in the road and splashing water roared. "They were supposed to immigrate to another planet on the summer solstice."

That was in two days. "Immigrate from where?"

"The mother told her they were going to the Sky Ranch. But we didn't know where that was."

"Tokpela! Tokpela Ranch. Sky in Hopi."

"Yeah. I figured that out today. How did you know?" "Lisa."

Something crashed as if Marlene had slammed a fist down. "She must have figured it out and they killed her to keep her quiet." Snakes knotted in Nora's stomach. "Warren? He's got a god syndrome and people think he's leading them to outer space. Crackpots like that come along all the time. Why would he have Lisa killed to keep her from telling anyone?"

"How the hell would I know?" Marlene yelled. She paused and continued, calmer now. "He's a crazy man. This family from Germany arrived at the ranch yesterday. Hans and his wife and kids. Hans's half-brother had immigrated a couple of weeks ago but Hans didn't tell

Warren he was related in case there were family quotas. When they got to the Sky Ranch, Hans's half-brother and family weren't in the bunker."

Nora swung the Jeep onto the highway and zoomed north. "A bunker?"

"Apparently there is a massive underground facility that can house a couple of thousand people and they've been gathering in the last week or so to wait for the solstice. Warren had it built at his family ranch. It must have been under constructions for years to complete it without anyone noticing."

As isolated as Tokpela Ranch seemed, building something on the sly would be possible. "This guy's brother from Germany went missing? Maybe he changed his mind and left."

"Yeah, I thought so, too. But Hans picked up clues from the other immigrants. They all give up their assets when they join. He's convinced his brother wanted to leave, but Warren's people didn't want him to spill the beans on their plans and they really didn't want to give him his money back. So they killed him. That's when Hans and his family snuck away."

People hiding underground in the desert waiting for the aliens to take them home—this couldn't be real. "Why did they come to you?"

"Hans tried to get another family to leave, too. They were too frightened, but they knew about the Underground Railroad so they gave him my name."

It sounded too far-fetched. "You believe him about all of this?"

"I don't know." She paused. "Yes, I guess I do. Until he showed up here today, I didn't know about the bunker or Topkela. Lisa did and now she's dead."

"Call the FBI. Tell them all of this and send them out to Lee's ranch."

Steel sounded in Marlene's voice. "I already did it an hour ago." Nora hung up and swung through Moab, speeding along the highway past the café and outfitter's office. She squealed her brakes to turn on the highway that ran alongside the river. Rain from afternoon monsoon storms upstream had swollen it and it raged muddy in the dusky shadow.

The only plan Nora could concoct was to go to Darrell. He had the resources to find Warren and stop him. She dialed him but it went straight to voicemail.

The rain smacked against the windshield and Nora felt time slipping by as she raced to Castle Valley. Full-on dark dropped before Nora whipped the Jeep from the highway onto the narrow road into the village.

A crack of lightning flared and she automatically counted until the boom of thunder followed. Four seconds. The storm would crash over them soon.

Her back tires skidded as she jerked the wheel to make the hard left into Lisa's lane. She gunned it down the sloshy tracks and slowed before rounding the last curve. A dark shape loomed ahead and she slammed on the brakes.

Darrell's 4Runner was parked along the road. He'd know who to call to help them find Abigail. Abbey jumped to his feet and put his front feet on her lap, ready to escape the Jeep after being cooped up so long.

She killed the engine and slipped from the Jeep. Abbey wanted out, but Nora held her hand up, blocking his exit. She pushed the Jeep door, snicking it closed instead of slamming it, though the roar of the wind would have masked a marching band.

She sprinted for the house but when she ran around the curve, she stopped. Lee's white pickup snugged up behind Rachel's Passat in front of the porch. Where was Darrell? Did he have Rachel and Lee subdued inside? Did they have him?

Hoping to avoid detection if Lee and Rachel were in the kitchen or living room or even on the front porch, Nora snuck around the cabin and came up the back. Maybe she'd be able to get some information about Abigail.

Wind tugged at her hair and whipped it into her face. She fumbled a ponytail elastic from her wrist and gathered her hair, twisting the tie around it while she ran. The rain still fell in fat drops, slapping the dirt and dampening the sage and pinion, letting off their spicy scents.

She slowed her pace as she neared the back deck. The wind continued its camouflaging racket and she sank to her knees. With great care, she moved as slowly as possible, careful not to draw attention to herself. Lying on her belly, she peered through the French doors into Lisa's office.

The office sat dark and empty. But lights in the kitchen shone on Rachel as she perched on a barstool facing the kitchen, her back to Nora.

Lee leaned against the sink, his black hat pushed back on his forehead. He wore his standard scowl and radiated a super-intense attitude. His lips moved and Rachel nodded as he talked, but Nora couldn't hear through the closed doors. She didn't see Darrell.

Nora backed away from the door and off the porch. She crawled along the side of the house, ducking under the open living room windows. The cabin blocked the full force of the wind and when Nora positioned herself directly under the window closest to Lee and Rachel, she could hear the hard notes of Rachel's voice.

"Nora's gone. She knows there's no film. She's not going to cause any more trouble." Yay, Rachel—sticking up for Nora's life.

"Darrell will find her and then it'll be all over." If Lee's voice had fingers, they'd be wrapped around Nora's neck.

Darrell was in on the Warren cult along with Rachel and Lee? That didn't make any sense. He must be playing along until he had the information needed to expose them.

"Darrell's not around, either. Maybe he's finally going to do what Warren ordered him to do and then we don't have anything to worry about." Warren must have ordered Darrell to kill Nora.

"Darrell won't do it." Disgust iced Lee's words. "He's never done Warren's bidding unless there was something in it for him. He won't put himself in danger just to please a dying man."

Of course Darrell wouldn't do it. He wasn't really working for Warren. But where was he?

Nora eased up to peer over the windowsill.

Rachel dropped her head to her folded arms on the counter. "We'll need to get them both."

Lee's mouth twisted as if he chewed on spoiled meat. "We'll take care of them."

Like they'd taken care of Lisa. Like Warren might take care of Abigail?

"Is Uncle Warren still determined to go through with this? It's crazy." Rachel said.

Lee stomped to the end of the kitchen and back, as though his hatred couldn't be contained. "It's not crazy. The Sky People are coming.

Uncle Warren's more determined than ever now that he's got his rightful heir."

Rachel sat up. "Why did she have to come here? Why did she have to know Lisa? If it wasn't for Nora and her precious film, Lisa wouldn't have died."

It sounded like Lee spit darts at Rachel. "Maybe Lisa died because of her unnatural ways. Maybe it's her punishment for leading you to sin."

Rachel let out a sob. "She should still be alive."

Lee leaned on the counter and his eyes drilled into Rachel. "Alive for what? For you to continue this sinful life?"

Rachel glared at him. "What kind of life do you think suits me better?"

Surprisingly, he sounded almost gentle. "You know." He reached out and touched her cheek. "You remember."

Rachel backed away. "I remember two good years." "It didn't have to end," he said.

She shook her head. "Even back then, you knew I wasn't the right wife for you."

He straightened and the rime of hatred lifted from his face. "That's not true. I loved you. I wanted you."

"That's just it. You wanted me, but I didn't want you in that same way. And you knew it."

"We could have worked it out."

Now her voice rose in near-hysteria. "I didn't want to work it out. And then you brought Tessa into our home. I didn't mind, really. In fact, it gave me a break from the part of our marriage I couldn't stand."

He studied her. "Then why?"

She swiped at tears. "Tessa was the younger sister. She loved me and is so easygoing. But then you brought Cassie. That ruined everything."

"She's your sister. And she was getting too old for anyone else. I thought I owed it to you, to your family. I thought you'd want your sisters with you."

"No woman wants to share her husband with her sisters!"

The rain intensified and Nora leaned closer to hear above the rumbling on the roof.

"You never asked me or even discussed it. You filled up our home with the others. They pushed me out. And when they started having babies, you never even looked at me anymore."

Lee reached out again and she backed up further. "Then I met Lisa. She was smart and wild and so pretty."

He flinched as if she had burned him.

"I finally knew what was wrong with me and Lisa didn't think it was wrong at all."

Lee looked like he wanted to stick his fingers in his ears. "It's wrong. It's against God's law."

"Whose God? A lot of people say what you do is a sin."

"You decided to love a woman because she paid attention to you and made you feel special." He said it as if she were a six-year-old who stole her friend's doll.

"No. I didn't decide. I discovered. One day, I was working at the farmer's market and Lisa was buying cheese. She used to come by the stand every week and we'd talk about everything and anything." Rachel drew in a shaky breath but smiled at the memory. "A mountain biking team walked by and they were tanned and muscled and nice looking. Lisa said, 'I can appreciate a good-looking man, and those are excellent bodies, but they don't do it for me.'" Lee let out a sound that might have been a wretch.

"And I thought, 'That's how I feel. It's how I've always felt.' I looked at Lisa and I knew why I always got tongue-tied when she stopped at the stand. I knew why I flushed when I saw her in the crowd and got all flustered when she left."

A whine at the screen made Rachel and Lee jerk their heads to the front door.

"Abbey?" Rachel said.

Lee swung his head to the window. He made eye contact with Nora before she spun around and sprinted from the cabin.

Once away from the protection of the eves, the wind and rain battered her. She swiveled her head to see Lee vault the front porch railing and land in the mud. He slipped in his cowboy boots, but pushed himself up and came after her.

Clay caked on the bottom of her boots and soon she carried what felt like ten extra pounds with each step. She pumped her arms and took off for the Jeep.

Lightning cracked and almost immediately, the thunder hit with a rumbling she felt in her bones. Another flash of lightning followed in rapid succession.

Her legs fought the sucking mud. The rain slashed at her face and her arms ripped through the sharp thorns of the wolfberry bush.

She barely made it out of the yard. The Jeep was a dark hulk camouflaged by rain. Lee grunted behind her. With the slick leather of his cowboy boots, he hadn't gathered the layers of clay to drag him down.

Fear fueled an extra surge of speed.

Something slammed into her back with the force of a freight train, knocking her down to splash in two inches of water and mud. Her cheek slammed into something hard and Lee landed on top of her. He felt like a solid lead skeleton—heavy, hard, and bony, grinding her into the grime and red slurry.

He pushed himself to his knees and grabbed a fistful of her T- shirt, hauling her up as he got to his feet. He didn't speak, just turned toward the house and started dragging her.

She pulled back, struggling and twisting. "Let me go!"

The night closed around them in deep darkness and the rain felt like a curtain. The illumination of the cabin flitted like a strobe light.

Lee slipped in the slick mud and Nora lurched back, ready to make another run. He reached out and closed long fingers around her ankle. He jerked and sent her to the mud bath again. Then Lee yanked her arm and pulled her to her feet. Without stopping, he grabbed her around her waist and hoisted her to his shoulder. With Nora's rear in the air, Lee struggled through the red soup toward the house. She knew her kicking and squirming wouldn't do much good. He had wrestled calves and cows meaner and stronger than Nora.

Rachel met them on the front porch. She held the door open and Lee shoved Nora inside. He followed her and Rachel came after him, shutting the heavy oak door against the rain and wind. Abbey closed in on her, wedging himself so close to her legs he nearly sent her sprawling. He panted and dripped saliva on the floor. Mud and rain slid from his fur. Thunder and lightning scared him and he must have panicked in the Jeep, throwing himself against the loosely latched door until it opened. She put a hand on his head to reassure him and he leaned against her.

Nora straightened and planted her dripping feet on the wood floor. She put her hand on her hips and demanded, "What have you done with my mother?"

"She's with Uncle Warren," Lee growled and took hold of her shoulder, forcing her to sit on a barstool.

Abbey pressed against her.

A gust of wind rattled against the windows, roaring its challenge to the night.

Abigail was alone with the man who'd raped her more than thirty years ago. She'd be terrified, assuming she was still alive. "What does he want with her?"

Lee pressed Nora's shoulders down, keeping her in the chair. "My best guess is that he's looking for you."

"Call him, tell him to let Abigail go." "Why would I do that?"

She glared at him. "If you don't, I'll go to the FBI."

He called over his shoulder to Rachel. "Get me some rope."

Nora jerked her arms but he didn't lose his grip. "I've got proof you killed Lisa. I found her camera and it shows you there."

He frowned. "Where?"

"Let me go and I'll give you the camera."

He ignored her and hollered for Rachel to bring the rope. Nora struggled against him but made little headway. Any knot

Lee tied would hold Nora for decades—or at least as long as it took for Warren to hurt Abigail.

Outside, lightning flashed and thunder sounded like a hungry lion. Abbey whined and put both front paws on Nora's thighs, lifting himself to standing. If she hadn't been propped on the barstool, he'd have crawled into her lap. The rain streamed down the windows in a black cascade.

Rachel appeared behind Lee, a roll of duct tape in her hands. "We don't have any rope. You can use this."

He grabbed it from Rachel with one hand while keeping a vise grip on Nora's shoulder. He held the roll to his mouth and peeled a corner loose with his teeth.

Rachel shifted from foot to foot. "You don't have to tape her up.

She'll stay here."

With the end of the tape in his mouth, he jerked the roll away from him, making it squawk. He lifted his hand from her shoulder.

Nora shoved her feet against the rungs of the stool and leaped from the chair. She had barely moved before Lee's fingers clamped around her wrist and yanked her back. Her arm twisted behind her and she cried out.

A German shepherd or Doberman pinscher might have taken her cry of pain as a sign to go for the jugular of her attacker. Abbey just appeared more agitated and frightened than ever.

Lee snapped her other wrist around. The tape roll dangled from his mouth. He used the same motions he'd probably practiced a million times for rodeo calf tying. Within seconds he'd whipped the end of the tape from his mouth, slapped it on her wrist, and wound the roll around both wrists to secure her.

He held her down by her shoulder again and hollered at Rachel. "Tape her ankles to the stool."

"This isn't necessary. We can take care of her without taping her up."

Rachel was right. How much strapping down does it take to hold someone still enough to shoot them? Or slit a throat, or bash in their brains with a rock?

"Besides, she can't go anywhere in this storm," Rachel said. "It's always this way with you. Always arguing, always questioning, needing to know why."

Maybe they'd strike up a lover's spat and Nora could bolt. But Rachel was right. The ground had been soup when they'd been outside. The rain had continued, driving down in sheets and running along the desert floor. Her Jeep might be stuck.

"We've got to keep her here," Lee said. "What if she gets away and Darrell finds her?"

"Damn it! Listen to me for once. Leave her alone. She's not going anywhere."

"Do you want to take that chance?"

If Darrell was here, he'd have made a move to rescue her by now.

Maybe Warren had him. Her last hope of help faded.

Rachel took the roll of tape and bent down to Nora's legs. Abbey licked her face and she gently pushed him aside. He crowded in close to her.

Nora twitched her legs back and forth to keep Rachel from binding them. Lee's face exploded with pent-up temper. He pulled one hand back to strike her. Rachel jumped up and grabbed it before he could swing. "No!"

He stared at Rachel, nostrils flaring.

Rachel's voice dipped low and slow. "As far as I know, you've never hit a woman. Don't start now."

Never hit a woman? She guessed snapping someone's neck and arranging her body to look like an accident didn't count as hitting.

Lee gritted his teeth and said to Nora, "Cooperate. This is for your own good."

Interesting what he thought was good for Nora. Maybe if she didn't fight, he wouldn't need to smack her around before he killed her.

She fought against the duct tape. It gave slightly, and in time, she'd probably be able to work free. But she needed something immediate. *Think!* She had nothing to bargain with. Or so she thought.

Inspiration struck. "I'll go to Warren. Trade me for Abigail." "You don't want anything to do with Warren," Rachel said. She secured one ankle and moved to the other.

Lightning split the sky. Hairs on Nora's neck tingled. Thunder *ca-whacked*, thrashing the walls and floor. Abbey whined again and jumped, his front paws brushing Nora. He slid to the floor and sat beside her chair, panting and dripping saliva.

Rachel huffed, nearly as frightened as Abbey. She closed her eyes for a second, then finished taping Nora's leg and stood. Lee released his grip on her shoulder, easing the crushing pressure, and plopped on the couch facing her. Seeing the chance to get closer to a human who might make the terrifying storm go away, Abbey trotted over and leaned into Lee, putting his face far up into Lee's lap. Lee put a hand on Abbey's head.

"Tell Warren I'll do whatever he wants," Nora pleaded.

Lee's fingers played in Abbey's fur. Rachel folded her arms on her chest and bit her lip. "You don't understand. We need to keep you here."

"I understand perfectly." If Nora's hands were free, she'd point her finger at Lee. "He needs to kill me so he can inherit everything. I swear I don't want Warren's money. He can have it all."

Bright crimson streaked Rachel's pale cheeks. "It's not just the money. It's the power. He's always craved it. That's why he killed Lisa, to keep her from telling anyone what she knew."

Pop. Sizzle. Ba-whump. Nature's artillery shells bombarded the cabin.

Nora narrowed her eyes at Lee but he stared ahead, deep in thought, stroking Abbey's head. Nora started to call out to him. She never got the words out.

The world erupted in chaos.

A freight train roared outside the cabin. The walls shook and the floor heaved. Rachel screamed.

Nora's heart flew to her throat as lightning flashed.

33

Lee sprang from the couch. Abbey let out a yelp and barked as if he couldn't decide to run and hide or take the offensive. Lee bounded across the room to the door and wrenched it open. The deafening noise increased. Rachel raced after Lee. They both disappeared into the darkness of the front porch amid the sound of a jet engine firing up.

"What is it?" Nora strained against the duct tape.

The house shook again and the windows rattled in the wind. Abbey lunged at Nora, trying to land in her sloping lap. He dropped to the floor and whined.

Lee and Rachel bolted inside. Together they shoved the door closed. Rachel's blonde hair was dark and hung limp with rain.

Lee swiped an arm across his face to dry it and strode to the window opposite Nora. His movements were jerky, as if he'd been zapped by electricity. He pressed his face to the glass. Rachel leaned against the door, pale and shaking.

"What?" Nora said.

No one answered. Another boom of thunder shook the floor. Rachel ducked her head between her shoulders and Lee drew in a sharp breath. "Dear Lord," he began, his words edged in razors of tension as he jerked his head toward Nora. "Cut her loose," he said to Rachel.

Rachel was too shocked to move. "What's happening?" Nora said.

Lee shouted at Rachel. "Do it. If this house is swept away, she deserves a fighting chance!"

Icy sweat sprang out on Nora's face. "The house can't get swept away. We're on a flat plain."

Lee's fiery eyes turned on her. "A plain in a valley with mountains on each side. This house sits in a channel—a flash flood wash."

Rachel hadn't moved from the door. Her lips were a white line. "Just cut her loose!" Lee bellowed.

Rachel sank to the floor, her eyes vacant, as if she'd retreated to some dark place for protection against the storm.

Lee rushed across the room. He reached into his pocket and fished out a knife. It took him only seconds to slice through the tape.

Nora leapt to her feet and sprang for the door. She had to shove Rachel out of the way before she could open it and run onto the porch. Even under the protection of the porch roof, rain pelted her face. The deck vibrated and she slipped on the inch-deep water that seemed to blanket the wooden surface.

Two inches.

Three.

Oh my God. Nora understood the roar, the shaking house, the wet deck. A flash flood raged in the black night just beyond the cabin. They were trapped here amid the swirling, roiling sea of mud and frenzied water.

She fled back inside and slammed the door, dripping with icy rain. How would she get away to help Abigail?

She stared at Lee. His grim expression met hers. Now there was no escape. He'd kill her. Gun, knife, garotte, bare hands—it was dealer's choice.

"Why did you do it?" she asked. He raised an eyebrow in response.

She pressed him. "Do you really believe space ships are coming to take you away?"

His shoulders drooped. "Is it so impossible to believe in life on other planets? So many things are unexplained. All the ancient religions mention people from the sky, even the Bible. Look at the rock art from thousands of years ago."

A shiver ran over her skin, the rain raising goose bumps on her arms. "Maybe, but how can you be sure they're coming back? And then pinpoint an exact day?"

His perpetual scowl deepened. "That's not for me to say. Uncle Warren has accomplished things that should have been impossible. He started out with nothing. How could he have risen so far without the hand of God interceding?"

"What has God and Mormonism got to do with space people and ancient Hopi prophecy?"

"We are all one," he said softly.

These words she knew. Lee could be reading from Benny's phrase book.

"The truth is there, and people from all nations, all corners of the Earth, know it. Why else would so many pilgrims follow the true prophet and gather in the desert?"

"What about the people in the bunkers who change their minds?" "Sometimes their doubts overcome them."

"So you kill them to keep their money?"

His mouth opened in shock. "We don't need their money. We simply keep them with us until they calm down again."

"You lock them in so they can't leave?" Nora was horrified. "They'll leave when the Sky People come for us. They chose freely.

They come from all over the world and they'll be the seeds of the Fifth World."

The walls creaked and the din from the raging water made it nearly impossible to hold a conversation. Nora's fingers cramped from clutching the chair and Rachel still huddled on the floor, but when she raised her eyes, Nora could see the focus coming back into them.

Lee strained to see out a window. The wind howled like an air raid siren. Rain blasted against the windows like bullets. The river attacked them, battering the house, rocking and crashing as debris smashed against it.

A deafening explosion erupted at the north wall. Rachel screamed again as the house shuddered. It sounded like cannonballs impacted against the cabin.

Rachel sprung from the floor to the kitchen. She clung to the counter as if it were a lifeboat. "The cabin is going to break apart! We need to get out!"

Lee left the window and hurried to Rachel. He grabbed her hands in a rough grip and pulled her close to him. He focused on her face, meeting her terrified eyes. "It's okay. We're safer in the house than in the water."

Lee was probably right. The raging swirl of mud and freezing water could sweep them away. It might only be a few feet deep, but they'd lose their footing in the swift current. They could get wrapped around a fence, pinned against a building, be bashed by debris, or get sucked under until their lungs burst and they drowned.

Rachel clutched Lee's hands and concentrated on his face.

Gradually her jaw unclenched and control seeped into her eyes.

The windows bowed and rattled while the wind roared with fury. Tree branches scratched against the house. The water rampaged as if sent to claim them for its own. Nora inched ever closer to the edge of control. The roar, accented by flashes of lightning and the boom of thunder, shredded her nerves.

Abbey whined and panted, lost in his own hell.

The house jerked and tilted. The lights died with a sizzle and a pop, the smell of ozone heavy in the air. Both women screamed as the scant light from the window limited their vision.

Rachel's face betrayed her battle to stay calm. "At least we'll be able to take care of her." She pointed her chin at Nora, her fingers still gripping Lee's.

"Darrell can't get to her in this flood," Lee agreed.

A shadow fell across the floor and Nora jerked her head toward the stairs.

"Unless he's already here," Darrell said. He stood midway up the stairs.

Thank God! He'd been here the whole time. Why hadn't he intervened earlier as Lee shoved Rachel behind him and leaped toward the stairs.

Darrell pulled his arm up, a gun clutched in his hand. Without hesitating, he fired at Lee. It happened so suddenly Nora hardly had time to register the shot. Lee cried out as he crumpled to the floor, blood blossoming across the shoulder of his plaid shirt.

"No!" Rachel threw herself at Darrell, knocking into him. He dropped the gun as he grappled with her. Nora flew to Lee and bent close to him in the gloom. Color drained from Lee's face as he gripped at his shoulder. Nora jumped up and raced to the kitchen. She grabbed a dish towel and ran back to him. She pulled his hand away from the gushing wound. Behind her, Darrell and Rachel grunted, still struggling. The house lurched and Nora thought she felt it slide a few inches. She pressed the towel to Lee's shoulder.

He opened his eyes. With surprising speed and strength, he gripped her hand. "Darrell..."

A terrible crashing interrupted him. Did Nora scream? Did Rachel? Or was it the chaos of the storm and the shriek of the cabin as it tore from its tenuous mooring? Timbers cracked and popped as dishes shattered. The kitchen window blew open and icy water, mixed with clay and grit in a swirling stew of mud and sticks and weeds, surged from the office into the living room.

Suddenly, Rachel appeared at Nora's side and together they heaved Lee from the water to the couch. The water was rapidly rising as the house jerked again. Nora scanned the room, looking for Darrell. She saw him sprawled out on the stairs. He had either fallen or had been knocked down by Rachel.

The gun rested a few steps above him and he reached for it as he pulled himself up. Rachel shoved Nora out of the way and leaned in close to Lee. He appeared weak and in pain. Nora knew the burning agony of being shot, but had no idea if it was a shallow wound or if it would prove to be fatal. She hoped Lee would survive, but he needed to get to a hospital.

The house convulsed again, coming to rest at a sharp angle. Something upstairs banged and the ceiling sounded like it might cave in. More glass shattered. Nora stood above Lee and Rachel, watching as Darrell pushed himself up another step and reached for the gun.

A hand grabbed her arm, yanking her backward. Rachel tried to tug Nora out the front door, now unhinged and hanging open. They struggled in the mud now blanketing the floor, each step proving to be a slipping struggle. Rachel shouted something at her but the rush of the flood and the rain and thunder masked her words. Nora tugged back, fighting to stay in the house.

With a deafening crash, one of the ceiling beams dislodged. The vibrations rocked the whole house and Rachel used the momentum to throw all of her weight against Nora. The perfect storm of motion knocked Nora off balance and she pitched headfirst to splash in the water on the floor. Rachel pulled on her arm again, dragging her through the front door.

Nora slid on her stomach, her arm wrenched high over her head. Rachel tugged her across the pitching front porch. With one last lunge, Rachel propelled them both off the porch and into the roiling waters. She lost her grip on Nora's arm and disappeared as the black rush of the freezing flood stole her away.

34

The confidence and power that had rushed through Warren earlier seeped away, leaving him frail. He huddled in the passenger seat of his Caddy, coughing and wheezing, fighting for every breath. His body burned with fever and he'd shed his expensive toupee hours ago, even though he hated for Abigail to see him bald.

He longed to give up, let his earthly body finally rest. But Warren knew God expected him to keep going. He had prepared a reward for Warren and he needed to show strength of spirit and mind. God hadn't made Warren's path easy, but He'd always rewarded him. He couldn't succumb to weakness now that the end grew near.

Abigail leaned forward over the steering wheel, peering into the inky night. The wipers slapped at high speed. She squinted. "I can't see anything."

He labored for breath. "Keep a light hand on the wheel. God will guide us."

She tightened her lips. "I've had enough of your God and His ridiculous plans. You're crazy. You've always been nuts, since the first moment we met you." She looked like his Abigail—the sweet, happy young girl without a harsh word—but she sounded more like Christine, who, despite having every advantage, felt disappointed with what life had given her.

"What happened to you to make you so hard?" he asked.

She frowned. "I had to get hard in a hurry. It's not easy to survive a rape, lose my dearly beloved husband, and raise a baby on my own."

He pushed himself to sit. "I loved you."

She said nothing, but her jaws clenched. Eventually she spoke. "Your nephew said Nora would be at the cabin?"

"She was on her way back from the reservation."

The rear of the Caddy fishtailed so she pulled her foot off the accelerator and coaxed the steering wheel in the opposite direction. They righted and she pressed the gas pedal. "You're sure?"

"My nephew wouldn't lie," he assured her.

He grabbed a plastic grocery bag and leaned over to wretch. Specks of blood and a tiny stream of foamy bile oozed from his heaving belly. His throat burned and his abdominal muscles ached with effort, but his stomach contained little. He heaved again, the sweat puddling in his armpits and filming his cold face.

He fell back on the seat and pushed the button to roll down the window. Warren forced the nearly empty bag through it and it was swept away by the rush of wind and rain. He rolled up the window and lay panting.

"What are you going to do with Nora?"

More questions. He closed his eyes, the effort it took to speak exhausting him. "I want to see her."

"You've already seen her."

He heard the weakness in his own voice. "I want to see her with the eyes of a father."

"You aren't her father. And even if you were, she wouldn't do what you want her to do."

He opened his eyes. "And what do you think I want her to do?"

She didn't take her eyes from the road or loosen her grip on the wheel. "I don't know. Take over your businesses? Be some grand poobah of the Mormon Church? I can't imagine what you want with her, but I know Nora and she won't have anything to do with you."

"I can offer her more than wealth," he began.

She frowned again. "It doesn't matter. I told her what you did to me."

Warren had been dragged through every bit of muck throughout his very public life. When a person acquired as much success as he had, it made him an easy target for resentment. Yet, no accusation hurt him the way Abigail's lies now ripped at his heart. The daughter he longed to see hadn't been conceived in anger or by force. Why couldn't Abigail realize that?

She slowed to a crawl and leaned so far forward her nose practically rested on the dash. She turned the wheel and they started up the road to Castle Valley. "Oh. Oh." She sounded so distressed Warren pulled himself up on the seat to see what was going on. He strained to see through the darkness outside his rain-streaked window, but finally he understood.

The valley below roiled and raged in a flash flood. What was once a peaceful sprawl of scraggly trees and homes was now a vengeful river, the red of the mud lightening the water so the flood's violence was even more obvious in the moonless night.

Abigail drove along the road to the turnoff that led down to Castle Valley. Of course, the road had been washed away. "The cabin ..." It sounded like she wanted to say more but couldn't form words.

He gripped the door handle and fought the terror pooling in the pit of his stomach. God wouldn't give him a daughter only to take her away at the last minute. Be calm and believe.

Abigail gasped. She pointed down the road where the headlights caused the raindrops to spark in the reflected glow. He squinted and saw a figure staggering in the rain. He reached for the glove box to pull out the gun he kept there. He prayed it was Nora but needed to prepare for the worst.

Abigail shoved her door open and scrambled into the storm, running toward the person. What if it was a looter or someone intending to harm them? A second passed before Warren identified it as a man making his slow progress in their direction. Warren gripped the dash as the man came into focus. Darrell.

This didn't feel right. He expected Lee, but hoped to see Rachel. He prayed Nora was safe. But he didn't know Darrell was out here.

Warren closed his eyes and summoned strength. There was so little left. His deepest desire was to lie down and stop fighting, let the good Lord have mercy on him and take him home. But it wasn't his time yet. First he needed to leave the kingdom in good hands. He pushed the door open. It felt like a stone blocking the entrance to a tomb. His legs shook trying to support his own meager weight, but he forced his feet to move. The rain dripped onto his bald head, cooling his fever but chilling him so that his teeth chattered.

Darrell shifted his focus from Abigail. Warren expected the man to rush to his side at the frail state of his leader. Instead, he waited as Warren staggered into the peripheral glow of the headlights.

Darrell's shirt clung to his chest, the tattered sleeves rippling in the wind. Blood and mud dripped from long scratches on his arms and his face was peppered with scrapes and bruises.

The storm was losing steam, but the flood continued roaring.

The frenzied water surged past with destructive energy. "Where's Nora?" Warren managed to ask.

Darrell's shoulders slumped as he looked at the ground. "I don't know. Rachel and Lee had her when the house collapsed. I only hope she survived."

Abigail gasped. "Oh my God! She's trapped in the flood?"

"I tried to save her. We would have been safe if we'd stayed in the house, even though it was badly damaged. But after Lee was injured, Rachel forced Nora into the water."

"Lee is injured? How bad?" Warren needed Lee. The colony needed his survivalist instincts, his faith, his intimate knowledge of the plan.

Darrell dropped his shoulders even more, his face a picture of sorrow. "I wish I didn't have to tell you this. But I shot Lee."

Abigail let out an alarmed gasp.

Warren stepped back a few paces to lean on the Caddy.

"He had Nora and he planned to kill her. I knew you needed Nora to carry on your legacy. There was no other way."

The firm grasp Warren had on the plan, the future, slipped from his fingers. Everything was spinning out of control. "You're brothers, a team. Together you were going to lead the faithful. You've always been my sons!"

Darrell's head shot up. "None of that is true. Now that you have a true heir, you plan on leaving it all to her."

Warren's knees buckled and he rested his bony rear on the bumper as the rain streamed down his face.

Darrell stepped forward, following the beam of light toward Warren. "Not brothers. Half-brothers. You know what that's like, don't you, Uncle Warren?"

Abigail stared at Darrell's sudden transformation. Warren should have known Darrell would break under the pressure. He usually had perfect instincts with people. But somehow he'd missed Darrell's weakness. And now his nephew was turning on him.

Darrell's feet sloshed in the muddy road as he continued his rant. "To be the son whose mother is not the favorite. The ugly mother. The one with the harsh tongue. The mother whose only son is kicked out when he's fourteen because there's only room for the favorite son at the homestead."

How could the situation be unraveling like this? "I took care of you. You never had to go through what I did. I paid for your college and law school and got you the best clerk positions. I helped you."

"Why? Was it because you loved me? Because you wanted what was best for me?"

Warren's skin burned and his eyes felt like flames. He wouldn't be able to hold his head up much longer.

Thinly contained rage packed Darrell's words. "It was because you needed me! Someone you could groom to follow in your insane footsteps. A captain to lead your troops and keep your crazy plan secret."

"Not crazy."

"I did keep it secret, though. I did everything you wanted. Did you know that on the morning I dealt with Lisa, Lee was on his way to save her? If I hadn't gotten there first, he would have helped her escape and she would have exposed you."

Warren struggled to maintain his breath. "Maybe she didn't need to die."

Darrell hardly paused. "I even played nice with Brother Lee and his disgusting family. Oh, you helped me with your contacts and a little money. But you could have done so much more. You never claimed me as you own."

Warren wretched into the mud, a thin string of blood dribbling from his lips before splashing into the road. "Couldn't."

"Right." Sarcasm soured Darrell's voice. "The polygamy. Can't let anyone know you came from that. You can cover up the past and help the young man of a single mother, but you can't admit he's from your family rooted in polygamy."

"What did you want?" Warren managed to ask.

"Money!" Darrell yelled into the night. "You have millions— billions, some say. And yet you couldn't buy me an election? Couldn't get me a decent car? Couldn't build Lee and his tribe a house? You stingy bastard."

"I needed it for..." Warren was interrupted by another heave. "For the plan. Building the bunker. Stocking it. Buying silence."

Darrell watched Warren raise his arm in slow motion to wipe the blood from his chin. It was clear he was in pain. "But it's not all gone. I know. Even a lunatic like you couldn't spend it all. Somewhere in the back of your mind, you know this whole thing is a joke."

No. Darrell believed. He had to believe. He'd killed Lisa Taylor to protect the plan.

"There is no space ship. There is no mystic connection with the Hopi and they won't be coming in two days to take the faithful."

Warren tried to lift his head to explain but he couldn't raise his chin from his chest.

"So the faithful will wait and when nothing happens, they'll know you lied to them."

Darrell stood in front of Warren, but Warren couldn't raise his eyes to see Darrell's face. He focused on the red mud caked on Darrell's shoes and the filth clinging to his dripping jeans. With slow, deliberate movements, Darrell slid his hand into his pocket and pulled out a pistol.

"Rachel and Nora will die in the flood. Lee is probably still in the cabin, dead. You're not going to last long and neither is she." He wagged his gun at Abigail. "No one is left to expose me."

Warren felt the shame of begging. "No. Please."

"And you know that will I prepared for you? The one you signed? I changed it after the fact." With feigned gratitude, he said, "You really shouldn't have been so generous to leave me what's left of your estate. Minus a small stipend for Christine, of course."

He'd failed. His life's work had crumbled in the grip of the evil man in front of him. The space ships would come, but the pilgrims couldn't get to them. Lee, his one faithful nephew, lay dead. His daughter, too—he'd never speak to her, never hold her.

Betrayed. Like his brother Jesus, Warren longed to cry out, "My God, my God, why hast thou forsaken me?"

Mud splashed as he heard the sound of footsteps. Good. He hoped Abigail was trying to escape.

But Darrell took a few strides then lunged, pinning Abigail to his chest with one arm. Warren prayed for the strength to protect her. He prayed God would listen to him, recognize the voice of his faithful servant, and grant him one last request. He needed to save her, the woman he had always loved. Just long enough to give her a name she'd know. The name to listen for when he called her across the veil. God didn't allow them to share this life, but surely He would grant them eternal life on their own planet. This had to be why He'd brought Abigail to him at this last moment. *God please. I'm trying. Please help.*

35

Nora's head plunged under the frothing wave of muddy water. She strained her neck, lifting her mouth to the air and filling her lungs. Grit choked her but she was able to breathe before dunking underneath the water and flipping herself over. Her spine scraped the desert floor and snagged on roots and branches. Sharp talons scratched at her face and the water tumbled debris against her to batter every part of her body.

She quickly lost contact with Rachel. She could only hope the surging water wouldn't drown them or smash them against a boulder or fence post and break them in two. The crushing pace of the water didn't diminish, but Nora choked back panic to form a plan. She dragged her rear on the sand, head pointed downstream. The water gushed around her chin and lapped into her mouth when she sucked a breath. She coughed and stretched herself flat so she could float along the surface. Kicking her legs and paddling with her hands, she worked her way to what she hoped was the north side of the flow.

The cold water penetrated her skin. If she stayed in the water much longer, she'd risk hypothermia. She lifted her head and opened her mouth for another gulp of air.

Nora couldn't see in the blackness that surrounded her, but the water felt more shallow here. She planted her hands in the sand behind her, with her feet out in front of her. She struggled but held her own against the current. Ten seconds ago, she hadn't been able to resist the deluge as it carried her toward destruction. She kept maneuvering herself to the shallower water, assuming she'd eventually reach the edge of the flood.

Nora pushed against the thick water, positioning her legs under her in a squat. Still facing the current, she resisted with her hands and legs, the water now to her knees and shoulders. Centering her weight, she stood and started to plow out of the main current. Planting her feet one step at a time, she made her way out of the river of muck. The rain had tapered to a few drops and the wind, while strong enough to make her teeth chatter with the cold, wasn't shrieking in her ears.

The black night closed around her as she felt her way around, sloshing in the ankle-deep mud, hoping she was headed for the bank that led to the road. She'd been tossed and tumbled so much she couldn't tell if she walked east or west.

Had Rachel made it? Maybe she shouldn't be so concerned with the fate of a woman who intended to kill her. But Nora didn't want to write Rachel off as an evil murderer just yet.

She kept picturing Rachel and Lisa together. A person couldn't fake the light in their eyes when their lover unexpectedly entered the room. Rachel never ignored an opportunity to touch Lisa and that kind of unconscious affection was hard to manufacture. Sure, people fall out of love. But that didn't lead to murder. Earlier, when Rachel spoke to Lee about Lisa, she had had the tone of a woman deeply in love.

The darkness in front of her solidified into the bank leading to the road. Saturated as it was, Nora struggled to climb. Her feet slid and she scraped her chin on the gravel and clay. Slowly, she crawled onto the road. Nora spotted lights about a quarter of a mile away. Headlights, she realized. Someone was out here and it meant help, warmth, and shelter.

She wanted to run, but her legs were too weak and she shivered so violently she did well just to keep moving, however slowly. She began to make out shapes in the headlights the closer she trudged. One very large person stood in the middle of the spotlight. It looked like another sat on the bumper. A few steps closer. The large person turned out to be two people standing close together, one holding the other up. An arm extended from the two person group.

Nora slowed her turtle-like pace and listened. "There is still time for you to do the right thing."

Oh my god. Abigail.

The dripping man holding her mother jerked her closer to him. "The right thing is that I get my reward for the humiliation and slave labor I've given him all my life."

Nora slid down the embankment so she could hide her approach, but kept her focus on the figures in the headlights. She crawled through the mud, her fingers numb and her teeth clenched against her trembling.

Darrell?

Darrell pointed his gun at the man slumped against the bumper. Warren. He didn't raise his head. His knees melted and he plopped into a puddle, whacking his head against the bumper.

The man who'd warned her against going to the cops. He'd told her he was taking care of Lee and Rachel. He had the gun trained on Warren. That was good. But he also threatened Abigail. Definitely not good.

Darrell lowered his gun. "You're finally getting what you deserve. Dying in the mud. How appropriate for the tenth richest man in the world." Darrell looked down at Abigail. "Come on." He jerked his head toward the bank and Nora ducked. "I think there's still enough water for a tragic drowning."

Had he heard her? Her heart hammered and she held her breath. Nora heard a scuffle in the mud and she poked her head above the rim of the bank. Darrell yanked Abigail toward the side of the road, only twenty feet from where Nora hid.

Abigail fought against him. "What do you hope to gain by this?" "Your silence." He grunted in effort as he dragged her along. "Even if I'm gone, Rachel and Nora will stop you."

"Rachel's had her chance. And Nora isn't going to make it through the night."

He succeeded in getting Abigail to the lip of the bank, but she didn't make it easy. Nora crouched well within his peripheral vision, but between the darkness and his struggle with Abigail, he didn't notice.

"I'm sure Nora has already called the cops." Abigail sounded strong for the fight.

"They won't help her. Most of them are packing their bags to join the faithful in the bunker."

Abigail freed one arm and swung her hand up to smack his face, but he dodged the blow. Nora waited until he had one foot down the bank, throwing off his center of gravity and making him unstable. She pushed off the thick mud to hurl herself at Darrell and send him sailing down the bank. But the mud sucked at her feet and she never got off the ground.

Her foot slipped and she tumbled backward, sliding down the bank with a grunt. Darrell spun toward her, pulling Abigail with him.

She lost her footing and shoved against Darrell. They toppled forward into the steep embankment. The turbulent water rushed below them. Darrell lost his grip on Abigail and she rolled down the bank toward the flood. She wasn't as strong as Nora and she'd be swept away. "Mother!" Nora's hands sank into the saturated hillside. She shoved with her feet, propelling herself toward Abigail. Abigail stopped rolling ten feet above the waves. Slathered in mud, she blended with the bank.

She twisted her head up and Nora swore she could read panic in her eyes, though it was impossible to tell in the dark.

"Hang on!" Nora yelled.

Lightning flashed, with a crack of thunder following. The rain resumed, falling in solid sheets. Darrell pushed himself to his knees as he raised his gun toward Abigail.

The slight ledge that had stopped Abigail's fall began to break loose and slide into the rampaging water. Abigail screamed and flailed her arms, looking for anything to grab hold of.

Nora didn't have time to think things through. She could either lunge for Abigail and hold her on the bank, letting Darrell get a shot off in close range, or dive for Darrell and leave Abigail to save herself.

Flash! Boom!

Abigail screamed. Her feet slid in slow motion and brushed the edge of the water. She slapped at the muddy bank, her fingers clawing at air.

Rain battered at them, carving mini-culverts of icy water in the bank. A deluge of liquid mud ran down Nora's face and into her mouth as she fought to stand. In one fluid motion, Nora dove head- first down the bank, her arm outstretched and her eyes focused on Abigail's frantically waving hand. She smacked into the mud, her fingers closing around air. Her mother's hand was just out of reach and slipping further away by the second.

Nora laid her head down, the rush of the flood splashing into her eyes and mouth. Abigail's legs kicked in the water as Nora saw her slide in past her knees. Her mother's sharp shriek sent lightning through Nora's veins and she scrambled through the mud, desperate to feel her mother's flesh. Nora had to concentrate in order to move her arms, legs, feet, and hands. The mud dragged on them, making them feel like leaden attachments instead of her own flesh and blood. She inched forward. Abigail slid another foot as the bank gave way beneath her hips. "No!" Not knowing or caring where she got the strength, Nora lunged forward and this time, she felt the grasping answer of her mother's fingers close on hers. Nora braced her free hand underneath her body and pulled backward. At first, they remained mired in the muck, the rain stinging against their skin. Nora gritted her teeth and doubled her effort.

Darrell's bullet would rip into her any second. She'd die drenched in mud, never seeing Cole's face again. Abigail would slide into the torrent, not possessing the strength to fight it.

Slowly, though, they moved up the bank, fighting for each inch until Abigail's feet were no longer submerged in the swirling river. Nora struggled into a sitting position, hauling Abigail to her and hugging her close. Abigail gasped and sobbed and flung her arms around Nora. The mud made it feel like a sandpaper embrace, but the love flowed strong. She knew this would be their last hug and tried to shield Abigail with her body.

Darrell stood above them on the bank. His arm held the gun steady, aimed at Nora. Why hadn't he shot them while they struggled on the bank?

He shook his head. "Nice rescue. But it won't save you. You should have let her drown. Now I'll have to break her neck to look like she died from flood injuries."

"You have experience with that," she yelled at him, desperate to keep him talking until she could figure out how to stop him.

"I didn't enjoy killing Lisa. I offered her a compromise and lots of money. But she had her principles."

"Maybe my mother and I are less principled." Nora kept her voice above the noise of the storm.

"I will not ... " Abigail started to say. Nora tightened her arm around her and cut off the rest.

"Liar." He steadied the gun and took a deep breath.

This was it. The bullet would rip into her heart. She thrust Abigail behind her and squeezed her eyes shut.

The shot rang in her ears.

She waited for the shock to wear off and the pain to hit. She inhaled her last breath.

And waited.

"Oh, thank god!" Abigail cried. Nora opened her eyes.

Darrell lay face down in the mud. His gun arm extended above his head, the gun flung down the slope.

Nora's eyes moved up the bank.

Warren stood on the edge of the road. His head hung down on a neck too weak to keep it up, and his eyes were closed. His arm was limp at his side, a gun dangling from his finger. A second later, it dropped into a puddle with a splash. He opened his eyes and found Nora with what appeared to be grueling effort. His lips moved as pinkish foam bubbled from his mouth. He sank to his knees, his mouth still opening and closing.

Maybe it was the rain or maybe tears streamed down his face.

He finally croaked one word. "Daughter."

He folded in on himself and splashed onto the road.

EPILOGUE

Bright sunshine toasted the top of Nora's head and warmed her arms. The wrens twittered along with the sparrows. Humid air rose from the damp red sand under her boots where pinpricks of green already battled their way through the flood fallout.

Nora breathed with care, making sure not to pant after the short hike up the washed-out trail. The doctor assured her the ribs were bruised and not broken, but the difference seemed negligible. She couldn't move without pain shooting through her. Even with a black eye, a purple bruise the size of a Volkswagen on her thigh, and more sore muscles than she thought possible, she still fared better than Rachel.

Rachel leaned heavily on one crutch, her head hanging down with her thin blonde hair shielding her face. Along with her fractured ankle, Rachel sported a bandage wrapped around her forehead. She hadn't complained much, but the doctor told Nora that Rachel's headaches had to be epic.

Still, Rachel had insisted they come here this morning. Before them, the creek burbled on a calm and happy note. Two days ago, while Nora and Rachel had been tossed like marbles in a box down the raging flood in Castle Valley, this canyon at Moonflower had also exploded in floodwaters. The tough willows and cottonwoods survived, red silt covered the ground, and now the creek flowed in denial of the incident.

Abbey had waited out the storm in the cabin. Terrified and alone, he'd come through without a physical scratch, though Nora figured storms would always be an ordeal for him. He rested under the shade of a willow.

Rachel didn't look up. "The last of the immigrants left this morning."

Nora focused on a tiny yellow bud poking through the sand, amazed it fought back so quickly. "Did they get their assets returned?"

Rachel's shoulders drooped. "Lee's not a monster, you know." Nora didn't know whether she agreed.

Rachel defended him. "Why wouldn't Lee believe Warren's lies? You don't know what it's like to be raised in isolation, where you're told only what they want you to know. Whatever they don't like, they label as sin and fill you with such terror of Hell, you don't dare rebel."

Nora said softly, "That's what happened to you?"

A sob caught in Rachel's throat. "Until I met Lisa. She saved me." They stood in silence, then Rachel continued. "I knew about Warren's plans. I could have stopped it. But I felt loyal to my family. And I honestly didn't think it would hurt anyone. The immigrants would wait, the space ships wouldn't come, then everyone would go home." More silence. "I should have known Lisa better. It's my fault she's gone."

The box Nora held felt too heavy.

"But that doesn't mean Lee was bad. He has a good heart. Warren and Darrell's death have broken it, maybe even broken him."

They stood in silence for several moments.

Rachel lifted her chin. "Okay. We came out here to say goodbye.

We might as well do it."

Nora set the box of ashes on the sand. She pulled the screwdriver from the back pocket of her shorts and worked at prying the lid off. Abbey stood and trotted over to stick his cold nose on her cheek.

Rachel bent over and scratched his ears and he sat back to lean on her legs.

Nora set the screwdriver down and pulled the lid off to reveal a plastic bag. "Thank you for letting me be here."

Rachel's throat worked before strained words came out. "I couldn't do it alone."

Nora closed her fingers on the plastic bag full of course gray ashes. She lifted it and stepped toward the creek.

Rachel hobbled after her and they stood together on a smooth rock on the bank at a bend in the creek. Nora slid the top of the bag open and offered it to Rachel.

Tears streamed down Rachel's face and she shook her head. She mouthed the words "I can't" and broke down in sobs.

Nora pictured a laughing Lisa, her vitality and passion clear on her face. She considered the creek and slowly let Lisa's ashes sift into the running water and dissolve.

When the bag was empty, Nora wadded it up and stuffed it in her pocket. Rachel's sobs tapered off, and her fingers tentatively brushed Nora's hand.

Nora closed her hand on Rachel's and they stood together, watching the creek. Finally Rachel stirred. "My ankle is hurting and I need to rest. Can you bring Lisa's box?"

"Of course." Nora ached to think of Rachel picking up the threads of her life alone. She'd turned her back on her upbringing and now had no family.

Rachel hobbled down the trail, leaving Nora and Abbey. A few minutes later the rumble of voices pricked their ears. Abbey's tail wagged. If Nora had a tail, hers would be doing the same.

Footsteps on damp sand kept tempo with her heart. Nora limped a few feet from the creek toward the trail. She couldn't stop the goofy grin she knew was spreading over her face.

Cole's sandy hair and broad shoulders emerged from the cottonwoods along the trail. Nora was barely aware of her swollen knee and bruised hip as she shuffled toward him.

Cole squinted into the sun and searched the clearing. When he spotted her, he broke into a wide grin and jogged toward her. In mere seconds, he threw his arms around her, lifting her into the air and crushing her against him.

Pain from a hundred wounds zapped through her. She didn't care.

She clung to him with all her strength. She buried her face in the warmth of his neck and breathed in his comforting scent.

They pulled apart and he bent to pat Abbey. "Your mother told me where you were."

"You didn't need to come all the way out here, but I'm glad you did."

He slid his arms around her again. "I had to make sure you're really okay."

"I'm sort of okay. Lots of bruises, and of course, I have major work to do if I'm going to present Canyonlands' case to the board."

"Of course." He chuckled. "But first, can I buy you some lunch?"

"A girl's gotta eat, right?" She hurried to retrieve Lisa's box. She leaned down to heft it up when her gaze was drawn to a splash of blue showing through the sand. Her breath left her lungs and she stood motionless for several seconds.

When her heart resumed, a smile danced on her lips. She brushed the sand away. The bright blue of the sash, as well as the feathers secured in his hand, identified the fist-sized kachina as hers.

She didn't bother looking around for who might have left the doll. She reached for the wooden figure. Energy surged through her fingers as she grasped him.

She belonged.

* * *

If you enjoyed these books, please leave a brief review on Amazon.

Review the Nora Abbott series at

Shannon-Baker.com/Nora-Abbott-Box-Set-Review

THE DESERT BEHIND ME

The mind never truly forgets. Even when it wants to.

When a teenaged girl goes missing in Arizona, retired New York cop Jamie Butler is frantic to find her. Haunted by the brutal murder of her own daughter, Jamie is convinced that this girl has been abducted in the same way.

But while others are slow to take alarm—the girl's mother believes she is merely off on a lark—Jamie sees inexplicable similarities to her own daughter's abduction. Connections that seem impossible. Because her daughter's killer is long-dead...

Already doubting her own grief-fractured mind, Jamie struggles to convince those around her of what she fears to be true. And as her search for the missing teen intensifies, new evidence comes to light.

Evidence that implicates Jamie, herself.

In a race to save the missing girl Jamie must finally confront her dark memories and unearth the long-suppressed secrets of her forgotten past.

Perfect for fans of *Girl on the Train* and *Into the Water.*

Shannon Baker delivers a dark psychological thriller filled with twists and turns. Gripping and sharply suspenseful, *The Desert Behind Me* will keep you guessing until the very end.

ABOUT THE AUTHOR

Shannon Baker lives on the edge of the desert in Tucson with her crazy Weimaraner and her favorite human. Baker spent 20 years in the Nebraska Sandhills, where cattle outnumber people by more than 50:1. She lived in Flagstaff for several years and worked for the Grand Canyon Trust, a hotbed of environmentalists who, usually, don't resort to murder. She is the proud recipient of the Rocky Mountain Fiction Writers 2014 and 2017-18 Writer of the Year Award.

A lover of the great outdoors, she can be found backpacking, traipsing to the bottom of the Grand Canyon, skiing mountains and plains, kayaking lakes, river running, hiking, cycling, and scuba diving whenever she gets a chance. Arizona sunsets notwithstanding, Baker is, and always will be a Nebraska Husker. Go Big Red.

You can find Shannon online at www.Shannon-Baker.com, and connect with her on Facebook at AuthorShannonBaker or Instagram at ShannonBaker5328.